WAR AND PEACE
BOOK 2

Count Leo Nikolayevich Tolstoy was born on the family estate of Yasnaya Polyana in the province of Tula in 1828, into a family ennobled by Peter the Great. He was educated privately and then studied law and Oriental languages at Moscow and Kazan Universities. He returned to Yasnaya where he remained until 1851, after which he enlisted in the Army of the Caucasus. Here he began to see the problems of the Russian society structure, and a year later he started his autobiographical trilogy, *Childhood, Boyhood* and *Youth*. He served in the Crimean War but retired from the Army after the fall of Sevastopol. Several years in St Petersburg society followed before he returned to Yasnaya and married Sophie Andreyevna Behrs in 1862. It was a very happy marriage and during the first fifteen years they had thirteen children.

War and Peace was begun in 1862 and finished seven years later. *Anna Karenina* was completed in two years, in 1877. After these two great novels, Tolstoy abandoned his beliefs and way of living for the simplicity of peasant life, and described the changeover in *Confession*, published in 1882. Several other books followed including *The Death of Ivan Ilyich* and *Resurrection*. Because of his new beliefs, family life became unbearable and in October 1910 Tolstoy escaped from home with Alexandra, his youngest daughter and only confidante. He became ill at a little railway station in central Russia and died in the stationmaster's room in early November.

LEO TOLSTOY
WAR AND PEACE
BOOK 2

translated from the Russian by
Constance Garnett

RUPA

Published by
Rupa Publications India Pvt. Ltd 2016
7/16, Ansari Road, Daryaganj
New Delhi 110002

Sales centres:
Allahabad Bengaluru Chennai
Hyderabad Jaipur Kathmandu
Kolkata Mumbai

Edition copyright © Rupa Publications India 2016

This is a work of fiction. Names, characters, places and incidents are either the product of the author's imagination or are used fictitiously, and any resemblance to any actual persons, living or dead, events or locales is entirely coincidental.

All rights reserved.
No part of this publication may be reproduced, transmitted, or stored in a retrieval system, in any form or by any means, electronic, mechanical, photocopying, recording or otherwise, without the prior permission of the publisher.

ISBN: 978-81-291-2905-5

Second impression 2019

10 9 8 7 6 5 4 3 2

The moral right of the author has been asserted.

Printed at BB Press, Noida

This book is sold subject to the condition that it shall not, by way of trade or otherwise, be lent, resold, hired out, or otherwise circulated, without the publisher's prior consent, in any form of binding or cover other than that in which it is published.

War and Peace
Book 2

The Chief Families in the novel and several important characters. The names most frequently used are in bold.

THE BEZUHOVS

Count Cyril **Bezuhov**
Pierre, his son, legitimised after his father's death, becomes Count Peter **Bezuhov**
Princess **Katish**, Pierre's cousin

THE ROSTOVS

Count Ilya Andreitch **Rostov**
Countess Nataly **Rostov,** his wife
Court **Nikolay** Rostov (**Nikolushka**), their elder son
Count Peter Rostov (**Petya**), their second son
Countess **Vera** Rostov, their elder daughter
Countess Nataly Rostov (**Natasha**), their younger daughter
Sonya, a poor member of the Rostov family circle
Berg, Alphonse Karlitch, an officer of German extraction, who marries Vera

THE BOLKONSKYAS

Prince Nikolay **Bolkonsky,** a retired General-in-Chief
Prince Andrey Bokonsky, his son
Princess Marya Bolkonsky, his daughter
Princess Elizabeth Bolkonsky (**Liza**), Andrey's wife
Tihon, Prince Nikolay's attendant
Alpatitch, his steward

THE KURAGINS

Prince Vassily Kuragin
Prince **Ippolit Kuragin**, his elder son
Prince **Anatole** Kuragin, his younger son
Princess **Ellen** Kuragin, his daughter, who marries Pierre

Princess **Anna Mihalovna** Drubetskoy
Prince **Boris** Drubetskoy, her son
Julie Karagin, an heiress who marries Boris
Anna Pavlovna Scherer, Maid of honour to the ex-Empress Mariya Fyodorovna
Dolohov (Fedya), an officer and desperado
Marya Dmitryevna Ahrosimov (le terrible dragon)
Denison, Vaska, a hussar officer
Platon **Karataev**, a peasant

PART IX

I

TOWARDS the end of the year 1811, there began to be greater activity in levying troops and in concentrating the forces of Western Europe, and in 1812 these forces—millions of men, reckoning those engaged in the transport and feeding of the army—moved from the west eastward, towards the frontiers of Russia, where, since 1811, the Russian forces were being in like manner concentrated.

On the 12th of June the forces of Western Europe crossed the frontier, and the war began, that is, an event took place opposed to human reason and all human nature. Millions of men perpetrated against one another so great a mass of crime—fraud, swindling, robbery, forgery, issue of counterfeit money, plunder, incendiarism, and murder—that the annals of all the criminal courts of the world could not muster such a sum of wickedness in whole centuries, though the men who committed those deeds did not at that time look on them as crimes.

What led to this extraordinary event? What were its causes? Historians, with simple-hearted conviction, tell us that the causes of this event were the insult offered to the Duke of Oldenburg, the failure to maintain the continental system, the ambition of Napoleon, the firmness of Alexander, the mistakes of the diplomatists, and so on.

According to them, if only Metternich, Rumyantsev, or Talleyrand had, in the interval between a levée and a court ball, really taken pains and written a more judicious diplomatic note, or if only Napoleon had written to Alexander, 'I consent to restore the duchy to the Duke of Oldenburg,' there would have been no war.

We can readily understand that being the conception of the war that presented itself to contemporaries. We can understand Napoleon's supposing the cause of the war to be the intrigues of England (as he said, indeed, in St. Helena); we can understand how to the members of the English House of Commons the cause of the war seemed to be Napoleon's ambition; how to the Duke of Oldenburg the war seemed due to the outrage done him; how to the trading class the war seemed due to the continental system that was ruining Europe; to the old soldiers and generals the chief reason for it seemed their need of active service; to the regiments of the period, the necessity of re-establishing *les bons principes*; while the diplomatists of the time set it down to the alliance of Russia with Austria in 1809 not having been with sufficient care concealed from Napoleon, and the memorandum, No. 178, having been awkwardly worded. We may well understand contemporaries believing in those causes, and in a countless, endless number more, the multiplicity of which is due to the infinite variety of men's points of view. But to us of a later generation, contemplating in all its vastness the immensity of the accomplished fact, and seeking to penetrate its simple and fearful significance, those explanations must appear insufficient. To us it is inconceivable that millions of Christian men should have killed and tortured each other, because Napoleon was ambitious, Alexander firm, English policy crafty, and the Duke of Oldenburg hardly treated. We cannot grasp the connection between these circumstances and the bare fact of murder and violence, nor why the duke's wrongs should induce thousands of men from the other side of Europe to pillage and murder the inhabitants of the Smolensk and Moscow provinces and to be slaughtered by them.

For us of a later generation, who are not historians led away by the process of research, and so can look at the facts with common-sense unobscured, the causes of this war appear innumerable in their multiplicity. The more deeply we search out the causes the more of them we discover; and every cause, and even a whole class of causes taken separately, strikes us as being equally true in itself, and equally deceptive through its insignificance in comparison with the immensity of the result, and its inability to produce (without all the other causes that concurred with it) the effect that followed. Such a cause, for instance, occurs to us as Napoleon's refusal to withdraw his troops beyond the Vistula, and to restore the duchy of Oldenburg; and then again we remember the readiness or the reluctance of the first chance French corporal to serve on a second campaign; for had he been unwilling to serve, and a second and a third, and thousands of corporals and soldiers had shared that reluctance, Napoleon's army would have been short of so many men, and the war could not have taken place.

If Napoleon had not taken offence at the request to withdraw beyond the Vistula, and had not commanded his troops to advance, there would have been no war. But if all the sergeants had been unwilling to serve on another campaign, there could have been no war either.

And the war would not have been had there been no intrigues on the part of England, no Duke of Oldenburg, no resentment on the part of Alexander; nor had there been no autocracy in Russia, no French

Revolution and consequent dictatorship and empire, nor all that led to the French Revolution, and so on further back: without any one of those causes, nothing could have happened. And so all those causes—myriads of causes—coincided to bring about what happened. And consequently nothing was exclusively the cause of the war, and the war was bound to happen, simply because it was bound to happen. Millions of men, repudiating their common-sense and their human feelings, were bound to move from west to east, and to slaughter their fellows, just as some centuries before hordes of men had moved from east to west to slaughter their fellows.

The acts of Napoleon and Alexander, on whose words it seemed to depend whether this should be done or not, were as little voluntary as the act of each soldier, forced to march out by the drawing of a lot or by conscription. This could not be otherwise, for in order that the will of Napoleon and Alexander (on whom the whole decision appeared to rest) should be effective, a combination of innumerable circumstances was essential, without any one of which the effect could not have followed. It was essential that the millions of men in whose hands the real power lay—the soldiers who fired guns and transported provisions and cannons—should consent to carry out the will of those feeble and isolated persons, and that they should have been brought to this aquiescence by an infinite number of varied and complicated causes.

We are forced to fall back upon fatalism in history to explain irrational events (that is those of which we cannot comprehend the reason). The more we try to explain those events in history rationally, the more irrational and incomprehensible they seem to us. Every man lives for himself, making use of his free-will for attainment of his own objects, and feels in his whole being that he can do or not do any action. But as soon as he does anything, that act, committed at a certain moment in time, becomes irrevocable and is the property of history, in which it has a significance, predestined and not subject to free choice.

There are two aspects to the life of every man: the personal life, which is free in proportion as its interests are abstract, and the elemental life of the swarm, in which a man must inevitably follow the laws laid down for him.

Consciously a man lives on his own account in freedom of will, but he serves as an unconscious instrument in bringing about the historical ends of humanity. An act he has once committed is irrevocable, and that act of his, coinciding in time with millions of acts of others, has an historical value. The higher a man's place in the social scale, the more connections he has with others, and the more power he has over them, the more conspicuous is the inevitability and predestination of every act he commits. 'The hearts of kings are in the hand of God.' The king is the slave of history.

History—that is the unconscious life of humanity in the swarm, in the community—makes every minute of the life of kings its own, as an instrument for attaining its ends.

Although in that year, 1812, Napoleon believed more than ever that to shed or not to shed the blood of his peoples depended entirely on his will (as Alexander said in his last letter to him), yet then, and more than at any time, he was in bondage to those laws which forced him, while to himself he seemed to be acting freely, to do what was bound to be his share in the common edifice of humanity, in history.

The people of the west moved to the east for men to kill one another. And by the law of the coincidence of causes, thousands of petty causes backed one another up and coincided with that event to bring about that movement and that war: resentment at the non-observance of the continental system, and the Duke of Oldenburg, and the massing of troops in Prussia—a measure undertaken, as Napoleon supposed, with the object of securing armed peace—and the French Emperor's love of war, to which he had grown accustomed, in conjunction with the inclinations of his people, who were carried away by the grandiose scale of the preparations, and the expenditure on those preparations, and the necessity of recouping that expenditure. Then there was the intoxicating effect of the honours paid to the French Emperor in Dresden, and the negotiations too of the diplomatists, who were supposed by contemporaries to be guided by a genuine desire to secure peace, though they only inflamed the *amour-propre* of both sides; and millions upon millions of other causes, chiming in with the fated event and coincident with it.

When the apple is ripe and falls—why does it fall? Is it because it is drawn by gravitation to the earth, because its stalk is withered, because it is dried by the sun, because it grows heavier, because the wind shakes it, or because the boy standing under the tree wants to eat it?

Not one of those is the cause. All that simply makes up the conjunction of conditions under which every living, organic, elemental event takes place. And the botanist who says that the apple has fallen because the cells are decomposing, and so on, will be just as right as the boy standing under the tree who says the apple has fallen because he wanted to eat it and prayed for it to fall. The historian, who says that Napoleon went to Moscow because he wanted to, and was ruined because Alexander desired his ruin, will be just as right and as wrong as the man who says that the mountain of millions of tons, tottering and undermined, has been felled by the last stroke of the last workman's pickaxe. In historical events great men—so called—are but the labels that serve to give a name to an event, and like labels, they have the least possible connection with the event itself.

Every action of theirs, that seems to them an act of their own free-will, is in an historical sense not free at all, but in bondage to the whole course of previous history, and predestined from all eternity.

II

ON the 29th of May Napoleon left Dresden, where he had been spending three weeks surrounded by a court that included princes, dukes, kings, and even one emperor. Before his departure, Napoleon took a gracious leave of the princes, kings, and emperor deserving of his favour, and sternly upbraided the kings and princes with whom he was displeased. He made a present of his own diamonds and pearls—those, that is, that he had taken from other kings—to the Empress of Austria. He tenderly embraced the Empress Marie Louise—who considered herself his wife, though he had another wife still living in Paris—and left her, so his historian relates, deeply distressed and hardly able to support the separation. Although diplomatists still firmly believed in the possibility of peace, and were zealously working with that object, although the Emperor Napoleon, with his own hand, wrote a letter to the Emperor Alexander calling him '*Monsieur mon frère*,' and assuring him with sincerity that he had no desire of war, and would always love and honour him, he set off to join the army, and at every station gave fresh commands, hastening the progress of his army from west to east. He drove in a travelling carriage, drawn by six horses and surrounded by pages, adjutants, and an armed escort, along the route by Posen, Thorn, Dantzig, and Königsberg. In each of these towns he was welcomed with enthusiasm and trepidation by thousands of people.

The army was moving from west to east, and he was driven after it by continual relays of six horses. On the 10th of June he overtook the army and spent the night in the Vilkovik forest, in quarters prepared for him on the property of a Polish count.

The following day Napoleon drove on ahead of the army, reached the Niemen, put on a Polish uniform in order to inspect the crossing of the river, and rode out on the river bank.

When he saw the Cossacks posted on the further bank and the expanse of the steppes—in the midst of which, far away, was the holy city, Moscow, capital of an empire, like the Scythian empire invaded by Alexander of Macedon—Napoleon surprised the diplomatists and contravened all rules of strategy by ordering an immediate advance, and his troops began crossing the Niemen next day.

Early on the morning of the 12th of June he came out of his tent, which had been pitched that day on the steep left bank of the Niemen, and looked through a field-glass at his troops pouring out of the Vilkovik forest, and dividing into three streams at the three bridges across the river. The troops knew of the Emperor's presence, and were on the look-out for him. When they caught sight of his figure in his greatcoat and hat standing apart from his suite in front of his tent on the hill opposite, they threw up their caps and shouted, 'Vive l'Empereur!' And one regiment after another, in a continuous stream, flowed out of the immense forest that had concealed them, and split up to cross the river by the three bridges. 'We shall make some way this time. Oh, when he takes a hand himself things begin to get warm! ... Name of God! ... There he is! ... Hurrah for the Emperor! So those are the Steppes of Asia! A nasty country it is, though. Good-bye, Beauché; I'll keep the finest palace in Moscow for you. Good-bye! good-luck! ... Have you seen the Emperor? Hurrah for the Emperor! If they make me Governor of the Indies, Gérard, I'll make you Minister of Cashmere, that's settled. Hurrah for the Emperor! Hurrah! hurrah! hurrah! The rascally Cossacks, how they are running. Hurrah for the Emperor! There he is! Do you see him? I have seen him twice as I am seeing you. The little corporal ... I saw him give the cross to one of the veterans. ... Hurrah for the Emperor!' Such was the talk of old men and young, of the most diverse characters and positions in society. All the faces of those men wore one common expression of joy at the commencement of a long-expected campaign, and enthusiasm and devotion to the man in the grey coat standing on the hill opposite.

On the 13th of June Napoleon mounted a small thoroughbred Arab horse and galloped towards one of the bridges over the Niemen, deafened all the while by shouts of enthusiasm, which he obviously endured simply because they could not be prevented from expressing in such shouts their love for him. But those shouts, invariably accompanying him everywhere, wearied him and hindered his attending to the military problems which beset him from the time he joined the army. He rode over a swaying bridge of boats to the other side of the river, turned sharply to the left, and galloped in the direction of Kovno, preceded by horse guards, who were breathless with delight and enthusiasm, as they cleared the way before him. On reaching the broad river Niemen, he pulled up beside a regiment of Polish Uhlans on the bank.

'Vive l'Empereur!' the Poles shouted with the same enthusiasm, breaking their line and squeezing against each other to get a view of him. Napoleon looked up and down the river, got off his horse, and sat down on a log that lay on the bank. At a mute sign from him, they handed him the field-glass. He propped it on the back of a page who ran up delighted. He began looking at the other side, then, with absorbed attention, scrutinised the map that was unfolded on the logs. Without raising his head he said something, and two of his adjutants galloped off to the Polish Uhlans.

'What? what did he say?' was heard in the ranks of the Polish Uhlans as an adjutant galloped up to them. They were commanded to look for a fording-place and to cross to the other side. The colonel of the Polish Uhlans, a handsome old man, flushing red and stammering from excitement, asked the adjutant whether he would be permitted to swim across the river with his men instead of seeking for a ford. In obvious dread of a refusal, like a boy asking permission to get on a horse, he asked to be allowed to swim across the river before the Emperor's eyes. The adjutant replied that probably the Emperor would not be displeased at this excess of zeal.

No sooner had the adjutant said this than the old whiskered officer, with happy face and sparkling eyes, brandished his sabre in the air shouting *'Vive l'Empereur!'* and commanding his men to follow him, he set spurs to his horse, and galloped down to the river. He gave a vicious thrust to his horse, that floundered under him, and plunged into the water, making for the most rapid part of the current. Hundreds of Uhlans galloped in after him. It was cold and dangerous in the middle in the rapid current. The Uhlans clung to one another, falling off their horses. Some of the horses were drowned, some, too, of the men; the others struggled to swim across, some in the saddle, others clinging to their horse's manes. They tried to swim straight across, and although there was a ford half a verst away they were proud to be swimming and drowning in the river before the eyes of that man sitting on the log and not even looking at what they were doing. When the adjutant, on going back, chose a favourable moment and ventured to call the Emperor's attention to the devotion of the Poles to his person, the little man in the grey overcoat got up, and summoning Berthier, he began walking up and down the bank with him, giving him instructions, and casting now and then a glance of displeasure at the drowning Uhlans who had interrupted his thoughts.

It was no new conviction for him that his presence in any quarter of the earth, from Africa to the steppes of Moscow, was enough to impress men and impel them to senseless acts of self-sacrifice. He sent for his horse and rode back to his bivouac.

Forty Uhlans were drowned in the river in spite of the boats sent to their assistance. The majority struggled back to the bank from which they had started. The colonel, with several of his men, swam across the river and with difficulty clambered up the other bank. But as soon as they clambered out in drenched and streaming clothes they shouted *'Vive l'Empereur!'* looking ecstatically at the place where Napoleon had stood, though he was no longer there, and at that moment thought themselves happy.

In the evening between giving two orders—one for hastening the arrival of the counterfeit rouble notes that had been prepared for circulation in Russia, and the other for shooting a Saxon who had been caught with a letter containing a report on the disposition of the French army—Napoleon gave a third order for presenting the colonel, who had quite unnecessarily flung himself in the river, the order of the Légion d'Honneur, of which he was himself the head. *Quos vult perdere, dementat.*

III

THE Russian Emperor had meanwhile been spending more than a month in Vilna, holding reviews and inspecting manoeuvres. Nothing was in readiness for the war, which all were expecting, though it was to prepare for it that the Tsar had come from Petersburg. There was no general plan of action. The vacillation between all the plans that were proposed and the inability to fix on any one of them, was more marked than ever after the Tsar had been for a month at headquarters. There was a separate commander-in-chief at the head of each of the three armies; but there was no commander with authority over all of them, and the Tsar did not undertake the duties of such a commander-in-chief himself.

The longer the Tsar stayed at Vilna, the less ready was the Russian army for the war, which they had grown weary of expecting. Every effort of the men who surrounded the Tsar seemed to be devoted to making their sovereign spend his time pleasantly and forget the impending war.

Many balls and fêtes were given by the Polish magnates, by members of the court, and by the Tsar himself; and in the month of June it occurred to one of the Polish generals attached to the Tsar's staff that all the generals on the staff should give a dinner and a ball to the Tsar. The suggestion was eagerly taken up. The Tsar gave his consent. The generals on the staff subscribed the necessary funds. The lady who was most likely to please the Tsar's taste was selected as hostess for the ball.

Count Bennigsen, who had land in the Vilna province, offered his house in the outskirts for this fête, and the 13th of June was the day fixed for a ball, a dinner, with a regatta and fireworks at Zakreta, Count Bennigsen's suburban house.

On the very day on which Napoleon gave the order to cross the Niemen, and the vanguard of his army crossed the Russian frontier, driving back the Cossacks, Alexander was at the ball given by the generals on his staff at Count Bennigsen's house.

It was a brilliant and festive entertainment. Connoisseurs declared that rarely had so many beauties been gathered together at one place. Countess Bezuhov, who had been among the Russian ladies who had followed the Tsar from Petersburg to Vilna, was at that ball, her heavy, Russian style of beauty—as it is called—overshadowing the more refined Polish ladies. She was much noticed, and the Tsar had deigned to bestow a dance upon her.

Boris Drubetskoy, who had left his wife at Moscow, and was living 'en garçon,' as he said, at Vilna, was also at that ball; and although he was not a general on the staff, he had subscribed a large sum to the ball. Boris was now a wealthy man who had risen to high honours. He no longer sought patronage, but was on an equal footing with the most distinguished men of his age. At Vilna he met Ellen, whom he had not seen for a long while. As Ellen was enjoying the good graces of a very important personage indeed, and Boris had so recently been married, they made no allusion to the past, but met as good-natured, old friends.

At midnight dancing was still going on. Ellen happening to have no suitable partner had herself proposed a mazurka to Boris. They were the third couple. Boris was looking coldly at Ellen's splendid bare shoulders, which rose out of her dress of dark gauze and gold, and was talking to her of old acquaintances, and yet though others and himself too were unaware of it, he never for a second ceased observing the Tsar who was in the same room. The Tsar was not dancing; he was standing in the doorway, stopping one person after the other with the gracious words he alone knew how to utter.

At the beginning of the mazurka, Boris saw that a general of the staff, Balashov, one of the persons in closest attendance on the Tsar, went up to him, and, regardless of court etiquette, stopped close to him, while he conversed with a Polish lady. After saying a few words to the lady, the Tsar glanced inquiringly at Balashov, and apparently seeing that he was behaving like this only because he had weighty reasons for doing so, he gave the lady a slight nod and turned to Balashov. The Tsar's countenance betrayed amazement, as soon as Balashov had begun to speak. He took Balashov's arm and walked across the room with him, unconsciously clearing a space of three yards on each side of him as people hastily drew back. Boris noticed the excited face of Araktcheev as the Tsar walked up the room with Balashov. Araktcheev, looking from under his brows at the Tsar, and sniffing with his red nose, moved forward out of the crowd as though expecting the Tsar to apply to him. (Boris saw that Araktcheev envied Balashov and was displeased at any important news having reached the Tsar not through him.) But the Tsar and Balashov walked out by the door into the lighted garden, without noticing Araktcheev. Araktcheev, holding his sword and looking wrathfully about him, followed twenty paces behind them.

Boris went on performing the figures of the mazurka, but he was all the while fretted by wondering what the news could be that Balashov had brought, and in what way he could find it out before other people. In the figure in which he had to choose a lady, he whispered to Ellen that he wanted to choose Countess Pototsky, who had, he thought, gone out on to the balcony, and gliding over the parquet, he flew to the door that opened into the garden, and seeing the Tsar and Balashov coming into the verandah, he stood still there. The Tsar and Balashov moved towards the door. Boris, with a show of haste, as though he had not time to move away, squeezed respectfully up to the doorpost and bowed his head. The Tsar in the tone of a man resenting a personal insult was saying:

'To enter Russia with no declaration of war! I will consent to conciliation only when not a single enemy under arms is left in my country,' he said.

It seemed to Boris that the Tsar liked uttering these words: he was pleased with the form in which he had expressed his feelings, but displeased at Boris overhearing them.

'Let nobody know of it!' the Tsar added, frowning.

Boris saw that this was aimed at him, and closing his eyes, inclined his head a little. The Tsar went back to the ballroom, and remained there another half hour.

Boris was the first person to learn the news that the French troops had crossed the Niemen; and, thanks to that fact, was enabled to prove to various persons of great consequence, that much that was hidden from others was commonly known to him, and was thereby enabled to rise even higher than before in the opinion of those persons.

The astounding news of the French having crossed the Niemen seemed particularly unexpected from coming after a month's uninterrupted expectation of it, and arriving at a ball! At the first moment of amazement and resentment on getting the news, Alexander hit on the declaration that has since become famous—a declaration which pleased him and fully expressed his feelings. On returning home after the ball at two o'clock in the night, the Tsar sent for his secretary Shishkov, and told him to write a decree to the army and a rescript to Field-Marshal Prince Saltykov; and he insisted on the words being inserted that he would never make peace as long as one Frenchman under arms remained in Russia.

The next day the following letter was written to Napoleon:

MONSIEUR MON FRÈRE,—I learnt yesterday that in spite of the loyalty with which I have kept my engagements with your Majesty, your troops have crossed the frontiers of Russia, and I have this moment received from Petersburg the note in which Count Lauriston informs me as cause of this invasion that your Majesty considers us to be in hostile relations ever since Prince Kurakin asked for his passport. The causes on which the Duc de Bassano based his refusal to give these passports would never have led me to suppose that the action of my ambassador could serve as a ground for invasion. And, indeed, he received no authorisation from me in his action, as has been made known by him; and as soon as I heard of it I immediately expressed my displeasure to Prince Kurakin, commanding him to perform the duties entrusted to him as before. If your Majesty is not inclined to shed the blood of your subjects for such a misunderstanding, and if you consent to withdraw your troops from Russian territory, I will pass over the whole incident unnoticed, and agreement between us will be possible. In the opposite case, I shall be forced to repel an invasion which has been in no way provoked on my side. Your Majesty has it in your power to preserve humanity from the disasters of another war.—I am, etc.,   (Signed) ALEXANDER.

IV

AT two o'clock in the night of the 13th of June, the Tsar sent for Balashov, and, reading him his letter to Napoleon, commanded him to go in person and give the letter to the French Emperor. As he dismissed Balashov, he repeated to him his declaration that he would never make peace as long as a single enemy under arms remained on Russian soil, and told him to be sure to repeat those words to Napoleon. The Tsar had not inserted them in his letter to Napoleon, because, with his characteristic tact he felt that those words would be inappropriate at the moment when the last efforts were being made for conciliation; but he expressly charged Balashov to repeat that message by word of mouth to Napoleon.

Balashov rode out on the night between the 13th and the 14th, accompanied by a trumpeter and two Cossacks; and at dawn he reached the French outposts at the village of Rykonty on the Russian side of the Niemen. He was stopped by the sentinels of the French cavalry.

A French subaltern of hussars, in a crimson uniform and a fur cap, shouted to Balashov to stop. Balashov did not immediately obey, but went on advancing along the road at a walking pace.

The subaltern, with scowls and muttered abuse, swooped down upon Balashov, drew his sword, and shouted rudely to the Russian general: 'Was he deaf that he did not hear when he was spoken to?' Balashov gave him his name. The subaltern sent a soldier to his superior officer.

Paying no further attention to Balashov, the subaltern began talking with his comrades about regimental matters, without looking at the Russian general. It was an exceedingly strange sensation for Balashov, who was used at all times to the dignities of his position, was always in contact with the highest power and authority, and only three hours before had been conversing with the Tsar, to be brought here on Russian soil into collision with this hostile, and still more, disrespectful display of brute force.

The sun was only beginning to rise behind storm-clouds, the air was fresh and dewy. A herd of cattle was being driven along the road from the village. Larks sprang up trilling one after another in the fields, like bubbles rising to the surface of water.

Balashov looked about him, awaiting the arrival of the officer from the village. The Russian Cossacks and trumpeter and the French hussars looked at one another now and then in silence.

A French colonel of hussars, evidently only just out of bed, came riding out of the village on a handsome, sleek, grey horse, accompanied by two hussars. The officers, the soldiers, and the horses all looked smart and well satisfied.

In this early stage of the campaign the troops were well in a state of good discipline, in good, almost parade, order, and engaged in peaceful pursuits, with a shade of martial swagger in their dress, and a shade of the gaiety and spirit of adventure in their temper that always accompanies the commencement of a war.

The French colonel had much ado to suppress his yawns, but was courteous in his manner, and evidently understood all the importance of Balashov's position. He led him past the line of outposts, and informed him that his desire to be presented to the Emperor would in all probability immediately be satisfied, as the Emperor's quarters were, he believed, not far off.

They rode through the village of Rykonty, past French picket ropes, sentinels, and soldiers, who saluted their colonel and stared with curiosity at the Russian uniform. They came out on the other side of the village, and the colonel told Balashov that they were only two kilomètres from the commander of the division, who would receive him and conduct him to his destination.

The sun had by now fully risen and was shining cheerfully on the bright green fields.

They had just passed an inn and were riding uphill when a party of horsemen came riding downhill towards them. The foremost figure was a tall man, in a hat with plumes, mounted on a raven horse, with trappings glittering in the sun. He had a scarlet cloak, and curly black hair, that floated on his shoulders, and he rode in the French fashion, with his long legs thrust out in front. This personage galloped towards Balashov, with his jewels and gold lace and feathers all fluttering and glittering in the bright June sun.

Balashov was some ten yards from this majestically theatrical figure in bracelets, feathers, necklaces, and gold, when Julner, the French colonel, whispered to him reverentially, 'The King of Naples!' It was in fact Murat, who was now styled the 'King of Naples.' Though it was utterly incomprehensible that he should be the King of Naples, he was addressed by that title, and was himself persuaded of his royal position, and consequently behaved with an air of greater solemnity and dignity than heretofore. So firmly did he believe that he really was the King of Naples, that when, just before leaving Naples, he was greeted by some Italians with shouts of 'Long live the King!' when walking in the streets with his wife, he turned to her with a pensive smile and said, 'Poor fellows, they don't know I am quitting them tomorrow.'

But though he believed so implicitly that he was King of Naples, and sympathised with his subjects' grief at losing him, after he had been commanded to return to the service, and especially after his interview with Napoleon at Dantzig, when his most august brother-in-law had said, 'I have made you king that you may rule in my way, and not in your own,' he had cheerfully resumed his familiar duties; and, like a well-fed, but not over-fed stallion feeling himself in harness, prancing in the shafts, and decked out in all possible motley magnificence, he went galloping along the roads of Poland, with no notion where or why he was going.

On seeing the Russian general he made a royal, majestic motion of his head with his floating curls, and looked inquiringly at the French colonel. The colonel deferentially informed his Majesty of the mission of Balashov, whose name he could not pronounce. 'De Bal-macheve!' said the King, resolutely attacking and vanquishing the colonel's difficulty. 'Charmed to make your acquaintance, general,' he added, with a gesture of royal condescension. As soon as the King spoke loudly and rapidly, all his royal dignity instantly deserted him, and, without himself being aware of it, he passed into the tone of good-humoured familiarity natural to him. He laid his hand on the forelock of Balashov's horse. 'Well, general, everything looks like war,' he said, as it were regretting a circumstance on which he could not offer an opinion. 'Your Majesty,' answered Balashov, 'the Emperor, my master, does not desire war, and as your Majesty sees.' Balashov declined 'your majesty' in all its cases, using the title with an affectation inevitable in addressing a personage for whom such a title was a novelty.

Murat's face beamed with foolish satisfaction as he listened to 'Monsieur de Balacheff.' But royalty has its obligations. He felt it incumbent on him to converse with Alexander's envoy on affairs of state as a king and an ally. He dismounted, and taking Balashov's arm, and moving a little away from the suite, who remained respectfully waiting, he began walking up and down with him, trying to speak with grave significance. He mentioned that the Emperor Napoleon had been offended at the demand that his troops should evacuate Prussia, especially because that demand had been made public, and was so derogatory to the dignity of France. Balashov said that there was nothing derogatory in that demand, seeing that . . . Murat interrupted him.

'So you consider that the Emperor Alexander is not responsible for the commencement of hostilities?' he said suddenly, with a foolish and good-humoured smile.

Balashov began to explain why he did consider that Napoleon was responsible for the war.

'Ah, my dear general,' Murat interrupted him again, 'with all my heart I wish that the emperors would settle the matter between themselves; and that the war, which has been begun by no desire of mine, may be concluded as quickly as possible,' he said in the tone in which servants speak who are anxious to remain on friendly terms though their masters have quarrelled. And he changed the subject; inquiring after the health of the Grand Duke, and recalling the agreeable time he had spent with him in Naples. Then suddenly, as though recollecting his royal dignity, Murat drew himself up majestically, threw himself into the pose in which he had stood at his coronation, and waving his right arm, said: 'I will detain you no longer, general; I wish you success in your mission.' And, with a flutter of his scarlet cloak and his feathers, and a flash of his precious stones, he rejoined the suite, who were respectfully awaiting him.

Balashov rode on further, expecting from Murat's words that he would be very shortly brought before Napoleon himself. But at the next village he was detained by the sentinels of Davoust's infantry corps, just as he had been at the outposts. An adjutant of the commander of that corps was sent for to conduct him to the village to see Marshal Davoust.

V

DAVOUST was to the Emperor Napoleon what Araktcheev was to Alexander. Davoust was not like Araktcheev a coward, but he was as exacting and as cruel, and as unable to express his devotion except by cruelty.

In the mechanism of the state organism these men are as necessary as wolves in the organism of nature. And they are always to be found in every government; they always make their appearance and hold their own, incongruous as their presence and their close relations with the head of the state may appear. It is only on the theory of this necessity that one can explain the fact that a man so cruel—capable of pulling out grenadiers' moustaches with his own hand—though unable, from the weakness of his nerves, to face danger, so uncultured, so boorish as Araktcheev, was able to retain such influence with a sovereign of chivalrous tenderness and nobility of character like Alexander.

Balashov found Davoust sitting on a tub in a barn adjoining a peasant's hut. He was occupied in writing, auditing accounts. An adjutant was standing beside him. Better quarters could have been found, but Marshal Davoust was one of these people who purposely put themselves into the most dismal conditions of life in order to have a right to be dismal. For the same reason they always persist in being busy and in a hurry.

'How could one be thinking of the bright side of life when, as you see, I am sitting on a tub in a dirty barn, hard at work?' was what his face expressed.

The great desire and delight of such people on meeting others enjoying life is to throw their own gloomy, dogged activity into their faces. Davoust gave himself that satisfaction when Balashov was brought in. He appeared even more deeply engrossed in his work when the Russian general entered, and glancing through his spectacles at the face of Balashov, who looked cheerful from the brightness of the morning and his talk with Murat, he did not get up, did not stir even, but scowled more than before, and grinned malignantly.

Observing the disagreeable impression made on Balashov by this reception, Davoust raised his head, and asked him frigidly what he wanted.

Assuming that such a reception could only be due to Davoust's being unaware that he was a general on the staff of Alexander, and his representative indeed before Napoleon, Balashov hastened to inform him of his rank and his mission. But, contrary to his expectations, Davoust became even surlier and ruder on hearing Balashov's words.

'Where is your despatch?' he said. 'Give it to me. I will send it to the Emperor.'

Balashov said that he was under orders to hand the document to the Emperor in person.

'The commands of your Emperor are obeyed in your army; but here,' said Davoust, 'you must do what you are told.'

And, as though to make the Russian general still more sensible of his dependence on brute force, Davoust sent the adjutant for the officer on duty.

Balashov took out the packet that contained the Tsar's letter, and laid it on the table (a table consisting of a door laid across two tubs with the hinges still hanging on it). Davoust took the packet and read the address on it.

'You are perfectly at liberty to show me respect or not, as you please,' said Balashov. 'But, permit me to observe that I have the honour to serve as a general on the staff of his Majesty . . .'

Davoust glanced at him without a word, and plainly derived satisfaction from signs of emotion and confusion on Balashov's face.

'You will be shown what is fitting,' he said, and putting the envelope in his pocket he walked out of the barn.

A minute later an adjutant of the marshal's, Monsieur de Castre, came in and conducted Balashov to the quarters that had been assigned him.

He dined that day in the barn with the marshal, sitting down to the door laid across the tubs.

Next day Davoust went out early in the morning, but before starting he sent for Balashov, and told him peremptorily that he begged him to remain there, to move on with the baggage-wagons should the command be given to do so, and to have no conversation with any one but Monsieur de Castre.

After four days spent in solitude and boredom, with a continual sense of dependence and insignificance, particularly galling after the position of power which he had hitherto occupied, after several marches with the marshal's baggage and the French troops, who were in possession of the whole district, Balashov was brought back to Vilna, now occupied by the French, and re-entered the town by the very gate by which he had left it four days earlier.

Next day the Emperor's gentleman-in-waiting, Count Turenne, came to Balashov with a message that it was the Emperor Napoleon's pleasure to grant him an audience.

Four days before sentinels of the Preobrazhensky regiment had been on guard before the very house to which Balashov was conducted. Now two French grenadiers were on duty before it, wearing fur caps and blue uniforms open over the breast, while an escort of hussars and Uhlans, and a brilliant suite of adjutants, pages, and generals were waiting for Napoleon to come out, forming a group round his saddle-horse at the steps and his Mameluke, Rustan. Napoleon received Balashov in the very house in Vilna from which Alexander had despatched him.

VI

Though Balashov was accustomed to the pomp of courts, he was impressed by the splendour and luxury of Napoleon's court.

Count de Turenne led him into the great reception-room, where a number of generals, gentlemen-in-waiting, and Polish magnates were waiting to see the Emperor. Many of them Balashov had seen at the court of the Russian Emperor. Duroc told him that the Emperor Napoleon would receive the Russian general before going out for his ride.

After a delay of several moments, a gentleman-in-waiting came into the great reception-room, and bowing courteously to Balashov, invited him to follow him.

Balashov went into the little reception-room, from which one door led to the study, the room where he had received the Russian Emperor's last charges before setting off. Balashov stood for a couple of minutes waiting. Hurried steps were audible through the door. Both halves of the door were swiftly thrown open, and in the complete stillness that followed other firm and resolute steps could be heard from the study: it was Napoleon. He had only just finished dressing for his ride. He was wearing a blue uniform, open over a white waistcoat, that came low down over his round belly, riding-boots, and white doeskin breeches, fitting tightly over his fat, short legs. His short hair had evidently just been brushed, but one lock hung down in the middle of his broad forehead. His plump, white neck stood out in sharp contrast to the black collar of his uniform; he smelt of eau-de-cologne. His still young-looking, full face, with its prominent chin, wore an expression of imperial graciousness and majestically condescending welcome.

He walked out with a quivering strut, his head thrown a little back. His whole stout, short figure, with his broad, fat shoulders and his prominent stomach and chest, had that imposing air of dignity common in men of forty who live in comfort. It was evident, too, that he happened that day to be in a particularly good humour.

He nodded in acknowledgment of Balashov's low and respectful bow, and going up to him, began to talk at once like a man who values every minute of his time, and will not deign to preface what he is going to say, as he is sure of always speaking well and saying the right thing.

'Good day, general!' said he. 'I have received the Emperor Alexander's letter that you brought, and I am very glad to see you.' He glanced at Balashov's face with his large eyes, and immediately looked past him.

It was obvious that he took no interest in Balashov's personality. It was plain that only what was passing in *his* soul had for him any interest. All that was outside him had no significance for him, because everything in the world depended, as he fancied, on his will.

'I do not, and did not, desire war,' he said, 'but you have forced me to it. Even *now*' (he threw emphasis on the word) 'I am ready to receive any explanations you can give me.' And he began briefly and clearly explaining the grounds of his displeasure with the Russian government.

Judging from the studiously composed and amicable tone of the French Emperor, Balashov was thoroughly persuaded that he was desirous of peace, and intended to enter into negotiations.

'Sire! The Emperor, my sovereign,' Balashov began, meaning to utter the speech he had prepared long before as soon as Napoleon had finished speaking, and looked inquiringly at him. But the look the Emperor turned upon him disconcerted him. 'You are embarrassed; recover yourself,' Napoleon seemed to say, as with a hardly perceptible smile he scanned Balashov's sword and uniform. Balashov regained his composure, and began to speak. He said that the Emperor Alexander did not regard Kurakin's asking for his passport a sufficient cause for war; that Kurakin had acted on his own initiative without the Tsar's consent; that the Tsar did not desire war, and that he had no relations with England.

'Not *as yet*,' Napoleon put in, and as though afraid to abandon himself to his feelings, he frowned and nodded slightly as a sign to Balashov that he might continue.

After saying all he had been instructed to say, Balashov wound up by saying that the Emperor Alexander was desirous of peace, but that he would not enter into negotiations except upon condition that ... At that point Balashov hesitated; he recollected the words the Emperor Alexander had not written in his letter, but had insisted on inserting in the rescript to Saltykov, and had commanded Balashov to repeat to Napoleon. Balashov remembered those words: 'As long as a single enemy under arms remains on Russian soil,' but some complicated feeling checked his utterance of them. He could not utter those words, though he tried to do so. He stammered, and said: 'On condition the French troops retreat beyond the Niemen.'

Napoleon observed Balashov's embarrassment in the utterance of those last words: his face quivered, and the calf of his left leg began twitching ryhthmically. Not moving from where he stood, he began speaking in a louder and more hurried voice than before. During the speech that followed Balashov could not help staring at the twitching of Napoleon's left leg, which grew more marked as his voice grew louder.

'I am no less desirous of peace than the Emperor Alexander,' he began. 'Haven't I been doing everything for the last eighteen months to obtain it? For eighteen months I have been waiting for an explanation, but before opening negotiations, what is it that's required of me?' he said, frowning and making a vigorous gesticulation with his fat, little white hand.

'The withdrawal of the forces beyond the Niemen, sire,' said Balashov.

'Beyond the Niemen?' repeated Napoleon. 'So now you want me to retreat beyond the Niemen—only beyond the Niemen?' repeated Napoleon, looking straight at Balashov.

Balashov bowed his head respectfully.

Four months before he had been asked to withdraw from Pomerania; now withdrawal beyond the Niemen was all that was required. Napoleon turned quickly away, and began walking up and down the room.

'You say that I am required to withdraw beyond the Niemen before opening negotiations; but two months ago I was required in the same way to withdraw beyond the Oder and the Vistula, and in spite of that you agree to enter into negotiations.'

He strode in silence from one corner of the room to the other and stopped again, facing Balashov. Balashov noticed that his left leg was twitching more rapidly than ever, and his face looked as though petrified with its stern expression. Napoleon was aware of this twitching. 'The vibration of my left calf is a great sign with me,' he said in later days.

'Such demands as to retire beyond the Oder and the Vistula may be made to a prince of Baden, but not to me,' Napoleon almost screamed, quite to his own surprise. 'If you were to give me Petersburg and Moscow I wouldn't accept such conditions. You say: I began the war. But who was the first to join his army? The Emperor Alexander, and not I. And you offer me negotiations when I have spent millions, when you are in alliance with England, and when your position is weak—you offer me negotiations! What is the object of your alliance with England? What has it given you?' he asked hurriedly. The motive of his words was obviously now not to enlarge on the benefits of peace and to consider its possibility, but simply to prove his own rectitude, and his own power, and point out the duplicity and the errors of Alexander.

He had plainly intended in entering on this conversation to point out the advantages of his own position, and to signify that in spite of them he would entertain the proposal of negotiations. But he had begun talking, and the more he talked the less able was he to control the tenor of his words.

The whole gist of his words now was obviously to glorify himself and to insult Alexander, precisely what he had least intended doing at the beginning of the interview.

'I am told you have concluded a peace with the Turks?'

Balashov bent his head affirmatively. 'Peace has been concluded...' he began. But Napoleon did not allow him to speak. He clearly did not wish any one to speak but himself, and he went on with the unrestrained volubility and irritability to which people spoilt by success are so prone.

'Yes, I know you have made peace with the Turks without gaining Moldavia and Wallachia. I would have given your Emperor those provinces just as I gave him Finland. Yes,' he went on, 'I promised, and would have given the Emperor Alexander Moldavia and Wallachia, but now he will not possess those fair provinces. He might have united them to his empire, however, and he would have enlarged the frontiers of Russia from the Gulf of Bothnia to the mouths of the Danube. Catherine the Great could have done no more,' Napoleon declared, growing hotter and hotter as he walked up and down the room, and repeated to Balashov almost the words he had used to Alexander himself at Tilsit. 'All that he would have owed to my friendship. Ah, what a fine reign! what a fine reign *might have been* that of the Emperor Alexander. Oh, what a grand reign,' he repeated several times. He stopped, took a gold snuff-box out of his pocket, and greedily put it to his nose.

He turned a commiserating glance on Balashov, and as soon as he would have made some observation, he hurriedly interrupted him again.

'What could he desire and look for that he would not have gained from my friendship? . . .' said Napoleon, shrugging his shoulders with an air of perplexity. 'No, he has thought better to surround himself with my enemies. And with whom?' he went on. 'He has gathered round him the Steins, the Armfeldts, the Bennigsens, the Wintzengerodes. Stein is a traitor, driven out of his own country; Armfeldt an intriguing debauchee; Wintzengerode a renegade French subject; Bennigsen is, indeed, rather more of a soldier than the rest, but still he's incompetent; he could do nothing in 1807, and I should have thought he must recall painful memories to the Emperor Alexander. . . . Even supposing he might make use of them if they were competent,' Napoleon went on, his words hardly able to keep pace with the rush of ideas that proved to him his right or his might (which to his mind meant the same), 'but they are not even that! They are no more use for war or for peace! Barclay, I'm told, is more capable than all of them, but I shouldn't say so, judging from his first manoeuvres. And what are they doing, what are all these courtiers doing? Pfuhl is making propositions, Armfeldt is quarrelling, Bennigsen is considering, while Barclay, who has been sent for to act, can come to no decision, and is wasting time and doing nothing. Bagration is the only one that is a real general. He is stupid, but he has experience, judgment, and determination. . . . And what part does your young Emperor play in this unseemly crowd? They compromise him and throw upon him the responsibility of all that happens. A sovereign ought not to be with the army except when he is a general,' he said, obviously uttering these words as a direct challenge to the Tsar. Napoleon knew how greatly Alexander desired to be a great general. 'It's a week now since the campaign commenced, and you haven't even succeeded in defending Vilna. You have been divided in two and driven out of the Polish provinces. Your army is discontented . . .'

'On the contrary, your Majesty,' said Balashov, who scarcely had time to recollect what had been said to him, and had difficulty in following these verbal fireworks, 'the troops are burning with eagerness . . .'

'I know all that,' Napoleon cut him short; 'I know all that, and I know the number of your battalions as exactly as I know my own. You have not two hundred thousand troops, while I have three times as many. I give you my word of honour,' said Napoleon, forgetting that his word of honour could carry no weight—'my word of honour that I have five hundred and thirty thousand men this side of the Vistula. The Turks will be no help to you; they are good for nothing, and have proved it by making peace with you. As for the Swedes, it's their destiny to be governed by mad kings. Their king was mad. They changed him for another Bernadotte, who promptly went mad; for no one not a madman could, being a Swede, ally himself with Russia.'

Napoleon laughed malignantly, and again put his snuff-box to his nose.

To each of Napoleon's phrases Balashov had a reply ready, and tried to utter it. He was continually making gestures indicative of a desire to speak, but Napoleon always interrupted him. To his remarks on the insanity of the Swedes, Balashov would have replied that Sweden was as good as an island with Russia to back her. But Napoleon shouted angrily to drown his voice. Napoleon was in that state of exasperation when a man wants to go on talking and talking simply to prove to himself that he is right. Balashov began to feel uncomfortable. As an envoy, he was anxious to keep up his dignity, and felt it essential to make some reply. But as a man he felt numb, repelled by the uncontrolled, irrational fury to which Napoleon abandoned himself. He knew that nothing Napoleon might say now had any significance and believed that he would himself on regaining his composure be ashamed of his words. Balashov remained standing, looking with downcast eyes at Napoleon's fat legs as they moved to and fro. He tried to avoid his eyes.

'And what are your allies to me?' said Napoleon. 'I have allies too—the Poles. There are eighty thousand of them and they fight like lions. And there will be two hundred thousand.'

He was probably still more exasperated at having told this obvious falsehood and at Balashov's standing mutely before him in that pose of resignation to his fate. He turned sharply round and going right up to Balashov, gesticulating rapidly and vigorously with his white hands close to his face, he almost shouted: 'Let me tell you, if you stir Prussia up against me, let me tell you, I'll wipe her off the map of Europe,' he said, his face pale and distorted with anger, as he smote one little hand vigorously against the other. 'Yes, I'll thrust you beyond the Dwina, beyond the Dnieper, and I'll restore the frontier that Europe was criminal and blind to let you overstep. Yes, that's what's in store for you, that's what you will gain by alienating me,' he said, and he walked in silence several times up and down the room, his thick shoulders twitching. He put the snuff-box in his waistcoat pocket, pulled it out again, held it several times to his nose, and stood still facing Balashov. He paused, looked sarcastically straight into Balashov's face and said in a low voice: 'And yet what a fine reign your master *might have had*.'

Balashov, feeling it incumbent upon him to reply, said Russia did not look at things in such a gloomy light. Napoleon was silent, still looking ironically at him and obviously not listening to him. Balashov said that in Russia the best results were hoped for from the war. Napoleon nodded condescendingly, as though to say, 'I know it's your duty to say that, but you don't believe in it yourself; you are convinced by me.' Towards the end of Balashov's speech, Napoleon pulled out his snuff-box again, took a sniff from it and tapped twice with his foot on the ground as a signal. The door opened, a gentleman-in-waiting, threading his way in respectfully, handed the Emperor his hat and gloves, another handed him a pocket-handkerchief. Napoleon, without bestowing a glance upon them, turned to Balashov.

'Assure the Emperor Alexander from me,' he said, taking his hat, 'that I am devoted to him as before; I know him thoroughly, and I prize very highly his noble qualities. I detain you no longer, general; you shall receive my letter to the Emperor.' And Napoleon walked rapidly to the door. There was a general stampede from the great reception-room down the staircase.

VII

AFTER all Napoleon had said to him, after those outbursts of wrath, and after the last frigidly uttered words, 'I will not detain you, general; you shall receive my letter,' Balashov felt certain that Napoleon would not care to see him again, would avoid indeed seeing again the envoy who had been treated by him with contumely, and had been the eyewitness of his undignified outburst of fury. But to his surprise Balashov received through Duroc an invitation to dine that day at the Emperor's table.

There were present at dinner, Bessières, Caulaincourt, and Berthier.

Napoleon met Balashov with a good-humoured and friendly air. He had not the slightest embarrassment or regret for his outbreak in the morning. On the contrary he seemed trying to encourage Balashov. It was evident that it had long been Napoleon's conviction that no possibility existed of his making mistakes. To his mind all he did was good, not because it was in harmony with any preconceived notion of good or bad, but simply because it was *he* who did it.

The Emperor was in excellent spirits after his ride about Vilna, greeted and followed with acclamations by crowds of the inhabitants. From every window in the streets through which he had passed draperies and flags with his monogram had been hanging, and Polish ladies had been waving handkerchiefs to welcome him.

At dinner he sat Balashov beside him, and addressed him affably. He addressed him indeed as though he regarded Balashov as one of his own courtiers, as one of the people, who would sympathise with his plans and be sure to rejoice at his successes. He talked, among other things, of Moscow, and began asking Balashov questions about the ancient Russian capital, not simply as a traveller of inquiring mind asks about a new place he intends to visit, but apparently with the conviction that Balashov as a Russian must be flattered at his interest in it.

'How many inhabitants are there in Moscow, how many horses? Is it true that Moscow is called the holy city? How many churches are there in Moscow?' he asked.

And when he was told there were over two hundred churches, he said:

'Why is there such a great number of churches?'

'The Russians are very religious,' replied Balashov.

'A great number, however, of monasteries and churches is always a sign of the backwardness of a people,' said Napoleon, looking at Caulaincourt for appreciation of this remark.

Balashov ventured respectfully to differ from the opinion of the French Emperor.

'Every country has its customs,' he observed.

'But there's nothing like that anywhere else in Europe,' said Napoleon.

'I beg your Majesty's pardon,' said Balashov; 'besides Russia, there is Spain, where there is also a great number of churches and monasteries.'

This reply of Balashov's, which suggested a covert allusion to the recent discomfiture of the French in Spain, was highly appreciated when Balashov repeated it at the court of the Emperor Alexander, though at the time at Napoleon's dinner-table it was very little appreciated and passed indeed unnoticed.

From the indifferent and perplexed faces of the marshals present it was obvious that they were puzzled to discover wherein lay the point of the retort, suggested by Balashov's intonation. 'If there were a point, we fail to catch it, or the remark was perhaps really pointless,' their expression seemed to say. So little effect had this retort that Napoleon indeed certainly saw nothing in it; and he naïvely asked Balashov through what towns the direct road from Vilna to Moscow passed. Balashov, who had been all dinner-time on his guard, replied that as, according to the proverb, every road leads to Rome, every road leads to Moscow; that there were very many roads, and among them was the road to *Poltava*, the one selected by Charles XII. Balashov could not help flushing with delight at the felicity of this reply. Balashov had hardly uttered the last word 'Poltava' when Caulaincourt began talking of the badness of the road from Petersburg to Moscow and his own Petersburg reminiscences.

After dinner they went to drink coffee into Napoleon's study, which had four days before been the study of the Emperor Alexander. Napoleon sat down, stirring his coffee in a Sèvres cup, and motioned Balashov to a seat beside him.

There is a well-known after-dinner mood which is more potent than any rational consideration in making a man satisfied with himself and disposed to regard every one as a friend. Napoleon was under the influence of this mood. He fancied himself surrounded by persons who adored him. He felt no doubt that Balashov too after his dinner was his friend and his worshipper. Napoleon addressed him with an amicable and rather ironical smile.

'This is the very room I am told in which the Emperor Alexander used to sit. Strange, isn't it, general?' he said, obviously without the slightest misgiving that this remark could be other than agreeable to the Russian, since it afforded a proof of his, Napoleon's, superiority over Alexander.

Balashov could make no reply to this, and he bowed in silence.

'Yes, four days ago, Wintzengerode and Stein were deliberating in this very room,' Napoleon continued, with the same confident and ironic smile. 'What I can't understand,' he said, 'is the Emperor Alexander's gathering round him all my personal enemies. That I do not understand. Didn't he consider that I might do the same?' he asked Balashov; and obviously the question brought him back to a reminiscence of the morning's anger, which was still fresh in him. 'And let him know that I will do so,' Napoleon said, getting up and pushing away his cup. 'I'll drive all his kith and kin out of Germany—the Würtembergs and Badens and Weimars... Yes, I'll drive them out. Let him get a refuge ready for them in Russia.'

Balashov bowed his head, with an air that indicated that he would be glad to withdraw, and was simply listening because he had no alternative but to listen to what was said to him. Napoleon did not notice this expression. He was addressing Balashov now, not as the envoy of his enemy, but as a man now quite devoted to him and certain to rejoice at the humiliation of his former master.

'And why has the Emperor Alexander taken the command of his troops? What's that for? War is my profession, but his work is to reign and not to command armies. What has induced him to take such a responsibility on himself?'

Napoleon again took his snuff-box, walked several times in silence up and down the room, and all at once surprised Balashov by coming close up to him. And with a faint smile, as confidently, rapidly, and swiftly, as though he were doing something that Balashov could not but regard as an honour and a pleasure, he put his hand up to the face of the Russian general of forty, and gave him a little pinch on the ear with a smile on his lips.

To have the ear pulled by the Emperor was regarded as the greatest honour and mark of favour at the French court.

'Well, you say nothing, admirer and courtier of the Emperor Alexander,' he said, as though it were comic that there should be in his presence a courtier and worshipper of any man other than him, Napoleon. 'Are the horses ready for the general?' he added, with a slight nod in acknowledgment of Balashov's bow. 'Give him mine; he has *a long way to go....*'

The letter taken back by Balashov was Napoleon's last letter to Alexander. Every detail of the conversation was transmitted to the Russian Emperor, and the war began.

VIII

AFTER his interview with Pierre in Moscow, Prince Andrey went away to Petersburg, telling his family that he had business there. In reality his object was to meet Anatole Kuragin there. He thought it necessary to meet him, but on inquiring for him when he reached Petersburg, he found he was no longer there. Pierre had let his brother-in-law know that Prince Andrey was on his track. Anatole Kuragin had promptly obtained a commission from the minister of war, and had gone to join the army in Moldavia. While in Petersburg Prince Andrey met Kutuzov, his old general, who was always friendly to him, and Kutuzov proposed that he should accompany him to Moldavia, where the old general was being sent to take command of the army. Prince Andrey received an appointment on the staff of the commander, and went to Turkey.

Prince Andrey did not think it proper to write to Kuragin to challenge him to a duel. He thought that a challenge coming from him, without any new pretext for a duel, would be compromising for the young Countess Rostov; and therefore he was seeking to encounter Kuragin in person in order to pick a quarrel with him that would serve as a pretext for a duel. But in the Turkish army too Prince Andrey failed to come across Kuragin. The latter had returned to Russia shortly after Prince Andrey reached the Turkish army. In a new country, amid new surroundings, Prince Andrey found life easier to bear. After his betrothed's betrayal of him, which he felt the more keenly, the more studiously he strove to conceal its effect on him from others, he found it hard to bear the conditions of life in which he had been happy, and felt still more irksome the freedom and independence he had once prized so highly. He could not now think the thoughts that had come to him for the first time on the field of Austerlitz, that he had loved to develop with Pierre, and that had enriched his solitude at Bogutcharovo, and later on in Switzerland and in Rome. Now he dreaded indeed those ideas that had then opened to him boundless vistas of light. Now he was occupied only with the most practical interests lying close at hand, and in no way associated with those old ideals. He clutched at these new interests the more eagerly the more the old ideals were hidden from him. It was as though the infinite, fathomless arch of heaven that had once stood over him had been suddenly transformed into a low, limited vault weighing upon him, with everything in it clear, but nothing eternal and mysterious.

Of the pursuits that presented themselves, military service was the simplest and the most familiar to him. He performed the duties of a general on duty on Kutuzov's staff with zeal and perseverance, surprising Kutuzov by his eagerness for work and his conscientiousness. When he missed Kuragin in Turkey, Prince Andrey did not feel it necessary to gallop back to Russia in search of him. Yet in spite of all his contempt for Kuragin, in spite of all the arguments by which he sought to persuade himself that Kuragin was not worth his stooping to quarrel with him, he knew that whatever length of time might elapse, when he did meet him, he would be unable to help challenging him, as a starving man cannot help rushing upon food. And the consciousness that the insult was not yet avenged, that his wrath had not been expended, but was still stored up in his heart, poisoned the artificial composure, which Prince Andrey succeeded in obtaining in Turkey in the guise of studiously busy and somewhat ambitious and vain energy.

In 1812, when the news of the war with Napoleon reached Bucharest (where Kutuzov had been fourteen months, spending days and nights together with his Wallachian mistress), Prince Andrey asked to be transferred to the western army. Kutuzov, who was by now sick of Bolkonsky's energy, and felt it a standing reproach to his sloth, was very ready to let him go, and gave him a commission for Barclay de Tolly.

Before joining the army of the west, which was in May encamped at Drissa, Prince Andrey went to Bleak Hills, which was directly in his road, only three versts from the Smolensk high-road. The last three years of Prince Andrey's life had been so full of vicissitudes, he had passed through such changes of thought and feeling, and seen such varied life (he had travelled both in the east and the west), that it struck him as strange and amazing to find at Bleak Hills life going on in precisely the same routine as ever. He rode up the avenue to the stone gates of the house, feeling as though it were the enchanted, sleeping castle. The same sedateness, the same cleanliness, the same silence reigned in the house; there was the same furniture, the same walls, the same sounds, the same smell, and the same timid faces, only a little older. Princess Marya was just the same timid, plain girl, no longer in her first youth, wasting the best years of her life in continual dread and suffering, and getting no benefit or happiness out of her existence. Mademoiselle Bourienne was just the same self-satisfied, coquettish girl, enjoying every moment of her life, and filled with the most joyous hopes for the future. She seemed only to have gained boldness, so Prince Andrey thought. The tutor he had brought back from Switzerland, Dessalle, was wearing a coat of Russian cut, and talked broken Russian to the servants, but he was just the same narrow-minded, cultivated, conscientious, pendantic preceptor. The only physical change apparent in the old prince was the loss of a tooth, that left a gap at the side of his mouth. In character he was the same as ever, only showing even more irritability and scepticism as to everything that happened in the world. Nikolushka was the only one who had changed: he had grown taller, and rosy, and had curly dark hair. When he was merry and laughing, he unconsciously lifted the upper lip of his pretty little mouth, just as his dead mother, the little princess, used to do. He was the only one not in bondage to the law of sameness that reigned in that spellbound sleeping castle. But though externally all was exactly as of old, the inner relations of all the persons concerned had changed since Prince Andrey had seen them last. The household was split up into two hostile camps, which held aloof from one another, and only now came together in his presence, abandoning their ordinary habits on his account. To one camp belonged the old prince, Mademoiselle Bourienne, and the architect; to the other—Princess Marya, Dessalle, Nikolushka, and all the nurses.

During his stay at Bleak Hills all the family dined together, but every one was ill at ease, and Prince Andrey felt that he was being treated as a guest for whom an exception was being made, and that his presence made all of them feel awkward. The first day Prince Andrey could not help being aware of this at dinner, and sat in silence. The old prince noticed his unnatural dumbness, and he, too, preserved a sullen silence, and immediately after dinner withdrew to his own room. Later in the evening when Prince Andrey went in to him, and began telling him about the campaign of the young Prince Kamensky to try and rouse him, the old prince, to his surprise, began talking about Princess Marya, grumbling at her superstitiousness, and her dislike of Mademoiselle Bourienne, who was, he said, the only person really attached to him.

The old prince declared that it was all Princess Marya's doing if he were ill; that she plagued and worried him on purpose, and that she was spoiling little Prince Nikolay by the way she petted him, and the silly tales she told him. The old prince knew very well that he tormented his daughter, and that her life was a very hard one. But he knew, too, that he could not help tormenting her, and considered that she deserved it. 'Why is it Andrey, who sees it, says nothing about his sister?' the old prince wondered. 'Why, does he suppose I'm a scoundrel or an old fool to be alienated from my daughter and friendly with this Frenchwoman for no good reason? He doesn't understand, and so I must explain it to him; he must hear what I have to say about it,' thought the old prince, and so he began to explain the reason why he could not put up with his daughter's unreasonable character.

'If you ask me,' said Prince Andrey, not looking at his father (it was the first time in his life that he had blamed his father), 'I did not wish to speak of it—but, if you ask me, I'll tell you my opinion frankly in regard to the whole matter. If there is any misunderstanding and estrangement between you and Masha, I can't blame her for it—I know how she loves and respects you. If you ask me,' Prince Andrey continued, losing his temper, as he very readily did in these latter days, 'I can only say one thing; if there are misunderstandings, the cause of them is that worthless woman, who is not fit to be my sister's companion.'

The old man stared for a moment at his son, and a forced smile revealed the loss of a tooth, to which Prince Andrey could not get accustomed, in his face.

'What companion, my dear fellow? Eh! So you've talked it over already! Eh?'

'Father, I had no wish to judge you,' said Prince Andrey, in a hard and spiteful tone, 'but you have provoked me, and I have said, and shall always say, that Marie is not to blame, but the people to blame—the person to blame—is that Frenchwoman...'

'Ah, he has passed judgment!... he has passed judgment!' said the old man, in a low voice, and Prince Andrey fancied, with embarrassment. But immediately after he leapt up and screamed, 'Go away, go away! Let me never set eyes on you again!...'

Prince Andrey would have set off at once, but Princess Marya begged him to stay one more day. During that day Prince Andrey did not see his father, who never left his room, and admitted no one to see him but Mademoiselle Bourienne and Tihon, from whom he inquired several times whether his son had gone. The following day before starting, Prince Andrey went to the part of the house where his son was to be found. The sturdy little boy, with curls like his mother's, sat on his knee. Prince Andrey began telling him the story of Bluebeard, but he sank into dreamy meditation before he had finished the story. He was not thinking of the pretty boy, his child, even while he held him on his knee; he was thinking of himself. He sought and was horrified not to find in himself either remorse for having provoked his father's anger, or regret at leaving home (for the first time in his life) on bad terms with him. What meant still more to him was that he could not detect in himself a trace of the tender affection he had once felt for his boy, and had hoped to revive in his heart, when he petted the child and put him on his knee.

'Come, tell me the rest,' said the boy. Prince Andrey took him off his knee without answering, and went out of the room.

As soon as Prince Andrey gave up his daily pursuits, especially to return to the old surroundings in which he had been when he was happy, weariness of life seized upon him as intensely as ever, and he made haste to escape from these memories, and to find some work to do as quickly as possible.

'Are you really going, Andrey?' his sister said to him.

'Thank God that I can go,' said Prince Andrey. 'I am very sorry you can't too.'

'What makes you say that?' said Princess Marya. 'How can you say that when you are going to this awful war, and he is so old? Mademoiselle Bourienne told me he keeps asking about you....' As soon as she spoke of that, her lips quivered, and tears began to fall. Prince Andrey turned away and began walking up and down the room.

'Ah, my God! my God!' he said. 'And to think what and who—what scum can be the cause of misery to people!' he said with a malignance that terrified Princess Marya.

She felt that when he uttered the word 'scum,' he was thinking not only of Mademoiselle Bourienne, who was the cause of her misery, but also of the man who had ruined his own happiness. 'Andrey, one thing I beg, I beseech of you,' she said, touching his elbow and looking at him with eyes that shone through her tears. 'I understand you.' (Princess Marya dropped her eyes.) 'Don't imagine that sorrow is the work of men. Men are His instruments.' She glanced upwards a little above Prince Andrey's head with the confident, accustomed glance with which one looks towards a familiar portrait. 'Sorrow is sent by Him, and not by men. Men are the instrument of His will, they are not to blame. If it seems to you that some one has wronged you—forget it, and forgive. We have no right to punish. And you will know the happiness of forgiveness.'

'If I were a woman, I would, Marie. That's a woman's virtue. But a man must not, and cannot, forgive and forget,' he said, and though till that minute he had not been thinking of Kuragin, all his unsatisfied revenge rose up again in his heart. 'If Marie is beginning to persuade me to forgive, it means that I ought long ago to have punished him,' he thought.

And making no further reply to Princess Marya, he began dreaming now of the happy moment of satisfied hate when he would meet Kuragin. He knew he was with the army.

Princess Marya besought her brother to stay another day, telling him how wretched her father would be, she knew, if Andrey went away without being reconciled to him. But Prince Andrey answered that he would probably soon be back from the army, that he would certainly write to his father, and that their quarrel would only be more embittered by his staying longer now. 'Remember that misfortunes come from God, and that men are never to blame,' were the last words he heard from his sister, as he said good-bye to her.

'So it must be so!' thought Prince Andrey, as he drove out of the avenue. 'She, poor innocent creature, is left to be victimised by an old man, who has outlived his wits. The old man feels he is wrong, but he can't help himself. My boy is growing up and enjoying life in which he will be deceived or deceiving like every one else. I am going to the army—what for? I don't know myself; and I want to meet that man whom I despise, so as to give him a chance to kill me and sneer at me!' All the conditions of life had been the same before, but before they had all seemed to him coherent, and now they had all fallen apart. Life seemed to Prince Andrey a series of senseless phenomena following one another without any connection.

IX

PRINCE ANDREY reached the headquarters of the army at the end of June. The first army, with which the Tsar was, was stationed in a fortified camp at Drissa. The second army was retreating, striving to effect a junction with the first army, from which—so it was said—it had been cut off by immense forces of the French. Every one was dissatisfied with the general course of events in the Russian army. But no one even dreamed of any danger of the Russian provinces being invaded, no one imagined the war could extend beyond the frontiers of the western Polish provinces.

Prince Andrey found Barclay de Tolly, to whom he was sent, on the bank of the Drissa. Since there was not one large village nor dwelling-place in the neighbourhood of the camp, the immense multitude of generals and courtiers accompanying the army were distributed about the neighbourhood for ten versts round in the best houses of the villages on both sides of the river. Barclay de Tolly was staying four versts away from the Tsar. He gave Bolkonsky a dry and frigid reception, and said in his German accent that he would mention him to the Tsar so that a definite appointment might be given him, and that meanwhile he begged him to remain on his staff. Anatole Kuragin, whom Prince Andrey had expected to find in the army, was not here. He was in Petersburg, and Bolkonsky was glad to hear it. He was absorbed in the interest of being at the centre of the immense war that was in progress, and he was relieved to be free for a time from the irritability produced in him by the idea of Kuragin. The first four days, during which he was not called upon to do anything, he spent in riding round the whole of the fortified camp, and by the aid of his experiences and his conversations with persons of greater experience he tried to form a definite idea about it. But the question whether such a camp were of use at all or not remained an open one in his mind. He had already, from his own military experience, formed the conviction that in war the most deeply meditated plans are of no avail (as he had seen at Austerlitz), that everything depends on how unexpected actions of the enemy, actions that cannot possibly be foreseen, are met; that all depends on how, and by whom, the battle is led. In order to settle this last question to his own satisfaction, Prince Andrey took advantage of his position and his acquaintances to try to get an insight into the character of the persons and parties who had a hand in the organisation of the army. This was the general idea he gained of the position of affairs.

While the Tsar had been at Vilna, the army had been divided into three. The first army was under the command of Barclay de Tolly, the second under the command of Bagration, and the third under the command of Tormasov. The Tsar was with the first army, but not in the capacity of commander-in-chief. In the proclamations, it was announced that the Tsar would be with the army, but it was not announced that he would take the command. Moreover, there was in attendance on the Tsar personally not a commander-in-chief's staff, but the staff of the imperial headquarters. The chief officer of the imperial staff was General-Quartermaster Volkonsky, and it contained generals, aides-de-camp, diplomatic officials, and an immense number of foreigners, but it was not a military staff. The Tsar had also in attendance on him in no definite capacity, Araktcheev, the late minister of war; Count Bennigsen, by seniority the first of the generals; the Tsarevitch, Konstantin Pavlovitch; Count Rumyantsev, the chancellor; Stein, the former Prussian minister; Armfeldt, the Swedish general; Pfuhl, the chief organiser of the plan of the campaign; Paulucci, a Sardinian refugee, who had been made a general-adjutant; Woltzogen; and many others. Though those personages had no definite posts in the army, yet, from their position, they had influence, and often the commander of a corps, or even one of the commanders-in-chief, did not know in what capacity Bennigsen or the Tsarevitch or Araktcheev or Prince Volkonsky addressed some advice or inquiry to him, and could not tell whether some command in the form of advice came directly from the person who got it or through him from the Tsar, and whether he ought or ought not to obey it. But all this formed simply the external aspect of the situation; the inner import of the presence of the Tsar and all these great personages was, from a courtier's point of view (and in the presence of a monarch all men become courtiers), plain to all. All grasped the fact that though the Tsar was not formally assuming the position of commander-in-chief, he did, in fact, hold the supreme control of all the armies in his hands, and the persons about him were his councillors. Araktcheev was a trusty administrator, a stern upholder of discipline, and careful of the safety of the Tsar. Bennigsen was a landholder in the neighbourhood, and seemed to feel it his function to entertain the Tsar there; while he was in reality, too, a good general, useful as an adviser, and useful to have in readiness to replace Barclay at any time. The Tsarevitch was there because he thought fit to be. The former Prussian minister, Stein, was there because his advice might be useful, and the Emperor Alexander had a high opinion of his personal qualities. Armfeldt was a bitter enemy of Napoleon, and had self-confidence, which never failed to have influence with Alexander. Paulucci was there because he was bold and decided in his utterances. The generals on the staff were there because they were always where the Emperor was; and the last and principal figure, Pfuhl, was there because he had created a plan of warfare against Napoleon, and having made Alexander believe in the consistency of this plan, was now conducting the plan of the whole campaign. Pfuhl was accompanied by Woltzogen, who put Pfuhl's ideas into a more easily comprehensible form than could be done by Pfuhl himself, who was a rigid theorist, with an implicit faith in his own views, and an absolute contempt for everything else.

The above-mentioned were the most prominent personages about the Tsar, and among them the foreigners were in the ascendant, and were every day making new and startling suggestions with the audacity characteristic of men who are acting in a sphere not their own. But, besides those, there were many more persons of secondary importance, who were with the army because their principals were there.

In this vast, brilliant, haughty, and uneasy world, among all these conflicting voices, Prince Andrey detected the following sharply opposed parties and differences of opinion.

The first party consisted of Pfuhl and his followers; military theorists, who believed in a science of war, having its invariable laws—laws of oblique movements, out-flanking, etc. Pfuhl and his adherents demanded that the army should retreat into the heart of the country in accordance with the exact principles laid down by their theory of war, and in every departure from this theory they saw nothing but barbarism, ignorance, or evil intention. To this party belonged Woltzogen, Wintzengerode, and others—principally Germans.

The second party was in direct opposition to the first. As is always the case where there is one extreme opinion, representatives had come forward of the opposite extreme. This party had urged an advance from Vilna into Poland regardless of all previous plans. This party, while advocating bold action, consisted of the representatives of nationalism, which made them even more one-sided in their views. They were Russians: Bagration, Yermolov, who was just beginning to make his mark, and some others. Yermolov's well-known joke was much quoted at the time—a supposed petition to the Tsar for promotion to be a 'German.' The members of this party, recalling Suvorov, maintained that what was wanted was not reasoning and sticking pins into maps, but fighting, beating the enemy, preventing the enemy from getting into Russia, and keeping up the spirits of the army.

To the third party, in which the Tsar was disposed to place most confidence, belonged the courtiers, who tried to effect a compromise between the two contending sides. The members of this party—to which Araktcheev belonged—were mostly not military men, and they spoke and reasoned as men usually do who have no convictions, but wish to pass for having them. They admitted that a war with such a genius as Bonaparte (they called him Bonaparte again now) did undoubtedly call for the profoundest tactical considerations and thorough scientific knowledge, and that on that side Pfuhl was a genius. But, at the same time, they acknowledged that it could not be denied that theorists were often one-sided, and so one should not put implicit confidence in them, but should listen too to what Pfuhl's opponents urged, and also to the views of practical men who had experience, and should take a middle course. They advocated maintaining the camp at Drissa on Pfuhl's plan, but altering his disposition of the other two armies. Though by this course of action neither aim could be attained, this seemed to the party of compromise the best line to adopt.

Of the fourth section of opinions, the most prominent representative was the Grand Duke, and heir-apparent, who could not get over his rude awakening at Austerlitz. He had ridden out at the head of his guards in helmet and cuirass as though to a review, expecting gallantly to rout the French, and finding himself unexpectedly just in the line of the enemy's fire, had with difficulty escaped in the general disorder. The members of this party had at once the merit and the defect of sincerity in their convictions. They feared Napoleon; they saw his strength and their own weakness, and frankly admitted it. They said: 'Nothing but a huge disgrace and ruin can come of the war! We have abandoned Vilna, and abandoned Vitebsk, and we are abandoning the Drissa too. The only sensible thing left for us to do is to conclude peace, and as soon as possible, before we have been driven out of Petersburg!'

This view was widely diffused in the higher military circles, and found adherents, too, in Petersburg—one of them being the chancellor Rumyantsev, who advocated peace on other political considerations.

A fifth section were the adherents of Barclay de Tolly, not so much from his qualities as a man, as a minister of war and commander-in-chief. 'Whatever he may be,' they always began, 'he is an honest, practical man, and there is nobody better. Let him have sole responsibility, since war can never be prosecuted successfully under divided authority, and he will show what he can do, as he did in Finland. We owe it simply to Barclay that our army is strong and well organised, and has retreated to the Drissa without disaster. If Barclay is replaced by Bennigsen now, everything will be lost; for Bennigsen has proved his incapacity already in 1807.' Such was the line of argument of the fifth party.

The sixth party, the partisans of Bennigsen, maintained on the contrary that there was after all no one more capable and experienced than Bennigsen, and that whatever else were done they would have to come back to him. They maintained that the whole Russian retreat to Drissa had been an uninterrupted series of shameful disasters and blunders. 'Let them blunder now if they will,' they said; 'the more blunders the better, at least it will teach them all the sooner that we can't go on like this. And we want none of your Barclays, but a man like Bennigsen, who showed what he was in 1807, so that Napoleon himself had to do him justice, and a man, too, is needed to whom all would readily intrust authority, and Bennigsen is the only such man.'

The seventh class were persons such as are always found in courts, and especially in the courts of young sovereigns, and were particularly plentiful in the suite of Alexander—generals and adjutants, who were passionately devoted to the Tsar, not merely as an emperor, but sincerely and disinterestedly adored him as a man, as Rostov had adored him in 1805, and saw in him every virtue and good quality of humanity. These persons, while they were ecstatic over the modesty of the Tsar in declining the chief command of the army, deplored that excess of modesty, and desired and urged one thing only, that their adored Tsar, conquering his excessive diffidence, would openly proclaim that he put himself at the head of the army, would gather the staff of the commander-in-chief about him, and, consulting experienced theorists and practical men where necessary, would himself lead his forces, who would be excited to the highest pitch of enthusiasm by this step.

The eighth and largest group, numbering ninety-nine to every one of the others, consisted of people who were eager neither for peace nor for war, neither for offensive operations nor defensive camps, neither at Drissa nor anywhere else; who did not take the side of Barclay, nor of the Tsar, nor of Pfuhl, nor of Bennigsen, but cared only for the one thing most essential—their own greatest gain and enjoyment. In the troubled waters of those cross-currents of intrigue, eddying about the Tsar's headquarters, success could be attained in very many ways that would have been inconceivable at other times. One courtier, with the single-hearted motive of retaining a lucrative position, would agree to-day, with Pfuhl, and tomorrow with his opponents, and the day after tomorrow would declare that he had no opinion on the subject in question, simply to avoid responsibility and to gratify the Tsar. Another, in the hope of bettering his position, would seek to attract the Tsar's attention by loudly clamouring a suggestion hinted at by the Tsar on the previous day, by quarrelling noisily at the council, striking himself on the chest and challenging opponents to a duel to prove his readiness to sacrifice himself for the common good. A third simply took advantage of the absence of enemies between two councils to beg a grant from the Single Assistance Fund for his faithful service, knowing there would be no time now for a refusal. A fourth took care to place himself where the Tsar might quite casually find him deeply engrossed in work. A fifth tried to reach the long-desired goal of his ambition—a dinner at the Tsar's table—by violently espousing one side or another and collecting more or less true and valid arguments in support of it.

All the members of this party were on the hunt after roubles, crosses, and promotions; and in that chase they simply followed the scent given them by the fluctuations of imperial favour. As soon as they saw the imperial weather-cock shifting to one quarter the whole swarm of these drones began buzzing away in that direction, making it more difficult for the Tsar to shift his course back again. In the uncertainty of the position, with the menace of serious danger, which gave a peculiarly intense character to everything, in this whirlpool of ambitions, of conflicting vanities, and views, and feelings, and different nationalities, this eighth and largest party, absorbed only in the pursuit of personal interests, greatly increased the complexity and confusion. Whatever question arose, the swarm of drones, still humming over the last subject, flew to the new one, and by their buzzing drowned and confused the voices of sincere disputants.

At the time when Prince Andrey reached the army yet another—a ninth party—was being formed out of all the rest, and was just making its voice heard. It consisted of sensible men of age and political experience, sharing none of the conflicting opinions, and able to take a general view of all that was being done at headquarters, and to consider means for escaping from the vagueness, uncertainty, confusion, and feebleness.

The members of this party thought and said that the whole evil was primarily due to the presence of the Tsar with his military court in the army; that it brought into the army that indefinite, conditional, and fluctuating uncertainty of relations which is in place in a court, but mischievous in an army; that it was for the Tsar to govern and not to lead his troops; that the only escape from the position was the departure of the Tsar and his court from the army; that the simple presence of the Tsar paralysed fifty thousand troops, which must be retained to secure his personal safety; that the worst commander-in-chief, acting independently, would be better than the best commander-in-chief with his hands tied by the presense and authority of the Tsar.

While Prince Andrey was staying, with nothing to do, at Drissa, Shishkov, the secretary of state, one of the leading representatives of this last group, wrote to the Tsar a letter to which Balashov and Araktcheev agreed to add their signatures. In this letter he took advantage of the Tsar's permitting him to offer his opinion on the general question, and respectfully suggested the sovereign's leaving the army, urging as a pretext for his doing so the absolute necessity of his presence to rouse public feeling in the capital.

To appeal to the people, and to rouse them in defence of their fatherland, was represented as urgently necessary to the Tsar, and was accepted by him as a sufficient reason for leaving. The outburst of patriotism that followed that appeal (so far indeed as it can be said to have been produced by the Tsar's visit to Moscow) was the principal cause of the subsequent triumph of Russia.

X

THIS letter had not yet been given to the Tsar, when Barclay, at dinner one day, informed Bolkonsky that his Majesty would be graciously pleased to see Prince Andrey in person, to ask him some questions about Turkey, and that Prince Andrey was to present himself at Bennigsen's quarters at six o'clock in the evening.

That day news had reached the Tsar's quarters of a fresh advance on Napoleon's part that might be regarded as menacing the army—news that turned out in the sequel to be false. And that morning Colonel Michaud had accompanieed the Tsar on a tour of inspection about the Drissa fortifications; and had tried to convince the Tsar that the fortified camp, constructed on Pfuhl's theory, and hitherto regarded as the *chef d'œuvre* of tactical science, destined to overthrow Napoleon—that that camp was a senseless absurdity that would lead to the destruction of the Russian army.

Prince Andrey arrived at Bennigsen's quarters, a small manor-house on the very bank of the river. Neither Bennigsen nor the Tsar were there; but Tchernishev, the Tsar's aide-de-camp, received Bolkonsky, and informed him that the Tsar had set off with General Bennigsen and Marchese Paulucci to make his second inspection that day of the fortifications of the Drissa camp, of the utility of which they were beginning to entertain grave doubts.

Tchernishev sat in the window of the outer room with a French novel. This room had once probably been the main hall; there was still an organ in it, on which were piled rugs of some sort, and in one corner of the room was a folding bedstead belonging to Bennigsen's adjutant. The owner of the bedstead, too, was there. Apparently exhausted by work or festivities, he sat dozing on the folded bed. Two doors led from the room: one straight in front opening into the drawing-room, another on the right opening into the study. From the first door came the sound of voices speaking German and occasionally French. In the drawing-room there was being held, by the Tsar's desire, not a military council —the Tsar loved to have things vague—but a meeting of a few persons, whose opinions he wished to hear in the present difficult position. It was not a military council, but a sort of council for the elucidation of certain questions for the benefit of the Tsar personally. To this sort of semi-council had been bidden the Swedish general, Armfeldt, the general on the staff Woltzogen, Wintzengerode (whom Napoleon had called a renegade French subject), Michaud, Toll, Count Stein—by no means a military man—and finally Pfuhl, who was, so Prince Andrey had heard, *la cheville ouvrière* of everything. Prince Andrey had the opportunity of getting a good view of him, as Pfuhl came in shortly after his arrival and stopped for a minute to say a few words to Tchernishev before going on into the drawing-room.

At the first glance Pfuhl, in his badly cut uniform of a Russian general, which looked out of keeping, like some fancy dress costume on him, seemed to Prince Andrey like a familiar figure, though he had never seen him before. He was of the same order as Weierother, and Mack, and Schmidt, and many other German generals, men of theory, whom Prince Andrey had seen in the war of 1808; but he was a more perfect type of the class than any of them. Such a typical German theorist, combining in himself all the characteristics of those other Germans, Prince Andrey had never seen before.

Pfuhl was short and very thin, but broad-boned, of a coarsely robust build, with broad hips and projecting shoulder-blades. His face was wrinkled; he had deep-set eyes; his hair had obviously been hastily brushed smooth in front, but stuck out behind in quaint wisps. Looking nervously and irritably about him, he walked in as though he were afraid of everything in the great room he had entered. With a clumsy gesture, holding his sword, he turned to Tchernishev, asking him where the Tsar was. He was unmistakably eager to get through the rooms, to get the bows and greetings over as quickly as possible, and to sit down to work at a map, where he would feel at home. He gave a hurried nod in response to Tchernishev's words, and smiled ironically on hearing that the Tsar was inspecting the fortifications that he, Pfuhl, had planned in accordance with his theory. He muttered something in the jerky bass, in which conceited Germans often speak, 'silly fool . . .' or 'damn the whole business . . .' or 'some idiocy's sure to come of that.' Prince Andrey did not catch his words, and would have passed on, but

Tchernishev introduced him to Pfuhl, observing that he had just come from Turkey, where the war had been so successfully concluded. Pfuhl barely glanced, not at, but across Prince Andrey, and commented, laughing: 'A model that war must have been of every principle of tactics!' And, laughing contemptuously, he went on into the room, from which the sound of voices came.

It was evident that Pfuhl—disposed at all times to be irritable and sarcastic—was that day particularly irritated at their having dared to inspect his camp and to criticise it without him. Thanks to his Austerlitz experiences, Prince Andrey could from this one brief interview form a clear idea of the man's character. Pfuhl was one of those hopelessly, immutably conceited men, ready to face martyrdom for their own ideas, conceited as only Germans can be, just because it is only a German's conceit that is based on an abstract idea—science, that is, the supposed possession of absolute truth. The Frenchman is conceited from supposing himself mentally and physically to be inordinately fascinating both to men and to women. An Englishman is conceited on the ground of being a citizen of the best-constituted state in the world, and also because he as an Englishman always knows what is the correct thing to do, and knows that everything that he, as an Englishman, does do is indisputably the correct thing. An Italian is conceited from being excitable and easily forgetting himself and other people. A Russian is conceited precisely because he knows nothing and cares to know nothing, since he does not believe it possible to know anything fully. A conceited German is the worst of them all, and the most hardened of all, and the most repulsive of all; for he imagines that he possesses the truth in a science of his own invention, which is to him absolute truth.

Pfuhl was evidently one of these men. He had a science—the theory of the oblique attack—which he had deduced from the wars of Frederick the Great; and everything he came across in more recent military history seemed to him imbecility, barbarism, crude struggles in which so many blunders were committed on both sides that those wars could not be called war at all. They had no place in his theory and could not be made a subject for science at all.

In 1806 Pfuhl had been one of those responsible for the plan of campaign that ended in Jena and Auerstadt. But in the failure of that war he did not see the slightest evidence of the weakness of his theory. On the contrary, the whole failure was to his thinking entirely due to the departures that had been made from his theory, and he used to say with his characteristic gleeful sarcasm: 'Didn't I always say the whole thing was going to the devil?' Pfuhl was one of those theorists who so love their theory that they lose sight of the object of the theory—its application to practice. His love for his theory led him to hate all practical considerations, and he would not hear of them. He positively rejoiced in failure, for failure, being due to some departure in practice from the purity of the abstract theory, only convinced him of the correctness of his theory.

He said a few words about the present war to Prince Andrey and Tchernishev with the expression of a man who knows beforehand that everything will go wrong, and is not, indeed, displeased at this being so. The uncombed wisps of hairs sticking out straight from his head behind, and the hurriedly brushed locks in front, seemed to suggest this with a peculiar eloquence.

He went on into the next room, and the querulous bass notes of his voice were at once audible there.

XI

PRINCE ANDREY had hardly seen the last of Pfuhl when Count Bennigsen came hurrying into the room, and bestowing a nod on Bolkonsky, went straight through to the study, giving some instruction to his adjutant. The Tsar was following him, and Bennigsen had hurried on to prepare something, and to be in readiness to meet him. Tchernishev and Prince Andrey went out into the porch. The Tsar, looking tired out, was dismounting from his horse. Marchese Paulucci was saying something to him. Turning his head to the left, the Tsar was listening with a look of displeasure to Paulucci, who was speaking with peculiar warmth. The Tsar moved, evidently anxious to end the conversation; but the Italian, flushed and excited, followed him, still talking, and oblivious of etiquette.

'As for the man who has counselled the camp at Drissa,' Paulucci was saying just as the Tsar, mounting the steps and noticing Prince Andrey, was looking more intently at his unfamiliar face. 'As for him, sire,' Paulucci persisted desperately, as though unable to restrain himself, 'I see no alternative but the madhouse or the gallows.'

Not attending, and appearing not to hear the Italian, the Tsar recognised Bolkonsky and addressed him graciously:

'I am very glad to see you. Go in where they are meeting and wait for me.'

The Tsar passed on into the study. He was followed by Prince Pyotr Mihalovitch Volkonsky and Baron Stein, and the study door was closed after them. Prince Andrey, taking advantage of the Tsar's permission to do so, accompanied Paulucci, whom he had met in Turkey, into the drawing-room where the council had assembled.

Prince Pyotr Mihalovitch Volkonsky was performing the duties of a sort of informal head of the Tsar's staff. Volkonsky came out of the study and bringing out maps laid them on the table, and mentioned the questions on which he wished to hear the opinion of the gentlemen present. The important fact was that news (which afterwards proved to be false) had been received in the night of movements of the French with the object of making a circuit round the camp at Drissa.

The first to begin speaking was General Armfeldt, who unexpectedly proposed, as a means of avoiding the present difficulty, a quite new project, inexplicable except as a proof of his desire to show that he, too, had a suggestion of his own. His idea was that the army should move into a position away from the Petersburg and Moscow roads, and, united there, await the enemy. It was evident that this project had been formed by Armfeldt long before, and that he brought it forward now not so much with the object of meeting the present problem, to which it presented no solution, as of seizing the opportunity of explaining its merits. It was one of the millions of suggestions which might be made, one as reasonable as another, so long as no one had any idea what form the war would take. Some of those present attacked his idea, others supported it. The young Colonel Toll criticised the Swedish general's project with more heat than any one; and in the course of his remarks upon it drew out of a side pocket a manuscript, which he asked leave to read aloud. In this somewhat diffuse note, Toll proposed another plan of campaign—entirely opposed to Armfeldt's, and also to Pfuhl's plan. Paulucci, in raising objections to Toll's scheme, proposed a plan of direct advance and attack, which he declared to be the only means of extricating us from our present precarious position, and from the trap (so he called the Drissa camp) in which we were placed. During all this discussion, Pfuhl and his interpreter Woltzogen (who was his mouthpiece in the court world) were silent. Pfuhl merely snorted contemptuously and turned his back to indicate that he would never stoop to reply to the rubbish he was hearing. But when Prince Volkonsky, who presided over the debate, called upon him to give his opinion, he simply said: 'Why ask me? General Armfeldt has proposed an excellent position with the rear exposed to the enemy. Or why not the attack suggested by this Italian gentleman? A fine idea! Or a retreat? Excellent, too. Why ask me?' said he. 'You all know better than I do, it appears.'

But when Volkonsky, frowning, said that it was in the Tsar's name that he asked his opinion, Pfuhl rose, and growing suddenly excited, began to speak:

'You have muddled and spoilt it all. You would all know better than

I, and now you come to me to ask how to set things right. There is nothing that needs setting right. The only thing is to carry out in exact detail the plan laid down by me,' he said, rapping his bony fingers on the table. 'Where's the difficulty? It's nonsense; child's play!' He went up to the map, and began talking rapidly, pointing with his wrinkled finger about the map, and proving that no sort of contingency could affect the adaptability of the Drissa camp to every emergency, that every chance had been foreseen, and that if the enemy actually did make a circuit round it, then the enemy would infallibly be annihilated.

Paulucci, who did not know German, began to ask him questions in French. Woltzogen came to the assistance of his leader, who spoke French very badly, and began translating his utterances, hardly able to keep pace with Pfuhl, who was proceeding at a great rate to prove that everything, not only what was happening, but everything that possibly could happen, had been provided for in his plan, and that if difficulties had arisen now, they were due simply to the failure to carry out that plan with perfect exactitude. He was continually giving vent to a sarcastic laugh as he went on proving, and at last scornfully abandoned all attempt to prove, his position, as a mathematician will refuse to establish by various different methods a problem he has once for all proved to be correctly solved. Woltzogen took his place, continuing to explain his views in French, and occasionally referring to Pfuhl himself: 'Is that not true, your excellency?' But Pfuhl, as a man in the heat of the fray will belabour those of his own side, shouted angrily at his own follower—at Woltzogen, too.

'To be sure, what is there to explain in that?'

Paulucci and Michaud fell simultaneously on Woltzogen in French. Armfeldt addressed Pfuhl himself in German. Toll was interpreting to Prince Volkonsky in Russian. Prince Andrey listened and watched them in silence.

Of all these men the one for whom Prince Andrey felt most sympathy was the exasperated, determined, insanely conceited Pfuhl. He was the only one of all the persons present who was unmistakably seeking nothing for himself, and harbouring no personal grudge against anybody else. He desired one thing only—the adoption of his plan, in accordance with the theory that was the fruit of years of toil. He was ludicrous; he was disagreeable with his sarcasm, but yet he roused an involuntary feeling of respect from his boundless devotion to an idea.

Apart from this, with the single exception of Pfuhl, every speech of every person present had one common feature, which Prince Andrey had not seen at the council of war in 1805—that was, a panic dread of the genius of Napoleon, a dread which was involuntarily betrayed in every utterance now, in spite of all efforts to conceal it. Anything was assumed possible for Napoleon; he was expected from every quarter at once, and to invoke his terrible name was enough for them to condemn each other's suggestions. Pfuhl alone seemed to look on him too, even Napoleon, as a barbarian, like every other opponent of his theory; and Pfuhl roused a feeling of pity, too, as well as respect, in Prince Andrey. From the tone with which the courtiers addressed him, from what Paulucci had ventured to say to the Tsar, and above all from a certain despairing expression in Pfuhl himself, it was clear that others knew, and he himself felt, that his downfall was at hand. And for all his conceit and his German grumpy irony, he was pitiful with his flattened locks on his forehead and his wisps of uncombed hair sticking out behind. Though he tried to conceal it under a semblance of anger and contempt, he was visibly in despair that the sole chance left him of testing his theory on a vast scale and proving its infallibility to the whole world was slipping away from him.

The debate lasted a long while, and the longer it continued the hotter it became, passing into clamour and personalities, and the less possible it was to draw any sort of general conclusion from what was uttered. Prince Andrey simply wondered at what they were all saying as he listened to the confusion of different tongues, and the propositions, the plans, the shouts, and the objections. The idea which had long ago and often occurred to him during the period of his active service, that there was and could be no sort of military science, and that therefore there could not be such a thing as military genius, seemed to him now to be an absolutely obvious truth. 'What theory and science can there be of a subject of which the conditions and circumstances are uncertain and can never be definitely known, in which the strength of the active forces engaged can be even less definitely measured? No one can, or possibly could, know the relative positions of our army and the enemy's in another twenty-four hours, and no one can gauge the force of this or the other detachment. Sometimes when there is no coward in front to cry, "We are cut off!" and to run, but a brave, spirited fellow leads the way, shouting "Hurrah!" a detachment of five thousand is as good as thirty thousand, as it was at Schöngraben, while at times fifty thousand will run from eight thousand, as they did at Austerlitz. How can there be a science of war in which, as in every practical matter, nothing can be definite, and everything depends on countless conditions, the influence of which becomes manifest all in a moment, and no one can know when that moment is coming. Armfeldt declares that our army is cut off, while Paulucci maintains that we have caught the French army between two fires; Michaud asserts that the defect of the Drissa camp is having the river in its rear, while Pfuhl protests that that is what constitutes its strength; Toll proposes one plan, Armfeldt suggests another; and all are good and all are bad, and the suitability of any proposition can only be seen at the moment of trial. And why do they all talk of military genius? Is a man to be called a genius because he knows when to order biscuits to be given out, and when to march his troops to the right and when to the left? He is only called a genius because of the glamour and authority with which the military are invested, and because masses of sycophants are always ready to flatter power, and to ascribe to it qualities quite alien to it. The best generals I have known are, on the contrary, stupid or absent-minded men. The best of them is Bagration—Napoleon himself admitted it. And Bonaparte himself! I remember his fatuous and limited face on the field of Austerlitz. A good general has no need of genius, nor of any great qualities; on the contrary, he is the better for the absence of the finest and highest of human qualities—love, poetry, tenderness, philosophic and inquiring doubt. He should be limited, firmly convinced that what he is doing is of great importance (or he would never have patience to go through with it), and only then will he be a gallant general. God forbid he should be humane, should feel love and compassion, should pause to think what is right and wrong. It is perfectly comprehensible that the theory of their genius should have been elaborated long, long ago, for the simple reason that they are the representatives of power. The credit of success in battle is not by right theirs; for victory or defeat depends in reality on the soldier in the ranks who first shouts "Hurrah!" or "We are lost!" And it is only in the ranks that one can serve with perfect conviction, that one is of use!'

Such were Prince Andrey's reflections as he heard the discussion going on around him, and he was only roused from his musing when Paulucci called to him and the meeting was breaking up.

Next day at the review the Tsar asked Prince Andrey where he desired to serve; and Bolkonsky ruined his chances for ever in the court world by asking to be sent to the front, instead of begging for a post in attendance on the Tsar's person.

XII

BEFORE the beginning of the campaign Rostov had received a letter from his parents, in which they informed him briefly of Natasha's illness and the breaking off of her engagement, and again begged him to retire from the army and come home to them. Natasha had, they explained, broken off the engagement by her own wish. On receiving this letter Nikolay did not even attempt to retire from the army or to obtain leave, but wrote to his parents that he was very sorry to hear of Natasha's illness and her rupture with her betrothed, and that he would do everything in his power to follow their wishes. To Sonya he wrote separately.

'Adored friend of my heart,' he wrote; 'nothing but honour could avail to keep me from returning to the country. But now, at the beginning of a campaign, I should feel myself dishonoured in my comrades' eyes, as well as my own, if I put my own happiness before my duty and my love for my country. But this shall be our last separation. Believe me, immediately after the war, if I be living and still loved by thee, I shall throw up everything and fly to thee to press thee for ever to my ardent breast.'

It was, in fact, only the outbreak of the war that detained Rostov and hindered him from returning home, as he had promised, and marrying Sonya. The autumn at Otradnoe with the hunting, and the winter with the Christmas festivities and Sonya's love had opened before his imagination a vista of peace and quiet country delights unknown to him before, and this prospect now lured him back. 'A charming wife, children, a good pack of hounds, ten to twelve leashes of swift harriers, the estate to look after, the neighbours, election to offices, perhaps, by the provincial nobility,' he mused. But now war was breaking out, and he had to remain with his regiment. And since this had to be, Nikolay Rostov was characteristically able to be content too with the life he led in the regiment, and to make that life a pleasant one.

On his return from his leave, Nikolay had been joyfully welcomed by his comrades and sent off for remounts. He succeeded in bringing back from Little Russia some first-rate horses that gave him great satisfaction, and won him the commendation of his superior officers. In his absence he had been promoted to be captain, and when the regiment was being made ready with reinforcements for active service, he was again put in command of his old squadron.

The campaign was beginning, pay was doubled, the regiment was reinforced with new officers, new men, and fresh horses, and had moved into Poland. The temper of eager cheerfulness, always common at the beginning of a war, was general in the army, and Rostov, fully conscious of his improved position in the regiment, gave himself up heart and soul to the pleasures and interests of the army, though he knew that sooner or later he would have to leave it.

The army had been compelled to retreat from Vilna owing to various complex considerations of state, of policy, and tactics. Every step of that retreat had been accompanied by a complicated play of interests, arguments, and passions at headquarters. For the hussars of the Pavlograd regiment, however, this whole march in the finest part of the summer, with ample supplies of provisions, was a most simple and agreeable business. Depression, uneasiness, and intrigue were possible only at headquarters; the rank and file of the army never even wondered where and why they were going. If the retreat was a subject of regret, it was simply owing to the necessity of leaving quarters one had grown used to or a pretty Polish hostess. If the idea did occur to any one that things were amiss, he tried, as a good soldier should, to put a cheerful face on it; and to keep his thoughts fixed on the duty that lay nearest, and not on the general progress of the war. At first they had been very pleasantly stationed near Vilna, where they made acquaintance with the Polish gentry of the neighbourhood, prepared for reviews, and were reviewed by the Tsar and various commanders of high authority. Then came the command to retreat to Sventsyany, and to destroy all the stores that could not be carried away. Sventsyany was memorable to the hussars simply as the *drunken camp*, the name given to the encampment there by the whole army, and as the scene of many complaints against the troops, who had taken advantage of orders to collect stores, and under the head of stores had carried off horses and carriages and carpets from the Polish landowners. Rostov remembered Sventsyany, because on the very day of his arrival there he had dismissed his quartermaster and did not know how to manage the men of his squadron, who had, without his knowledge, carried off five barrels of strong old ale and were all drunk. From Sventsyany they had fallen further back, and then further again, till they reached Drissa; and from Drissa they retreated again, till they were getting near the frontiers of Russia proper.

On the 13th of July the Pavlograd hussars took part in their first serious action.

On the previous evening there had been a violent storm of rain and hail. The summer of 1812 was remarkably stormy throughout.

The two Pavlograd squadrons were bivouacking in the midle of a field of rye, which was already in ear, but had been completely trodden down by the cattle and horses. The rain was falling in torrents, and Rostov was sitting with a young officer, Ilyin, a protégé of his, under a shanty, that had been hastily rigged up for them. An officer of their regiment, adorned with long moustaches, that hung down from his cheeks, was caught in the rain on his way back from visiting the staff, and he went into Rostov's shanty for shelter.

'I'm on my way from the staff, count. Have you heard of Raevsky's exploit?' And the officer proceeded to relate to them details of the Saltanov battle that had been told him at the staff.

Rostov smoked his pipe, and wriggled his neck, down which the water was trickling. He listened with little interest, looking from time to time at the young officer Ilyin, who was squatting beside him. Ilyin, a lad of sixteen, who had lately joined the regiment, took now with Nikolay the place Nikolay had taken seven years before with Denisov. Ilyin tried to imitate Rostov in everything and adored him, as a girl might have done.

The officer with the double moustaches, Zdrzhinsky, in a very high-flown manner, described the dyke at Saltanov as the Russian Thermopylae, and the heroic deed of General Raevsky on that dyke as worthy of antiquity. Zdrzhinsky told then how Raevsky had thrust his two sons forward on the dyke under a terrific fire, and had charged at their side. Rostov listened to the tale, and said nothing betokening sympathy with Zdrzhinsky's enthusiasm. He looked, indeed, as though ashamed of what he was told, but not intending to gainsay it. After Austerlitz and the campaign of 1807, Rostov knew from his own experience that men always lie when they describe deeds of battle, as he did himself indeed. He had had too sufficient experience to know that everything in battle happens utterly differently from our imagination and description of it. And so he did not like Zdrzhinsky's story, and did not, indeed, like Zdrzhinsky himself, who had, besides his unprepossessing moustaches, a habit of bending right over into the face of the person he was speaking to. He was in their way in the cramped little shanty. Rostov looked at him without speaking. 'In the first place, on the dyke they were charging there must have been such a crowd and confusion that, if Raevsky really thrust his sons forward, it would have had no effect except on the dozen men closest to him,' thought Rostov; 'the rest could not have even seen who were with Raevsky on the dyke. And those who did see it were not likely to be greatly affected by it, for what thought had they to spare for Raevsky's tender, parental feelings, when they had their own skins to think of saving? And besides the fate of the country did not depend on whether that dyke was taken or not, as we are told the fate of Greece did depend on Thermopylae. And then what was the object of such a sacrifice? Why do your own children a mischief in war? I wouldn't put Petya, my brother, in a place of danger; no, even Ilyin here, who's nothing to me but a good-natured lad, I would do my best to keep safe and sheltered,' Rostov mused, as he listened to Zdrzhinsky. But he did not give utterance to his thoughts, he had experience of that too. He knew that this tale redounded to the glory of our arms, and therefore one must appear not to doubt its truth: and he acted accordingly.

'I can't stand this, though,' said Ilyin, noticing that Rostov did not care for Zdrzhinsky's story; 'stockings and shirt, and all—I'm wet through. I'm going to look for shelter. I fancy the rain's not so heavy.' Ilyin ran out and Zdrzhinsky rode away.

Five minutes later Ilyin came splashing through the mud to the shanty.

'Hurrah! Rostov, make haste and come along. I have found an inn, two hundred paces or so from here; a lot of our fellows are there already. We can get dry anyway, and Marya Hendrihovna's there.'

Marya Hendrihovna was the wife of the regimental doctor; a pretty young German woman, whom he had married in Poland. Either from lack of means or disinclination to part from his young wife in the early days of their marriage, the doctor had brought her with him in the regiment, and his jealousy was a favourite subject for the jibes of the hussars.

Rostov flung on a cape, shouted to Lavrushka to follow them with their things, and went off with Ilyin, slipping in the mud, and splashing through the pools in the drizzling rain and the darkness, which was rent at intervals by distant lightning.

'Rostov, where are you?'

'Here. What a flash!' they called to one another as they went.

XIII

IN the inn, before which was standing the doctor's covered cart, there were already some half-dozen officers. Marya Hendrihovna, a plump, flaxen-headed little German in a dressing-jacket and nightcap, was sitting on a broad bench in the foremost corner. Her husband, the doctor, lay asleep behind her. Rostov and Ilyin entered the room, welcomed with merry shouts and laughter.

'I say! You are having a jolly time here!' said Rostov, laughing.

'And what are you yawning over?'

'Pretty figures you look! There's a perfect waterfall from them! Don't swamp our drawing-room.'

'Mind you don't spatter Marya Hendrihovna's dress,' chimed in voices.

Rostov and Ilyin made haste to look for a retreat where, without offence to the modesty of Marya Hendrihovna, they might change their wet clothes. They went behind a partition wall to change; but in the little recess were three officers, who completely filled it up. They were sitting playing cards by the light of a single candle on an empty box, and nothing would induce them to budge from their places. Marya Hendrihovna lent them her petticoat to be hung by way of a curtain; and screened by it, Rostov and Ilyin took off their wet things and put on dry clothes, with the aid of Lavrushka, who had brought their packages.

They made up a fire in the broken-down stove. They got hold of a board, propped it on two saddles, and covered it with a horse-cloth; then brought out a little samovar, a case of wine, and half a bottle of rum. All crowded round Marya Hendrihovna, begging her to preside. One offered her a clean handkerchief, to wipe her charming hands; another put his tunic under her little feet, to keep them from the damp floor; a third hung a cape over the window, to screen her from the draught; while a fourth brushed the flies off her husband's face, to prevent their waking him.

'Let him alone,' said Marya Hendrihovna, with a timid and happy smile; 'he will sleep well anyhow after being up all night.'

'Oh no, Marya Hendrihovna,' answered the officer, 'one must look after the doctor well! Anything may happen; and he will be kind to me, I dare say, when he has to cut off my leg or my arm.'

There were only three glasses; the water was so dirty that there was no telling whether the tea were strong or weak, and the samovar would only hold water enough for six glasses. But that made it all the more fun to take turns in order of seniority to receive a glass from the plump, short-nailed, and not over clean fingers of Marya Hendrihovna. All the officers seemed indeed to be genuinely in love for that evening with Marya Hendrihovna. Even the officers who had been playing cards behind the screen soon threw up their game, and gathered round the samovar, catching the general mood, and joining in the homage paid to Marya Hendrihovna. The latter, seeing herself surrounded by these spendid and devoted young men, beamed with delight, which she sought in vain to conceal, though she was unmistakably alarmed at every movement made by her husband, who was slumbering behind her. There was only one spoon; sugar there was in plenty, but it took so long for all to stir their glasses, that it was settled that Marya Hendrihovna must stir the sugar for each in turn. Rostov took his glass of tea, and adding rum to it, begged Marya Hendrihovna to stir it for him.

'But you take it without sugar?' she said, smiling all the while as though whatever she said or the others said had a quite different and very amusing meaning.

'I don't care about sugar, all I want is for you to stir it with your little hand.'

Marya Hendrihovna began looking for the spoon, which some one had pounced upon.

'Use your little finger, Marya Hendrihovna,' said Rostov; 'it will be all the sweeter.'

'It's hot,' said Marya Hendrihovna, blushing with pleasure.

Ilyin took the bucket of water, and pouring a few drops of rum in it, went up to Marya Hendrihovna, begging her to stir it with her finger.

'This is my cup,' he said. 'Only dip your finger in and I'll drink it all up.'

When the samovar was empty, Rostov took up the cards and proposed a game of 'Kings' with Marya Hendrihovna. They tossed to decide which was to have the lady for a partner. Rostov proposed as a rule of the game that the one who was 'king' should have the right to kiss Marya Hendrihovna's hand, and the one who was left knave should have to fetch another samovar for the doctor, when he waked.

'Well, but what if Marya Hendrihovna is king?' asked Ilyin.

'She is our queen already! And her commands are law.'

The game was just beginning when the doctor's dishevelled head popped up behind his wife. He had been awake for some time and listening to the conversation, and apparently he saw nothing agreeable, funny, or amusing in what was being said and done. His face looked depressed and weary. He did not greet the officers, but scratching himself, he asked them to move to let him pass. As soon as he had left the room, all the officers broke into loud peals of laughter, and Marya Hendrihovna blushed till the tears came, making her even more charming in the eyes of the officers. Coming in again from the yard, the doctor told his wife (who had lost her radiant smile, and looked at him in dismay in expectation of the sentence in store for her) that the rain was over and they must spend the night in their covered cart, or they would have all their things stolen.

'But I'll put an orderly on guard . . . two, indeed!' said Rostov. 'That's nonsense, doctor.'

'I'll be sentinel myself!' said Ilyin.

'No, gentlemen, you have had plenty of sleep, but I have been up those two nights,' said the doctor, and he sat gloomily by his wife's side, waiting for the end of the game.

Looking at the doctor's gloomy face and sidelong glances at his wife, the officers grew even more lively, and many of them could not suppress their laughter, for which they hastily sought presentable pretexts. When the doctor had led his wife away, and settled himself with her in their cart, the officers lay down in the inn, covering themselves with their wet overcoats. But for a long while they stayed awake, chatting, recalling the dismay of the doctor, and the delight of the doctor's wife, or running out on to the steps to report on what was going on in the cart. Several times Rostov muffled his head up and tried to go to sleep. But again some remark roused him, again a conversation sprang up, and again there were peals of causeless, merry, childish laughter.

XIV

IT was past two o'clock, no one was yet asleep, when the quartermaster appeared, bringing a command to advance upon a little place called Ostrovna. Still with the same chatter and laughter the officers began hurriedly getting ready; again the samovar was filled up with dirty water. But Rostov, without waiting for tea, went off to his squadron. It was already light; the rain had ceased, and the clouds were parting. It was chill and damp, especially in their still wet clothes. As they came out of the inn, in the twilight of the dawn, Rostov and Ilyin both glanced at the leather cover of the doctor's cart, still glistening from the rain. The doctor's feet were sticking out from under the cover, and in the middle of the cart they caught a glimpse of his wife's nightcap, and heard sleepy breathing.

'She's really very charming,' said Rostov to Ilyin.

'An exquisite woman!' responded Ilyin, with all the gravity of a boy of sixteen.

Half an hour later the squadron stood drawn up on the road. The word of command was heard, 'Mount!' and the soldiers crossed themselves and got on their horses. Rostov, riding ahead of them, gave the word: 'Forward!' and drawing out four abreast, the hussars started with a sound of subdued talk, splashing hoofs, and jingling sabres. They trotted along the broad high road, with birch-trees on each side of it, following the infantry and artillery, who had gone on before.

The broken, purplish-blue clouds, flushed red by the sunrise, were scudding before the wind. It grew lighter and lighter. They could see distinctly, still glistening from the rain, the feathery grass which always grows beside by-roads. The drooping branches of the birch-trees swayed in the wind, and dripped bright drops aslant across the road. The faces of the soldiers showed more and more distinctly. Rostov, with Ilyin, who would not drop behind, rode on one side of the road between the two rows of birch-trees.

On active service Rostov allowed himself the indulgence of riding a Cossack horse instead of the regimental horse, broken in for parade. He was a connoisseur and lover of horses, and had lately obtained a big sorrel horse with white tail and mane, a fine spirited beast of the Don breed, on whom he could out-gallop every one. It was an enjoyment to Rostov to ride this horse. He rode on, thinking of the horse, of the morning, of the doctor's wife, and never once giving a thought to the danger awaiting him.

In former days Rostov had felt fear when he was going into an engagement; now he had not the slightest feeling of fear. He had not lost his fears from growing used to being under fire (one can never get accustomed to danger) but from gaining control of his feelings in face of danger. He had schooled himself when going into action to think of anything except what one would have supposed to be more interesting than anything else—the danger in store for him. Earnestly as he strove to do this, and bitterly as he reproached himself for cowardice, he could not at first succeed in this. But with years it had come of itself. He rode now beside Ilyin, between the birch-trees, stripping leaves off the twigs that met his hand, sometimes touching his horse's side with his foot, handing the pipe he had finished to an hussar behind, without turning his head, all with as calm and careless an air as though he were out for a ride. He felt sorry to see the excited face of Ilyin, who talked a great deal nervously. He knew by experience the agonising state of anticipation of terror and of death, in which the cornet was plunged, and he knew that nothing but time could help him out of it.

As soon as the sun appeared in the clear strip of sky under the storm clouds, the wind sank, as though not daring to spoil the beauty of the summer morning after the storm; the trees still dripped, but the drops fell vertically now—and all was hushed. The sun rose completely above the horizon, and vanished in a long, narrow cloud that hung over it. A few minutes later the sun showed even more brightly on the upper side of the cloud, tearing its edge. Everything grew bright and shining. And with the bright light, as though in response to it, rang out shots in front of them.

Rostov had not time to collect his thoughts and decide how far off these shots were, when an adjutant of Count Osterman-Tolstoy galloped up from Vitebsk, bringing the order to advance at full speed along the road.

The squadron overtook and passed the infantry and the battery, who were also quickening their pace. Then the hussars raced downhill, passed through an empty and deserted village, and trotted uphill again. The horses were beginning to get in a lather and the men looked flushed.

'Halt! in line!' said the officer in command of the division. 'Left about face, walking pace!' sounded the command in advance.

And the hussars passed along the lines of the other troops to the left flank of the position, and halted behind our Uhlans, who formed the front line. On the right was a dense column of our infantry—they formed the reserves; on the hill above them, in the pure, clear air, in the brilliant, slanting, morning sunshine, could be seen our cannons on the very horizon line. In front, beyond a hollow dale, could be seen the enemy's columns and cannons. In the dale could be heard our advance pickets, already keeping up a lively interchange of shots with the enemy.

Rostov felt his spirits rise at those sounds, so long unheard, as though they had been the liveliest music. Trap-ta-ta-tap! rang out several shots, first together, then in rapid succession. All sank into silence again, and again there was a sound as of popping squibs.

The hussars remained for about an hour in the same spot. The cannons began firing. Count Osterman, with his suite behind the squadron, rode up; he stopped to say a word to the colonel of the regiment, and rode off to the cannons on the hill.

After Osterman had ridden away, the command rang out among the Uhlans 'Form in column; make ready to charge!' The infantry in front parted in two to let the cavalry pass through. The Uhlans galloped off, the streamers on their lances waving, and trotted downhill towards the French cavalry, who came into sight below on the left.

As soon as the Uhlans had started downhill, the hussars received the order to ride off uphill to cover the battery. Just as the hussars were moving into the place of the Uhlans, there came flying from the outposts some cannon-balls, hissing and whistling out of the distance, and hitting nothing.

This sound, which he had not heard for so long, had an even more inspiring and cheering effect on Rostov than the report of the muskets. Drawing himself up, he surveyed the field of battle, as it opened out before him riding uphill, and his whole heart went with the movements of the Uhlans. They were swooping down close upon the French dragoons; there was some confusion yonder in the smoke, and five minutes later the Uhlans were dashing back, not towards the spot where they had been posted, but more to the left. Between the ranks of Uhlans on the chestnut horses, and in a great mass behind them, could be seen blue French dragoons on grey horses.

XV

ROSTOV, with his keen sportsman's eye, was one of the first to descry these blue dragoons pursuing our Uhlans. Nearer and nearer flew the disordered crowds of the Uhlans and the French dragoons in pursuit of them. He could see now separate figures, looking small at the bottom of the hill, fighting, overtaking one another, and waving their arms and their swords.

Rostov gazed at what was passing before him as at a hunt. He felt instinctively that if he were to charge with his hussars on the French dragoons now, they could not stand their ground; but if he were to charge it must be that very minute or it would be too late. He looked round. The captain standing beside him had his eyes too fixed on the cavalry below.

'Andrey Sevastianitch,' said Rostov, 'we could close them in, surely . . .'

'And a smart job, too,' said the captain, 'and indeed . . .'

Rostov, without waiting for his answer, set spurs to his horse and galloped off in front of his squadron. Before he had time to give the command, the whole squadron, sharing his feeling, flew after him. Rostov himself could not have said how or why he did it. He did it all, as he did everything in a wolf hunt, without thinking or considering. He saw that the dragoons were near, that they were galloping in no order, he knew they could not stand their ground; he knew there was only one minute to act in, which would not return if he let it slip. The cannonballs were hissing and whistling so inspiritingly about him, his horse pulled so eagerly forward that he could not resist it. He spurred his horse, shouted the command, and the same instant flew full trot downhill towards the dragoons, hearing the tramp of his squadron behind him. As they dashed downhill, the trot insensibly passed into a gallop that became swifter and swifter, as they drew nearer their Uhlans and the French dragoons pursuing them. The dragoons were close now. The foremost, seeing the hussars, began turning back; the hindmost halted. With the same feeling with which he had dashed off to cut off the wolf's escape, Rostov, letting his Don horse go at his utmost speed, galloped to cut off the broken ranks of the dragoons. One Uhlan halted; another, on foot, flung himself to the ground to avoid being knocked down; a riderless horse was carried along with the hussars. Almost all the dragoons were galloping back. Rostov picked out one of them on a grey horse and flew after him. On the way he rode straight at a bush; his gallant horse cleared it; and Nikolay was hardly straight in the saddle again when he saw in a few seconds he would overtake the enemy he had pitched upon as his aim. The Frenchman, probably an officer from his uniform, sat crouched upon his grey horse, and urging it on with his sword. In another instant Rostov's horse dashed up against the grey horse's hindquarters, almost knocking it over, and at the same second Rostov, not knowing why he did so, raised his sword, and aimed a blow at the Frenchman.

The instant he did this all Rostov's eagerness suddenly vanished. The officer fell to the ground, not so much from the sword cut, for it had only just grazed his arm above the elbow, as from fright and the shock to his horse. As Rostov pulled his horse in, his eyes sought his foe to see what sort of man he had vanquished. The French officer was hopping along on the ground, with one foot caught in the stirrup. Screwing up his eyes, as though expecting another blow every instant, he glanced up at Rostov frowning with an expression of terror. His pale, mud-stained face—fair and young, with a dimple on the chin and clear blue eyes—was the most unwarlike, most good-natured face, more in place by a quiet fireside than on the field of battle. Before Rostov could make up his mind what to do with him, the officer shouted, 'I surrender.' He tried hurriedly and failed to extricate his foot from the stirrup, and still gazed with his frightened blue eyes at Rostov. The hussars, galloping up, freed his foot, and got him into his saddle. The hussars were busily engaged on all sides with the dragoons; one was wounded, but though his face was streaming with blood he would not let go of his horse; another put his arms round an hussar as he sat perched up behind on his horse; a third was clambering on to his horse, supported by an hussar. The French infantry were in front, firing as they ran. The hussars galloped hastily back with their prisoners. Rostov galloped back with the rest, conscious of some disagreeable sensation, a kind of ache at his heart. A glimpse of something vague and confused, of which he could not get a clear view, seemed to have come to him with the capture of that French officer and the blow he had dealt him.

Count Osterman-Tolstoy met the hussars on their return, summoned Rostov, thanked him and told him he would report his gallant action to the Tsar and would recommend him for the cross of St. George. When Rostov was called up to Count Osterman, bethinking himself that he had received no command to charge, he had no doubt that his commanding officer sent for him to reprimand him for this breach of discipline. Osterman's flattering words and promise of a reward, should, therefore, have been a pleasant surprise to Rostov; but he still suffered from that unpleasant vague feeling of moral nausea. 'Why, what on earth is it that's worrying me?' he wondered, as he rode away from the general. 'Ilyin? No, he's all right. Did I do anything disgraceful? No, that's not it either!' Something else fretted him like a remorse. 'Yes, yes, that officer with the dimple. And I remember clearly how my hand paused when I had lifted it.'

Rostov saw the prisoners being led away, and galloped after them to look at his Frenchman with the dimple in his chin. He was sitting in his strange uniform on one of the spare horses, looking uneasily about him.

The sword-cut in his arm could hardly be called a wound. He looked at Rostov with a constrained smile, and waved his hand by way of greeting. Rostov still felt the same discomfort and vague remorse.

All that day and the next Rostov's friends and comrades noticed that, without being exactly depressed or irritable, he was silent, dreamy, and preoccupied. He did not care to drink, tried to be alone, and seemed absorbed in thought. Rostov was still pondering on his brilliant exploit, which, to his amazement, had won him the St. George's Cross and made his reputation indeed for fearless gallantry. There was something he could not fathom in it. 'So they are even more frightened than we are,' he thought. 'Why, is this all that's meant by heroism? And did I do it for the sake of my country? And was he to blame with his dimple and his blue eyes? How frightened he was! He thought I was going to kill him. Why should I kill him? My hand trembled. And they have given me the St. George's Cross. I can't make it out, I can't make it out!'

But while Nikolay was worrying over these questions in his heart and unable to find any clear solution of the doubts that troubled him, the wheel of fortune was turning in his favour, as so often happens in the service. He was brought forward after the affair at Ostrovna, received the command of a battalion of hussars, and when an officer of dauntless courage was wanted he was picked out.

XVI

COUNTESS ROSTOV had not recovered her strength when she received the news of Natasha's illness. Weak as she still was, she set out at once for Moscow with Petya and the whole household, and the Rostovs moved from Marya Dmitryevna's into their own house, where the whole family were installed.

Natasha's illness was so serious that, luckily for herself and her parents, all thought of what had caused it, of her conduct and of the breaking off of her engagement, fell into the background. She was so ill that no one could consider how far she was to blame for all that had happened, while she could not eat nor sleep, was growing visibly thinner, coughed, and was, as the doctors gave them to understand, in actual danger. Nothing could be thought of but how to make her well again. Doctors came to see Natasha, both separately and in consultation. They said a great deal in French, in German, and in Latin. They criticised one another, and prescribed the most diverse remedies for all the diseases they were familiar with. But it never occurred to one of them to make the simple reflection that they could not understand the disease from which Natasha was suffering, as no single disease can be fully understood in a living person; for every living person has his individual peculiarities and always has his own peculiar, new, complex complaints unknown to medicine—not a disease of the lungs, of the kidneys, of the skin, of the heart, and so on, as described in medical books, but a disease that consists of one out of the innumerable combinations of ailments of those organs. This simple reflection can never occur to doctors (just as a sorcerer cannot entertain the idea that he is unable to work magic spells) because it is the work of their life to undertake the cure of disease, because it is for that that they are paid, and on that that they have wasted the best years of their life. And what is more, that reflection could not occur to the doctors because they saw that they unquestionably were of use; and they certainly were of use to all the Rostov household. They were of use, not because they made the patient swallow drugs, mostly injurious (the injury done by them was hardly perceptible because they were given in such small doses). They were of use, were needed, were indispensable in fact (for the same reason that there have always been, and always will be, reputed healers, witches, homoeopaths, and allopaths), because they satisfied the moral cravings of the patient and those who loved her. They satisfied that eternal human need of hope for relief, that need for sympathetic action that is felt in the presence of suffering, that need that is shown in its simplest form in the little child, who must have the place rubbed when it has hurt itself. The child is hurt, and runs at once to the arms of its mother or nurse for them to kiss or rub the tender spot, and it feels better for the kissing and rubbing. The child cannot believe that these stronger, cleverer creatures have not the power to relieve its pain. And the hope of relief and the expressions of sympathy as the mother rubs it comfort it. To Natasha the doctors took the place of the mother, kissing and rubbing her 'bobo,' when they declared that all the trouble would soon be over, if the coachman were to drive to the chemist's shop, in Arbasky Place, and buy—for a rouble and seventy kopecks—those powders and pills in a pretty little box, and if those powders were given to the patient in boiled water precisely every two hours, neither more nor less.

What would Sonya, and the count, and the countess have done, how could they have felt if they had taken no steps, if they had not had those pills at certain hours, and the warm beverage, and the chicken cutlets, and all the detailed régime laid down by the doctors, which gave occupation and consolation to all of them. How could the count have borne his dearly loved daughter's illness if he had not known that it was costing him a thousand roubles, and that he would not grudge thousands more, if that would do her any good; if he had not known that, in case she did not get better, he would spend thousands more on taking her abroad and consulting doctors there; if he had not been able to tell people how Metivier and Feller had failed to diagnose the complaint, but Friez had fathomed it, and Mudrov had succeeded even better in defining it? What would the countess have done if she had not sometimes been able to scold her sick Natasha for not following the doctor's orders quite faithfully?

'You can never get well like this,' she would say, finding a refuge from her grief in anger, 'if you won't listen to the doctors and take your medicine properly? We can't have any nonsense, when it may turn to pneumonia,' said the countess, and in pronouncing that—not to her only —mysterious word, she found great comfort. What would Sonya have done, had she not had the glad consciousness that at first she had not had her clothes off for three nights running, so as to be in readiness to carry out the doctor's orders, and that now she did not sleep at night for fear of missing the exact hour at which the innocuous pills were to be given out of the gilt pill-box? Even Natasha herself, though she did declare that no medicines could do her any good, and that it was all nonsense, was glad to see so many sacrifices being made for her, and glad to have to take medicines at certain hours. And she was even glad, indeed, to be able by her disregard of the doctor's prescription to show how little faith she put in them, and how little she cared for life.

The doctor came every day, felt her pulse, looked at her tongue, and made jokes, regardless of her dejected face. But then when he had gone into the next room, and the countess had hastily followed him, he assumed a serious face, and shaking his head gravely, said that though there was indeed danger, he had hopes from the effect of the most recent medicine, and that they could only wait and see; that the illness was more due to moral than physical causes, but . . . The countess slipped some gold into his hand, trying to conceal the action from herself and from him, and always went back to the sick-room with a lighter heart.

The symptoms of Natasha's illness were loss of appetite, sleeplessness, a cough, and continual depression. The doctors declared that she must have medical treatment, and therefore kept her in the stifling atmosphere of the town. And all the summer of 1812 the Rostovs did not visit the country.

In spite of the numerous little bottles and boxes of pills, drops, and powders, of which Madame Schoss, who had a passion for them, made a complete collection, in spite of the loss of the country life to which she was accustomed, youth gained the upper hand; Natasha's grief began to be covered up by the impressions of daily life; it ceased to lie like an aching load on her heart; it began to fade into the past; and Natasha began to return to physical health again.

XVII

NATASHA was calmer, but no happier. She did not merely shun every external form of amusement—balls, skating, concerts, and theatres—but she never even laughed without the sound of tears behind her laughter. She could not sing. As soon as she began to laugh or attempted to sing all by herself, tears choked her: tears of remorse; tears of regret for that time of pure happiness that could never return; tears of vexation that she should so wantonly have ruined her young life, that might have been so happy. Laughter and singing especially seemed to her like scoffing at her grief. She never even thought of desiring admiration; she had no impulse of vanity to restrain. She said and felt at that time that all men were no more to her than Nastasya Ivanovna, the buffoon. An inner sentinel seemed to guard against every sort of pleasure. And, indeed, she seemed to have lost all the old interests of her girlish, careless life, that had been so full of hope. Most often, and with most pining, she brooded over the memory of those autumn months, the hunting, the old uncle, and the Christmas holidays spent with Nikolay at Otradnoe. What would she not have given to bring back one single day of that time! But it was all over for ever. Her presentiment at the time had not deceived her, that such a time of freedom and readiness for every enjoyment would never come again. But yet she had to live.

It comforted her to think, not that she was better, as she had once fancied, but worse, far worse than any one, than any one in the whole world. But that meant little to her. She believed it; but then she asked: 'And what next?' And there was nothing to come. There was no gladness in life, but life was passing. All Natasha tried after was plainly to be no burden to others, and not to hinder other people's enjoyment; but for herself she wanted nothing. She held aloof from all the household. It was only with her brother, Petya, that she felt at ease. She liked being with him better than being with the rest, and sometimes even laughed when she was alone with him. She hardly left the house to go anywhere; and of the guests who came to the house she was only glad to see one person—Pierre. No one could have been more tender, circumspect, and at the same time serious, than Count Bezuhov in his manner to her. Natasha was unconsciously aware of this tenderness, and it was owing to it that she found more pleasure in his society. But she was not even grateful to him for it. Nothing good in him seemed to her due to an effort on Pierre's part. It seemed so natural to Pierre to be kind that there was no merit in his kindness. Sometimes Natasha noticed some confusion or awkwardness in Pierre in her presence, especially when he was trying to do something for her pleasure or afraid something in the conversation might suggest to her painful reminiscences. She observed this, and put it down to his general kindliness and shyness, which she supposed would be the same with every one else. Ever since those unforeseen words—that if he had been free, he would have asked on his knees for her hand and her love—uttered in a moment full of violent emotion for her, Pierre had said nothing of his feelings to Natasha; and it seemed to her clear that those words, which had so comforted her, had been uttered, just as one says any meaningless nonsense to console a weeping child. It was not because Pierre was a married man, but because Natasha felt between herself and him the force of that moral barrier—of the absence of which she had been so conscious with Kuragin—that the idea never occurred to her that her relations with Pierre might develop into love on her side, and still less on his, or even into that tender, self-conscious, romantic friendship between a man and a woman, of which she had known several instances.

Towards the end of St. Peter's fast, Agrafena Ivanovna Byelov, a country neighbour of the Rostovs, came to Moscow to pay her devotions to the saints there. She suggested to Natasha that she should prepare herself for the Sacrament, and Natasha caught eagerly at the suggestion. Although the doctors forbade her going out early in the morning, Natasha insisted on keeping the fast, and not simply as it was kept in the Rostovs' household, by taking part in three services in the house, but keeping it as Agrafena Ivanovna was doing, that is to say for a whole week, not missing a single early morning service, or litany, or vesper.

The countess was pleased at these signs of religious fervour in Natasha. After the poor results of medical treatment, at the bottom of her heart she hoped that prayer would do more for her than medicine; and though she concealed it from the doctors and had some inward misgivings, she fell in with Natasha's wishes, and intrusted her to Madame Byelov.

Agrafena Ivanovna went in to wake Natasha at three o'clock in the night, and frequently found her not asleep. Natasha was afraid of sleeping too late for the early morning service. Hurriedly washing, and in all humility putting on her shabbiest dress and old mantle, Natasha, shuddering at the chill air, went out into the deserted streets, in the limpid light of the early dawn. By the advice of Agrafena Ivanovna, Natasha did not attend the services of her own parish church, but went to a church where the priest was esteemed by the devout Madame Byelov as being of a particularly severe and exemplary life.

There were few people in the church. Natasha and Madame Byelov always took the same seat before an image of the Mother of God, carved at the back of the left choir; and a new feeling of humility before the great mystery came over Natasha, as at that unusual hour in the morning she gazed at the black outline of the Mother of God, with the light of the candles burning in front of it, and the morning light falling on it from the window. She listened to the words of the service, and tried to follow and understand them. When she did understand them, all the shades of her personal feeling blended with her prayer; when she did not understand, it was still sweeter for her to think that the desire to understand all was pride, that she could not comprehend all; that she had but to believe and give herself up to God, Who was, she felt, at those moments guiding her soul. She crossed herself, bowed to the ground, and when she did not follow, simply prayed to God to forgive her everything, everything, and to have mercy on her, in horror at her own vileness. The prayer into which she threw herself heart and soul was the prayer of repentance. On the way home in the early morning, when they met no one but masons going to their work, or porters cleaning the streets, and every one was asleep in the houses, Natasha had a new sense of the possibility of correcting herself of her sins and leading a new life of purity and happiness.

During the week she spent in this way, that feeling grew stronger with every day. And the joy of 'communication,' as Agrafena Ivanovna liked to call taking the Communion, seemed to her so great that she fancied she could not live till that blissful Sunday.

But the happy day did come. And when on that memorable Sunday Natasha returned from the Sacrament wearing a white muslin dress, for the first time for many months she felt at peace, and not oppressed by the life that lay before her.

The doctor came that day to see Natasha, and gave directions for the powders to be continued that he had begun prescribing a fortnight ago. 'She must certainly go on taking them morning and evening,' he said, with visible and simple-hearted satisfaction at the success of his treatment. 'Please, don't forget them. You may set your mind at rest, countess,' the doctor said playfully, as he deftly received the gold in the hollow of his palm. 'She will soon be singing and dancing again. The last medicine has done her great, great good. She is very much better.'

The countess looked at her finger-nails and spat, to avert the ill-omen of such words, as with a cheerful face she went back to the drawing-room.

XVIII

At the beginning of July the rumours as to the progress of the war current in Moscow became more and more alarming; and there was talk of the Tsar's appeal to the people, and the Tsar himself was said to be coming from the army to Moscow. And as up to the 11th of July the manifesto and appeal to the people had not been received, the most exaggerated reports about them and the position of Russia were common. It was said that the Tsar was coming away because the army was in danger; it was said that Smolensk had surrendered; that Napoleon had millions of troops, and that nothing short of a miracle could save Russia.

On Saturday, the 11th of July, the manifesto was received, but was not yet in print; and Pierre, who happened to be at the Rostovs', promised to come next day, Sunday, to dinner, and to bring the manifesto, which he could obtain from Count Rastoptchin.

That Sunday the Rostovs attended service as usual in the private chapel of the Razumovskys. It was a hot July day. Even by ten o'clock, when the Rostovs got out of their carriage before the chapel, the sultry air, the shouts of the street hawkers, the gay, light summer dresses of the crowd, the dusty leaves of the trees on the boulevard, the martial music and white trousers of the battalion marching by to parade, the rattle of the pavements, and the brilliant, hot sunshine, were all full of that summer languor, that content and discontent with the present, which is felt particularly vividly on a bright, hot day in town. All the fashionable world of Moscow, all the Rostovs' acquaintances were in the chapel. A great number of wealthy families, who usually spent the summer in the country, were staying on in Moscow that year, as though in vague anticipation of something.

As Natasha walked beside her mother, behind a footman in livery, who made way for them through the crowd, she heard the voice of some young man speaking in too loud a whisper about her:

'That's the young Countess Rostov, the very girl!'

'She's ever so much thinner, but still pretty!' she caught, and fancied that the names of Kuragin and Bolkonsky were mentioned. But that was always happening. She was always fancying that any one who looked at her could be thinking of nothing but what happened to her. With a sinking heart, wretched as she always was now in a crowd, Natasha, in her lilac silk dress, trimmed with black lace, walked on, as only women know how to do, with an air of ease and dignity all the greater for the pain and shame in her heart. She knew for a fact that she was pretty, but that did not give her pleasure now, as once it had. On the contrary, it had been a source of more misery than anything of late, and especially so on this bright, hot summer day in town. 'Another Sunday, another week,' she said to herself, recalling how she had been here on that memorable Sunday; 'and still the same life that is no life, and still the same circumstances in which life used to seem so easy once. Young and pretty, and I know that now I am good, and before I was wicked! But now I am good,' she mused, 'but yet the best years, the best of my life, are all being wasted, and no good to any one.' She stood by her mother's side, and nodded to the acquaintances who were standing near. From force of habit Natasha scrutinised the dresses of the ladies, and criticised the *tenue* of a lady standing near her, and the awkward and cramped way in which she was crossing herself. Then she thought with vexation that she was herself being criticised again, and was criticising others; and at the first sounds of the service she was horrified at her sinfulness, horrified that her purity of heart should be lost again.

A handsome, clean-looking old priest read the service with the mild solemnity that has such an elevating and soothing effect on the souls of those who pray. The sanctuary doors were closed, the curtain was slowly drawn, and a voice, mysteriously subdued, uttered some word from it. Tears, that she could not herself have explained, rose to Natasha's eyes, and a feeling of joyful agitation came upon her.

'Teach me what to do, how to live my life, how to conquer my sins for ever, for ever!' . . . she prayed. The deacon came out to the steps before the altar screen; with his thumb held out apart from the rest, he pulled his long hair out from under his surplice, and laying the cross on his breast, he began in a loud voice solemnly reading the prayer:

'As one community let us pray to the Lord.'

'As one community, all together without distinction of class, free from enmity, all united in brotherly love, let us pray,' thought Natasha.

'For the world above and the salvation of our souls!'

'For the world of angels and the souls of all spiritual beings who live above us,' prayed Natasha.

When they prayed for the army, she thought of her brother and Denisov. When they prayed for all travelling by sea and by land, she thought of Prince Andrey, and prayed for him, and prayed that God would forgive her the wrong she had done him. When they prayed for all who love us, she prayed for all her family, her father and mother, and Sonya —for the first time feeling all the shortcomings in her behaviour to them, and all the strength of her own love for them. When they prayed for those who hate us, she tried to think of enemies, to pray for them. She reckoned as enemies all her father's creditors, and every one who had business relations with him; and always at the thought of enemies who hated her she thought of Anatole, who had done her so cruel an injury, and though he had not hated her, she prayed gladly for him, as an enemy. It was only at her prayers that she felt able to think calmly and clearly either of Prince Andrey or of Anatole, with a sense that her feelings for them were as nothing compared with her feeling of worship and awe of God. When they prayed for the Imperial family and the Synod, she bowed and crossed herself more devoutly than ever, telling herself that if she did not comprehend, she could not doubt, and anyway loved the Holy Synod and prayed for it.

When the litany was over, the deacon crossed his stole over his breast and pronounced:

'Ourselves and our life we offer up to Christ the Lord!'

'Ourselves we offer up to God,' Natasha repeated in her heart. 'My God, I give myself unto Thy keeping!' she thought. 'I ask for nothing, I desire nothing; teach me how to act, how to do Thy will! Yes, take me; take me to Thee!' Natasha said, with devout impatience in her heart. She did not cross herself, but stood with her thin arms hanging down, as though in expectation every moment that an unseen force would come and carry her off and rescue her from herself, from her regrets and desires and remorse and hopes and sins.

Several times during the service the countess looked round at her daughter's devout face and shining eyes, and prayed to God to help her.

To the general surprise, in the middle of the service, which Natasha knew so well, the deacon brought forward the little bench, from which they repeated the prayers, kneeling, on Trinity Day, and set it before the sanctuary doors. The priest advanced in his lilac velvet calotte, threw back his hair, and, with an effort, dropped on his knees. All the congregation did the same, looking at one another in surprise. There followed the prayer, which had just been received from the Synod, the prayer for the delivery of Russia out of the hands of the enemy.

'Lord God of our might, God of our salvation,' began the priest in that clear, mild, unemphatic voice, that is only used by the Slavonic priesthood, and has such an indescribable effect on the Russian heart.

'Lord God of might, God of our salvation! Look in grace and blessing on Thy humble people, and hear with loving kindness, and spare and have mercy on us. The foe is confounding Thy land, and is fain to rise up against all the earth and lay it waste. These lawless men are gathered together to overwhelm Thy kingdom, to destroy Thy holy Jerusalem, Thy beloved Russia: to defile Thy temples, to overturn the altars and violate our holy shrines. How long, O Lord, how long shall the wicked prevail? How long shall they wreak their sinful will?

'Almighty God! Hear us when we pray to Thee, strengthen with Thy might our most gracious and supreme sovereign, Emperor Alexander Pavlovitch. Be mindful of his truth and mercy, recompense him according to his good deeds, and let them preserve Thy chosen Israel. Bless his counsels, his undertakings, and his deeds; fortify his kingdom with Thy Almighty hand, and vouchsafe him victory over the enemy, even as Thou gavest Moses victory over Amalek, and Gideon over Midian, and David over Goliath. Preserve his army; put weapons of brass in the hands that wage war in Thy name, and gird them about with strength for the battle. Take Thou the lance and shield, and rise up to succour us, and put to shame and to confusion them that devise evil against us, and let them be scattered before the face of Thy faithful armament like dust before the wind; and may Thy mighty angel put them to flight and to confusion. And let the net ensnare them when they wot not of it, and their plots that they have hatched in secret be turned against them. And let them be laid low before the feet of Thy servants and vanquished by our hosts. Lord! it is nought for Thee to save both great and small. Thou art God, and man can do nought against Thee!

'God of our Fathers! Remember Thy mercy and loving-kindness, that are everlasting. Turn not Thy face away from us; be gracious to our unworthiness; but in the greatness of Thy mercy and the infinity of Thy goodness, overlook our transgressions and our iniquities. Purify our hearts, and renew the true spirit within us; strengthen us all by faith in Thee; fortify us with hope; breathe into us true love for one another; arm us with unity of spirit in the righteous defence of the heritage Thou hast given us and our fathers; and let not the sceptre of the unrighteous be exalted above the destinies of Thy holy people.

'O Lord our God, in Whom we believe, and in Whom we put our trust, let us not be confounded in our faith in Thy mercy, and give us a sign for our blessing that they that hate us and our holy faith may see it and be put to shame and confusion, and that all lands may know that the Lord is Thy Name, and we are Thy people. Show Thy mercy upon us this day, O Lord, and grant us Thy salvation. Rejoice the hearts of Thy servants with Thy mercy; strike down our enemies and trample them swiftly under the feet of Thy faithful. Thou art the defence, the succour, and the victory of them that put their trust in Thee; and to Thee be the glory, to Father, and to Son, and to Holy Ghost, now and ever has been, for ever and ever. Amen!'

In Natasha's religiously impressionable state, this prayer affected her strongly. She heard every word about Moses's victory over Amalek, and Gideon's over Midian, and David's over Goliath, and about the destruction of Thy Jerusalem; and she prayed to God with all the tenderness and fervour with which her heart was overflowing, but she had no distinct idea what she was asking for in this prayer. With all her soul she joined in the petition for the true spirit, for the strengthening of hearts with faith and hope, and the breathing into them of love. But she could not pray for the trampling of her enemies underfoot, when she had only a few minutes before been wishing she had more of them to forgive and pray for. But yet she could have no doubts of the righteousness of this prayer that had been read by the priest on his knees. She felt in her heart a thrill of awe and horror at the punishment in store for men's sins, and especially for her sins, and prayed to God to forgive them all, and her too, and give them all and her peace and happiness. And it seemed to her that God heard her prayer.

XIX

EVER since the day when Pierre had looked up at the comet in the sky, on his way home from the Rostovs', and recalling Natasha's grateful look, had felt as though some new vista was opening before him, the haunting problem of the vanity and senselessness of all things earthly had ceased to torment him. That terrible question: Why? what for? which had till then haunted him in the midst of every occupation, was not now replaced by any other question, nor by an answer to the old question; its place was filled by the image of *her*. If he heard or talked of trivialities, or read or was told of some instance of human baseness or folly, he was not cast down as of old; he did not ask himself why people troubled, when all was so brief and uncertain. But he thought of her as he had seen her last, and all his doubts vanished; not because she had answered the questions that haunted him, but because her image lifted him instantly into another bright realm of spiritual activity, in which there could be neither right nor wrong, into a region of beauty and love, which was worth living for. Whatever infamy he thought of, he said to himself, 'Well, let so and so rob the state and the Tsar, while the state and the Tsar heap honours on him; but she smiled at me yesterday, and begged me to come, and I love her, and nobody will ever know it,' he thought.

Pierre still went into society, drank as much, and led the same idle and aimless life, because, apart from the hours he spent at the Rostovs', he had to get through the rest of his time somehow, and the habits and the acquaintances he had made in Moscow drew him irresistibly into the same life. But of late, since the reports from the seat of war had become more and more disquieting, and Natasha's health had improved, and she had ceased to call for the same tender pity, he had begun to be more and more possessed by a restlessness that he could not explain. He felt that the position he was in could not go on for long, that a catastrophe was coming that would change the whole course of his life, and he sought impatiently for signs of this impending catastrophe. One of his brother masons had revealed to Pierre the following prophecy relating to Napoleon, and taken from the Apocalypse of St. John.

In the Apocalypse, chapter thirteen, verse seventeen, it is written: 'Here is wisdom; let him that hath understanding, count the number of the beast; for it is the number of a man, and his number is six hundred threescore and six.'

And in the fifth verse of the same chapter: 'And there was given unto him a mouth speaking great things and blasphemies, and power was given unto him to continue forty and two months.'

If the French alphabet is treated like the Hebrew system of enumeration, by which the first ten letters represent the units, and the next the tens, and so on, the letters have the following value:

a b c d e f g h i k l m n o p q r s t u v w x y z
1 2 3 4 5 6 7 8 9 10 20 30 40 50 60 70 80 90 100 110 120 130 140 150 160

Turning out the words *l'empereur Napoléon* into ciphers on this system, it happens that the sum of these numbers equals 666, and Napoleon is thereby seen to be the beast prophesied in the Apocalypse. Moreover, working out in the same way the words *quarante-deux*, that is the term for which the beast was permitted to continue, the sum of these numbers again equals 666, from which it is deduced that the term of Napoleon's power had come in 1812, when the French Emperor reached his forty-second year. This prophecy made a great impression on Pierre. He frequently asked himself what would put an end to the power of the beast, that is, of Napoleon; and he tried by the same system of turning letters into figures, and reckoning them up to find an answer to this question. He wrote down as an answer, *l'empereur Alexandre? La nation russe?* He reckoned out the figures, but their sum was far more or less than 666. Once he wrote down his own name 'Counte Pierre Bezuhov,' but the sum of the figure was far from being right. He changed the spelling, putting s for z, added 'de,' added the article 'le,' and still could not obtain the desired result. Then it occurred to him that if the answer sought for were to be found in his name, his nationality ought surely to find a place in it too. He tried *Le russe Besuhof*, and adding up the figure made the sum 671. This was only five too much; the 5 was denoted by the letter 'e,' the letter dropped in the article in the expression *l'empereur Napoléon*. Dropping the 'e' in a similar way, though of course incorrectly, Pierre obtained the answer he sought in *L'russe Besuhof*, the letters of which on that system added up to 666. This discovery greatly excited him. How, by what connection, he was associated with the great event foretold in the Apocalypse, he could not tell. But he did not for a moment doubt of that connection. His love for Natasha, Antichrist, Napoleon's invasion, the comet, the number 666, *l'empereur Napoléon*, and *l'russe Besuhof*—all he thought were to develop, and come to some crisis together to extricate him from that spellbound, trivial round of Moscow habits, to which he felt himself in bondage, and to lead him to some great achievement and great happiness.

The day before that Sunday on which the new prayer had been read in the churches, Pierre had promised the Rostovs to call on Count Rastoptchin, whom he knew well, and to get from him the Tsar's appeal to the country, and the last news from the army. On going to Count Rastoptchin's in the morning, Pierre found there a special courier, who had only just arrived from the army. The courier was a man whom Pierre knew, and often saw at the Moscow balls.

'For mercy's sake, couldn't you relieve me of some of my burden,' said the courier; 'I have a sack full of letters to parents.'

Among these letters was a letter from Nikolay Rostov to his father. Pierre took that; and Count Rastoptchin gave him a copy of the Tsar's appeal to Moscow, which had just been printed, the last announcements in the army, and his own last placard. Looking through the army announcements, Pierre found in one of them, among lists of wounded, killed and promoted, the name of Nikolay Rostov, rewarded with the order of St. George, of the fourth degree, for distinguished bravery in the Ostrovna affair, and in the same announcement the appointment of Prince Andrey Bolkonsky to the command of a regiment of light cavalry. Though he did not want to remind the Rostovs of Bolkonsky's existence, Pierre could not resist the inclination to rejoice their hearts with the news of their son's decoration. Keeping the Tsar's appeal, Rastoptchin's placard, and the other announcement to bring with him at dinner-time, Pierre sent the printed announcement and Nikolay's letter to the Rostovs.

The conversation with Rastoptchin, and his tone of anxiety and hurry, the meeting with the courier, who had casually alluded to the disastrous state of affairs in the army, the rumours of spies being caught in Moscow, of a sheet circulating in the town stating that Napoleon had sworn to be in both capitals before autumn, of the Tsar's expected arrival next day—all combined to revive in Pierre with fresh intensity that feeling of excitement and expectation, that he had been conscious of ever since the appearance of the comet, and with even greater force since the beginning of the war.

The idea of entering the army had long before occurred to Pierre, and he would have acted upon it, but that, in the first place, he was pledged by his vow to the Masonic brotherhood, which preached universal peace and the abolition of war; and secondly, when he looked at the great mass of Moscow gentlemen, who put on uniforms, and professed themselves patriots, he felt somehow ashamed to take the same step. A cause that weighed with him even more in not entering the army was the obscure conception that he, *l'russe Besuhof*, had somehow the mystic value of the number of the beast, 666, that his share in putting a limit to the power of the beast, 'speaking great things and blasphemies,' had been ordained from all eternity, and that therefore it was not for him to take any step whatever; it was for him to wait for what was bound to come to pass.

XX

A FEW intimate friends were, as usual on Sundays, dining with the Rostovs.

Pierre came early, hoping to find them alone.

Pierre had that year grown so stout, that he would have been grotesque, had he not been so tall, so broad-shouldered, and so powerfully built that he carried off his bulky proportions with evident ease.

Puffing, and muttering something to himself, he went up the stairs. His coachman did not even ask whether he should wait. He knew that when the count was at the Rostovs', it was till midnight. The Rostovs' footmen ran with eager welcome to take off his cloak, and take his stick and hat. From the habit of the club, Pierre always left his stick and hat in the vestibule.

The first person he saw at the Rostovs' was Natasha. Before he saw her, while taking off his cloak, he heard her. She was practising her sol-fa exercises in the hall. He knew she had given up singing since her illness, and so he was surprised and delighted at the sound of her voice. He opened the door softly, and saw Natasha, in the lilac dress she had worn at the service, walking up and down the room singing.

She had her back turned to him as he opened the door; but when she turned sharply round and saw his broad, surprised face, she flushed and ran quickly up to him.

'I want to try and sing again,' she said. 'It's something to do, any way,' she added as though in excuse.

'Quite right too!'

'How glad I am you have come! I'm so happy today,' she said with the old eagerness that Pierre had not seen for so long. 'You know, Nikolenka has got the St. George's cross. I'm so proud of him.'

'Of course, I sent you the announcement. Well, I won't interrupt you,' he added, and would have gone on to the drawing-room.

Natasha stopped him.

'Count, is it wrong of me to sing?' she said, blushing, but still keeping her eyes fixed inquiringly on Pierre.

'No.... Why should it be? On the contrary.... But why do you ask me?'

'I don't know myself,' Natasha answered quickly; 'but I shouldn't like to do anything you wouldn't like. I trust you in everything. You don't know how much you are to me, and what a great deal you have done for me!'... She spoke quickly, and did not notice how Pierre flushed at these words. 'I saw in that announcement, *he*, Bolkonsky' (she uttered the word in a rapid whisper), 'he is in Russia, and in the army again. What do you think,' she said hurriedly, evidently in haste to speak because she was afraid her strength would fail her, 'will he ever forgive me? Will he not always have an evil feeling for me? What do you think? What do you think?'

'I think...' said Pierre. 'He has nothing to forgive... If I were in his place...' From association of ideas, Pierre was instantly carried back in imagination to the time when he had comforted her by saying that if he were not himself, but the best man in the world and free, he would beg on his knees for her hand, and the same feeling of pity, tenderness, and love took possession of him, and the same words rose to his lips. But she did not give him time to utter them.

'Yes, you—you,' she said, uttering that word *you* with enthusiasm, 'that's a different matter. Any one kinder, more generous than you, I have never known—no one could be. If it had not been for you then, and now too... I don't know what would have become of me, because...' Tears suddenly came into her eyes: she turned away, held her music before her eyes, and began again singing and walking up and down the room.

At that moment Petya ran in from the drawing-room.

Petya was by now a handsome, rosy lad of fifteen, with full red lips, very like Natasha. He was being prepared for the university, but had lately resolved in secret with his comrade, Obolensky, to go into the hussars.

Petya rushed up to his namesake, Pierre, to talk to him of this scheme.

He had begged him to find out whether he would be accepted in the hussars.

Pierre walked about the drawing-room, not heeding Petya.

The boy pulled him by the arm to attract his attention.

'Come, tell me about my plan, Pyotr Kirillitch, for mercy's sake! You're my only hope,' said Petya.

'Oh yes, your plan. To be an hussar? I'll speak about it; today I'll tell them all about it.'

'Well, my dear fellow, have you got the manifesto?' asked the old count. 'My little countess was at the service in the Razumovsky's chapel; she heard the new prayer there. Very fine it was, she tells me.'

'Yes, I have got it,' answered Pierre. 'The Tsar will be here tomorrow.... There's to be an extraordinary meeting of the nobility and a levy they say of ten per thousand. Oh, I congratulate you.'

'Yes, yes, thank God. Well, and what news from the army?'

'Our soldiers have retreated again. They are before Smolensk, they say,' answered Pierre.

'Mercy on us, mercy on us!' said the count. 'Where's the manifesto?'

'The Tsar's appeal? Ah, yes!' Pierre began looking for the papers in his pockets, and could not find them. Still slapping his pockets, he kissed the countess's hand as she came in, and looked round uneasily, evidently expecting Natasha, who had left off singing now, but had not come into the drawing-room. 'Good Heavens, I don't know where I have put it,' he said.

'To be sure, he always mislays everything,' said the countess.

Natasha came in with a softened and agitated face and sat down, looking mutely at Pierre. As soon as she came into the room, Pierre's face, which had been overcast, brightened, and while still seeking for the paper, he looked several times intently at her.

'By God, I'll drive round, I must have forgotten them at home. Of course . . .'

'Why, you will be late for dinner.'

'Oh! and the coachman has not waited.'

But Sonya had gone into the vestibule to look for the papers, and there found them in Pierre's hat, where he had carefully put them under the lining. Pierre would have read them.

'No, after dinner,' said the old count, who was obviously looking forward to the reading of them as a great treat.

At dinner they drank champagne to the health of the new cavalier of St. George, and Shinshin told them of the news of the town, of the illness of the old Georgian princess, and of the disappearance of Metivier from Moscow, and described how a German had been brought before Rastoptchin by the people, who declared (so Count Rastoptchin told the story) that he was a *champignon*, and how Count Rastoptchin had bade them let the *champignon* go, as he was really nothing but an old German mushroom.

'They keep on seizing people,' said the count. 'I tell the countess she ought not to speak French so much. Now's not the time to do it.'

'And did you hear,' said Shinshin, 'Prince Galitzin has engaged a Russian teacher—he's learning Russian. It begins to be dangerous to speak French in the streets.'

'Well, Count Pyotr Kirillitch, how if they raise a general militia, you will have to mount a horse too, ah?' said the old count addressing Pierre.

Pierre was dreamy and silent all dinner-time. He looked at the count as though not understanding.

'Yes, yes, for the war,' he said. 'No! A fine soldier I should make! And yet everything's so strange; so strange! Why, I don't understand it myself. I don't know, I am far from being military in my taste, but in these days no one can answer for himself.'

After dinner the count settled himself comfortably in a low chair, and with a serious face asked Sonya, who enjoyed the reputation of a good reader, to read the Tsar's appeal.

'To our metropolitan capital Moscow. The enemy has entered our border with an immense host and comes to lay waste our beloved country,' Sonya read conscientiously in her thin voice. The count listened with closed eyes, heaving abrupt sighs at certain passages.

Natasha sat erect, looking inquisitively and directly from her father to Pierre.

Pierre felt her eyes on him and tried not to look round. The countess shook her head disapprovingly and wrathfully at every solemn expression in the manifesto. In all these words she saw nothing but that the danger menacing her son would not soon be over. Shinshin, pursing his lips up into a sarcastic smile, was clearly preparing to make a joke at the first subject that presented itself: at Sonya's reading, the count's next remark, or even the manifesto itself, if no better pretext should be found.

After reading of the dangers threatening Russia, the hopes the Tsar rested upon Moscow, and particularly on its illustrious nobility, Sonya, with a quiver in her voice, due principally to the attention with which they were listening to her, read the last words: 'We shall without delay be in the midst of our people in the capital, and in other parts of our empire, for deliberation, and for the guidance of all our militia levies, both those which are already barring the progress of the foe, and those to be formed for conflict with him, wherever he may appear. And may the ruin with which he threatens us recoil on his own head, and may Europe, delivered from bondage, glorify the name of Russia!'

'That's right!' cried the count, opening his wet eyes, and several times interrupted by a sniff, as though he had put a bottle of strong smelling-salts to his nose. He went on, 'Only let our sovereign say the word, we will sacrifice everything without grudging.'

Before Shinshin had time to utter the joke he was ready to make on the count's patriotism, Natsha had jumped up from her seat and run to her father.

'What a darling this papa is!' she cried, kissing him, and she glanced again at Pierre with the unconscious coquetry that had come back with her fresh interest in life.

'Oh, what a patriot she is!' said Shinshin.

'Not a patriot at all, but simply . . .' Natasha began, nettled. 'You think everything funny, but this isn't at all a joke . . .'

'A joke,' repeated the count. 'Only let him say the word, we will all go . . . We're not a set of Germans!'

'Did you notice,' said Pierre, 'the words, "for deliberation . . ."'

'Yes, to be sure, for whatever might come . . .'

Meanwhile Petya, to whom no one was paying attention, went up to his father, and very red, said in a voice that passed abruptly from gruffness to shrillness, 'Well, now, papa, I tell you positively—and mamma too, say what you will—I tell you you must let me go into the army, because I cannot . . . and that's all about it.'

The countess in dismay turned her eyes up to heaven, clasped her hands, and said angrily to her husband:

'See, what your talk has brought us to!'

But the count recovered the same instant from his excitement.

'Come, come,' he said. 'A fine warrior you'd make! Don't talk nonsense: you have your studies to attend to.'

'It's not nonsense, papa. Fedya Obolensky's younger than I am, and he's going too; and what's more, I can't anyhow study now, when . . .' Petya stopped, flushed till his face was perspiring, yet stoutly went on . . . 'when the country's in danger.'

'Hush, hush, nonsense! . . .'

'Why, but you said yourself you would sacrifice everything.'

'Petya! I tell you be quiet,' cried the count, looking at his wife, who was gazing with a white face and fixed eyes at her younger son.

'Let me say . . . Pyotr Kirillovitch here will tell you . . .'

'I tell you, it's nonsense; the milk's hardly dry on his lips, and he wants to go into the army! Come, come, I tell you,' and the count, taking the papers with him, was going out of the room, probably to read them once more in his study before his nap.

'Pyotr Kirillovitch, let us have a smoke. . .'

Pierre felt embarrassed and hesitating. Natasha's unusually brilliant and eager eyes, continually turned upon him with more than cordiality in them, had reduced him to this condition.

'No; I think I'll go home. . . .'

'Go home? But you meant to spend the evening with us. . . . You come rarely enough, as it is. And this girl of mine,' said the count good-humouredly, looking towards Natasha, 'is never in spirits but when you are here. . .'

'But I have forgotten something. I really must go home. . . . Business. . . .' Pierre said hurriedly.

'Well, good-bye then,' said the count as he went out of the room.

'Why are you going away? Why are you so upset? What for?' Natasha asked Pierre, looking with challenging eyes into his face.

'Because I love you!' he wanted to say, but he did not say it. He crimsoned till the tears came, and dropped his eyes.

'Because it is better for me not to be so often with you. . . . Because . . . no, simply I have business. . . .'

'What for? No, do tell me,' Natasha was beginning resolutely, and she suddenly stopped. Both in dismay and embarrassment looked at one another. He tried to laugh, but could not; his smile expressed suffering, and he kissed her hand and went out without a word.

Pierre made up his mind not to visit the Rostovs again.

XXI

AFTER the uncompromising refusal he had received, Petya went to his own room, and there locking himself in, he wept bitterly. All his family behaved as though they noticed nothing when he came in to tea, silent and depressed with tear-stained eyes.

Next day, the Tsar arrived in Moscow. Several of the Rostovs' servants asked permission to go out to see the Tsar. That morning Petya spent a long time dressing. He combed his hair and arranged his collar like a grown-up man. He screwed up his eyes before the looking-glass, gesticulated, shrugged his shoulders, and finally, without saying anything to any one, he put on his cap and went out of the house by the back way, trying to escape observation. Petya had resolved to go straight to where the Tsar was, and to explain frankly to some gentleman-in-waiting (Petya fancied that the Tsar was always surrounded by gentlemen-in-waiting) that he, Count Rostov, wished, in spite of his youth, to serve his country, that youth could be no hindrance to devotion, and that he was ready . . . Petya had, while he was dressing, prepared a great many fine speeches to make to the gentleman-in-waiting.

Petya reckoned on the success of his presentation to the Tsar simply because he was a child (Petya dreamed, indeed, of how they would wonder at his youth), and yet in his arrangement of his collar, and his hair, and in the sedate, deliberate walk he adopted, he tried to act the part of an elderly man. But the further he went, the more interested he became in the growing crowds about the Kremlin, and he forgot to keep up the sedateness and deliberation characteristic of grown-up people. As he got closer to the Kremlin, he began to try to avoid being crushed, and with a resolute and threatening mien, stuck his elbows out on each side of him. But in spite of his determined air, in the Toistsky Gate the crowd, probably unaware of his patriotic object in going to the Kremlin, so pushed him against the wall, that he was obliged to submit and stand still, while carriages drove in with a rumbling sound under the archway. Near Petya stood a peasant woman, a footman, two merchants, and a discharged soldier. After standing for some time in the gateway, Petya, not caring to wait for all the carriages to pass, tried to push on before the rest, and began resolutely working away with his elbows, but the peasant woman standing next him, who was the first person he poked, shouted angrily to him:

'Why are you shoving away, little master? You see everybody's standing still. What do you want to push for?'

'What, if every one were to push then!' said the footman; and he too setting to work with his elbows shoved Petya into the stinking corner of the gateway.

Petya rubbed the sweat off his face with his hands, and set straight the soaking collar, that he had so carefully arranged at home like a grown-up person's.

Petya felt that he looked unpresentable, and was afraid that if he showed himself in this guise to the gentlemen-in-waiting, they would not admit him to the Tsar's presence. But the crush gave him no possibility of setting himself straight or getting into another place. One of the generals who rode by was an acquaintance of the Rostovs. Petya wanted to ask him for help, but considered this would be below his manly dignity. When all the carriages had driven by, the crowd made a rush, and swept Petya along with it into the square, which was already full of people. Not only in the square, but on the slopes, and the roofs, and everywhere there were crowds of people. As soon as Petya got into the square, he heard the ringing of bells and the joyous hum of the crowd filling the whole Kremlin.

For a while the crush was less in the square, but all at once all heads were bared, and there was another rush forward. Petya was so crushed that he could hardly breathe, and there was a continual shouting: 'Hurrah! hurrah! hurrah!'

Petya tiptoed, pushed, and pinched, but he could see nothing but the crowd around him.

All the faces wore the same expression of excitement and enthusiasm. A shopkeeper's wife standing near Petya sobbed, and tears flowed down her cheeks.

'Father, angel!' she kept saying, wiping her tears with her fingers.

'Hurrah!' shouted the crowd on all sides.

For a minute the crowd remained stationary; then there was another rush forward.

Petya, beside himself with excitement, clenched his teeth, and rolling his eyes savagely, rushed forward, elbowing his way and shouting 'Hurrah!' as though he were prepared to kill himself and every one else at that moment, but just as savage faces pushed on each side of him with the same shouts of 'hurrah!'

'So this is the Tsar!' thought Petya. 'No, I could never give him the petition myself, it would be too bold!'

In spite of that, he still forced his way forward as desperately, and over the backs of those in front of him caught a glimpse of open space with a passage covered with red cloth in the midst of it. But at that moment the crowd began heaving back; the police in front were forcing back those who had pressed too close to the procession. The Tsar was passing from the palace to the Uspensky Sobor. Petya received such a sudden blow in the ribs, and was so squeezed, that all at once a mist passed before his eyes, and he lost consciousness. When he came to himself, a clerical personage, with a mane of grey hair on his shoulders, in a shabby blue cassock—probably a deacon—was holding him up with one arm, while with the other he kept off the crowd.

'A young gentleman's been crushed!' the deacon was saying. 'Mind what you're about! ... easy there! ... you're crushing him, you're crushing him!'

The Tsar had entered the Uspensky Sobor. The crowd spread out again, and the deacon got Petya pale and breathless on to the big cannon. Several persons pitied Petya; and suddenly quite a crowd noticed his plight, and began to press round him. Those who were standing near him looked after him, unbuttoned his coat, sat him on the highest part of the cannon, and scolded those who were squeezing too close to him.

'Any one may be crushed to death like that. What next! Killing people! Why, the poor dear's as white as a sheet,' said voices.

Petya soon recovered, and the colour came back into his face; the pain was over, and by this temporary inconvenience he had gained a seat on the cannon, from which he hoped to see the Tsar, who was to walk back. Petya thought no more now of presenting his petition. If only he could see him, he would think himself lucky! During the service in the Uspensky Sobor, in celebration of the Tsar's arrival, and also in thanksgiving for the peace with the Turks, the crowd dispersed about the square, and hawkers appeared crying kvass, gingerbread, and poppyseed sweets—of which Petya was particularly fond—and he could hear the usual talk among the people. One shopkeeper's wife was showing her torn shawl, and saying how much she had paid for it; while another observed that all silk things were very dear nowadays. The deacon who had rescued Petya was talking to a clerk of the different priests who were taking part in the service today with the most reverend bishop. The deacon several times repeated the word '*soborne*,' which Petya did not understand. Two young artisans were joking with some servant-girls, cracking nuts. All these conversations, especially the jokes with the servant-girls—which would have seemed particularly attractive at his age to Petya—did not interest him now. He sat on his high perch on the cannon, still in the same excitement at the thought of the Tsar and his love for him. The blending of the feeling of pain and fright when he was crushed with the feeling of enthusiasm intensified his sense of the gravity of the occasion.

Suddenly cannon shots were heard from the embankment—the firing was in celebration of the peace with the Turks—and the crowd made a dash for the embankment to see the firing. Petya, too, would have liked to run there, but the deacon, who had taken the young gentleman under his protection, would not let him. The firing still continued, when officers, generals, and gentlemen-in-waiting came running out of the Uspensky Sobor. Then others came out with less haste, and again caps were lifted, and those who had run to look at the cannons, ran back. At last four men in uniforms and decorations came out from the doors of the Sobor. 'Hurrah! hurrah!' the crowd shouted again.

'Which? which one?' Petya asked in a weeping voice of those around him, but no one answered him. Every one was too much excited, and Petya, picking out one of the four, and hardly able to see him for the tears that started into his eyes, concentrated all his enthusiasm on him, though it happened not to be the Tsar. He shouted 'Hurrah!' in a voice of frenzy, and resolved that tomorrow, come what might of it, he would join the army. The crowd ran after the Tsar, accompanied him to the palace, and began to disperse. It was late, and Petya had had nothing to eat, and the sweat was dripping from his face. But he did not go home. He remained with a smaller, though still considerable, crowd before the palace during the Tsar's dinner-time. He gazed up at the palace windows, expecting something to happen, and envying equally the grand personages who drove up to the entrance to dine with the Tsar, and the footmen waiting at table, of whom he caught glimpses at the window.

At the Tsar's dinner, Valuev said, looking out of the window:

'The people are still hoping to get a sight of your majesty.'

The dinner was almost over, the Tsar got up, and still munching a biscuit, came out on the balcony. The crowd, with Petya in the midst, rushed towards the balcony.

'Angel, father! Hurrah!' . . . shouted the crowd, and with it Petya. And again women, and in a less degree some men—among them Petya —shed tears of happiness.

A good sized piece of the biscuit in the Tsar's hand broke off, fell on the balcony railing, and from the railing to the ground. A coachman in a jerkin, who stood nearest, pounced on the piece of biscuit and snatched it up. Several persons rushed at the coachman. Noticing this the Tsar asked for a plate of biscuits, and began dropping them from the balcony. Petya's eyes almost started out of his head; the danger of being crushed excited him more than ever, and he rushed at the biscuits. He did not know why, but he felt he must have a biscuit from the Tsar's hands, and he must not give in. He made a dash and upset an old woman, who was just about to seize a biscuit. But the old woman refused to consider herself beaten, though she was on the ground; she snatched at the biscuits on her hands and knees. Petya pushed her hand away with his knee, snatched up a biscuit, and as though afraid of being late, hastily shouted again, 'Hurrah!' in a hoarse voice.

The Tsar went in, and after that the greater part of the crowd dispersed.

'There, I said if only we waited—and so it was,' was the delighted comment on various sides in the crowd.

Happy as Petya was, he felt sad to go home, and to feel that all the enjoyment of that day was over. From the Kremlin, Petya went not home, but to his comrade Obolensky's. He was fifteen, and he, too, was going into the army. On getting home, Petya announced with decision and firmness that if they would not let him do so too, he would run away. And next day, though Count Ilya Andreitch had not quite yielded, he went to inquire if a commission could be obtained for Petya somewhere where there would be little danger.

XXII

ON the morning of the 15th, the next day but one, a great number of carriages stood outside the Slobodsky palace.

The great halls were full. In the first were the noblemen in their uniforms; in the second there were merchants with medals and long beards, wearing blue, full-skirted coats. The first room was full of noise and movement. The more important personages were sitting on high-backed chairs at a big table under the Tsar's portrait; but the greater number of the noblemen were walking about the hall.

The noblemen, whom Pierre saw every day either at the club or at their houses, were all in uniforms; some in those of Catherine's court, some in those of the Emperor Pavel, and some in the new uniforms of Alexander's reign, others in the common uniforms of the nobility, and the general character of their dress gave a strange and fantastic look to these old and young, most diverse and familiar faces. Particularly striking were the older men, dim-eyed, toothless, bald, and thin, with faces wrinkled or lost in yellow fat. They sat still for the most part and were silent, or if they walked and talked, attached themselves to someone younger. Just like the faces Petya had seen in the crowd, all these faces, in their universal expectation of something solemn, presented a striking contrast with their everyday, yesterday's aspect, when talking over their game of boston, Petrushka the cook, the health of Zinaida Dmitryevna, etc, etc.

Pierre, who had been since early morning in an uncomfortable uniform, that had become too tight for him, was in the room. He was in a state of excitement; this extraordinary assembly, not only of the nobility, but of the merchant class too—the estates, *états généraux*—called up in him a whole series of ideas of the *Contrat Social* and the French Revolution, ideas imprinted deeply on his soul, though they had long been laid aside. The words he had noticed in the manifesto, that the Tsar was coming to the capital *for deliberation* with his people, confirmed him in this chain of thought. And supposing that something of importance in that direction was near at hand, that what he had long been looking for was coming, he looked and listened attentively, but he saw nowhere any expression of the ideas that engrossed him.

The Tsar's manifesto was read, and evoked enthusiasm; and then all moved about, talking. Apart from their everyday interests, Pierre heard discussion as to where the marshals were to stand when the Tsar should come in, when the ball was to be given for the Tsar, whether they were to be divided according to districts or the whole province together ... and so on. But as soon as the war and the whole object of their meeting together was touched upon, the talk was uncertain and hesitating. Every one seemed to prefer listening to speaking.

A manly looking, handsome, middle-aged man, wearing the uniform of a retired naval officer, was speaking, and a little crowd was gathered about him in one of the rooms. Pierre went up to the circle that had formed round him, and began to listen. Count Ilya Andreitch, in his uniform of Catherine's time, was walking about with a pleasant smile among the crowd, with all of whom he was acquainted. He too approached this group, and began to listen with a good-humoured smile, as he always did listen, nodding his head approvingly in token of his agreeing with the speaker. The retired naval officer was speaking very boldly (that could be seen from the expression on the faces of the listeners and from the fact that some persons, known to Pierre as particularly submissive and timid, drew back from him in disapprobation or expressed dissent). Pierre pushed his way into the middle of the circle, listened, and gained the conviction that the speaker certainly was a liberal, but in quite a different sense from what Pierre was looking for. The naval officer spoke in the peculiarly mellow, sing-song baritone of a Russian nobleman, with peculiar burring of the r's and suppression of the consonants, in the voice in which men shout: 'Waiter, a pipe!' and such phrases. He talked with the habit of riotous living and of authority in his voice.

'What if the Smolensk people have offered the Emperor a levy of militia. Are the Smolensk people any rule for us? If the nobility of the Moscow province thinks fit, it can show its devotion to our sovereign the Emperor by other means. Have we forgotten the militia in the year 1807? It was only the beggarly priests' sons and thieves made a good thing of it....'

Count Ilya Andreitch, smiling blandly, nodded his head in approval.

'And were our militiamen of any service to the state? Not the slightest! They only ruined our agriculture. Even conscription is better.... As it is, a man comes back to you neither soldier nor peasant, nothing, but only demoralised. The nobility don't grudge their lives. We will go ourselves to a man; take recruits, too; and the Tsar has but to say the word, and we will all die for him,' added the orator, warming up.

Ilya Andreitch's mouth was watering with satisfaction, and he nudged Pierre, but Pierre wanted to speak too. He moved forward, feeling stirred, though he did not yet know why nor what he would say. He was just opening his mouth to speak when he was interrupted by a perfectly toothless senator with a shrewd and wrathful face, who was standing close by the last orator. Evidently accustomed to lead debates and bring forward motions, he began speaking in a low but audible voice:

'I imagine, my dear sir,' said the senator, mumbling with his toothless mouth, 'that we are summoned here not to discuss which is more suitable for the country at the present moment—conscription or the militia. We are summoned to reply to the appeal which our sovereign the Emperor graciously deigns to make to us. And to judge which is the fitter means—recruiting or a levy for militia—we leave to a higher power....'

Pierre suddenly found the right outlet for his excitement. He felt exasperated with the senator, who introduced this conventional and narrow view of the duties that lay before the nobility. Pierre stepped forward and cut him short. He did not know himself what he was going to say, but he began eagerly, using bookish Russian, and occasionally relapsing into French.

'Excuse me, your excellency,' he began (Pierre was well acquainted with this senator, but he felt it necessary on this occasion to address him formally), 'though I differ from the gentleman . . .' (Pierre hesitated; he would have liked to say *mon très honorable préopinant*) 'with the gentleman . . . whom I have not the honour of knowing; but I imagine the estate of the nobility, apart from the expression of its sympathy and enthusiasm, has been convoked also to deliberate upon the measures by which we can assist our country. I imagine,' said Pierre, growing warmer, 'that the Tsar would himself be displeased if he should find in us only the owners of peasants, whom we give up to him, and *chair à canon*, which we offer in ourselves—and should not find in us co . . . co . . . counsel....'

Many persons moved a little away from the circle, noticing the disdainful smile of the senator and the freedom of Pierre's words. Ilya Andreitch was the only person pleased at what Pierre said, just as he had been pleased with the naval officer's speech and the senator's, as he always was with the last speech he had heard.

'I consider that before discussing these questions,' Pierre continued, 'we ought to ask the Emperor, most respectfully to ask his Majesty, to communicate to us what forces we have, what is the position of our men and our army, and then ...'

Pierre had hardly uttered these words when he was promptly attacked on three sides at once. The most violent onslaught was made upon him by an old acquaintance and partner at boston, who had always been on the friendliest terms with him, Stepan Stepanovitch Adraksin. Stepan Stepanovitch was, of course, in uniform, and whether it was due to the uniform or to other causes, Pierre saw before him quite a changed man. Stepan Stepanovitch, with an old man's anger in his face, screamed at Pierre:

'In the first place, let me tell you that we have no right to ask such questions of the Emperor; and secondly, if the nobility had any such right, the Emperor could not answer such questions. The movements of the troops depend on the movements of the enemy; the troops are augmented and decreased ...'

Another voice interrupted Adraksin. The speaker was a man of forty, of medium height, whom Pierre had seen in former days at the gypsies' entertainments, and knew as a bad card-player. But now he, too, was quite transformed by his uniform, as he moved up to Pierre.

'Yes, and it's not the time for deliberation,' said this nobleman. 'What's needed is action; there is war in Russia. Our foe comes to ruin Russia, to desecrate the tombs of our fathers, to carry away our wives and children.' The gentleman struck himself a blow on the chest. 'We will all rise up; we will all go to a man, we will follow our father the Tsar!' he cried, rolling his bloodshot eyes. Several approving voices could be heard in the crowd. 'We are Russians and we do not grudge our blood for the defence of our faith, our throne, and our country. But we must put a stop to idle talk, if we are true sons of our fatherland. We will show Europe how Russia can defend Russia!' shouted this gentleman.

Pierre tried to reply, but he could not get in a word. He felt that the sound of his words, apart from any meaning they conveyed, was less audible than the sound of his excited adversary's voice.

In the rear of the group, Ilya Andreitch was nodding approval; several of the audience turned their shoulders briskly to the orator at the conclusion of a phrase and said:

'That's so, that's so, indeed!'

Pierre wanted to say that he was by no means averse to the sacrifice of his money, or his peasants, or himself, but that one ought to know the true position of affairs, in order to be able to assist, but he could not speak.

A number of voices were speaking and shouting together, so much so that Ilya Andreitch had not time to nod approval to all of them. And the group grew larger and broke up into knots, re-formed again, and moved all together with a hum of talk to the big table in the big room. Pierre was not allowed to speak; they rudely interrupted him, indeed hustled him and turned their backs on him as though he were the common foe. This was not really due to their dislike of the tenor of his speech, which they had forgotten, indeed, after the great number of speeches that followed it. But a crowd is always pleased to have a concrete object for its love or its hatred. Pierre furnished it with the latter.

Many orators spoke after the eager nobleman, but all spoke in the same tone. Some spoke eloquently and originally.

The editor of the *Russian Messenger*, Glinka, who was recognised and greeted with shouts of 'the author, the author!' said that hell must be driven back by hell, that he had seen a child smiling at the lightning flash and the thunder clap, but we would not be like that child.

'Yes, yes, at the thunder clap!' was repeated with approval at the back of the crowd.

The crowd approached the great table, where grey or bald old noblemen of seventy were sitting, wearing uniforms and decorations. Almost all of them Pierre had seen with their buffoons in their own homes or playing boston at the club. The crowd drew near the table, still with the same buzz of talk. The orators, squeezed in behind the high chair backs by the surging crowd, spoke one after another and sometimes two at once. Those who stood further back noticed what the speaker had left unsaid and hastened to supply the gap. Others were busy in the heat and crush, ransacking their brains to find some idea and hurriedly uttering it. The old grandees at the table sat looking from one to another, and their expression for the most part betrayed nothing but that they were very hot. Pierre however felt excited, and the general feeling of desire to show that they were ready for anything, expressed for the most part more in tones and looks than in the tenor of the speeches, infected him too. He did not disavow his ideas, but felt himself somehow in fault and tried to defend himself.

'I only said that we could make sacrifices to better purpose when we know what is needed,' he cried, trying to shout down the other voices.

One old man close by him looked round, but his attention was immediately called off by a shout at the other end of the table.

'Yes, Moscow will be surrendered! She will be the expiation!' one man was shouting.

'He is the enemy of mankind!' another shouted.

'Allow me to say . . .'

'Gentlemen, you are crushing me! . . .'

XXIII

At that moment Count Rastoptchin, with his prominent chin and alert eyes, strode in rapidly through the parting crowd, wearing the uniform of a general and a ribbon over his shoulder.

'Our sovereign the Emperor will be here immediately,' said Rastoptchin. 'I have just come from him. I presume that in the position in which we are placed, there is no need of much discussion. The Emperor has graciously seen fit to summon us and the merchants,' said Count Rastoptchin. 'They will pour out their millions' (he pointed to the merchants' hall); 'it is our duty to raise men and not to spare ourselves.... It is the least we can do.'

A consultation took place between the great noblemen at the table only. The whole consultation was more than subdued, it seemed even mournful, when, after all the hubbub that had gone before, the old voices could be heard, one at a time, saying 'agreed,' or for the sake of variety, 'I am of the same opinion.'

The secretary was told to write down the resolution of the Moscow nobility: that the nobles of Moscow, like those of Smolensk, would furnish a levy of ten men in every thousand, with their complete equipment.

The gentlemen, who had been sitting, got up with an air of relief; there was a scraping of chairs and the great noblemen walked about to stretch their legs, taking their friends' arms and chatting together.

'The Tasr! the Tsar!' was suddenly heard all through the rooms, and the whole crowd rushed towards the entrance.

The Tsar walked in along the wide, free space left for him, between walls of noblemen close packed on each side. Every face expressed reverent and awe-stricken curiosity. Pierre was some distance, and could not quite catch all the Tsar said. He knew from what he did hear that the Tsar was speaking of the danger in which the empire was placed, and the hopes he rested on the Moscow nobility. The Tsar was answered by a voice informing him of the resolution just passed by the nobility.

'Gentlemen!' said the trembling voice of the Tsar. A stir passed through the crowd, and then a hush fell on it again, and Pierre distinctly heard the voice of the Tsar, warmly humane and deeply touched: 'I have never doubted of the devotion of the Russian nobility. But this day it has surpassed my expectations. I thank you in the name of the fatherland. Gentlemen, let us act—time is more precious than anything....'

The Tsar ceased speaking; the crowd began pressing round him, and cries of enthusiasm were heard on all sides.

'Yes, more precious than anything . . . a royal saying,' said the voice of Ilya Andreitch with a sob. He had heard nothing, but understood everything in his own way.

From the nobility's room the Tsar went into the merchants' room. He was there for about ten minutes. Pierre amongst the rest saw the Tsar coming back from the merchants' room with tears of emotion in his eyes. They learned afterwards that the Tsar had hardly begun to speak to the merchants when the tears gushed from his eyes and he continued in a trembling voice. When Pierre saw the Tsar come out, he was accompanied by two merchants. One of them Pierre knew, a stout contractor; the other was the mayor, with a thin, yellow face and narrow beard. Both were weeping. The tears stood in the thin man's eyes, but the stout contractor was sobbing like a child and continually repeating:

'Take life and property too, your Majesty!'

Pierre felt nothing at that moment but the desire to show that nothing was too much for him and that he was ready to sacrifice everything. The constitutional tenor of his speech weighed on him like a sin; he sought an opportunity of glossing it over. On hearing that Count Mamonov was furnishing a regiment, Bezuhov at once told Count Rastoptchin that he would furnish one thousand men and their equipment.

Old Rostov could not tell his wife what had passed without tears, and he agreed at once to Petya's wishes, and went himself to enter his name.

Next day the Tsar went away. All the assembled noblemen went back to their homes and their clubs, took off their uniforms, and with some groans gave orders to their stewards to raise the levy, wondering themselves at what they had done.

PART X

I

NAPOLEON BEGAN THE war with Russia because he could not help going to Dresden, being dazzled by the homage paid him there, putting on the Polish uniform, yielding to the stimulating influence of a June morning, and giving way to an outburst of fury in the presence of Kurakin and afterwards of Balashev.

Alexander refused all negotiations because he felt himself personally insulted. Barclay de Tolly did his utmost to command the army in the best way possible, so as to do his duty and gain the reputation of a great general. Rostov charged the French because he could not resist the temptation to gallop across the level plain. And all the innumerable persons who took part in the war acted similarly, in accordance with their personal peculiarities, habits, circumstances, and aims. They were all impelled by fear or vanity, enjoyment, indignation, or rational consideration, supposing that they knew what they were about and that they were acting independently, while they were all the involuntary tools of history and were working out a result concealed from themselves but comprehensible to us. Such is the invariable fate of all practical leaders, and the higher their place in the social hierarchy, the less free they are.

Now the leading men of 1812 have long left their places; their personal interests have vanished, leaving no trace, and nothing remains before us but the historical results of the time.

But once let us admit that the people of Europe under Napoleon's leadership *had* to make their way into the heart of Russia and there to perish, and all the self-contradictory, meaningless, cruel actions of the men who took part in this war become intelligible to us.

Providence compelled all those men in striving for the attainment of their personal aims to combine in accomplishing one immense result, of which no one individual man (not Napoleon, not Alexander, still less any one taking practical part in the campaign) had the slightest inkling.

Now it is clear to us what was the cause of the destruction of the French army in 1812. No one disputes that the cause of the loss of

Napoleon's French forces was, on one hand, their entering at too late a season upon a winter march in the heart of Russia without sufficient preparation; and on the other, the character the war had assumed from the burning of Russian towns and the hatred the enemy aroused in the peasantry. But obvious as it seems now, no one at the time foresaw that this was the only means by which the best army in the world, eight hundred thousand strong, led by the best of generals, could be defeated in a conflict with the inexperienced Russian army of half the strength, led by inexperienced generals. Not only was this utterly unforeseen, but every effort indeed was being continually made *on the Russian side* to hinder the one means that could save Russia; and in spite of the experience and so-called military genius of Napoleon, every effort was made *on the French side* to push on to Moscow at the end of the summer, that is to do the very thing bound to bring about their ruin.

In historical works on the year 1812, the French writers are very fond of saying that Napoleon was aware of the danger of lengthening out his line, that he sought a decisive engagement, that his marshals advised him to stay at Smolensk, and similar statements to show that even at the time the real danger of the campaign was seen. The Russian historians are still fonder of declaring that from the beginning of the campaign there existed a plan of Scythian warfare by leading Napoleon on into the heart of Russia. And this plan is ascribed by some writers to Pfuhl, by others to some Frenchman, and by others to Barclay de Tolly; while other writers give the credit of this supposed scheme to the Emperor Alexander himself, supporting their view by documents, proclamations, and letters, in which such a course of action certainly is hinted at. But all these hints at foreseeing what actually did happen on the French as well as on the Russian side are only conspicuous now because the event justified them. If the event had not come to pass, these hints would have been forgotten, as thousands and millions of suggestions and suppositions are now forgotten that were current at the period, but have been shown by time to be unfounded and so have been consigned to oblivion. There are always so many pre-suppositions as to the cause of every event that, however the matter ends, there are always people who will say: 'I said at the time that it would be so': quite oblivious of the fact that among the numerous suppositions they made there were others too suggesting just the opposite course of events.

The notion that Napoleon was aware of the danger of extending his line, and that the Russians had a scheme for drawing the enemy into the heart of Russia, obviously belong to the same category; and only historians with a great bias can ascribe such reflections to Napoleon and his marshals, or such plans to the Russian generals. All the facts are directly opposed to such a view. Far from desiring to lure the French into the heart of Russia, the Russians did their utmost to arrest their progress thoughout the war from the time they crossed the frontier. And far from dreading the extension of his line of communications, Napoleon rejoiced at every step forward as a triumph, and did not seek pitched battles as eagerly as he had done in his previous campaigns.

At the very beginning of the campaign, our armies were divided up, and the sole aim for which we strove was to unite them; though there was no benefit to be derived from uniting them, if our object was to retreat and draw the enemy into the heart of the country. The Emperor was with the army to inspire it not to yield an inch of Russian soil and on no account to retreat. An immense camp was fortified at Drissa in accordance with Pfuhl's plan, and it was not proposed to retreat further. The Tsar reprimanded the commander-in-chief for every retreat. The Tsar can never have anticipated the burning of Moscow, or even the enemy's presence at Smolensk, and when the armies had been reunited, the Tsar was indignant at the taking and burning of Smolensk without a general engagement having been fought before its walls. Such was the Tsar's feeling, but the Russian generals, and the whole Russian people were even more indignant at the idea of our men retreating.

Napoleon, after dividing up the army, moved on into the heart of the country, letting slip several opportunities of an engagement. In August he was in Smolensk and thinking of nothing but advancing further, though, as we see now, that advance meant inevitable ruin.

The facts show perfectly clearly that Napoleon foresaw no danger in the advance on Moscow, and that Alexander and the Russian generals did not dream at the time of luring Napoleon on, but aimed at the very opposite. Napoleon was drawn on into Russia, not through any plans—no one dreamed of the possibility of it—but simply through the complex play of intrigues and desires and motives of the actors in the war, who had no conception of what was to come and of what was the sole means of saving Russia. Everything came to pass by chance. The army was split up early in the campaign. We tried to effect a junction between the parts with the obvious intention of fighting a battle and checking the enemy's advance; and in this effort to effect a junction, avoiding a battle with a far stronger enemy, we were forced to retreat at an acute angle, and so drew the French after us to Smolensk. But it is not enough to say that both parts of the army retreated on lines inclined at an acute angle, because the French were advancing between the two armies. The angle was made the more acute and we retreated further because Barclay de Tolly, an unpopular German, was detested by Bagration, and the latter, in command of the second half of the army, did his utmost to delay a junction with Barclay de Tolly in order to avoid being under his command. Bagration delayed the junction of the armies, though this was the chief aim of all the authorities, because he believed that he would expose his army to danger on the march, and that it would be more advantageous for him to retreat more to the left and the south, annoying the enemy on the flank and rear, and reinforcing his army in Ukraine. And he believed this, because he did not want to put himself under the command of the German Barclay, who was his junior in the service, and personally disliked by him.

The Emperor accompanied the army in order to excite its patriotic ardour; but his presence and inability to decide on any course of action and the immense number of counsellors and plans that swarmed about him, nullified all action on the part of the first army, and that army too had to retreat.

At the camp at Drissa it was proposed to take a stand. But the energy of Paulucci, scheming to become a leading general, affected Alexander; and Pfuhl's whole plan was abandoned, and the scheme of campaign intrusted to Barclay. But as the latter did not inspire complete confidence, his power too was limited. The armies were split up, there was no unity, no supreme command: Barclay was unpopular. But on one side the confusion and division and unpopularity of the German commander-in-chief led to vacillation and to avoiding a battle, which would have been inevitable had the armies been united and any one but Barclay in command of them. And on the other hand, it all led to a growing indignation with the Germans and a growing fervour of patriotism.

At last the Tsar left the army, and, as the only suitable excuse to get rid of him, the happy suggestion was made that he must rouse up the people in the capitals to wage the war on a truly national scale. And the Tsar's visit to Moscow did in fact treble the forces of the Russian army. The Tsar left the army in the hope that the commander-in-chief would be able to act alone, and that more decisive measures would be taken. But the commander's position became weaker and even more difficult. Bennigsen, the Grand Duke, and a swarm of adjutant generals, remained with the army to watch over the actions of the commander-in-chief, and to urge him to greater activity; and Barclay, feeling less than ever free to act under the watchful gaze of all these 'eyes of the Tsar,' became still more cautious and anxious to avoid a pitched battle, and clung to a prudent inaction. The Grand Duke hinted at treachery, and demanded a general engagement. Lubomirsky, Bronnitsky, Vlotsky, and others of the same sort, helped to swell the clamour to such a point that Barclay, on the pretext of sending papers to the Tsar in Petersburg, got rid of the Polish generals, and entered into open conflict with Bennigsen and the Grand Duke.

In Smolensk, in spite of Bagration's wishes to the contrary, the armies were at last united.

Bagration drove up in his carriage to the house occupied by Barclay. Barclay put on his official scarf, and came out to greet and to present his report to his senior officer, Bagration. Bagration, to rival his magnanimity, acknowledged Barclay as his superior officer, in spite of his own seniority; but he was less in accord with him than ever. At the Tsar's command, he sent reports personally to him, and wrote to Araktcheev: 'My sovereign's will is law, but I can do nothing acting with the *minister*' (so he called Barclay). 'For God's sake, send me somewhere else, if only in command of a regiment, for here I can do nothing. The headquarters are crammed full of Germans, there's no living here for a Russian, and no making head or tail of anything. I supposed I was serving my sovereign and my country, but in practice it comes to serving Barclay. I must own I do not care to.'

The swarm of Bronnitskys, Wintzengerodes, and others like them, embittered the feud between the commanders still further, and there was less unity than ever. Preparations were made to attack the French before Smolensk. A general was sent to review the position. This general, detesting Barclay, visits a friend of his own, a commander of a corps, and after spending the day with him, returns and condemns on every point the proposed field of battle without having seen it.

While disputes and intrigues were going on as to the suitable spot for a battle, and while we were looking for the French and mistaking their line of advance, the French fell upon Nevyerovsky's division, and advanced upon the walls of Smolensk itself.

We were surprised into having to fight at Smolensk to save our communications. A battle was fought. Thousands were slain on both sides.

Smolensk was abandoned against the will of the Tsar and the whole people. But Smolensk was burnt by its own inhabitants, who had been deceived by their governor. And those ruined inhabitants, after setting an example to the rest of Russia, full of their losses, and burning with hatred of the enemy, moved on to Moscow. Napoleon advances; we retreat; and so the very result is attained that is destined to overthrow Napoleon.

II

THE day after his son's departure, Prince Nikolay Andreitch sent for Princess Marya.

'Well, now are you satisfied?' he said to her. 'You have made me quarrel with my son! Are you satisfied? That was all you wanted! Satisfied? . . . It's a grief to me, a grief. I'm old and weak, and it was your wish. Well, now, rejoice over it. . . .' And after that, Princess Marya did not see her father again for a week. He was ill and did not leave his study.

Princess Marya noticed to her surprise that during this illness the old prince excluded Mademoiselle Bourienne too from his room. Tihon was the only person who looked after him.

A week later the prince reappeared, and began to lead the same life as before, showing marked energy in the laying out of farm buildings and gardens, and completely breaking off all relations with Mademoiselle Bourienne. His frigid tone and air with Princess Marya seemed to say: 'You see, you plotted against me, told lies to Prince Andrey of my relations with that Frenchwoman, and made me quarrel with him, but you see I can do without you, and without the Frenchwoman too.'

One half of the day Princess Marya spent with Nikolushka, giving him his Russian lessons, following his other lessons, and talking to Dessalle. The rest of the day she spent in reading, or with her old nurse and 'God's folk,' who came by the back stairs sometimes to visit her. The war Princess Marya looked on as women do look on war. She was apprehensive for her brother who was at the front, and was horrified, without understanding it, at the cruelty of men, that led them to kill one another. But she had no notion of the significance of this war, which seemed to her exactly like all the preceding wars. She had no notion of the meaning of this war, although Dessalle, who was her constant companion, was passionately interested in the course of the war, and tried to explain his views on the subject to her, and although 'God's folk' all, with terror, told her in their own way of the rumours among the peasantry of the coming of Antichrist, and although Julie, now Princess Drubetskoy, who had renewed her correspondence with her, was continually writing her patriotic letters from Moscow.

'I write to you in Russian, my sweet friend,' Julie wrote, 'because I feel a hatred for all the French and for their language too; I can't bear to hear it spoken. . . . In Moscow we are all wild with enthusiasm for our adored Emperor.

'My poor husband is enduring hardships and hunger in wretched

Jewish taverns, but the news I get from him only increases my ardour.

'You have doubtless heard of the heroic action of Raevsky, who embraced his two sons and said, "We will die together, but we will not flinch!" And though the enemy were twice as strong, we did not in fact flinch. We kill time here as best we can; but in war, as in war. Princess Alina and Sophie spend whole days with me, and we, unhappy widows of living husbands, have delightful talks over scraping lint. We only want you, my darling, to make us complete,' etc. etc.

The principal reason why Princess Marya failed to grasp the significance of the war was that the old prince never spoke of it, refused to recognise its existence, and laughed at Dessalle when he mentioned the war at dinner-time. The prince's tone was so calm and confident that Princess Marya put implicit faith in him.

During the whole of July the old prince was excessively active and even lively. He laid out another new garden and a new wing for the servants. The only thing that made Princess Marya anxious about him was that he slept badly, and gave up his old habit of sleeping in his study, and had a bed made up for him in a new place every day. One night he would have his travelling bedstead set up in the gallery, the next night he would spend dozing dressed on the sofa or in the lounge-chair in the drawing-room, while the lad Petruskha, who had replaced Mademoiselle Bourienne in attendance on him, read aloud to him; then he would try spending a night in the dining-room.

On the first of August a second letter came from Prince Andrey. In his first letter, which had been received shortly after he left home, Prince Andrey had humbly asked his father's forgiveness for what he had permitted himself to say to him, and had begged to be restored to his favour. To this letter, the old prince had sent an affectionate answer, and from that time he had kept the Frenchwoman at a distance. Prince Andrey's second letter was written under Vitebsk, after the French had taken it. It consisted of a brief account of the whole campaign, with a plan sketched to illustrate it, and of reflections on the probable course it would take in the future. In this letter Prince Andrey pointed out to his father the inconvenience of his position close to the theatre of war, and in the direct line of the enemy's advance, and advised him to move to Moscow.

At dinner that day, on Dessalle's observing that he had heard that the French had already entered Vitebsk, the old prince recollected Prince Andrey's letter.

'I have heard from Prince Andrey today,' he said to Princess Marya; 'have you read the letter?'

'No, *mon père*,' the princess answered timidly. She could not possibly have read the letter, of which indeed she had not heard till that instant.

'He writes about this war,' said the prince, with the contemptuous smile that had become habitual with him in speaking of the present war.

'It must be very interesting,' said Dessalle. 'Prince Andrey is in a position to know....'

'Ah, very interesting!' said Mademoiselle Bourienne.

'Go and get it for me,' said the old prince to Mademoiselle Bourienne. 'You know, on the little table under the paper-weight.'

Mademoiselle Bourienne jumped up eagerly.

'Ah, no,' he shouted, frowning. 'You run, Mihail Ivanitch!' Mihail Ivanitch got up and went to the study. But he had hardly left the room when the old prince, looking about him nervously, threw down his dinner napkin and went himself.

'They never can do anything, always make a muddle.'

As he went out, Princess Marya, Dessalle, Mademoiselle Bourienne, and even little Nikolushka, looked at one another without speaking. The old prince accompanied by Mihail Ivanitch came back with a hurried step, bringing the letter and a plan, which he laid beside him, and did not give to any one to read during dinner.

When they went into the drawing-room, he handed the letter to Princess Marya, and spreading out before him the plan of his new buildings, he fixed his eyes upon it, and told her to read the letter aloud.

After reading the letter, Princess Marya looked inquiringly at her father. He was gazing at the plan, evidently engrossed in his own ideas.

'What do you think about it, prince?' Dessalle ventured to inquire.

'I? eh?...' said the old prince, seeming to rouse himself with a painful effort, and not taking his eyes from the plan of the building.

'It is very possible that the field of operations may be brought so close to us...'

'Ha-ha-ha! The field of operations indeed!' said the old prince. 'I have always said, and I say still, that the field of operations is bound to be Poland, and the enemy will never advance beyond the Niemen.' Dessalle looked in amazement at the prince, who was talking of the Niemen, when the enemy was already at the Dnieper. But Princess Marya, forgetting the geographical position of the Niemen, supposed that what her father said was true.

'When the snows thaw they'll drown in the marshes of Poland. It's only that they can't see it,' said the old prince, obviously thinking of the campaign of 1807, which seemed to him so recent. 'Bennigsen ought to have entered Prussia earlier, and things would have taken quite another turn....'

'But, prince!' said Dessalle timidly, 'the letter speaks of Vitebsk....'
'Ah, the letter? Yes, ...' said the prince, with displeasure. 'Yes ... yes ...' His face suddenly assumed a gloomy expression. He paused. 'Yes, he writes, the French have been beaten. On what river was it?'
Dessalle dropped his eyes. 'The prince says nothing about that,' he said gently.
'What, doesn't he? Why, you don't suppose I imagined it.'
Every one was for a long time silent.
'Yes ... yes ... Well, Mihail Ivanitch,' he said suddenly raising his head and pointing to the plan of the building, 'tell me how you propose to make that alteration....'
Mihail Ivanitch went up to the plan, and the old prince, talking to him about it, went off to his own room, casting a wrathful glance at Princess Marya and Dessalle.
Princess Marya saw Dessalle's embarrassed and amazed expression as he looked at her father. She noticed his silence and was struck by the fact that her father had left his son's letter forgotten on the drawing-room table. But she was afraid to speak of it, to ask Dessalle the reason of his embarrassed silence, afraid even to think about it.
In the evening Mihail Ivanitch was sent by the prince to Princess Marya to ask for the letter that had been forgotten on the table. Princess Marya gave him the letter, and much as she disliked doing so, she ventured to ask what her father was doing.
'Still very busy,' said Mihail Ivanitch, in a tone of deferential irony, that made her turn pale. 'Worrying very much over the new wing. Been reading a little: but now'—Mihail Ivanitch dropped his voice—'he's at his bureau looking after his will, I expect.' One of the old prince's favourite occupations of late had been going over the papers which he meant to leave at his death, and called his 'will'.
'And is Alpatitch being sent to Smolensk?' asked Princess Marya.
'To be sure; he's been waiting a long while for his orders.'

III

WHEN Mihail Ivanitch went back to the study with the letter, the old prince was sitting in his spectacles with a shade over his eyes and shades on the candles, at his open bureau, surrounded by papers, held a long distance off. He was in a rather solemn attitude, reading the papers (the 'remarks,' as he called them) which were to be given to the Tsar after his death.

When Mihail Ivanitch went in, there were tears in his eyes, called up by the memory of the time when he had written what he was now reading. He took the letter out of Mihail Ivanitch's hand, put it in his pocket, folded up his papers and called in Alpatitch, who had been waiting a long while to see him.

He had noted down on a sheet of paper what he wanted in Smolensk, and he began walking up and down the room, as he gave his instructions to Alpatitch, standing at the door.

'First, letter paper, do you hear, eight quires, like this pattern, you see; gilt edged . . . take the pattern, so as to be sure to match it; varnish, sealing-wax—according to Mihail Ivanitch's list.'

He walked up and down the room and glanced at the memorandum.

'Then deliver the letter about the enrolment to the governor in person.'

Then bolts for the doors of the new building were wanted, and must be of a new pattern, which the old prince had himself designed. Then an iron-bound box was to be ordered for keeping his will in.

Giving Alpatitch his instructions occupied over two hours. The prince still would not let him go. He sat down, sank into thought, and closing his eyes, dropped into a doze. Alpatitch made a slight movement.

'Well, go along, go along,' said the prince; 'if anything is wanted, I'll send.'

Alpatitch went away. The prince went back again to the bureau; glancing into it, he passed his hand over his papers, closed it again, and sat down to the table to write to the governor.

It was late when he sealed the letter and got up. He was sleepy, but he knew he would not sleep, and that he would be haunted by most miserable thoughts in bed. He called Tihon, and went through the rooms with him, to tell him where to make up his bed for that night. He walked about, measuring every corner.

There was no place that pleased him, but worst of all was the couch in the study that he had been used to. That couch had become an object of dread to him, probably from the painful thoughts he had thought lying on it. No place was quite right, but best of them all was the corner in the divan-room, behind the piano; he had never slept there yet.

Tihon brought the bedstead in with the footmen, and began putting it up.

'That's not right, that's not right!' cried the old prince. With his own hands he moved the bed an inch further from the corner, and then closer to it again.

'Well, at last, I have done everything; now I shall rest,' thought the prince, and he left it to Tihon to undress him.

Frowning with vexation at the effort he had to make to take off his coat and trousers, the prince undressed, dropped heavily down on his bed, and seemed to sink into thought, staring contemptuously at his yellow, withered legs. He was not really thinking, but simply pausing before the effort to lift his legs up and lay them in the bed. 'Ugh, how hard it is! Ugh, if these toils could soon be over, and if *you* would let me go!' he mused. Pinching his lips tightly, he made that effort for the twenty thousandth time, and lay down. But he had hardly lain down, when all at once the bed seemed to rock regularly to and fro under him, as though it were heaving and jolting. He had this sensation almost every night. He opened his eyes that were closing of themselves.

'No peace, damn them!' he grumbled, with inward rage at some persons unknown. 'Yes, yes, there was something else of importance—something of great importance I was saving up to think of in bed. The bolts? No, I did speak about them. No, there was something, something in the drawing-room. Princess Marya talked some nonsense. Dessalle—he's a fool—said something, something in my pocket—I don't remember.'

'Tishka! what were we talking about at dinner?'

'About Prince Mihail . . .'

'Stay, stay'—the prince slapped his hand down on the table. 'Yes, I know, Prince Andrey's letter. Princess Marya read it. Dessalle said something about Vitebsk. I'll read it now.'

He told Tihon to get the letter out of his pocket, and to move up the little table with the lemonade and the spiral wax candle on it, and putting on his spectacles he began reading. Only then in the stillness of the night, as he read the letter, in the faint light under the green shade, for the first time he grasped for an instant its meaning. 'The French are at Vitebsk, in four days' march they may be at Smolensk; perhaps they are there by now. Tishka!' Tihon jumped up. 'No, nothing, nothing!' he cried.

He put the letter under the candlestick and closed his eyes. And there rose before his mind the Danube, bright midday, the reeds, the Russian camp, and he, a young general, without one wrinkle on his brow, bold, gay, ruddy, entering Potyomkin's gay-coloured tent, and the burning sensation of envy of the favourite stirs within him as keenly as at the time. And he recalls every word uttered at that first interview with Potyomkin. And then he sees a plump, short woman with a sallow, fat face, the mother empress, her smiles, and words at her first gracious reception of him; and then her face as she lay on the bier, and the quarrel with Zubov over her coffin for the right to kiss her hand.

'Oh, to make haste, to make haste back to that time, and oh, that the present might soon be over and they might leave me in peace!'

IV

BLEAK HILLS, the estate of Prince Nikolay Andreitch Bolkonsky, was sixty versts from Smolensk, a little to the rear of it, and three versts from the main road to Moscow.

The same evening on which the old prince gave Alpatitch his instructions, Dessalle asked for a few words with Princess Marya, and told her that since the prince was not quite well and was taking no steps to secure his own safety, though from Prince Andrey's letter it was plain that to stay on at Bleak Hills was not free from danger, he respectfully advised her to write herself, and send by Alpatitch a letter to the governor at Smolensk, and to ask him to let her know the position of affairs and the degree of danger they were running at Bleak Hills. Dessalle wrote the letter to the governor for Princess Marya and she signed it, and the letter was given to Alpatitch with instructions to give it to the governor, and in case there was danger, to come back as quickly as possible.

When he had received all his orders, Alpatitch put on his white beaver hat—a gift from the prince—and carrying a stick in his hand, like the prince, went out, accompanied by all his household, to get into the leather gig harnessed to three sleek, roan horses.

The bells were tied up and stuffed with paper. The prince allowed no one at Bleak Hills to drive with bells. But Alpatitch loved to have bells ringing when he went a long journey. All Alpatitch's satellites, the counting-house clerk, the servants' cook and the head cook, two old women, a footboy, coachman, and various other servants saw him off.

His daughter put chintz-covered, down pillows under him and behind his back. His old sister-in-law slyly popped in a kerchief full of things. One of the coachmen helped him to get in.

'There, there, women's fuss! Women folk, women folk!' said Alpatitch, puffing and talking rapidly, just as the old prince used to talk. He sat down in the gig, giving the counting-house clerk his last directions about the work to be done in the fields; and then dropping his imitation of the prince, Alpatitch took his hat off his bald head and crossed himself three times.

'If there's anything . . . you turn back, Yakov Alpatitch; for Christ's sake, think of us,' his wife called to him, alluding to the rumours of war and of the enemy near.

'Ah, these women and their fuss!' Alpatitch muttered to himself as he drove off, looking about him at the fields. He saw rye turning yellow, thick oats still green, and here and there patches still black, where they were only just beginning the second ploughing. Alpatitch drove on, admiring the crop of corn, singularly fine that season, staring at the rye fields, in some of which reaping was already beginning, meditating like a true husbandsman on the sowing and the harvest, and wondering whether he had forgotten any of the prince's instructions. He stopped twice to feed his horses on the way, and towards the evening of the 4th of August reached the town.

All the way Alpatitch had met and overtaken wagons and troops, and as he drove into Smolensk he heard firing in the distance, but he scarcely heeded the sound. What struck him more than anything was that close to Smolensk he saw a splendid field of oats being mown down by some soldiers evidently for forage; there was a camp, too, pitched in the middle of it. This did make an impression upon Alpatitch, but he soon forgot it in thinking over his own affairs.

All the interests of Alpatitch's life had been for over thirty years bounded by the will of the prince, and he never stepped outside that limit. Anything that had nothing to do with carrying out the prince's orders had no interest, had in fact no existence, for Alpatitch.

On reaching Smolensk on the evening of the 4th of August, Alpatitch put up where he had been in the habit of putting up for the last thirty years, at a tavern kept by a former house-porter, Ferapontov, beyond the Dnieper in the Gatchensky quarter. Twelve years before, Ferapontov had profited by Alpatitch's good offices to buy timber from the old prince, and had begun going into trade; and by now he had a house, an inn and a corn-dealer's shop in the town. Ferapontov was a stout, dark, ruddy peasant of forty, with thick lips, a thick, knobby nose, similar knobby bumps over his black, knitted brows, and a round belly.

He was standing in his print shirt and his waistcoat in front of his shop, which looked into the street. He saw Alpatitch, and went up to him.

'You're kindly welcome, Yakov Alpatitch. Folk are going out of the town, while you come into it,' said he.

'How's that? Out of town?' said Alpatitch.

'To be sure, I always say folks are fools. Always frightened of the French.'

'Women's nonsense, women's nonsense!' replied Alpatitch.

'That's just what I think, Yakov Alpatitch. I say there's a notice put up that they won't let them come in, so to be sure that's right. But the peasants are asking as much as three roubles for a cart and horse—they've no conscience!'

Yakov Alpatitch heard without heeding. He asked for a samovar, and for hay for his horses; and after drinking tea lay down to sleep.

All night long the troops were moving along the street by the tavern. Next day Alpatitch put on a tunic, which he kept for wearing in town, and went out to execute his commissions. It was a sunny morning, and by eight o'clock it was hot. 'A precious day for the harvest,' as Alpatitch thought. From early morning firing could be heard from beyond the town.

At eight o'clock the boom of cannon mingled with the rattle of musketry. The streets were thronged with people, hurrying about, and also with soldiers, but drivers plied for hire, the shopkeepers stood at their shops, and services were being held in the churches just as usual. Alpatitch went to the shops, to the government offices, to the post and to the governor's. Everywhere that he went every one was talking of the war, and of the enemy who was attacking the town. All were asking one another what was to be done, and trying to calm each other's fears.

At the governor's house, Alpatitch found a great number of people, and saw Cossacks, and a travelling carriage belonging to the governor at the entrance. On the steps Yakov Alpatitch met two gentlemen, one of whom he knew. This gentleman, a former police-captain, was speaking with great heat.

'Well, this is no jesting matter,' he said. 'Good luck for him who has only himself to think of. It's bad enough for one alone, but when one has a family of thirteen and a whole property.... Things have come to such a pass that we shall all be ruined; what's one to say of the government after that?... Uh, I'd hang the brigands....'

'Come, come, hush!' said the other.

'What do I care! let him hear! Why, we're not dogs!' said the former police-captain, and looking round, he caught sight of Alpatitch.

'Ah, Yakov Alpatitch, how do you come here?'

'By command of his excellency to his honour the governor,' answered Alpatitch, lifting his head proudly and putting his hand into his bosom, as he always did when he mentioned the old prince.... 'His honour was pleased to bid me inquire into the position of affairs,' he said.

'Well, you may as well know then,' cried the gentleman: 'they have brought matters to such a pass that there are no carts to be got, nothing!... That's it again, do you hear?' he said, pointing in the direction from which the sounds of firing came.

'They have brought us all to ruin ... the brigands!' he declared again, and he went down the steps.

Alpatitch shook his head and went up. The waiting-room was full of merchants, women, and clerks, looking dumbly at one another. The door of the governor's room opened, all of them got up and made a forward movement. A clerk ran out of the room, said something to a merchant, called a stout official with a cross on his neck to follow him, and vanished again, obviously trying to avoid all the looks and the questions addressed to him. Alpatitch moved forward, and the next time the same clerk emerged, he put his hand into his buttoned coat, and addressed him, handing him the two letters.

'To his honour the Baron Ash from the general-in-chief Prince Bolkonsky,' he boomed out with so much pomposity and significance that the clerk turned to him and took the letters. A few minutes afterwards Alpatitch was shown into the presence of the governor, who said to him hurriedly, 'Inform the prince and the princess that I knew nothing about it. I acted on the highest instructions—here. . . .'

He gave Alpatitch a document.

'Still, as the prince is not well my advice to him is to go to Moscow. I'm setting off myself immediately. Tell them . . .' But the governor did not finish; a dusty and perspiring officer ran into the room and began saying something in French. A look of horror came into the governor's face.

'You can go,' he said, nodding to Alpatitch, and he put some questions to the officer. Eager, panic-stricken, helpless glances were turned upon Alpatitch when he came out of the governor's room. Alpatitch could not help listening now to firing, which seemed to come closer and to be getting hotter, as he hurried back to the inn. The document the governor had given to Alpatitch ran as follows:

'I guarantee that the town of Smolensk is not in the slightest danger, and it is improbable that it should be threatened in any way. I myself from one side, and Prince Bagration from the other, will effect a junction before Smolensk on the 22nd instant, and both armies will proceed with their joint forces to defend their compatriots of the province under your government, till their efforts beat back the enemies of our country, or till their gallant ranks are cut down to the last warrior. You will see from this that you have a perfect right to reassure the inhabitants of Smolensk, as they are defended by two such valiant armies and can be confident of their victory.

('By order of Barclay de Tolly to the civil governor of Smolensk, Baron Ash. 1812.')

Crowds of people were moving uneasily about the streets. Wagons, loaded up with household crockery, chairs, and cupboards, were constantly emerging from the gates of houses, and moving along the streets.

Carts were standing at the entrance of the house next to Ferapontov's, and women were wailing and exchanging good-byes. The yard dog was frisking about the horses, barking.

Alpatitch's step was more hurried than usual as he entered the yard, and went straight under the shed to his horses and cart. The coachman was asleep; he waked him up, told him to put the horses in, and went into the outer room of the house. In the private room of the family, he heard the wailing of children, the heartrending sobs of a woman, and the furious, husky shouting of Ferapontov. The cook came fluttering into the outer room like a frightened hen, just as Alpatitch walked in.

'He's beating her to death—beating the mistress! ... He's beaten her so, thrashed her so! ...'

'What for?' asked Alpatitch.

'She kept begging to go away. A woman's way! Take me away, says she; don't bring me to ruin with all my little children; folks are all gone, says she, what are we about? So he fell to beating her ... beating and thrashing her!'

Alpatitch nodded his head, apparently in approval at those words; and not caring to hear more he went toward the door on the opposite side leading to the room in which his purchases had been left.

'Wretch, villain,' screamed a thin, pale woman, bursting out at that moment with a child in her arms and her kerchief torn off her head. She ran down the steps into the yard. Ferapontov was going after her, but seeing Alpatitch, he pulled down his waistcoat, smoothed his hair, yawned and followed Alpatitch into the room.

'Do you want to be getting off already?' he asked. Without answering the question or looking round at him, Alpatitch collected his purchases and asked how much he owed him.

'We'll reckon up! Been at the governor's, eh?' asked Ferapontov. 'What did you hear?'

Alpatitch replied that the governor had told him nothing definite.

'How are we to pack up and go with our business?' said Ferapontov. 'Seven roubles to pay for cartage to Dorogobuzh. What I say is: they have no conscience!' said he. 'Selivanov, he did a good turn on Friday, sold flour to the army for nine roubles the sack. What do you say to some tea?' he added. While the horses were being harnessed, Alpatitch and Ferapontov drank tea and discussed the price of corn, the crops, and the favourable weather for the harvest.

'It's getting quieter though,' said Ferapontov, getting up after drinking three cups of tea. 'I suppose, our side has got the best of it. It's been said they won't let them in. So we're in force it seems. . . . The other day they were saying Matvey Ivanitch Platov drove them into the river Marina: eighteen thousand of them he drowned in one day.'

Alpatitch gathered up his purchases, handed them to the coachman, and settled his accounts with Ferapontov. There was the sound of wheels and hoofs and the ringing of bells as the gig drove out of the gates.

It was by now long past midday, half the street lay in shadow, while half was in brilliant sunshine. Alpatitch glanced out of the window and went to the door. All of a sudden there came a strange sound of a faraway hiss and thump, followed by the boom of cannons, mingling into a dim roar that set the windows rattling.

Alpatitch went out into the street; two men were running along the street towards the bridge. From different sides came the hiss and thud of cannon-balls and the bursting of grenades, as they fell in the town. But these sounds were almost unheard, and the inhabitants scarcely noticed them, in comparison with the boom of the cannons they heard beyond the town. It was the bombardment, which Napoleon had ordered to be opened upon the town at four o'clock from one hundred and thirty cannons. The people did not at first grasp the meaning of this bombardment.

The sounds of the dropping grenades and cannon-balls at first only excited the curiosity of the people. Ferapontov's wife, who had till then been wailing in the shed, ceased, and with the baby in her arms went out to the gate, staring in silence at the people, and listening to the sounds.

The cook and shopman came out to the gate. All of them were trying with eager curiosity to get a glimpse of the projectiles as they flew over their heads. Several persons came round the corner in eager conversation.

'What force!' one was saying; 'roof and ceiling were smashed up to splinters.'

'Like a pig routing into the earth, it went!' said another.

'Isn't it first-rate? Wakes one up!' he said laughing.

'It's as well you skipped away or it would have flattened you out.'

Others joined this group. They stopped and described how a cannon-ball had dropped on a house close to them. Meanwhile other projectiles —now a cannon-ball, with a rapid, ominous hiss, and now a grenade with a pleasant whistle—flew incessantly over the people's heads: but not one fell close, all of them flew over. Alpatitch got into his gig. Ferapontov was standing at the gate.

'Will you never have done gaping!' he shouted to the cook, who in her red petticoat, with her sleeves tucked up and her bare elbows swinging, had stepped to the corner to listen to what was being said.

'A wonder it is!' she was saying, but hearing her master's voice, she came back, pulling down her tucked-up skirt.

Again something hissed, but very close this time, like a bird swooping down; there was a flash of fire in the middle of the street, the sound of a shot, and the street was filled with smoke.

'Scoundrel, what are you about?' shouted Ferapontov, running up to the cook.

At the same instant there rose a piteous wailing from the women; the baby set up a terrified howling, and the people crowded with pale faces round the cook. Above them all rose out of the crowd the moans and cries of the cook.

'O-o-oy, good kind souls, blessed friends! don't let me die! Good kind souls! . . .'

Five minutes later no one was left in the street. The cook, with her leg broken by the bursting grenade, had been carried into the kitchen. Alpatitch, his coachman, Ferapontov's wife and children and the porter were sitting in the cellar listening. The thunder of the cannon, the hiss of the balls, and the piteous moaning of the cook, which rose above all the noise, never ceased for an instant. Ferapontov's wife alternately dandled and soothed her baby, and asked in a frightened whisper of every one who came into the cellar where was her husband, who had remained in the street. The shopman told her the master had gone with the crowd to the cathedral, where they were raising on high the wonder-working, holy picture of Smolensk.

Towards dusk the cannonade began to subside. Alpatitch came out of the cellar and stood in the doorway.

The clear evening sky was all overcast with smoke. And a new crescent moon looked strange, shining high up in the sky, through that smoke. After the terrible thunder of the cannons had ceased, a hush seemed to hang over the town, broken only by the footsteps, which seemed all over the town, the sound of groans and distant shouts, and the crackle of fires. The cook's moans had ceased now. On two sides black clouds of smoke from fires rose up and drifted away. Soldiers in different uniforms walked and ran about the streets in different directions, not in ranks, but like ants out of a disturbed ant heap. Several of them ran into Ferapontov's yard before Alpatitch's eyes. He went out to the gate. A regiment, crowded and hurrying, blocked up the street, going back.

'The town's surrendered; get away, get away,' said an officer noticing his figure; and turning immediately to the soldiers, he shouted, 'I'll teach you to run through the yards!'

Alpatitch went back to the house, and calling the coachman told him to set off. Alpatitch and the coachman were followed out by all the household of Ferapontov. When they saw the smoke and even the flames of burning houses, which began to be visible now in the dusk, the women, who had been silent till then, broke into a sudden wail, as they gazed at the fires. As though seconding them, similar wails rose up in other parts of the street. Alpatitch and the coachman with trembling hands pulled out the tangled reins and the traces of the horses under the shed.

As Alpatitch was driving out of the gate, he saw about a dozen soldiers in loud conversation in Ferapontov's open shop. They were filling their bags and knapsacks with wheaten flour and sunflower seeds. At that moment Ferapontov returned and went into the shop. On seeing the soldiers, he was about to shout at them, but all at once he stopped short, and clutching at his hair broke into a sobbing laugh.

'Carry it all away, lads! Don't leave it for the devils,' he shouted, snatching up the sacks himself and pitching them into the street. Some of the soldiers ran away in a fright, others went on filling up their bags. Seeing Alpatitch, Ferapontov turned to him.

'It's all over with Russia!' he shouted. 'Alpatitch! it's all over! I'll set fire to it myself. It's over . . .' Ferapontov ran into the house.

An unbroken stream of soldiers was blocking up the whole street, so that Alpatitch could not pass and was obliged to wait. Ferapontov's wife and children were sitting in a cart too, waiting till it was possible to start.

It was now quite dark. There were stars in the sky, and from time to time the new moon shone through the veil of smoke. Alpatitch's and his hostess's vehicles moved slowly along in the rows of soldiers and of other conveyances, and on the slope down to the Dnieper they had to halt altogether. In a lane not far from the cross-roads where the traffic had come to a full stop, there were shops and a house on fire. The fire was by now burning down. The flame died down and was lost in black smoke, then flared up suddenly, lighting up with strange distinctness the faces of the crowd at the cross-roads. Black figures were flitting about before the fire, and talk and shouts could be heard above the unceasing crackling of the flames. Alpatitch, seeing that it would be some time before his gig could move forward, got out and went back to the lane to look at the fire. Soldiers were scurrying to and fro before the fire; and Alpatitch saw two soldiers with a man in a frieze coat dragging burning beams from the fire across the street to a house near, while others carried armfuls of hay.

Alpatitch joined a great crowd of people standing before a high corn granary in full blaze. The walls were all in flames; the back wall had fallen in; the plank roof was breaking down, and the beams were glowing. The crowd were evidently watching for the moment when the roof would fall in. Alpatitch too waited to see it.

'Alpatitch!' the old man suddenly heard a familiar voice calling to him.

'Mercy on us, your excellency,' answered Alpatitch, instantly recognising the voice of his young master.

Prince Andrey, wearing a cape, and mounted on a black horse, was in the crowd, and looking at Alpatitch.

'How did you come here?' he asked.

'Your . . . your excellency!' Alpatitch articulated, and he broke into sobs.... 'Your, your ... is it all over with us, really? Master ...'

'How is it you are here?' repeated Prince Andrey. The flames flared up at that instant, and Alpatitch saw in the bright light his young master's pale and worn face. Alpatitch told him how he had been sent to the town and had difficulty in getting away.

'What do you say, your excellency, is it all over with us?' he asked again.

Prince Andrey, making no reply, took out his note-book, and raising his knee, scribbled in pencil on a leaf he had torn out. He wrote to his sister:

'Smolensk has surrendered,' he wrote. 'Bleak Hills will be occupied by the enemy within a week. Set off at once for Moscow. Let me know at once when you start; send a messenger to Usvyazh.'

Scribbling these words, and giving Alpatitch the paper, he gave him further directions about sending off the old prince, the princess and his son with his tutor, and how and where to let him hear, a soon as they had gone. Before he had finished giving those instructions, a staff officer, followed by his suite, galloped up to him.

'You a colonel,' shouted the staff officer in a voice Prince Andrey knew, speaking with a German accent. 'Houses are being set on fire in your presence and you stand still! What's the meaning of it? You will answer for it,' shouted Berg, who was now assistant to the head of the staff of the assistant of the chief officer of the staff of the commander of the left flank of the infantry of the first army, a very agreeable and prominent position, so Berg said.

Prince Andrey stared at him, and without making any reply went on addressing Alpatitch:

'Tell them then that I shall wait for an answer till the 10th, and if I don't receive news by the 10th, that they have all gone away, I shall be obliged to throw up everything and go myself to Bleak Hills.'

'Prince,' said Berg, recognizing Prince Andrey, 'I only speak because it's my duty to carry out my instructions, because I always do exactly carry out... You must please excuse me,' Berg tried to apologise.

There was a crash in the fire. The flames subsided for an instant; black clouds of smoke rolled under the roof. There was another fearful crash, and the falling of some enormous weight.

'Ooo-roo!' the crowd yelled, as the ceiling of the granary fell in, and a smell of baked cakes rose from the burning wheat. The flames flared up again, and lighted up the delighted and careworn faces of the crowd around it.

The man in the frieze coat, brandishing his arms in the air, was shouting:

'First-rate! Now she's started! First-rate, lads! . . .' 'That's the owner himself,' murmured voices.

'So you tell them everything I have told you,' said Prince Andrey, addressing Alpatitch. And without bestowing a word on Berg, who stood mute beside him, he put spurs to his horse and rode down the lane.

V

FROM Smolensk the troops continued to retreat. The enemy followed them. On the 10th of August the regiment of which Prince Andrey was in command was marching along the high-road past the avenue that led to Bleak Hills. The heat and drought had lasted more than three weeks. Every day curly clouds passed over the sky, rarely covering the sun; but towards evening the sky cleared again and the sun set in a glowing, red mist. But a heavy dew refreshed the earth at night. The wheat left in the fields was burnt up and dropping out of the ear. The marshes were dry. The cattle lowed from hunger, finding nothing to graze on in the sun-baked meadows. Only at night and in the woods, as long as the dew lasted, it was cool. But on the road, on the high-road along which the troops marched, there was no coolness even at night, and even where the road passed through the woods. The dew was imperceptible on the sandy dust of the road, more than a foot deep. As soon as it was daylight, the soldiers began to move. The transports and artillery moved noiselessly, buried up to their axles, and the infantry sank to their ankles in the soft, stifling, burning dust, that never got cool even at night. The sandy dust clung to their legs and to the wheels, rose in a cloud over their heads, and got into the eyes and hair and nostrils and lungs of the men and beasts that moved along the road. The higher the sun rose, the higher rose the cloud of dust, and through the fine, burning dust the sun in the cloudless sky looked like a purple ball, at which one could gaze with undazzled eyes. There was no wind, and the men gasped for breath in the stagnant atmosphere. They marched with handkerchiefs tied over their mouths and noses. When they reached the villages, there was a rush for the wells. They fought over the water and drank it down to the mud.

Prince Andrey was in command of a regiment; and the management of the regiment, the welfare of his men, the necessity of receiving and giving orders occupied his mind. The burning and abandonment of Smolensk made an epoch in Prince Andrey's life. A new feeling of intense hatred of the enemy made him forget his own sorrow. He was devoted heart and soul to the interests of his regiment; he was careful of the welfare of his men and his officers, and cordial in his manner with them. They called him in the regiment 'our prince', were proud of him, and loved him. But he was kind and gentle only with his own men, with Timohin, and others like him, people quite new to him, belonging to a different world, people who could have no notion of his past. As soon as he was brought into contact with any of his old acquaintances, any of the staff officers, he bristled up again at once, and was vindictive, ironical, and contemptuous. Everything associated by memories with the past was repulsive to him, and so, in his relations with that old world, he confined himself to trying to do his duty, and not to be unfair.

Prince Andrey, in fact, saw everything in the darkest, gloomiest light, especially after Smolensk, which he considered could and should have been defended, had been abandoned, on the 6th of August, and his invalid father had been forced, as he supposed, to flee to Moscow, leaving Bleak Hills, the house that he had so loved, that he had designed and settled with his peasants, to be plundered. But in spite of that, thanks to his position, Prince Andrey had another subject to think of, quite apart from all general questions, his regiment. On the 10th of August, the column of which his regiment formed part reached the turning leading off to Bleak Hills. Two days before Prince Andrey had received the news that his father, his son, and his sister had gone away to Moscow. Though there was nothing for Prince Andrey to do at Bleak Hills, he decided, with characteristic desire to aggravate his own sufferings, that he must ride over there.

He ordered his horse to be saddled, and turned off from the main line of march towards his father's house, where he had been born and had spent his childhood. As he rode by the pond, where there always used to be dozens of peasant women gossiping, rinsing their linen or beating it with washing bats, Prince Andrey noticed that there was no one by the pond, and that the platform where they used to stand had been torn away, and was floating sideways in the middle of the pond, half under water. Prince Andrey rode up to the keeper's lodge. There was no one to be seen at the stone gates and the door was open. The paths of the garden were already overgrown with weeds, and cattle and horses were straying about the English park. Prince Andrey rode up to the conservatory: the panes were smashed, and some of the trees in tubs were broken, others quite dried up. He called Taras, the gardener. No one answered. Going round the conservatory on the terrace, he saw that the paling-fence was all broken down, and branches of the plum-trees had been pulled off with the fruit. An old peasant, whom Prince Andrey used to see in his childhood at the gate, was sitting on the green garden seat plaiting bast shoes.

He was deaf, and did not hear Prince Andrey's approach. He was sitting on the seat on which the old prince liked to sit, and near him the bast was hanging on the branches of a broken and dried-up magnolia.

Prince Andrey rode up to the house. Several lime-trees in the old garden had been cut down; a piebald mare and a colt were among the rose-trees just before the house. The shutters were all up in the house, except on one open window downstairs. A servant lad caught sight of Prince Andrey and ran into the house.

Alpatitch had sent his family away, and was staying on alone at Bleak Hills. He was sitting indoors, reading the *Lives of the Saints*. On hearing that Prince Andrey had come, he ran out, spectacles on nose, buttoning himself up, hurried up to the prince, and without uttering a word, burst into tears, kissing his knee.

Then he turned away in anger at his own weakness, and began giving him an account of the position of affairs. Everything precious and valuable had been moved to Bogutcharovo. Corn to the amount of a hundred measures had been carried away, but the hay, and the wheat—an extraordinary crop that season, so Alpatitch said—had been cut green and carried off by the troops. The peasants were ruined: some of them, too, had gone to Bogutcharovo; a small number remained. Prince Andrey, not heeding his words, asked, 'When did my father and sister go?' meaning when had they set off for Moscow. Alpatitch, assuming he was asking about the removal to Bogutcharovo, answered that they had set off on the 7th, and began going off again into details about the crops, asking for instructions.

'Is it your honour's orders that I let the oats go on getting a receipt from the officers?' asked Alpatitch. 'We have still six hundred measures left.'

'What am I to say to him?' Prince Andrey wondered, looking at the old man's bald head shining in the sun, and reading in his face the consciousness that he knew himself the untimeliness of those questions, and asked them only to stifle his own grief.

'Yes, let it go,' he said.

'If your excellency noticed any disorder in the garden,' said Alpatitch, 'it could not be prevented; three regiments have been here and spent the night. The dragoons were the worst; I noted down the name and rank of the commanding officer to lodge a complaint.'

'Well, and what are you going to do? Shall you stay, if the enemy occupies the place?' Prince Andrey asked him.

Alpatitch turned his face towards Prince Andrey and looked at him; then all at once, with a solemn gesture, he lifted his hand upwards: 'He is my protector, and His will be done!' he said. A group of peasants and house-serfs were coming across the meadow, uncovering their heads as they drew near Prince Andrey.

'Well, good-bye!' said Prince Andrey, bending over to Alpatitch. 'Go away yourself; take what you can; and tell the peasants to set off for the Ryazan estate or the property near Moscow.'

Alpatitch hugged his leg and broke into sobs. Prince Andrey gently moved him away, and spurring his horse galloped down the garden walk.

On the terrace the old man was still sitting as before, as uninterested as a fly on some beloved dead face, knocking on the sole of the bast shoe. And two little girls came running from the plum-trees in the conservatories with their skirts full of plums. They ran almost against Prince Andrey, and seeing their young master, the elder one clutched her younger companion by the hand, with a panic-stricken face, and hid with her behind a birch tree not stopping to pick up the green plums they had dropped.

Prince Andrey turned away from them in nervous haste, afraid of letting them notice that he had seen them. He was sorry to have frightened the pretty child. He was afraid to glance at her, but yet he felt an irresitible inclination to do so. A new soothing and consolatory feeling came upon him, as gazing at the little girls, he became aware of the existence of other human interests, utterly remote from him, and as legitimate as his own. Those little girls were evidently possessed by one passionate desire to carry off and devour those green plums without being caught, and Prince Andrey wished them success in their enterprise. He could not resist glancing at them once more. Fancying themselves already secure, they had darted out of their hiding-place, and piping something in their shrill, little voices, and holding up their skirts, they ran gaily and swiftly through the grass with their bare, sunburnt little feet.

Prince Andrey was somewhat refreshed by his ride outside the region of the dust of the high-road along which the troops were marching. But he rode back into the road not far from Bleak Hills, and overtook his regiment at the halting-place near the dike of a small pond. It was about two o'clock in the afternoon. The sun, a red ball through the dust, baked and scorched his back intolerably in his black coat. The dust stood as immovably as ever over the buzzing, halting troops. There was not a breath of wind. As he rode towards the dike, Prince Andrey smelt the fresh, muddy smell of the pond. He longed to be in the water, however muddy it might be. He looked round at the pond, from which he heard shrieks and laughter. The small pond, thickly covered with green slime, was visibly half a yard higher and overflowing the dam, because it was full of white, naked human bodies, with brick-red hands and heads and necks, all plunging about in it. All that bare, white human flesh was splashing about with shrieks and laughter, in the muddy pool, like carp floundering in a net. There was a ring of merriment in that splashing, and that was what made it peculiarly sad.

One fair-haired young soldier – Prince Andrey knew him – of the third company, with a strap round the calf of his leg, stepped back, crossing himself, to get a good run, and plunge into the water. Another swarthy and very tousle-headed sergeant up to his waist in the water, bending his fine, muscular figure, was snorting with enjoyment, as he poured the water over his head with his blackened hands. There was a sound of them slapping each other, and shrieks and cries.

On the banks, on the dike, in the pond, everywhere there was white, healthy, muscular flesh. Timohin, the officer with the red nose, was rubbing himself with a towel on the dike, and was abashed at seeing Prince Andrey, but made up his mind to address him.

'It's pleasant, really, your excellency; you should try it!' he said.

'It's dirty,' said Prince Andrey, grimacing.

'We will clear it out for you in a minute.' And undressed as he was, Timohin ran to clear the men out. 'The prince wants to come.'

'What prince? Our prince?' cried voices, and all of them were in such haste to make way for him that Prince Andrey hardly had time to check them. He thought it would be better for him to have a bath in a barn. 'Flesh, meat, *chair à canon*,' he thought, looking too at his own naked body and shuddering, not so much from cold as from the repulsion and horror, mysterious to himself, that he had felt at the sight of that immense multitude of naked bodies floundering in the muddy water.

On the 7th of August, Prince Bagration, at his halting-place at Mihalovka on the Smolensk road, had written a letter to Araktcheev. Though the letter was addressed to Araktcheev, he knew it would be read to the Tsar, and therefore he weighed every word, so far as he was capable of doing so.

'DEAR COUNT ALEXEY ANDREEVITCH,—I presume that the minister has already reported the abandonment of Smolensk to the enemy. It is sad, it is pitiable, and the whole army is in despair at the most important place having been wantonly abandoned. I for my part begged him personally in the most urgent manner, and finally wrote to him; but nothing would persuade him. I swear to you on my honour that Napoleon was in a greater fix than he has ever been, and he might have lost half his army, but could not have taken Smolensk. Our troops have fought and are fighting as never before. With fifteen thousand men I have held the enemy in check for thirty-five hours and beaten them, but he wouldn't hold his ground for fourteen hours. It is a shame and a stain on our army, and as for himself, I consider he ought not to be alive. If he reports that our losses were great, it is false; perhaps about four thousand, not that, but that is nothing: if it had been ten thousand, what of it, that's war. But on the other hand the enemy's losses were immense.

'What would it have cost him to hold his ground for a couple of days? In any case they must have retired of their own accord; for they had no water for their men or their horses. He gave me his word he would not retreat, but all of a sudden sent an announcement that he was withdrawing in the night. We cannot fight in this way, and we may soon bring the enemy on to Moscow....

'There is a rumour afloat that you are thinking of peace. To make peace, God preserve us! After all the sacrifices that have been made and after such mad retreats – to make peace, you will set all Russia against you, and every one of us will feel it a disgrace to wear the uniform. If it has come to that, we ought to fight as long as Russia can, and as long as there are men able to stand....

'There must be one man in command, not two. Your minister, may be, is very well in the ministry; but as a general, he's not simply useless, but contemptible, and the fate of all our fatherland has been put in his hands ... I am frantic, truly, with rage; forgive me for writing abusively. It is plain that the man does not love his sovereign, and desire the ruin of us all, who advises peace to be concluded and the minister to be put in command of the army. And so I write to you plainly: get the militia ready. For the minister is leading our visitors to the capital in the most skilful manner. The object of chief suspicion to the whole army is the aide-de-camp Woltzogen. They say he's more for Napoleon than for us, and everything the minister does is by his advice. I am not merely civil to him, but obey him like a corporal, though I am his senior. It is hard: but loving my sovereign and benefactor, I obey. And I grieve for the Tsar that he intrusts his gallant army to such a man. Consider that on our retreat we have lost more than fifteen thousand men from fatigue, or left sick in the hospitals; if we had attacked, that would not have been so. Tell me for God's sake what will Russia—our mother—say at our displaying such cowardice, and why are we abandoning our good and gallant country to the rabble and rousing the hatred and shame of every Russian. Why are we in a panic? what are we afraid of? It is not my fault that the minister is vacillating, cowardly, unreasonable, dilatory, and has every vice. All the army is bewailing it and loading him with abuse....'

VI

AMONG the innumerable categories into which it is possible to classify the phenomena of life, one may classify them all into such as are dominated by matter and such as are dominated by form. To the latter class one may refer the life of Petersburg, especially in its drawing-rooms, as distinguished from the life of the country, of the district, of the province, or even of Moscow. That life of the drawing-rooms is unchanging.

Between the year 1805 and 1812 we had made peace with Bonaparte and quarrelled with him again; we had made new constitutions and unmade them again, but the salons of Anna Pavlovna and of Ellen were precisely as they had been—the former seven, the latter five years —before. Anna Pavlovna's circle were still speaking with incredulous wonder of Bonaparte's successes; and saw in his successes, and in the submissive attitude of the sovereigns of Europe, a malicious conspiracy, the sole aim of which was to give annoyance and anxiety to the court circle of which Anna Pavlovna was the representative. The set that gathered about Ellen, whom no less a person than Rumyantsev condescended to visit, and looked on as a remarkably intelligent woman, talked in 1812 with the same enthusiasm as in 1808, of the 'great nation', and the 'great man,' and regretted the breach with France, which must, they believed, shortly end in peace.

Of late after the Tsar's return from the army, some increase of excitement was perceptible in these antagonistic salons, and they made something like demonstrations of hostility to one another, but the bias of each circle remained unaffected. Anna Pavlovna's set refused to admit any French people but the most unimpeachable legitimists; and in her drawing-room the patriotic view found expression that the French theatre ought not to be patronised, and that the maintenance of the French company there cost as much as the maintenance of a whole army corps. The progress of the war was eagerly followed, and rumours greatly to the advantage of our army were circulated. In the circle of Ellen, of Rumyantsev, the French circle, the reports of the enemy's cruelty and barbarous methods of warfare were discredited; and all sorts of conciliatory efforts on the part of Napoleon were discussed. This set discountenanced the premature counsels of those who advised preparations for the removal to Kazan of the court and the girls' schools, that were under the protection of the empress mother. The whole war was in fact regarded in Ellen's salon as a series of merely formal demonstrations, very shortly to be terminated by peace; and the view prevailed, expressed by Bilibin, who was now in Petersburg and constantly seen at Ellen's, as every man of wit was sure to be, that the war would be ended not by gunpowder by but those who had invented it. The patriotic fervour of Moscow, of which tidings reached Petersburg with the Tsar, was in Ellen's salon a subject of ironical, and very witty, though circumspect, raillery.

In Anna Pavlovna's circle on the contrary these patriotic demonstrations roused the greatest enthusiasm, and were spoken of as Plutarch speaks of his ancient Romans. Prince Vassily, who still filled the same important positions, constituted the connecting link between the two circles. He used to visit 'my good friend Anna Pavlovna,' and was also seen in the 'diplomatic salon of my daughter'; and often was led into blunders from his frequent transitions from one to the other, and said in one drawing-room what should have been reserved for the other.

Soon after the Tsar's arrival, Prince Vassily, in conversation about the progress of the war at Anna Pavlovna's, severely criticised Barclay de Tolly, and expressed himself unable to decide who should be appointed commander-in-chief. One of the guests, usually spoken of as a 'man of great abilities,' described how he had that day seen the newly elected commander of the Petersburg militia, Kutuzov, presiding over the enrolment of militiamen in the Court of Exchequer, and ventured discreetly to suggest that Kutuzov would be the man who might satisfy all requirements.

Anna Pavlovna smiled mournfully, and observed that Kutuzov had done nothing but cause the Tsar annoyance.

'I have said so over and over again in the assembly of nobility,' interposed Prince Vassily, 'but they wouldn't listen to me. I said that his election to the command of the militia would not be pleasing to his Majesty. They wouldn't listen to me. It's all this mania for being in the opposition,' he went on. 'And to what public are they playing, I should like to know. It's all because we are trying to ape the silly enthusiasm of Moscow,' said Prince Vassily, forgetting for a moment that it was at

Ellen's that that enthusiasm was jeered at, while at Anna Pavlovna's it was as well to admire it. But he hastened to retrieve his mistake. 'Is it suitable for Kutuzov, the oldest general in Russia, to be presiding in the court? *Et il en restera pour sa peine!* Did any one hear of such a thing as appointing a man commander-in-chief who cannot sit a horse, who drops asleep at a council—a man, too, of the lowest morals! A pretty reputation he gained for himself in Bucharest! To say nothing of his qualities as a general, can we appoint, at such a moment, a man decrepit and blind—yes, simply blind! A fine idea—a blind general! He sees nothing. Playing blind-man's buff—that's all he's fit for!'

No one opposed that view.

On the 24th of July it was accepted as perfectly correct. But on the 29th Kutuzov received the title of prince. The bestowal of this title might be taken to indicate a desire to shelve him, and therefore Prince Vassily's dictum still remained correct, though he was in no such hurry now to express it. But on the 8th of August a committee, consisting of General Field-Marshal Saltykov, Araktcheev, Vyazmitinov, Lopuhin, and Kotchubey was held to consider the progress of the war. This committee decided that the disasters were due to divided authority; and although the members of the committee were aware of the Tsar's dislike of Kutuzov, after a deliberation they advised the appointment of Kutuzov commander-in-chief. And that same day Kutuzov was appointed commander-in-chief of the army, and intrusted with unlimited authority over the whole region occupied by the troops.

On the 9th of August Prince Vassily once more met the 'man of great abilities' at Anna Pavlovna's. The latter gentleman was assiduous in his attendance at Anna Pavlovna's, in the hope of receiving, through her influence, an appointment on one of the institutions of female education. Prince Vassily strode into the room with the air of a victorious general, of a man who has succeeded in attaining the object of his desires.

'Well, you know the great news! Prince Kutuzov is marshal!' All differences of opinion are at an end. I am so glad, so delighted!' said Prince Vassily. 'At last here is a man!' he declared, looking sternly and significantly at all the company. In spite of his desire to secure the post he coveted, the 'man of great abilities' could not refrain from reminding Prince Vassily of the view he had expressed shortly before. (This was a breach of civility to Prince Vassily in Anna Pavlovna's drawing-room, and also to Anna Pavlovna, who had received the tidings with equal enthusiasm; but he could not refrain.)

'But they say he is blind, prince,' he said to recall to Prince Vassily his own words.

'*Allez donc, il y voit assez*,' said Prince Vassily, with the rapid bass voice and the cough with which he always disposed of all difficulties. 'He sees quite enough,' he repeated. 'And what I'm particularly glad of,' he went on, 'is that the Emperor has given him unlimited authority over all the troops, over the whole region, an authority no commander-in-chief has ever had before. It's another autocrat,' he concluded, with a victorious smile.

'God grant it may be,' said Anna Pavlovna.

The 'man of great abilities,' a novice in court society, was anxious to flatter Anna Pavlovna by maintaining her former opinion against this new view of the position. He said: 'They say the Emperor was unwilling to give Kutuzov such authority. They say he blushed like a young lady to whom Joconde is read, saying to him, "The sovereign and the country decree you this honour."'

'Perhaps the heart was not of the party,' said Anna Pavlovna.

'Oh no, no,' Prince Vassily maintained warmly. Now he would not put Kutuzov second to any one. To hear Prince Vassily now Kutuzov was not simply a good man in himself, but idolised by every one. 'No, that's impossible, for the sovereign has always known how to appreciate him,' he added.

'God only grant that Prince Kutuzov may take the control of things into his own hands,' said Anna Pavlovna, 'and not permit *any one* to put a spoke in his wheel.'

Prince Vassily knew at once who was meant. He whispered, 'I know for a fact that Kutuzov made it an express condition that the Tsarevitch should not be with the army. *Vous savez ce qu'il a dit à l'Empereur.*' And Prince Vassily repeated the words said to have been spoken by Kutuzov to the Tsar: '"I can neither punish him if he does wrong, nor reward him if he does well." Oh! he's a shrewd fellow, Prince Kutuzov. I have known him a long while.'

'They do say,' observed the 'man of great abilities,' who had not acquired a courtier's tact, 'that his excellency even made it an express condition that the Emperor himself should not be with the army.'

He had hardly uttered the words when Anna Pavlovna and Prince Vassily simultaneously turned their backs on him, and looked mournfully at one another, with a sigh at his naïveté.

VII

AT the time when this was taking place in Petersburg, the French had passed through Smolensk, and were moving closer and closer to Moscow. Napoleon's historian, Thiers, like others of Napoleon's historians, tries to justify his hero by maintaining that he was drawn on to the walls of Moscow against his will. He is as right as any historians who seek the explanation of historic events in the will of a man; he is as right as the Russian historians, who assert that Napoleon was lured to Moscow by the skilful strategy of the Russian generals. In this case, apart from the law of 'retrospectiveness,' which makes all the past appear a preparation for the subsequent facts, the element of mutual interaction, too, comes in, confusing the whole subject. A good chess-player, who has lost a game, is genuinely convinced that his failure is due to his blunders, and he seeks the blunder at the commencement of the game, forgetting that at every move during the whole game there were similar errors, that not one piece has been played as perfectly as possible. The blunder on which he concentrates his attention attracts his notice simply because his opponent took advantage of it. How much more complex is the game of war, which must be played within certain limits of time, in which there is not one will controlling lifeless toys, in which the whole is the resultant of the innumerable *collisions* of diverse individual wills!

After Smolensk, Napoleon tried to force on a battle beyond Dorogobuzh, at Vyazma, and then at Tsavero-Zaimishtche. But the Russians could not give battle, owing to innumerable combinations of circumstances, till Borodino, one hundred and twelve versts from Moscow. From Vyazma Napoleon gave instructions for an advance straight upon Moscow.

'Moscow, the Asiatic capital of this great empire, the holy city of the peoples of Alexander, Moscow, with its innumerable churches in the form of Chinese pagodas!'

This Moscow would not let Napoleon's imagination rest. On the march from Vyazma to Tsarevo-Zaimishtche Napoleon was riding on his cream-coloured English horse, accompanied by his guards, and sentinels, and pages, and adjutants. The commander of the staff, Berthier, had dropped behind to put questions to a Russian prisoner taken by the cavalry. Accompanied by the interpreter, Lelorme d'Ideville, he galloped after Napoleon, and pulled his horse up with an amused expression.

'Well?' said Napoleon.

'A Cossack of Platov's detachment says Platov is effecting a junction with the main army, and that Kutuzov has been appointed commander-in-chief. He is very shrewd and talkative.'

Napoleon smiled, and bade them give the Cossack a horse and bring him before him. He wished to talk to him himself. Several adjutants galloped off, and within an hour Denisov's serf Lavrushka, whom his master had left with Rostov, rode up to Napoleon, sitting on a French cavalry saddle, wearing an orderly's short jacket, and looking sly, tipsy, and mirthful. Napoleon bade him ride at his side and began questioning him.

'Are you a Cossack?'

'Yes; a Cossack, your honour.'

'The Cossack, ignorant in whose company he was, since Napoleon's plain appearance had nothing to suggest to the Oriental imagination the presence of a monarch, talked with extraordinary familiarity of the incidents of the war,' says Thiers, relating this episode. In reality Lavrushka, who had been drunk the previous evening, and had left his master without dinner, had been thrashed for it, and sent to the village in quest of fowls, where he was tempted on by plunder till he got caught by the French. Lavrushka was one of those coarse, impudent lackeys, who have seen a good deal of life, look on it as a duty to do nothing without cunning and trickery, are ready to do any kind of service for their masters, and are particularly keen in scenting out the baser impulses of their superiors, especially on the side of vanity and pettiness. On coming into the presence of Napoleon, whom he easily and confidently recognised, Lavrushka was not in the least taken aback, and only did his utmost to win the favour of his new master.

He was very well aware that this was Napoleon, and Napoleon's presence impressed him no more than Rostov's or the quartermaster's with the rod in his hand, because he had nothing of which either the quartermaster or Napoleon could not deprive him.

He had repeated all the gossip that was talked among the officers' servants. Much of it was true. But when Napoleon asked him whether the Russians expected to conquer Bonaparte or not, Lavrushka screwed up his eyes and thought a bit.

He saw in the question a sharp piece of cunning, as cunning fellows, like Lavrushka, always do in everything. He frowned and paused a minute.

'Well, if it does come to a battle,' he said thoughtfully, 'and pretty soon, then yours will win. That's a sure thing. But if now, three days and there's a battle after that, well then, I say, that same battle will be a long job.' This was translated to Napoleon. 'If a battle is fought within three days the French will win it, but if later, God knows what will come of it,' Lelorme d'Ideville put it, smiling. Napoleon did not smile, though he was evidently in high good humour, and told him to repeat the words.

Lavrushka noticed that, and to entertain him further, said, pretending not to know who he was:

'We know, you have got your Bonaparte; he has conquered every one in the world, ay, but with us it will be a different story . . .' himself hardly aware how and why this bit of bragging patriotism slipped out. The interpreter translated these words without the conclusion; and Bonaparte smiled. 'The young Cossack brought a smile on to the lips of his august companion,' says Thiers. After a few paces in silence, Napoleon turned to Berthier, and said he should like to try the effect '*sur cet enfant du Don*' of learning that the man with whom he was speaking was the Emperor himself, the very Emperor who had carved his immortally victorious name on the Pyramids. The fact was communicated. Lavrushka—discerning that this was done to test him, and that Napoleon expected him to be panic-stricken—tried to gratify his new masters by promptly affecting to be astounded, struck dumb; he opened round eyes, and made the sort of face usual with him when he was being led off to be thrashed. 'Hardly,' says Thiers, 'had Napoleon's interpreter spoken, than the Cossack was struck dumb with amazement; he did not utter another word, and walked with his eyes constantly fixed on the great conqueror, whose fame had reached him across the steppes of the East. All his loquacity suddenly vanished, and was replaced by a naïve and silent awe. Napoleon made the Cossack a present, and ordered him to be set at liberty like *un oiseau qu'on rend aux champs qui l'ont vu naître.*'

Napoleon rode on, dreaming of that Moscow that filled his imagination, while the bird returning to the fields that had seen him born, galloped back to the outposts, inventing the tale he would tell his comrades. What had really happened he did not care to relate, simply because it seemed to him not worth telling. He rode back to the Cossacks, inquired where was his regiment, now forming part of Platov's detachment; and towards evening found his master, Nikolay Rostov, encamped at Yankovo. Rostov was just mounting his horse to ride through the villages near with Ilyin. He gave Lavrushka another horse and took him with them.

VIII

PRINCESS MARYA was not in Moscow and out of danger as Prince Andrey supposed.

After Alpatitch's return from Smolensk, the old prince seemed as though he had suddenly waked out of a sleep. He gave orders for the militiamen to assemble out of the villages, and to be armed; and wrote a letter to the commander-in-chief, in which he informed him of his intention to remain at Bleak Hills to the last and to defend himself, leaving it to his discretion to take steps or not for the defence of Bleak

Hills, where he said one of the oldest Russian generals would be taken prisoner or die. He announced to his household that he should remain at Bleak Hills.

But though resolved himself to remain, the prince made arrangements for sending the princess with Dessalle and the little prince to Bogutcharovo, and from there on to Moscow. Frightened at her father's feverish, sleepless energy, following on his previous apathy, Princess Marya could not bring herself to leave him alone, and for the first time in her life ventured not to obey him. She refused to go, and a fearful tempest of wrath burst upon her. The prince reminded her of every previous instance of injustice to her. Trying to find pretexts for reviling her, he said she had done everything to worry him, that she had estranged him from his son, that she harboured the vilest suspicions of him, that she made it the object of her life to poison his existence. He drove her out of his study, telling her that he did not care if she did not go away. He told her that he did not want to hear of her existence, but gave her fair warning not to dare to show herself before him. Princess Marya was relieved that he had not, as she had dreaded, ordered her to be forcibly removed from Bleak Hills, but had simply commanded her not to show herself. She knew that this meant that in the secret recesses of his soul he was glad she was staying at home.

The day after Nikolushka had left, the old prince dressed himself in the morning in full uniform, and prepared to make a call on the commander-in-chief. The carriage was standing ready. Princess Marya saw him in his uniform, with all his orders on his breast, walk out of the house and go down the garden to inspect the armed peasants and house serfs. Princess Marya sat at the window listening to his voice resounding from the garden. Suddenly several men came running up the avenue with panic-stricken faces.

Princess Marya ran out on to the steps, along the flower-bed path, and into the avenue. A great crowd of militiamen and servants were coming down it towards her, and in the middle of that crowd several men were holding up and dragging along a little old man in a uniform and decorations. Princess Marya ran towards him, and in the dancing, tiny rings of light that filtered through the shade of the lime-tree avenue, she could form no distinct impression of the change in his face. The only thing she could see was that the stern and determined expression of his face had changed to a look of timidity and submission. On seeing his daughter, he tried to move his powerless lips, and uttered a hoarse sound. It was impossible to understand what he meant. He was lifted up, carried into his study, and laid on the couch, which had been such an object of dread to him of late.

The doctor, who was brought over the same night, bled him, and declared that the prince had had a stroke, paralysing his right side.

To remain at Bleak Hills was becoming more and more dangerous, and the next day they moved the prince to Bogutcharovo. The doctor travelled with him.

When they reached Bogutcharovo, they found Dessalle had already set off for Moscow with the little prince.

For three weeks the old prince lay stricken with paralysis, getting neither better nor worse, in the new house Prince Andrey had planned at Bogutcharovo. The old prince was unconscious; he lay like a deformed corpse. He muttered incessantly, twitching his eyebrows and lips, and it was impossible to tell whether he understood his surroundings or not. Only one thing could be said for certain: that was, that he was suffering, and had a craving to express something. But what that was no one could tell: whether it were some sick and half-crazy whim; whether it related to public affairs or family circumstances.

The doctor said that this uneasiness meant nothing; that it was due to physical causes. But Princess Marya believed (and the fact that her presence seemed to intensify the restlessness, confirmed her supposition) that he wanted to tell her something.

He was evidently suffering both physically and mentally. There was no hope of recovery. It was impossible to move him. What if he were to die on the road? 'Wouldn't it be better if it were over, if all were over?' Princess Marya thought sometimes. Day and night, almost without sleep, she watched him, and, terrible to say, she watched him, not in the hope of finding symptoms of a change for the better, but often in the hope of seeing symptoms of the approaching end.

Strange as it was for the princess to own it to herself, she had this feeling in her heart. And what was still more horrible to Princess Marya was the fact that ever since her father's illness (if not even before, when she resolved to stay with him, in vague expectation of something) all the forgotten hopes and desires slumbering within her had awakened. Ideas that had not entered her head for years—dreams of a life free from the terror of her father, even of the possibility of love and a happy married life, haunted her imagination like temptations of the devil. In vain she tried to drive away the thought; questions were continually in her mind how she would order her life now, after *this*. It was a temptation of the devil, and Princess Marya knew it. She knew that the sole weapon of avail against *him* was prayer, and she strove to pray. She threw herself into the attitude of prayer, gazed at the holy pictures, repeated the words of the prayer, but still she could not pray. She felt herself carried off into a new world of real life, of labour and free activity, utterly opposed to the moral atmosphere in which she had been kept in bondage, and in which the one consolation was prayer. She could not pray and could not weep, and practical cares absorbed her mind.

To remain at Bogutcharovo was becoming unsafe. Rumours came from all sides of the French being near, and in one village, fifteen versts from Bogutcharovo, a house had been sacked by French marauders. The doctor insisted on the necessity of moving the prince; the marshal of the province sent an official to Princess Marya to persuade her to get away as quickly as possible. The captain of the police visited Bogutcharovo to insist on the same thing, telling her that the French were only forty versts away; that French proclamations were circulating in the villages, and that if the princess did not move her father before the 15th, he could not answer for the consequences.

The princess made up her mind to leave on the 15th. The preparations and giving all the necessary instructions, for which every one applied to her, kept her busy the whole of the previous day. The night of the 14th she spent as usual, without undressing, in the room next to the one where the old prince lay. Several times she waked up, hearing his groaning and muttering, the creak of the bedstead, and the steps of Tihon and the doctor moving him. Several times she listened at the door, and it seemed to her that he was muttering more loudly than usual and turning more restlessly. She could not sleep, and several times she went to the door, listening, tempted to go in, but unable to make up her mind to do so. Although he could not speak, Princess Marya saw and knew how he disliked any expression of anxiety about him. She had noticed how he turned in displeasure away from her eyes, which were sometimes unconsciously fixed persistently on him. She knew her going in at night, at an unusual time, would irritate him.

But never had she felt so sorry for him; never had she felt it so dreadful to lose him. She went over all her life with him, and in every word, every action, she saw an expression of his love for her. Occasionally these reminiscences were interrupted by the temptation of the devil; dreams came back to her imagination of what would happen after his death, and how she would order her new independent existence. But she drove away such thoughts with horror. Towards morning he was quieter, and she fell asleep.

She waked up late. The perfect sincerity, which often accompanies the moment of waking, showed her unmistakably what it was that was of most interest to her in her father's illness. She waked up, listened to what was passing through the door, and catching the sound of his muttering, she told herself with a sigh that there was no change.

'But what should there be? What did I hope for? I hope for his death,' she cried, with inward loathing of herself.

She washed, dressed, said her prayers, and went out on to the steps. At the entrance the carriages in which their luggage was packed were standing without horses.

The morning was warm and grey. Princess Marya lingered on the steps, still horrified at her own spiritual infamy, and trying to get her ideas into shape before going in to see him.

The doctor came downstairs and out to her.

'He is a little better today,' said the doctor. 'I was looking for you. One can make out a little of what he says. His head is clearer. Come in. He is asking for you . . .'

Princess Marya's heart beat so violently at this news that she turned pale and leaned against the door to keep from falling. To see him, to talk to him, to be under his eyes now, when all her soul was filled with these fearful, sinful imaginings was full of an agonising joy and terror for her.

'Let us go in,' said the doctor.

Princess Marya went in to her father, and went up to his bedside. He was lying raised high on his back; his little bony hands, covered with knotted purple veins, were laid on the quilt; his left eye was gazing straight before him, while the right eye was distorted, and his lips and eyebrows were motionless. He looked so thin, so small, and pitiable. His face looked withered up or melted away; his features all seemed smaller. Princess Marya went up and kissed his hand. His left hand clasped her hand in a way that showed he had long been wanting her. He twitched her hand, and his eyebrows and lips quivered angrily.

She looked at him in dismay, trying to fathom what he wanted of her. When she changed her position so that his left eye could see her, he seemed satisfied, and for several seconds kept his eye fixed on her. Then his lips and tongue twitched; sounds came, and he tried to speak, looking with imploring timidity at her, evidently afraid she would not understand him.

Princess Marya strained every faculty of attention as she gazed at him. The comic effort with which he strove to make his tongue work made Princess Marya drop her eyes, and she had much ado to stifle the sobs that rose in her throat. He was saying something, several times repeating his words. Princess Marya could not understand them; but she tried to guess what he was saying, and repeated interrogatively the words she supposed him to be uttering.

'O . . . o . . . aye . . . aye . . . !' he repeated several times. It was impossible to interpret these sounds. The doctor thought he had guessed it, and asked:

'The princess is afraid?'

He shook his head, and again repeated the same sounds.

'The soul, the soul is in pain!' Princess Marya guessed. He grunted affirmatively, took her hand, and began pressing it to different parts of his breast as though seeking the right place for it.

'Always thinking!—about you . . . thinking . . . !' he articulated, far more intelligibly than before now that he felt sure of being understood. Princess Marya pressed her head against his arm, trying to hide her sobs and tears.

He passed his hand over her hair.

'I called for you all night . . .' he articulated.

'If I had only known . . .' she said, through her tears. 'I was afraid to come in.'

He pressed her hand.

'Weren't you asleep?'

'No, I couldn't sleep,' said Princess Marya, shaking her head.

Unconsciously imitating her father, she tried to speak more by signs, as he spoke, as though she, too, had a difficulty in articulating.

'Darling!' . . . or 'dear one!' . . . Princess Marya could not distinguish the word; but from the expression of his eyes she had no doubt what was said was a word of caressing tenderness such as he had never used to her before. 'Why didn't you come?'

'And I was wishing, wishing for his death!' thought Princess Marya.

He paused.

'Thanks . . . to you . . . child, dear one! for all, for all . . . forgive! . . . thanks! . . . forgive! . . . thanks! . . .' And tears flowed from his eyes. 'Call Andryusha,' he said suddenly, and a look of childish and deprecating misgiving came into his face at the question. He seemed to be himself aware that his question had no meaning. So at least it seemed to Princess Marya.

'I have had a letter from him,' answered Princess Marya.

He looked at her with timid wonder.

'Where is he?'

'He's with the army, father, at Smolensk.'

He was silent for a long while, closing his eyes. Then, as though to answer his doubts, and to assert that now he understood it all and remembered, he nodded his head and opened his eyes.

'Yes,' he said, softly and distinctly. 'Russia is lost! They have lost her!'

And again he broke into sobs, and tears flowed from his eyes. Princess Marya could restrain herself no more, and wept too as she looked at his face.

He closed his eyes again. His sobs ceased. He pointed to his eyes; and Tihon, understanding him, wiped away his tears.

Then he opened his eyes, and said something, which, for a long while, no one could understand; and at last Tihon understood and interpreted. Princess Marya looked for the drift of his words in the direction in which he had been speaking a minute before. She supposed he was speaking of Russia; then of Prince Andrey, of herself, of his grandson, then of his own death. And this was just why she could not understand his words.

'Put on your white dress. I like it,' he had said.

When she understood those words Princess Marya sobbed louder than ever, and the doctor, taking her on his arm, led her out of the room on to the terrace, trying to persuade her to calm down, and to devote herself to preparations for the journey. After Princess Marya had left the prince, he began talking again of his son, of the war, of the Tsar, twitched his eyebrows angrily, began to raise his hoarse voice, and was seized by a second and final stroke.

Princess Marya stayed on the terrace. The day had become brilliantly fine, sunny, and warm. She could grasp nothing, could think of nothing, and feel nothing but her passionate love for her father, of which it seemed to her that she had not been aware till that minute. She ran out into the garden, and ran sobbing towards the pond along the paths planted with young lime-trees by Prince Andrey.

'Yes ... I ... I ... I longed for his death! Yes, I wanted it soon to be over ... I wanted to be at peace ... And what will become of me? What use will peace be to me when he is gone?' Princess Marya muttered aloud, walking with rapid steps through the garden, and pressing her hands to her bosom, which heaved with convulsive sobs. Going round the garden in a circle, which brought her back again to the house, she saw coming towards her Mademoiselle Bourienne (who was remaining at Bogutcharovo, preferring not to move away), and with her an unknown gentleman. It was the district marshal, who had come to call on the princess, to urge upon her the necessity of her immediate departure. Princess Marya listened and did not take in what he said. She took him into the house, offered him lunch, and sat down with him. Then asking him to excuse her, she went to the old prince's door. The doctor came out with a perturbed face and told her she could not go in.

'Go away, princess; go away!'

Princess Marya went out again into the garden, and by the pond at the bottom of the hill she sat down on the grass, in a place where no one could see her. She could not have said how long she was there. A woman's footsteps running along the path made her look round She got up and saw Dunyasha, her maid, evidently running to look for her, stop short, as though in alarm, on seeing her mistress.

'Come, please, princess ... the prince ...' said Dunyasha, in a breaking voice.

'I'm coming, I'm coming!' the princess cried hurriedly, not letting Dunyasha have time to say what she meant to; and trying to avoid seeing her, she ran into the house.

'Princess, it is God's will! You must be prepared for the worst,' said the marshal, meeting her at the door into the house.

'Let me be; it's not true!' she cried angrily at him.

The doctor tried to stop her. She pushed him away and ran to the door. 'What are these people with scared faces stopping me for? I don't want any of them! What are they doing here?' she thought. She opened the door, and the bright daylight in the room, always hitherto darkened, frightened her. Her old nurse and other women were in the room. They all drew back from the bed, making way for her. He was still lying on the bed as before; but the stern look on his calm face arrested Princess Marya on the threshold.

'No, he is not dead, it cannot be!' Princess Marya said to herself. She went up to him, and struggling with the terror that came upon her, she pressed her lips to his cheek. But she started back from him at once. Instantaneously all the tenderness she had been feeling for him vanished, and was followed by a feeling of horror for what lay before her. 'No, no, he is no more! He is no more, and here in the place where he was, is something unfamiliar and sinister, some fearful, terrifying, and repulsive secret!' And hiding her face in her hands, Princess Marya sank into the arms of the doctor, who supported her.

In the presence of Tihon and the doctor, the women washed what had been the prince, bound a kerchief round the head that the mouth might not become rigidly open, and bound another kerchief round the limbs. Then the uniform with the decorations was put on, and the little dried-up body was laid on the table. There was no telling when or who took thought for all this; it seemed to be done of itself. Towards night candles were lighted round the coffin, a pall was laid over it, juniper was strewn on the floor, a printed prayer was put under the dead withered head, and a deacon sat in the corner reading aloud the Psalter.

Like horses crowding, snorting, and starting round a dead horse numbers of familiar and unfamiliar figures crowded round the coffin—

the marshal, and the village elder, and peasant women, and all with scared and fascinated eyes, crossed themselves, and bowed down and kissed the cold, stiff hand of the old prince.

IX

UNTIL Prince Andrey's stay at Bogutcharovo, the estate had never had an owner in residence, and the Bogutcharovo peasants were of quite a different character from the peasants of Bleak Hills. They differed from them in speech, in dress, and in manners. They said they came from the steppes. The old prince praised them for their industry when they came to Bleak Hills for harvesting, or digging ponds and ditches; but he did not like them because of their savage manners.

Prince Andrey's residence at Bogutcharovo, and his innovations—his hospitals and schools and the lowering of their rent—had not softened their manners, but, on the contrary, had intensified their traits of character, which the old prince called their savagery.

Obscure rumours were always current among them: at one time a belief that they were all to be carried off to be made Cossacks, then that they were to be converted to some new religion, then rumours of some supposed proclamations of the Tsar, or of the oath to the Tsar Pavel Petrovitch in 1797 (which was said to have granted freedom to the peasants, and to have been withdrawn by the gentry later); then of the expected return of the Tsar Peter Fedorovitch, who was to rise again from the dead in seven years, and to bring perfect freedom, and to make an end of the existing order of things. Rumours of the war, and Bonaparte and his invasion, were connected in their minds with vague conceptions of Antichrist, of the end of the world, and perfect freedom.

In the vicinity of Bogutcharovo were large villages inhabited by Crown serfs, or peasants who paid rent to absentee owners. There were very few resident landowners in the neighbourhood, and consequently very few house-serfs or peasants able to read and write. And among the peasants of that part of the country there could be seen more distinctly and strongly marked than among others those mysterious undercurrents in the life of the Russian peasantry, which are so baffling to contemporaries. Twenty years before, there had been a movement among the peasants of the district to emigrate to certain supposed warm rivers. Hundreds of peasants, among them those of Bogutcharovo, had suddenly begun selling their cattle and moving away with their families towards the south-west. Like birds flying to unknown realms over the ocean, these men with their wives and children turned towards the south-west, where no one of them had been. They set off in caravans, redeemed their freedom one by one, ran and drove and walked to the unknown region of the warm springs. Many were punished; some sent to Siberia; many died of cold and hunger on the road; many came back of their own accord; and the movement died down as it had begun without obvious cause. But the undercurrents still flowed among the people, and were gathering force for some new manifestation, destined to appear as strangely, unexpectedly, and at the same time simply, naturally, and forcibly. In 1812 any one living in close relations with the peasants might have observed that there was a violent ferment working below the surface, and an outbreak of some kind was at hand.

Alpatitch, who came to Bogutcharovo a little while before the old prince's death, noticed that there was some excitement among the peasants; and noticed that, unlike the Bleak Hills district, where within a radius of sixty versts all the peasants had moved away, abandoning their villages to be wasted by the Cossacks, in the Bogutcharovo steppe country the peasants had entered, it was said, into communication with the French, and were remaining in their homes, and there were some mysterious documents circulating among them. He learned through serfs who were attached to him that the peasant Karp, a man of great influence in the village, had a few days previously accompanied a government transport, and had returned with the news that the Cossacks were destroying the deserted villages, while the French would not touch them. He knew that another peasant had on the previous day even brought from the hamlet of Vislouhovo, where the French were encamped, a proclamation from the French general that no harm would be done to the inhabitants, and that everything taken from them would be paid for, if they would remain. In token of good faith, the peasant brought from Vislouhovo a hundred-rouble note (he did not know it was false), paid him in advance for hay.

And last, and most important of all, Alpatitch learned that on the day on which he had given the village elder orders to collect carts to move the princess's luggage from Bogutcharovo, there had been a meeting in the village at which it was resolved to wait and not to move. Meanwhile, time was pressing. On the day of the prince's death, the 15th of August, the marshal urged Princess Marya to move the same day, as it was becoming dangerous. He said that he could not answer for what might happen after the 16th. He drove away that evening, promising to return next morning for the funeral. But next day he could not come, as he received information of an expected advance of the French, and was only just in time to get his family and valuables moved away from his own estate.

For nearly thirty years Bogutcharovo had been under the direction of the village elder, Dron, called by the old prince, Dronushka.

Dron was one of those physically and morally vigorous peasants, who grow a thick beard as soon as they are grown up, and go on almost unchanged till sixty or seventy, without a grey hair or the loss of a tooth, as upright and vigorous at sixty as at thirty.

Shortly after the attempted migration to the warm rivers, in which he had taken part with the rest, Dron was made village elder and overseer of Bogutcharovo, and had filled those positions irreproachably for twenty-three years. The peasants were more afraid of him than of their master. The old prince and the young one and the steward respected him, and called him in joke the minister. Dron had never once been drunk or ill since he had been appointed elder; he had never after sleepless nights or severe labour shown the slightest sign of fatigue; and though he could not read or write, he never forgot an account of the pounds of flour in the huge wagon-loads he sold, and of the money paid for them, nor missed a sheaf of wheat on an acre of Bogutcharovo fields.

This peasant Dron it was for whom Alpatitch sent on coming from the plundered estate at Bleak Hills. He ordered him to get ready twelve horses for the princess's carriages, and eighteen conveyances for the move which was to be made from Bogutcharovo. Though the peasants paid rent instead of working as serfs, Alpatitch expected to meet no difficulty on their part in carrying out this order, since there were two hundred and thirty efficient families in Bogutcharovo, and the peasants were well-to-do. But Dron, on receiving the order, dropped his eyes and made no reply. Alpatitch mentioned the names of peasants from whom he told him to take the carts.

Dron replied that the horses belonging to those peasants were away on hire. Alpatitch mentioned the names of other peasants. They too, according to Dron, had no horses available: some were employed in government transport, others had gone lame, and others had died through the shortness of forage. In Dron's opinion, there was no hope of getting horses enough for the princess's carriages, not to speak of the transport of baggage.

Alpatitch looked intently at Dron and scowled. Dron was a model village elder, but Alpatitch had not been twenty years managing the prince's estates for nothing, and he too was a model steward. He possessed in the highest degree the faculty of divining the needs and instincts of the peasants, with whom he had to deal, and was consequently an excellent steward. Glancing at Dron, he saw at once that his answers were not the expression of his own ideas, but the expression of the general drift of opinion in the Bogutcharovo village, by which the elder had already been carried away. At the same time, he knew that Dron, who had saved money and was detested by the village, must be hesitating between two camps —the master's and the peasants'. He detected the hesitation in his eyes, and so frowning he came closer to Dron.

'Now, Dronushka,' he said, 'you listen to me! Don't you talk nonsense to me. His excellency, Prince Andrey Nikolaevitch, himself gave me orders to move the folk away, and not leave them with the enemy, and the Tsar has issued a decree that it is to be so. Any one that stays is a traitor to the Tsar. Do you hear?'

'I hear,' answered Dron, not raising his eyes.

Alpatitch was not satisfied with his reply.

'Ay, Dron, there'll be trouble!' said Alpatitch, shaking his head.

'It's for you to command!' said Dron dejectedly.

'Ay, Dron, drop it!' repeated Alpatitch, taking his hand out of the bosom of his coat, and pointing with a solemn gesture to the ground under Dron's feet. 'I can see right through you; and more than that, I can see three yards into the earth under you,' he said, looking at the ground under Dron's feet.

Dron was disconcerted; he looked furtively at Alpatitch, and dropped his eyes again.

'You drop this nonsense, and tell the folks to pack up to leave their homes and go to Moscow, and to get ready carts tomorrow morning for the princess's luggage; and don't you go to the meeting. Do you hear?'

All at once Dron threw himself at his feet.

'Yakov Alpatitch, discharge me! Take the keys from me; discharge me, for Christ's sake!'

'Stop that!' said Alpatitch sternly. 'I can see through you three yards into the earth,' he repeated, knowing that his skill in bee-keeping, his knowledge of the right day to sow the oats, and his success in pleasing the old prince for twenty years had long ago gained him the reputation of a wizard, and that power of seeing for three yards under a man is ascribed to wizards.

Dron got up, and would have said something, but Alpatitch interrupted him.

'What's this you've all got in your head? Eh? . . . What are you thinking about? Eh?'

'What am I to do with the people?' said Dron. 'They're all in a ferment. I do tell them . . .'

'Oh, I dare say you do,' said Alpatitch. 'Are they drinking?' he asked briefly.

'They're all in a ferment, Yakov Alpatitch; they have got hold of another barrel.'

'Then you listen to me. I'll go to the police-captain and you tell them so, and tell them to drop all this and get the carts ready.'

'Certainly,' answered Dron.

Yakov Alpatitch did not insist further. He had much experience in managing the peasants, and knew that the chief means for securing obdience was not to show the slightest suspicion that they could do anything but obey. Having wrung from Dron a submissive 'certainly,' Yakov Alpatitch rested content with it, though he had more than doubts —he had a conviction—that the carts would not be provided without the intervention of the military authorities.

And as a fact when evening came, the carts had not been provided. There had been again a village meeting at the tavern, and at the meeting it had been resolved to drive the horses out into the forest and not to provide the conveyances. Without saying a word of all this to the princess, Alpatitch ordered his own baggage to be unloaded from the wagons that had come from Bleak Hills and the horses to be taken from them for the princess's carriage, while he rode off himself to the police authorities.

X

AFTER her father's funeral Princess Marya locked herself in her room and would not let any one come near her. A maid came to the door to say that Alpatitch had come to ask for instructions in regard to the journey. (This was before Alpatitch had talked to Dron.) Princess Marya got up from the sofa on which she was lying, and through the closed door replied that she was never going away, and begged to be left in peace.

The windows of the room in which Princess Marya lay looked to the west. She lay on the sofa facing the wall, and fingering the buttons on the leather bolster, she saw nothing but that bolster, and her thoughts were concentrated obscurely on one subject. She thought of the finality of death and of her spiritual baseness, of which she had had no idea till it showed itself during her father's illness. She longed to pray, but dared not; dared not, in the spiritual state she was in, turn to God. For a long while she lay in that position.

The sun was setting, and the slanting rays lighted up the room through the open window, and threw a glow on part of the morocco cushion at which Princess Marya was looking. The current of her thoughts was suddenly arrested. She unconsciously sat up, smoothed her hair, stood up, and walked to the window, involuntarily drawing a deep breath of the refreshing coolness of the clear, windy evening.

'Yes, now you can admire the sunset at your ease! He is not here, and there is no one to hinder you,' she said to herself, and sinking into a chair, she let her head fall on the window-sill.

Some one spoke her name in a soft and tender voice from the garden and kissed her on the head. She looked up. It was Mademoiselle Bourienne in a black dress and *pleureuses*. She softly approached Princess Marya, kissed her with a sigh, and promptly burst into tears. Princess Marya looked round at her. All her old conflicts with her, her jealousy of her, recurred to Princess Marya's mind. She remembered too that *he* had changed of late to Mademoiselle Bourienne, could not bear the sight of her, and therefore how unjust had been the censure that she had in her heart passed upon her. 'Yes, and is it for me, after desiring his death, to pass judgment on any one?' she thought.

Princess Marya pictured vividly to herself Mademoiselle Bourienne's position, estranged from her of late, though dependent on her, and living among strangers. And she felt sorry for her. She looked at her in gentle inquiry and held out her hand to her. Mademoiselle Bourienne at once began kissing her hand with tears and talking of the princess's sorrow making herself a partner in that sorrow. She said that her only consolation in her sorrow was that the princess permitted her to share it with her. She said that all their former misunderstandings must sink into nothing before their great sorrow; that she felt herself guiltless in regard to every one, and that *he* from above saw her love and gratitude. The princess heard her without heeding her words, though she looked at her now and then and listened to the sound of her voice.

'Your position is doubly dreadful, dear princess,' said Mademoiselle Bourienne. 'I know you could not and cannot think of yourself; but with my love for you I am bound to do so. . . . Has Alpatitch been with you? Has he spoken to you of moving?' she asked.

Princess Marya did not answer. She did not understand who was to move and where. 'Was it possible to undertake anything now, to think of anything? Could anything matter?' she wondered. She made no reply.

'Do you know, *chère Marie*,' said Mademoiselle Bourienne, 'that we are in danger, that we are surrounded by the French; it is dangerous to move now. If we move, we are almost certain to be taken prisoner, and God knows . . .'

Princess Marya looked at her companion, with no notion what she was saying.

'Oh, if any one knew how little anything matters to me now,' she said. 'Of course, I would not on any account move away from *him* . . . Alpatitch said something about going away. . . . You talk to him . . . I can't do anything, and I don't want . . .'

'I have been talking to him. He hopes that we may manage to get away tomorrow; but I think it would be better now to remain here,' said Mademoiselle Bourienne. 'Because you will agree, *chère Marie,* that to fall into the hands of the soldiers or of rioting peasants on the road would be awful.'

Mademoiselle Bourienne took out of her reticule a document, not on the usual Russian paper. It was the proclamation of General Rameau, announcing that protection would be given by the French commanders to all inhabitants who did not abandon their homes. She handed it to the princess.

'I imagine the best thing would be to appeal to this general,' said Mademoiselle Bourienne. 'I am convinced that all proper respect would be shown you.'

Princess Marya read the document and her face worked with tearless sobs.

'Through whom did you get this?' she asked.

'They probably found out I was French from my name,' said Mademoiselle Bourienne, flushing.

With the proclamation in her hand, Princess Marya got up from the window, and with a pale face walked out of the room into Prince Andrey's former study.

'Dunyasha! send Alpatitch to me, Dronushka, or somebody!' said Princess Marya. 'And tell Amalya Karlovna not to come to me,' she added, hearing Mademoiselle Bourienne's voice. 'To set off at once! as quick as possible!' said Princess Marya, appalled at the idea that she might be left in the power of the French.

'That Prince Andrey should know that she was in the power of the French! That she, the daughter of Prince Nikolay Andreitch Bolkonsky, should stoop to ask General Rameau to grant her his protection, and should take advantage of his good offices.' The idea appalled her, made her shudder and turn crimson. She felt a rush of vindictive wrath and pride of which she had had no conception. All the bitterness, and still more the humiliation, of her position rose vividly to her imagination. 'They, the French, would take up their quarters in the house: M. le Général Rameau would occupy Prince Andrey's study; would amuse himself by looking through and reading his letters and papers; Mademoiselle Bourienne would do the honours of Bogutcharovo; I should be given a room as a favour; the soldiers would break open my father's newly dug grave to take his crosses and decorations; they would tell me of their victories over the Russians, would affect hypocritical sympathy with my grief, . . .' thought Princess Marya, thinking not the thoughts natural to her, but feeling it a duty to think as her father and brother would have done. To her personally it did not matter where she stayed and what happened to her, but, at the same time she felt herself the representative of her dead father and Prince Andrey. Unconsciously she thought their thoughts and felt their feelings. What they would have said, what they would have done now, she felt it incumbent upon her to do. She went into Prince Andrey's study, and trying to enter completely into his ideas, thought over her situation.

The exigencies of life, which she had regarded as of no consequence since her father's death, all at once rose up about Princess Marya with a force she had known nothing of before, and swept her away with them.

Flushed and excited she walked about the room, sending first for Alpatitch, then for Mihail Ivanitch, then for Tihon, then for Dron. Dunyasha, the old nurse, and the maids could not tell her how far Mademoiselle Bourienne's statements had been correct. Alpatitch was not in the house; he had gone to the police authorities. Mihail Ivanitch, the architect, came with sleepy eyes on being sent for, but could tell Princess Marya nothing. With the same smile of acquiescence with which he had been accustomed during the course of fifteen years to meet the old prince's remarks without committing himself, he now met the princess's questions, so that there was no getting any definite answer out of him. The old valet, Tihon, whose wan and sunken face wore the stamp of inconsolable grief, answered 'Yes, princess,' to all Princess Marya's questions, and could scarcely restrain his sobs as he looked at her.

Lastly, the village elder, Dron, came into the room, and bowing low to the princess, took up his position near the doorway.

Princess Marya walked up and down the room and stood still facing him.

'Dronushka,' she said, seeing in him a staunch friend, the Dronushka who had every year brought back from the fair at Vyazma the same gingerbreads she connected with him, and had presented them to her with the same smile, 'Dronushka, now, after our misfortune,' . . . she began, and paused, unable to proceed.

'We are all in God's hands,' he said, with a sigh.

They were silent.

'Dronushka, Alpatitch has gone off somewhere, I have no one to turn to. Is it true, as I'm told, that it is impossible for me to go away?'

'Why shouldn't you go away, your excellency? you can go,' said Dron.

'I have been told there is danger from the enemy. My good friend, I can do nothing, I know nothing about it, I have nobody. I want to set off without fail tonight or tomorrow morning early.'

Dron did not speak. He looked up from under his brows at Princess Marya.

'There are no horses,' he said. 'I have told Yakov Alpatitch so already.'

'How is that?' said the princess.

'It's all the visitation of the Lord,' said Dron. 'Some horses have been carried off for the troops, and some are dead; it's a bad year, it is. If only we don't die of hunger ourselves, let alone feeding the horses! Here they've been three days without a bit of bread. There's nothing, they have been plundered to the last bit.'

Princess Marya listened attentively to what he said to her.

'The peasants have been plundered? They have no bread?' she asked.

'They are dying of hunger,' said Dron; 'no use talking of horses and carts.'

'But why didn't you say so, Dronushka? Can't they be helped? I'll do everything I can . . .' It was strange to Princess Marya to think that at such a moment, when her heart was overflowing with such a sorrow, there could be rich people and poor, and that the rich could possibly not help the poor. She vaguely knew that there was a store of 'seignorial corn,' and that it was sometimes given to the peasants. She knew, too, that neither her brother nor her father would refuse the peasants in their need; she was only afraid of making some mistake in the wording of the order for this distribution. She was glad that she had an excuse for doing something in which she could, without scruple, forget her own grief. She began to question Dronushka about the peasants' needs, and to ask whether there was a 'seignorial store' at Bogutcharovo.

'I suppose we have a store of wheat of my brother's?' she asked.

'The wheat is all untouched,' Dron declared with pride. 'The prince gave me no orders about selling it.'

'Give it to the peasants, give them all they need; I give you leave in my brother's name,' said Princess Marya.

Dron heaved a deep sigh and made no answer.

'You distribute the corn among them, if it will be enough for them. Distribute it all. I give you the order in my brother's name; and tell them, what's ours is theirs. We would grudge nothing for them. Tell them so.'

Dron watched the princess intently all the while she was speaking.

'Discharge me, ma'am, for God's sake, bid them take the keys from me,' said he. 'I have served twenty-three years, and done no wrong; discharge me, for God's sake.'

Princess Marya had no notion what he wanted of her and why he asked her to discharge him. She answered that she had never doubted his fidelity, and that she was ready to do everything for him and for the peasants.

XI

AN hour later Dunyasha came in to the princess with the news that Dron had come, and all the peasants by the princess's orders were assembled at the granary and desirous of speaking with their mistress.

'But I did not send for them,' said Princess Marya. 'I merely told Dronushka to give them the corn.'

'Only, for God's sake, your excellency, order them to be sent away and don't go to them. It's all a plot,' said Dunyasha, 'and Yakov Alpatitch will come and we will start ... and pray ...'

'How a plot?' asked the princess in surprise.

'Why, I know all about it, only do listen to me, for God's sake. Ask old nurse too. They say they won't agree to move away at your orders.'

'You are making some mistake. Why, I have never given them orders to go away ...' said Princess Marya. 'Call Dronushka.'

Dron on coming in confirmed Dunyasha's words; the peasants had come by the princess's instructions.

'But I have never sent for them,' said the princess. 'You must have given them my message wrong. I only said that you were to give them the corn.'

Dron sighed without replying.

'If so you command, they will go away,' he said.

'No, no, I'll go out to them,' said Princess Marya.

In spite of Dunyasha's and the old nurse's attempts to dissuade her, Princess Marya went out on to the steps. Dronushka, Dunyasha, the old nurse, and Mihail Ivanitch followed her.

'They probably imagine I am offering them the corn to keep them here while I go away myself, leaving them at the mercy of the French,' thought Princess Marya. 'I will promise them monthly rations and lodgings on the Moscow estate. I am sure Andrey would do more for them in my place,' she thought, as she went out in the twilight towards the crowd, waiting on the pasture near the granary.

The crowd stirred, huddling closer, and rapidly took off their hats. Princess Marya came closer to them, her eyes cast down and her feet tripping over her gown. So many different eyes, old and young, were fixed upon her, there were so many different faces that Princess Marya did not see a single one of them, and feeling it necessary to address all at once, did not know how to set about it. But again the sense that she was the representative of her father and brother gave her strength, and she boldly began her speech.

'I am very glad you have come,' she began, not raising her eyes and feeling the rapid and violent beating of her heart. 'Dronushka has told me that the war has ruined you. That is our common trouble, and I will grudge nothing to aid you. I am going away myself because it is dangerous here . . . and the enemy is near . . . because . . . I give you everything, my friends, and I beg you to take everything, all our corn, that you may not suffer want. But if you have been told that I am giving you corn to keep you here, it is false. On the contrary, I beg you to move away with all your belongings to our Moscow estate, and there I undertake and promise you that you shall not be in want. You shall be given houses and bread.' The princess stopped. Nothing was to be heard from the crowd but sighs.

'I don't do this on my own account,' the princess went on; 'I do it in the name of my dead father, who was a good master to you, and for my brother and his son.'

She paused again. No one broke the silence.

'We have trouble in common, and we will share it all equally. All that is mine is yours,' she said, looking up at the faces before her. All the eyes were gazing at her with the same expression, the meaning of which she could not fathom. Whether it were curiosity, devotion, gratitude, or apprehension, and distrust, the expression on all the faces was alike.

'Very thankful for your kindness, only it's not for us to take the master's corn,' said a voice from the back.

'But why not?' said the princess. No one answered, and Princess Marya, looking up at the crowd, noticed that now all the eyes dropped at once on meeting hers.

'Why don't you want to?' she asked again.

No one replied.

Princess Marya was oppressed by the silence; she tried to catch somebody's eye.

'Why don't you speak?' she said, addressing a very old man who was standing near her, his arms propped on his stick. 'Tell me if you think something more is needed. I will do anything,' she said, catching his eye. But as though angered by her doing so, he bent his head, and said :

'Why should we agree? We don't want your corn.'

'Why are we to give up everything? We're not willing . . . Not willing. It's not with our consent. We are sorry for you, but we are not willing. You go away by yourself, alone . . .' was protested from different parts of the crowd. And again all the faces in the crowd wore the same expression; and now it was unmistakably not an expression of curiosity and gratitude, but an expression of exasperated determination.

'But you misunderstand me,' said Princess Marya, with a melancholy smile. 'Why don't you want to move away? I promise to settle you, to provide for you. And here the enemy will plunder you . . .' But her voice was drowned by the voices of the crowd.

'We're not willing, let him plunder us! We won't take your corn, we won't agree!'

Princess Marya tried again to catch some one's eye in the crowd, but no one was looking at her; their eyes unmistakably avoided hers. She felt strange and awkward.

'To be sure, she would school us, . . . a good dodge, . . . follow her into slavery. Pull down your house and go into bondage. I dare say! I'll give you corn, says she!' voices were saying in the crowd.

Princess Marya moved out of the ring, and went to the house with a dejected countenance. Repeating her command to Dron that horses were to be ready next day for her to start, she went away to her own room and remained alone with her own thoughts.

XII

FOR a long while Princess Marya sat at the open window of her room listening to the sound of the peasants' voices floating across from the village, but she was not thinking of them. She felt that she could not understand them however long she thought of them. She thought all the while of one thing—of her sorrow, which now after the break made by anxiety about the present, already seemed to belong to the past. Now she could remember, could weep, and could pray. With the setting of the sun the wind sank. The night was still and fresh. At midnight the voices in the village began to die down; a cock crowed; the full moon rose from behind a lime-tree; there rose a fresh, white, dewy mist, and stillness reigned over the village and the house.

One after another pictures of the immediate past—her father's illness and last moments—rose before her imagination. And with mournful gladness she let her mind now rest on those images, only shunning with horror the one last scene which she felt she had not the strength to contemplate even in fancy at that still and mysterious hour of the night. And those images rose with such clearness and in such detail before her, that they seemed to her now in the actual present, now in the past, and now in the future.

She had a vivid picture of the moment when he was first stricken down and was being dragged in from the garden at Bleak Hills, and he had muttered something, twitching his grey eyebrows, and looking timidly and uneasily at her. 'Even then he wanted to tell me what he told me on the day of his death,' she thought. 'He always thought what he told me then.'

And then she recalled with every detail the night at Bleak Hills before his stroke, when, with a presentiment of trouble, she had remained with him against his will. She had not slept; and at night she had stolen down on tiptoe, and going to the door of the conservatory room where her father was spending that night, she had listened to his voice. He was talking in a weary, harassed voice to Tihon. He was saying something about the Crimea, about the warm nights, about the Empress. Evidently he wanted to talk to some one. 'And why didn't he send for me? Why didn't he let me be there in Tihon's place?' Princess Marya had thought then and thought again now. 'Now he will never tell any one all that was in his heart. Now the moment will never return when he might have told me all he longed to express, and I and not Tihon might have heard and understood. Why didn't I go into his room then?' she thought. 'Perhaps he would have said to me then what he said on the day of his death. Even then talking to Tihon he asked about me twice. He was longing to see me while I was standing there behind the door. He was sad and weary talking to Tihon, who did not understand him. I remember how he spoke to him of Liza as though she were living—he forgot that she was dead, and Tihon reminded him that she was no more, and he cried, "Fool!" He was miserable. I heard from the door how he lay down groaning on the bed and cried out aloud, "My God!" Why didn't I go in then? What could he have done to me? What could I have lost? And, perhaps, then he would have been comforted, he would have said that word to me.' And Princess Marya uttered aloud that caressing word he had said to her on the day of his death. 'Da-ar-ling!' Princess Marya repeated the word and broke into sobs that relieved her heart. She could see his face before her now. And not the face she had known ever since she could remember and had always seen at a distance; but the weak and timid face she had seen on the last day when, bending to his lips to catch what he said, she had, for the first time, looked at it quite close with all its wrinkles.

'Darling,' she repeated.

'What was he thinking when he uttered that word? What is he thinking now?' was the question that rose suddenly to her mind; and in answer to it she saw him with the expression she had seen on the face bound up with a white handkerchief in the coffin. And the horror that had overcome her at the moment when she had touched him, and felt that it was not he but something mysterious and horrible, came over her now. She tried to think of something else, tried to pray, and could do nothing. With wide eyes she gazed at the moonlight and the shadows, every instant expecting to see his dead face, and feeling as though she were held spellbound in the stillness that reigned without and within the house.

'Dunyasha!' she whispered. 'Dunyasha!' she shrieked wildly, and tearing herself out of the stillness, she ran towards the maids' room, meeting the old nurse and the maids running out to meet her.

XIII

ON the 17th of August Rostov and Ilyin, accompanied by Lavrushka, who had just come back from being taken prisoner by the French, and an hussar on orderly duty, rode out from Yankovo, fifteen versts from Bogutcharovo. They meant to try a new horse that Ilyin had bought, and to find out whether there was hay to be had in the village.

Bogutcharovo had been for the last three days between the two hostile armies, so that the Russian rearguard could reach the village as easily as the French vanguard; and therefore Rostov, like a careful officer, was anxious to anticipate the French in securing any provisions that might be left there.

Rostov and Ilyin were in the liveliest spirits. On the way to Bogutcharovo, which they knew to be an estate belonging to a prince, with a manor-house, where they hoped to find a large household, and, perhaps, pretty servant-girls, they questioned Lavrushka about Napoleon, and laughed at his stories; then raced their horses to test Ilyin's new purchase. Rostov had no notion that the village to which he was going was the property of the very Prince Bolkonsky who had been betrothed to his sister.

Rostov and Ilyin had just let their horses race till they were weary for the last time before Bogutcharovo, and Rostov, outstripping Ilyin, was the first to gallop into the village street.

'You started in front,' said Ilyin, flushed.

'Yes, always in front, in the meadow and here too,' answered Rostov, patting his foaming Don horse.

'And on my Frenchy, your excellency,' said Lavrushka from behind, meaning the wretched cart-horse he was riding, 'I could have overtaken you, only I didn't want to put you to shame.'

They rode at a walking pace towards the granary, where there was a great crowd of peasants standing. Several of the peasants took off their caps, others stared at them without taking off their caps. Two old peasants with wrinkled faces and scanty beards, came out of the tavern, reeling and singing a tuneless song, and advanced with smiles towards the officers. 'They're fine fellows!' said Rostov, laughing. 'Well, have you any hay?'

'And so alike, somehow...' said Ilyin.

'Ma ... a ... aking mer ... ry in my sum ... sum ... mer. ..' chanted the peasant, with a blissful smile.

A peasant came out of the crowd and went up to Rostov.

'Which part will you be from?' asked the peasant.

'We're French,' answered Ilyin, laughing. 'And this is Napoleon himself,' he said, pointing to Lavrushka.

'I suppose you are Russians then?' the peasant inquired.

'And have you many troops here?' asked another short peasant, approaching.

'A great many,' answered Rostov. 'But why are you all assembled here?' he added. 'Is it a holiday or what?'

'The old men are met about the village business,' answered the peasant, moving away from him.

At that moment there came into sight two women and a man in a white hat running from the prince's house towards the officers.

'The one in pink's mine; hands off, beware!' said Ilyin, noticing Dunyasha running resolutely towards them.

'She'll be the girl for us!' said Lavrushka, winking to Ilyin.

'What is it you want, my pretty?' said Ilyin, smiling.

'The princess sent me to ask of what regiment are you, and what is your name?'

'This is Count Rostov, the commander of the squadron, and I am your humble servant.'

'Mer ... mer ... mer ... arbour!' chanted the drunken peasant, smiling blissfully, and gazing at Ilyin as he talked to the girl. Alpatitch followed Dunyasha, taking off his hat to Rostov as he approached.

'I make bold to trouble your honour,' he said, putting one hand in his bosom, and speaking with a respectfulness in which there was a shade of contempt for the officer's youth. 'My mistress, the daughter of general-in-chief Prince Nikolay Andreitch Bolkonsky, who died on the 15th of this month, being in difficulties owing to the coarse ignorance of those people'—he pointed to the peasants—'begs you to come

... Would you not be pleased,' said Alpatitch, with a melancholy smile, 'to move a little away, as it is not so convenient before ...' Alpatitch indicated two peasants, who were hovering about him, like gadflies about a horse.

'Ay! ... Alpatitch! ... Ay! Yakov Alpatitch! first-rate job! h? ... for Christ's sake, forgive us. First-rate! ay?' cried the peasants, smiling gleefully at him.

Rostov looked at the drunken peasants, and smiled.

'Or possibly this entertains your excellency?' said Yakov Alpatitch, with a sober air, pointing with his other hand to the old peasants.

'No, there's nothing very entertaining in that,' said Rostov, and he moved away. 'What is the matter?' he inquired.

'I make bold to submit to your excellency that the rude peasants here will not let their lady leave the estate, and threaten to take the horses out of her carriage, so that everything has been packed since morning, yet her excellency cannot get away.'

'Impossible!' cried Rostov.

'I have the honour of submitting to you the simple truth,' said Alpatitch.

Rostov got off his horse, and giving it to the orderly, walked with Alpatitch to the house, questioning him further about the state of affairs.

The princess's offer of corn, and her interview with Dron and with the peasants, had, in fact, made the position so much worse that Dron had finally given up the keys of office, joined the peasants, and refused to appear when Alpatitch sent for him. In the morning when the princess ordered the horses to be put in for her to set off, the peasants had come out in a great crowd to the granary, and had sent to say that they would not let the princess go out of the village; that there was an edict that people were not to leave their houses, and that they would unharness the horses. Alpatitch went out to lecture them; in reply they told him (a certain Karp was the principal speaker, Dron kept in the background in the crowd) that the princess could not be allowed to go, that there was an edict forbidding it, but that only let her stay, and they would serve her and obey her in everything as before.

At the moment when Rostov and Ilyin were galloping along the village street, regardless of the efforts of Alpatitch, the old nurse, and the maid to dissuade her, Prince Marya had just ordered the horses to be put in, and was intending to start. But seeing the horsemen galloping up, the coachmen took them for the French, and ran away, and a great lamentation arose among the women of the household.

'Kind sir! Protector! God has sent thee,' cried voices, with much feeling, as Rostov crossed the vestibule. Princess Marya was sitting helpless and distraught in the hall, when Rostov was shown in to see her. She did not know who he was, or what brought him there, or what was happening to her. Seeing his Russian face, and recognising him at his first words and gait for a man of her own rank, she looked at him, with her deep, luminous gaze, and began speaking in a voice, broken and trembling with emotion. Rostov at once conceived a romance in this meeting. 'A defenceless girl, crushed by sorrow, alone, abandoned to the mercy of coarse, rebellious peasants! And what strange destiny has brought me here!' thought Rostov, as he listened to her and looked at her. 'And what mildness, what nobility in her features and expression!' he thought, as he listened to her timid story.

When she began to tell him that all this had happened the day after her father's funeral, her voice trembled. She turned away, and as though afraid Rostov might ascribe her words to a desire to work on his feelings, she glanced at him with a look of apprehensive inquiry. There were tears in Rostov's eyes. Princess Marya noticed it, and looked at him with the luminous eyes that made one forget the plainness of her face.

'I cannot express how glad I am, princess, that I happened to come this way, and am able to serve you in anything,' said Rostov, rising. 'I trust you will start at once, and I answer for it on my honour, no person shall dare to cause you annoyance, if you will only permit me to escort you,' and making a deep bow, such as are made to ladies of the royal family, he turned to the door.

By the respectfulness of his tone, Rostov tried to show that though he would consider it a happiness to be acquainted with her, he did not wish to take advantage of her misfortunes to force an acquaintanceship upon her.

Princess Marya felt and appreciated this tone.

'I am very, very grateful to you,' she said to him in French; 'but I hope it was all only a misunderstanding, and that no one is to blame.' She began all at once to cry.

'Excuse me,' she said.

Rostov, knitting his brows, bowed low once more, and went out of the room.

XIV

'WELL, is she pretty? But, my boy, my pink girl's charming; her name is Dunyasha.' . . . But glancing into Rostov's face, Ilyin paused. He saw his hero and superior officer was absorbed in a very different train of thought.

Rostov looked angrily at Ilyin, and without replying, strode off rapidly to the village.

'I'll teach them; I'll pay them out; the scoundrels,' he muttered to himself.

Alpatitch followed Rostov at a quick trot, which he could only just keep from breaking into a run.

'What decision has your honour come to?' he said, overtaking him. Rostov stopped short, and clenching his fists moved suddenly up to Alpatitch with a menacing gesture.

'Decision? What decision, old shuffler?' he shouted. 'What have you been thinking about? Eh? The peasants are unruly and you don't know how to manage them? You're a traitor yourself. I know you. I'll flog the skin off the lot of you . . .' And, as though afraid of wasting the energy of his anger, he left Alpatitch and went quickly ahead. Alpatitch, swallowing his wounded feelings, hurried with a swaying step after Rostov, still giving him the benefit of his reflections on the subject. He said that the peasants were in a very stubborn state, that at the moment it was imprudent to *oppositionise* them, without an armed force, and would it not be better first to send for armed force.

'I'll give them armed force. . . . I'll oppositionise them . . .' Nikolay muttered meaninglessly, choking with irrational animal rage and desire to vent that rage on some one. Without considering what he was going to do, unconsciously, he moved with a rapid, resolute step up to the crowd. And the nearer he approached, the more Alpatitch felt that his imprudent action might produce the happiest results. The peasants in the crowd were feeling the same thing as they watched his firm and rapid step and determined, frowning face.

After the hussars had entered the village and Rostov had gone in to see the princess, a certain hesitation and division of opinion had become apparent in the crowd. Some of the peasants began to say that the horsemen were Russians, and it might be expected they would take it amiss that they had not let their young lady go. Dron was of that opinion; but as soon as he expressed it, Karp and others fell upon him.

'How many years have you been fattening on the village?' shouted Karp. 'It's all one to you! You'll dig up your pot of money and make off with it. What is it to you if our homes are ruined or not?'

'We were told everything was to be in order and no one to leave their homes, and not a thing to be moved away—and that's all about it!' shouted another.

'It was your son's turn; but you spared your fat youngster,' a little old man suddenly burst out, pouncing upon Dron, 'and sent my Vanka to be shaved for a soldier. Ugh, and yet we all have to die!'

'To be sure, we all have to die!'

'I'm not one to go against the mir,' said Dron.

'Not one to go against it; you have grown fat off it! ...'

Two lanky peasants said their say. As soon as Rostov, accompanied by Ilyin, Lavrushka, and Alpatitch approached the crowd, Karp, thrusting his fingers into his sash, walked forward with a slight smile. Dron, on the contrary, retreated to the back, and the crowd huddled closer together.

'Hey! who is elder among you here?' shouted Rostov, walking quickly up to the crowd.

'The elder? What do you want him for? ...' asked Karp. But he hardly had time to get the words out when his hat was sent flying off his head, and he was sent reeling from a violent blow on the head.

'Caps off, traitors!' shouted Rostov's full-blooded voice. 'Where is the elder?' he roared furiously.

'The elder, the elder's wanted. Dron Zaharitch, he calls you,' voices were heard saying, hurriedly subservient, and caps were taken off.

'We can't be said to be unruly; we're following the orders,' declared Karp. And several voices at the back began at the same instant:

'It's as the elders settle; there are too many of you giving orders ...'

'Talking? ... Mutiny! ... Scoundrels! Traitors!' Rostov shouted, without thinking, in a voice unlike his own, as he seized Karp by the collar. 'Bind him, bind him!' he shouted, though there was no one to bind him but Lavrushka and Alpatitch.

Lavrushka, however, ran up to Karp and seized his arms from behind.

'Shall I call our fellows from below the hill, your honour?' he shouted.

Alpatitch turned to the peasants, calling upon two of them by name to bind Karp. The peasants obediently stepped out of the crowd and began undoing their belts.

'Where's the village elder?' shouted Rostov.

Dron, with a pale and frowning face, stepped out of the crowd.

'Are you the elder? Bind him, Lavrushka,' shouted Rostov, as though the order could meet with no sort of opposition. And in fact two peasants did begin binding Dron, who took off his sash, and gave it them as though to assist in the operation.

'And all of you, listen to me,' Rostov turned to the peasants. 'March straight to your homes this minute, and don't let me hear your voices again.'

'Why, we haven't done any harm. It was all, do you see, through foolishness. Only a bit of nonsense . . . I always said that it wasn't the right thing,' said voices, blaming one another.

'Didn't I tell you,' said Alpatitch, resuming his rightful position. 'You've done wrong, lads.'

'It was our foolishness, Yakov Alpatitch,' answered voices, and the crowd at once began to break up and to disperse about the village.

The two peasants who were bound they took to the manor-house. The two drunken peasants followed them.

'Ay, now look at you!' said one of them, addressing Karp.

'Do you suppose you can talk to the gentry like that? What were you thinking about? You are a fool,' put in the other; 'a regular fool'.

Within two hours the horses and carts required were standing in the courtyard of the Bogutcharovo house. The peasants were eagerly hurrying out and packing in the carts their owners' goods; and Dron, who had at Princess Marya's desire, been released from the lumber-room, where they had shut him up, was standing in the yard, giving directions to the men.

'Don't pack it so carelessly,' said one of the peasants, a tall man with a round, smiling face, taking a casket out of a housemaid's hands. 'It's worth money too, you may be sure. Why if you fling it down like that or put it under the cord, it will get scratched. I don't like to see things done so. Let everything be done honestly, according to rule, I say. There, like this, under the matting, and cover it up with hay; there, that's first-rate.'

'Mercy on us, the books, the books,' said another peasant, bringing out Prince Andrey's bookshelves. 'Mind you don't stumble! Ay, but it's heavy, lads; the books are stout and solid!'

'Yes, they must have worked hard to write them!' said a tall, round-faced peasant pointing with a significant wink to a lexican lying uppermost.

Rostov, not wishing to force his acquaintanceship on the princess, did not go back to the house, but remained at the village waiting for her to drive out. When Princess Marya's carriage drove out from the house, Rostov mounted his horse and escorted her as far as the road occupied by our troops, twelve versts from Bogutcharovo. At the inn at Yankovo he parted from her respectfully, for the first time permitting himself to kiss her hand.

'How can you speak of it!' he said, blushing in response to Princess Marya's expression of gratitude to him for saving her, as she called it. 'Any police officer would have done as much. If we only had to wage war with peasants, we would not have let the enemy advance so far,' he said, trying with a sort of bashfulness to change the conversation. 'I am only happy to have had the opportunity of making your acquaintance. Good-bye, princess. I trust you may find happiness and consolation, and I hope I may meet you again in happier circumstances. If you don't want to make me blush, please don't thank me.'

But if the princess thanked him no more in words, she thanked him with the whole expression of her face, which was radiant with gratitude and warmth. She could not believe that she had no cause to thank him. On the contrary, to her mind it was an incontestable fact that had it not been for him, she must inevitably have fallen a victim to the rebellious peasants or the French; that *he*, to save her, had exposed himself to obvious and fearful danger; and even more certain was the fact that he was a man of noble and lofty soul, able to sympathise with her position and her grief. His kindly and honest eyes, with tears starting to them at the moment when weeping herself she had spoken of her loss, haunted her imagination. When she had said good-bye to him and was left alone, Princess Marya suddenly felt tears in her eyes, and then—not for the first time—the question occurred to her: 'Was she in love with him?' On the rest of the way to Moscow, though the princess's position was by no means a joyful one, Dunyasha, who was in the carriage with her, noticed that her mistress's face wore a vaguely happy and pensive smile, as she looked out of the window.

'Well, what if I have fallen in love with him?' Though she was ashamed at acknowledging to herself that she had fallen in love with a man who would perhaps never care for her, she comforted herself with the reflection that no one would ever know it, and she was not to blame, if she loved in secret for the first and last time and for her whole life long.

Sometimes she recalled his looks, his sympathy, his words, and happiness seemed to her not quite impossible. And then it was that Dunyasha noticed that she looked out of the window smiling.

'And to think that he should come to Bogutcharovo and at that very moment!' thought Princess Marya. 'And that his sister should have refused Andrey!' And in all that, Princess Marya saw the hand of Providence.

The impression made on Rostov by Princess Marya was a very agreeable one. When he thought of her, he felt pleased. And when his comrades, hearing of his adventure at Bogutcharovo, rallied him on having gone to look for hay, and having picked up one of the greatest heiresses in Russia, it made him angry. He was angry just because the idea of marrying the gentle, and, to his mind, charming Princess Marya with her enormous fortune had more than once, against his own will, occurred to his mind. As far as he personally was concerned, Nikolay could have asked nothing better than to have Princess Marya for his wife. To marry her would make the countess, his mother, happy, and would repair his father's broken fortunes. And it would even—Nikolay felt it—make the happiness of the princess herself.

But Sonya? And his promise? And that was why it made Rostov angry to be rallied about the Princess Bolkonsky.

XV

ON receiving the chief command of the army, Kutuzov remembered Prince Andrey and sent him a summons to headquarters.

Prince Andrey reached Tsarevo-Zaimishtche on the very day and at the very hour when Kutuzov was making his first inspection of the troops. Prince Andrey stopped in the village at the house of the priest, where the commander-in-chief's carriage was standing, and sat down on a bench at the gate to await his highness, as every one now called Kutuzov. From the plain beyond the village came the sounds of regimental music, and the roar of a vast multitude, shouting 'Hurrah!' to the new commander-in-chief. At the gate, some ten paces from Prince Andrey, stood two orderlies, a courier, and a butler, taking advantage of their master's absence to enjoy the fine weather. A swarthy, little lieutenant-colonel of hussars, his face covered with bushy moustaches and whiskers, rode up to the gate, and glancing at Prince Andrey asked whether his highness were putting up here and whether he would soon be back.

Prince Andrey told him that he did not belong to his highness's staff, but had only just arrived. The lieutenant-colonel of hussars turned to the smart orderly, and the orderly told him with the peculiar scornfulness with which commander-in-chiefs' orderlies do speak to officers:

'His highness? We expect him back immediately. What is your business?'

The officer grinned in his moustaches at the orderly's tone, dismounted, gave his horse to a servant, and went up to Bolkonsky with a slight bow.

Bolkonsky made room for him on the bench. The hussar sat down beside him.

'You, too, waiting for the commander-in-chief?' he began. 'They say he is willing to see any one, thank God! It was a very different matter with the sausage-makers! Yermolov might well ask to be promoted a German. Now, I dare say, Russians may dare to speak again.

And devil knows what they have been about. Nothing but retreating and retreating. Have you been in the field?' he asked.

'I have had the pleasure,' said Prince Andrey, 'not only of taking part in the retreat, but also of losing everything I valued in the retreat —not to speak of my property and the home of my birth ... my father, who died of grief. I am a Smolensk man.'

'Ah! ... Are you Prince Bolkonsky? Very glad to make your acquaintance. Lieutenant-colonel Denisov, better known by the name of Vaska,' said Denisov, pressing Prince Andrey's hand and looking into his face with a particularly kindly expression. 'Yes, I had heard about it,' he said sympathetically, and after a brief pause he added: 'Yes, this is Scythian warfare. It's all right, but not for those who have to pay the piper. So you are Prince Andrey Bolkonsky?' He shook his head. 'I am very glad, prince; very glad to make your acquaintance,' he added, pressing his hand again with a melancholy smile.

Prince Andrey knew of Denisov from Natasha's stories of her first suitor. The recollection of them—both sweet and bitter—carried him back to the heart-sickness of which he had of late never thought, though it still lay buried within him. Of late so many different and grave matters, such as the abandonment of Smolensk, his visit to Bleak Hills, the recent news of his father's death—so many emotions had filled his heart that those memories had long been absent, and when they returned did not affect him nearly so violently. And for Denisov, the associations awakened by the name of Bolkonsky belonged to a far-away, romantic past, when, after supper and Natasha's singing, hardly knowing what he was doing, he had made an offer to the girl of fifteen. He smiled at the recollection of that time and his love for Natasha, and passed at once to what he was just now intensely and exclusively interested in. This was a plan of campaign he had formed while on duty at the outposts during the retreat. He had laid the plan before Barclay de Tolly, and now intended to lay it before Kutuzov. The plan was based on the fact that the line of the French operations was too extended, and on the suggestion that, instead of or along with a frontal attack, barring the advance of the French, attacks should be made on their communications. He began explaining his plan to Prince Andrey.

'They are not able to defend all that line; it's impossible. I'll undertake to break through them. Give me five hundred men and I would cut their communications, that's certain! The one system to adopt is partisan warfare.'

Denisov got up and began with gesticulations to explain his plans to Bolkonsky. In the middle of his exposition they heard the shouts of the army, mingling with music and song, and apparently coming from detached groups scattered over a distance. From the village came cheers and the tramp of horses' hoofs.

'Himself is coming,' shouted the Cossack, who stood at the gate; 'he's coming!'

Bolkonsky and Denisov moved up to the gate, where there stood a knot of soldiers (a guard of honour), and they saw Kutuzov coming down the street mounted on a low bay horse. An immense suite of generals followed him. Barclay rode almost beside him; a crowd of officers was running behind and around them shouting 'hurrah!'

His adjutants galloped into the yard before him. Kutuzov impatiently kicked his horse, which ambled along slowly under his weight, and continually nodded his head and put his hand up to his white horseguard's cap, with a red band and no peak. When he reached the guard of honour, a set of stalwart grenadiers, mostly cavalry men, saluting him, he looked at them for a minute in silence, with the intent, unflinching gaze of a man used to command; then he turned to the group of generals and officers standing round him. His face suddenly wore a subtle expression; he shrugged his shoulders with an air of perplexity. 'And with fellows like that retreat and retreat!' he said. 'Well, goodbye, general,' he added, and spurred his horse into the gateway by Prince Andrey and Denisov.

'Hurrah! hurrah! hurrah!' rang out shouts behind him.

Since Prince Andrey had seen him last Kutuzov had grown stouter and more corpulent than ever; he seemed swimming in fat. But the familiar scar, and the white eye, and the expression of weariness in his face and figure were unchanged. He was wearing a white horseguard's cap and a military coat, and a whip on a narrow strap was slung over his shoulder. He sat heavily swaying on his sturdy horse.

'Fugh! . . . fugh! . . . fugh! . . .' he whistled, hardly audibly, as he rode into the courtyard. His face expressed the relief of a man who looks forward to resting after a performance. He drew his left foot out of the stirrup, and with a lurch of his whole person, frowning with the effort, brought it up to the saddle, leaned on his knee, and with a groan let himself drop into the arms of the Cossacks and adjutants, who stood ready to support him.

He pulled himself together, looked round with half-shut eyes, glanced at Prince Andrey, and evidently not recognising him, moved with his shambling gait towards the steps.

'Fugh! . . . fugh! . . . fugh!' he whistled, and again looked round at Prince Andrey. As is often the case with the aged, the impression of Prince Andrey's face did not at once call up the memory of his personality. 'Ah, how are you, how are you, my dear boy, come along . . .' he said wearily, and walked heavily up the steps that creaked under his weight. He unbuttoned his coat and sat down on the seat in the porch.

'Well, how's your father?'

'The news of his death reached me yesterday,' said Prince Andrey briefly.

Kutuzov looked at him with eyes opened wide with dismay, then he took off his cap, and crossed himself. 'The peace of heaven be with him! And may God's will be done with all of us!' He heaved a heavy sigh and paused. 'I loved him deeply and respected him, and I feel for you with all my heart.' He embraced Prince Andrey, pressed him to his fat breast, and for some time did not let him go. When he released him, Prince Andrey saw that Kutuzov's thick lips were quivering and there were tears in his eyes. He sighed and pressed his hands on the seat to help himself in rising from it.

'Come in, come in, we'll have a chat,' he said; but at that moment Denisov, who stood as little in dread of the authorities as he did of the enemy, walked boldly up, his spurs clanking on the steps, regardless of the indignant whispers of the adjutants, who tried to prevent him. Kutuzov, his hands still pressed on the seat to help him up, looked ruefully at Denisov. Denisov, mentioning his name, announced that he had to communicate to his highness a matter of great importance for the welfare of Russia. Kutuzov bent his weary eyes on Denisov, and, lifting his hands with a gesture of annoyance, folded them across his stomach, and repeated, 'For the welfare of Russia? Well, what is it? Speak.' Denisov blushed like a girl (it was strange to see the colour come on that hirsute, time-worn, hard-drinking face), and began boldly explaining his plan for cutting the enemy's line between Smolensk and Vyazma. Denisov's home was in that region, and he knew the country well. His plan seemed unquestionably a good one, especially with the energy of conviction that was in his words. Kutuzov stared at his own feet, and occasionally looked round towards the yard of the next cottage, as though he were expecting something unpleasant to come from it. From the cottage there did in fact emerge, during Denisov's speech, a general with a portfolio under his arm.

'Eh?' Kutuzov inquired in the middle of Denisov's exposition, 'are you ready now?'

'Yes, your highness,' said the general. Kutuzov shook his head with an air that seemed to say, 'How is one man to get through it all?' and gave his attention again to Denisov.

'I give you my word of honour as a Russian officer,' Denisov was saying, 'that I will cut Napoleon's communications.'

'Is Kirill Andreevitch Denisov, the ober-intendant, any relation of yours?' Kutuzov interposed.

'My uncle, your highness.'

'Oh! we used to be friends,' said Kutuzov, more cheerily. 'Very good, very good, my dear boy; you stay here on the staff; we'll have a talk tomorrow.' Nodding to Denisov, he turned away and put out his hand for the papers Konovnitsyn had brought him.

'Will not your highness be pleased to walk into the house?' said the general on duty in a discontented voice; 'it's necessary to look through the plans and to sign some papers.' An adjutant appeared at the door to announce that everything was in readiness within. But apparently Kutuzov preferred to be rid of business before going indoors. He paused...

'No; have a table placed here, my dear boy; I'll look through them here,' he said. 'Don't you go away,' he added, addressing Prince Andrey. Prince Andrey remained in the porch listening to the general on duty.

While the latter was presenting his report Prince Andrey heard the whisper of a woman's voice and the rustle of a woman's silk dress at the door. Several times glancing in that direction he noticed behind the door a plump, rosy-faced, good-looking woman in a pink dress with a lilac silk kerchief on her head. She had a dish in her hand, and was apparently waiting for the commander-in-chief to enter. Kutuzov's adjutant explained to Prince Andrey in a whisper that this was the priest's wife, the mistress of the house, who intended to offer his highness bread and salt, the emblems of welcome, on his entrance. Her husband had met his highness with the cross in church, and she intended to welcome him to the house.... 'She's very pretty,' added the adjutant with a smile. Kutuzov looked round at the words. He heard the general's report, the subject of which was chiefly a criticism of the position of the troops before Tsarevo-Zaimishtche, just as he had heard Denisov, and just as, seven years before, he had heard the discussions of the military council before Austerlitz. He was obviously hearing it simply because he had ears, and although one of them was stuffed up with cotton-wool they could not help hearing. But it was obvious that nothing that general could possibly say could surprise or interest him, that he knew beforehand all he would be told, and listened only because he had to listen to it, just as one has to listen to the litany being sung. All Denisov had said was practical and sensible. What the general was saying was even more practical and sensible, but apparently Kutuzov despised both knowledge and intellect, and knew of something else that would settle things—something different, quite apart from intellect and knowledge. Prince Andrey watched the commander-in-chief's face attentively, and the only expression he could detect in it was an expression of boredom, of curiosity to know the meaning of the feminine whispering at the door, and of a desire to observe the proprieties. It was obvious that Kutuzov despised intellect and learning, and even the patriotic feeling Denisov had shown; but he did not despise them through intellect, nor through sentiment, nor through learning (for he made no effort to display anything of the kind), he despised them through something else—through his old age, through his experience of life. The only instruction of his own that Kutuzov inserted in the report related to acts of marauding by Russian troops. The general, at the end of the report, presented his highness a document for signature relating to a petition for damages from a landowner for the cutting of his oats by certain officers.

Kutuzov smacked his lips together and shook his head, as he listened to the matter.

'Into the stove . . . into the fire with it! And I tell you once for all, my dear fellow,' he said, 'all such things put into the fire. Let them cut the corn and burn the wood to their hearts' content. It's not by my orders and it's not with my permission, but I can't pursue the matter. It can't be helped. You can't hew down trees without the chips flying.' He glanced once more at the paper. 'Oh, this German preciseness,' he commented, shaking his head.

XVI

'WELL, now, that's all,' said Kutuzov, as he signed the last paper, and rising clumsily, and straightening his fat, white neck, he went to the door with a more cheerful countenance.

The priest's wife, with the colour rushing to her face, snatched up the dish, and though she had been so long preparing, she did not succeed in presenting it at the right moment. With a low bow she offered it to Kutuzov. Kutuzov screwed up his eyes. He smiled, chucked her under the chin, and said:

'And what a pretty face! Thank you, my dear!'

He took some gold coins out of his trouser pocket, and put them on the dish. 'Well, and how are we getting on?' he said, going towards the room that had been assigned him. The priest's wife, with smiling dimples on her rosy face, followed to show him the room. The adjutant came out to Prince Andrey in the porch, and invited him to lunch. Half an hour later Kutuzov sent for Prince Andrey. He was reclining in a low chair, still in the same unbuttoned military coat. He had a French novel in his hand, and at Prince Andrey's entrance laid a paper-knife in it and put it aside. It was *Les Chevaliers du Cygne*, a work by Madame de Genlis, as Prince Andrey saw by the cover.

'Well, sit down; sit down here. Let us have a little talk,' said Kutuzov. 'It's sad; very sad. But remember, my dear, think of me as a father, another father, to you ...!'

Prince Andrey told Kutuzov all he knew about his father's end, and what he had seen at Bleak Hills.

'To think what we have been brought to!' Kutuzov cried suddenly, in a voice full of feeling, Prince Andrey's story evidently bringing vividly before him the position of Russia.

'Wait a bit; wait a bit!' he added, with a vindictive look in his face, and apparently unwilling to continue a conversation that stirred him too deeply, he said:

'I sent for you to keep you with me.'

'I thank your highness!' answered Prince Andrey, 'but I am afraid I am no more good for staff work,' he said, with a smile, which Kutuzov noticed. He looked at him inquiringly. 'And the great thing is,' added Prince Andrey, 'I am used to my regiment. I like the officers; and I think the men have come to like me. I should be sorry to leave the regiment. If I decline the honour of being in attendance on you, believe me ...'

Kutuzov's podgy face beamed with a shrewd, good-natured, and yet subtly ironical expression. He cut Bolkonsky short.

'I'm sure you would have been of use to me. But you're right; you're right. It's not here that we want men. There are always a multitude of counsellors; but men are scarce. The regiments wouldn't be what they are if all the would-be counsellors would serve in them like you. I remember you at Austerlitz. I remember, I remember you with the flag!' said Kutuzov, and a flush of pleasure came into Prince Andrey's face at this reminiscence. Kutuzov held out his hand to him, offering him his cheek to kiss, and again Prince Andrey saw tears in the old man's eyes. Though Prince Andrey knew Kutuzov's tears were apt to come easily, and that he was particularly affectionate and tender with him from the desire to show sympathy with his loss, yet he felt this reminder of Austerlitz agreeable and flattering.

'Go your own way, and God bless you in it.... I know your path is the path of honour!' He paused. 'I missed you at Bucharest. I wanted some one to send ...' And changing the subject, Kutuzov began talking of the Turkish war, and of the peace that had been concluded. 'Yes, I have been roundly abused,' he said, 'both for the war and the peace ...

but it all happened in the nick of time. "Everything comes in time for him who knows how to wait,"' he said, quoting the French proverb. 'And there were as many counsellors there as here, . . .' he went on, returning to the superfluity of advisers, a subject which evidently occupied his mind. 'Ugh, counsellors and counsellors!' he said. 'If we had listened to all of them, we should be in Turkey now. We should not have made peace, and the war would never have been over. Always in haste, and more haste, worse speed. Kamensky would have come to grief there, if he hadn't died. He went storming fortresses with thirty thousand men. It's easy enough to take fortresses, but it's hard to finish off a campaign successfully. Storms and attacks are not what's wanted, but *time* and *patience*. Kamensky sent his soldiers to attack Rustchuk, but I trusted to them alone—time and patience—and I took more fortresses than Kamensky, and made the Turks eat horseflesh!' He shook his head. 'And the French shall, too. Take my word for it,' cried Kutuzov, growing warmer and slapping himself on the chest, 'I'll make them eat horseflesh!' And again his eyes were dim with tears.

'We shall have to give battle, though, shan't we?' said Prince Andrey.

'We must, if every one wants to; there is no help for it. . . But, mark my words, my dear boy! The strongest of all warriors are these two—time and patience. They do it all, and our wise counsellors *n'entendent pas de cette oreille, voilà le mal.* Some say ay, and some say no. What's one to do?' he asked, evidently expecting a reply. 'Come, what would you have me do?' he repeated, and his eyes twinkled with a profound, shrewd expression. 'I'll tell you what to do,' he said, since Prince Andrey still did not answer. 'I'll tell you what to do, and what I do. *Dans le doute, mon cher*—he paused—'*abstiens-toi.*' He articulated deliberately the French saying.

'Well, good-bye, my dear. Remember, with all my heart, I feel for your sorrow, and that for you I'm not his highness, nor prince, nor commander-in-chief, but simply a father to you. If you want anything, come straight to me. Good-bye, my dear boy!' Again he embraced and kissed him.

And before Prince Andrey had closed the door, Kutuzov settled himself comfortably with a sigh, and renewed the unfinished novel of Madame Genlis, *Les Chevaliers du Cygne*.

How, and why it was, Prince Andrey could not explain, but after this interview with Kutuzov, he went back to his regiment feeling reassured as to the future course of the war, and as to the man to whom its guidance was intrusted. The more clearly he perceived the absence of everything personal in the old leader, who seemed to have nothing left of his own but habits of passions, and instead of an intellect grasping events and making plans, had only the capacity for the calm contemplation of the course of events, the more confident he felt that all would be as it should be. 'He will put in nothing of himself. He will contrive nothing, will undertake nothing,' thought Prince Andrey; 'but he will hear everything, will think of everything, will put everything in its place, will not hinder anything that could be of use, and will not allow anything that could do harm. He knows that there is something stronger and more important than his will—that is the inevitable march of events, and he can see them, can grasp their significance, and, seeing their significance, can abstain from meddling, from following his own will, and aiming at something else. 'And the chief reason,' thought Prince Andrey, 'why one believes in him is that he's Russian, in spite of Madame Genlis's novel and the French proverbs, that his voice shook when he said, "What we have been brought to!" and that he choked when he said "he would make them eat horseflesh!"'

It was this feeling, more or less consciously shared by all, that determined the unanimous approval given to the appointment of Kutuzov to the chief command, in accordance with national sentiment, and in opposition to the intrigues at court.

XVII

AFTER the Tsar had left Moscow, the life of that city flowed on in its old accustomed channel, and the current of that life ran so much as usual that it was difficult to remember the days of patriotic fervour and enthusiasm, and hard to believe that Russia actually was in danger, and that the members of the English club were also her devoted sons, ready to make any sacrifice for her sake. The one thing that recalled the general patriotic fervour of the days of the Tsar's presence in Moscow was the call for contributions of men and money, and these demands were presented at once in a legal, official form, so that they seemed inevitable. As the enemy drew nearer to Moscow the attitude taken by its inhabitants in regard to their position did not become more serious, but, on the contrary, more frivolous, as is always the case with people who see a great danger approaching. At the approach of danger there are always two voices that speak with equal force in the heart of man: one very reasonably tells the man to consider the nature of the danger and the means of avoiding it; the other even more reasonably says that it is too painful and harassing to think of the danger, since it is not in a man's power to provide for everything and escape from the general march of events; and that it is therefore better to turn aside from the painful subject till it has come, and to think of what is pleasant. In solitude a man generally yields to the first voice; in society to the second. So it was now with the inhabitants of Moscow. It was long since there had been so much gaiety in Moscow as that year.

Rastoptchin's posters, with a print at the top of a gin-shop, a potman, and the Moscow artisan, Karpushka Tchigirin, 'who, having gone into the militia, heard that Bonaparte meant to come to Moscow, was mightily wrath thereat, used very bad language about all the French, came out of the gin-shop and began to address the people assembled under the eagles,' were as much read and discussed as the last *bouts rimés* of Vassily Lvovitch Pushkin.

In the corner room of the club the members gathered together to read these posters; and some liked the way Karpushka was made to jeer at the French, saying that 'they would be blown out with Russian cabbage, that Russian porridge would rip their guts open, and cabbage soup would finish them off; that they were all dwarfs, and a village lass could toss three of them on her pitchfork single-handed!'

Some people did not approve of this tone, and said it was vulgar and stupid. People said that Rastoptchin had sent all Frenchmen, and even foreigners, out of Moscow, and that there had been spies and agents of Napoleon among them. But they talked of this principally in order to repeat the witticisms uttered by Rastoptchin on the occasion. The foreigners had been put on a barque sailing to Nizhny, and Rastoptchin had said to them: 'Keep yourselves to yourselves, get into the barque, and take care it does not become the barque of Charon to you.' People talked too of all the government offices having been removed from Moscow, and added Shinshin's joke, that for that alone Moscow ought to be grateful to Napoleon. People said that Mamonov's regiment was costing him eight hundred thousand; that Bezuhov was spending even more on his; but that the noblest proof of Bezuhov's patriotism was that he was going to put on the uniform himself and ride at the head of his regiment, without any charge for seats to spectators.

'You have no mercy on any one,' said Julie Drubetskoy, gathering up a pinch of scraped lint in her slender fingers covered with rings.

Julie was intending to leave Moscow next day, and was giving a farewell *soirée*.

'Bezuhov *est ridicule*, but he is so good-natured, so nice; how can you take pleasure in being so *caustique*?'

'Forfeit!' said a young man in a volunteer's uniform, whom Julie called '*mon chevalier*,' and was taking with her to Nizhny.

In Julie's circle, as in many circles in Moscow, it was a principle now to speak nothing but Russian, and those who made a mistake by speaking

French had to pay a forfeit for the benefit of the committee of voluntary subscriptions.

'Another forfeit for a Gallicism,' said a Russian writer who happened to be present. '"Take pleasure!" is not Russian.'

'You have no mercy on any one,' Julie went on to the volunteer, paying no attention to the remark of the author.

'*Caustique*, I admit,' she said, 'and I'll pay for the pleasure of telling you the truth. I am ready to pay even more; but I am not responsible for Gallicisms,' she said to the writer. 'I have neither the time nor the money to engage a teacher and learn Russian like Prince Galitzin. Ah, here he is!' added Julie. '*Quand on* . . . No, no,' she protested to the volunteer, 'you're not going to catch me. When one speaks of the sun, one sees its rays. We were just talking of you,' she said, smiling affably to Pierre, and adding, with the easy lying characteristic of society women, 'We were saying your regiment was certain to be a finer one than Mamonov's.'

'Oh, don't talk to me about my regiment,' answered Pierre, kissing his hostess's hand, and sitting down beside her. 'I am so heartily sick of it!'

'You will take the command of it yourself, of course?' said Julie, with a sly and sarcastic look towards the volunteer.

The latter was by no means so ready to be caustic in Pierre's presence, and his countenance betokened perplexity as to what Julie's smile could signify. In spite of his absentmindedness and good nature, Pierre's presence never failed to cut short any attempt at ridicule at his expense.

'No,' answered Pierre, laughing and looking at his huge, bulky figure; 'I should make too good a target for the French, and indeed I'm afraid I could hardly scramble on to a horse's back.'

Among the people picked out as subjects for gossip, Julie's friends happened to pitch on the Rostovs. 'Their pecuniary position is very serious, I am told,' said Julie. 'And the count is so unreasonable. The Razumovskys wanted to buy his house and his estate in the environs, and the matter is still dragging on. He will ask too much.'

'No, I fancy purchase will be concluded in a few days,' said some one. 'Though it's madness to buy anything in Moscow just now.'

'Why so?' said Julie. 'Surely you don't suppose that Moscow is in any danger.'

'Why are you leaving it then?'

'I? That's a strange question. I am going because . . . well, because everybody's going, and I am not a Jeanne d'Arc nor an Amazon.'

'Oh, oh! Give me another strip of linen to scrape.'

'He ought to be able to pay off all his debts, if he sets about it properly,' the volunteer observed of Count Rostov.

'He's a good-hearted old fellow, but very foolish.'

'And why are they staying on here so long? They were meaning to leave for the country long ago. Natalie is quite well again now, I suppose?' Julie asked Pierre, with a sly smile.

'They are waiting for their younger son,' said Pierre. 'He went into Obolensky's Cossacks, and was sent off to Byela Tserkov. The regiment is being formed there. But now they have transferred him to my regiment, and he is expected every day. The count wanted to get away long ago, but nothing would induce the countess to leave Moscow till her son's return.'

'I saw them the day before yesterday at the Arharovs. Natalie has quite recovered her looks and her spirits. She sang a song. How easily some people get over everything!'

'Get over what?' Pierre asked, looking displeased.

Julie smiled.

'Oh count, you know, such chivalrous knights as you are only to be found in Madame Suza's novels.'

'Knights! What do you mean?' Pierre asked blushing.

'Come now, my dear count. *C'est la fable de tout Moscou. Je vous admire, ma parole d'honneur.*'

'Forfeit! forfeit!' said the volunteer.

'Oh, very well. One cannot talk, what a bore it is!'

'What is the talk of all Moscow?' said Pierre angrily, rising to his feet.

'Nonsense, count, you know!'

'I know nothing about it,' said Pierre.

'I know what great friends you have always been with Natalie, and so . . . But, I was always more friendly with Vera. That darling Vera.'

'No, madam,' Pierre persisted in a tone of annoyance. 'I have by no means taken upon myself the rôle of Countess Rostov's knight; indeed, it's almost a month since I have been near them. But I cannot understand the cruelty . . .'

'*Qui s'excuse s'accuse,*' cried Julie, smiling, and waving the lint triumphantly, and that she might have the last word, she promptly changed the subject. 'By the way, I have heard poor Marie Bolkonsky arrived in Moscow yesterday. Have you heard she has lost her father?'

'Really? Where is she? I should like to see her,' said Pierre.

'I spent the evening with her yesterday. She is going on today or tomorrow morning to their estate in the province with her nephew.'

'Well, how is she? Tell me,' said Pierre.

'Oh, she is well, but very sad. But do you know who rescued her? It is quite a romance. Nikolay Rostov. She was surrounded; they tried to kill her and wounded her servants. He rushed in and saved her....'

'Another romance,' said the volunteer. 'This general flight is evidently intended to marry off all the old maids. Katish is one, Princess Bolkonsky another.'

'You know, I really do believe she's *un petit peu amoureuse du jeune homme.*'

'Forfeit! forfeit! forfeit!

'But how is one to say that in Russian?'

XVIII

WHEN Pierre returned home, he was handed two new placards of Rastoptchin's that had just appeared.

The first declared that the rumour, that it was forbidden to leave Moscow by Count Rastoptchin's order, was false, and that, on the contrary, he was glad that ladies and merchants' wives were leaving the town. 'There will be less panic and less false news,' said the notice; 'but I will stake my life on it that the miscreant will never enter Moscow.'

These words first showed Pierre clearly that the French certainly would enter Moscow. In the second placard it was announced that our headquarters were at Vyazma, that Count Wittgenstein had defeated the French, but that since many of the inhabitants of Moscow were desirous of arming themselves, weapons had been provided to meet their wishes in the arsenal: swords, pistols, and guns could all be procured there at a low rate.

The tone of this notice was not as jocose as the former supposed discourses of Tchigirin. The two placards made Pierre ponder. It was evident to him that the menacing storm cloud, for the advent of which his whole soul longed, though it roused an involuntary thrill of horror, it was evident that that cloud was coming closer.

'Shall I enter the service and join the army or wait here?' Pierre thought, a question he had put to himself a hundred times already. He took up a pack of cards that lay on the table to deal them for a game of patience.

'If I succeed in this game of patience,' he said to himself, shuffling the pack as he held it in his hand and looked upwards; 'if I succeed, it means ... what does it mean?' ... He had not time to decide this question when he heard at the door of his study the voice of the eldest princess, asking whether she might come in. 'Then it will mean that I must set off to join the army,' Pierre told himself. 'Come, come in,' he said to the princess.

The eldest of his cousins, the one with the long waist and the stony face, was the only one still living in Pierre's house; the two younger sisters had both married.

'Excuse my coming to you, cousin,' she said in a tone of reproach and excitement. 'Some decision really must be come to, you know. What is going to happen? Every one has left Moscow, and the populace are becoming unruly. Why are we staying on?'

'On the contrary, everything seems going on satisfactorily, *'ma cousine*,' said Pierre in the habitually playful tone he had adopted with his cousin, to carry off the embarrassment he always felt at being in the position of a benefactor to her.

'Oh yes, satisfactorily . . . highly satisfactory, I dare say. Varvara Ivanovna told me today how our troops are distinguishing themselves. It is certainly a credit to them. And the populace, too, is in complete revolt, they won't obey any one now; even my maid has begun to be insolent. If it goes on like this, they will soon begin killing us. One can't walk about the streets. And the worst of it is, in another day or two the French will be here. Why are we waiting for them? One favour I beg of you, *mon cousin*,' said the princess, 'give orders for me to be taken to Petersburg; whatever I may be, any way I can't live under Bonaparte's rule.'

'But what nonsense, *ma cousine*! where do you get your information from? On the contrary . . .'

'I'm not going to submit to your Napoleon. Other people may do as they like. . . . If you won't do this for me . . .'

'But I will, I'll give orders for it at once.'

The princess was obviously annoyed at having no one to be angry with. Muttering something, she sat down on the edge of the chair.

'But you have been incorrectly informed,' said Pierre. 'All's quiet in the town, and there's no sort of danger. See I have just read . . .' Pierre showed the princess the placards. 'The count writes that he will stake his life on it that the enemy will never be in Moscow.'

'Ah, your count,' the princess began spitefully 'he's a hypocrite, a miscreant who has himself stirred the mob on to disorder. Didn't he write in his idiotic placards that they were to take anybody whoever it might be and drag by the hair to the lock-up (and how silly it is!). Honour and glory, says he, to the man who does so. And this is what he has brought us to. Varvara Ivanovna told me the mob almost killed her for speaking French.'

'Oh, well, well . . . You take everything too much to heart,' said Pierre, and he began dealing out the patience.

Although he did succeed in the game, Pierre did not set off to join the army, but stayed on in Moscow, now rapidly emptying, and was still in the same agitation, uncertainty and alarm, and, at the same time, joyful expectation of something awful.

Next day the princess set off in the evening, and Pierre's head-steward came to inform him that it was impossible to raise the money he required for the equipment of his regiment unless he sold one of his estates. The head-steward impressed on Pierre generally that all this regimental craze would infallibly bring him to ruin. Pierre could hardly conceal a smile as he listened to the head-steward.

'Well, sell it then,' he said. 'There's no help for it, I can't draw back now!'

The worse the position of affairs, and especially of his own affairs, the better pleased Pierre felt, and the more obvious it was to him that the catastrophe he expected was near at hand. Scarcely any of Pierre's acquaintances were left in the town. Julie had gone, Princess Marya had gone. Of his more intimate acquaintances the Rostovs were the only people left; but Pierre did not go to see them.

To divert his mind that day, Pierre drove out to the village of Vorontsovo, to look at a great air balloon which was being constructed by Leppich to use against the enemy, and the test balloon which was to be sent up the following day. The balloon was not yet ready; but as Pierre learned it was being constructed by the Tsar's desire. The Tsar had written to Count Rastoptchin about it in the following terms:

'As soon as Leppich is ready, get together a crew for his car consisting of thoroughly trustworthy and intelligent men, and send a courier to General Kutuzov to prepare him for it. I have mentioned it to him. Impress upon Leppich, please, to take careful note where he descends the first time, that he may not go astray and fall into the hands of the enemy. It is essential that he should regulate his movements in accordance with the movements of the commander-in-chief.'

On his way home from Vorontsovo, Pierre drove through Bolotny Square, and seeing a crowd at Lobnoye Place, stopped and got out of his chaise. The crowd were watching the flogging of a French cook, accused of being a spy. The flogging was just over, and the man who had administered it was untying from the whipping-post a stout, red-whiskered man in blue stockings and a green tunic, who was groaning piteously. Another victim, a thin, pale man, was standing by. Both, to judge by their faces, were Frenchmen. With a face of sick dread like that of the thin Frenchman, Pierre pushed his way in among the crowd.

'What is it? Who are they? What for?' he kept asking. But the attention of the crowd—clerks, artisans, shopkeepers, peasants, women in pelisses and jackets—was so intently riveted on what was taking place on the Lobnoye Place that no one answered. The stout man got up, shrugged his shoulders frowning, and evidently trying to show fortitude, began putting on his tunic without looking about him. But all at once his lips quivered and to his own rage he began to cry, as grown-up men of sanguine temperament do cry. The crowd began talking loudly, to drown a feeling of pity in themselves, as it seemed to Pierre.

'Some prince's cook...'

'Eh, monsieur, Russian sauce is a bit strong for a French stomach... sets the teeth on edge,' said a wrinkled clerk standing near Pierre, just when the Frenchman burst into tears. The clerk looked about him for signs of appreciation of his jest. Several persons laughed, but some were still gazing in dismay at the man who was undressing the second Frenchman and about to flog him.

Pierre choked, scowled, and turning quickly, went back to his chaise, still muttering something to himself as he went, and took his seat in it. During the rest of the way he several times started, and cried out so loudly that the coachman at last asked him what he desired.

'Where are you driving?' Pierre shouted to the coachman as he drove to Lubyanka.

'You told me to drive to the governor's,' answered the coachman.

'Fool! dolt!' shouted Pierre, abusing his coachman, a thing he very rarely did. 'I told you home; and make haste, blockhead! This very day I must set off,' Pierre said to himself.

At the sight of the tortured Frenchman and the crowd round the Lobnoye Place, Pierre had so unhesitatingly decided that he could stay no longer in Moscow, and must that very day set off to join the army, that it seemed to him either that he had told the coachman so, or that the coachman ought to know it of himself.

On reaching home Pierre told his omniscient and omnipotent head-coachman, Yevstafitch, who was known to all Moscow, that he was going to drive that night to Mozhaisk to the army, and gave orders for his saddle horses to be sent on there. All this could not be arranged in one day, and therefore by Yevstafitch's representations Pierre was induced to defer his departure till next day to allow time for relays of horses to be sent on ahead.

The 24th was a bright day after a spell of bad weather, and after dinner on that day Pierre set out from Moscow. Changing horses in the night at Perhushkovo, Pierre learned that a great battle had been fought that evening. He was told that the earth had been vibrating there at

Perhushkovo from the cannon. No one could answer Pierre's question whether the battle were a victory or a defeat. This was the battle of the 24th at Shevardino. Towards dawn Pierre approached Mozhaisk.

Troops were quartered on all the houses in Mozhaisk, and at the inn, where Pierre was met by his coachman and postillion, there was not a room to spare; the whole place was full of officers.

From Mozhaisk onwards troops were halting or marching everywhere. Cossacks, foot soldiers, horse soldiers, wagons, gun-carriages, and cannons were everywhere.

Pierre pushed on as fast as possible, and the further he got and the more deeply he plunged into this ocean of soldiers, the stronger became the thrill of uneasiness and of a new pleasurable sensation. It was a feeling akin to what he had felt at the Slobodsky Palace on the Tsar's visit, a sense of the urgent necessity of taking some step and making some sacrifice. He was conscious now of a glad sense that all that constitutes the happiness of life, comfort, wealth, even life itself, were all dust and ashes, which it was a joy to fling away in comparison with something else.... What that something else was Pierre could not have said, and indeed he did not seek to get a clear idea, for whose sake and for what object he found such peculiar joy in sacrificing all. He was not interested in knowing the object of the sacrifice, but the sacrifice itself afforded him a new joyful sensation.

XIX

O N the 24th was fought the battle before the redoubt of Shevardino; on the 25th not a shot was fired on either side; on the 26th was fought the battle of Borodino.

How and with what object were the battles of Shevardino and Borodino fought? Why was the battle of Borodino fought? There was not the slightest sense in it, either for the French or for the Russians. The immediate result of it was, and was bound to be, for the Russians, that we were brought nearer to the destruction of Moscow (the very thing we dreaded above everything in the world); and for the French, that they were brought nearer to the destruction of their army (which they, too, dreaded above everything in the world). That result was at the time perfectly obvious, and yet Napoleon offered battle, and Kutuzov accepted it.

If military leaders were guided by reasonable considerations only, it would seem that it must have been clear to Napoleon that in advancing two thousand versts into the heart of the country and giving battle, with the probable contingency of losing a quarter of his men, he was going to certain destruction; and that it must have been equally clear to Kutuzov that in accepting that battle and risking the loss of a fourth of his army, he would infallibly lose Moscow. For Kutuzov this was mathematically clear, as clear as it is at chess, that if I have one piece less than my adversary and I exchange pieces, I am certain to be a loser by it, and therefore must avoid exchanging pieces. When my adversary has sixteen pieces and I have fourteen, I am only one-eighth weaker than he; but when we have exchanged thirteen pieces, he is three times as strong as I am.

Up to the battle of Borodino our forces were approximately five-sixths of the French, but after that battle they were only one-half—that is, before the battle a hundred thousand against a hundred and twenty thousand, and after the battle fifty thousand against a hundred thousand. And yet the shrewd and experienced Kutuzov fought the battle. Napoleon, a military genius, as he is called, gave battle, losing a fourth of his army and drawing his line of communications out further than ever. If we are told that he expected the taking of Moscow to complete the campaign, as the taking of Vienna had done, we may say that there are many evidences to the contrary. Napoleon's historians themselves tell us that he wanted to halt as soon as he reached Smolensk; that he knew the danger of his extended line, and that he knew that the taking of Moscow would not be the end of the campaign, because from Smolensk he had learned in what condition the towns were left when abandoned to him, and he had not received a single reply to his reiterated expressions of a desire to open negotiations.

In giving and accepting battle at Borodino, Kutuzov and Napoleon acted without design or rational plan. After the accomplished fact historians have brought forward cunningly devised evidences of the foresight and genius of the generals, who of all the involuntary instruments of the world's history were the most slavish and least independent agents.

The ancients have transmitted to us examples of epic poems in which the whole interest of history is concentrated in a few heroic figures; and under their influence we are still unable to accustom our minds to the idea that history of that kind is meaningless at our stage in the development of humanity.

In answer to the next question, how the battles of Borodino and Shevardino came to be fought, we have also a very definite, well-known, and utterly false account. All the historians describe the affair thus:

The Russian army, they say, in its retreat from Smolensk sought out the best position for a general engagement, and such a position they found in Borodino. The Russians, they say, fortified the position beforehand, to the left of the road (from Moscow to Smolensk) at right angles to it, from Borodino to Utitsa, at the very place where the battle was fought.

In front of this position, they tell us, a fortified earthwork was thrown up on the Shevardino redoubt as an outpost for observation of the enemy's movements.

On the 24th, we are told, Napoleon attacked this redoubt, and took it. On the 26th he attacked the whole Russian army, which had taken up its position on the plain of Borodino.

This is what we are told in the histories, and all that is perfectly incorrect, as any one may easily see who cares to go into the matter.

The Russians did not seek out the best position; on the contrary, on their retreat they had passed by many positions better than Borodino. They did not make a stand at one of these positions, because Kutuzov did not care to take up a position he had not himself selected, because the popular clamour for a battle had not yet been so strongly expressed, because Miloradovitch had not yet arrived with reinforcements of militia, and for countless other reasons.

The fact remains that there were stronger positions on the road the Russian army had passed along, and that the plain of Borodino, on which the battle was fought, is in no respect a more suitable position than any other spot in the Russian empire to which one might point at hazard on the map.

Far from having fortified the position on the left at right angles to the road—that is the spot on which the battle was fought—the Russians never, till the 25th of August 1812, dreamed of a battle being possible on that spot. The proof of this is, first, that there were no fortifications there before the 25th, and that the earthworks begun on that day were not completed by the 26th; and, secondly, the Shevardino redoubt, owing to its situation in front of the position on which the battle was actually fought, was of no real value. With what object was that redoubt more strongly fortified than any of the other points? And with what object was every effort exhausted and six thousand men sacrificed to defend it till late at night on the 24th? A picket of Cossacks would have been enough to keep watch on the enemy's movements. And a third proof that the position of the battlefield was not foreseen, and that the redoubt of Shevardino was not the foremost point of that position, is to be found in the fact that Barclay de Tolly and Bagration were, till the 25th, under the impression that the Shevardino redoubt was the left flank of the position, and that Kutuzov himself, in the report written in hot haste after the battle, speaks of Shevardino as the left flank of the position. Only a good time later, when reports of the battle were written at leisure, the incorrect and strange statement was invented (probably to cover the blunders of the commander-in-chief, who had, of course, to appear infallible) that the Shevardino redoubt served as an advance post, though it was in reality simply the fortified point of the left flank, and that the battle of Borodino was fought by us on a fortified position selected beforehand for it, though it was in reality fought on a position quite unforeseen, and almost unfortified.

The affair obviously took place in this way. A position had been pitched upon on the stream Kolotcha, which intersects the high-road, not at a right angle, but at an acute angle, so that the left flank was at Shevardino, the right near the village of Novoe, and the centre at Borodino, near the confluence of the Kolotcha and the Voina. Any one looking at the plain of Borodino, and not considering how the battle actually was fought, would pick out this position, covered by the Kolotcha, as the obvious one for an army, whose object was to check the advance of an enemy marching along the Smolensk road towards Moscow.

Napoleon, riding up on the 24th to Valuev, did not (we are told in the histories) see the position of the Russians from Utitsa to Borodino (he could not have seen that position since it did not exist), and did not see the advance posts of the Russian army, but in the pursuit of the Russian rearguard stumbled upon the left flank of the Russian position at the redoubt of Shevardino, and, to the surprise of the Russians, his troops crossed the Kolotcha. And the Russians, since it was too late for a general engagement, withdrew their left wing from the position they had intended to occupy, and took up a new position, which had not been foreseen, and was not fortified. By crossing to the left bank of the Kolotcha, on the left of the road, Napoleon shifted the whole battle from right to left (looking from the Russian side), and transferred it to the plain between Utitsa, Semyonovskoye and Borodino—a plain which in itself was a no more favourable position than any other plain in Russia—and on that plain was fought the whole battle of the 26th. A rough outline map of the supposed and of the actual battle is given.

Had Napoleon not reached the Kolotcha on the evening of the 24th, and had he not ordered the redoubt to be attacked at once that evening, had he begun the attack next morning, no one could have doubted that the Shevardino redoubt was the left flank of the Russian position; and the battle would have been fought as we expected. In that case we should probably have defended the Shevardino redoubt by our left flank even more obstinately; we should have attacked Napoleon in the centre or on the right, and the general engagement would have been fought on the 24th on the position prepared and fortified for it. But as the attack was made on our left flank in the evening after the retreat of our rearguard, that is, immediately after the action at Gridnevo, and as the Russian generals would not, or could not, begin the general engagement on the evening of the 24th, the first and most important action of the battle of Borodino was lost on the 24th, and that loss led inevitably to the loss of the battle fought on the 26th.

After the loss of the Shevardino redoubt, we found ourselves on the morning of the 25th with our left flank driven from its position, and were forced to draw in the left wing of our position and hurriedly fortify it where we could.

So that on the 26th of August the Russian troops were only defended by weak, unfinished earthworks, and the disadvantage of that position was aggravated by the fact that the Russian generals, not fully recognising the facts of the position (the loss of the position on the left flank, and the shifting of the whole field of the coming battle from right to left), retained their extended formation from Novoe to Utitsa, and, consequently, had to transfer their troops from right to left during the battle. Consequently, we had during the whole battle to face the whole French army attacking our left wing, with our forces of half the strength.

(Ponyatovsky's action facing Utitsa and Uvarov's action against the French right flank were quite independent of the general course of the battle.)

And so the battle of Borodino was fought, not at all as, in order to cover the blunders of our commanders, it is described by our historians, whose accounts, consequently, diminish the credit due to the Russian army and the Russian people. The battle of Borodino was not fought on a carefully picked and fortified position, with forces only slightly weaker on the Russian side. After the loss of the Shevardino redoubt, the Russians fought on an open, almost unfortified position, with forces half the strength of the French, that is, in conditions in which it was not merely senseless to fight for ten hours and gain a drawn battle, but incredibly difficult to keep the army for three hours together from absolute rout and flight.

XX

ON the morning of the 25th Pierre drove out of Mozhaisk. On the slope of an immense, steep, and winding hill, leading out of the town, Pierre got out of the carriage, and walked by a cathedral on the right of the hill, where a service was being performed. A cavalry regiment followed him down the hill, the singers of the regiment in front. A train of carts came up the hill towards them, filled with wounded from the previous day's engagement. The peasant drivers kept running from side to side, shouting and whipping the horses. The carts, in each of which three or four wounded soldiers were lying or sitting, jolted up and down on the stones that had been thrown on the steep ascent to mend the road. The wounded men, pale and bandaged up, with compressed lips and knitted brows, clung to the sides, as they were shaken and jolted in the carts. Almost all of them stared with naïve and childlike curiosity at Pierre's white hat and green coat.

Pierre's coachman shouted angrily at the train of wounded men to keep to one side of the road. The cavalry regiment, coming down the hill in time to their song, overtook Pierre's chaise and blocked the road. Pierre stopped, keeping close to the edge of the road that had been hollowed out in the hill. The sun did not reach over the side of the hill to the road, and there it felt cold and damp. But overhead it was a bright August morning, and the chimes rang out merrily. One cart full of wounded men came to a standstill at the edge of the road quite close to Pierre. The driver, in bast shoes, ran panting up to his cart, thrust a stone under the hind wheels, which were without tires, and began setting straight the breech on his horse.

An old wounded soldier, with his arm in a sling, walking behind the cart, caught hold of it with his uninjured arm, and looked round at Pierre.

'Well, fellow-countryman, are we to be put down here or taken on to Moscow?' he said.

Pierre was so lost in thought that he did not hear the question. He looked from the cavalry regiment, which was now meeting the train of wounded, to the cart by which he stood, with the two wounded men sitting, and one lying down in it. One of the soldiers sitting in the cart had probably been wounded in the cheek. His whole head was done up in bandages, and one cheek was swollen as large as a baby's head. All his mouth and nose were on one side. This soldier was looking at the cathedral and crossing himself. Another, a young fellow, a light-haired recruit, as white as though there were not a drop of blood in his thin face, gazed with a fixed, good-natured smile at Pierre. The third lay so that his face could not be seen. The singers of the cavalry regiment passed close by the cart.

'A! za-pro-pa-la...'

they sang the military dance tune. As though seconding them, though in a different tone of gaiety, clanged out the metallic notes of the chimes at the top of the hill. And the hot rays of the sun bathed the top of the opposite slope with sunshine sparkling with another suggestion of gaiety. But where Pierre stood under the hillside, by the cart full of wounded soldiers, and the panting, little nag, it was damp, overcast, and dismal.

The soldier with the wounded cheek looked angrily at the singing horse soldiers.

'Oh, the smart fellows!' he murmured reproachfully.

'It's not soldiers only, but peasants, too, I have seen today! Peasants, too, they are hunting up,' said the soldier standing by the cart, addressing himself to Pierre, with a melancholy smile. 'They can't pick and choose now. . . . They want to mass all the people together—it's a matter of Moscow, you see. There is only one thing to do now.' In spite of the vagueness of the soldier's words, Pierre fully grasped his meaning, and nodded his head approvingly.

The road was clear once more, and Pierre walked downhill, and drove on further.

Pierre drove on, looking on both sides of the road for familiar faces, and meeting none but unfamiliar, military faces, belonging to all sorts of regiments, and all staring with the same surprise at his white hat and green coat.

After driving four versts, for the first time he met an acquaintance, and greeted him joyfully. This was a doctor, one of the heads of the medical staff. He drove to meet Pierre in a covered gig, with a young doctor sitting beside him; and recognising Pierre, he called to the Cossack, who sat on the driver's seat, and told him to stop.

'Count, your excellency, how do you come here?' asked the doctor.

'Oh, I wanted to have a look . . .'

'Oh well, there will be something to look at . . .' Pierre got out of his carriage, and stopped to have a talk with the doctor, explaining to him his plan for taking part in the battle.

The doctor advised Bezuhov to go straight to his highness.

'Why, you would be God knows where during the battle, out of sight,' he said, with a glance at his young companion; 'and his highness knows you anyway, and will give you a gracious reception. That's what I should do, my friend,' said the doctor.

The doctor seemed tired and hurried.

'So you think. . . . But one thing more I wanted to ask you, where is the position exactly?' said Pierre.

'The position?' said the doctor; 'well, that's not in my line. Drive on to Tatarinovo, there's a great deal of digging going on there. There you'll come out on a mound; from there you get a view,' said the doctor.

'A view from it? ... If you would ...

But the doctor interrupted, and moved toward his gig.

'I would have shown you the way, but by God, you see' (the doctor made a significant gesture), 'I'm racing to the commander of the corps. We're in such a fix you see ... You know, count, there's to be a battle tomorrow; with a hundred thousand troops, we must reckon on twenty thousand wounded at least; and we haven't the stretchers, nor beds, nor attendants, nor doctors for six thousand. There are ten thousand carts; but we want other things; one must manage as one can.'

The strange idea that of those thousands of men, alive and well, young and old, who had been staring with such light-hearted amusement at his hat, twenty thousand were inevitably doomed to wounds and death (perhaps the very men whom he had seen) made a great impression on Pierre.

'They will die, perhaps, tomorrow; how can they think of anything but death?' And suddenly, by some latent connection of ideas, he saw a vivid picture of the hillside of Mozhaisk, the carts of wounded men, the chimes, the slanting sunshine, and the singing of the cavalry regiment.

'They were going into battle, and meeting wounded soldiers, and never for a minute paused to think what was in store for them, but went by and winked at their wounded comrades. And of all those, twenty thousand are doomed to death, and they can wonder at my hat! Strange!' thought Pierre, as he went on towards Tatarinovo.

Carriages, waggons, and crowds of orderlies and sentinels were standing about a gentleman's house on the left side of the road. The commander-in-chief was putting up there. But when Pierre arrived, he found his highness and almost all the staff were out. They had all gone to the church service. Pierre pushed on ahead to Gorky; and driving uphill into a little village street, Pierre saw for the first time the peasants of the militia in white shirts, with crosses on their caps. With loud talk and laughter, eager and perspiring, they were working on the right of the road at a huge mound overgrown with grass.

Some of them were digging out the earth, others were carrying the earth away in wheelbarrows, while a third lot stood doing nothing.

There were two officers on the knoll giving them instructions. Seeing these peasants, who were unmistakably enjoying the novelty of their position as soldiers, Pierre thought again of the wounded soldiers at Mozhaisk, and he understood what the soldier had tried to express by the words 'they want to mass all the people together.' The sight of these bearded peasants toiling on the field of battle with their queer, clumsy boots, with their perspiring necks, and here and there with shirts unbuttoned showing their sun-burnt collar-bones, impressed Pierre more strongly than anything he had yet seen and heard with the solemnity and gravity of the moment.

XXI

PIERRE got out of his carriage, and passing by the toiling peasants, clambered up the knoll from which the doctor had told him he could get a view of the field of battle.

It was eleven o'clock in the morning. The sun was a little on the left, and behind Pierre, and in the pure, clear air, the huge panorama that stretched in an amphitheatre before him from the rising ground lay bathed in brilliant sunshine.

The Smolensk high-road ran winding through that amphitheatre, intersecting it towards the left at the top, and passing through a village with a white church, which lay some five hundred paces before and below the knoll. This was Borodino. The road passed below the village, crossed a bridge, and ran winding uphill and downhill, mounting up and up to the hamlet of Valuev, visible six versts away, where Napoleon now was. Behind Valuev the road disappeared into a copse turning yellow on the horizon. In this copse of birch- and pine-trees, on the right of the road, could be seen far away the shining cross and belfry of the Kolotsky monastery. Here and there in the blue distance, to right and to left of the copse and the road, could be seen smoking camp-fires and indistinct masses of our troops and the enemy's. On the right, along the course of the rivers Kolotcha and Moskva, the country was broken and hilly. Through the gaps between the hills could be seen the villages of Bezzubovo and Zaharino. On the left the ground was more level; there were fields of corn and a smoking village that had been set on fire—Semyonovskoye.

Everything Pierre saw was so indefinite, that in no part of the scene before him could he find anything fully corresponding to his preconceptions. There was nowhere a field of battle such as he had expected to see, nothing but fields, dells, troops, woods, camp-fires, villages, mounds, and streams. With all Pierre's efforts, he could not discover in the living landscape a military position. He could not even distinguish between our troops and the enemy's.

'I must ask some one who understands it,' he thought, and he addressed the officer, who was looking with curiosity at his huge, unmilitary figure.

'Allow me to ask,' Pierre said, 'what village is that before us?'

'Burdino, isn't it called?' said the officer, turning inquiringly to his comrade.

'Borodino,' the other corrected.

The officer, obviously pleased at an opportunity for conversation, went nearer to Pierre.

'Are these our men there?' asked Pierre.

'Yes, and away further, those are the French,' said the officer. 'There they are, there you can see them.'

'Where? where?' asked Pierre.

'One can see them with the naked eye. Look!' The officer pointed to smoke rising on the left beyond the river, and the same stern and grave expression came into his face that Pierre had noticed in many of the faces he had met.

'Ah, that's the French! And there? . . .' Pierrre pointed to a knoll on the left about which troops could be seen.

'Those are our men.'

'Oh, indeed! And there? . . .' Pierre pointed to another mound in the distance, with a big tree on it, near a village that could be seen in a gap between the hills, where there was a dark patch and the smoke of camp-fires.

'Ah! that's *he* again!' said the officer. (It was the redoubt of Shevardino.) 'Yesterday that was ours, but now it's *his*.'

'So what is our position, then?'

'Our position?' said the officer, with a smile of satisfaction. 'I can describe it very clearly, because I have had to do with the making of almost all our fortifications. There, our centre, do you see, is here at Borodino.' He pointed to the village with the white church, in front of them. 'There's the ford across the Kolotcha. Here, do you see, where the rows of mown hay are still lying in the low ground, there's the bridge. That's our centre. Our right flank is away yonder' (he pointed to the right, far away to the hollows among the hills), 'there is the river Moskva, and there we have thrown up three very strong redoubts. The left flank . . .' there the officer paused. 'It's hard to explain, you see. . . . Yesterday our left flank was over there, at Shevardino, do you see, where the oak is. But now we have drawn back our left wing, now it's over there,—you see the village and the smoke—that's Semyonovskoye, and here—look,' he pointed to Raevsky's redoubt. 'Only the battle won't be there, most likely. *He* has moved his troops here, but that's a blind; *he* will probably try to get round on the right. Well, but however it may be, there'll be a lot of men missing at roll-call tomorrow!' said the officer.

The old sergeant, who came up during the officer's speech, had waited in silence for his superior officer to finish speaking. But at this point he interrupted him in undisguised annoyance at his last words.

'We have to send for gabions,' he said severely.

The officer seemed abashed, as though he were fully aware that though he might think how many men would be missing next day, he ought not to talk about it.

'Well, send the third company again,' he said hurriedly. 'And who are you, not one of the doctors?'

'No, I am nothing in particular,' answered Pierre. And he went downhill again, passing the peasant militiamen.

'Ah, the damned beasts!' said the officer, pinching his nose, and hurrying past them with Pierre.

'Here they come! ... They are bringing her, they are coming. ... Here she is ... they'll be here in a minute,' cried voices suddenly, and officers, soldiers, and peasants ran forward along the road.

A church procession was coming up the hill from Borodino. In front of it a regiment of infantry marched smartly along the dusty road, with their shakoes off and their muskets lowered. Behind the infantry came the sounds of church singing.

Soldiers and peasants came running down bareheaded to meet it, overtaking Pierre.

'They are bringing the Holy Mother! Our defender ... the Holy Mother of Iversky! ...'

'The Holy Mother of Smolensk ...' another corrected.

The militiamen who had been in the village and those who had been working at the battery, flinging down their spades, ran to meet the procession. The battalion marching along the dusty road was followed by priests in church robes, a little old man in a hood with attendant deacons and choristers. Behind them came soldiers and officers bearing a huge holy picture, with tarnished face in a setting of silver. This was the holy icon that had been brought away from Smolensk, and had accompanied the army ever since. Behind, before, and all round it, walked or ran crowds of soldiers with bared heads, bowing to the earth.

On top of the hill the procession stopped; the men bearing the holy picture on a linen cloth were relieved by others; the deacons relighted their censers, and the service began. The burning rays of the sun beat vertically down on the crowds; a faint, fresh breeze played with the hair of their bare heads, and fluttered the ribbons with which the holy picture was decked; the singing sounded subdued under the open sky. An immense crowd—officers, soldiers, and militiamen— stood round, all with bare heads. In a space apart, behind the priests and deacons, stood the persons of higher rank. A bald general, with the order of St. George on his neck, stood directly behind the priest. He was unmistakably a German, for he stood, not crossing himself, patiently waiting for the end of the service, to which he thought it right to listen, probably as a means of arousing the patriotism of the Russian peasantry; another general stood in a martial pose and swung his arm before his chest, looking about him as he made the sign of the cross. Pierre, standing among the peasants, recognised in this group of higher rank several persons he knew. But he did not look at them; his whole attention was engrossed by the serious expression of the faces in the crowd, soldiers and peasants alike, all gazing with the same eagerness at the holy picture. As soon as the weary choristers (it was their twentieth service) began languidly singing their habitual chant, 'O Mother of God, save Thy servants from calamity,' and priest and deacon chimed in, 'For to Thee we all fly as our invincible Bulwark and Protectress,' there was a gleam on every face of that sense of the solemnity of the coming moment, which he had seen on the hill at Mozhaisk and by glimpses in so many of the faces meeting him that morning. And heads were bowed lower, while locks of hair fluttered in the breeze, and there was the sound of sighing and beating the breast as the soldiers crossed themselves.

The crowd suddenly parted and pressed upon Pierre. Some one, probably a very great person, judging by the promptitude with which they made way for him, was approaching the holy picture.

It was Kutuzov, who had been making the round of the position. On his way back to Tatarinovo, he joined the service. Pierre at once recognised him from his peculiar figure, which marked him out at once.

In a long military coat, with his enormously stout figure and bent back, with his white head uncovered, and his blind white eye, conspicuous in his puffy face, Kutuzov walked with his waddling, swaying gait into the ring and stood behind the priest. He crossed himself with an habitual gesture, bent down, with his hand touching the earth, and, sighing heavily, bowed his grey head. Kutuzov was followed by Bennigsen and his suite. In spite of the presence of the commander-in-chief, which drew the attention of all persons of higher rank, the militiamen and soldiers went on praying without looking at him.

When the service was over, Kutuzov went up to the holy picture, dropped heavily down on his knees, bowing to the earth, and for a long time he attempted to get up, and was unable from his weakness and heavy weight. His grey head twitched with the strain. At last he did get up, and putting out his lips in a naïvely, childlike way kissed the holy picture, and again bowed down, with one hand touching the ground.

The other generals followed his example; then the officers, and after them the soldiers and militiamen ran up with excited faces, pushing each other, and shoving breathlessly forward.

XXII

STAGGERING from the crush of the crowd that carried him along with it, Pierre looked about him.

'Count! Pyotr Kirillitch! How did you come here?' said a voice. Pierre looked round.

Boris Drubetskoy, brushing his knee with his hand (he had probably made it dusty in his devotions before the holy picture) came up to Pierre smiling. Boris was elegantly dressed, though his get-up was of a style appropriate to active service. He wore a long military coat and had a riding-whip slung across his shoulder, as Kutuzov had.

Kutuzov had meanwhile reached the village, and sat down in the shade of the nearest house, on a bench which one Cossack went to fetch him, and another hastily covered with a rug. An immense retinue of magnificent officers surrounded him.

The procession was moving on further, accompanied by the crowd. Pierre stood still about thirty paces from Kutuzov, talking to Boris.

He explained to him his desire to take part in the battle and to inspect the position.

'I tell you what you had better do,' said Boris. 'I will do the honours of the camp for you. You will see everything best of all from where Count Bennigsen is to be. I am in attendance on him. I will mention it to him. And if you like to go over the position, come along with us; we are just going to the left flank. And then when we come back, I beg you will stay the night with me, and we will make up a game of cards. You know Dmitry Sergeitch, of course. He is staying there.' He pointed to the third house in Gorky.

'But I should have liked to have seen the right flank. I'm told it is very strong,' said Pierre. 'I should have liked to go from the river Moskva through the whole position.'

'Well, that you can do later, but the great thing is the left flank.'

'Yes, yes. And where is Prince Bolkonsky's regiment? can you point it out to me?' asked Pierre.

'Andrey Nikolaevitch's? We shall pass it. I will take you to him.'

'What about the left flank?' asked Pierre.

'To tell you the truth, between ourselves, there's no making out how things stand with the left flank,' said Boris confidentially, dropping his voice. 'Count Bennigsen had proposed something quite different. He proposed to fortify that knoll over there, not at all as it has . . . but . . .' Boris shrugged his shoulders. 'His highness would not have it so, or he was talked over. You see . . .' Boris did not finish because Kaisarov, Kutuzov's adjutant, at that moment came up to Pierre. 'Ah, Paisy Sergeitch,' said Boris to him, with an unembarrassed smile, 'I am trying, you see, to explain the position to the count. It's amazing how his highness can gauge the enemy's plans so accurately!'

'Do you mean about the left flank?' said Kaisarov.

'Yes, yes; just so. Our left flank is now extremely strong.'

Although Kutuzov had made a clearance of the superfluous persons on the staff, Boris had succeeded, after the change he had made, in retaining a post at headquarters. Boris was in attendance on Count Bennigsen. Count Bennigsen, like every one on whom Boris had been in attendance, looked on young Prince Drubetskoy as an invaluable man. Among the chief officers of the army there were two clearly defined parties: Kutuzov's party and the party of Bennigsen, the chief of staff. Boris belonged to the latter faction, and no one succeeded better than he did in paying the most servile adulation to Kutuzov, while managing to insinuate that the old fellow was not good for much, and that everything was really due to the initiative of Bennigsen. Now the decisive moment of battle had come, which must mean the downfall of Kutuzov and the transfer of the command to Bennigsen, or if Kutuzov should gain the battle, the credit of it must be skilfully put down to Bennigsen. In any case many promotions were bound to be made, and many new men were certain to be brought to the front after the morrow. And Boris was consequently in a state of nervous exhilaration all that day.

Others of Pierre's acquaintances joined him; and he had not time to answer all the questions about Moscow that were showered upon him, nor to listen to all they had to tell him. Every face wore a look of excitement and agitation. But it seemed to Pierre that the cause of the excitement that was betrayed by some of those faces was to be found in questions of personal success, and he could not forget that other look of excitement he had seen in the other faces, that suggested problems, not of personal success, but the universal questions of life and death.

Kutuzov noticed Pierre's figure and the group gathered about him.

'Call him to me,' said Kutuzov.

An adjutant communicated his highness's desire, and Pierre went towards the bench. But a militiaman approached Kutuzov before him. It was Dolohov.

'How does that man come to be here?' asked Pierre.

'Oh, he's such a sly dog, he pokes himself in everywhere!' was the answer he received. 'He has been degraded to the ranks, you know. Now he wants to pop up again. He has made plans of some sort and spies in the enemy's lines at night... but he's a plucky fellow...'

Pierre took off his hat and bowed respectfully to Kutuzov.

'I decided that if I were to lay the matter before your highness you might dismiss me or say that you were aware of the facts and then I shouldn't lose anything,' Dolohov was saying.

'To be sure.'

'And if I were right, I should do a service for my fatherland, for which I am ready to die.'

'To be sure... to be sure...'

'And if your highness has need of a man who would not spare his skin, graciously remember me... perhaps I might be of use to your highness...'

'To be sure... to be sure...' repeated Kutuzov, looking with a laughing, half-closed eye at Pierre.

Meanwhile Boris, with his courtier-like tact, had moved close to the commander-in-chief with Pierre, and in the most natural manner, in a quiet voice, as though continuing his previous conversation, he said to Pierre:

'The peasant militiamen have simply put on clean, white shirts to be ready to die. What heroism, count!'

Boris said this to Pierre with the evident intention of being overheard by his excellency. He knew Kutuzov's attention would be caught by those words, and his highness did in fact address him.

'What are you saying about the militia?' he said to Boris.

'They have put on white shirts, your highness, by way of preparing for tomorrow, to be ready for death.'

'Ah!... A marvellous, unique people,' said Kutuzov, and closing his eyes he shook his head. 'A unique people!' he repeated, with a sigh.

'Do you want a sniff of powder?' he said to Pierre. 'Yes; a pleasant smell. I have the honour to be one of your wife's worshippers; is she quite well? My quarters are at your service.' And Kutuzov began, as old people often do, gazing abstractedly about him, as though forgetting all he had to say or do. Apparently recollecting the object of his search, he beckoned to Andrey Sergeitch Kaisorov, the brother of his adjutant.

'How was it, how do they go, those verses of Marin? How do they go? What he wrote on Gerakov: "You will be teacher in the corps...." Tell me, tell me,' said Kutuzov, his countenance relaxing in readiness for a laugh. Kaisarov repeated the lines ... Kutuzov, smiling, nodded his head to the rhythm of the verse.

When Pierre moved away from Kutuzov, Dolohov approached and took his hand.

'I am very glad to meet you here, count,' he said, aloud, disregarding the presence of outsiders, and speaking with a marked determination and gravity. 'On the eve of a day which God knows who among us will be destined to survive I am glad to have the chance of telling you that I regret the misunderstandings there have been between us in the past; and I should be glad to think you had nothing against me. I beg you to forgive me.'

Pierre looked with a smile at Dolohov, not knowing what to say to him. With tears starting into his eyes, Dolohov embraced and kissed Pierre.

Boris had said a few words to his general, and Count Bennigsen addressed Pierre, proposing that he should accompany them along the line.

'You will find it interesting,' he said.

'Yes, very interesting,' said Pierre.

Half an hour later Kutuzov was on his way back to Tatarinovo, while Bennigsen and his suite, with Pierre among them, were inspecting the position.

XXIII

FROM Gorky Bennigsen went down the high-road to the bridge, which the officer on the knoll had pointed out to Pierre as the centre of the position, where by the riverside lay rows of sweet-scented, new-mown hay. They crossed the bridge to the village of Borodino, then turned to the left, and passing immense numbers of men and cannons, came out on to the high knoll on which militiamen were at work excavating. This was the redoubt, as yet unnamed, afterwards called Raevsky's redoubt, or the battery on the mound.

Pierre did not take special notice of this redoubt. He did not dream that that spot would be more memorable for him than any other part of the plain of Borodino. Then they crossed a hollow to Semyonovskoye, where the soldiers were dragging away the last logs of the huts and barns. Then they rode on downhill and uphill again, across a field of rye, trampled and laid as though by hail, along the track newly made by the artillery, over the ridges of the ploughed field, to the earthworks, at which the men were still at work.

Bennigsen halted at the earthworks, and looked in front at the redoubt of Shevardino, which had been ours the day before. Several horsemen could be descried upon it. The officers said that Napoleon and Murat were there. And all gazed eagerly at the little group of horsemen. Pierre too stared at them, trying to guess which of the scarcely discernible figures was Napoleon. At last the group of horsemen descended the hill and passed out of sight.

Bennigsen began explaining to a general who had ridden up to him the whole position of our troops. Pierre listened to his words, straining every faculty of his mind to grasp the essential points of the coming battle, but to his mortification he felt that his faculties were not equal to the task. He could make nothing of it. Bennigsen finished speaking, and noticing Pierre's listening face, he said, turning suddenly to him:

'It's not very interesting for you, I expect.'

'Oh, on the contrary, it's very interesting,' Pierre repeated, not quite truthfully.

From the earthworks they turned still more to the left of the road that ran winding through a thick, low-growing, birch wood. In the middle of the wood a brown hare with white feet popped out on the road before them, and was so frightened by the tramp of so many horses, that in its terror it hopped along the road just in front of them for a long while, rousing general laughter, and only when several voices shouted at it, dashed to one side and was lost in the thicket. After a couple of versts of woodland, they came out on a clearing, where were the troops of Tutchkov's corps, destined to protect the left flank.

At this point, at the extreme left flank, Bennigsen talked a great deal with much heat; and gave instructions, of great importance from a military point of view, as it seemed to Pierre. Just in front of the spot where Tutchkov's troops were placed there rose a knoll, which was not occupied by troops. Bennigsen was loud in his criticism of this oversight, saying that it was insane to leave a height that commanded the country round unoccupied and place troops just below it. Several generals expressed the same opinion. One in particular, with martial warmth, declared that they were doomed there to certain destruction. Bennigsen, on his own responsibility, ordered the troops to be moved on to the high-road.

This change of position on the left flank made Pierre more than ever doubtful of his capacity for comprehending military matters. As he heard Bennigsen and the other generals criticising the position of the troops at the foot of the hill, Pierre fully grasped and shared their views. But that was why he could not imagine how the man who had placed them there could have made so gross and obvious a blunder.

Pierre did not know that the troops had not been placed there to defend their position, as Bennigsen supposed, but had been stationed in that concealed spot in ambush, in order unobserved to deal a sudden blow at the enemy unawares. Bennigsen, ignorant of this project, moved the troops into a prominent position without saying anything about this change to the commander-in-chief.

XXIV

PRINCE ANDREY was on that bright August evening lying propped on his elbow in a broken-down barn in the village of Knyazkovo, at the further end of the encampment of his regiment. Through a gap in the broken wall he was looking at the line of thirty-year-old pollard birches in the hedge, at the field with sheaves of oats lying about it, and at the bushes where he saw the smoke of camp-fires, at which the soldiers were doing their cooking.

Cramped and useless and burdensome as his life seemed now to Prince Andrey, he felt nervously excited and irritable on the eve of battle, just as he had felt seven years earlier before Austerlitz.

He had received and given all orders for the next day's battle. He had nothing more to do. But thoughts—the simplest, most obvious, and therefore most awful—would not leave him in peace. He knew that the battle next day would be the most awful of all he had taken part in, and death, for the first time, presented itself to him, not in relation to his actual manner of life, or to the effect of it on others, but simply in relation to himself, to his soul, and rose before him simply and awfully with a vividness that made it like a concrete reality. And from the height of this vision everything that had once occupied him seemed suddenly illumined by a cold, white light, without shade, without perspective or outline. His whole life seemed to him like a magic lantern, at which he had been looking through the glass and by artificial light. Now he saw suddenly, without the glass, in the clear light of day, those badly daubed pictures. 'Yes, yes, there are they; there are the cheating forms that excited torments and ecstasies in me,' he said to himself, going over in imagination the chief pictures of the magic lantern of his life, looking at them now in the cold, white daylight of a clear view of death. 'These are they, these coarsely sketched figures which seemed something splendid and mysterious. Glory, the good of society, love for a woman, the fatherland—what grand pictures they used to seem to me, with what deep meaning they seemed to be filled! And it is all so simple, so colourless and coarse in the cold light of the day that I feel is dawning for me.' The three chief sorrows of his life held his attention especially. His love for a woman, his father's death, and the invasion of the French—now in possession of half of Russia. 'Love! . . . That little girl, who seemed to me brimming over with mysterious forces. How I loved her! I made romantic plans of love, of happiness with her! O simple-hearted youth!' he said aloud bitterly. 'Why, I believed in some ideal love which was to keep her faithful to me for the whole year of my absence! Like the faithful dove in the fable, she was to pine away in my absence from me! And it was all so much simpler. . . . It is all so horribly simple and loathsome!'

'My father, too, laid out Bleak Hills, and thought it was his place, his land, his air, his peasants. But Napoleon came along, and without even knowing of his existence, swept him away like a chip out of his path, and his Bleak Hills laid in the dust, and all his life with it brought to nought. Princess Marya says that it is a trial sent from above. What is the trial for, since he is not and never will be? He will never come back again! He is not! So for whom is it a trial! Fatherland, the spoiling of Moscow! But tomorrow I shall be killed; and not by a Frenchman even, maybe, by one of our own men, like the soldier who let off his gun close to my ear yesterday; and the French will come and pick me up by my head and my heels and pitch me into a hole that I may not stink under their noses; and new conditions of life will arise, and I shall know nothing of them, and I shall not be at all.'

He gazed at the row of birch-trees with their motionless yellows and greens, and the white bark shining in the sun. 'To die then, let them kill me tomorrow, let me be no more . . . let it all go on, and let me be at an end.' He vividly pictured his own absence from that life. And those birch-trees, with their light and shade, and the curling clouds and the smoke of the fires, everything around seemed suddenly transformed into something weird and menacing. A shiver ran down his back. Rising quickly to his feet, he went out of the barn, and began to walk about.

He heard voices behind the barn.

'Who's there?' called Prince Andrey.

The red-nosed Captain Timohin, once the officer in command of Dolohov's company, now in the lack of officers promoted to the command of a battlion, came shyly into the barn. He was followed by an adjutant and the paymaster of the regiment.

Prince Andrey got up hurriedly, listened to the matters relating to their duties that the officers had come to him about, gave a few instructions, and was about to dismiss them, when he heard a familiar, lisping voice behind the barn.

'*Que diable!*' said the voice of some one stumbling over something.

Prince Andrey, peeping out of the barn, saw Pierre, who had just hit against a post lying on the ground, and had almost fallen over. Prince Andrey always disliked seeing people from his own circle, especially Pierre, who reminded him of all the painful moments he had passed through on his last stay at Moscow.

'Well!' he cried. 'What fate has brought you? I didn't expect to see you.'

While he said this there was in his eyes and his whole face more than coldness, positive hostility, which Pierre noticed at once. He had approached the barn with the greatest eagerness, but now, on seeing Prince Andrey's face, he felt constrained and ill at ease.

'I have come . . . you know . . . simply . . . I have come . . . it's interesting,' said Pierre, who had so many times already that day repeated that word 'interesting' without meaning it. 'I wanted to see the battle!'

'Yes, yes; but your mason brethren, what do they say of war? How would they avert it?' said Prince Andrey sarcastically. 'Well, tell me about Moscow. And my people? Have they reached Moscow at last?' he asked seriously.

'Yes. Julie Drubetskoy told me so. I went to call, but missed them. They had started for your Moscow estate.'

XXV

THE officers would have taken leave, but Prince Andrey, apparently unwilling to be left alone with his friend, pressed them to stay and have some tea. Benches were set, and tea was brought. With some astonishment the officers stared at Pierre's huge, bulky figure, and heard him talk of Moscow, and of the position of our troops, which he had succeeded in getting a view of. Prince Andrey did not speak, and his face was so forbidding that Pierre addressed his remarks more to the simple-hearted Timohin than to Bolkonsky.

'So you understand the whole disposition of the troops?' Prince Andrey put in.

'Yes. At least, how do you mean?' said Pierre. 'As I am not a military man, I can't say I do fully; but still I understand the general arrangement.'

'Well, then, you know more than anybody else,' said Prince Andrey.

'Oh!' said Pierre incredulously, looking over his spectacles at Prince Andrey. 'Well, and what do you say of the appointment of Kutuzov?' he asked.

'I was very glad of his appointment; that's all I know,' said Prince Andrey.

'Well, tell me of your opinion of Barclay de Tolly. In Moscow they are saying all kinds of things about him. What do you think of him?'

'Ask them,' said Prince Andrey, indicating the officers.

With the condescendingly doubtful smile with which every one addressed him, Pierre looked at Timohin.

'It was a gleam of light in the dark, your excellency, when his highness took the command,' said Timohin, stealing shy glances continually at his colonel.

'Why so?' asked Pierre.

'Well, as regards firewood and food, let me tell you. Why, all the way we retreated from Sventsyan not a twig, nor a wisp of hay, nor anything, dare we touch. We were retreating, you see, so *he* would get it, wouldn't he, your excellency?' he said, turning to his prince, 'but we mustn't dare to. In our regiment two officers were court-martialled for such things. Well, since his highness is in command, it's all straightforward as regards that. We see daylight . . .'

'Then why did he forbid it?'

Timohin looked round in confusion, at a loss how to answer such a question. Pierre turned to Prince Andrey with the same inquiry.

'Why, so as not to waste the country we were leaving for the enemy,' said Prince Andrey, with angry sarcasm. 'That's a first principle: never to allow pillage and accustom your men to marauding. And at Smolensk too he very correctly judged that the French were the stronger and might overcome us. But he could not understand,' cried Prince Andrey in a voice suddenly shrill, 'he could not understand that for the first time we were fighting on Russian soil, that there was a spirit in the men such as I had never seen before, that we had twice in succession beaten back the French, and that success had multiplied our strength tenfold. He ordered a retreat, and all our efforts and our curses were in vain. He had no thought of treachery; he tried to do everything for the best and thought over everything well. But for that very reason he was no good. He is no good now just because he considers everything soundly and accurately as every German must. How can I explain to you. . . . Well, your father has a German valet, say, and he's an excellent valet and satisfies all his requirements better than you can do, and all's well and good; but if your father is sick unto death, you'll send away the valet and wait on your father yourself with your awkward, unpractised hands, and be more comfort to him than a skilful man who's a stranger. That's how we have done with Barclay. While Russia was well, she might be served by a stranger, and an excellent minister he was, but as soon as she's in danger, she wants a man of her own kith and kin. So you in your club have been making him out to be a traitor! They slander him now as a traitor; and afterwards, ashamed of their false accusations, they will suddenly glorify him as a hero or genius, which would be even more unfair to him. He's an honest and conscientious German ...'

'They say he's an able general, though,' said Pierre.

'I don't know what's meant by an able general,' Prince Andrey said ironically.

'An able general,' said Pierre; 'well, it's one who foresees all contingencies ... well, divines the enemy's projects.'

'But that's impossible,' said Prince Andrey, as though of a matter long ago settled.

Pierre looked at him in surprise.

'But you know they say,' he said, 'that war is like a game of chess.'

'Yes,' said Prince Andrey, 'only with this little difference, that in chess you may think over each move as long as you please, that you are not limited as to time, and with this further difference that a knight is always stronger than a pawn and two pawns are always stronger than one, while in war a battalion is sometimes stronger than a division, and sometimes weaker than a company. No one can ever be certain of the relative strength of armies. Believe me,' he said, 'if anything did depend on the arrangements made by the staff, I would be there, and helping to make them, but instead of that I have the honour of serving here in the regiment with these gentlemen here, and I consider that the day really depends upon us tomorrow and not on them. . . . Success never has depended and never will depend on position, on arms, nor even on numbers; and, least of all, on position.'

'On what then?'

'On the feeling that is in me and him,' he indicated Timohin, 'and every soldier.'

Prince Andrey glanced at Timohin, who was staring in alarm and bewilderment at his colonel. In contrast to his usual reserved taciturnity, Prince Andrey seemed excited now. Apparently he could not refrain from expressing the ideas that suddenly rose to his mind. 'The battle is won by the side that has firmly resolved to win. Why did we lose the battle of Austerlitz? Our losses were almost equalled by the French losses; but we said to ourselves very early in the day that we were losing the battle, and we lost it. And we said so because we had nothing to fight for then; we wanted to get out of fighting as quick as we could. "We are defeated; so let us run!" and we did run. If we had not said that till evening, God knows what might not have happened.

But tomorrow we shan't say that. You talk of our position of the left flank being weak, and the right flank too extended,' he went on; 'all that's nonsense; that's all nothing. But what awaits us tomorrow? A hundred millions of the most diverse contingencies, which will determine on the instant whether they run or we do; whether one man is killed and then another; but all that's being done now is all mere child's play. The fact is that these people with whom you have been inspecting the positions do nothing towards the progress of things; they are a positive hindrance. They are entirely taken up with their own petty interests.'

'At such a moment?' said Pierre reproachfully.

'*At such a moment*,' repeated Prince Andrey. 'To them this is simply a moment on which one may score off a rival and win a cross or ribbon the more. To my mind what is before us tomorrow is this: a hundred thousand Russian and a hundred thousand French troops have met to fight, and the fact is that these two hundred thousand men will fight, and the side that fights most desperately and spares itself least will conquer. And if you like, I'll tell you that whatever happens, and whatever mess they make up yonder, we shall win the battle tomorrow; whatever happens we shall win the victory.'

'Your excellency, that's the truth of it, the holy truth,' put in Timohin; 'who would spare himself now! The soldiers in my battalion, would you believe it, wouldn't drink their vodka; this isn't an ordinary day, they say.'

All were silent.

The officers rose. Prince Andrey went with them out of the barn, giving the last instructions to the adjutant. When the officers had gone, Pierre came nearer to Prince Andrey, and was just about to begin talking when they heard the tramp of hoofs not far away on the road, and glancing in that direction Prince Andrey recognized Wolzogen and Klausewitz, accompanied by a Cossack. They rode close by them, still talking, and Pierre and Prince Andrey could not help overhearing the following phrases in German:

'The war ought to be carried on over a wide extent of country. I cannot sufficiently strongly express that view of the matter,' one said in German.

'Oh yes,' said another voice, 'since the object is to wear out the enemy, one must not consider the losses of private persons.'

'Certainly not,' acquiesced the first voice.

'Carried into a wide extent of country,' Prince Andrey repeated with a wrathful snort, when they had ridden by. 'In that open country I had a father and son and sister at Bleak Hills. He doesn't care about that.

That's just what I was saying to you: these excellent Germans won't win the battle tomorrow, they will only make a mess of it, so far as they are able, because they have nothing in their German noddles but calculations that are not worth a rotten egg, and they haven't in their heart the one thing that's wanted for tomorrow, that Timohin has. They have given all Europe up to *him*, and now they have come to teach us—fine teachers!' he added, his voice growing shrill again.

'So you think the battle tomorrow will be a victory,' said Pierre.

'Yes, yes,' said Prince Andrey absently. 'There's one thing I would do, if I were in power,' he began again. 'I wouldn't take prisoners. What sense is there in taking prisoners? That's chivalry. The French have destroyed my home and are coming to destroy Moscow; they have outraged and are outraging me at every second. They are my enemies, they are all criminals to my way of thinking. They must be put to death. Since they are my enemies, they can't be my friends, whatever they may have said at Tilsit.'

'Yes, yes,' said Pierre, looking with shining eyes at Prince Andrey. 'I entirely agree with you!'

The question that had been disturbing Pierre all that day, since the Mozhaisk hill, now struck him as perfectly clear and fully solved. He saw now all the import and all the gravity of the war and the impending battle. All he had seen that day, all the stern, grave faces of which he had had glimpses, appeared to him in a new light now. He saw, to borrow a term from physics, the latent heat of patriotism in all those men he had seen, and saw in it the explanation of the composure and apparent levity with which they were all preparing for death. 'We ought not to take prisoners,' said Prince Andrey. 'That change alone would transform the whole aspect of war and would make it less cruel. But playing at war, that's what's vile; and playing at magnanimity and all the rest of it. That magnanimity and sensibility is like the magnanimity and sensibility of the lady who turns sick at the sight of a slaughtered calf—she is so kindhearted she can't see blood—but eats fricasseed veal with a very good appetite. They talk of the laws of warfare, of chivalry, of flags of truce, and humanity to the wounded, and so on. That's all rubbish. I saw enough in 1805 of chivalry and flags of truce: they duped us, and we duped them. They plunder other people's homes, issue false money, and, worse than all, kill my children, my father, and then talk of the laws of warfare, and generosity to a fallen foe. No prisoners; and go to give and to meet death! Any one who has come to think this as I have, through the same sufferings...'

Prince Andrey, who had thought that he did not care whether they took Moscow as they had taken Smolensk, was suddenly pulled up in his speech by a nervous catch in his throat. He walked to and fro several times in silence, but his eyes blazed with feverish brilliance and his lip quivered, as he began to speak again.

'If there were none of this playing at generosity in warfare, we should never go to war, except for something worth facing death for, as now. Then there would not be wars because Pavel Ivanitch had insulted Mihail Ivanitch. But if there is war as now, let it be really war. And then the intensity of warfare would be something quite different. All these Westphalians and Hessians Napoleon is leading against us would not have come to fight us in Russia, and we should not have gone to war in Austria and in Prussia without knowing what for. War is not a polite recreation, but the vilest thing in life, and we ought to understand that and not play at war. We ought to accept it sternly and solemnly as a fearful necessity. It all comes to this: have done with lying, and if it's war, then it's war and not a game, or else warfare is simply the favourite pastime of the idle and frivolous.... The military is the most honoured calling. And what is war, what is needed for success in war, what are the morals of the military world? The object of warfare is murder; the means employed in warfare—spying, treachery, and the encouragement of it, the ruin of a country, the plundering of its inhabitants and robbery for the maintenance of the army, trickery and lying, which are called military strategy; the morals of the military class—absence of all independence, that is, discipline, idleness, ignorance, cruelty, debauchery, and drunkenness. And in spite of all that, it is the highest class, respected by every one. All sovereigns, except the Chinese, wear a military uniform, and give the greatest rewards to the man who succeeds in killing most people.... They meet together to murder one another, as we shall do tomorrow; they slaughter and mutilate tens of thousands of men, and then offer up thanksgiving services for the number of men they have killed (and even add to it in the telling), and glorify the victory, supposing that the more men have been slaughtered the greater the achievement. How God can look down from above and hear them!' shrieked Prince Andrey in a shrill, piercing voice. 'Ah, my dear boy, life has been a bitter thing for me of late. I see that I have come to understand too much. And it is not good for man to taste of the tree of the knowledge of good and evil.... Ah, well, it's not for long!' he added. 'But you are getting sleepy and it's time I was in bed too. Go back to Gorky,' said Prince Andrey suddenly.

'Oh no!' answered Pierre, gazing with eyes full of scared sympathy at Prince Andrey.

'You must be off; before a battle one needs to get a good sleep,' repeated Prince Andrey. He went quickly up to Pierre, embraced and kissed him. 'Good-bye, be off,' he cried, 'whether we see each other again or not . . .' and turning hurriedly, he went off into the barn.

It was already dark, and Pierre could not distinguish whether the expression of his face was exasperated or affectionate.

Pierre stood for some time in silence, hesitating whether to go after him or to return to Gorky. 'No; he does not want me!' Pierre made up his mind, 'and I know this is our last meeting!' He heaved a deep sigh and rode back to Gorky.

Prince Andrey lay down on a rug in the barn, but he could not sleep.

He closed his eyes. One set of images followed another in his mind. On one mental picture he dwelt long and joyfully. He vividly recalled one evening in Petersburg. Natasha with an eager, excited face had been telling him how in looking for mushrooms the previous summer she had lost her way in a great forest. She described incoherently the dark depths of the forest, and her feelings, and her talk with a bee-keeper she met, and every minute she broke off in her story, saying: 'No, I can't, I'm not describing it properly; no, you won't understand me,' although Prince Andrey tried to assure her that he understood and did really understand all she wanted to convey to him. Natasha was dissatisfied with her own words; she felt that they did not convey the passionately poetical feeling she had known that day and tried to give expression to. 'It was all so exquisite, that old man, ánd it was so dark in the forest . . . and such a kind look in his . . . no, I can't describe it,' she had said, flushed and moved.

Prince Andrey smiled now the same happy smile he had smiled then, gazing into her eyes. 'I understood her,' thought Prince Andrey, 'and more than understood her: that spiritual force, that sincerity, that openness of soul, the very soul of her, which seemed bound up with her body, the very soul it was I loved in her . . . loved so intensely, so passionately . . .' And all at once he thought how his love had ended. '*He* cared nothing for all that. *He* saw nothing of it, had no notion of it. He saw in her a pretty and *fresh* young girl with whom he did not deign to unite his life permanently. And I? . . . And he is still alive and happy.' Prince Andrey jumped up as though suddenly scalded, and began walking to and fro before the barn again.

XXVI

ON the 25th of August, on the eve of the battle of Borodino, the prefect of the French Emperor's palace, M. de Beausset, and Colonel Fabvier, arrived, the former from Paris, and the latter from Madrid, at Napoleon's encampment at Valuev.

After changing into court uniform M. de Beausset ordered the package he had brought for the Emperor to be carried before him, and walked into the first compartment of Napoleon's tent, where he busied himself while conversing with the aides-de-camp in unpacking the box.

Fabvier stood talking with generals of his acquaintance in the entrance of the tent.

The Emperor Napoleon had not yet left his bedroom, he was finishing his toilet. With snorts and grunts of satisfaction, he was turning first his stout back and then his plump, hirsute chest towards the flesh-brush with which a valet was rubbing him down. Another valet, holding a bottle with one finger on it, was sprinkling eau de cologne on the Emperor's pampered person with an expression which seemed to say that he alone knew where and how much eau de cologne must be sprinkled. Napoleon's short hair was wet and matted on his brow. But his face, though puffy and yellow, expressed physical satisfaction.

'Go on, hard, go on . . .' he said, shrugging and clearing his throat, to the valet brushing him. An adjutant, who had come into the bedroom to report to the Emperor the number of prisoners taken in the last engagement, was standing at the door, after giving his message, awaiting permission to withdraw. Napoleon, frowning, glanced up from under his brows at the adjutant. 'No prisoners,' he repeated the adjutant's words. 'They are working their own destruction. So much the worse for the Russian army,' said he. 'Harder, brush harder,' he said, hunching his fat shoulders before the valet. 'Good. Let Beausset come in and Fabvier too,' he said to the adjutant, nodding.

'I obey, sire,' and the adjutant disappeared.

The two valets rapidly dressed his Majesty, and in the blue uniform of the guards he walked into the reception-room with firm, rapid steps.

Beausset meanwhile was in great haste setting up the present he had brought from the Empress on two chairs just before the Emperor as he entered. But the Emperor had been so unaccountably rapid over getting dressed and coming in that he had not time to have the surprise ready for him.

Napoleon at once noticed what they were about, and guessed they were not ready. He did not want to deprive them of the pleasure of preparing an agreeable surprise for him. He pretended not to see M. de Beausset, and beckoned Fabvier to him. Napoleon, frowning sternly, listened in silence to what Fabvier was saying of the gallantry and devotion of his army, fighting before Salamanca, at the other end of Europe; they had, he said, but one dream—to be worthy of their Emperor, and one fear—to displease him. The result of the battle had been disastrous. Napoleon made ironical remarks during Fabvier's account of it, as though he had not expected it to be otherwise in his absence.

'I must make up for it at Moscow,' said Napoleon. '*A tantôt*,' he added, and summoned Beausset, who had by this time succeeded in preparing his effect, had stood something on the chairs and thrown a cover over it.

Beausset made a courtier's low bow, such as only the old retainers of the Bourbons knew how to make, and approached him, handing him a letter.

Napoleon addressed him gaily, and pinched him by the ear.

'You have been quick, delighted to see you. Well, what is Paris saying?' he said, his look of sternness suddenly changing to the most cordial expression.

'Sire, all Paris is regretting your absence,' answered Beausset, as in duty bound. But though Napoleon knew Beausset was bound to say this or something like it, though at his lucid moments he knew it was all false, he was glad to hear this from him. He condescended to pinch his ear again.

'I am very sorry to have made you to travel so far,' he said.

'Sire, I expected to find you at least at the gates of Moscow,' said Beausset.

Napoleon smiled, and lifting his head absently looked round to the right. An adjutant approached obsequiously with a gold snuff-box and offered it. Napoleon took it.

'Yes, it's a happy chance for you,' he said, putting the open snuff-box to his nose. 'You are fond of travelling, and in three days you will see Moscow. You probably did not expect to see the Asiatic capital. You will have a delightful journey.'

Beausset bowed with gratitude for this interest in his tastes for travel (of which he had till that moment been unaware).

'Ah! what's this?' said Napoleon, observing that all the courtiers were gazing at something concealed under a covering. Beausset with courtier-like agility retired two steps with a half turn, not showing his back, and at the same moment twitched off the covering, saying: 'A present to your majesty from the Empress.'

It was a portrait, painted in brilliant colours by Gerard, of the child of Napoleon and the daughter of the Austrian Emperor, the little boy whom every one for some unknown reason called the King of Rome.

The very pretty, curly-headed child, with eyes like the Christ with the Sistine Madonna, had been portrayed playing cup and ball. The ball represented the terrestrial globe and the cup in the other hand was a sceptre.

Though it was not altogether clear what the painter had intended to express by representing the so-called King of Rome tossing the terrestrial globe on a sceptre, the allegory apparently seemed to Napoleon, as it had to every one who had seen it in Paris, quite clear and extremely pleasing.

'The King of Rome!' he said, pointing with a graceful gesture to the portrait. ' 'Admirable!' With the characteristic Italian facility for changing his expression at will, he went up to the portrait and assumed an air of pensive tenderness. He felt that what he might say or do at that moment would be historical. And it struck him that the best line he could take at that moment, at the height of his grandeur—so great that his child was playing cup and ball with the earth—would be to display, in contrast with that grandeur, the simplest, fatherly tenderness. His eyes were veiled by emotion; he moved up, looked round for a chair (a chair seemed to spring up under him), and sat down, facing the portrait. At a single gesture from him all withdrew on tiptoe, leaving the great man to himself and his feelings. After sitting there a little while and passing his fingers, he could not have said why, over the rough surface of the painting, he got up and again sent for Beausset and the officer on duty. He gave orders for the portrait to be carried out in front of his tent, so that the Old Guard, standing about his tent, might not be deprived of the happiness of seeing the King of Rome, the son and heir of their adored Emperor.

While he sat at breakfast with M. de Beausset—whom he had honoured by an invitation to join him—he heard, as he had expected, enthusiastic shouts from the soldiers and officers of the Old Guard, who had run up to see the portrait.

'*Vive l'Empereur! Vive le roi de Rome! Vive l'Empereur!*' shouted enthusiastic voices.

After breakfast, in Beausset's presence, Napoleon dictated his proclamation to the army.

'*Courte et énergique!*' Napoleon pronounced it, when he had read over the proclamation that he had dictated straight off without corrections. It was as follows:

'Soldiers! This is the battle you have so greatly desired. Victory is in our hands. It is essential for us; it will give us everything we need: comfortable quarters and a speedy return to our own country. Behave as you behaved at Austerlitz, Friedland, Vitebsk, and Smolensk. May posterity recall with pride your achievement on this day! And may they say of each of you: he was at the great battle before Moscow!'

'Before Moscow,' repeated Napoleon, and inviting M. de Beausset, so fond of travel, to accompany him on his ride, he went out of the tent to the saddled horses awaiting them outside.

'Your Majesty is too kind,' said Beausset, in response to the invitation to accompany the Emperor. He was very sleepy. He could not ride well, and was afraid of horses.

But Napoleon nodded to the traveller, and Beausset had to mount. When Napoleon came out of the tent the shouts of the Guards before his son's portrait were redoubled. Napoleon frowned.

'Take him away,' he said, with a gracefully majestic gesture, pointing to the portrait. 'It is too early yet for him to look upon the field of battle.'

Beausset, dropping his eyelids, and bowing his head, heaved a deep sigh, to testify how well he was able to appreciate and comprehend the Emperor's words.

XXVII

THE whole of that day, the 25th of August, Napoleon spent, so his historians relate, on horseback, inspecting the locality, criticising the plans submitted to him by his marshals, and giving commands in person to his generals.

The original line of the Russian disposition, along the Kolotcha, had been broken through, and, in consequence of the taking of the Shevardino redoubt on the previous day, part of that line—the left flank—had been drawn further back. That part of the line had not been strengthened, was no longer protected by the river, and more open and level ground lay before it. It was obvious to any man, military or nonmilitary, that it was that part of the line that the French should attack. One would have thought that no great deliberation would be necessary to reach this conclusion; that all the care and anxiety of the Emperor and his marshals were unnecessary, and that there was absolutely no need of that peculiar high degree of talent called genius, which they are so fond of ascribing to Napoleon. But the historians, who described the battle afterwards, and the men surrounding Napoleon at the time, and he himself, thought otherwise.

Napoleon rode about the field, gazing with a profound air at the country, wagging his head approvingly or dubiously to himself, and without communicating to the generals around him the profound chain of reasoning that guided him in his decisions, conveyed to them merely the final conclusions in the form of commands. Upon the suggestion being made by Davoust, now styled Duke of Eckmühl, for turning the Russian left flank, Napoleon said there was no need to do this, without explaining why there was no need. But to the proposal of General Compans (who was to attack the advanced earthworks), to lead his division through the forest, Napoleon signified his assent, although the so-called Duke of Elchingen, that is, Ney, ventured to observe that to move troops through woodland is risky, and might break up the formation of the division.

After examining the nature of the country opposite the Shevardino redoubt, Napoleon pondered a little while in silence and pointed to the spots where two batteries were to be placed by the morrow for action against the Russian fortifications, and the spots where, in a line with them, the field artillery was to be arranged.

After giving these and other commands, he went back to his quarters, and the disposition of the troops was written down from his dictation.

This disposition, of which the French speak with enthusiasm, and other historians with profound respect, consisted of the following instructions:

'Two new batteries, to be placed during the night on the plain occupied by the Duke of Eckmühl, will open fire at dawn on the two opposite batteries of the enemy.

'At the same time General Pernetti, in command of the artillery of the 1st corps, with thirty cannon of Compans's division, and all the howitzers of Desaix and Friant's division, will move forwards, open fire, and shower shells on the enemy's battery, against which there will be at once in action:

24 cannons of the artillery of the Guards,
30 cannons of Compans's division, and
8 cannons of Friant and Desaix's division

In all 62 cannons.

'General Fouché, in command of the artillery of the 3rd corps, will place all the sixteen howitzers of the 3rd and 8th corps at the flanks of the battery, told off to bombard the left fortification, making forty guns in all aimed against it.

'General Sorbier is to be in readiness to advance on the word being given, with all the howitzers of the artillery of the Guards against either of the enemy's fortifications.

'During the cannonade Prince Poniatovsky is to advance to the village in the wood, and to turn the enemy's position.

'General Compans will cross the wood to gain possession of the first fortification.

'After the attack has begun on these lines, further commands will be given in accordance with the enemy's movements.

'The cannonade on the left flank will begin as soon as the cannons of the right are heard. The sharpshooters of Morand's division and of the viceroy's division will open a hot fire on seeing the beginning of the attack of the right wing.

'The viceroy will take possession of the village of Borodino, and cross by its three bridges, advancing to the same height with Morand's and Gérard's divisions, which under his leadership will advance to the redoubt and come into line with the other troops of the army.

'All this is to be done in good order (*le tout se fera avec ordre et methode*), preserving as far as possible troops in reserve.

'The imperial camp, near Mozhaisk, September 6, 1812.'

These instructions—which strike one as exceedingly confused and obscure, if one ventures to throw off the superstitious awe for Napoleon's genius in treating of his disposition of his troops—may be condensed into four points—four commands. Not one of those instructions was or could be carried out.

In the first place the instruction is given: *That the batteries placed on the spot selected by Napoleon, with the cannons of Pernetti and Fouché, which were to join them, in all one hundred and two cannons, were to open fire and shell the Russian earthworks and redoubts.* This could not be done, since from the spots fixed on by Napoleon the shells did not carry so far as the Russian earthworks, and these one hundred and two cannons fired in the air till such time as the nearest officer in command ordered them to advance, in opposition to Napoleon's instructions.

The second instruction given is that *Poniatovsky, advancing to the village in the wood, should turn the Russian left flank.* This was not, and could not be, done, as Poniatovsky, on advancing to the village in the wood, found Tutchkov there barring his way, and did not, and could not, turn the Russian position.

The third instruction is: *General Compans will move into the wood to take possession of the first Russian fortification.* Compans's division did not take the first fortification, but was beaten back, because, as it came out of the wood, it had to form under a fire of grapeshot, of which Napoleon knew nothing.

The fourth instruction is: *That the viceroy will take possession of the village (Borodino), and crossing by its three bridges, and following to the same high ground as Morand's and Friant's divisions* (nothing is said of whence and when they were to advance), *which under his leadership will advance to the redoubt and form in a line with the other troops*. As far as one can make out, not so much from this confused paragraph, as from the attempts made by the viceroy to carry out the orders given him, he was to advance through Borodino from the left to the redoubt, and the divisions of Morand and Friant were to advance simultaneously from the front. All this, like the other instructions, was impossible to carry out. After passing through Borodino the viceroy was beaten back at the Kolotcha, and could advance no further. The divisions of Morand and Friant did not take the redoubt, but were driven back, and at the end of the day the redoubt was captured by the cavalry (in an action probably unforeseen by Napoleon, and not heard of by him).

And not one of the instructions given was, or could be, carried into effect. But in the disposition was the statement, that after the battle had begun, further instructions would be given in accordance with the enemy's movements; and so it might be supposed that all necessary instructions had been given by Napoleon during the battle. But this was not, and could not be, the case, because, during the whole battle, Napoleon was so far from the scene of action that (as it turned out later) he knew nothing of the course of the battle, and not a single instruction given by him during the fight could possibly be executed.

XXVIII

MANY historians assert that the French failed at Borodino because Napoleon had a cold in his head; that if he had not had a cold the orders given by him before and during the battle would have been even more remarkable for their genius, and Russia would have been lost and the face of the world would have been changed. To historians, who can maintain that Russia was transformed at the will of one man—Peter the Great—and that France, from a republic, became an empire, and that the French army marched into Russia at the will of one man—Napoleon—the conclusion that Russia has remained a power because Napoleon had a bad cold on the 26th of August may seem indisputable and convincing. Had it depended on Napoleon's will to fight, or not to fight, at Borodino, or had it depended on his will whether he gave this order or that, it is evident that a cold, affecting the manifestation of his will, might be the saving of Russia, and consequently the valet, who forgot to put on Napoleon's waterproof boots on the 24th, would be the saviour of Russia. On that method of reasoning such a deduction is inevitable; as inevitable as the contention which Voltaire maintains in jest (unconscious what he was ridiculing) that the Massacre of St. Bartholomew was due to an attack of dyspepsia from which Charles IX was suffering. But for minds that cannot admit that Russia was transformed at the will of one man—Peter the Great—and that the French empire was created, and the war with Russia begun, at the will of one man—Napoleon—such a contention will seem not merely unsound and irrational, but contrary to the whole nature of humanity. The question, What constitutes the cause of historical events? will suggest to them another answer, resting on the idea that the course of earthly events is predestined from on high, depends on the combination of all the wills of the men taking part in those events, and that the predominant influence of Napoleon in those events is purely external and fictitious.

Strange at first sight as appears the proposition that the Massacre of St. Bartholomew, the order for which was given by Charles IX, was not the result of his will, and that it was only in his fancy that the command he had given was the cause of it, and that the Borodino slaughter of eighty thousand men was not due to Napoleon's will (though he gave the order for the commencement of the battle), and that it was only his fancy that it was his doing, strange as this proposition appears, yet human dignity, that tells us that every one of us is neither more nor less a man than Napoleon, bids us admit that solution of the question, and historical researches abundantly confirm the proposition.

At the battle of Borodino Napoleon did not fire at any one, nor kill any one. All that was done by his soldiers. Therefore it was not he who killed those men. The soldiers of the French army went out to slay their fellow-men at Borodino, not owing to Napoleon's commands, but through their own desire to do so. The whole army—French, Italians, Germans, Poles—hungry, ragged, and exhausted by the march, felt at the sight of an army, barring their way to Moscow: the wine is drawn, it must be drunk. Had Napoleon forbidden them at that point to fight the Russians, they would have killed him, and have proceeded to fight the Russians, because it was inevitable for them.

When they heard Napoleon's proclamation, offering them as consolation for maiming and death the reminder that posterity would say that they had been at the battle before Moscow, they shouted, '*Vive l'Empereur*,' just as they shouted '*Vive l'Empereur*' at the sight of the picture of the little boy playing cup and ball with the earth, and just as they shouted '*Vive l'Empereur*' at every absurdity that was said. There was nothing left for them to do but to shout '*Vive l'Empereur!*' and to fight so as to get food and rest as conquerors in Moscow. Therefore it was not owing to Napoleon's commands that they killed their fellow-men.

And it was not Napoleon who ordained the course of the battle, because none of his instructions were put into execution, and he knew nothing of what was passing before him. Therefore the manner in which these men slaughtered one another did not depend on Napoleon's will, but proceeded independently of him, from the wills of the hundreds of thousands of men who took part in the affair. It *only seemed* to Napoleon that all this was due to his will. And therefore the question whether Napoleon had or had not a cold in his head is of no more interest to history than the cold of the lowest soldier of the commissariat.

The contention of some writers, that Napoleon's cold was the reason of his previous instructions and commands during the battle being weaker than usual, is completely groundless.

The instructions that have been reproduced here are by no means inferior, are indeed superior, to many similar arrangements by which he had gained victories in the past. His supposed instructions during the day were also in no way inferior to the commands he had given in previous battles, but were much the same as usual. But these instructions are supposed to be inferior, simply because Borodino was the first battle in which Napoleon was not victorious. The finest and profoundest combinations seem very poor, and every military student can criticise them with a consequential air, when the battle has not been won by means of them; and the stupidest combinations will seem exceedingly ingenious, and serious writers will fill volumes in proving their excellence, when the battle that followed chances to have been a victory.

The plan composed by Weierother at Austerlitz was a model of perfection in its own line, but it has yet been condemned, and condemned for its very perfection, for its over-minuteness in detail.

At Borodino Napoleon played his part as the representative of supreme power as well, or even better, than he had done at previous battles. He did nothing likely to hinder the progress of the battle; he yielded to the most sensible advice; he was not confused, did not contradict himself, did not lose his presence of mind, nor run away from the field of battle, but with his great tact and military experience, he performed calmly and with dignity his role of appearing to be in supreme control of it all.

XXIX

ON returning from a second careful inspection of the lines, Napoleon said:

'The pieces are on the board, the game will begin tomorrow.'

He ordered some punch, and sending for Beausset began talking of Paris with him, discussing various changes he intended to make in the

Empress's household, and surprising the prefect by his memory of the minutest details of court affairs.

He showed interest in trifles, jested at Beausset's love of travel, and chatted carelessly, as some renowned, skilful and confident surgeon will often chat playfully while he tucks up his sleeves and puts on his apron, and the patient is being bound down on the operating-table. 'I have the whole business at my finger-tips, and it's all clear and definite in my head. When I have to set to work, I will do it as no one else could, but now I can jest, and the more serenely I jest the more calm and confidence and admiration for my genius you ought to feel.'

After emptying a second glass of punch, Napoleon went to seek repose before the grave business which, as he imagined, lay before him next day.

He was so preoccupied with what lay before him that he could not sleep, and in spite of his cold, which got worse with the damp of evening, he got up at three o'clock, went out into the principal compartment of the tent, sneezing violently. He asked whether the Russians had not retreated. He was told that the enemy's fires were still in the same places. He nodded approval.

The adjutant on duty came into the tent.

'Well, Rapp, do you think we shall do good business today?' he said to him.

'Without doubt, sire!' answered Rapp.

Napoleon looked at him.

'Do you remember what you did me the honour to say at Smolensk?' said Rapp: 'the wine is drawn, it must be drunk.'

Napoleon frowned, and sat for a long while in silence, his head in his hand.

'This poor army, it has greatly diminished since Smolensk. *La fortune est une franche courtisane*, Rapp. I have always said so, and I begin to feel it; but the Guard, Rapp, the Guard is intact?' he said inquiringly.

'Yes, sire,' replied Rapp.

Napoleon took a lozenge, put it in his mouth, and looked at his watch. He was not sleepy, and morning was still far off; and there were no instructions to be drawn up to get through the time, for all had been already given, and were even now being put into execution.

'Have the biscuits and the rice been distributed to the regiments of the Guard?' Napoleon asked severely.

'Yes, sire.'

'The rice too?'

Rapp answered that he had given the Emperor's orders about the rice; but Napoleon shook his head with a dissatisfied air, as though he doubted whether his command had been carried out. A servant came in with punch. Napoleon ordered another glass for Rapp, and took a few sips from his own in silence. 'I have neither taste nor smell,' he said, sniffing at the glass. 'I am sick of this cold. They talk about medicine. What is medicine, when they can't cure a cold? Corvisart gave me these lozenges, but they do no good. What can they cure? They can't cure anything. Our body is a machine for living. It is organised for that, it is its nature; leave life to it unhindered, let life defend itself in it; it will do more than if you paralyse it, encumbering it with remedies. Our body is a perfect watch, meant to go for a certain time; the watchmaker has not the power of opening it, he can only handle it in fumbling fashion, blindfold. Our body is a machine for living, that's all.' And apparently because he had dropped into making definitions, which he had a weakness for doing, he suddenly hazarded one on a fresh subject. 'Do you know, Rapp, what the military art consists in?' he asked. 'It is the art of being stronger than the enemy at a given moment. That is all.'

Rapp made no reply.

'Tomorrow we shall have to do with Kutuzov,' said Napoleon. 'We shall see! Do you remember, he was in command at Braunau, and never once in three weeks mounted a horse to inspect his entrenchments. We shall see!'

He looked at his watch. It was still only four o'clock. He was not sleepy; the punch was finished, and there was still nothing to do. He got up, walked up and down, put on a warm coat and hat and went out of the tent. The night was dark and damp; a slight drizzle was falling almost inaudibly. Close by in the French Guard, the camp-fires burned dimly, and far away they were blazing brightly through the smoke along the Russian line. The air was still, and a faint stir and tramp could be distinctly heard from the French troops beginning to move to occupy the position.

Napoleon walked to and fro before the tent, looked at the fires, listened to the tramp, and passed by a tall guardsman in a fur cap, a sentinel at his tent, who drew himself up like a black post on seeing the Emperor. The latter stood still, facing him.

'Since what year have you served? he asked, with that affectation of military bluntness and geniality with which he always addressed the soldiers. The soldier answered.

'Ah! one of the veterans! Have you all had rice in the regiment?'

'Yes, your Majesty.'

Napoleon nodded and walked away.

At half-past five Napoleon rode to the village of Shevardino.

It began to get light; the sky cleared, only a single storm cloud lay on the eastern horizon. The deserted camp-fires burned down in the pale light of morning.

A solitary, deep cannon shot boomed out on the right, hovered in the air, and died away in the stillness. Several minutes passed. A second, and a third shot was heard, the air was full of vibration; a fourth and a fifth boomed out majestically, closely on the right.

The first shots had not died away, when others rang out, and more and more, their notes blending and overtaking one another.

Napoleon rode with his suite to the Shevardino redoubt, and dismounted there. The game had begun.

XXX

PIERRE, on returning to Gorky from seeing Prince Andrey, gave directions to his postillion to have horses ready and to call him early next morning, and promptly fell fast asleep in the corner behind a screen which Boris had put at his disposal.

When Pierre was fully awake next morning, there was no one in the hut. The panes were rattling in the little windows. The postillion was at his side, shaking him. 'Your excellency, your excellency, your excellency . . .' the groom kept saying persistently, shaking him by the shoulder, without even looking at him, apparently having lost all hope of ever waking him up.

'Eh, has it begun? Is it time?' said Pierre, waking up.

'Listen to the firing, your excellency,' said the postillion, an old soldier; 'all the gentlemen are gone already; his highness set off long ago.'

Pierre dressed in haste, and ran out into the porch. It was a bright, fresh, dewy, cheerful morning. The sun had just broken through the cloud that had screened it, and its rays filtered through the rent clouds, and over the roofs of the street opposite on to the dew-drenched dust of the road, on to the fences and the windows of the houses, and Pierre's horses standing by the cottage. The roar of the cannon could be heard more distinctly in the open air. An adjutant galloped down the street, followed by a Cossack.

'It's time, count, it's time!' cried the adjutant. Pierre gave orders that he should be followed with a horse, and walked along the street to the knoll from which he had viewed the field of battle the day before. On this knoll was a crowd of officers, and Pierre heard the French chatter of the staff, and saw Kutuzov's grey head sunk in his shoulders, and his white cap, with red braiding on it. Kutuzov was looking through a field-glass along the high-road before him.

Mounting the steps of the approach to the mound, Pierre glanced before him, and felt a thrill of delight at the beauty of the spectacle. It was the same scene that he had admired from that mound the day before. But now the whole panorama was filled with troops and the smoke of the guns, and in the pure morning air the slanting rays of the sun, behind Pierre on the left, shed on it a brilliant light full of gold and pink tones, and broken up by long, dark shadows. The distant forests that bounded the scene lay in a crescent on the horizon, looking as though carved out of some precious yellow-green stone, and through their midst behind Valuev ran the great Smolensk road, all covered with troops. In the foreground lay golden fields and copses glittering in the sun. Everywhere, to right, to life, and in front were soldiers. The whole scene was inspiriting, impressive, and unexpected; but what struck Pierre most of all was the aspect of the field of battle itself, of Borodino, and the hollow on both sides of the Kolotcha.

About the Kolotcha, in Borodino, and both sides of it, especially to the left where the Voina runs through swampy ground into the Kolotcha, a mist still hung over the scene, melting, parting, shimmering with light in the bright sunshine, and giving fairy-like beauty to the shapes seen through it. The smoke of the guns mingled with this mist, and everywhere gleams of sunlight sparkled in it from the water, from the dew, from the bayonets of the soldiers crowding on the river banks and in Borodino. Through this mist could be seen a white church, here and there roofs of cottages in Borodino, and fitful glimpses came of compact masses of soldiers, and green ammunition-boxes and cannons. And the whole scene moved, or seemed to move, as the mist and smoke trailed over the wide plain. In this low ground about Borodino in the mist, and above it, and especially along the whole line to the left, in the copses, in the meadows below, and on the tops of the heights, clouds of smoke were incessantly springing out of nothing, now singly, now several at once, then at longer intervals, then in rapid succession. These clouds of smoke, puffing, rolling, melting into one another, and sundering apart, trailed all across the wide plain. These puffs of smoke, and the reports that followed them, were, strange to say, what gave the chief charm to the scene.

'*Poooff!*' suddenly there flew up a round, compact ball of smoke, with shades of purple, grey, and milk-white in it, and '*booom!*' followed the roar of the cannon a minute later.

'*Poooff-poooff!*' two clouds of smoke rose, meeting and mingling into one; and '*boom-boom,*' the sound repeated what the eye had seen.

Pierre looked round at the first puff of smoke, which he had seen a second before a round, compact ball, and already in its place were wreaths of smoke trailing away to one side, and *pooff* . . . (then a pause) *pooff-pooff*—three more flew up, and another four at once, and at the same intervals after each other *boom* . . . *boom-boom-boom,* rang out the sonorous, resolute, unfailing sounds. At one moment it seemed that those clouds of smoke were scudding across the plain, at the next, that they were stationary, and the copses, fields, and glittering bayonets were flying by them. From the left side these great clouds of smoke were incessantly flying over the fields and bushes, with the stately roar resounding after each of them. Still nearer, in the low meadows and copses, there darted up from the musket-fire tiny puffs that hardly formed into balls of smoke, and each of these, too, had its tiny report echoing after it. Tra-ta-ta-ta sounded the crack of the muskets at frequent intervals, but thin and irregular in comparison with the rhythmic roar of the cannon.

Pierre longed to be there in the midst of the smoke, the glittering bayonets, the movement, and the noise. He looked round at Kutuzov and his suite to compare his own impression with that of others. All like him were looking before them at the field, and, he fancied, with the same feeling. Every face now was lighted up by that *latent heat* of feeling that Pierre had noticed the day before, and understood perfectly after his talk with Prince Andrey.

'Go, my dear fellow, go, and Christ be with you!' said Kutuzov, never taking his eyes off the field of battle, to a general standing beside him. The general, who received this order, ran by Pierre down the descent from the mound.

'To ride across! . . .' the general said coldly and severely, in answer to a question from one of the staff.

'And I too, I too,' thought Pierre, and he went in the same direction.

The general mounted a horse, led up to him by a Cossack. Pierre went up to the groom, who was holding his horses. Asking him which was the quietest, Pierre got on it, clutched at the horse's mane, pressed his heels into the beast's stomach, and feeling that his spectacles were slipping off, and that he was incapable of leaving go of the mane and the reins, he galloped after the general, followed by smiles from the staff officers staring at him from the mound.

XXXI

THE general after whom Pierre galloped trotted downhill, turned off sharply to the left, and Pierre, losing sight of him, galloped into the middle of a battalion of infantry marching ahead of him. He tried to get away from them, turning to left and to right; but there were soldiers everywhere, all with the same anxious faces, preoccupied with some unseen, but evidently serious, business. They all looked with the same expression of annoyed inquiry at the stout man in the white hat, who was, for some unknown reason, trampling them under his horse's feet.

'What does he want to ride into the middle of a battalion for?' one man shouted at him. Another gave his horse a shove with the butt-end of his gun; and Pierre, leaning over on the saddle bow, and scarcely able to hold in his rearing horse, galloped out to where there was open space in front of the soldiers.

Ahead of him he saw a bridge, and at the bridge stood the soldiers firing. Pierre rode towards them. Though he did not know it, he rode up to the bridge over the Kolotcha, between Gorky and Borodino, which was attacked by the French in one of the first actions. Pierre saw there was a bridge in front of him, and that the soldiers were doing something in the smoke on both sides of the bridge, and in the meadow among the new-mown hay he had noticed the day before. But in spite of the unceasing fire going on there, he had no notion that this was the very centre of the battle. He did not notice the bullets whizzing on all sides, and the shells flying over him; he did not see the enemy on the other side of the river, and it was a long time before he saw the killed and wounded, though many fell close to him. He gazed about him with a smile still on his face.

'What's that fellow doing in front of the line?' some one shouted at him again.

'To the left,' 'to the right,' men shouted to him. Pierre turned to the right, and unwittingly rode up to an adjutant of General Raevsky's, with whom he was acquainted. The adjutant glanced wrathfully at Pierre; and he, too, was apparently about to shout at him, but recognising him, he nodded.

'How did you come here?' he said, and galloped on. Pierre, feeling out of place and of no use, and afraid of getting in some one's way again, galloped after him.

'What is it, here? Can I go with you?' he asked.

'In a minute, in a minute,' answered the adjutant, and galloping up to a stout colonel in the meadow, he gave him some message, and then addressed Pierre. 'What has brought you here, count?' he said to him, with a smile. 'Are you still curious?'

'Yes, yes,' said Pierre. But the adjutant, turning his horse's head, rode on further.

'Here it's all right,' said the adjutant; 'but on the left flank, in Bagration's division, it's fearfully hot.'

'Really?' said Pierre. 'Where's that?'

'Why, come along with me to the mound; we can get a view from there. But it's still bearable at our battery,' said the adjutant. 'Are you coming?'

'Yes, yes, I'll go with you,' said Pierre, looking about him, trying to see his groom. It was only then for the first time that Pierre saw wounded men, some staggering along and some borne on stretchers. In the meadow with the rows of sweet-scented hay, through which he had ridden the day before, there lay motionless across the rows one soldier with his shako off, and his head thrown awkwardly back. 'And why haven't they taken that one?' Pierre was beginning, but seeing the adjutant's set face looking in the same direction, he was silent.

Pierre did not succeed in finding his groom, and rode along the hollow with the adjutant towards Raevsky's redoubt. His horse dropped behind the adjutant's, and jolted him at regular intervals.

'You are not used to riding, count, I fancy?' asked the adjutant.

'Oh no, it's all right; but it does seem to be hopping along somehow,' said Pierre, with a puzzled look.

'Ay! . . . but he's wounded,' said the adjutant, 'the right fore-leg above the knee. A bullet, it must have been. I congratulate you, count,' he said, 'you have had your baptism of fire now.'

After passing in the smoke through the sixth corps behind the artillery, which had been moved forward and was keeping up a deafening cannonade, they rode into a small copse. There it was cool and still and full of the scents of autumn. Pierre and the adjutant got off their horses and walked on foot up the hill.

'Is the general here?' asked the adjutant on reaching the redoubt.

'He was here just now; he went this way,' some one answered, pointing to the right.

The adjutant looked round at Pierre, as though he did not know what to do with him.

'Don't trouble about me,' said Pierre. 'I'll go up on to the mound; may I?'

'Yes, do; you can see everything from there, and it's not so dangerous, and I will come to fetch you.'

Pierre went up to the battery, and the adjutant rode away. They did not see each other again, and only much later Pierre learned that that adjutant had lost an arm on that day.

The mound—afterwards known among the Russians as the battery mound, or Raevsky's battery, and among the French as 'the great redoubt,' 'fatal redoubt,' and 'central redoubt'—was the celebrated spot at which tens of thousands of men were killed, and upon which the French looked as the key of the position.

The redoubt consisted of a mound, with trenches dug out on three sides of it. In the entrenchments stood ten cannons, firing through the gaps left in the earthworks.

In a line with the redoubt on both sides stood cannons, and these too kept up an incessant fire. A little behind the line of cannons were troops of infantry. When Pierre ascended this mound, he had no notion that this place, encircled by small trenches and protected by a few cannons, was the most important spot in the field.

He fancied, indeed (simply because he happened to be there), that it was a place of no importance whatever.

Pierre sat down on the end of the earthwork surrounding the battery and gazed at what was passing around him with an unconscious smile of pleasure. At intervals Pierre got up, and with the same smile on his face walked about the battery, trying not to get in the way of the soldiers, who were loading and discharging the cannons and were continually running by him with bags and ammunition. The cannons were firing continually, one after another, with deafening uproar, enveloping all the country round in clouds of smoke.

In contrast to the painful look of dread in the infantry soldiers who were guarding the battery, here in the battery itself, where a limited number of men were busily engaged in their work, and shut off from the rest of the trench, there was a general feeling of eager excitement, a sort of family feeling shared by all alike.

The appearance of Pierre's unmartial figure and his white hat at first impressed this little group favourably. The soldiers cast sidelong glances of surprise and even alarm at him, as they ran by. The senior artillery officer, a tall, long-legged, pock-marked man, approached Pierre, as though he wanted to examine the action of the cannon at the end, and stared inquisitively at him.

A boyish, round-faced, little officer, quite a child, evidently only just out of the cadets' school, and very conscientious in looking after the two cannons put in his charge, addressed Pierre severely.

'Permit me to ask you to move out of the way, sir,' he said. 'You can't stay here.'

The soldiers shook their heads disapprovingly as they looked at Pierre. But as the conviction gained ground among them that the man in the white hat was doing no harm, and either sat quietly on the slope of the earthwork, or, making way with a shy and courteous smile for the soldiers to pass, walked about the battery under fire as calmly as though he were strolling on a boulevard, their feeling of suspicious ill-will began to give way to a playful and kindly cordiality akin to the feeling soldiers always have for the dogs, cocks, goats, and other animals who share the fortunes of the regiment. The soldiers soon accepted Pierre in their own minds as one of their little circle, made him one of themselves, and gave him a name: 'our gentleman' they called him, and laughed good-humouredly about him among themselves.

A cannon-ball tore up the earth a couple of paces from Pierre. Brushing the earth off his clothes, he looked about him with a smile.

'And how is it you're not afraid, sir, upon my word?' said a broad, red-faced soldier, showing his strong, white teeth in a grin.

'Why, are you afraid then?' asked Pierre.

'Why, to be sure!' answered the soldier. 'Why, she has no mercy on you. She smashes into you, and your guts are sent flying. Nobody could help being afraid,' he said laughing.

Several soldiers stood still near Pierre with amused and kindly faces. They seemed not to expect him to talk like any one else, and his doing so delighted them.

'It's our business—we're soldiers. But for a gentleman—it's surprising. It's queer in a gentleman!'

'To your places!' cried the little officer-boy to the soldiers, who had gathered round Pierre. It was evidently the first, or at most, the second time, this lad had been on duty as an officer, and so he behaved with the utmost punctiliousness and formality both to the soldiers and his superior officer.

The roar of cannon and the rattle of musketry was growing louder all over the field, especially on the left, where Bagration's earthworks were, but from where Pierre was, hardly anything could be seen for the smoke. Moreover, watching the little fraternal group of men, shut off from all the world on the battery, engrossed all Pierre's attention. His first unconscious delight in the sights and sounds of the battlefield had given way to another feeling, ever since he had seen the solitary dead soldier lying on the hayfield. Sitting now on the slope of the earthwork, he watched the figures moving about him.

By ten o'clock some twenty men had been carried away from the battery; two cannons had been disabled, and more and more frequently shells fell on the battery, and cannon-balls came with a hiss and whir, flying out of the distance. But the men on the battery did not seem to notice this: merry chatter and jokes were to be heard on all sides.

'Not this way, my pretty,' shouted a soldier to a grenade that came whistling towards them.

'Give the infantry a turn!' another added with a chuckle, as the grenade flew across and fell among the ranks of the infantry.

'What, see a friend coming, do you?' another soldier jeered at a peasant, who had ducked low at the sight of a flying cannon-ball.

Several soldiers gathered together at the earthwork, looking at what was being done in front.

'And they've taken the outposts, see, they're retreating,' they said, pointing over the earthwork.

'Mind your own business,' the old sergeant shouted to them. 'If they have come back, it's because they have something to do further back.' And the sergeant, taking one of the soldiers by the shoulder, gave him a shove with his knee. There was the sound of laughter.

'Fifth cannon, roll away!' they were shouting on one side.

'Now then, a good pull, all together!' shouted the merry voices of the men charging the cannon.

'Ay, she almost snatched "our gentleman's" hat off,' the red-faced, jocose soldier laughed, showing his teeth. 'Hey, awkward hussy!' he added reproachfully to a cannon-ball that hit a wheel and a man's leg. 'Now, you foxes there!' laughed another, addressing the peasant militiamen, who were creeping in and out among the guns after the wounded. 'Don't you care for our porridge, hey? Ah, the crows! that pulls them up!' they shouted at the militiamen, who hesitated at the sight of the soldier whose leg had been torn off. 'Oo . . . oo . . . lad,' they cried, mimicking the peasants, 'we don't like it at all, we don't!'

Pierre noticed that after every ball that fell in their midst, after every loss, the general elation became more and more marked.

The closer the storm cloud swooped down upon them, the more bright and frequent were the gleams of latent fire that glowed like lightning flashes on those men's faces, called up, as it were, to meet and resist their danger.

Pierre did not look in front at the field of battle; he took no more interest in what was going on there. He was entirely engrossed in the contemplation of that growing fire, which he felt was burning in his own soul too.

At ten o'clock the infantry, who had been in advance of the battery, in the bushes and about the stream Kamenka, retreated. From the battery they could see them running back past them, bearing their wounded on their guns. A general with a suite came on to the redoubt, and after talking to the colonel and looking angrily at Pierre, went away again, ordering the infantry standing behind the battery guarding it to lie down, so as to be less exposed to fire. After that a drum was heard in the ranks of the infantry, more to the right of the battery, and shouts gave the word of command, and from the battery they could see the ranks of infantry moving forward.

Pierre looked over the earthwork. One figure particularly caught his eye. It was the officer, walking backwards with a pale, boyish face. He held his sword downwards and kept looking uneasily round.

The rows of infantry soldiers vanished into the smoke, but they could hear a prolonged shout from them and a rapid musketry fire. A few minutes later crowds of wounded men and a number of stretchers came back from that direction. Shells fell more and more often in the battery. Several men lay on the ground, not picked up. The soldiers bustled more busily and briskly than ever about the cannons. No one took any notice of Pierre now. Twice he was shouted at angrily for being in the way. The senior officer strode rapidly from one cannon to another with a frowning face. The officer-boy, his cheeks even more crimson, gave the soldiers their orders more scrupulously than ever. The soldiers served out the charges, turned round, loaded, and did all their work with exaggerated smartness. They moved as though worked by springs.

The storm cloud was swooping closer; and more brightly than ever glowed in every face that fire which Pierre was watching. He was standing near the senior officer. The little officer-boy ran up, his hand to his shako, saluting his superior officer.

'I have the honour to inform you, colonel, only eight charges are left; do you command to continue firing?' he asked.

'Grape-shot!' the senior officer shouted, looking away over the earthwork.

Suddenly something happened; the boy-officer groaned, and whirling round sat down on the ground, like a bird shot on the wing. All seemed strange, indistinct, and darkened before Pierre's eyes.

One after another the cannon-balls came whistling, striking the breastwork, the soldiers, the cannons. Pierre, who had scarcely heard those sounds before, now could hear nothing else. On the right side of the battery, soldiers, with shouts of 'hurrah,' were running, not forward, it seemed to Pierre, but back.

A cannon-ball struck the very edge of the earthwork, before which Pierre was sitting, and sent the earth flying; a dark, round mass flashed just before his eyes, and at the same instant flew with a thud into something. The militiamen, who had been coming into the battery, ran back.

'All with grape-shot!' shouted the officer.

The sergeant ran up to the officer, and in a frightened whisper (just as at a dinner the butler will sometimes tell the host that there is no more of some wine asked for) said that there were no more charges.

'The scoundrels, what are they about?' shouted the officer, turning to Pierre. The senior officer's face was red and perspiring, his piercing eyes glittered. 'Run to the reserves, bring the ammunition-boxes!' he shouted angrily, avoiding Pierre with his eyes, and addressing the soldier.

'I'll go,' said Pierre. The officer, making no reply, strode across to the other side.

'Cease firing.... Wait!' he shouted.

The soldier who had been commanded to go for the ammunition ran against Pierre.

'Ah, sir, it's no place for you here,' he said, as he ran away.

Pierre ran after the soldier, avoiding the spot where the boy-officer was sitting.

One cannon-ball, a second and a third flew over him, hitting the ground in front, on each side, behind Pierre as he ran down. 'Where am I going?' he suddenly wondered, just as he ran up to the green ammunition-boxes. He stopped short in uncertainty whether to go back or forward. Suddenly a fearful shock sent him flying backwards on to the ground. At the same instant a flash of flame dazed his eyes, and a roar, a hiss, and a crash set his ears ringing.

When he recovered his senses, Pierre found himself sitting on the ground leaning on his hands. The ammunition-box, near which he had been, had gone; there were a few charred green boards and rags lying scattered about on the scorched grass. A horse was galloping away with broken fragments of the shafts clattering after it; while another horse lay, like Pierre, on the ground, uttering a prolonged, piercing scream.

XXXII

PIERRE, beside himself with terror, jumped up and ran back to the battery as the one refuge from the horrors encompassing him.

Just as Pierre ran up to the redoubt, he noticed that there was no sound of firing from the battery, but that there were men there doing something or other. He had not time to make out what men they were. He caught sight of the senior officer lying with his back towards him on the earth wall, as though gazing intently at something below; and he noticed one soldier, who, tearing himself away from the men who were holding him, shouted 'Mates!' and he saw something else that was strange.

But before he had time to grasp that the colonel had been killed, that the soldier shouting 'Mates!' was a prisoner, another soldier was stabbed in the back by a bayonet before his eyes. He had hardly run up into the redoubt when a thin man with a yellow, perspiring face, in a blue uniform, ran up to him with a sword in his hand, shouting something. Pierre, instinctively defending himself, as they came full tilt against each other, put out his hands and clutched the man (it was a French officer) by the shoulder and the throat. The officer, dropping his sword, seized Pierre by the collar.

For several seconds both gazed with frightened eyes at each other's unfamiliar-looking faces, and both were bewildered, not knowing what they were doing or what they were to do. 'Am I taken prisoner or am I taking him prisoner?' each of them was wondering. But the French officer was undoubtedly more disposed to believe he was taken prisoner, because Pierre's powerful hand, moved by instinctive terror, was tightening its grip on his throat. The Frenchman tried to speak, when suddenly a cannon-ball flew with a fearful whiz close over their heads, and it seemed to Pierre that the Frenchman's head had been carried off by it, so swiftly had he ducked it.

Pierre, too, ducked and let go with his hands. Giving no more thought to the question which was taken prisoner, the Frenchman ran back to the battery, while Pierre dashed downhill, stumbling over the dead and wounded, who seemed to him to be clutching at his feet.

But before he had reached the bottom he was met by dense crowds of Russian soldiers, who, stumbling against each other and tripping up, were running in wild merriment towards the battery. (This was the attack of which Yermolov claimed the credit, declaring that it was only his valour and good luck that made this feat of arms possible; it was the attack in which he is supposed to have strewn the redoubt with the St. George's crosses that were in his pocket.)

The French, who had captured the battery, fled. Our soldiers pursued them so far beyond the battery that they were with difficulty stopped. They were bringing the prisoners down from the battery, among them a wounded French general, surrounded by officers. Crowds of wounded, both French and Russians—among them men Pierre recognised—walked, or crawled, or were borne on stretchers from the battery, their faces distorted by suffering.

Pierre went up into the battery, where he had spent over an hour; and found no one left of that little fraternal group that had accepted him as one of themselves. There were many dead there, whom he had not seen before. But several he recognised. The boy-officer was still sitting huddled up in a pool of blood at the edge of the earth wall. The red-faced, merry soldier was still twitching convulsively; but they did not carry him away.

Pierre ran down the slope.

'Oh, now they will stop it, now they will be horrified at what they have done!' thought Pierre, aimlessly following the crowds of stretchers moving off the battlefield.

But the sun still stood high behind the veil of smoke, and in front, and even more so to the left, about Semyonovskoye, there was still a turmoil seething in the smoke; and the roar of cannon and musketry, far from slackening, grew louder and more desperate, like a man putting all his force into one deafening outcry as a last despairing effort.

XXXIII

THE chief action of the battle of Borodino was fought on the space seven thousand feet in width between Borodino and Bagration's flèches. Outside that region, on one side there was the action on the part of Uvarov's cavalry in the middle of the day; on the other side, behind Utitsa, there was the skirmish between Poniatovsky and Tutchkov; but those two actions were detached and of little importance in comparison with what took place in the centre of the battlefield. The chief action of the day was fought in the simplest and the most artless fashion on the open space, visible from both sides, between Borodino and the fleches by the copse.

The battle began with a cannonade from several hundreds of guns on both sides. Then, when the whole plain was covered with smoke, on the French side the two divisions of Desaix and Compans advanced on the right upon the flèches, and on the left the viceroy's regiments advanced upon Borodino. The flèches were a verst from the Shevardino redoubt, where Napoleon was standing; but Borodino was more than two versts further, in a straight line, and therefore Napoleon could not see what was passing there, especially as the smoke, mingling with the fog, completely hid the whole of that part of the plain. The soldiers of Desaix's division, advancing upon the flèches, were in sight till they disappeared from view in the hollow that lay between them and the flèches. As soon as they dropped down into the hollow, the smoke of the cannon and muskets on the flèches became so thick that it concealed the whole slope of that side of the hollow. Through the smoke could be caught glimpses of something black, probably men, and sometimes the gleam of bayonets. But whether they were stationary or moving, whether they were French or Russian, could not be seen from Shevardino.

The sun had risen brightly, and its slanting rays shone straight in Napoleon's face as he looked from under his hand towards the flèches. The smoke hung over the flèches, and at one moment it seemed as though it were the smoke that was moving, at the next, the troops moving in the smoke. Sometimes cries could be heard through the firing, but it was impossible to tell what was being done there.

Napoleon, standing on the redoubt, was looking through a field-glass, and in the tiny circle of the glass saw smoke and men, sometimes his own, sometimes Russians. But where what he had seen was, he could not tell when he looked again with the naked eye.

He came down from the redoubt, and began walking up and down before it.

At intervals he stood still, listening to the firing and looking intently at the battlefield.

It was not simply impossible from below, where he was standing, and from the redoubt above, where several of his generals were standing, to make out what was passing at the flèches; but on the flèches themselves, occupied now together, now alternately by French and Russians, living, dead, and wounded, the frightened and frantic soldiers had no idea what they were doing. For several hours together, in the midst of incessant cannon and musket fire, Russians and French, infantry and cavalry, had captured the place in turn: they rushed upon it, fell, fired, came into collision, did not know what to do with each other, screamed, and ran back again.

From the battlefield adjutants were continually galloping up to Napoleon with reports from his marshals of the progress of the action. But all those reports were deceptive; both because in the heat of battle it is impossible to say what is happening at any given moment, and because many of the adjutants never reached the actual battlefield, but simply repeated what they heard from others, and also because, while the adjutant was galloping the two or three versts to Napoleon, circumstances had changed, and the news he brought had already become untrue. Thus an adjutant came galloping from the viceroy with the news that Borodino had been taken and the bridge on the Kolotcha was in the hands of the French. The adjutant asked Napoleon should the troops cross the bridge. Napoleon's command was to form on the further side and wait; but long before he gave that command, when the adjutant indeed had only just started from Borodino, the bridge had been broken down and burnt by the Russians in the very skirmish Pierre had taken part in at the beginning of the day.

An adjutant, galloping up from the flèches with a pale and frightened face, brought Napoleon word that the attack had been repulsed, and Compans wounded and Davoust killed; while meantime the flèches had been captured by another division of the troops, and Davoust was alive and well, except for a slight bruise. Upon such inevitably misleading reports Napoleon based his instructions, which had mostly been carried out before he made them, or else were never, and could never, be carried out at all.

The marshals and generals who were closer to the scene of action, but, like Napoleon, not actually taking part in it, and only at intervals riding within bullet range, made their plans without asking Napoleon, and gave their orders from where and in what direction to fire, and where the cavalry were to gallop and the infantry to run. But even their orders, like Napoleon's, were but rarely, and to a slight extent, carried out.

For the most part what happened was the opposite of what they commanded to be done. The soldiers ordered to advance found themselves under grape-shot fire, and ran back. The soldiers commanded to stand still in one place seeing the Russians appear suddenly before them, either ran away or rushed upon them; and the cavalry unbidden galloped in after the flying Russians. In this way two cavalry regiments galloped across the Semyonovkoye hollow, and as soon as they reached the top of the hill, turned and galloped headlong back again. The infantry, in the same way, moved sometimes in the direction opposite to that in which they were commanded to move.

All decisions as to when and where to move the cannons, when to send infantry to fire, when to send cavalry to trample down the Russian infantry—all such decisions were made by the nearest officers in the ranks, without any reference to Ney, Davoust, and Murat, far less to Napoleon himself. They did not dread getting into trouble for nonfulfilment of orders, nor for assuming responsibility, because in battle what is at stake is what is most precious to every man—his own life; and at one time it seems as though safety is to be found in flying back, sometimes in flying forward; and these men placed in the very thick of the fray acted in accordance with the temper of the moment.

In reality all these movements forward and back again hardly improved or affected the position of the troops. All their onslaughts on one another did little harm; the harm, the death and disablement was the work of the cannon-balls and bullets, that were flying all about the open space, where those men ran to and fro. As soon as they got out of that exposed space, over which the balls and bullets were flying, their superior officer promptly formed them in good order, and restored discipline, and under the influence of that discipline led them back under fire again; and there again, under the influence of the terror of death, they lost all discipline, and dashed to and fro at the chance promptings of the crowd.

XXXIV

NAPOLEON'S generals, Davoust, Ney, and Murat, who were close to that region of fire, and sometimes even rode into it, several times led immense masses of orderly troops into that region. But instead of what had invariably happened in all their previous battles, instead of hearing that the enemy were in flight, the disciplined masses of troops came back in undisciplined, panic-stricken crowds. They formed them in good order again, but their number was steadily dwindling. In the middle of the day Murat sent his adjutant to Napoleon with a request for reinforcements.

Napoleon was sitting under the redoubt, drinking punch, when Murat's adjutant galloped to him with the message that the Russians would be routed if his Majesty would let them have another division.

'Reinforcements?' said Napoleon, with stern astonishment, staring, as though failing to comprehend his words, at the handsome, boyish adjutant, who wore his black hair in floating curls, like Murat's own. 'Reinforcements!' thought Napoleon. 'How can they want reinforcements when they have half the army already, concentrated against one weak, unsupported flank of the Russians!'

'Tell the King of Naples,' said Napoleon sternly, 'that it is not midday, and I don't yet see clearly over my chess-board. You can go.'

The handsome, boyish adjutant with the long curls heaved a deep sigh, and still holding his hand to his hat, galloped back to the slaughter.

Napoleon got up, and summoning Caulaincourt and Berthier, began conversing with them of matters not connected with the battle.

In the middle of the conversation, which began to interest Napoleon, Berthier's eye was caught by a general, who was galloping on a steaming horse to the redoubt, followed by his suite. It was Beliard. Dismounting from his horse, he walked rapidly up to the Emperor, and, in a loud voice, began boldly explaining the absolute necessity of reinforcements. He swore on his honour that the Russians would be annihilated if the Emperor would let them have another division.

Napoleon shrugged his shoulders, and continued walking up and down, without answering. Beliard began loudly and eagerly talking with the generals of the suite standing round him.

'You are very hasty, Beliard,' said Napoleon, going back again to him. 'It is easy to make a mistake in the heat of the fray. Go and look again and then come to me.' Before Beliard was out of sight another messenger came galloping up from another part of the battlefield.

'Well, what is it now?' said Napoleon, in the tone of a man irritated by repeated interruptions.

'Sire, the prince . . .' began the adjutant.

'Asks for reinforcements?' said Napoleon, with a wrathful gesture. The adjutant bent his head affirmatively, and was proceeding to give his message, but the Emperor turned and walked a couple of steps away, stopped, turned back, and beckoned to Berthier. 'We must send the reserves,' he said with a slight gesticulation. 'Whom shall we send there? what do you think?' he asked Berthier, that 'gosling I have made an eagle,' as he afterwards called him.

'Claparède's division, sire,' said Berthier, who knew all the divisions, regiments, and battalions by heart.

Napoleon nodded his head in assent.

The adjutant galloped off to Claparède's division. And a few moments later the Young Guards, stationed behind the redoubt, were moving out. Napoleon gazed in that direction in silence.

'No,' he said suddenly to Berthier, 'I can't send Claparède. Send Friant's division.'

Though there was no advantage of any kind in sending Friant's division rather than Claparède's, and there was obvious inconvenience and delay now in turning back Claparède and despatching Friant, the order was carried out. Napoleon did not see that in relation to his troops he played the part of the doctor, whose action in hindering the course of nature with his nostrums he so truly gauged and condemned.

Friant's division vanished like the rest into the smoke of the battlefield. Adjutants still kept galloping up from every side, and all, as though in collusion, said the same thing. All asked for reinforcements; all told of the Russians standing firm and keeping up a hellish fire, under which the French troops were melting away.

Napoleon sat on a camp-stool, plunged in thought. M. de Beausset, the reputed lover of travel, had been fasting since early morning, and approaching the Emperor, he ventured respectfully to suggest breakfast to his Majesty.

'I hope that I can already congratulate your Majesty on a victory,' he said.

Napoleon shook his head. Supposing the negative to refer to the victory only and not to the breakfast, M. de Beausset permitted himself with respectful playfulness to observe that there was no reason in the world that could be allowed to interfere with breakfast when breakfast was possible.

'Go to the . . .' Napoleon jerked out gloomily, and he turned his back on him. A saintly smile of sympathy, regret, and ecstasy beamed on M. de Beausset's face as he moved with his swinging step back to the other generals.

Napoleon was experiencing the bitter feeling of a lucky gambler, who, after recklessly staking his money and always winning, suddenly finds, precisely when he has carefully reckoned up all contingencies, that the more he considers his course, the more certain he is of losing.

The soldiers were the same, the generals the same, there had been the same preparations, the same disposition, the same proclamation, *courte et énergique.* He was himself the same,—he knew that; he knew that he was more experienced and skilful indeed now than he had been of old. The enemy even was the same as at Austerlitz and Friedland. But the irresistible wave of his hand seemed robbed of its might by magic.

All the old manoeuvres that had invariably been crowned with success: the concentration of the battery on one point, and the advance of the reserves to break the line, and the cavalry attack of 'men of iron', all these resources had been employed; and far from victory being secure, from all sides the same tidings kept pouring in of killed or wounded generals, of reinforcements needed, of the troops being in disorder, and the Russians impossible to move.

Hitherto, after two or three orders being given, two or three phrases delivered, marshals and adjutants had galloped up with radiant faces and congratulations, announcing the capture as trophies of whole corps of prisoners, of bundles of flags and eagles, of cannons and stores, and Murat had asked leave to let the cavalry go to capture the baggage. So it had been at Lodi, Marengo, Arcole, Jena, Austerlitz, Wagram, and so on, and so on. But now something strange was coming over his men.

In spite of the news of the capture of the flèches, Napoleon saw that things were not the same, not at all the same as at previous battles. He saw that what he was feeling, all the men round him, experienced in military matters, were feeling too. All their faces were gloomy; all avoided each other's eyes. It was only a Beausset who could fail to grasp the import of what was happening. Napoleon after his long experience of war knew very well all that was meant by an unsuccessful attack after eight hours' straining every possible effort. He knew that this was almost equivalent to a defeat, and that the merest chance might now, in the critical point the battle was in, be the overthrow of himself and his troops.

When he went over in his own mind all this strange Russian campaign, in which not a single victory had been gained, in which not a flag, nor a cannon, nor a corps had been taken in two months, when he looked at the concealed gloom in the faces round him, and heard reports that the Russians still held their ground—a terrible feeling, such as is experienced in a nightmare, came over him, and all the unlucky contingencies occurred to him that might be his ruin. The Russians might fall upon his left wing, might break through his centre; a stray ball might even kill himself. All that was possible. In his former battles he had only considered the possibilities of success, now an immense number of unlucky chances presented themselves, and he expected them all. Yes, it was like a nightmare, when a man dreams that an assailant is attacking him, and in his dream he lifts up his arm and deals a blow with a force at his assailant that he knows must crush him, and feels that his arm falls limp and powerless as a rag, and the horror of inevitable death comes upon him in his helplessness.

The news that the Russians were attacking the left flank of the French army aroused that horror in Napoleon. He sat in silence on a camp-stool under the redoubt, his elbows on his knees, and his head sunk in his hands. Berthier came up to him and suggested that they should inspect the lines to ascertain the position of affairs.

'What? What do you say?' said Napoleon. 'Yes, tell them to bring my horse.' He mounted a horse and rode to Semyonovskoye.

In the slowly parting smoke, over the whole plain through which Napoleon rode, men and horses, singly and in heaps, were lying in pools of blood. Such a fearful spectacle, so great a mass of killed in so small a space, had never been seen by Napoleon nor any of his generals. The roar of the cannon that had not ceased for ten hours, exhausted the ear and gave a peculiar character to the spectacle (like music accompanying living pictures). Napoleon rode up to the height of Semyonovskoye, and through the smoke he saw ranks of soldiers in uniforms of unfamiliar hues. They were the Russians.

The Russians stood in serried ranks behind Semyonovskoye and the redoubt, and their guns kept up an incessant roar and smoke all along their lines. It was not a battle. It was a prolonged massacre, which could be of no avail either to French or Russians. Napoleon pulled up his horse, and sank again into the brooding reverie from which Berthier had roused him. He could not stay that thing that was being done before him and about him, and that was regarded as being led by him and as depending on him, that thing for the first time, after ill success, struck him as superfluous and horrible. One of the generals, riding up to Napoleon, ventured to suggest to him that the Old Guards should advance into action. Ney and Berthier, standing close by, exchanged glances and smiled contemptuously at the wild suggestion of this general.

Napoleon sat mute with downcast head.

'Eight hundred leagues from France, I am not going to let my Guard be destroyed,' he said, and turning his horse, he rode back to Shevardino.

XXXV

KUTUZOV, with his grey head hanging, and his heavy, corpulent frame sunk into a heap, was sitting on a bench covered with a rug, in the same place in which Pierre had seen him in the morning. He issued no orders, and simply gave or withheld his assent to what was proposed to him.

'Yes, yes, do so,' he would say in reply to various suggestions. 'Yes, yes, go across, my dear boy, and see,' he would cry first to one and then to another of the adjutants near him; or, 'No, better not; we'd better wait a bit,' he would say. He listened to the reports brought him, and gave orders, when they were asked for. But as he heard the reports, he seemed to take little interest in the import of the words spoken; something else in the expression of the face, in the tone of the voice of the speaker, seemed to interest him more. From long years of military experience he had learned, and with the wisdom of old age he had recognised, that one man cannot guide hundreds of thousands of men struggling with death; that the fate of battles is not decided by the orders given by the commander-in-chief, nor the place in which the troops are stationed, nor the number of cannons, nor of killed, but by that intangible force called the spirit of the army, and he followed that force and led it as far as it lay in his power.

The general expression of Kutuzov's face was concentrated, quiet attention and intensity, with difficulty overcoming his weak and aged body.

At eleven o'clock they brought him the news that the French had been driven back again from the flèches they had captured, but that Bagration was wounded. Kutuzov groaned, and shook his head.

'Ride over to Prince Pyotr Ivanovitch and find out exactly about it,' he said to one of the adjutants, and then he turned to the Prince of Würtemburg, who was standing behind him:

'Will your highness be pleased to take the command of the first army?'

Soon after the prince's departure—so soon that he could not yet have reached Semyonovskoye—his adjutant came back with a message from him asking Kutuzov for more troops.

Kutuzov frowned, and sent Dohturov orders to take the command of the first army, and begged the prince to come back, saying that he found he could not get on without him at such an important moment. When news was brought that Murat had been taken prisoner, and the members of the staff congratulated Kutuzov, he smiled.

'Wait a little, gentlemen,' he said. 'The battle is won, and Murat's being taken prisoner is nothing very extraordinary. But we had better defer our rejoicings.' Still he sent an adjutant to take the news to the troops.

When Shtcherbinin galloped up from the left flank with the report of the capture of the flèche, and Semyonovskoye by the French, Kutuzov, guessing from the sounds of the battlefield and Shtcherbinin's face, that the news was bad, got up as though to stretch his legs, and taking Shtcherbinin by the arm drew him aside.

'You go, my dear boy,' he said, to Yermolov, 'and see whether something can't be done.'

Kutuzov was in Gorky, the centre of the Russian position. The attack on our left flank had been several times repulsed. In the centre the French did not advance beyond Borodino. Uvarov's cavalry had sent the French flying from the left flank.

At three o'clock the attacks of the French ceased. On the faces of all who came from the battlefield, as well as of those standing round him, Kutuzov read an expression of effort, strained to the utmost tension. He was himself satisfied with the success of the day beyond his expectations. But the old man's physical force was failing him. Several times his head sank, as though he were falling, and he dropped asleep. Dinner was brought him.

The adjutant-general, Woltzogen, the man whom Prince Andrey had overheard saying that the war ought to be '*im Raum verlegen*,' and whom Bagration so particularly detested, rode up to Kutuzov while he was at dinner. Woltzogen had come from Barclay to report on the progress of the fight on the left flank. The sagacious Barclay de Tolly, seeing crowds of wounded men running back, and the ranks in disorder, and weighing all the circumstances of the case, made up his mind that the battle was lost, and sent his favourite adjutant to the commander-in-chief to tell him so.

Kutuzov was with difficulty chewing roast chicken, and his eyes were screwed up with a more cheerful expression as he glanced at Woltzogen.

With a half-contemptuous smile Woltzogen walked carelessly up to Kutuzov, scarcely touching the peak of his cap.

He behaved to his highness with a certain affected negligence, which aimed at showing that he, as a highly trained military man, left it to the Russians to make a prodigy of this useless old person, and was himself well aware what kind of a man he had to deal with. 'The "old gentleman"—this was how Kutuzov was always spoken of in Woltzogen's German circle—'is making himself quite comfortable,' he thought; and glancing severely at the dishes before Kutuzov, he began reporting to the old gentleman Barclay's message and his own impressions and views. 'Every point of our position is in the enemy's hands, and they cannot be driven back, because there are not the troops to do it; the men run away and there's no possibility of stopping them,' he submitted.

Kutuzov, stopping short in his munching, stared at Woltzogen in amazement, as though not understanding what was said to him. Woltzogen, noticing the old gentleman's excitement, said with a smile:

'I did not consider I had a right to conceal from your highness what I saw.... The troops are completely routed....'

'You saw? You saw?...' cried Kutuzov, getting up quickly, and stepping up to Woltzogen. 'How... how dare you!...' making a menacing gesture with his trembling hands, he cried, with a catch in his breath. 'How dare you, sir, tell *me* that? You know nothing about it. Tell General Barclay from me that his information is incorrect, and that I, the commander-in-chief, know more of the course of the battle than he does.'

Woltzogen would have made some protest, but Kutuzov interrupted him.

'The enemy has been repulsed on the left and defeated on the right flank. If you have seen amiss, sir, do not permit yourself to speak of what you do not understand. Kindly return to General Barclay and inform him of my unhesitating intention to attack the French tomorrow,' said Kutuzov sternly.

All were silent, and nothing was to be heard but the heavy breathing of the gasping old general. 'Repulsed at all points, for which I thank God and our brave men. The enemy is defeated, and tomorrow we will drive him out of the holy land of Russia!' said Kutuzov, crossing himself; and all at once he gave a sob from the rising tears.

Woltzogen, shrugging his shoulders, and puckering his lips, walked away in silence, marvelling *'über diese Eingenommenheit des alten Herrn'*.

'Ah, here he is, my hero!' said Kutuzov, as a stoutish, handsome, black-haired general came up the hillside. It was Raevsky, who had spent the whole day at the most important part of the battlefield.

Raevsky reported that the men were standing their ground firmly, and that the French were not venturing a further attack.

When he had heard him out, Kutuzov said in French: 'You do not think, like some others, that we are obliged to retreat?'

'On the contrary, your highness, in indecisive actions it is always the most obstinate who remains victorious,' answered Raevsky; 'and in my opinion ...'

'Kaisarov,' Kutuzov called to his adjutant, 'sit down and write the order for tomorrow. And you,' he turned to another, 'ride along the line and announce that tomorrow we attack.'

While he was talking to Raevsky and dictating the order, Woltzogen came back from Barclay and announced that General Barclay de Tolly would be glad to have a written confirmation of the order given by the field-marshal.

Kutuzov, without looking at Woltzogen, ordered an adjutant to make out this written order, which the former commander-in-chief very prudently wished to have to screen himself from all responsibility. And through the undefinable, mysterious link that maintains through a whole army the same temper, called the spirit of the army, and constituting the chief sinew of war, Kutuzov's words, his order for the battle next day, were transmitted instantaneously from one end of the army to the other.

The words and the phrases of the order were by no means the same when they reached the furthest links in the chain. There was, indeed, not a word in the stories men were repeating to one another from one end of the army to the other, that resembled what Kutuzov had actually said; but the drift of his words spread everywhere, because what Kutuzov had said was not the result of shrewd considerations, but the outflow of a feeling that lay deep in the heart of the commander-in-chief, and deep in the heart of every Russian.

And learning that tomorrow we were to attack the enemy, hearing from the higher spheres of the army the confirmation of what they wanted to believe, the worn-out, wavering men took comfort and courage again.

XXXVI

PRINCE ANDREY'S regiment was in the reserves, which were until two o'clock stationed behind Semyonovskoye in complete inaction, under a hot artillery fire. Before two o'clock the regiment, which had already lost over two hundred men, was moved forward into the trampled oat-field, in that space between Semyonovskoye and the battery redoubt, on which thousands of men were killed that day, and on which, about two o'clock, there was directed the concentrated fire of several hundreds of the enemy's cannons.

Not leaving that spot, nor discharging a single round of ammunition, the regiment lost here another third of its men. In front, and especially on the right side, the cannons kept booming in the smoke that never lifted, and from the mysterious region of the smoke that hid all the country in front, there came flying swiftly hissing cannon-balls and slowly whizzing grenades. Sometimes, as though to give them a breathing space, for a whole quarter of an hour all the cannon-balls and grenades flew over them, but at other times, in the course of a single minute, several men out of the regiment would be swept off, and they were busy the whole time dragging away the dead and carrying off the wounded.

With every fresh stroke the chances of life grew less and less for those who were not yet killed. The regiment was divided into battalions three hundred paces apart; but in spite of that, all the regiment was under the influence of the same mood. All the men of the regiment were alike gloomy and silent. At rare intervals there was the sound of talk in the ranks, but that sound was hushed every time the falling thud and the cry of 'stretchers!' was heard. For the greater part of the time, by command of the officers, the men sat on the ground. One, taking off his shako, carefully loosened and then drew up the folds of it; another, crumbling the dry clay in his hands, rubbed up his bayonet with it; another shifted and fastened the buckle of his shoulder straps; while another carefully undid, and did up again, his leg bandages, and changed his boots. Some built little houses of clods of the ploughed field, or plaited straws of stubble. All of them appeared entirely engrossed in these pursuits. When men were killed or wounded, when the stretchers trailed by, when our troops retreated, when immense masses of the enemy came into view through the smoke, no one took any notice of these circumstances. When our artillery or cavalry advanced, when our infantry could be seen moving, approving observations could be heard on all sides. But quite extraneous incidents that had nothing to do with the battle were what attracted most notice; as though the attention of these morally overstrained men found a rest in the commonplace incidents of everyday life. Some batteries of artillery passed in front of their line. In one of the ammunition carriages a horse had put its leg through the traces.

'Hey! look at the trace-horse! . . . Take her leg out! She'll fall! . . . Hey! they don't see! . . .' Shouts rose from the ranks all through the regiment.

Another time the attention of all was attracted by a little brown dog, with its tail in the air, who had come no one knew from where, and was running about fussily in front of the ranks. All at once a cannon-ball fell near it, and it squealed and dashed away with its tail between its legs! Roars and shrieks of laughter rang out from the whole regiment. But distractions of this kind did not last more than a minute, and the men had been eight hours without food or occupation, with the terror of death never relaxing for an instant, and their pale and haggard faces grew paler and more haggard.

Prince Andrey, pale and haggard like every one else in the regiment, walked to and fro in the meadow next to the oat-field from one boundary-line to the other, with his hands clasped behind his back, and his eyes fixed on the ground. There was no need for him to give orders, and nothing for him to do everything was done of itself. The killed were dragged behind the line; the wounded were removed, and the ranks closed up. If any soldiers ran away, they made haste to return at once. At first Prince Andrey, thinking it his duty to keep up the spirits of the men, and set them an example, had walked about among the ranks. But soon he felt that there was nothing he could teach them. All his energies, like those of every soldier, were unconsciously directed to restraining himself from contemplating the horror of his position. He walked about the meadow, dragging one leg after the other, making the grass rustle, and watching the dust, which covered his boots. Then he strode along, trying to step on the traces of the footsteps of the mowers on the meadow; or counting his steps, calculated how many times he would have to walk from one boundary rut to another to make a verst; or cut off the flowers of wormwood growing in the rut, and crushing them in his hands, sniffed at the bitter-sweet, pungent odour. Of all the thoughts of the previous day not a trace remained. He thought of nothing at all. He listened wearily to the sounds that were ever the same, the whiz of the shells above the booming of the cannon, looked at the faces of the men of the first battalion, which he had gazed at to weariness already, and waited. 'Here it comes . . . this one's for us again!' he thought, listening to the whiz of something flying out of the region of smoke. 'One, another! More! Fallen' . . . He stopped short and looked towards the ranks. 'No; it has flown over. But that one has fallen!' And he fell to pacing up and down again, trying to reach the next boundary in sixteen steps.

A whiz and a thud! Five paces from him the dry soil was thrown up, as a cannon-ball sank into the earth. A chill ran down his back. He looked at the ranks. Probably a number had been struck: the men had gathered in a crowd in the second battalion.

'M. l'aide-de-camp,' he shouted, 'tell the men not to crowd together.'

The adjutant, having obeyed this instruction, was approaching Prince Andrey. From the other side the major in command of the battalion came riding up.

'Look out!' rang out a frightened cry from a soldier, and like a bird, with swift, whirring wings alighting on the earth, a grenade dropped with a dull thud a couple of paces from Prince Andrey, near the major's horse. The horse, with no question of whether it were right or wrong to show fear, snorted, reared, almost throwing the major, and galloped away. The horse's terror infected the men.

'Lie down!' shouted the adjutant, throwing himself on the ground. Prince Andrey stood in uncertainty. The shell was smoking and rotating like a top between him and the recumbent adjutant, near a bush of wormwood in the rut between the meadow and the field.

'Can this be death?' Prince Andrey wondered, with an utterly new, wistful feeling, looking at the grass, at the wormwood, and at the thread of smoke coiling from the rotating top. 'I can't die, I don't want to die, I love life, I love this grass and earth and air . . .'

He thought this, and yet at the same time he did not forget that people were looking at him.

'For shame, M. l'aide-de-camp!' he said to the adjutant; 'what sort of . . .' He did not finish. Simultaneously there was a tearing, crashing sound, like the smash of broken crockery, a puff of stifling fumes, and Prince Andrey was sent spinning over, and flinging up one arm, fell on his face.

Several officers ran up to him. A great stain of blood was spreading over the grass from the right side of his stomach.

The militiamen stood with their stretchers behind the officers. Prince Andrey lay on his chest, with his face sunk in the grass; he was still breathing in hard, hoarse gasps.

'Well, why are you waiting, come along!'

The peasants went up and took him by the shoulders and legs, but he moaned piteously, and they looked at one another, and laid him down again.

'Pick him up, lay him on, it's all the same!' shouted some one. They lifted him by the shoulders again and laid him on the stretcher.

'Ah, my God! my God! what is it? . . . The stomach! It's all over then! Ah, my God!' could be heard among the officers. 'It almost grazed my ear,' the adjutant was saying. The peasants, with the stretcher across their shoulders, hurried along the path they had trodden to the ambulance station.

'Keep step! . . . Aie! . . . these peasants!' cried an officer, seizing them by the shoulders, as they jogged along, jolting the stretcher.

'Drop into it, Fyodor, eh?' said the foremost peasant.

'That's it, first-rate,' said the hindmost, falling into step.

'Your excellency? Eh, prince?' said the trembling voice of Timohin, as he ran up and peeped over the stretcher.

Prince Andrey opened his eyes, and looked at the speaker from the stretcher, through which his head had dropped, and closed his eyelids again.

The militiamen carried Prince Andrey to the copse, where there were vans and an ambulance station. The ambulance station consisted of three tents, pitched at the edge of a birch copse. In the wood stood the ambulance wagons and horses. The horses in nose-bags were munching oats, and the sparrows flew up to them and picked up the grains they dropped. Some crows, scenting blood, flitted to and fro among the birches, cawing impatiently. For more than five acres round the tents there were sitting or lying men stained with blood, and variously attired. They were surrounded by crowds of dejected-looking and intently observant soldiers, who had come with stretchers. Officers, trying to keep order, kept driving them away from the place; but it was of no use. The soldiers, heedless of the officers, stood leaning against the stretchers, gazing intently at what was passing before their eyes, as though trying to solve some difficult problem in this spectacle. From the tents came the sound of loud, angry wailing, and piteous moans. At intervals a doctor's assistant ran out for water, or to point out those who were to be taken in next. The wounded, awaiting their turn at the tent, uttered hoarse groans and moans, wept, shouted, swore, or begged for vodka. Several were raving in delirium. Prince Andrey, as a colonel, was carried through the crowd of wounded not yet treated, and brought close up to one of the tents, where his bearers halted awaiting instructions. Prince Andrey opened his eyes, and for a long while could not understand what was passing around him. The meadow, the wormwood, the black, whirling ball, and his passionate rush of love for life came back to his mind. A couple of paces from him stood a tall, handsome, dark-haired sergeant, with a bandaged head, leaning against a branch. He had been wounded in the head and in the leg, and was talking loudly, attracting general attention. A crowd of wounded men and stretcher-bearers had gathered round him, greedily listening to his words.

'We regularly hammered him out, so he threw up everything; we took the king himself,' the soldier was shouting, looking about him with feverishly glittering black eyes. 'If only the reserves had come up in the nick of time, my dear fellow, there wouldn't have been a sign of him left, for I can tell you . . .'

Prince Andrey, like all the men standing round the speaker, gazed at him with bright eyes, and felt a sense of comfort. 'But isn't it all the same now?' he thought. 'What will be there, and what has been here? Why was I so sorry to part with life? There was something in this life that I didn't understand, and don't understand.'

XXXVII

ONE of the doctors came out of the tent with a blood-stained apron, and small, blood-stained hands, in one of which he had a cigar, carefully held between his thumb and little finger, that it might not be stained too. This doctor threw his head up, and looked about him, but over the level of the wounded crowd. He was evidently longing for a short respite. After turning his head from right to left for a few minutes, he sighed and dropped his eyes again.

'All right, immediately,' he said in reply to an assistant, who pointed him out Prince Andrey, and he bade the bearers carry him into the tent.

A murmur rose in the crowd of wounded men waiting.

'Even in the next world it's only the gentry who will have a good time,' said one.

Prince Andrey was carried in, and laid on a table that had just been cleared, and was being rinsed over by an assistant. He could not make out distinctly what was in the tent. The pitiful groans on all sides, and the excruciating pain in his thigh, his stomach, and his back distracted his attention. Everything he saw around melted for him into a single general impression of naked, blood-stained, human flesh, which seemed to fill up the whole low-pitched tent, as, a few weeks before, on that hot August day, the bare human flesh had filled up the dirty pond along the Smolensk road. Yes, it was the same flesh, the same *chair a canon*, the sight of which had aroused in him then a horror, that seemed prophetic of what he felt now.

There were three tables in the tent. Two were occupied, on the third they laid Prince Andrey. For some time he was left alone an involuntary witness of what was being done at the other tables. On the table nearest sat a Tatar, probably of a Cossack regiment, judging from the uniform that had been thrown down close by. Four soldiers were holding him. A doctor in spectacles was cutting something in his brown, muscular back.

'Ooh! ooh! ooh! . . .' the Tatar, as it were, grunted, and all of a sudden, throwing up his broad, swarthy, sun-burned face, and showing his white teeth, he began wriggling, twitching, and shrieking a piercingly shrill, prolonged scream. On the other table, round which a number of persons were standing, a big, stout man lay on his back, with his head flung back. The colour and curliness of the hair and the shape seemed strangely familiar to Prince Andrey. Several assistants were holding him, and weighing on his chest. One white, plump leg was incessantly moving with a rapid, spasmodic twitching. This man was sobbing and choking convulsively. Two doctors – one was pale and trembling – were mutely engaged in doing something with the other red, gory leg. Having finished with the Tatar, over whom a cloak was thrown, the doctor in spectacles came up to Prince Andrey, wiping his hands.

He glanced at his face, and hurriedly turned away. 'Undress him! Why are you dawdling?' he shouted angrily to the assistant.

His earliest, remotest childhood came back to Prince Andrey, when the assistant, with tucked-up sleeves, hurriedly unbuttoned his buttons, and took off his clothes. The doctor bent close down over the wound, felt it, and sighed deeply. Then he made a sign to some one. And the excruciating pain inside his stomach made Prince Andrey lose consciousness. When he regained consciousness, the broken splinters of his thighbone had been removed, the bits of ragged flesh had been cut off, and the wound bound up. Water was sprinkled on his face. As soon as Prince Andrey opened his eyes, the doctor bent over him, kissed him on the lips without speaking, and hurried away.

After the agony he had passed through, Prince Andrey felt a blissful peace, such as he had not known for very long. All the best and happiest moments of his life, especially his earliest childhood, when he had been undressed and put to bed, when his nurse had sung lullabies over him, when, burying his head in the pillows, he had felt happy in the mere consciousness of life, rose before his imagination, not like the past even, but as though it were the actual present.

The doctors were busily engaged with the wounded man, whose head had seemed somehow familiar to Prince Andrey: they were lifting him up and trying to soothe him.

'Show it to me . . . oo! o! ooo!' he could hear his frightened, abjectly suffering moans, broken by sobs. Hearing his moans, Prince Andrey wanted to cry. Either because he was dying thus without glory, or because he was sorry to part with life, or from these memories of a childhood that could never return, or because he was in pain, or because others were suffering, and that man was moaning so piteously, he longed to weep childlike, good, almost happy, tears.

They showed the wounded man the leg that had been amputated, wearing a boot, and covered with dry gore. 'O! oooo!' he sobbed like a woman. The doctor who had been standing near him, screening his face, moved away.

'My God! How's this? Why is he here?' Prince Andrey wondered.

In the miserable, sobbing, abject creature, whose leg had just been cut off, he recognised Anatole Kuragin. It was Anatole they were holding up in their arms and offering a glass of water, the edge of which he could not catch with his trembling, swollen lips. Anatole drew a sobbing, convulsive breath. 'Yes, it is he; yes, that man is somehow closely and painfully bound up with me,' thought Prince Andrey, with no clear understanding yet of what was before him. 'What is the connection between that man and my childhood, my life?' he asked himself, unable to find the clue. And all at once a new, unexpected memory from that childlike world of purity and love rose up before Prince Andrey. He remembered Natasha, as he had seen her for the first time at the ball in 1810, with her slender neck and slender arms, and her frightened, happy face, ready for ecstatic enjoyment, and a love and tenderness awoke in his heart for her stronger and more loving than ever. He recalled now the bond that existed between him and this man, who was looking vaguely at him through the tears that filled his swollen eyes. Prince Andrey remembered everything, and a passionate pity and love for that suffering man filled his happy heart.

Prince Andrey could restrain himself no more and wept tears of love and tenderness over his fellow-men, over himself, and over their errors and his own. 'Sympathy, love for our brothers, for those who love us, love for those who hate us, love for our enemies; yes, the love that God preached upon earth, that Marie sought to teach me, and I did not understand, that is why I am sorry to part with life, that is what was left me if I had lived. But now it is too late. I know that!'

XXXVIII

THE fearful spectacle of the battlefield, heaped with dead and wounded, in conjunction with the heaviness of his head, the news that some twenty generals he knew well were among the killed or wounded, and the sense of the impotence of his once mighty army, made an unexpected impression on Napoleon, who was usually fond of looking over the dead and wounded, proving thereby, as he imagined, his dauntless spirit. On that day, the awful spectacle of the battlefield overcame this dauntless spirit, which he looked upon as a merit and a proof of greatness. He hastened away from the field of battle and returned to Shevardino. With a yellow, puffy, heavy face, dim eyes, a red nose, and a husky voice, he sat on a camp-stool, looking down and involuntarily listening to the sounds of the firing. With sickly uneasiness he awaited the end of this action, in which he considered himself the prime mover, though he could not have stopped it. The personal, human sentiment for one brief moment gained the ascendant over the artificial phantasm of life, that he had served so long. He imagined in his own case the agonies and death he had seen on the battlefield. The heaviness of his head and chest reminded him of the possibility for him too of agony and death. At that minute he felt no longing for Moscow, for victory or for glory. (What need had he for more glory?) The one thing he desired now was repose, tranquillity, and freedom. But when he was on the height above Semyonovskoye, the officer in command of the artillery proposed to him to bring several batteries up on to that height to increase the fire on the Russian troops before Knyazkovo. Napoleon assented, and gave orders that word should be brought him of the effect produced by this battery.

An adjutant came to say that by the Emperor's orders two hundred guns had been directed upon the Russians, but that they were still holding their ground.

'Our fire is mowing them down in whole rows, but they stand firm,' said the adjutant.

'They want more of it!' said Napoleon in his husky voice.

'Sire?' repeated the adjutant, who had not caught the words.

'They want even more!' Napoleon croaked hoarsely, frowning. 'Well, let them have it then.'

Already, without orders from him, what he did not really want was being done, and he gave the order to do it simply because he thought the order was expected of him. And he passed back again into his old artificial world, peopled by the phantoms of some unreal greatness, and again (as a horse running in a rolling wheel may imagine it is acting on its own account) he fell back into submissively performing the cruel, gloomy, irksome, and inhuman part destined for him.

And not for that hour and day only were the mind and conscience darkened in that man, on whom the burden of all that was being done lay even more heavily than on all the others who took part in it. Never, down to the end of his life, had he the least comprehension of good, of beauty, of truth, of the significance of his own acts, which were too far opposed to truth and goodness, too remote from everything human for him to be able to grasp their significance. He could not disavow his own acts, that were lauded by half the world, and so he was forced to disavow truth and goodness and everything human.

Not on that day only, as he rode about the battlefield, piled with corpses and mutilated men (the work, as he supposed, of his will) he reckoned as he gazed at them how many Russians lay there for each Frenchman, and cheated himself into finding matter for rejoicing in the belief that there were five Russians for every Frenchman. Not on that day only he wrote to Paris that *'le champ de bataille a été superbe,'* because there were fifty thousand corpses on it. Even in St. Helena, in the peaceful solitude where he said he intended to devote his leisure to an account of the great deeds he had done, he wrote:

'The Russian war ought to have been the most popular of modern times: it was the war of good sense and real interests, of the repose and security of all: it was purely pacific and conservative.

'It was for the great cause, the end of uncertainties and the beginning of security. A new horizon, new labours were unfolding, all full of welfare and prosperity for all. The European system was established; all that remained was to organise it.

'Satisfied on these great points and tranquil everywhere, I too should have had my *congress* and my *holy alliance*. These are ideas stolen from me. In this assembly of great sovereigns, we could have treated of our interests like one family and have reckoned, as clerk with master, with the peoples.

'Europe would soon in that way have made in fact but one people, and every one, travelling all over it, would always have found himself in the common fatherland. I should have required all the rivers to be open for the navigation of all; the seas to be common to all; and the great standing armies to be reduced henceforth simply to the bodyguard of the sovereigns.

'Returning to France, to the bosom of the great, strong, magnificent, tranquil, and glorious fatherland, I should have proclaimed its frontiers immutable, all future war purely *defensive,* all fresh aggrandisement *anti-national*. I should have associated my son in the empire; my *dictatorship* would have been over, and his constitutional reign would have begun...

'Paris would have been the capital of the world, and the French the envy of the nations!...

'My leisure then and my old age would have been consecrated, in company with the Empress, and during the royal apprenticeship of my son, to visiting in leisurely fashion with our own horses, like a genuine country couple, every corner of the empire, receiving complaints, redressing wrongs, scattering monuments and benefits on all sides.'

He, predestined by Providence to the gloomy, slavish part of executioner of the peoples, persuaded himself that the motive of his acts had been the welfare of the peoples, and that he could control the destinies of millions, and make their prosperity by the exercise of his power.

'Of the four hundred thousand men who crossed the Vistula,' he wrote later of the Russian war, 'half were Austrians, Prussians, Saxons, Poles, Bavarians, Würtembergers, Mecklenburgers, Spaniards, Italians, Neapolitans. The Imperial army, properly so-called, was one third composed of Dutch, Belgians, inhabitants of the Rhineland, Piedmontese, Swiss, Genevese, Tuscans, Romans, inhabitants of the thirty-second military division, of Bremen, Hamburg, etc. It reckoned barely a hundred and forty thousand men speaking French. The Russian expedition cost France itself less than fifty thousand men. The Russian army in the retreat from Vilna to Moscow in the different battles lost four times as many men as the French army. The fire in Moscow cost the lives of one hundred thousand Russians, dead of cold and want in the woods; lastly, in its march from Moscow to the Oder, the Russian army, too, suffered from the inclemency of the season: it only reckoned fifty thousand men on reaching Vilna, and less than eighteen thousand at Kalisch.'

He imagined that the war with Russia was entirely due to his will, and the horror of what was done made no impression on his soul. He boldly assumed the whole responsibility of it all; and his clouded intellect found justification in the fact that among the hundreds of thousands of men who perished, there were fewer Frenchmen than Hessians and Bavarians.

XXXIX

S O M E tens of thousands of men lay sacrificed in various postures and uniforms on the fields and meadows belonging to the Davidov family and the crown serfs, on those fields and meadows where for hundreds of years the peasants of Borodino, Gorky, Shevardino, and Semyonov-skoye had harvested their crops and grazed their cattle. At the ambulance stations the grass and earth were soaked with blood for two acres round. Crowds of men, wounded and unwounded, of various arms, with panic-stricken faces, dragged themselves, on one side back to Mozhaisk, on the other to Valuev. Other crowds, exhausted and hungry, were led forward by their officers. Others still held their ground, and went on firing.

Over all the plain, at first so bright and gay with its glittering bayonets and puffs of smoke in the morning sunshine, there hung now a dark cloud of damp mist and smoke, and a strange, sour smell of saltpetre and blood. Storm clouds had gathered, and a drizzling rain began to fall on the dead, on the wounded, on the panic-stricken, and exhausted, and hesitating soldiers. It seemed to say: 'Enough, enough; cease. . . . Consider. What are you doing?'

To the men on both sides, alike exhausted from want of food and rest, the doubt began to come whether they should still persist in slaughtering one another; and in every face could be seen hesitation, and in every heart alike there rose the question: 'For what, for whom am I to slay and be slain? Slay whom you will, do what you will, but I have had enough!' This thought took shape towards evening in every heart alike. Any minute all those men might be horror-stricken at what they were doing, might throw up everything and run anywhere.

But though towards the end of the battle the men felt all the horror of their actions, though they would have been glad to cease, some unfathomable, mysterious force still led them on, and the artillerymen—the third of them left—soaked with sweat, grimed with powder and blood, and panting with weariness, still brought the charges, loaded, aimed, and lighted the match; and the cannon-balls flew as swiftly and cruelly from each side and crushed human flesh, and kept up the fearful work, which was done not at the will of men, but at the will of Him who sways men and worlds.

Any one looking at the disorder in the rear of the Russian army would have said that the French had but to make one slight effort more and the Russian army would have been annihilated; and any one seeing the rear of the French army would have said that the Russians need but make a slight effort more and the French would be overthrown. But neither French nor Russians made that effort, and the flame of the battle burnt slowly out.

The Russians did not make this effort, because they were not attacking the French. At the beginning of the battle they merely stood on the road to Moscow, barring it to the French; and they still stood at the end of the battle as they had at the beginning. But even if it had been the aim of the Russians to drive back the French, they could not have made this final effort, because all the Russian troops had been routed; there was not a single part of the army that had not suffered in the battle, and the Russians, without being driven from their position, lost ONE HALF of their army.

For the French, with the memory of fifteen years of victories, with confidence in Napoleon's all-vanquishing genius, with the consciousness of having taken a part of the battlefield, of having only lost a fourth of their men, and of having a body of twenty thousand—the Guards intact—it would have been an easy matter to make this effort. The French, attacking the Russian army with the object of driving it from its position, ought to have made this effort, because as long as the Russians still barred the way to Moscow, as before the battle, the aim of the French had not been attained, and all losses and exertions had been in vain. But the French did not make that effort. Some historians assert that if Napoleon had only let his Old Guard advance, the battle would have been gained. To talk of what might have happened if Napoleon had let his Guard advance is much the same as to talk of what would happen if spring came in autumn. That could not have been. Napoleon did not do so, not because he did not want to, but because it was impossible to do so. All the generals, officers, and soldiers of the French army knew that it was impossible to make this final effort, because the flagging spirit of the troops did not allow of it.

It was not Napoleon alone who had that nightmare feeling that the mighty arm was stricken powerless: all the generals, all the soldiers of the French army, those who fought and those who did not, after all their experiences of previous battles (when after one-tenth of the effort the enemy had always run), showed the feeling of horror before this foe, who, after losing ONE HALF of the army, still stood its ground as dauntless at the end as at the beginning of the battle. The moral force of the French, the attacking army, was exhausted. Not the victory, signalised by the capture of rags on the end of sticks, called flags, or of the ground on which the troops were standing, but a moral victory, that which compels the enemy to recognise the moral superiority of his opponent, and his own impotence, was won by the Russians at Borodino. The French invading army, like a ravening beast that has received its death-wound in its onslaught, felt its end near. But it could not stop, no more than the Russian army—of half its strength—could help retreating. After that check, the French army could still drag on to Moscow, but there, without fresh effort on the part of the Russian army, its ruin was inevitable, as its life-blood ebbed away from the deadly wound dealt it at Borodino. The direct consequence of the battle of Borodino was Napoleon's causeless flight from Moscow, his return by the old Smolensk road, the ruin of the invading army of five hundred thousand men, and the downfall of the Napoleonic rule, on which for the first time at Borodino, was laid the hand of a foe of stronger spirit.

PART XI

I

FOR THE HUMAN mind the absolute continuity of motion is inconceivable. The laws of motion of any kind only become comprehensible to man when he examines units of this motion, arbitrarily selected. But at the same time it is from this arbitrary division of continuous motion into discontinuous units that a great number of human errors proceeds.

We all know the so-called sophism of the ancients, proving that Achilles would never overtake the tortoise, though Achilles walked ten times as fast as the tortoise. As soon as Achilles passes over the space separating him from the tortoise, the tortoise advances one-tenth of that space: Achilles passes over that tenth, but the tortoise has advanced a hundredth, and so on to infinity. This problem seemed to the ancients insoluble. The irrationality of the conclusion (that Achilles will never overtake the tortoise) arises from the arbitrary assumption of disconnected units of motion, when the motion both of Achilles and the tortoise was continuous.

By taking smaller and smaller units of motion we merely approach the solution of the problem, but we never attain it. It is only by assuming an infinitely small magnitude, and a progression rising from it up to a tenth, and taking the sum of that geometrical progression, that we can arrive at the solution of the problem. A new branch of mathematics, dealing with infinitely small quantities, gives now in other more complex problems of dynamics solutions of problems that seemed insoluble.

This new branch of mathematics, unknown to the ancients, by assuming infinitely small quantities, that is, such as secure the chief condition of motion (absolute continuity), corrects the inevitable error which the human intellect cannot but make, when it considers disconnected units of motion instead of continuous motion.

In the investigation of the laws of historical motion precisely the same mistake arises.

The progress of humanity, arising from an innumerable multitude of individual wills, is continuous in its motion.

The discovery of the laws of this motion is the aim of history. But in order to arrive at the laws of the continuous motion due to the sum of all these individual wills, the human mind assumes arbitrary, disconnected units. The first proceeding of the historian is taking an arbitrary series of continuous events to examine it apart from others, while in reality there is not, and cannot be, a beginning to any event, but one event flows without any break in continuity from another. The second proceeding is to examine the action of a single person, a sovereign, or a general, as though it were equivalent to the sum of many individual wills, though the sum of individual wills never finds expression in the action of a single historical personage.

Historical science as it advances is continually taking smaller and smaller units for analysis, and in this way strives to approximate to the truth. But however small the units of which history takes cognisance, we feel that the assumption of a unit, disconnected from another, the assumption of a *beginning* of any phenomenon, and the assumption that the individual wills of all men find expression in the actions of a single historical personage, are false in themselves.

Every conclusion of history can, without the slightest effort on the part of the critic, be dissipated like dust, leaving no trace, simply through criticism selecting, as the object of its analysis, a greater or smaller disconnected unit, which it has a perfect right to do, seeing that the unit of history is always selected arbitrarily.

Only by assuming an infinitely small unit for observation—a differential of history—that is, the homogeneous tendencies of men, and arriving at the integral calculus (that is, taking the sum of those infinitesimal quantities), can we hope to arrive at the laws of history.

The first fifteen years of the nineteenth century present the spectacle of an extraordinary movement of millions of men. Men leave their habitual pursuits; rush from one side of Europe to the other; plunder, slaughter one another, triumph and despair; and the whole current of life is transformed and presents a quickened activity, first moving at a growing speed, and then slowly slackening again. What was the cause of that activity, or from what laws did it arise? asks the human intellect.

The historians, in reply to that inquiry, lay before us the sayings and doings of some dozens of men in one of the buildings of the city of Paris, summing up those doings and sayings by one word—revolution. Then they give us a detailed biography of Napoleon, and of certain persons favourably or hostilely disposed to him; talk of the influence of some of these persons upon others; and then say that this it is to which that activity is due, and these are its laws.

But the human intellect not only refuses to believe in that explanation, but flatly declares that the method of explanation is not a correct one, because in this explanation a smaller phenomenon is taken as the cause of a greater phenomenon. The sum of men's individual wills produced both the revolution and Napoleon; and only the sum of those wills endured them and then destroyed them.

'But whenever there have been wars, there have been great military leaders; whenever there have been revolutions in states, there have been great men,' says history. 'Whenever there have been great military leaders there have, indeed, been wars,' replies the human reason; 'but that does not prove that the generals were the cause of the wars, and that the factors leading to warfare can be found in the personal activity of one man.'

Whenever, looking at my watch, I see the hand has reached the figure x, I hear the bells beginning to ring in the church close by. But from the fact that the watch hand points to ten whenever the bells begin to ring, I have not the right to infer that the position of the hands of my watch is the cause of the vibration of the bells.

Whenever I see a steam-engine move, I hear the whistle, I see the valve open and the wheels turn; but I have no right to conclude from that that the whistle and the turning of the wheels are the causes of the steam-engine's moving.

The peasants say that in the late spring a cold wind blows because the oak-buds are opening, and, as a fact, a cold wind does blow every spring when the oak is coming out. But though the cause of a cold wind's blowing just when the oaks are coming out is unknown to me, I cannot agree with the peasants that the cause of the cold wind is the opening of the oak-buds, because the force of the wind is altogether outside the influence of the buds. I see in this simply such a coincidence of events as is common in every phenomenon of life, and I see that however long and minutely I might examine the watch hand, the valve, and the wheel of the steam-engine and the oak-bud, I shall not discover the cause of the bells ringing, of the steam-engine moving, and of the spring wind. To do that I must completely change my point of observation and study the laws of the motion of steam, of the bells, and of the wind. History must do the same. And efforts have already been made in this direction.

For the investigation of the laws of history, we must completely change the subject of observations, must let kings and ministers and generals alone, and study the homogeneous, infinitesimal elements by which masses are led. No one can say how far it has been given to man to advance in that direction in understanding of the laws of history. But it is obvious that only in that direction lies any possibility of discovering historical laws; and that the human intellect has hitherto not devoted to that method of research one millionth part of the energy that historians have put into the description of the doings of various kings, ministers, and generals, and the exposition of their own views on those doings.

II

THE armed forces of twelve different nationalities of Europe invade Russia. The Russian army and population fall back, avoiding a battle, to Smolensk, and from Smolensk to Borodino. The French army moves on to Moscow, its goal, with continually increasing impetus. The impetus of its advance is increased as it approaches its goal, just as the velocity of a falling body increases as it gets nearer the earth. Behind them thousands of versts of famine-stricken, hostile country; before them some dozens of versts between them and their goal. Every soldier of Napoleon's army feels it, and the expedition advances of itself, by the force of its own impetus.

In the Russian troops the spirit of fury, of hatred of the foe, burns more and more fiercely during their retreat; it gathers strength and concentration as they draw back. At Borodino the armies meet. Neither army is destroyed, but the Russian army, immediately after the conflict, retreats as inevitably as a ball rebounds after contact with another ball flying with greater impetus to meet it. And just as inevitably (though parting with its force in the contact) the ball of the invading army is carried for a space further by the energy, not yet fully spent, within it.

The Russians retreat one hundred and twenty versts beyond Moscow; the French reach Moscow and there halt. For five weeks after this there is not a single battle. The French do not move. Like a wild beast mortally wounded, bleeding and licking its wounds, for five weeks the French remain in Moscow, attempting nothing; and all at once, with nothing new to account for it, they flee back; they make a dash for the Kaluga road (after a victory, too, for they remained in possession of the field of battle at Maley Yaroslavets); and then, without a single serious engagement, fly more and more rapidly back to Smolensk, to Vilna, to the Berezina, and beyond it.

On the evening of the 26th of August, Kutuzov and the whole Russian army were convinced that the battle of Borodino was a victory. Kutuzov wrote to that effect to the Tsar. He ordered the troops to be in readiness for another battle, to complete the defeat of the enemy, not because he wanted to deceive any one, but because he knew that the enemy was vanquished, as every one who had taken part in the battle knew it.

But all that evening and next day news was coming in of unheard-of losses, of the loss of one-half of the army, and another battle turned out to be physically impossible.

It was impossible to give battle when information had not yet come in, the wounded had not been removed, the ammunition stores had not been filled up, the slain had not been counted, new officers had not been appointed to replace the dead, and the men had had neither food nor sleep. And meanwhile, the very next morning after the battle, the French army of itself moved down upon the Russians, carried on by the force of its own impetus, accelerated now in inverse ratio to the square of the distance from its goal. Kutuzov's wish was to attack next day, and all the army shared this desire. But to make an attack it is not sufficient to desire to do so; there must also be a possibility of doing so, and this possibility there was not. It was impossible not to retreat one day's march, and then it was as impossible not to retreat a second and a third day's march, and finally, on the 1st of September, when the army reached Moscow, despite the force of the growing feeling in the troops, the force of circumstances compelled those troops to retreat beyond Moscow. And the troops retreated one more last day's march, and abandoned Moscow to the enemy.

Persons who are accustomed to suppose that plans of campaigns and of battles are made by generals in the same way as any of us sitting over a map in our study make plans of how we would have acted in such and such a position, will be perplexed by questions why Kutuzov, if he had to retreat, did not take this or that course, why he did not take up a position before Fili, why he did not at once retreat to the Kaluga road, leaving Moscow, and so on. Persons accustomed to think in this way forget, or do not know, the inevitable conditions which always limit the action of any commander-in-chief. The action of a commander-in-chief in the field has no sort of resemblance to the action we imagine to ourselves, sitting at our ease in our study, going over some campaign on the map with a certain given number of soldiers on each side, in a certain known locality, starting our plans from a certain moment. The general is never in the position of the *beginning* of any event, from which we always contemplate the event. The general is always in the very middle of a changing series of events, so that he is never at any moment in a position to deliberate on all the bearings of the event that is taking place. Imperceptibly, moment by moment, an event takes shape in all its bearings, and at every moment in that uninterrupted, consecutive shaping of events the commander-in-chief is in the centre of a most complex play of intrigues, of cares, of dependence and of power, of projects, counsels, threats, and conceptions, with one thing depending on another, and is under the continual necessity of answering the immense number of mutually contradictory inquiries addressed to him.

We are, with perfect seriousness, told by those learned in military matters that Kutuzov ought to have marched his army towards the Kaluga road long before reaching Fili; that somebody did, indeed, suggest such a plan. But the commander of an army has before him, especially at a difficult moment, not one, but dozens of plans. And each of those plans, based on the rules of strategy and tactics, contradicts all the rest. The commander's duty would, one would suppose, be merely to select one out of those plans; but even this he cannot do. Time and events will not wait. It is suggested to him, let us suppose, on the 28th to move towards the Kaluga road, but at that moment an adjutant gallops up from Miloradovitch to inquire whether to join battle at once with the French or to retire. He must be given instructions at once, at the instant. And the order to retire hinders us from turning to the Kaluga road. And then after the adjutant comes the commissariat commissioner to inquire where the stores are to be taken, and the ambulance director to ask where the wounded are to be moved to, and a courier from Petersburg with a letter from the Tsar, not admitting the possibility of abandoning Moscow, and the commander's rival, who is trying to cut the ground from under his feet (and there are always more than one such) proposes a new project, diametrically opposed to the plan of marching upon the Kaluga road. The commander's own energies, too, require sleep and support. And a respectable general, who has been overlooked when decorations were bestowed, presents a complaint, and the inhabitants of the district implore protection, and the officer sent to inspect the locality comes back with a report utterly unlike that of the officer sent on the same commission just previously; and a spy, and a prisoner, and a general who has made a reconnaissance, all describe the position of the enemy's army quite differently. Persons who forget, or fail to comprehend, those inevitable conditions under which a commander has to act, present to us, for instance, the position of the troops at Fili, and assume that the commander-in-chief was quite free on the 1st of September to decide the question whether to abandon or to defend Moscow, though, with the position of the Russian army, only five versts from Moscow, there could no longer be any question on the subject. When was that question decided? At Drissa, and at Smolensk, and most palpably of all on August the 24th at Shevardino, and on the 26th at Borodino, and every day and hour and minute of the retreat from Borodino to Fili.

III

THE Russian army, retreating from Borodino, halted at Fili. Yermolov, who had been inspecting the position, rode up to the commander-in-chief.

'There is no possibility of fighting in this position,' he said.

Kutuzov looked at him in wonder, and made him repeat the words he had just uttered. When he had done so, he put out his hand to him.

'Give me your hand,' he said; and turning it so as to feel his pulse, he said: 'You are not well, my dear boy. Think what you are saying.'

Kutuzov could not yet take in the idea of its being possible to retreat, abandoning Moscow without a battle.

On the Poklonnaya Hill, six versts from Dorogomilovsky gate, Kutuzov got out of his carriage and sat down on a bench by the side of the road. A great crowd of generals gathered about him. Count Rastoptchin, who had come out from Moscow, joined them. All this brilliant company broke up into several circles, and talked among themselves of the advantages and disadvantages of the position, of the condition of the troops, of the plans proposed, of the situation of Moscow—in fact, of military questions generally. All felt that though they had not been summoned for the purpose, it was really, if not ostensibly, a military council. All conversation was confined to public questions. If any one did repeat or inquire any piece of personal news, it was in a whisper, and the talk passed at once back to general topics. There was not a jest, not a laugh, not even a smile, to be seen among all these men. They were all making an obvious effort to rise to the level of the situation. And all the groups, while talking among themselves, tried to keep close to the commander-in-chief, whose bench formed the centre of the whole crowd, and tried to talk so that he might hear them. The commander-in-chief listened, and sometimes asked what had been said near him, but did not himself enter into conversation or express any opinion. For the most part, after listening to the talk of some group, he turned away with an air of disappointment, as though they were not speaking of anything he cared to hear about at all. Some were discussing the position, criticising not so much the position itself as the intellectual qualifications of those who had selected it. Others argued that a blunder had been made earlier, that a battle ought to have been fought two days before. Others talked of the battle of Salamanca, which a Frenchman, Crosart, wearing a Spanish uniform, was describing to them. (This Frenchman, who had just arrived, had with one of the German princes serving in the Russian army been criticising the siege of Saragossa, foreseeing a possibility of a similar defence of Moscow.) In the fourth group, Count Rastoptchin was saying that he, with the Moscow city guard, was ready to die under the walls of the city, but that still he could not but complain of the uncertainty in which he had been left, and that had he known it earlier, things would have been different. . . . A fifth group was manifesting the profundity of their tactical insight by discussing the direction the troops should certainly take now. A sixth group were talking arrant nonsense.

Kutuzov's face grew more and more careworn and gloomy. From all this talk Kutuzov saw one thing only: the defence of Moscow was a *physical impossibility* in the fullest sense of the words. It was so utterly impossible that even if some insane commander were to give orders for a battle, all that would follow would be a muddle, and no battle would be fought. There would be no battle, because all the officers in command, not merely recognised the position to be impossible, but were only engaged now in discussing what was to be done after the inevitable abandonment of that position. How could officers lead their men to a field of battle which they considered it impossible to hold? The officers of lower rank, and even the soldiers themselves (they too form their conclusions), recognised that the position could not be held, and so they could not advance into battle with the conviction that they would be defeated. That Bennigsen urged the defence of this position, and others still discussed it, was a fact that had no significance in itself, but only as a pretext for dissension and intrigue. Kutuzov knew that.

Bennigsen was warmly manifesting his Russian patriotism (Kutuzov could not listen to him without wincing), by insisting on the defence of Moscow. To Kutuzov, his object was as clear as daylight: in case of the defence being unsuccessful, to throw the blame on Kutuzov, who had brought the army as far as the Sparrow Hills without a battle; in case of its being successful, to claim the credit; in case of it not being attempted, to clear himself of the crime of abandoning Moscow.

But these questions of intrigue did not occupy the old man's mind now. One terrible question absorbed him. And to that question he heard no reply from any one. The question for him now was this: 'Can it be that I have let Napoleon get to Moscow, and when did I do it? When did it happen? Was it yesterday, when I sent word to Platov to retreat, or the evening before when I had a nap and bade Bennigsen give instructions? Or earlier still? . . . When, when was it this fearful thing happened? Moscow must be abandoned. The army must retire, and I must give the order for it.'

To give that terrible order seemed to him equivalent to resigning the command of the army. And apart from the fact that he loved power, and was used to it (the honours paid to Prince Prozorovsky, under whom he had been serving in Turkey, galled him), he was convinced that he was destined to deliver Russia, and had only for that cause been chosen commander-in-chief contrary to the Tsar's wishes by the will of the people. He was persuaded that in these difficult circumstances he was the one man who could maintain his position at the head of the army, that he was the only man in the world capable of meeting Napoleon as an antagonist without panic. And he was in terror at the idea of having to resign the command. But he must decide on some step, he must cut short this chatter round him, which was beginning to assume too free a character.

He beckoned the senior generals to him.

'Ma tête, fût-elle bonne ou mauvaise, n'a qu'à s'aider d'elle-même,' he said, getting up from his bench, and he rode off to Fili, where his carriages were waiting.

IV

IN the large best room of the peasant Andrey Savostyanov's cottage, at two o'clock, a council met. The men and women and children of the peasant's big family all crowded together in the room on the other side of the passage. Only Andrey's little grandchild, Malasha, a child of six, whom his highness had petted, giving her sugar while he drank his tea, stayed behind by the big stove in the best room. Malasha peeped out from near the stove with shy delight at the faces, the uniforms, and the crosses of the generals, who kept coming into the room one after another, and sitting in a row on the broad benches in the best corner under the holy images. 'Grandad' himself, as Malasha in her own mind called Kutuzov, was sitting apart from the rest in the dark corner behind the stove. He sat sunk all of a heap in a folding armchair, and was continually clearing his throat and straightening the collar of his coat, which, though it was unbuttoned, still seemed to gall his neck. The generals, as they came in one after another, walked up to the commander-in-chief: he shook hands with some, to others he merely nodded.

The adjutant, Kaisarov, would have drawn back a curtain from the window facing Kutuzov, but the latter shook his hand angrily at him, and Kaisarov saw that his highness did not care for them to see his face.

Round the peasant's deal table, on which lay maps, plans, pencils, and papers, there was such a crowd that the orderlies brought in another bench, and set it near the table. Yermolov, Kaisarov, and Toll seated themselves on this bench. In the foremost place, under the holy images, sat Barclay de Tolly, with his Order of St. George on his neck, with his pale, sickly face and high forehead that met his bald head. He had been in the throes of fever for the last two days, and was shivering and shaking now. Beside him sat Usarov, speaking to him with rapid gesticulation in the same low voice in which everybody spoke. Little chubby Dohturov was listening attentively with his eyebrows raised and his hands clasped over his stomach. On the other side, resting his broad head on his hand, sat Count Osterman-Tolstoy, with his bold features and brilliant eyes, apparently plunged in his own thoughts. Raevsky sat twisting his black curls on his temples, as he always did, and looking with impatience from Kutuzov to the door. Konovnitsyn's firm, handsome, good-humoured face was bright with a sly and kindly smile. He caught Malasha's eye, and made signs to her with his eyes, that set the little girl smiling.

They were all waiting for Bennigsen, who, on the pretext of a fresh inspection of the position, was engaged in finishing his luxurious dinner. They waited for him from four to six o'clock, and all that time did not enter on their deliberations, but talked of extraneous matters in subdued tones.

Only when Bennigsen had entered the hut, Kutuzov moved out of his corner and came up to the table, but sat there so that his face did not come within the light of the candles on it.

Bennigsen opened the council by the question: Whether to abandon the holy and ancient capital of Russia, or to defend it?

A prolonged silence followed. Every face was knitted, and in the stillness Kutuzov could be heard angrily coughing and clearing his throat. All eyes were fixed on him. Malasha too gazed at 'Grandad'.

She was nearest of all to him, and saw that his face was working; he seemed to be going to cry. But that did not last long.

'*The holy and ancient capital of Russia!*' he cried suddenly, in a wrathful voice, repeating Bennigsen's words, and thereby underlining the false note in them. 'Allow me to tell your Excellency that that question has no meaning to a Russian.' (He lurched his unwieldy figure forward.) 'Such a question cannot be put; there is no sense in such a question. The question I have asked these gentlemen to meet to discuss is the question of the war. 'The question is: The safety of Russia lies in her army. Is it better to risk the loss of the army and of Moscow by giving battle, or to abandon Moscow without a battle? That is the question on which I desire to learn your opinion.' He lurched back into his low chair again.

A debate began. Bennigsen did not yet consider that the game was lost. Overruled by the opinion of Barclay and others into admitting the impossibility of maintaining a defensive position at Fili, he proceeded to prove his Russian patriotism and devotion to Moscow by proposing to move the army during the night from the right to the left flank of the position, and to aim a blow at the French right flank next day. Opinions were divided, and arguments were advanced for and against this project. Yermolov, Dohturov, and Raevsky sided with Bennigsen. Led by a feeling that a sacrifice was called for before abandoning the city, and by other personal considerations, these generals seemed unable to grasp that the council then sitting could not affect the inevitable course of events, and that Moscow was already in effect abandoned. The other generals understood this, and leaving the question of Moscow on one side, talked of the direction the army ought to take in retreating.

Malasha, who kept her eyes fixed on what was passing before her, saw the council in quite a different light. It seemed to her that the whole point at issue was a personal struggle between 'Grandad' and 'Longcoat,' as she called Bennigsen to herself. She saw that they were angry when they spoke to one another, and in her heart she was on 'Grandad's' side. In the middle of the conversation, she caught the swift, subtle glance that 'Grandad' gave Bennigsen, and immediately after, she noted with glee that 'Grandad's' words had put 'Longcoat' down. Bennigsen suddenly flushed, and strode angrily across the room. The words that had thus affected Bennigsen were Kutuzov's quietly and softly uttered comment on his proposal to move the troops from the right to the left flank in the night in order to attack the French right.

'I cannot approve of the count's plan, gentlemen,' said Kutuzov. 'Movements of troops in close proximity to the enemy are always risky, and military history affords many examples of disasters arising from them. For instance . . .' (Kutuzov seemed to ponder, seeking an example, and then looking with a frank, naïve expression at Bennigsen) . . . 'well, the battle of Friedland, which, as I have no doubt the count remembers, was not . . . completely successful owing to the change of the position of the troops in too close proximity to the enemy . . .'

A momentary silence followed that seemed lengthy to all.

The debate was renewed; but pauses often interrupted it, and it was felt that there was nothing to talk about.

In one of these pauses Kutuzov heaved a heavy sigh, as though preparing to speak. All looked round at him.

'Well, gentlemen, I see that it is I who will have to pay for the broken pots,' he said. And slowly rising from his seat, he walked up to the table. 'Gentlemen, I have heard your opinions. Some of you will not agree with me. But I' (he stopped), 'by the authority entrusted me by my Tsar and my country, give the order to retire.'

After that the generals began to disperse with the solemnity and circumspect taciturnity with which people separate after a funeral. Several of the generals made some communication to the commander-in-chief in a low voice, pitched in quite a different scale from that in which they had been talking at the council.

Malasha, who had long been expected in the other room to supper, dropped backwards down from the stove, her bare toes clinging to the projections of the stove, and slipping between the generals' legs, she darted out at the door.

After dismissing the generals, Kutuzov sat a long while with his elbows on the table, pondering that terrible question: 'When, when had it become inevitable that Moscow should be abandoned? When was the thing done that made it inevitable, and who is to blame for it?'

'This I did not expect!' he said to the adjutant, Schneider, who came in to him late at night; 'this I did not expect! This I never thought of!'

'You must rest, your highness,' said Schneider.

'Yes; but they shall eat horse-flesh like the Turks!' Kutuzov cried, not heeding him, as he brought his podgy fist down on the table. 'They, too, shall eat it, if only...!'

V

MEANWHILE, in an event of even greater importance than the retreat of the army without a battle, in the abandonment and burning of Moscow, Count Rastoptchin, whom we conceive as taking the lead in that event, was acting in a very different manner from Kutuzov.

This event—the abandonment and burning of Moscow—was, after the battle of Borodino, as inevitable as the retreat of the army without fighting.

Every Russian could have foretold what happened, not as a result of any train of intellectual deductions, but from the feeling that lies at the bottom of our hearts, and lay at the bottom of our fathers'!

In every town and village on Russian soil, from Smolensk onwards, without the assistance of Count Rastoptchin and his placards, the same thing took place as happened in Moscow. The people awaited the coming of the enemy without disturbance; did not display excitement; tore nobody to pieces, but calmly awaited their fate, feeling in themselves the power to find what they must do in the moment of difficulty.

And as soon as the enemy came near, the wealthier elements of the population went away, leaving their property behind; the poorer remained, and burnt and destroyed all that was left.

The sense that this would be so, and always would be so, lay, and lies, at the bottom of every Russian's heart. And a sense of this, and more, a foreboding that Moscow would be taken by the enemy, lay in the Russian society of Moscow in 1812. Those who had begun leaving Moscow in July and the beginning of August had shown that they expected it. Those who left the city with what they could carry away, abandoning their houses and half their property, did so in consequence of that latent patriotism, which finds expression, not in phrases, not in giving one's children to death for the sake of the fatherland, and such unnatural exploits, but expresses itself imperceptibly in the most simple, organic way, and so always produces the most powerful results.

'It's a disgrace to fly from danger; only the cowards are flying from Moscow,' they were told. Rastoptchin, in his placards, urged upon them that it was base to leave Moscow. They were ashamed at hearing themselves called cowards; they were ashamed of going away; but still they went away, knowing that it must be so. Why did they go away? It cannot be supposed that Rastoptchin had scared them with tales of the atrocities perpetrated by Napoleon in the countries he conquered. The first to leave were the wealthy, educated people, who knew very well that Vienna and Berlin remained uninjured, and that the inhabitants of those cities, when Napoleon was in occupation of them, had spent their time gaily with the fascinating Frenchmen, of whom all Russians, and especially the ladies, had at that period been so fond.

They went away because to Russians the question whether they would be comfortable or not under the government of the French in Moscow could never occur. To be under the government of the French was out of the question; it was worse than anything. They were going away even before Borodino, and still more rapidly after Borodino; regardless of the calls to defend the city, regardless of the proclamations of the governor of Moscow; of his intention of going with the Iversky Virgin into battle, and of the air-balloons which were to demolish the French, and all the nonsense with which Rastoptchin filled his placards. They knew that it was for the army to fight, and if the army could not, it would be of no use to rush out with young ladies and house-serfs to fight Napoleon on the Three Hills, and so they must make haste and get away, sorry as they were to leave their possessions to destruction. They drove away without a thought of the vast consequences of this immense wealthy city being abandoned by its inhabitants, and being inevitably thereby consigned to the flames. To abstain from destroying and burning empty houses would never occur to the Russian peasantry. They drove away, each on his own account, and yet it was only in consequence of their action that the grand event came to pass that is the highest glory of the Russian people. The lady who in June set off with her negroes and her buffoons from Moscow for her Saratov estates, with a vague feeling that she was not going to be a servant of Bonaparte's, and a vague dread that she might be hindered from going by Rastoptchin's orders, was simply and genuinely doing the great deed that saved Russia.

Count Rastoptchin at one time cried shame on those who were going, then removed all the public offices, then served out useless weapons to the drunken rabble, then brought out the holy images, and prevented Father Augustin from removing the holy relics and images, then got hold of all the private conveyances that were in Moscow, then in one hundred and thirty-six carts carried out the air-balloon made by Leppich, at one time hinted that he should set fire to Moscow, at one time described how he had burnt his own house, and wrote a proclamation to the French in which he solemnly reproached them for destroying the home of his childhood. He claimed the credit of having set fire to Moscow, then disavowed it; he commanded the people to capture all spies, and bring them to him, then blamed the people for doing so; he sent all the French residents out of Moscow, and then let Madame Aubert-Chalmy, who formed the centre of French society in Moscow, remain. For no particular reason he ordered the respected old postmaster, Klucharov, to be seized and banished. He got the people together on the Three Hills to fight the French, and then, to get rid of them, handed a man over to them to murder, and escaped himself by the back door. He vowed he would never survive the disaster of Moscow, and later on wrote French verses in albums on his share in the affair.[1]

This man had no inkling of the import of what was happening. All he wanted was to do something himself, to astonish people, to perform some heroic feat of patriotism, and, like a child, he frolicked about the grand and inevitable event of the abandonment and burning of Moscow, trying with his puny hand first to urge on, and then to hold back, the tide of the vast popular current that was bearing him along with it.

VI

E L L E N had accompanied the court on its return from Vilna to Petersburg, and there found herself in a difficult position.

In Petersburg Ellen had enjoyed the special patronage of a great

---

[1] *"Je suis né Tartare*
Je voulus être Romain
Les Français m'appelèrent barbare,
Les Russes—George Dandin

personage, who occupied one of the highest positions in the government. In Vilna she had formed a liaison with a young foreign prince.

When she returned to Petersburg the prince and the great dignitary were both in that town; both claimed their rights, and Ellen was confronted with a problem that had not previously arisen in her career—the preservation of the closest relations with both, without giving offence to either.

What might have seemed to any other woman a difficult or impossible task never cost a moment's thought to Countess Bezuhov, who plainly deserved the reputation she enjoyed of being a most intelligent woman. Had she attempted concealment; had she allowed herself to get out of her awkward position by subterfuges, she would have spoilt her own case by acknowledging herself the guilty party. But like a truly great man, who can always do everything he chooses, Ellen at once assumed the rectitude of her own position, of which she was indeed genuinely convinced, and the guilty responsibility of every one else concerned.

The first time the young foreign prince ventured to reproach her, she lifted her beautiful head, and, with a haughty tone towards him, said firmly:

'This is the egoism and the cruelty of men. I expected nothing else. Woman sacrifices herself for you; she suffers, and this is her reward. What right have you, your highness, to call me to account for my friendships, my affections? He is a man who has been more than a father to me!'

The prince would have said something. Ellen interrupted him.

'Well, yes, perhaps he has sentiments for me other than those of a father, but that is not a reason I should shut my door on him. I am not a man to be ungrateful. Know, your highness, that in all that relates to my private sentiments I will account only to God and to my conscience!' she concluded, laying her hand on her beautiful, heaving bosom, and looking up to heaven.

'But listen to me, in God's name!'...

'Marry me, and I will be your slave!'

'But it is impossible.'

'You do not deign to stoop to me, you...' Ellen burst into tears.

The prince attempted to console her. Ellen, as though utterly distraught, declared through her tears that there was nothing to prevent her marrying; that there were precedents (they were but few at that time, but Ellen quoted the case of Napoleon and some other persons of exalted rank); that she had never been a real wife to her husband; that she had been dragged an unwilling victim into the marriage.

'But the law, religion ...' murmured the prince, on the point of yielding.

'Religion, laws ... what can they have been invented for, if they are unable to manage that?' said Ellen.

The prince was astonished that so simple a reflection had never occurred to him, and applied to the council of the brotherhood of the Society of Jesus, with which he was in close relations.

A few days later, at one of the fascinating fêtes Ellen used to give at her summer villa at Kamenny Ostrov, a certain fascinating M. Jobert was presented to her; a man no longer young, with snow-white hair and brilliant black eyes, *un Jésuite à robe courte*, who walked for a long while with Ellen among the illuminations in the garden to the strains of music, conversing with her of the love of God, of Christ, of the heart of the Holy Mother, and of the consolations afforded in this life and the next by the one true Catholic faith. Ellen was touched, and several times tears stood both in her eyes and in M. Jobert's, and their voices trembled. A dance, to which her partner fetched Ellen away, cut short her conversation with the future 'director of her conscience,' but the next evening M. Jobert came alone to see Ellen, and from that day he was a frequent visitor.

One day he took the countess into a Catholic church, where she fell on her knees before the altar, up to which she was conducted. The fascinating, middle-aged Frenchman laid his hands on her head, and as she herself afterwards described it, she felt something like a breath of fresh air, which seemed wafted into her soul. It was explained to her that this was the 'grace of God.'

Then an abbé *à robe longue* was brought to her; he confessed her, and absolved her from her sins. Next day a box was brought containing the Sacred Host, and left for her to partake of at her house. Several days later Ellen learned to her satisfaction that she had now been admitted into the true Catholic Church, and that in a few days the Pope himself would hear of her case, and send her a document of some sort.

All that was done with her and around her at this period, the attention paid her by so many clever men, and expressed in such agreeable and subtle forms, and her dovelike purity during her conversion (she wore nothing but white dresses and white ribbons all the time)—all afforded her gratification. But this gratification never led her for one instant to lose sight of her object. And, as always happens in contests of cunning, the stupid person gains more than the cleverer; Ellen, fully grasping that the motive of all these words and all this manoeuvring was by her conversion to Catholicism to get a round sum from her for the benefit of the Jesuit order (this was hinted at, indeed), held back the money, while insisting steadily on the various operations that would set her free from her conjugal bonds. To her notions, the real object of every religion was to provide recognised forms of propriety for the satisfaction of human desires. And with this end in view, she insisted, in one of her conversations with her spiritual adviser, on demanding an answer to the question how far her marriage was binding.

They were sitting in the drawing-room window. It was dusk. There was a scent of flowers from the window. Ellen wore a white dress, transparent over the bosom and shoulders. The sleek, well-fed abbé, with his plump, clean-shaven chin, his amiable, strong mouth, and his white hands, clasped mildly on his knees, was sitting close by Ellen. With a subtle smile on his lips, and a look of discreet admiration in his eyes, he gazed from time to time at her face, as he expounded his views on the subject. Ellen, with a restless smile, stared at his curly hair and his smooth-shaven, blackish cheeks, and seemed every minute to be expecting the conversation to take a new turn. But the abbé, though unmistakably aware of the beauty of his companion, was also interested in his own skilful handling of the question. The spiritual adviser adopted the following chain of reasoning:

'In ignorance,' said he, 'of the significance of your promise, you took a vow of conjugal fidelity to a man who, on his side, was guilty of sacrilege in entering on the sacrament of matrimony with no faith in its religious significance. That marriage had not the dual binding force it should have had. But in spite of that, your vow was binding upon you. You broke it. What did you commit? Venial sin or mortal sin? A venial sin, because you committed it with no intention of acting wrongly. If now, with the object of bearing children, you should enter into a new marriage, your sin might be forgiven. But the question again falls into two divisions. First . . .'

'But, I imagine,' Ellen, who was getting bored, said suddenly, with her fascinating smile, 'that after being converted to the true religion, I cannot be bound by any obligations laid upon me by a false religion.'

Her spiritual adviser was astounded at the simplicity of this solution, as simple as the solution of Columbus's egg. He was enchanted at the unexpected rapidity of his pupil's progress, but could not abandon the edifice of subtle argument that had cost him mental effort.

'Let us understand each other,' he said, with a smile; and began to find arguments to refute his spiritual daughter's contention.

VII

ELLEN perceived that the matter was very simple and easy from the ecclesiastical point of view, but that her spiritual counsellors raised difficulties simply because they were apprehensive of the way in which it might be looked at by the temporal authorities.

And, consequently, Ellen decided in her own mind that the way must be paved for society to look at the matter in the true light. She excited the jealousy of the old dignitary, and said the same thing to him as she had to her other suitor—that is, gave him to understand that the sole means of obtaining exclusive rights over her was to marry her. The elderly dignitary was, like the young foreign prince, for the first moment taken aback at this proposal of marriage from a wife whose husband was living. But Ellen's unfaltering confidence in asserting that it was a matter as simple and natural as the marriage of an unmarried girl had its effect on him too. Had the slightest traces of hesitation, shame, or reserve been perceptible in Ellen herself, her case would have been undoubtedly lost. But far from it; with perfect directness and simple-hearted naïveté, she told her intimate friends (and that term included all Petersburg), that both the prince and the dignitary had made her proposals of marriage, and that she loved both, and was afraid of grieving either.

The rumour was immediately all over Petersburg—not that Ellen wanted a divorce from her husband (had such a rumour been discussed very many persons would have set themselves against any such illegal proceeding)—but that the unhappy, interesting Ellen was in hesitation which of her two suitors to marry. The question was no longer how far any marriage was possible, but simply which would be the more suitable match for her, and how the court would look at the question. There were, indeed, certain strait-laced people who could not rise to the high level of the subject, and saw in the project a desecration of the sanctity of marriage; but such persons were few in number, and they held their tongues; while the majority were interested in the question of Ellen's happiness, and which would be the better match for her. As to whether it were right or wrong for a wife to marry when her husband was alive, that was not discussed, as the question was evidently not a subject of doubt for persons 'wiser than you and me' (as was said), and to doubt the correctness of their decision would be risking the betrayal of one's ignorance and absence of *savoir faire*.

Marya Dmitryevna Ahrosimov, who had come that summer to Petersburg to see one of her sons, was the only person who ventured on the direct expression of a contrary opinion. Meeting Ellen at a ball, Marya Dmitryevna stopped her in the middle of the room, and in the midst of a general silence said to her, in her harsh voice:

'So you are going to pass on from one husband to another, I hear! You think, I dare say, it's a new fashion you are setting. But you are not the first, madam. That's a very old idea. They do the same in all the . . .' And with these words, Marya Dmitryevna tucked up her broad sleeves with her usual menacing action, and looking severely round her, walked across the ballroom.

Though people were afraid of Marya Dmitryevna, yet in Petersburg they looked on her as a sort of buffoon, and therefore of all her words they noticed only the last coarse one, and repeated it to one another in whispers, supposing that the whole point of her utterance lay in that.

Prince Vassily had of late dropped into very frequently forgetting what he had said, and repeating the same phrase a hundred times; and every time he happened to see his daughter he used to say:

'Ellen, I have a word to say to you,' he would say, drawing her aside, and pulling her arm downwards. 'I have got wind of certain projects relative to . . . you know. Well, my dear child, you know how my father's heart rejoices to know you are . . . You have suffered so much. But, my dear child, consult only your heart. That's all I tell you.' And concealing an emotion identical on each occasion, he pressed his cheek to his daughter's cheek and left her.

Bilibin, who had not lost his reputation as a wit, was a disinterested friend of Ellen's; one of those friends always to be seen in the train of brilliant women, men friends who can never pass into the rank of lovers. One day, in a 'small and intimate circle,' Bilibin gave his friend Ellen his views on the subject.

'*Écoutez*, Bilibin' (Ellen always called friends of the category to which Bilibin belonged by their surnames), and she touched his coat-sleeve with her white, beringed fingers. 'Tell me, as you would a sister, what ought I to do? Which of the two?'

Bilibin wrinkled up the skin over his eyebrows, and pondered with a smile on his lips.

'You do not take me unawares, you know,' he said. 'As a true friend, I have thought, and thought again of your affair. You see, if you marry the prince'—(the younger suitor) he crooked his finger—'you lose for ever the chance of marrying the other, and then you displease the court. (There is a sort of relationship, you know.) But if you marry the old count, you make the happiness of his last days. And then as widow of the great . . . the prince will not be making a *mésalliance* in marrying you . . .' and Bilibin let the wrinkles run out of his face.

'That's a real friend!' said Ellen beaming, and once more touching Bilibin's sleeve. 'But the fact is I love them both, and I don't want to make them unhappy. I would give my life for the happiness of both,' she declared.

Bilibin shrugged his shoulders to denote that for such a trouble even he could suggest no remedy.

'*Une maîtresse-femme!* That is what's called putting the question squarely. She would like to be married to all three at once,' thought Bilibin.

'But do tell me what is your husband's view of the question?' he said, the security of his reputation saving him from all fear of discrediting himself by so naïve a question. 'Does he consent?'

'Oh, he is so fond of me!' said Ellen, who, for some unknown reason, fancied that Pierre too adored her. '*Il fera tout pour moi.*'

Bilibin puckered up his face in preparation of the coming *mot*.

'*Même le divorce?*' he said.

Ellen laughed.

Among the persons who ventured to question the legality of the proposed marriage was Ellen's mother, Princess Kuragin. She had constantly suffered pangs of envy of her daughter, and now when the ground for such envy was the one nearest to her own heart, she could not reconcile herself to the idea of it.

She consulted a Russian priest to ascertain how far divorce and re-marriage was possible for a woman in her husband's lifetime. The priest assured her that this was impossible; and to her delight referred her to the text in the Gospel in which (as it seemed to the priest) re-marriage during the lifetime of the husband was directly forbidden.

Armed with these arguments, which seemed to her irrefutable, Princess Kuragin drove round to her daughter's early one morning in order to find her alone.

Ellen heard her mother's protests to the end, and smiled with bland sarcasm.

'You see it is plainly said: "He who marryeth her that is divorced..."'

'O mamma, don't talk nonsense. You don't understand. In my position I have duties...' Ellen began, passing out of Russian into French, for in the former language she always felt a lack of clearness about her case.

'But, my dear...'

'O mamma, how is it you don't understand that the Holy Father, who has the right of granting dispensations...'

At that moment the lady companion, who lived in Ellen's house, came in to announce that his highness was in the drawing-room, and wished to see her.

'No, tell him I don't want to see him, that I am furious with him for not keeping his word.'

'Countess, there is mercy for every sin,' said a young man with fair hair and a long face and long nose.

The old princess rose respectfully and curtsied at his entrance. The young man took no notice of her. Princess Kuragin nodded to her daughter, and swam to the door.

'Yes, she is right,' thought the old princess, all of whose convictions had been dissipated by the appearance of his highness on the scene. 'She is right; but how was it in our youth—gone now for ever—we knew nothing of this? And it is so simple,' thought Princess Kuragin, as she settled herself in her carriage.

At the beginning of August Ellen's affairs were settled, and she wrote to her husband (who, as she supposed, was deeply attached to her) a letter, in which she made known to him her intention of marrying N. N. She informed him also of her conversion to the one true faith, and begged him to go through all the necessary formalities for obtaining a divorce, of which the bearer of the letter would give him further details. 'On which I pray God to have you in His holy and powerful keeping. Your friend, Ellen.'

This letter was brought to Pierre's house at the time when he was on the field of Borodino.

VIII

AT the end of the day of Borodino, Pierre ran for a second time from Raevsky's battery, and with crowds of soldiers crossed the ravine on the way to Knyazkovo. There he reached an ambulance tent, and seeing blood and hearing screams and groans, he hurried on, caught up in a mob of soldiers.

The one thing Pierre desired now with his whole soul was to get away from the terrible sensations in which he had passed that day, to get back into the ordinary conditions of life, and to go to sleep quietly indoors in his own bed. He felt that only in the ordinary conditions of life would he be fit to understand himself and all he had seen and felt. But the ordinary conditions of life were nowhere to be found.

Though bullets and cannon-balls were not whistling here on the road along which he was striding, still he saw here on all sides the same sights as on the field of battle. There were everywhere the same suffering, exhausted, and sometimes strangely indifferent faces; everywhere the same blood and soldiers' overcoats, the same sound of firing at a distance, yet still rousing the same horror. There was heat and dust besides.

After walking about three versts along the Mozhaisk road, Pierre sat down by the roadside.

The shadows of night were beginning to fall over the earth, and the roar of cannon died down. Pierre lay leaning on his elbow, and lay so a long while, gazing at the shadows passing by him in the dusk. He was continually fancying that a cannon-ball was swooping down upon him with a fearful whiz. He started and sat up. He had no idea how long he had been there. In the middle of the night, three soldiers, dragging branches after them, settled themselves near him and began making a fire.

Casting sidelong glances at Pierre, the soldiers lighted the fire, set a pot on it, broke up their biscuits into it, and put in some lard. The pleasant odour of the savoury and greasy mess blended with the smell of smoke. Pierre raised himself and sighed. The soldiers (there were three of them) were eating and talking among themselves, without taking any notice of Pierre.

'And what lot will you be one of?' one of the soldiers suddenly asked Pierre, evidently suggesting in this inquiry precisely what Pierre was thinking about. 'If you are hungry we'll give you some, only tell us whether you're a true man.'

'I?' . . . said Pierre, feeling the necessity of minimising his social position as far as possible, so as to be closer to the soldiers and more within their range. 'I am really a militia officer, but my company's nowhere about; I came to the battle and lost sight of my comrades.'

'Well! Fancy that!' said one of the soldiers.

Another soldier shook his head.

'Well, you can have some of the mash, if you like!' said the first, and licking a wooden spoon he gave it to Pierre.

Pierre squatted by the fire, and fell to eating the mess in the pot, which seemed to him the most delicious dish he had ever tasted. While he was bending over the pot, helping himself to big spoonfuls and greedily munching one after another, the soldiers stared at him in silence.

'Where do you want to go? Tell us!' the first of them asked again.

'To Mozhaisk.'

'You're a gentleman, then?'

'Yes.'

'And what's your name?'

'Pyotr Kirillovitch.'

'Well, Pyotr Kirillovitch, come along, we'll take you there.'

In the pitch dark the soldiers and Pierre walked to Mozhaisk.

The cocks were crowing when they reached Mozhaisk, and began ascending the steep hill into the town.

Pierre walked on with the soldiers, entirely forgetting that his inn was at the bottom of the hill and he had passed it. He would not have been aware of this—so preoccupied was he—if he had not chanced half-way up the hill to stumble across his groom, who had been to look for him in the town, and was on his way back to the inn. The groom recognised Pierre by his hat, which gleamed white in the dark.

'Your excellency!' he cried, 'why, we had quite given you up. How is it you are on foot? And, mercy on us, where are you going?'

'Oh, to be sure...' said Pierre.

The soldiers halted.

'Well, found your own folks then?' said one of them.

'Well, good-bye to you—Pyotr Kirillovitch, wasn't it?'

'Good-bye, Pyotr Kirillovitch!' said the other voices.

'Good-bye,' said Pierre, and with the groom he turned in the direction of the inn.

'I ought to give them something!' thought Pierre, feeling for his pocket. 'No, better not,' some inner voice prompted him.

There was not a room at the inn: all were full. Pierre went out into the yard, and muffling his head up, lay down in his carriage.

IX

PIERRE had hardly put his head on the pillow when he felt that he was dropping asleep. But all of a sudden he heard, almost with the distinctness of reality, the sound of the boom, boom, boom of the cannon, the groans and shrieks and dull thud of the falling shell, smelt the blood and powder; and the feeling of horror, of the dread of death came over him. He opened his eyes in a panic, and put his head out from the cloak. All was quiet in the yard. The only sound came from a servant of some sort talking with the porter at the gate, and splashing through the mud. Over Pierre's head, under the dark, wooden eaves, he heard pigeons fluttering, startled by the movement he had made in sitting up. The whole yard was pervaded by the strong smell of a tavern —full of peaceful suggestion and soothing relief to Pierre—the smell of hay, of dung, and of tar. Between two dark sheds he caught a glimpse of the pure, starlit sky.

'Thank God, that is all over!' thought Pierre, covering his head up again. 'Oh, how awful terror is, and how shamefully I gave way to it! But they ... *they* were firm and calm all the while up to the end ...' he thought. *They*, in Pierre's mind, meant the soldiers, those who had been on the battery, and those who had given him food, and those who had prayed to the holy picture. *They*—those strange people, of whom he had known nothing hitherto—*they* stood out clearly and sharply in his mind apart from all other people.

'To be a soldier, simply a soldier!' thought Pierre as he fell asleep. 'To enter with one's whole nature into that common life, to be filled with what makes them what they are. But how is one to cast off all that is superfluous, devilish in one's self, all the burden of the outer man? At one time I might have been the same. I might have run away from my father as I wanted to. After the duel with Dolohov too I might have been sent for a soldier.'

And into Pierre's imagination flashed a picture of the dinner at the club, at which he had challenged Dolohov, then the image of his benefactor at Torzhok. And there rose before his mind a solemn meeting of the lodge. It was taking place at the English Club. And some one he knew, some one near and dear to him, was sitting at the end of the table. 'Why, it is he! It is my benefactor. But surely he died?' thought Pierre. 'Yes, he did die, but I didn't know he was alive. And how sorry I was when he died, and how glad I am he is alive again!' On one side of the table were sitting Anatole, Dolohov, Nesvitsky, Denisov, and others like them (in Pierre's dream these people formed as distinct a class apart as those other men who he had called *them* to himself), and those people, Anatole and Dolohov, were loudly shouting and singing. But through their clamour the voice of his benefactor could be heard speaking all the while, and the sound of his voice was as weighty and as uninterrupted as the din of the battlefield, but it was pleasant and comforting. Pierre did not understand what his benefactor was saying, but he knew (the category of his ideas, too, was distinct in his dream) that he was talking of goodness, of the possibility of being like *them*. And *they* with their simple, good, plucky faces were surrounding his benefactor on all sides. But though they were kindly, they did not look at Pierre; they did not know him. Pierre wanted to attract their notice, and to speak to them. He got up, but at the same instant became aware that his legs were bare and chill.

He felt ashamed, and put his arm over his legs, from which his cloak had in fact slipped off. For an instant Pierre opened his eyes as he pulled up the cloak, and saw the same roofs, and posts, and yard, but it was now full of bluish light, and glistening with dew or frost.

'It's getting light,' thought Pierre. 'But that's not the point. I want to hear and understand the benefactor's words.'

He muffled himself in the cloak again, but the masonic dinner and his benefactor would not come back. All that remained were thoughts, clearly expressed in words, ideas; some voice was speaking, or Pierre was thinking.

When he recalled those thoughts later, although they had been evoked by the impressions of that day, Pierre was convinced that they were uttered by some one outside himself. It seemed to him that he had never been capable of thinking those thoughts and expressing them in that form in his waking moments.

'The most difficult thing is the subjection of man's will to the law of God,' said the voice. 'Simplicity is the submission to God; there is no escaping from Him. And *they* are simple. *They* do not talk, but act. A word uttered is silver, but unuttered is golden. No one can be master of anything while he fears death. And all things belong to him who fears it not. If it were not for suffering, a man would know not his limits, would know not himself. The hardest thing' (Pierre thought or heard in his dream) 'is to know how to unite in one's soul the significance of the whole. To unite the whole?' Pierre said to himself. 'No, not to unite. One cannot unite one's thoughts, but to *harness* together all those ideas, that's what's wanted. Yes, one *must harness* together, *harness* together,' Pierre repeated to himself with a thrill of ecstasy, feeling that those words, and only those words, expressed what he wanted to express, and solved the whole problem fretting him.

'Yes, one must *harness* together; it's time to *harness* . . .'

'We want to harness the horses; it's time to harness the horses, your excellency! Your excellency,' some voice was repeating, 'we want to harness the horses; it's time . . .'

It was the groom waking Pierre. The sun was shining full in Pierre's face. He glanced at the dirty tavern yard; at the well in the middle of it soldiers were watering their thin horses; and wagons were moving out of the gate.

He turned away with repugnance, and shutting his eyes, made haste to huddle up again on the seat of the carriage. 'No, I don't want that; I don't want to see and understand that; I want to understand what was revealed to me in my sleep. Another second and I should have understood it all. But what am I to do? To harness, but how harness all together?' And Pierre felt with horror that the whole meaning of what he had seen and thought in his dream had slipped away.

The groom, the coachman, and the porter told Pierre that an officer had come with the news that the French were advancing on Mozhaisk and our troops were retreating.

Pierre got up, and ordering the carriage to be got out and to drive after him, crossed the town on foot.

The troops were marching out, leaving tens of thousands of wounded behind. The wounded could be seen at the windows of the houses, and were crowding the yards and streets. Screams, oaths, and blows could be heard in the streets about the carts which were to carry away the wounded. Pierre put his carriage at the service of a wounded general of his acquaintance, and drove with him to Moscow. On the way he was told of the death of his brother-in-law, Anatole, and of the death of Prince Andrey.

X

ON the 30th Pierre returned to Moscow. Almost at the city gates he was met by an adjutant of Count Rastoptchin's.

'Why, we have been looking for you everywhere,' said the adjutant. 'The count urgently wants to see you. He begs you to come to him at once on very important business.' Instead of going home, Pierre hailed a cab-driver and drove to the governor's.

Count Rastoptchin had only that morning arrived from his summer villa at Sokolniky. The ante-room and waiting-room in the count's house were full of officials, who had been summoned by him, or had come to him for instructions. Vassiltchekov and Platov had already seen the count, and informed him that the defence of Moscow was out of the question, and the city would be surrendered. Though the news was being concealed from the citizens, the heads of various departments and officials of different kinds knew that Moscow would soon be in the hands of the enemy, just as Count Rastoptchin knew it. And all of them to escape personal responsibility had come to the governor to inquire how to act in regard to the offices in their charge.

At the moment when Pierre went into the waiting-room, a courier from the army was just coming out from an interview with the count.

The courier waved his hand with a hopeless air at the questions with which he was besieged, and walked across the room.

While he waited, Pierre watched with weary eyes the various officials —young, old, military, and civilian, important and insignificant—who were gathered together in the room. All seemed dissatisfied and uneasy. Pierre went up to one group of functionaries, among whom he recognised an acquaintance. After greeting him, they went on with their conversation.

'Well, to send out and bring back again would be no harm; but in the present position of affairs there's no answering for anything.'

'But look here, what he writes,' said another, pointing to a printed paper he held in his hand.

'That's a different matter. That's necessary for the common people,' said the first.

'What is it?' asked Pierre.

'The new proclamation.'

Pierre took it and began to read.

'His highness the prince has passed Mozhaisk, so as to unite with the troops that are going to join him, and has taken up a strong position, where the enemy cannot attack him suddenly. Forty-eight cannon with shells have been sent him from here, and his highness declares that he will defend Moscow to the last drop of blood, and is ready even to fight in the streets. Don't mind, brothers, that the courts of justice are closed; we must take our measures, and we'll deal with miscreants in our own fashion. When the time comes, I shall have need of some gallant fellows, both of town and country. I will give the word in a couple of days; but now there's no need, and I hold my peace. The axe is useful; the pike, too, is not to be despised; but best of all is the three-pronged fork: a Frenchman is no heavier than a sheaf of rye. Tomorrow after dinner, I shall take the Iversky Holy Mother to St. Catherine's Hospital to the wounded. There we will consecrate the water; they will soon be well again. I, too, am well now; one of my eyes was bad, but now I look well out of both.'

'Why, I was told by military men,' said Pierre, 'that there could be no fighting in the town itself, and the position . . .'

'To be sure, that's just what we are saying,' said the first speaker.

'But what does that mean: "One of my eyes was bad, but now I look out of both"?' asked Pierre.

'The count had a sty in his eye,' said the adjutant smiling; 'and he was very much put out when I told him people were coming to ask what was the matter. And oh, count,' he said suddenly, addressing Pierre with a smile, 'we have been hearing that you are in trouble with domestic anxieties, that the countess, your spouse . . .'

'I have heard nothing about it,' said Pierre indifferently. 'What is it you have heard?'

'Oh, you know, stories are so often made up. I only repeat what I hear.'

'What have you heard?'

'Oh, they say,' said the adjutant again with the same smile; 'that the countess, your wife, is preparing to go abroad. It's most likely nonsense.'

'It may be,' said Pierre, looking absent-mindedly about him. 'Who is that?' he asked, indicating a tall old man in a clean blue overcoat, with a big, snow-white beard and eyebrows and a ruddy face.

'That? Oh, he's a merchant; that is, he's the restaurant-keeper, Vereshtchagin. You have heard the story of the proclamation, I dare say?'

'Oh, so that's Vereshtchagin!' said Pierre, scrutinising the firm, calm face of the old merchant, and seeking in it some token of treachery.

'That's not the man himself. That's the father of the fellow who wrote the proclamation,' said the adjutant. 'The young man himself is in custody, and I fancy it will go hardly with him.'

A little old gentleman with a star, and a German official with a cross on his neck, joined the group.

'It's a complicated story, you see,' the adjutant was relating. 'The proclamation appeared two months ago. It was brought to the count. He ordered inquiry to be made. Well, Gavrilo Ivanitch made investigations; the proclamation had passed through some sixty-three hands. We come to one and ask, From whom did you get it? From so and so. And the next refers us on to so and so; and in that way they traced it to Vereshtchagin . . . a half-educated merchant's son, one of those pretty dears you know,' said the adjutant smiling. 'He too was asked, From whom did you get it? And we knew very well from whom he had it really. He could have had it from no one but the director of the post-office. But it was clear there was an understanding between them. He says he got it from no one, but had composed it himself. And threaten him and question him as they would, he stuck to it, he had written it himself. So the matter was reported, and the count had him sent for. "From whom did you get the proclamation?" "I wrote it myself." Well! you know the count,' said the adjutant, with a smile of pride and delight. 'He was fearfully angry; and only fancy the insolence, and lying, and stubbornness!'

'Oh! the count wanted him to say it was from Klutcharyov, I understand,' said Pierre.

'Oh no, not at all,' said the adjutant in dismay. 'Klutcharyov had sins enough to answer for without that, and that's why he was banished. But any way, the count was very indignant. "How could you write it?" says the count. He took up the *Hamburg Gazette* that was on the table. "Here it is. You did not compose it, but translated it, and very badly too, because you don't even know French, you fool." What do you think? "No," says he, "I have never read any gazettes; I made it up."

"But if so, you're a traitor, and I'll hand you over for judgment, and you will be hanged." "Tell us from whom you got it." "I have not seen any gazettes; I composed it." So the matter rests. The count sent for the father; he sticks to the same story. And they had him tried, and he was sentenced, I believe, to hard labour. Now the father has come to petition in his favour. But he is a worthless young scamp! You know the style of spoilt merchant's son, a regular dandy and lady-killer; has attended lectures of some sort, and so fancies that he's above everybody. A regular young scamp! His father has an eating-house here on the Kamenny bridge; and in the shop, you know, there is a great picture of God the Supporter of All, represented with a sceptre in one hand and the empire in the other; well, he took that picture home for a few days, and what do you suppose he did! He got hold of some wretched painter...'

XI

IN the middle of this new story Pierre was summoned to the governor.

He went into Count Rastoptchin's study. Rastoptchin, frowning, passed his hand across his forehead and eyes as Pierre entered. A short man was saying something, but as soon as Pierre walked in he stopped, and went out.

'Ah! greetings to you, valiant warrior,' said Rastoptchin as soon as the other man had left the room. 'We have been hearing about your *prouesses*! But that's not the point. *Mon cher, entre nous*, are you a mason?' said Count Rastoptchin in a severe tone, that suggested that it was a crime to be so, but that he intended to pardon it. Pierre did not speak. '*Mon cher, je suis bien informé*; but I know that there are masons and masons, and I hope you don't belong to those among them who, by way of regenerating the human race, are trying to ruin Russia.'

'Yes, I am a mason,' answered Pierre.

'Well then, look here, my dear boy. You are not unaware, I dare say, of the fact that Speransky and Magnitsky have been sent—to their proper place—and the same has been done with Klutcharyov and the others who, under the guise of building up the temple of Solomon, have been trying to destroy the temple of their fatherland. You may take it for granted there are good reasons for it, and that I could not have banished the director of the post-office here if he had not been a dangerous person. Now, it has reached my ears that you sent him your carriage to get out of the town, and that you have even taken charge of his papers. I like you, and wish you no harm, and as you are half my age, I advise you, as a father might, to break off all connection with people of that sort, and to get away from here yourself as quickly as you can.'

'But what was Klutcharyov's crime?' asked Pierre.

'That's my business; and it's not yours to question me,' cried Rastoptchin.

'If he is accused of having circulated Napoleon's proclamation, the charge has not been proved,' said Pierre, not looking at Rastoptchin. 'And Vereshtchagin ...'

'*Nous y voilà*,' Rastoptchin suddenly broke in, scowling and shouting louder than ever. 'Vereshtchagin is a traitor and a deceiver, who will receive the punishment he deserves,' he said, with the vindictiveness with which people speak at the recollection of an affront. 'But I did not send for you to criticise my actions, but in order to give you advice or a command, if you will have it so. I beg you to break off all connection with Klutcharyov and his set, and to leave the town. And I'll knock the nonsense out of them, wherever I may find it.' And, probably becoming conscious that he was taking a heated tone with Bezuhov, who was as yet guilty of no offence, he added, taking Pierre's hand cordially: 'We are on the eve of a public disaster, and I haven't time to say civil things to every one who has business with me. My head is at times in a perfect whirl. Well, what are you going to do, you personally?'

'Oh, nothing,' answered Pierre, with his eyes still downcast, and no change in the expression of his dreamy face.

The count frowned.

'*Un conseil d'ami, mon cher*. Decamp, and as soon as may be, that's my advice. *A bon entendeur, salut!* Good-bye, my dear boy. Oh, by the way,' he called after him at the door, 'is it true the countess has fallen into the clutches of the holy fathers of the Society of Jesus?'

Pierre made no answer. He walked out from Rastoptchin's room, scowling and wrathful as he had never been seen before.

By the time he reached home it was getting dark. Eight persons of different kinds were waiting on him that evening. A secretary of a committee, the colonel of his battalion of militia, his steward, his bailiff, and other persons with petitions. All of them had business matters with Pierre, which he had to settle. He had no understanding of their questions, nor interest in them, and answered them with the sole object of getting rid of these people. At last he was left alone, and he broke open and read his wife's letter.

'*They*—the soldiers on the battery, Prince Andrey killed ... the old man ... Simplicity is submission to God's will. One has to suffer ... the significance of the whole ... one must harness all together ... my wife is going to be married ... One must forget and understand ...'

And, without undressing, he threw himself on his bed and at once fell asleep.

When he waked up next morning his steward came in to announce that a police official was below, sent expressly by Count Rastoptchin to find out whether Count Bezuhov had gone, or was going away.

A dozen different people were waiting in the drawing-room to see Pierre on business. Pierre dressed in haste, and instead of going down to see them, he ran down the back staircase and out by the back entry to the gates.

From that moment till the occupation of Moscow was over, no one of Bezuhov's household saw him again, nor could discover his whereabouts, in spite of every effort to track him.

XII

THE Rostovs remained in Moscow till the 1st of September, the day before the enemy entered the city.

After Petya had joined Obolensky's regiment of Cossacks and had gone away to Byely Tserkov, where the regiment was being enrolled, the countess fell into a panic of terror. The idea that both her sons were at the war, that they had both escaped from under her wing, that any day either of them—and possibly even both at once, like the three sons of a lady of her acquaintance—might be killed, seemed for the first time that summer to strike her imagination with cruel vividness. She tried to get Nikolay back, wanted to go herself after Petya, or to obtain some post for him in Petersburg; but all these seemed equally impossible. Petya could not be brought back except by the return of his regiment, or through being transferred to another regiment on active service. Nikolay was somewhere at the front, and nothing had been heard from him since the letter in which he had given a detailed account of his meeting with Princess Marya. The countess could not sleep at nights, and when she did sleep, she dreamed that her sons had been killed. After much talking the matter over, and many consultations of friends, the count at last hit on a means for soothing the countess. He got Petya transferred from Obolensky's regiment to Bezuhov's, which was in formation near Moscow. Though, even so, Petya remained in the army, by this exchange the countess had the consolation of seeing one son at least again under her wing; and she hoped to manage not to let her Petya escape her again, but to succeed in getting him always appointed to places where there would be no risk of his being in battle. While Nikolay had been the only one in danger, the countess had fancied (and had suffered some pricks of conscience on the subject) that she loved her elder son better than the other children. But now that her younger boy, the scapegrace Petya, always idle at his lessons, always in mischief, and teasing every one, her little Petya, with his snub-nose, his merry black eyes, his fresh colour, and the soft down just showing on his cheeks, had slipped away into the company of those big, dreadful, cruel men, who were fighting away somewhere about something, and finding a sort of pleasure in it—now it seemed to the mother that she loved him more, far more, than all the rest. The nearer the time came for the return of her longed-for Petya to Moscow, the greater was the uneasiness of the countess. She positively thought she would never live to see such happiness. Not only Sonya's presence, even her favourite Natasha's, even her husband's company, irritated the countess. 'What do I want with them, I want no one but Petya!' she thought. One day towards the end of August, the Rostovs received a second letter from Nikolay. He wrote from the province of Voronezh, where he had been sent to procure remounts. This letter did not soothe the countess. Knowing that one son was out of danger, she seemed to feel even greater alarm on Petya's account.

Although by the 20th of August almost all the Rostovs' acquaintances had left Moscow; although everybody was trying to persuade the countess to get away as quickly as possible, she would not hear of leaving till her treasure, her idolised Petya, had come back. On the 28th of August Petya arrived. The morbidly passionate tenderness with which his mother received him was by no means gratifying to the sixteen-year-old officer. Though his mother concealed her intention of never letting him escape from under her wing again, Petya divined her plans, and instinctively afraid of his mother's making him too soft, of her 'making a ninny' of him (as he expressed it in his own mind), he treated her rather coolly, avoided being with her, and during his stay in Moscow devoted himself exclusively to Natasha, for whom he had always had the warmest brotherly affection, almost approaching adoration.

The count, with his characteristic carelessness, had by the 28th made no preparations for leaving, and the waggons that were to come from their Moscow and Ryazan estate to remove all their property out of the house only arrived on the 30th.

From the 28th to the 31st, Moscow was all bustle and movement. Every day thousands of wounded from the field of Borodino were brought in at the Dorogomilov gate and conveyed across Moscow, and thousands of vehicles, full of residents and their belongings, were driving out at the gates on the opposite side of the city. In spite of Rastoptchin's placards—either arising independently of them, or perhaps in consequence of them—the strangest and most contradictory rumours were circulating about the town. Some said that every one was forbidden to leave the city; others asserted that all the holy pictures had been taken from the churches, and every one was to be driven out of Moscow by force. Some said there had been another battle after Borodino, in which the French had been utterly defeated; others declared that the whole Russian army had been annihilated. Some talked of the Moscow militia, which was to advance, preceded by priests, to Three Hills; others whispered that Father Augustin had been forbidden to leave, that traitors had been caught, that the peasants were in revolt, and were plundering those who left the town, and so on. But all this was only talk: in reality even though the council at Fili, at which it was decided to abandon Moscow, had not yet taken place, all—those who were leaving and those who were staying—felt that Moscow would be surrendered, though they did not say so freely, and felt that they must make all haste to escape, and to save their property. There was a feeling that there must come a general crash and change, yet till the 1st of September everything went on unchanged. Like a criminal being led to the gallows, who knows in a minute he must die, and yet stares about, and puts straight the cap awry on his head, Moscow instinctively went on with the daily routine of life, though aware that the hour of ruin was approaching, when all the customary conditions of life would be at an end.

During the three days preceding the occupation of Moscow, the whole Rostov family was busily engaged in various practical ways. The head of the family, Count Ilya Andreitch, was continually driving about the town, picking up all the rumours that were in circulation, and while at home, gave superficial and hasty directions for the preparations for departure.

The countess superintended the sorting out of things to be packed; she was out of humour with every one, and was in continual pursuit of Petya, who was as continually escaping from her, and exciting her jealousy by spending all his time with Natasha. Sonya was the only person who really undertook the practical business of getting things packed. But Sonya had been particularly silent and melancholy of late. She had been present when Nikolay's letter mentioning Princess Marya had elicited the most delighted deductions from the countess, who saw in Nikolay's meeting with Princess Marya the direct intervention of Providence.

'I was never really happy,' said the countess, 'when Bolkonsky was engaged to Natasha, but I had always longed for Nikolay to marry the princess, and I have always had a presentiment about it. And what a good thing it would be!'

Sonya felt that this was true; that the only possibility of retrieving the Rostovs' position was by Nikolay's marriage to an heiress, and that the princess would be an excellent match for him. But this reflection was very bitter for her. In spite, or perhaps in consequence, of her sadness, she undertook the difficult task of seeing after the sorting and packing of the household goods, and for whole days together she was busily employed. The count and countess referred to her when they had any orders to give. Petya and Natasha, on the contrary, did nothing to help their parents, but were generally in every one's way, and were only a hindrance. And all day long the house resounded with their flying footsteps and shouts and shrieks of causeless mirth. They laughed and were gay, not in the least because there was reason for laughter. But they were gay and glad at heart, and so everything that happened was reason enough for gaiety and laughter in them. Petya was in high spirits because he had left home a boy, and come back (so every one told him) a fine young man, because he was at home, because he had left Byely Tserkov, where there seemed no hope of being soon on active service, and come to Moscow where there would be fighting in a few days, and above all, because Natasha, whose lead he always followed, was in high spirits. Natasha was gay, because she had too long been sad, and now nothing reminded her of the cause of her sadness, and she was quite strong again. She was gay too, because she needed some one to adore her (the adoration of others was like the grease on the wheels, without which her mechanism never worked quite smoothly), and Petya did adore her. And above all, they were both gay, because there was war at the very gates of Moscow, because there would be fighting at the barriers, because arms were being given out, and everybody was rushing about, and altogether something extraordinary was happening, which is always inspiriting, especially for the young.

XIII

ON Saturday, the 31st of August, the whole household of the Rostovs seemed turned upside down. All the doors stood wide open, all the furniture had been moved about or carried out, looking-glasses and pictures had been taken down. The rooms were littered up with boxes, with hay and packing paper and cord. Peasants and house-serfs were tramping about the parquet floors carrying out the baggage. The courtyard was crowded with peasants' carts, some piled high with goods and corded up, others still standing empty.

The voices and steps of the immense multitude of servants and of peasants, who had come with the carts, resounded through the courtyard and the house. The count had been out since early morning. The countess had a headache from the noise and bustle, and was lying down in the new divan-room with compresses steeped in vinegar on her head. Petya was not at home; he had gone off to see a comrade, with whom he was planning to get transferred from the militia to a regiment at the front. Sonya was in the great hall, superintending the packing of the china and glass. Natasha was sitting on the floor in her dismantled room among heaps of dresses, ribbons, and scarfs. She sat gazing immovably at the floor, holding in her hands an old ball-dress, the very dress, now out of fashion, in which she had been to her first Petersburg ball.

Natasha was ashamed of doing nothing when every one in the house was so busy, and several times that morning she had tried to set to work; but her soul was not in it; and she was utterly unable to do anything unless all her heart and soul were in it. She stood over Sonya while she packed the china, and tried to help; but soon threw it up, and went to her room to pack her own things. At first she had found it amusing to give away her dresses and ribbons to the maids, but afterwards when it came to packing what was left, it seemed a wearisome task.

'Dunyasha, you'll pack it all, dear? Yes? yes?'

And when Dunyasha readily undertook to do it all for her, Natasha sat down on the floor with the old ball-dress in her hands, and fell to dreaming on subjects far removed from what should have been occupying her mind then. From the reverie she had fallen into, Natasha was aroused by the talk of the maids in the next room and their hurried footsteps from their room to the backstairs. Natasha got up and looked out of the window. A huge train of carts full of wounded men had stopped in the street.

The maids, the footmen, the housekeeper, the old nurse, the cooks, the coachmen, the grooms, and the scullion-boys were all at the gates, staring at the wounded men.

Natasha flung a white pocket-handkerchief over her hair, and holding the corners in both hands, went out into the street.

The old housekeeper, Mavra Kuzminishna, had left the crowd standing at the gate, and gone up to a cart with a tilt of bast-mats thrown over it. She was talking to a pale young officer who was lying in this cart. Natasha took a few steps forward, and stood still timidly, holding her kerchief on and listening to what the housekeeper was saying.

'So you have no one then in Moscow?' Mavra Kuzminishna was saying. 'You'd be more comfortable in some apartment. . . . In our house even. The masters are all leaving.'

'I don't know if it would be allowed,' said the officer in a feeble voice.

'There's our chief officer ... ask him,' and he pointed to a stout major who had turned back and was walking along the row of carts down the street.

Natasha glanced with frightened eyes into the face of the wounded officer, and at once went to meet the major.

'May the wounded men stay in our house?' she asked.

The major with a smile put his hand to his cap.

'What is your pleasure, ma'mselle?' he said, screwing up his eyes and smiling.

Natasha quietly repeated her question, and her face and her whole manner, though she still kept hold of the corners of the pocket-handkerchief, was so serious, that the major left off smiling, and after a moment's pondering—as though asking himself how far it were possible—he gave her an affirmative answer.

'Oh yes, why not, they may,' he said.

Natasha gave a slight nod, and went back with rapid steps to Mavra Kuzminishna, who was still talking with commiserating sympathy to the young officer.

'They may; he said they might!' whispered Natasha.

The officer in the covered-cart turned into the Rostovs' courtyard, and dozens of carts of wounded men began at the invitation of the inhabitants to drive up to the entries of the houses in Povarsky Street. Natasha was evidently delighted at having to do with new people in conditions quite outside the ordinary routine of life. She joined Mavra Kuzminishna in trying to get as many as possible driven into their yard.

'We must ask your papa though,' said Mavra Kuzminishna.

'Nonsense, nonsense. What does it matter? For one day, we'll move into the drawing-room. We can give them all our half of the house.'

'What an idea! what next? The lodge, may be, the men's room, and old nurse's room; and you must ask leave for that.'

'Well, I will ask.'

Natasha ran indoors, and went on tiptoe to the half-open door of the divan-room, where there was a strong smell of vinegar and Hoffmann's drops.

'Are you asleep, mamma?'

'Oh, what chance is there of sleep!' said the countess, who had just dropped into a doze.

'Mamma, darling!' said Natasha, kneeling before her mother and leaning her face against her mother's. 'I am sorry, forgive me, I'll never do it again, I waked you. Mavra Kuzminishna sent me; they have brought some wounded men in, officers, will you allow it? They have nowhere to go; I know you will allow it, . . .' she said rapidly, not taking breath.

'Officers? Who have been brought in? I don't understand,' said the countess.

Natasha laughed, the countess too smiled faintly.

'I knew you would let me . . . so I will tell them so.' And Natasha, kissing her mother, got up and went to the door.

In the hall she met her father, who had come home with bad news.

'We have lingered on too long!' said the count, with unconscious anger in his voice; 'the club's shut up and the police are leaving.'

'Papa, you don't mind my having invited some of the wounded into the house?' said Natasha.

'Of course not,' said the count absently. 'But that's not to the point. I beg you now not to let yourself be taken up with any nonsense, but to help to pack and get off—to get off tomorrow . . .'

And the count gave his butler and servants the same orders. Petya came back at dinner-time, and he too had news to tell them.

He said that the mob was taking up arms today in the Kremlin; that though Rastoptchin's placard said he would give the word two days later, it had really been arranged that all the people should go next day in arms to the Three Hills, and there a great battle was to be fought.

The countess looked in timid horror at her son's eager, excited face, as he told them this. She knew that if she said a word to try and dissuade Petya from going to this battle (she knew how he was enjoying the prospect of it), he would say something about the duty of a man, about honour, and the fatherland—something irrational, masculine, and perverse—which it would be useless to oppose, and all hope of preventing him would be gone. And, therefore, hoping to succeed in setting off before this battle, and in taking Petya with her, to guard and protect them on the road, she said nothing to her son, but after dinner called her husband aside, and with tears besought him to take her away as soon as could be, that night if possible. With the instinctive, feminine duplicity of love, though she had till then shown not the slightest sign of alarm, she declared she should die of terror if they did not get away that very night. She was indeed without feigning afraid now of everything.

XIV

MADAME SCHOSS, who had gone out to visit her daughter, increased the countess's terrors by describing the scenes she had witnessed at a spirit dealer's in Myasnitsky Street. She entered that street on her way home, but could not pass through it owing to the drunken mob raging round the spirit dealer's. She had taken a cab and driven home by a circuitous route, and the driver had told her that the mob had broken open the casks of spirit, that orders had been given to that effect.

After dinner all the Rostov household set to work packing and preparing for their departure with eager haste. The old count, suddenly rousing himself to the task, spent the rest of the day continually trotting from the courtyard into the house and back again, shouting confused instructions to the hurrying servants, and trying to spur them on to even greater haste. Petya looked after things in the yard. Sonya was quite bewildered by the count's contradictory orders, and did not know what to do. The servants raced about the rooms, shouting, quarrelling, and making a noise. Natasha, too, suddenly set to work with the ardour that was characteristic of her in all she did. At first her intervention was sceptically received. No one expected anything serious from her or would obey her instructions. But with heat and perseverance, she insisted on being obeyed, got angry and almost shed tears that they did not heed her, and did at last succeed in impressing them. Her first achievement, which cost her immense effort, and established her authority, was the packing of the rugs. There were a number of costly Gobelin tapestries and Persian rugs in the house. When Natasha set to work, she found two boxes standing open in the hall: one packed almost full of china, the other full of rugs. There was a great deal more china left standing on the tables and there was more still to come from the storeroom. Another third box was needed, and the men had gone to get one.

'Sonya, wait a little, and we'll pack it all without that,' said Natasha.

'You cannot, miss; we have tried already,' said the footman.

'No, wait a minute, please.' And Natasha began taking out the plates and dishes, packed up in paper.

'The dishes would go better in here with the rugs,' she said.

'Why, there are rugs enough left that we shall hardly get into three boxes,' said the footman.

'But do wait a little, please.' And Natasha began rapidly and deftly sorting out the things. 'These we don't want,' she said of the plates of Kiev ware; 'this and this we can pack in the rugs,' she decided, fishing out the Saxony dishes.

'Come, let it alone, Natasha; come, that's enough, we'll pack them,' said Sonya reproachfully.

'What a young lady!' protested the footman.

But Natasha would not give in. She pulled everything out, and began rapidly packing them again, deciding that the commoner rugs and crockery should not be taken at all. When she had taken everything out, she began repacking what was to go; and by sorting out almost all the cheaper goods which were not worth taking, all that was of value was got into two boxes. Only the lid of the box full of rugs would not shut. A few things might have been taken out, but Natasha wanted to manage it in her own way. She unpacked, repacked, squeezed the things in, made the footman and Petya, whom she had drawn into assisting in the work, press on the lid, and herself tried desperately to do the same.

'That will do, Natasha,' Sonya said to her. 'I see you are quite right, but take out just the top one.'

'I won't,' cried Natasha, with one hand holding her disordered hair off her perspiring face, while with the other she squeezed down the rugs. 'Press it, Petya, press it! Vassilitch, press hard!' she cried. The rugs yielded, and the lid closed. Natasha, clapping her hands, shrieked with delight, and tears started into her eyes. But that lasted only a second. She set to work at once on a fresh job; and now the servants put complete faith in her, and the count did not take it amiss when they told him that Natalya Ilyinitshna had given some direction superseding his orders; and the servants came to Natasha to ask whether a cart was packed full enough and whether the loads were to be tied on. The packing went on fast now, thanks to Natasha's supervision; everything useless was left behind, and the most valuable goods were packed as compactly as possible.

But with all their exertions, even late at night everything was not ready. The countess had fallen asleep, and the count put off their departure till morning and went to bed.

Sonya and Natasha slept in the divan-room, without undressing.

That night another wounded officer was driven along Povarsky Street, and Mavra Kuzminishna, who was standing at the gate, had him brought into the Rostovs' yard. The wounded officer must, Mavra Kuzminishna thought, be a man of very great consequence. He was in a coach with the hood let down and a carriage apron completely covering it. An old man, a most respectable-looking valet, was sitting on the box with the driver. A doctor and two soldiers followed the carriage in another conveyance.

'Come into our house, come in. The masters are going away, the whole house is empty,' said the old woman, addressing the old servant.

'Well,' answered the valet, sighing, 'and indeed we have no hope of getting him home alive! We have a house of our own in Moscow, but it is a long way further, and there's no one living in it either.'

'Pray come in, our masters have plenty of everything, and you are welcome,' said Mavra Kuzminishna. 'Is the gentleman very bad, then?' she asked.

'There's no hope! I must ask the doctor.' And the valet got down and went to the vehicle behind.

'Very good,' said the doctor.

The valet went up to the coach again, peeped into it, shook his head, told the coachman to turn into the yard, and stood still beside Mavra Kuzminishna.

'Lord Jesus Christ, have mercy!' she murmured.

Mavra Kuzminishna suggested the wounded man being carried into the house.

'The masters won't say anything . . .' said she.

But they had to avoid lifting him up the steps, and so they carried the wounded man to the lodge, and put him in the room that had been Madame Schoss's. This wounded officer was Prince Andrey Bolkonsky.

XV

THE last day of Moscow had come. It was a bright, clear autumn day. It was Sunday. The bells were ringing for service in all the churches, just as on all other Sundays. No one seemed yet able to grasp what was awaiting Moscow.

There were only two indications in the condition of society that betrayed the position of Moscow: those were the rabble, that is, the poorer classes, and the prices of different objects. Factory hands, house-serfs, and peasants came out early that morning on to Three Hills in immense crowds, which were swelled by clerks, divinity students, and gentlemen. After staying there a while waiting for Rastoptchin, who did not come, and gaining the conviction that Moscow would be surrendered, this mob dispersed about the taverns and drink-shops of Moscow. Prices, too, on that day indicated the position of affairs. The prices of weapons, of carts and horses, and the value of gold rose higher and higher, while the value of paper-money and the prices of things useful in town were continually falling, so that by the middle of the day there were instances of cab-drivers carrying off at half-price expensive goods, like cloth; and while five hundred roubles was paid for a peasant's horse, furniture, mirrors, and bronzes were given away for nothing.

In the old-fashioned and decorous house of the Rostovs the collapse of all the usual conditions of life was very slightly perceptible. In the night three out of the immense retinue of servants did indeed disappear; but nothing was stolen, and the Rostovs were only aware of the change in the relative value of things from finding that the thirty carts from the country were of enormous value, for which they were envied by many, and offered enormous sums. Besides these would-be purchasers, all the previous evening and early in the morning of the 1st of September orderlies and servants were being continually sent into the Rostovs' courtyard from wounded officers, and wounded men were constantly dragging themselves there from the Rostovs' and neighbouring houses, to beseech the servants to try and get them a lift out of Moscow. The butler, to whom these requests were referred, resolutely refused, though he felt for the wounded men, and declared that he would never even dare to hint at such a thing to the count. Pitiable as the position of these wounded men was, it was obvious that if one gave up one cart to them, one might as well give all—and would even have to put the carriages too at their service. Thirty waggons could not save all the wounded, and in the general catastrophe one must think of oneself and one's family first. So the butler reasoned on his master's behalf.

On waking up that morning Count Ilya Andreitch slipped quietly out of his bedroom, so as not to wake his wife, who had been awake till morning, and in his lilac silk dressing-gown he came out on to the steps. The loaded waggons were standing in the courtyard. The carriages were drawn up at the steps. The butler was standing in the entrance talking with an old orderly and a pale young officer with his arm in a sling. The butler, seeing his master, made a significant and peremptory sign to them both to retire.

'Well, is everything ready, Vassilitch?' said the count, rubbing his bald head; and looking benignly at the officer and the orderly, he nodded to them. (The count was always attracted by new faces.)

'Ready to put the horses in immediately, your excellency.'

'Well, that's capital; the countess will soon be awake, and, please God, we set off! What can I do for you, sir?' he said, addressing the officer. 'You are staying in my house?'

The officer came closer. His pale face suddenly flushed crimson.

'Count, do me a great favour, allow me . . . for God's sake . . . to get into one of your waggons. I have nothing here with me. . . I can go quite well with the luggage . . .'

Before the officer finished speaking, the orderly came up to make the same request for his master.

'Oh! yes, yes, yes,' said the count hurriedly. 'I shall be very glad indeed. Vassilitch, you see to it; you have a waggon or two cleared, well . . . well . . . what's needed . . .?' The count murmured some vague orders. But the glowing look of gratitude on the officer's face instantly put the seal on the order. The count looked about him; everywhere—in the yard, at the gates, at the windows of the lodge—he saw wounded men and orderlies. They were all gazing at him and moving up towards the steps.

'Will you please walk into the gallery, your excellency; what are your orders about the pictures there?' said the butler. And the count went into the house with him, repeating his instructions that they were not to refuse the wounded men who begged to go with them.

'You can take something out of the loads, you know,' he added, in a subdued and mysterious voice, as though he were afraid of being overheard.

At nine o'clock the countess woke up, and Matrona Timofyevna, who had been her maid before her marriage, and now performed the duties of a sort of *chef de gendarmes* for the countess, came in to report to her that Madame Schoss was very much aggrieved, and that the young ladies' summer dresses could not possibly be left behind. On the countess inquiring the cause of Madame Schoss's resentment, it appeared that that lady's trunk had been taken out of the waggon, and that all the waggons were being unloaded, and that the luggage was being taken out, as the waggons were to be given up to the wounded men, whom the count, with his usual readiness to be imposed upon, had consented to take away with them. The countess sent for her husband to come to her.

'What's this, my dear? I hear the luggage is being unloaded.'

'Do you know, *ma chere*, I wanted to speak to you about it ... dear little countess ... an officer came up to me—they are imploring us to let them have a few waggons for the wounded. It's all a question of money loss to us, of course, but to be left behind ... think what it means to them! ... Here they are in our very yard; we asked them in ourselves; here are officers. ... You know, I really think, *ma chere* ... well, let them take them. We are in no hurry.'

The count spoke timidly, as he always did when the subject was in any way connected with money. The countess was used to that tone, which always ushered in some matter prejudicial to her children's interests, such as the building of a new gallery, or conservatory, or a new theatre in the house, or the training of an orchestra; and she made it a habit, and regarded it as a duty, to oppose everything that was communicated in that tone.

She assumed her air of tearful resignation, and said to her husband:

'Listen, count, you have mismanaged things so, that we are getting nothing for the house, and now you want to throw away all our—all the *children's*—property. Why, you told me yourself that we have a hundred thousand roubles' worth of valuables in the house. I protest, and protest, my love. What would you have! It's for the Government to look after the wounded. They know that. Only think, the Lopuhins opposite cleared everything to the last stick out of their house the day before yesterday. That's how other people manage. It's only we who are such fools. If you have no consideration for me, do at least think of your children.'

The count waved his hands in despair, and went out of the room without a word.

'Papa! why do you do that?' said Natasha, who had followed him into her mother's room.

'Nothing! It's no business of yours!' the count said angrily.

'But I heard,' said Natasha. 'Why won't mamma have it?'

'It's no business of yours!' cried the count.

Natasha walked away to the window and pondered.

'Papa, here's Berg coming to see us,' she said, looking out of window.

XVI

THE Rostovs' son-in-law, Berg, was by now a colonel, with the orders of Vladimir and Anne on his neck, and was still filling the same comfortable and agreeable post of assistant to the head of the staff of the assistant of the chief officer of the staff of the commander of the left flank of the infantry of the first army.

On the 1st of September he had come into Moscow from the army.

He had absolutely nothing to do in Moscow; but he noticed that every one in the army was asking leave to go into Moscow, and was busy doing something there. He, too, thought fit to ask leave of absence on account of urgent domestic and family affairs.

Berg drove up to his father-in-law's house in his spruce chaise, with his pair of sleek roans, precisely similar to those of a certain prince. He looked carefully at the luggage in the yard, and as he ran up the steps, he took out a clean pocket-handkerchief, and tied a knot in it.

Berg ran with a swimming, impatient step from the entry into the drawing-room, embraced the count, kissed Natasha's hand and Sonya's, and then hastened to inquire after mamma's health.

'Health, at a time like this! Come, tell us what news of the army!' said the count. 'Are they retreating, or will there be a battle?'

'Only Almighty God can tell what will be the fate of our Fatherland, papa,' said Berg. 'The army is animated by the most ardent spirit of heroism, and now its chiefs, so to speak, are sitting in council. No one knows what is coming. But I can tell you, papa, that our heroic spirit, the truly antique valour of the Russian army, which they—it, I mean,' he corrected himself—'showed in the fight of the 26th . . . well, there are no words that can do justice to it.' (He smote himself on the chest, just as he had seen a general do, who had used much the same phrases before him—but he was a little too late, for the blow on the chest should properly have been at the words, 'the Russian army.') 'I can assure you, papa, that we officers, so far from having to urge the soldiers on, or anything of the sort, had much ado to keep in check this . . . yes, these exploits recalling the valour of antiquity,' he rattled off. 'General Barclay de Tolly risked his life everywhere in front of his troops, I can assure you. Our corps was posted on the slope of a hill. Only fancy!' And Berg proceeded to recount all the stories he had heard repeated about the battle. Natasha stared at Berg, as though seeking the solution of some problem in his face, and her eyes disconcerted him.

'Altogether, the heroism shown by the Russian soldiers is beyond praise, and beyond description!' said Berg, looking at Natasha; and as though wishing to soften her, he smiled in response to her persistent stare . . . ' "Russia is not in Moscow, she lives in the hearts of her sons!" Eh, papa?' said Berg.

At that moment the countess came in from the divan-room with a look of weariness and annoyance on her face. Berg skipped up, kissed the countess's hand, asked after her health, and stood beside her, with a sympathetic shake of his head.

'Yes, mamma, to tell the truth, these are hard and sorrowful times for every Russian. But why should you be so anxious? You have still time to get away . . .'

'I can't make out what the servants are about,' said the countess, addressing her husband. 'They told me just now nothing was ready. Some one really must go and look after them. It's at such times one misses Mitenka. There will be no end to it.'

The count was about to make some reply; but with a visible effort to restrain himself, got up and went to the door without a word.

Berg, meanwhile, had taken out his handkerchief as though about to blow his nose, and, seeing the knot in it, he pondered a moment, shaking his head with mournful significance.

'And, do you know, papa, I have a great favour to ask . . .' he began.

'H'm?' said the count, pausing.

'I was passing by Yusupov's house just now,' said Berg, laughing. 'The steward, a man I know, ran out and asked me whether I wouldn't care to buy any of their things. I went in, you know, out of curiosity, and there is a little chiffonier and dressing-table. You know, just like what Verushka wanted, and we quarrelled about.' (Berg unconsciously passed into a tone expressive of his pleasure in his own excellent domestic arrangements.) 'And such a charming thing!—it moves forward, you know, with a secret English lock. And it's just what Verushka wanted. So I want to make it a surprise for her. I see what a number of peasants you have in the yard. Please, spare me one of them. I'll pay him well, and . . .'

The count frowned and sniffed.

'Ask the countess; I don't give the orders.'

'If it's troublesome, pray don't,' said Berg. 'Only I should have liked it on Vera's account.'

'Ah, go to damnation all of you, damnation! damnation! damnation!' cried the old count. 'My head's going round.' And he went out of the room.

The countess began to cry.

'Yes, indeed, these are terrible times, mamma!' said Berg.

Natasha went out with her father, and as though unable to make up her mind on some difficult question, she followed him at first, then turned and ran downstairs.

Petya was standing at the entrance, engaged in giving out weapons to the servants, who were leaving Moscow. The loaded waggons were still standing in the yards. Two of them had been uncorded, and on to one of these the wounded officer was clambering with the assistance of his orderly.

'Do you know what it was about?' Petya asked Natasha. (Natasha knew that he meant, what their father and mother had been quarrelling about.) She did not answer.

'It was because papa wanted to give up all the waggons to the wounded,' said Petya. 'Vassilitch told me. And what I think . . .'

'What I think,' Natasha suddenly almost screamed, turning a furious face on Petya, 'what I think is, that it's so vile, so loathsome . . . I don't know. Are we a lot of low Germans? . . .' Her throat was quivering with sobs, but afraid of being weak, or wasting the force of her anger, she turned and flew headlong up the stairs.

Berg was sitting beside the countess, trying with filial respectfulness to reassure her. The count was walking about the room with a pipe in his hand, when, with a face distorted by passion, Natasha burst like a tempest into the room, and ran with rapid steps up to her mother.

'It's vile! It's loathsome!' she screamed. 'It can't be true that it's your order.'

Berg and the countess gazed at her in alarm and bewilderment. The count stood still in the window listening.

'Mamma, it's impossible; look what's being done in the yard!' she cried; 'they are being left . . .'

'What's the matter? Who are they? What do you want?'

'The wounded! It's impossible, mamma, it's outrageous. . . . No, mamma, darling, it's all wrong; forgive me, please, darling . . . Mamma, what is it to us what we take away; you only look out into the yard. . . . Mamma! . . . It can't be done. . . .'

The count stood in the window, and listened to Natasha without turning his head. All at once he gave a sort of gulp, and put his face closer to the window.

The countess glanced at her daughter, saw her face full of shame for her mother, saw her emotion, felt why her husband would not look at her now, and looked about her with a distracted air.

'Oh, do as you please. Am I doing anything to hinder any one?' she said, not giving way all at once.

'Mamma, darling, forgive me.'

But the countess pushed away her daughter, and went up to the count.

'My dear, you order what is right. . . . I don't understand about it, you know,' she said, dropping her eyes with a guilty air.

'The eggs. . . . the eggs teaching the hen, . . .' the count murmured through tears of gladness, and he embraced his wife, who was glad to hide her ashamed face on his breast.

'Papa, mamma! may I give the order? May I? . . .' asked Natasha. 'We'll take all that's quite necessary all the same,' she added.

The count nodded; and Natasha, with the same swiftness with which she used to run at 'catch-catch,' flew across the hall into the vestibule, and down the steps into the yard.

The servants gathered round Natasha, and could hardly believe the strange order she gave them, till the count himself in his wife's name confirmed the order that all the waggons were to be placed at the disposal of the wounded, and the boxes were to be taken down to the storerooms. When they understood, the servants gleefully and busily set to this new task. It no longer seemed strange to the servants, it seemed to them, indeed, that no other course was possible; just as a quarter of an hour before they had not thought it strange to leave the wounded behind and take the furniture; had accepted that too, in fact, as the only course possible.

All the household set to work getting the wounded men into the waggons with the greatest zeal, as though to make up for not having espoused their cause earlier. The wounded soldiers came creeping out of their rooms, and crowded round the waggons, with pale, delighted faces. The news spread to the neighbouring houses, and wounded men began to come into the yard from other houses too. Many of the wounded soldiers begged them not to take out the boxes, but only to let them sit on the top of them. But when once the work of unloading had begun there was no stopping it; it seemed of little consequence whether all were left or half. The cases of china, of bronzes, of pictures and looking-glasses, which had been so carefully packed during the previous night lay in the yard, and still they sought and found possibilities of taking out more and more, and leaving more and more, for the wounded.

'We can take four more,' said the steward. 'I'll leave my luggage, or else what is to become of them?'

'Oh, let them have our wardrobe cart,' said the countess; 'Dunyasha will go with me in the carriage.'

The waggon packed with the ladies' wardrobe was unloaded, and sent to fetch wounded men from two doors off. All the family and the servants too were eager and merry. Natasha was in a state of ecstatic happiness, such as she had not known for a very long while.

'Where are we to fasten this on?' said the servant, trying to lay a trunk on the narrow footboard behind in the carriage. 'We must keep just one cart for it.'

'What is it?' asked Natasha.

'The count's books.'

'Leave it. Vassilitch will put it away. That's not necessary.'

The covered gig was full of people; they were only in doubt where Pyotr Ilyitch was to sit.

'He'll go on the box. You'll go on the box, won't you, Petya?' cried Natasha.

Sonya, too, worked with unflagging zeal; but the aim of her exertions was the opposite of Natasha's. She saw to the storing away of all that was left behind, made a list of them at the countess's desire, and tried to get as much as possible taken with them.

XVII

BY two o'clock the Rostovs' four carriages, packed and ready to start, stood in the approach. The waggon-loads of wounded were filing one after another out of the yard.

The coach in which Prince Andrey was being taken drove by the front door, and attracted the attention of Sonya, who was helping a maid to arrange the countess's seat comfortably in her huge, high carriage.

'Whose carriage is that?' asked Sonya, popping her head out of the carriage window.

'Why, haven't you heard, miss?' answered the maid. 'The wounded prince; he stayed the night in the house, and is going on with us.'

'Oh, who is he? what's his name?'

'Our betrothed that was . . . Prince Bolkonsky himself!' answered the maid, sighing. 'They say he is dying.'

Sonya jumped out of the carriage and ran in to the countess. The countess, dressed for the journey, in her hat and shawl, was walking wearily about the drawing-room, waiting for the rest of the household to come in and sit down with closed doors, for the usual silent prayer before setting out. Natasha was not in the room.

'Mamma,' said Sonya, 'Prince Andrey is here, wounded and dying. He is going with us.'

The countess opened her eyes in dismay, and clutching Sonya's arm, looked about her.

'Natasha,' she said.

Both to Sonya and the countess this news had for the first moment but one significance. They knew their Natasha, and alarm at the thought of the effect the news might have on her outweighed all sympathy for the man, though they both liked him.

'Natasha does not know yet, but he is going with us,' said Sonya.

'You say he is dying?'

Sonya nodded.

The countess embraced Sonya and burst into tears. 'The ways of the Lord are past our finding out!' she thought, feeling that in all that was passing now the Hand of the Almighty, hitherto unseen, was beginning to be manifest.

'Well, mamma, it's all ready. What is it? . . .' asked Natasha, running with her eager face into the room.

'Nothing,' said the countess. 'If we're ready, then do let us start.' And the countess bent over her reticule to hide her agitated face. Sonya embraced Natasha and kissed her.

Natasha looked inquisitively at her.

'What is it? What has happened?'

'Nothing, . . . oh, no, . . .'

Something very bad, concerning me? . . . What is it?' asked the keen-witted Natasha.

Sonya sighed, and made no reply. The count, Petya, Madame Schoss, Mavra Kuzminishna, and Vassilitch came into the drawing-room; and closing the doors, they all sat down, and sat so in silence, without looking at each other for several seconds.

The count was the first to get up. With a loud sigh he crossed himself before the holy picture. All the others did the same. Then the count proceeded to embrace Mavra Kuzminishna and Vassilitch, who were to remain in Moscow; and while they caught at his hand and kissed his shoulder, he patted them on the back with vaguely affectionate and reassuring phrases. The countess went off to the little chapel, and Sonya found her there on her knees before the holy pictures, that were still left here and there on the walls. All the holy pictures most precious through association with the traditions of the family were being taken with them.

In the porch and in the yard the servants who were going—all of whom had been armed with swords and daggers by Petya—with their trousers tucked in their boots, and their sashes or leather belts tightly braced, took leave of those who were left behind.

As is invariably the case at starting on a journey, a great many things were found to have been forgotten, or packed in the wrong place; and two grooms were kept a long while standing, one each side of the open carriage door, ready to help the countess up the carriage steps, while maids were flying with pillows and bags from the house to the carriages, the coach, and the covered gig, and back again.

'They will always forget everything as long as they live!' said the countess. 'You know that I can't sit like that.' And Dunyasha, with clenched teeth and an aggrieved look on her face, rushed to the carriage to arrange the cushions again without a word.

'Ah, those servants,' said the count, shaking his head.

The old coachman Efim, the only one whom the countess could trust to drive her, sat perched up on the box, and did not even look round at what was passing behind him. His thirty years' experience had taught him that it would be some time yet before they would say, 'Now, in God's name, start!' and that when they had said it, they would stop him at least twice again to send back for things that had been forgotten; and after that he would have to pull up once more for the countess herself to put her head out of window and beg him, for Christ's sake, to drive carefully downhill. He knew this, and therefore awaited what was to come with more patience than his horses, especially the left one, the chestnut Falcon, who was continually pawing the ground and champing the bit. At last all were seated; the carriage steps were pulled up, and the door slammed, and the forgotten travelling-case had been sent for, and the countess had popped her head out and given the usual injunctions. Then Efim deliberately took his hat off and began crossing himself. The postillion and all the servants did the same.

'With God's blessing!' said Efim, putting his hat on. 'Off!' The postillion started his horse. The right-shaft horse began to pull, the high springs creaked, and the carriage swayed. The footman jumped up on the box while it was moving. The carriage jolted as it drove out of the yard on to the uneven pavement; the other vehicles jolted in the same way as they followed in a procession up the street. All the occupants of the carriages, the coach and the covered gig, crossed themselves on seeing the church opposite. The servants, who were staying in Moscow, walked along on both sides of the carriages to see them off.

Natasha had rarely felt such a joyful sensation as she experienced at that moment sitting in the carriage by the countess and watching, as they slowly moved by her, the walls of forsaken, agitated Moscow. Now and then she put her head out of the carriage window and looked back, and then in front at the long train of waggons full of wounded soldiers preceding them. Foremost of them all she could see Prince Andrey's closed carriage. She did not know who was in it, and every time she took stock of the procession of waggons she looked out for that coach. She knew it would be the foremost. In Kudrino, and from Nikitsky Street, from Pryesny, and from Podnovinsky several trains of vehicles, similar to the Rostovs', came driving out, and by the time they reached Sadovoy Street the carriages and carts were two deep all along the road.

As they turned round Suharev Tower, Natasha, who was quickly and inquisitively scrutinising the crowd driving and walking by, uttered a cry of delight and surprise:

'Good Heavens! Mamma, Sonya, look! it's he!'

'Who? who?'

'Look, do look! Bezuhov,' said Natasha, putting her head out of the carriage window and staring at a tall, stout man in a coachman's long coat, obviously a gentleman disguised, from his carriage and gait. He was passing under the arch of the Suharev Tower beside a yellow-looking, beardless, little old man in a frieze cloak.

'Only fancy! Bezuhov in a coachman's coat, with a queer sort of old-looking boy,' said Natasha. 'Do look; do look!'

'No, it's not he. How can you be so absurd!'

'Mamma,' cried Natasha. 'On my word of honour, I assure you, it is he. Stop, stop,' she shouted to the coachman; but the coachman could not stop, because more carts and carriges were coming out of Myeshtchansky Street, and people were shouting at the Rostovs to move on, and not to keep the rest of the traffic waiting.

All the Rostovs did, however, though now at a much greater distance, see Pierre, or a man extraordinarily like him, wearing a coachman's coat, and walking along the street with bent head and a serious face beside a little, beardless old man, who looked like a footman. This old man noticed a face poked out of the carriage window staring at them, and respectfully touching Pierre's elbow, he said something to him, pointing towards the carriage. It was some time before Pierre understood what he was saying; he was evidently deeply absorbed in his own thoughts. At last he looked in the direction indicated, and recognising Natasha, he moved instantly towards the carriage, as though yielding to the first impulse. But after taking a dozen steps towards it, he stopped short, apparently recollecting something. Natasha's head beamed out of the carriage window with friendly mockery.

'Pyotr Kirillitch, come here! We recognised you, you see! It's a wonder!' she cried, stretching out a hand to him. 'How is it? Why are you like this?'

Pierre took her outstretched hand, and awkwardly kissed it as he ran beside the still moving carriage.

'What has happened, count?' the countess asked him, in a surprised and commiserating tone.

'Eh? why? Don't ask me,' said Pierre, and he looked up at Natasha, the charm of whose radiant, joyous eyes he felt upon him without looking at her.

'What are you doing, or are you staying in Moscow?'

Pierre was silent.

'In Moscow?' he queried. 'Yes, in Moscow. Good-bye.'

'Oh, how I wish I were a man, I would stay with you. Ah, how splendid that is!' said Natasha. 'Mamma, do let me stay.'

Pierre looked absently at Natasha, and was about to say something, but the countess interrupted him.

'You were at the battle, we have been told.'

'Yes, I was there,' answered Pierre. 'Tomorrow there will be a battle again . . .' he was beginning, but Natasha interposed:

'But what is the matter, count? You are not like yourself . . .'

'Oh, don't ask me, don't ask me, I don't know myself. Tomorrow . . . No! Good-bye; good-bye,' he said; 'it's an awful time!' And he left the carriage and walked away to the pavement.

For a long while Natasha's head was still thrust out of the carriage window, and she beamed at him with a kindly and rather mocking, joyous smile.

XVIII

FROM the time of his disappearance, two days before, Pierre had been living in the empty abode of his dead benefactor, Osip Bazdyev. This was how it had come to pass.

On waking up the morning after his return to Moscow and his interview with Count Rastoptchin, Pierre could not for some time make out where he was and what was expected of him. When the names of the persons waiting to see him were announced to him—among them a Frenchman, who had brought a letter from his wife, the Countess Elena Vassilyevna—he felt suddenly overcome by that sense of the hopelessness and intricacy of his position to which he was particularly liable. He suddenly felt that everything was now at an end, everything was in a muddle, everything was breaking down, that no one was right nor wrong, that there was no future before him, and that there was no possible escape from the position. Smiling unnaturally and muttering to himself, he sat on the sofa in a pose expressive of utter hopelessness, or got up, approached the door, and peeped through the crack into the reception-room, where his visitors were awaiting him, then turned back with a gesture of despair and took up a book. The butler came in for the second time with a message that the Frenchman who had brought the letter from the countess was very desirous of seeing him if only for a minute, and that they had sent from the widow of Osip Alexyevitch Bazdyev to ask him to take charge of some books, as Madame Bazdyev was going away into the country.

'Oh yes, in a minute; wait . . . No, no; go and say, I am coming immediately,' said Pierre.

As soon as the butler had left the room, Pierre had taken up his hat, which was lying on the table, and gone out by the other door. He found no one in the corridor. Pierre walked the whole length of the corridor to the staircase, and frowning and rubbing his forehead with both hands, he went down as far as the first story landing. The porter was standing at the front door. A second staircase led from the landing to the back entrance. Pierre went down the back stairs and out into the yard. No one had seen him. But as soon as he turned out at the gates into the street, the coachman, standing by the carriages, and the gate-porter saw him and took off their caps to him. Aware of their eyes fixed on him, Pierre did, as the ostrich does, hiding its head in a bush to escape being seen; ducking his head and quickening his pace he hurried along the street.

Of all the business awaiting Pierre that morning, the task of sorting the books and papers of Osip Alexyevitch seemed to him the most urgent.

He hailed the first cab-driver he came across, and told him to drive to Patriarch's Ponds, where was the house of the widow of Bazdyev.

Continually watching the loaded vehicles moving out of Moscow from all directions, and balancing his bulky person carefully not to slip out of the rickety old chaise, Pierre had the happy sensation of a runaway schoolboy, as he chatted with his driver.

The latter told him that today arms were being given out in the Kremlin, and that next day every one would be driven out beyond the Three Hills Gate, and there there was to be a great battle.

On reaching the Patriarch's Ponds, Pierre looked for Bazdyev's house, where he had not been for a long while past. He went up to a little garden gate. Gerasim, the yellow, beardless old man Pierre had seen five years before at Torzhok with Osip Alexyevitch, came out on hearing him knock.

'At home?' asked Pierre.

'Owing to present circumstances, Sofya Danilovna and her children have gone away into the country, your excellency.'

'I'll come in, all the same; I want to look through the books,' said Pierre.

'Pray do, you are very welcome; the brother of my late master—the heavenly kingdom be his!—Makar Alexyevitch has remained, but your honour is aware he is in feeble health,' said the old servant.

Makar Alexyevitch was, as Pierre knew, a brother of Osip Alexyevitch, a half-mad creature, besotted by drink.

'Yes, yes, I know. Let us go in,' said Pierre, and he went into the house. A tall, bald old man in a dressing-gown, with a red nose and goloshes on his bare feet, was standing in the vestibule; seeing Pierre, he muttered something angrily, and walked away into the corridor.

'He was a great intellect, but now, as your honour can see, he has grown feeble,' said Gerasim. 'Will you like to go into the study?' Pierre nodded. 'As it was sealed up, so it has remained. Sofya Danilovna gave orders that if you sent for the books they were to be handed over.'

Pierre went into the gloomy study, which he had entered with such trepidation in the lifetime of his benefactor. Now covered with dust, and untouched since the death of Osip Alexyevitch, the room was gloomier than ever.

Gerasim opened one blind, and went out of the room on tiptoe. Pierre walked round the study, went up to the bookcase, where the manuscripts were kept, and took one of the most important, at one time a sacred relic of the order. This consisted of the long Scottish acts of the order, with Bazdyev's notes and commentaries. He sat down to the dusty writing-table and laid the manuscripts down before him, opened and closed them, and at last, pushing them away, sank into thought, with his elbow on the table and his head in his hand.

Several times Gerasim peeped cautiously into the study and saw that Pierre was sitting in the same attitude.

More than two hours passed by. Gerasim ventured to make a slight noise at the door to attract Pierre's attention. Pierre did not hear him.

'Is the driver to be dismissed, your honour?'

'Oh yes,' said Pierre, waking up from his reverie, and hurriedly getting up. 'Listen,' he said, taking Gerasim by the button of his coat and looking down at the old man with moist, shining, eager eyes. 'Listen! You know that tomorrow there is to be a battle...'

'They have been saying so...' answered Gerasim.

'I beg you not to tell any one who I am. And do what I tell you...'

'Certainly, sir,' said Gerasim. 'Would your honour like something to eat?'

'No, but I want something else. I want a peasant dress and a pistol,' said Pierre, suddenly flushing red.

'Certainly, sir,' said Gerasim, after a moment's thought.

All the rest of that day Pierre spent alone in his benefactor's study, pacing restlessly from one corner to the other, as Gerasim could hear, and talking to himself; and he spent the night on a bed made up for him there.

Gerasim accepted Pierre's taking up his abode there with the imperturbability of a servant, who had seen many queer things in his time, and he seemed, indeed, pleased at having some one to wait upon. Without even permitting himself to wonder with what object it was wanted, he obtained for Pierre that evening a coachman's coat and cap, and promised next day to procure the pistol he required. Makar Alexyevitch twice that evening approached the door, shuffling in his goloshes, and stood there, gazing with an ingratiating air at Pierre. But as soon as Pierre turned to him, he wrapped his dressing-gown round him with a shamefaced and wrathful look, and hastily retreated. Pierre put on the coachman's coat, procured and carefully fumigated for him by Gerasim, and went out with the latter to buy a pistol at the Suharev Tower. It was there he had met the Rostovs.

XIX

ON the night of the 1st of September Kutuzov gave the Russian troops the command to fall back across Moscow to the Ryazan road.

The first troops moved that night, marching deliberately and in steady order. But at dawn the retreating troops on reaching the Dorogomilov bridge saw before them, crowding on the other side, and hurrying over the bridge, and blocking the streets and alleys on the same side, and bearing down upon them from behind, immense masses of soldiers. And the troops were overtaken by causeless panic and haste. There was a general rush forward towards the bridge, on to the bridge, to the fords and to the boats. Kutuzov had himself driven by back streets to the other side of Moscow.

At ten o'clock in the morning of the 2nd of September the only troops left in the Dorogomilov suburbs were the regiments of the rearguard, and the crush was over. The army was already on the further side of Moscow, and out of the town altogether.

At the same time, at ten o'clock in the morning of the 2nd of September, Napoleon was standing in the midst of his troops on Poklonny Hill, gazing at the spectacle that lay before him. From the 26th of August to the 2nd of September, from the day of Borodino to the entrance into Moscow, all that agitating, that memorable week, there had been that extraordinarily beautiful autumn weather, which always comes as a surprise, when though the sun is low in the sky it shines more warmly than in spring, when everything is glistening in the pure, limpid air, so that the eyes are dazzled, while the chest is braced and refreshed inhaling the fragrant autumn air; when the nights even are warm, and when in these dark, warm nights golden stars are continually falling from the sky, to the delight or terror of all who watch them.

At ten o'clock on the 2nd of September the morning light was full of the beauty of fairyland. From Poklonny Hill Moscow lay stretching wide below with her river, her gardens, and her churches, and seemed to be living a life of her own, her cupolas twinkling like stars in the sunlight.

At the sight of the strange town, with its new forms of unfamiliar architecture, Napoleon felt something of that envious and uneasy curiosity that men feel at the sight of the aspects of a strange life, knowing nothing of them. It was clear that that town was teeming with vigorous life. By those indefinable tokens by which one can infallibly tell from a distance a live body from a dead one, Napoleon could detect from Poklonny Hill the throb of life in the town, and could feel, as it were, the breathing of that beautiful, great being. Every Russian gazing at Moscow feels she is the mother; every foreigner gazing at her, and ignorant of her significance as the mother city, must be aware of the feminine character of the town, and Napoleon felt it.

'This Asiatic city with the innumerable churches, Moscow the holy. Here it is at last, the famous city! It was high time,' said Napoleon; and dismounting from his horse he bade them open the plan of Moscow before him, and sent for his interpreter, Lelorme d'Ideville.

'A city occupied by the enemy is like a girl who has lost her honour,' he thought (it was the phrase he had uttered to Tutchkov at Smolensk).

And from that point of view he gazed at the Oriental beauty who lay for the first time before his eyes. He felt it strange himself that the desire so long cherished, and thought so impossible, had at last come to pass. In the clear morning light he gazed at the town, and then at the plan, looking up its details, and the certainty of possessing it agitated and awed him.

'But how could it be otherwise?' he thought. 'Here is this capital, she lies at my feet awaiting her fate. Where is Alexander now, and what is he thinking? A strange, beautiful, and grand city! And a strange and grand moment is this! In what light must I appear to them?' he mused, thinking of his soldiers, 'Here is the city—the reward for all those of little faith,' he thought, looking round at his suite and the approaching troops, forming into ranks.

'One word of mine, one wave of my arm, and the ancient capital of the Tsar is no more. But my clemency is ever prompt to stoop to the vanquished. I must be magnanimous and truly great. But no, it is not true that I am in Moscow,' the idea suddenly struck him. 'She lies at my feet, though, her golden domes and crosses flashing and twinkling in the sun. But I will spare her. On the ancient monuments of barbarism and despotism I will inscribe the great words of justice and mercy ... Alexander will feel that more bitterly than anything; I know him.' (It seemed to Napoleon that the chief import of what had happened lay in his personal contest with Alexander.) 'From the heights of the Kremlin—yes, that's the Kremlin, yes—I will dictate to them the laws of justice, I will teach them the meaning of true civilisation, I will make the generations of boyards to enshrine their conqueror's name in love. I will tell the deputation that I have not sought, and do not seek, war; that I have been waging war only with the deceitful policy of their court; that I love and respect Alexander, and that in Moscow I will accept terms of peace worthy of myself and my peoples. I have no wish to take advantage of the fortune of war to humiliate their honoured Emperor. "Boyards," I will say to them, "I do not seek war; I seek the peace and welfare of all my subjects." But I know their presence will inspire me, and I shall speak to them as I always do, clearly, impressively, and greatly. But can it be true that I am in Moscow! Yes, there she is!'

'Let the boyards be brought to me,' he said, addressing his suite. A general, with a brilliant suite of adjutants, galloped off at once to fetch the boyards.

Two hours passed. Napoleon had lunched, and was again standing on the same spot on the Poklonny Hill, waiting for the deputation. His speech to the boyards had by now taken definite shape in his mind. The speech was full of dignity and of greatness, as Napoleon understood it. Napoleon was himself carried away by the magnanimity with which he intended to act in Moscow. In imagination he had already fixed the days for a *'reunion dans le palais des Czars,'* at which the great Russian nobles were to mingle with the courtiers of the French Emperor. In thought he had appointed a governor capable of winning the hearts of the people. Having heard that Moscow was full of religious instituttions, he had mentally decided that his bounty was to be showered on these institutions. He imagined that as in Africa he had had to sit in a mosque wearing a burnous, in Moscow he must be gracious and bountiful as the Tsars. And being, like every Frenchman, unable to imagine anything moving without a reference to *sa chère, sa tendre, sa pauvre mère*, he decided finally to touch the Russian heart, that he would have inscribed on all these charitable foundations in large letters, 'Dedicated to my beloved mother,' or simply, *'Maison de ma mère,'* he decided. 'But am I really in Moscow? Yes, there she lies before me; but why is the deputation from the city so long in coming?' he wondered.

Meanwhile a whispered and agitated consultation was being held among his generals and marshals in the rear of the suite. The adjutants sent to bring the deputation had come back with the news that Moscow was empty, that every one had left or was leaving the city. The faces of all the suite were pale and perturbed. It was not that Moscow had been abandoned by its inhabitants (grave as that fact appeared) that alarmed them. They were in alarm at the idea of making the fact known to the Emperor; they could not see how, without putting his Majesty into the terrible position, called by the French *ridicule*, to inform him that he had been waiting so long for the boyards in vain, that there was a drunken mob, but no one else in Moscow. Some of the suite maintained that come what may, they must anyway scrape up a deputation of some sort; others opposed this view, and asserted that the Emperor must be carefully and skilfully prepared, and then told the truth.

'We shall have to tell him all the same,' said some gentleman of the suite.... 'But gentlemen...'

The position was the more difficult as the Emperor, pondering on his magnanimous plans, was walking patiently up and down before the map of the city, shading his eyes to look from time to time along the road to Moscow, with a proud and happy smile.

'But it's awkward...' the gentlemen-in-waiting kept repeating, shrugging their shoulders and unable to bring themselves to settle the terrible word in their minds: *'le ridicule....'*

Meanwhile the Emperor, weary of waiting in vain, and with his actor's instinct feeling that the great moment, being too long deferred, was beginning to lose its grandeur, made a sign with his hand. A solitary cannon shot gave the signal, and the invading army marched into Moscow—at the Tver, the Kaluga, and the Dorogomilov gates. More and more rapidly, vying with one another, at a quick run and a trot, the troops marched in, concealed in the clouds of dust they raised, and making the air ring with their deafening shouts.

Tempted on by the advance of the army, Napoleon too rode as far as the Dorogomilov gate, but there he halted again, and dismounting walked about the Kamerkolezhsky wall for a long time, waiting for the deputation.

XX

MOSCOW meanwhile was empty. There were still people in the city; a fiftieth part of all the former inhabitants still remained in it, but it was empty.

It was deserted as a dying, queenless hive is deserted.

In a queenless hive there is no life left. Yet at a superficial glance it seems as much alive as other hives.

In the hot rays of the midday sun the bees soar as gaily around the queenless hive as around other living hives; from a distance it smells of honey like the rest, and bees fly into and out of it just the same. Yet one has but to watch it a little to see that there is no life in the hive. The flight of the bees is not as in living hives, the smell and the sound that meet the beekeeper are changed. When the beekeeper strikes the wall of the sick hive, instead of the instant, unanimous response, the buzzing of tens of thousands of bees menacingly arching their backs, and by the rapid stroke of their wings making that whirring, living sound, he is greeted by a disconnected, droning hum from different parts of the deserted hive. From the alighting board comes not as of old the spirituous, fragrant smell of honey and bitterness, and the whiff of heat from the multitudes within. A smell of chill emptiness and decay mingles with the scent of honey. Around the entrance there is now no throng of guards, arching their backs and trumpeting the menace, ready to die in its defence. There is heard no more the low, even hum, the buzz of toil, like the singing of boiling water, but the broken, discordant uproar of disorder comes forth. The black, long-shaped, honey-smeared workers fly timidly and furtively in and out of the hive: they do not sting, but crawl away at the sight of danger. Of old they flew in only with their bags of honey, and flew out empty; now they fly out with their burdens. The beekeeper opens the lower partition and peeps into the lower half of the hive. Instead of the clusters of black, sleek bees, clinging on each other's legs, hanging to the lower side of the partition, and with an unbroken hum of toil building at the wax, drowsy, withered bees wander listlessly about over the roof and walls of the hive. Instead of the cleanly glued-up floor, swept by the bees' wings, there are now bits of wax, excrement, dying bees feebly kicking, and dead bees lying not cleared away on the floor.

The beekeeper opens the upper door and examines the super of the hive. In place of close rows of bees, sealing up every gap left in the combs and fostering the brood, he sees only the skilful, complex edifice of combs, and even in this the virginal purity of old days is gone. All is forsaken; and soiled, black, stranger bees scurry swiftly and stealthily about the combs in search of plunder; while the dried-up, shrunken, listless, old-looking bees of the hive wander slowly about, doing nothing to hinder them, having lost every desire and sense of life. Drones, gadflies, wasps and butterflies flutter about aimlessly, brushing their wings against the walls of the hive. Here and there, between the cells full of dead brood and honey, is heard an angry buzz; here and there a couple of bees from old habit and custom, though they know not why they do it, are cleaning the hive, painfully dragging away a dead bee or a wasp, a task beyond their strength. In another corner two other old bees are languidly fighting or cleaning themselves or feeding one another, themselves unaware whether with friendly or hostile intent. Elsewhere a crowd of bees, squeezing one another, is falling upon some victim, beating and crushing it; and the killed or enfeebled bee drops slowly, light as a feather, on to the heap of corpses. The beekeeper parts the two centre partitions to look at the nursery. Instead of the dense, black rings of thousands of bees sitting back to back, watching the high mysteries of the work of generation, he sees hundreds of dejected, lifeless, and slumbering wrecks of bees. Almost all have died, unconscious of their coming end, sitting in the holy place, which they had watched—now no more. They reek of death and corruption. But a few of them still stir, rise up, fly languidly and settle on the hand of the foe, without the spirit to die stinging him: the rest are dead and as easily brushed aside as fishes' scales. The beekeeper closes the partition, chalks a mark on the hive, and choosing his own time, breaks it up and burns it.

So was Moscow deserted, as Napoleon, weary, uneasy and frowning, paced up and down at the Kamerkolezhsky wall awaiting that merely external, but still to his mind essential observance of the proprieties—a deputation.

Some few men were still astir in odd corners of Moscow, aimlessly following their old habits, with no understanding of what they were doing.

When, with due circumspectness, Napolon was informed that Moscow was deserted, he looked wrathfully at his informant, and turning his back on him, went on pacing up and down in silence.

'My carriage,' he said. He sat down in his carriage beside the adjutant on duty, and drove into the suburbs.

'Moscow deserted! What an incredible event!' he said to himself.

He did not drive right into the town, but put up for the night at an inn in the Dorogomilov suburb. The dramatic scene had not come off.

XXI

THE Russian troops were crossing Moscow from two o'clock at night to two o'clock in the day, and took with them the last departing inhabitants and wounded soldiers.

The greatest crush took place on the Kamenny bridge, the Moskvoryetsky bridge, and Yauzsky bridge. While the troops, parting into two about the Kremlin, were crowding on to the Moskvoryetsky and Kamenny bridges, an immense number of soldiers availed themselves of the stoppage and the block to turn back, and slipping stealthily and quietly by Vassily the Blessed, and under the Borovitsky gates, they made their way uphill to the Red Square, where some instinct told them they could easily carry off other people's property. Every passage and alley of the Gostinny bazaar was filled with a crowd, such as throngs there at sales. But there were no ingratiating, alluring voices of shopmen, no hawkers, no motley, female mob of purchasers—everywhere were the uniforms and overcoats of soldiers without guns, going out in silence with loads of booty, and coming in empty-handed. The shopkeepers and shopmen (they were few) were walking about among the soldiers, like men distraught, opening and shutting their shops, and helping their assistants to carry away their wares. There were drummers in the square before the bazaar beating the muster-call. But the roll of the drum made the pillaging soldiers not run up at the call as of old, but, on the contrary, run away from the drum. Among the soldiers in the shops and passages could be seen men in the grey coats, and with the shaven heads of convicts. Two officers, one with a scarf over his uniform, on thin, dark grey horse, the other on foot, wearing a military overcoat, stood at the corner of Ilyinka, talking. A third officer galloped up to them.

'The general has sent orders that they positively must all be driven out. Why, this is outrageous! Half the men have run off.'

'Why, are you off too? . . . Where are you fellows off to?' . . . he shouted to three infantry soldiers, who ran by him into the bazaar without guns, holding up the skirts of their overcoats. 'Stop, rascals!'

'Yes, you see, how are you going to get hold of them?' answered another officer. 'There's no getting them together; we must push on so that the last may not be gone, that's the only thing to do!'

'How's one to push on? There they have been standing, with a block on the bridge, and they are not moving. Shouldn't a guard be set to prevent the rest running off.'

'Why, come along! Drive them out,' shouted the senior officer.

The officer in the scarf dismounted, called up a drummer, and went with him into the arcade. Several soldiers in a group together made a rush away. A shopkeeper, with red bruises on his cheeks about his nose, with an expression on his sleek face of quiet persistence in the pursuit of gain, came hurriedly and briskly up to the officer gesticulating.

'Your honour,' said he, 'graciously protect us. We are not close-fisted —any trifle now . . . we shall be delighted! Pray, your honour, walk in, I'll bring out cloth in a moment—a couple of pieces even for a gentleman—we shall be delighted! For we feel how it is, but this is simple robbery! Pray, your honour! a guard or something should be set, to let us at least shut up . . .'

Several shopkeepers crowded round the officer.

'Eh! it's no use clacking,' said one of them, a thin man, with a stern face; 'when one's head's off, one doesn't weep over one's hair. Let all take what they please!' And with a vigorous sweep of his arm he turned away from the officer.

'It's all very well for you to talk, Ivan Sidoritch,' the first shopkeeper began angrily. 'If you please, your honour.'

'What's the use of talking!' shouted the thin man; 'in my three shops here I have one hundred thousand worth of goods. How's one to guard them when the army is gone? Ah, fellows, God's will is not in men's hands!'

'If you please, your honour,' said the first shopkeeper, bowing.

The officer stood in uncertainty, and his face betrayed indecision. 'Why, what business is it of mine!' he cried suddenly, and he strode on rapidly along the arcade. In one open shop he heard blows and high words, and just as the officer was going into it, a man in a grey coat, with a shaven head, was thrust violently out of the door.

This man doubled himself up and bounded past the shopkeepers and the officer. The officer pounced on the soldiers who were in the shop. But meanwhile fearful screams, coming from an immense crowd, were heard near the Moskvoryetsky bridge, and the officer ran out into the square.

'What is it? What is it?' he asked, but his comrade had already galloped off in the direction of the screams. The officer mounted his horse and followed him. As he drew near the bridge, he saw two cannons that had been taken off their carriages, the infantry marching over the bridge, a few broken-down carts, and some soldiers with frightened, and some with laughing, faces. Near the cannons stood a waggon with a pair of horses harnessed to it. Behind the wheels huddled four greyhounds in collars. A mountain of goods was piled up in the waggon, and on the very top, beside a child's chair turned legs uppermost, sat a woman, who was uttering shrill and despairing shrieks. The officer was told by his comrades that the screams of the crowd and the woman's shrieks were due to the fact that General Yermilov had come riding down on the crowd, and learning that the soldiers were straying away in the shops, and crowds of the townspeople were blocking the bridge, had commanded them to take the cannons out of their carriages, and to make as though they would fire them at the bridge. The crowd had made a rush; upsetting waggons, trampling one another, and screaming desperately, the bridge had been cleared, and the troops had moved on.

XXII

THE town itself meanwhile was deserted. There was scarcely a creature in the streets. The gates and the shops were all closed; here and there near pot-houses could be heard solitary shouts or drunken singing. No one was driving in the streets, and footsteps were rarely heard. Povarsky Street was perfectly still and deserted. In the immense courtyard of the Rostovs' house a few wisps of straw were lying about, litter out of the waggons that had gone away, and not a man was to be seen. In the Rostovs' house—abandoned with all its wealth—there were two persons in the great drawing-room. These were the porter, Ignat, and the little page, Mishka, the grandson of Vassilitch, who had remained in Moscow with his grandfather. Mishka had opened the clavichord, and was strumming with one finger. The porter, with his arms akimbo and a gleeful smile on his face, was standing before the great looking-glass.

'That's fine, eh, Uncle Ignat?' said the boy, beginning to bang with both hands at once on the keys.

'Ay, ay!' answered Ignat, admiring the broadening grin on his visage in the glass.

'Shameless fellows! Shameless, upon my word!' they heard behind them the voice of Mavra Kuzminishna, who had softly entered. 'The fat-faced fellow grinning at himself! So this is what you are at! It's not all cleared away down there, and Vassilitch fairly knocked up. You wait a bit!'

Ignat, setting his belt straight, left off smiling, and with eyes submissively downcast, walked out of the room.

'Auntie, I was only just touching ...' said the boy.

'I'll teach you only just to touch. Little rascal!' cried Mavra Kuzminishna, waving her hand at him. 'Go and set the samovar for your grandad.'

Brushing the dust off, she closed the clavichord, and sighing heavily went out of the drawing-room and closed the door. Going out into the yard Mavra Kuzminishna mused where she would go next: whether to drink tea in the lodge with Vassilitch, or to the storeroom to put away what still remained to be stored away.

There was a sound of rapid footsteps in the still street. The steps paused at the gate, the latch rattled as some hand tried to open it.

Mavra Kuzminishna went up to the little gate.

'Whom do you want?'

'The count, Count Ilya Andreitch Rostov.'

'But who are you?'

'I am an officer. I want to see him,' said a genial voice, the voice of a Russian gentleman.

Mavra Kuzminishna opened the gate. And there walked into the courtyard a round-faced officer, a lad of eighteen, whose type of face strikingly resembled the Rostovs'.

'They have gone away, sir. Yesterday, in the evening, their honours set off,' said Mavra Kuzminishna cordially. The young officer standing in the gateway, as though hesitating whether to go in or not, gave a click with his tongue expressive of disappointment.

'Ah, how annoying!' he said. 'Yesterday I ought to ... Ah, what a pity ...'

Meanwhile Mavra Kuzminishna was intently and sympathetically scrutinising the familiar features of the Rostov family in the young man's face, and the tattered cloak and trodden-down boots he was wearing. 'What was it you wanted to see the count for?' she asked.

'Well ... what am I to do now!' the officer cried, with vexation in his voice, and he took hold of the gate as though intending to go away. He stopped short again in uncertainty.

'You see,' he said all at once, 'I am a kinsman of the count's, and he has always been very kind to me. So do you see' (he looked with a merry good-humoured smile at his cloak and boots) 'I am in rags, and haven't a farthing; so I had meant to ask the count . . .'

Mavra Kuzminishna did not let him finish.

'Would you wait just a minute, sir. Only one minute,' she said. And as soon as the officer let go of the gate, Mavra Kuzminishna turned, and with her rapid, elderly step hurried into the back court to her lodge.

While she was running to her room, the officer, with downcast head and a faint smile, was pacing up and down the yard, gazing at his tattered boots.

'What a pity I have missed uncle! What a nice old body! Where has she run off to? And how am I to find out the nearest way for me to overtake the regiment, which must be at Rogozhsky by now?' the young officer was musing meanwhile. Mavra Kuzminishna came round the corner with a frightened and, at the same time, resolute face, carrying in her hands a knotted check handkerchief. A few steps from him, she untied the handkerchief, took out of it a white twenty-five rouble note, and gave it hurriedly to the officer.

'Had his excellency been at home, to be sure, he would have done a kinsman's part, but as it is . . . see, may be . . .' Mavra Kuzminishna was overcome with shyness and confusion. But the officer, with no haste nor reluctance, took the note, and thanked Mavra Kuzminishna. 'If only the count had been at home,' murmured Mavra Kuzminishna, as it were apologetically. 'Christ be with you, sir. God keep you safe,' she said, bowing and showing him out. The officer, smiling and shaking his head, as though laughing at himself, ran almost at a trot along the empty streets to overtake his regiment at Yauzsky bridge.

But for some time Mavra Kuzminishna remained standing with wet eyes before the closed gate, pensively shaking her head, and feeling a sudden rush of motherly tenderness and pity for the unknown boy-officer.

XXIII

IN an unfinished house in Varvarka, the lower part of which was a pothouse, there were sounds of drunken bawling and singing. Some ten factory hands were sitting on benches at tables in a little, dirty room. Tipsy, sweating, bleary-eyed, with wide-gaping mouths, bloated with drink, they were singing some sort of a song. They were singing discordantly, with toil, with labour, not because they wanted to sing, but simply to betoken that they were drunk, and were enjoying themselves.

One of them, a tall, flaxen-headed fellow, in a clean, blue long coat was standing over the rest. His face, with its straight, fine nose, would have been handsome, but for the thick, compressed, continually twitching lips and the lustreless, staring, and frowning eyes. He was standing over the singers, and, obviously with some notion in his head, was making solemn and angular passes over their heads with his bare, white arm, while he tried to spread his dirty fingers out unnaturally wide apart. The sleeve of his coat was incessantly slipping down, and the young fellow kept carefully tucking it up again with his left hand, as though there was something of special significance requiring that white, sinewy, waving arm to be bare. In the middle of the song, shouts and blows were heard in the passage and the porch. The tall fellow waved his arms.

'Shut up!' he shouted peremptorily. 'A fight, lads!' and still tucking up his sleeves, he went out to the porch.

The factory hands followed him. They had brought the tavern-keeper some skins that morning from the factory, had had drink given them for this service, and had been drinking under the leadership of the tall young man. The blacksmiths working in a smithy hard by heard the sounds of revelry in the pothouse, and supposing the house had been forcibly broken into, wanted to break in too. A conflict was going on in the porch.

The tavern-keeper was fighting with a blacksmith in the doorway, and at the moment when the factory hands emerged, the smith had reeled away from the tavern-keeper, and fallen on his face on the pavement.

Another smith dashed in at the door, staggering with his chest against the tavern-keeper.

The young man with the sleeve tucked up, as he went, dealt a blow in the face of the smith who had dashed in at the door, and shouted wildly:

'Lads! they are beating our mates!'

Meanwhile, the first smith got up from the ground, and, with blood spurting from his bruised face, cried in a wailing voice:

'Help! They have killed me . . .! They have killed a man! Mates! . . .'

'Oy, mercy on us, killed entirely, a man killed!' squealed a woman, coming out of the gates next door. A crowd of people gathered round the blood-stained smith.

'Haven't you ruined folks enough, stripping the shirts off their backs?' said a voice, addressing the tavern-keeper; 'and so now you have murdered a man! Blackguard!'

The tall young man standing on the steps turned his bleared eyes from the tavern-keeper to the smiths, as though considering with which to fight.

'Cut-throat!' he cried suddenly at the tavern-keeper. 'Lads, bind him!'

'Indeed, and you try and bind a man like me!' bawled the tavern-keeper, tearing himself away from the men who threw themselves on him, and taking off his cap, he flung it on the ground. As though this act had some mysterious and menacing significance, the factory hands, who had surrounded the tavern-keeper, stood still in uncertainty.

'I know the law, mate, very well, I do. I'll go to the police. Are you thinking I won't find them? Robbery's not the order of the day for any one!' bawled the tavern-keeper, picking up his cap.

'And go we will, so there!' . . . 'And go we will . . . so there!' the tavern-keeper and the tall fellow repeated after one another, and both together moved forward along the street. The blood-bespattered smith walked on a level with them. The factory-hands and a mob of outsiders followed them with talk and shouting.

At the corner of Maroseyka, opposite a great house with closed shutters, and the signboard of a bootmaker, stood a group of some twenty bootmakers, thin, exhausted-looking men, with dejected faces, in loose smocks, and torn coats.

'He ought to pay folks properly!' a thin boot hand, with a scant beard and scowling brows, was saying. 'He's sucked the life-blood out of us, and then he's quit of us. He's been promising and promising us all the week. And now he's driven us to the last point, and he's made off.'

Seeing the mob and the blood-bespattered smith, the man paused, and all the bootmakers with inquisitive eagerness joined the moving crowd.

'Where are the folks going?'

'Going to the police, to be sure.'

'Is it true we are beaten?'

'Why, what did you think? Look what folks are saying!'

Questions and answers were audible. The tavern-keeper, taking advantage of the increased numbers of the rabble, dropped behind the mob, and went back to his tavern.

The tall young fellow, not remarking the disappearance of his foe, the tavern-keeper, still moved his bare arm and talked incessantly, attracting the attention of all. The mob pressed about his figure principally, expecting to get from him some solution of the questions that were absorbing all of them.

'Let them show the order, let him show the law, that's what the government's for! Isn't it the truth I am saying, good Christian folk?' said the tall young man, faintly smiling.

'Does he suppose there's no government? Could we do without government? Wouldn't there be plenty to rob us, eh?'

'Why talk nonsense!' was murmured in the crowd. 'Why, will they leave Moscow like this! They told you a lot of stuff in joke, and you believed them. Haven't we troops enough? No fear, they won't let him enter! That's what the government's for. Ay, listen what folks are prating of!' they said, pointing to the tall fellow.

By the wall of the Kitay-Gorod there was another small group of people gathered about a man in a frieze coat, who held a paper in his hand.

'A decree, a decree being read! A decree is being read,' was heard in the crowd, and the mob surged round the reader.

The man in the frieze coat was reading the placard of the 31st of August. When the mob crowded round, he seemed disconcerted, but at the demand of the tall fellow who pressed close up to him, he began with a faint quiver in his voice reading the notice again from the beginning.

'Early tomorrow I am going to his highness the prince,' he read ('his highness!' the tall young man repeated, with a triumphant smile and knitted brows), 'to consult with him, to act and to aid the troops to exterminate the wretches; we, too, will destroy them root and branch...' the reader went on and paused ('D'ye see?' bawled the tall fellow with an air of victory. 'He'll unravel the whole evil for you...') 'and send our visitors packing to the devil; I shall come back to dinner, and we will set to work, we will be doing till we have done, and done away with the villains.'

These last words were uttered by the reader in the midst of complete silence. The tall fellow's head sank dejectedly. It was obvious that nobody had understood these last words. The words 'I shall come back to dinner' in especial seemed to offend both reader and audience. The faculties of the crowd were strained to the highest pitch, and this was too easy and unnecessarily simple; it was just what any one of them might have said, and what for that reason could not be said in a decree coming from a higher authority.

All stood in depressed silence. The tall fellow's lips moved, and he staggered.

'Ask him!... Isn't that himself?... How'd it be to ask him! Or else... He'll explain...' was suddenly heard in the back rows of the crowd, and the general attention turned to the chaise of the head of the police, which drove into the square, escorted by two mounted dragoons.

The head of the police, who had driven out that morning by Count Rastoptchin's command to set fire to the barques in the river, and had received for that commission a large sum of money, at that moment in his pocket, ordered his coachman to stop on seeing a crowd bearing down upon him.

'What are those people?' he shouted to the people, who timidly approached the chaise in detached groups. 'What is this crowd, I ask you?' repeated the head of police, receiving no reply.

'Your honour,' said the man in the frieze coat, 'it was their wish, your honour, not sparing their substance, in accord with his excellency the count's proclamation, to serve, and not to make a riot at all, as his excellency said . . .'

'The count has not gone, he is here, and will give orders about you,' said the head of police. 'Go on!' he said to his coachman. The crowd stood still, pressing round those who had heard what was said by the official, and looking at the departing chaise.

The head of the police meantime looked about him in alarm, and said something to his coachman; the horses trotted faster.

'Cheated, mates! Lead us to himself!' bawled the voice of the tall fellow. 'Don't let him go, lads! Let him answer for it! Keep him!' roared voices, and the crowd dashed full speed after the chaise.

The mob in noisy talk pursued the head of police to Lubyanka.

'Why, the gentry and the tradespeople are all gone, and we are left to perish. Are we dogs, pray?' was heard more frequently in the crowd.

XXIV

ON the evening of the 1st of September, Count Rastoptchin had come away from his interview with Kutuzov mortified and offended at not having been invited to the council of war, and at Kutuzov's having taken no notice of his offer to take part in the defence of the city, and astonished at the new view of things revealed to him in the camp, in which the tranquillity of the city and its patriotic fervour were treated as matters of quite secondary importance, if not altogether irrelevant and trivial. Mortified, offended, and astonished at all this, Count Rastoptchin had returned to Moscow. After supper, he lay down on a sofa without undressing, and at one o'clock was waked by a courier bringing him a letter from Kutuzov. The letter asked the count, since the troops were retreating to the Ryazan road behind Moscow, to send police officials to escort the troops through the town. The letter told Rastoptchin nothing new. He had known that Moscow would be abandoned not merely since his interview the previous day with Kutuzov on the Poklonny Hill, but ever since the battle of Borodino; since when all the generals who had come to Moscow had with one voice declared that another battle was impossible, and with Rastoptchin's sanction government property had been removed every night, and half the inhabitants had left. But nevertheless the fact, communicated in the form of a simple note, with a command from Kutuzov, and received at night, breaking in on his first sleep, surprised and irritated the governor.

In later days, Count Rastoptchin, by way of explaining his action during this time, wrote several times in his notes that his two great aims at that time were to maintain tranquillity in Moscow, and to make the inhabitants go out of it. If this twofold aim is admitted, every act of Rastoptchin's appears irreproachable. Why were not the holy relics, the arms, the ammunition, the powder, the stores of bread taken away? Why were thousands of the inhabitants deceived into a belief that Moscow would not be abandoned and so ruined? 'To preserve the tranquillity of the city,' replies Count Rastoptchin's explanation. Why were heaps of useless papers out of the government offices and Leppich's balloon and other objects carried away? 'To leave the town empty,' replies Count Rastoptchin's explanation. One has but to admit some menace to public tranquillity and every sort of action is justified.

All the horrors of terrorism were based only on anxiety for public tranquillity.

What foundation was there for Count Rastoptchin's dread of popular disturbance in Moscow in 1812? What reason was there for assuming a disposition to revolution in the city? The inhabitants were leaving it; the retreating troops were filling Moscow. Why were the mob likely to riot in consequence?

Not in Moscow only, but everywhere else in Russia nothing like riots took place at the approach of the enemy. On the 1st and 2nd of September more than ten thousand people were left in Moscow, and except for the mob that gathered in the commander-in-chief's courtyard, attracted there by himself, nothing happened. It is obvious that there would have been even less ground for anticipating disturbances among the populace if, after the battle of Borodino, when the surrender of Moscow became a certainty, or at least a probability, Rastoptchin had taken steps for the removal of all the holy relics, of the powder, ammunition, and treasury, and had told the people straight out that the town would be abandoned, instead of exciting the populace by posting up placards and distributing arms.

Rastoptchin, an impulsive, sanguine man, who had always moved in the highest spheres of the administration, was a patriot in feeling, but had not the faintest notion of the character of the people he supposed himself to be governing. From the time when the enemy first entered Smolensk, Rastoptchin had in his own imagination been playing the part of leader of popular feeling—of the heart of Russia. He did not merely fancy—as every governing official always does fancy—that he was controlling the external acts of the inhabitants of Moscow, but fancied that he was shaping their mental attitude by means of his appeals and placards, written in that vulgar, slangy jargon which the people despise in their own class, and simply fail to understand when they hear it from persons of higher station. The picturesque figure of leader of the popular feeling was so much to Rastoptchin's taste, and he so lived in it, that the necessity of abandoning it, the necessity of surrendering Moscow with no heroic effect of any kind, took him quite unawares; the very ground he was standing on seemed slipping from under his feet, and he was utterly at a loss what to do. Though he knew it was coming, he could not till the last minute fully believe in the abandonment of Moscow, and did nothing towards it. The inhabitants left the city against his wishes. If the courts were removed, it was only due to the insistence of the officials, to which Rastoptchin reluctantly gave way. He was himself entirely absorbed by the rôle he had assumed. As is often the case with persons of heated imagination, he had known for a long while that Moscow would be abandoned; but he had known it only with his intellect, and refused with his whole soul to believe in it, and could not mentally adapt himself to the new position of affairs.

The whole course of his painstaking and vigorous activity—how far it was beneficial or had influence on the people is another question—aimed simply at awakening in the people the feeling he was himself possessed by—hatred of the French and confidence in himself.

But when the catastrophe had begun to take its true historic proportions; when to express hatred of the French in words was plainly insufficient; when it was impossible to express that hatred even by a battle; when self-confidence was of no avail in regard to the one question before Moscow, when the whole population, as one man, abandoning their property, streamed out of Moscow, in this negative fashion giving proof of the strength of their patriotism;—then the part Rastoptchin had been playing suddenly became meaningless. He felt suddenly deserted, weak, and absurd, with no ground to stand on.

On being waked out of his sleep to read Kutuzov's cold and peremptory note, Rastoptchin felt the more irritated the more he felt himself to blame. There was still left in Moscow all that was under his charge, all the government property which it was his duty to have removed to safety. There was no possibility of getting it all away. 'Who is responsible for it? who has let it come to such a pass?' he wondered. 'Of course, it's not my doing. I had everything in readiness; I held Moscow in my hand—like this! And see what they have brought things to! Scoundrels, traitors!' he thought, not exactly defining who were these scoundrels and traitors, but feeling a necessity to hate these vaguely imagined traitors, who were to blame for the false and ludicrous position in which he found himself.

All that night Rastoptchin was giving instructions, for which people were continually coming to him from every part of Moscow. His subordinates had never seen the count so gloomy and irascible.

'Your excellency, they have come from the Estates Department, from the director for instructions.... From the Consistory, from the Senate, from the university, from the Foundling Hospital, the vicar has sent ... he is inquiring ... what orders are to be given about the fire brigade? The overseer of the prison ... the superintendent of the madhouse ...' all night long, without pause, messages were being brought to the count.

To all these inquiries he gave brief and wrathful replies, the drift of which was that his instructions were now not needed, that all his careful preparations had now been ruined by somebody, and that that somebody would have to take all responsibility for anything that might happen now.

'Oh, tell that blockhead,' he replied to the inquiry from the Estates Department, 'to stay and keep guard over his deeds. Well, what nonsense are you asking about the fire brigade? There are horses, let them go off to Vladimir. Don't leave them for the French.'

'Your excellency, the superintendent of the madhouse has come; what are your commands?'

'My commands? Let them all go, that's all.... And let the madmen out into the town. When we have madmen in command of our armies, it seems it's God's will they should be free.'

To the inquiry about the convicts in the prison, the count shouted angrily to the overseer:

'What, do you want me to give you two battalions for a convoy for them, when we haven't any battalions at all? Let them all go, and that settles it!'

'Your excellency, there are political prisoners—Myeshkov, Vereshtchagin...'

'Vereshtchagin! He is not yet hanged?' cried Rastoptchin. 'Send him to me.'

XXV

BY nine o'clock in the morning, when the troops were moving across Moscow, people had ceased coming to Rastoptchin for instructions. All who could get away were going without asking leave; those who stayed decided for themselves what they had better do.

Count Rastoptchin ordered his horses in order to drive to Sokolniky, and with a yellow and frowning face, sat in silence with folded arms in his study.

Every governing official in quiet, untroubled times feels that the whole population under his charge is only kept going by his efforts; and it is this sense of being indispensably necessary in which every governing official finds the chief reward for his toils and cares. It is easy to understand that while the ocean of history is calm, the governing official holding on from his crazy little skiff by a pole to the ship of the people, and moving with it, must fancy that it is his efforts that move the ship on to which he is clinging. But a storm has but to arise to set the sea heaving and the ship tossing upon it, and such error becomes at once impossible. The ship goes on its vast course unchecked, the pole fails to reach the moving vessel, and the pilot, from being the master, the source of power, finds himself a helpless, weak, and useless person.

Rastoptchin felt this, and it drove him to frenzy. The head of the police, who had got away from the crowd, went in to see him at the same time as an adjutant, who came to announce that his horses were ready. Both were pale, and the head of the police, after reporting that he had discharged the commission given to him, informed Count Rastoptchin that there was an immense crowd of people in his courtyard wanting to see him.

Without a word in reply, Count Rastoptchin got up and walked with rapid steps to his light, sumptuously furnished drawing-room. He went up to the balcony door, took hold of the door-handle, let go of it, and moved away to the window, from which the whole crowd could be better seen. The tall young fellow was standing in the front, and with a severe face, waving his arms and saying something. The blood-bespattered smith stood beside him with a gloomy air. Through the closed windows could be heard the roar of voices.

'Is the carriage ready?' said Rastoptchin, moving back from the window.

'Yes, your excellency,' said the adjutant.

Rastoptchin went again to the balcony door.

'Why, what is it they want?' he asked the head of the police.

'Your excellency, they say they have come together to go to fight the French, by your orders; they were shouting something about treachery. But it is an angry crowd, your excellency. I had much ado to get away. If I may venture to suggest, your excellency...'

'Kindly leave me; I know what to do without your assistance,' cried Rastoptchin angrily. He stood at the door of the balcony looking at the crowd. 'This is what they have done with Russia! This is what they have done with me!' thought Rastoptchin, feeling a rush of irrepressible rage against the undefined some one to whose fault what was happening could be set down. As is often the case with excitable persons, he was possessed by fury, while still seeking an object for it. 'Here is the populace, the dregs of the people,' he thought, looking at the crowd, 'that they have stirred up by their folly. They want a victim,' came into his mind, as he watched the waving arm of the tall fellow in front. And the thought struck him precisely because he too wanted a victim, an object for his wrath.

'Is the carriage ready?' he asked again.

'Yes, your excellency. What orders in regard to Vereshtchagin? He is waiting at the steps,' answered the adjutant.

'Ah!' cried Rastoptchin, as though struck by some sudden recollection.

And rapidly opening the door, he walked resolutely out on the balcony. The hum of talk instantly died down, caps and hats were lifted, and all eyes were raised upon the governor.

'Good-day, lads!' said the count, speaking loudly and quickly. 'Thanks for coming. I'll come out to you in a moment, but we have first to deal with a criminal. We have to punish the wretch by whose doing Moscow is ruined. Wait for me!' And as rapidly he returned to the apartment, slamming the door violently.

An approving murmur of satisfaction ran through the crowd. 'He'll have all the traitors cut down, of course. And you talk of the French ... he'll show us the rights and the wrongs of it all!' said the people, as it were reproaching one another for lack of faith.

A few minutes later an officer came hurriedly out of the main entrance, and gave some order, and the dragoons drew themselves up stiffly. The crowd moved greedily up from the balcony to the front steps. Coming out there with hasty and angry steps, Rastoptchin looked about him hurriedly, as though seeking some one.

'Where is he?' he said, and at the moment he said it, he caught sight of a young man with a long, thin neck, and half of his head shaven and covered with short hair, coming round the corner of the house between two dragoons. This young man was clothed in a fox-lined, blue cloth coat, that had once been foppish but was now shabby, and in filthy convict's trousers of fustian, thrust into uncleaned and battered thin boots. His uncertain gait was clogged by the heavy manacles hanging about his thin, weak legs.

'Ah!' said Rastoptchin, hurriedly turning his eyes away from the young man in the fox-lined coat and pointing to the bottom steps. 'Put him here!'

With a clank of manacles the young man stepped with effort on to the step indicated to him; putting his finger into the tight collar of his coat, he turned his long neck twice, and sighing, folded his thin, unworkman-like hands before him with a resigned gesture.

For several seconds, while the young man was taking up his position on the step, there was complete silence. Only at the back of the mass of people, all pressing in one direction, could be heard sighs and groans and sounds of pushing and the shuffling of feet.

Rastoptchin, waiting for him to be on the spot he had directed, scowled, and passed his hand over his face.

'Lads!' he said, with a metallic ring in his voice, 'this man, Vereshtchagin, is the wretch by whose doing Moscow is lost.'

The young man in the fox-lined coat stood in a resigned pose, clasping his hands together in front of his body, and bending a little forward. His wasted young face, with its look of hopelessness and the hideous disfigurement of the half-shaven head, was turned downwards. At the count's first words he slowly lifted his head and looked up from below at the count, as though he wanted to say something to him, or at least to catch his eye. But Rastoptchin did not look at him. The blue vein behind the young man's ear stood out like a cord on his long, thin neck, and all at once his face flushed crimson.

All eyes were fixed upon him. He gazed at the crowd, and, as though made hopeful by the expression he read on the faces there, he smiled a timid, mournful smile, and dropping his head again, shifted his feet on the step.

'He is a traitor to his Tsar and his country; he deserted to Bonaparte; he alone of all the Russians has disgraced the name of Russia, and through him Moscow is lost,' said Rastoptchin in a harsh, monotonous voice; but all at once he glanced down rapidly at Vereshtchagin, who still stood in the same submissive attitude. As though that glance had driven him to frenzy, flinging up his arms, he almost yelled to the crowd:

'You shall deal with him as you think fit! I hand him over to you!'

The people were silent, and only pressed closer and closer on one another. To bear each other's weight, to breathe in that tainted foulness, to be unable to stir, and to be expecting something vague, uncomprehended and awful, was becoming unbearable. The men in the front of the crowd, who saw and heard all that was passing before them, all stood with wide-open, horror-struck eyes and gaping mouths, straining all their strength to support the pressure from behind on their backs.

'Beat him! . . . Let the traitor perish and not shame the name of Russia!' screamed Rastoptchin. 'Cut him down! I give the command!' Hearing not the words, but only the wrathful tones of Rastoptchin's voice, the mob moaned and heaved forward, but stopped again.

'Count!' . . . the timid and yet theatrical voice of Vereshtchagin broke in upon the momentary stillness that followed. 'Count, one God is above us . . .' said Vereshtchagin, lifting his head, and again the thick vein swelled on his thin neck and the colour swiftly came and faded again from his face. He did not finish what he was trying to say.

'Cut him down! I command it! . . .' cried Rastoptchin, suddenly turning as white as Vereshtchagin himself.

'Draw sabres!' shouted the officer to the dragoons, himself drawing his sabre.

Another still more violent wave passed over the crowd, and reaching the front rows, pushed them forward, and threw them staggering right up to the steps. The tall young man, with a stony expression of face and his lifted arm rigid in the air, stood close beside Vereshtchagin. 'Strike at him!' the officer said almost in a whisper to the dragoons; and one of the soldiers, his face suddenly convulsed by fury, struck Vereshtchagin on the head with the flat of his sword.

Vereshtchagin uttered a brief 'Ah!' of surprise, looking about him in alarm, as though he did not know what this was done to him for. A similar moan of surprise and horror ran through the crowd.

'O Lord!' some one was heard to utter mournfully. After the exclamation of surprise that broke from Vereshtchagin he uttered a piteous cry of pain, and that cry was his undoing. The barrier of human feeling that still held the mob back was strained to the utmost limit, and it snapped instantaneously. The crime had been begun, its completion was inevitable. The piteous moan of reproach was drowned in the angry and menacing roar of the mob. Like the great seventh wave that shatters a ship, that last, irresistible wave surged up at the back of the crowd, passed on to the foremost ranks, carried them off their feet and engulfed all together. The dragoon who had struck the victim would have repeated his blow. Vereshtchagin, with a scream of terror, putting his hands up before him, dashed into the crowd. The tall young man, against whom he stumbled, gripped Vereshtchagin's slender neck in his hands, and with a savage shriek fell with him under the feet of the trampling, roaring mob. Some beat and tore at Vereshtchagin, others at the tall young man. And the screams of persons crushed in the crowd and of those who tried to rescue the tall young man only increased the frenzy of the mob. For a long while the dragoons were unable to get the bleeding, half-murdered factory workman away. And in spite of all the feverish haste with which the mob strove to make an end of what had once been begun, the men who beat and strangled Vereshtchagin and tore him to pieces could not kill him. The crowd pressed on them on all sides, heaved from side to side like one man with them in the middle, and would not let them kill him outright or let him go.

'Hit him with an axe, eh? . . . they have crushed him . . . Traitor, he sold Christ! . . . living . . . alive . . . serve the thief right. With a bar! . . . Is he alive? . . .'

Only when the victim ceased to struggle, and his shrieks had passed into a long-drawn, rhythmic death-rattle, the mob began hurriedly to change places about the bleeding corpse on the ground. Every one went up to it, gazed at what had been done, and pressed back horror-stricken, surprised, and reproachful.

'O Lord, the people's like a wild beast; how could he be alive!' was heard in the crowd. 'And a young fellow too . . . must have been a merchant's son, to be sure the people . . they do say it's not the right man . . . not the right man! . . . O Lord! . . . They have nearly murdered another man; they say he's almost dead . . . Ah, the people . . . who wouldn't be afraid of sin . . .' were saying now the same people, looking with rueful pity at the dead body, with the blue face fouled with dust and blood, and the long, slender, broken neck.

A punctilious police official, feeling the presence of the body unseemly in the courtyard of his excellency, bade the dragoons drag the body away into the street. Two dragoons took hold of the mutilated legs, and drew the body away. The dead, shaven head, stained with blood and grimed with dust, was trailed along the ground, rolling from side to side on the long neck. The crowd shrank away from the corpse.

When Vereshtchagin fell, and the crowd with a savage yell closed in and heaved about him, Rastoptchin suddenly turned white, and instead of going to the back entrance, where horses were waiting for him, he strode rapidly along the corridor leading to the rooms of the lower story, looking on the floor and not knowing where or why he was going. The count's face was white, and he could not check the feverish twitching of his lower jaw.

'Your excellency, this way . . . where are you going? . . . this way,' said a trembling, frightened voice behind him. Count Rastoptchin was incapable of making any reply. Obediently turning, he went in the direction indicated. At the back entrance stood a carriage. The distant roar of the howling mob could be heard even there. Count Rastoptchin hurriedly got into the carriage, and bade them drive him to his house at Sokolniky beyond the town. As he drove out into Myasnitsky Street and lost the sound of the shouts of the mob, the count began to repent. He thought with dissatisfaction now of the excitement and terror he had betrayed before his subordinates. 'The populace is terrible, it is hideous. They are like wolves that can only be appeased with flesh,' he thought. 'Count! there is one God over us!' Vereshtchagin's words suddenly recurred to him, and a disagreeable chill ran down his back. But that feeling was momentary, and Count Rastoptchin smiled contemptuously at himself. 'I had other duties. The people had to be appeased. Many other victims have perished and are perishing for the public good,' he thought; and he began to reflect on the social duties he had towards his family and toward the city intrusted to his care; and on himself—not as Fyodor Vassilyevitch Rastoptchin (he assumed that Fyodor Vassilyevitch Rastoptchin was sacrificing himself for *le bien publique*)—but as governor of Moscow, as the representative of authority entrusted with full powers by the Tsar. 'If I had been simply Fyodor Vassilyevitch, my course of action might have been quite different; but I was bound to preserve both the life and the dignity of the governor.'

Lightly swayed on the soft springs of the carriage, and hearing no more of the fearful sounds of the mob, Rastoptchin was physically soothed, and as is always the case simultaneously with physical relief, his intellect supplied him with grounds for moral comfort. The thought that reassured Rastoptchin was not a new one. Ever since the world has existed and men have killed one another, a man has never committed such a crime against his fellow without consoling himself with the same idea. That idea is *le bien publique*, the supposed public good of others.

To a man not swayed by passion this good never seems certain; but a man who has committed such a crime always knows positively where that public good lies. And Rastoptchin now knew this.

Far from reproaching himself in his meditations on the act he had just committed, he found grounds for self-complacency in having so successfully made use of an occasion so *à propos* for executing a criminal, and at the same time satisfying the crowd. 'Vereshtchagin had been tried and condemned to the death penalty,' Rastoptchin reflected (though Vereshtchagin had only been condemned by the senate to hard labour). 'He was a spy and a traitor; I could not let him go unpunished, and so I hit two birds with one stone. I appeased the mob by giving them a victim, and I punished a miscreant.'

Reaching his house in the suburbs, the count completely regained his composure in arranging his domestic affairs.

Within half an hour the count was driving with rapid horses across the Sokolniky plain, thinking no more now of the past, but absorbed in thought and plans for what was to come. He was approaching now the Yauzsky bridge, where he had been told that Kutuzov was. In his own mind he was preparing the biting and angry speeches he would make upbraiding Kutuzov for his deception. He would make that old court fox feel that the responsibility for all the disasters bound to follow the abandonment of Moscow, and the ruin of Russia (as Rastoptchin considered it), lay upon his old, doting head. Going over in anticipation what he would say to him, Rastoptchin wrathfully turned from side to side in the carriage, and angrily looked about him.

The Sokolniky plain was deserted. Only at one end of it, by the almshouse and lunatic asylum, there were groups of people in white garments, and similar persons were wandering about the plain, shouting and gesticulating.

One of them was running right across in front of Count Rastoptchin's carriage. And Count Rastoptchin himself and his coachman, and the dragoons, all gazed with a vague feeling of horror and curiosity at these released lunatics, and especially at the one who was running towards them.

Tottering on his long, thin legs in his fluttering dressing-gown, this madman ran at headlong speed, with his eyes fixed on Rastoptchin, shouting something to him in a husky voice, and making signs to him to stop. The gloomy and triumphant face of the madman was thin and yellow, with irregular tufts of beard growing on it. The black, agate-like pupils of his eyes moved restlessly, showing the saffron-yellow whites above. 'Stay! stop, I tell you!' he shouted shrilly, and again breathlessly fell to shouting something with emphatic gestures and intonations.

He reached the carriage and ran alongside it.

'Three times they slew me, three times I rose again from the dead. They stoned me, they crucified me ... I shall rise again ... I shall rise again ... I shall rise again. My body they tore to pieces. The kingdom of heaven will be overthrown ... Three times I will overthrow it, and three times I will set it up again,' he screamed, his voice growing shriller and shriller. Count Rastoptchin suddenly turned white, as he had turned white when the crowd fell upon Vereshtchagin. He turned away. 'G ... go on, faster!' he cried in a trembling voice to his coachman.

The carriage dashed on at the horses' topmost speed. But for a long while yet Count Rastoptchin heard behind him the frantic, desperate scream getting further away, while before his eyes he saw nothing but the wondering, frightened, bleeding face of the traitor in the fur-lined coat. Fresh as that image was, Rastoptchin felt now that it was deeply for ever imprinted on his heart. He felt clearly now that the bloody print of that memory would never leave him, that the further he went the more cruelly, the more vindictively, would that fearful memory rankle in his heart to the end of his life. He seemed to be hearing now the sound of his own words: 'Tear him to pieces, you shall answer for it to me!—Why did I say these words? I said it somehow without meaning to ... I might not have said them,' he thought, 'and then nothing would have happened.' He saw the terror-stricken, and then suddenly frenzied face of the dragoon who had struck the first blow, and the glance of silent, timid reproach cast on him by that lad in the fox-lined coat. 'But I didn't do it on my own account. I was bound to act in that way. *La plèbe ... le traître ... le bien publique,* ...' he mused.

The bridge over the Yauza was still crowded with troops. It was hot. Kutuzov, looking careworn and weary, was sitting on a bench near the bridge, and playing with a whip on the sand, when a carriage rattled noisily up to him. A man in the uniform of a general, wearing a hat with plumes, came up to Kutuzov. He began addressing him in French, his eyes shifting uneasily, with a look between anger and terror in them. It was Count Rastoptchin. He told Kutuzov that he had come here, for since Moscow was no more, the army was all that was left. 'It might have been very different if your highness had not told me you would not abandon Moscow without a battle; all this would not have been!' said he.

Kutuzov stared at Rastoptchin, and, as though not understanding the meaning of the words addressed to him, he strove earnestly to decipher the special meaning betrayed at that minute on the face of the man addressing him. Rastoptchin ceased speaking in discomfiture. Kutuzov slightly shook his head, and, still keeping his searching eyes on Rastoptchin's face, he murmured softly:

'Yes, I won't give up Moscow without a battle.'

Whether Kutuzov were thinking of something different when he uttered those words, or said them purposely, knowing them to be meaningless, Count Rastoptchin made him no reply, and hastily left him. And—strange to tell! the governor of Moscow, the proud Count Rastoptchin, picking up a horse whip, went to the bridge, and fell to shouting and driving on the crowded carts.

XXVI

AT four o'clock in the afternoon, Murat's troops entered Moscow. In front rode a detachment of Würtemburg hussars, behind, with an immense suite, rode the King of Naples himself.

Near the middle of Arbaty, close to Nikola Yavlenny, Murat halted to await information from the detachment in advance as to the condition in which the citadel of the city, '*le Kremlin*,' had been found.

A small group of inhabitants of Moscow had gathered about Murat. All stared with timid astonishment at the strange figure of the long-haired commander, decked in gold and feathers.

'Why is this their Tsar himself? Nought amiss with him,' voices were heard saying softly.

An interpreter approached the group of gazers.

'Caps . . . caps off,' they muttered, turning to each other in the little crowd. The interpreter accosted one old porter, and asked him if it were far to the Kremlin. The porter, listening with surprise to the unfamiliar Polish accent, and not recognising the interpreter's words for Russian, had no notion what was being said to him, and took refuge behind the others.

Murat approached the interpreter, and told him to ask where were the Russian troops. One of the Russians understood this question, and several voices began answering the interpreter simultaneously. A French officer from the detachment in advance rode up to Murat and reported that the gates into the citadel were blocked up, and that probably there was an ambush there.

'Good,' said Murat, and turning to one of the gentlemen of his suite, he commanded four light cannons to be moved forward, and the gates to be shelled upon.

The artillery came trotting out from the column following Murat, and advanced along Arbaty. When they reached the end of Vosdvizhenka the artillery halted and drew up in the square. Several French officers superintended the placing of the cannon some distance apart, and looked at the Kremlin through a field-glass. A bell was ringing in the Kremlin for evening service, and that sound troubled the French. They supposed that it was the call to arms. Several infantry soldiers ran to the Kutafyev gateway. A barricade of beams and planks lay across the gateway. Two musket shots rang out from the gates, just as an officer with some men were running up to them. The general standing by the cannons shouted some words of command to the officer, and the officer and the soldiers ran back.

Three more shots were heard from the gate. One shot grazed the leg of a French soldier, and a strange shout of several voices rose from behind the barricade. Instantaneously, as though at the word of command, the expression of good humour and serenity on the faces of the French general, officers, and men was replaced by a stubborn, concentrated expression of readiness for conflict and suffering. To all of them, from the marshal to the lowest soldier, this place was not Vosdvizhenka, Mohova, Kutaf, and the Troitsky gates; it was a new battlefield, likely to be the scene of a bloody conflict. And all were ready for that conflict. The shouts from the gates died away. The cannons were moved forward. The artillerymen quenched the burning linstocks. An officer shouted 'Fire!' and two whistling sounds of clinking tin rang out one after another. The grape-shot fell rattling on the stone of the gateway, on the beams and screens of planks, and two clouds of smoke rolled over the square.

Some instants after the echoes of the shots had died away over the stone Kremlin, a strange sound was heard over the heads of the French. An immense flock of jackdaws rose above the walls and swept round in the air with loud caws, and the whir of thousands of wings. Together with this sound, there rose a solitary human cry at the gate, and the figure of a man bareheaded, in a long peasant's coat, came into sight through the smoke. Holding a gun up, he took aim at the French. 'Fire!' repeated the artillery officer, and at the same instant one rifle shot and two cannon shots were heard. The gate was again hidden in smoke.

Nothing more stirred behind the barricade, and the French infantry soldiers with their officers passed in at the gate. In the gateway lay three men wounded and four dead. Two men in long peasant-coats had run away along the walls toward Znamenka.

'Clear this away,' said the officer, pointing to the beams and the corpses; and the French soldiers finished off the wounded, and flung the corpses over the fence below. Who these men were nobody knew. 'Clear this away!' was all that was said to them, and they were flung away that they might not stink. Thiers has indeed devoted some eloquent lines to their memories. 'These wretches had invaded the sacred citadel, had taken possession of the guns of the arsenal and fired (the wretches) on the French. Some of them were sabred, and the Kremlin was purged of their presence.'

Murat was informed that the way had been cleared. The French entered the gates, and began pitching their camp on Senate-house Square. The soldiers flung the chairs out of the windows of the Senate-house into the square, and began making fires.

Other detachments marched across the Kremlin and encamped in Moroseyka, Lubyanka, and Pokrovka. Others pitched their camps in Vosdvizhenka, Znamenka, Nikolskaya, and Tverskaya. Not finding citizens to entertain them, the French everywhere bivouacked as in a camp pitched in a town, instead of quartering themselves on the houses.

Tattered, hungry, and exhausted, as they were, and dwindled to one-third their original numbers, the French soldiers yet entered Moscow in good discipline. It was a harassed and exhausted, yet still active and menacing army. But it was an army only up to the moment when the soldiers of the army dispersed all over the town. As soon as the soldiers began to disperse about the wealthy, deserted houses, the army was lost for ever, and in its place was a multitude of men, neither citizens nor soldiers, but something nondescript between, known as marauders. When five weeks later these same men set out from Moscow, they no longer made up an army. They were a mob of marauders, each of whom carried or dragged along with him a mass of objects he regarded as precious and useful. The aim of each of these men on leaving Moscow was not, as it had been, to fight as a soldier, but simply to keep the booty he had obtained. Like the ape, who slipping his hand into the narrow neck of a pitcher, and snatching up a handful of nuts inside it, will not open his fist for fear of losing his prize, even to his own ruin, the French on leaving Moscow were inevitably bound to come to ruin, because they dragged their plunder along with them, and it seemed as impossible to them to fling away their booty as it seems to the ape to let go of the nuts. Ten minutes after the several French regiments had dispersed about the various quarters of Moscow, not a soldier nor an officer was left among them. At the windows of the houses men could be seen in military coats and Hessian boots, laughing and strolling through the rooms. In the cellars, in the storerooms similar men were busily looking after the provisions; in the courtyards they were unlocking or breaking open the doors of sheds and stables; in the kitchens they were making up fires, and with bare arms mixing, kneading, and baking, and frightening, or trying to coax and amuse, women and children. Men there were in plenty everywhere, in all the shops and houses; but the army was no more.

That day one order after another was issued by the French commanders forbidding the troops to disperse about the town, sternly forbidding violence to the inhabitants, and pillaging, and proclaiming that a general roll-call was to take place that evening. But in spite of all such measures the men, who had made up an army, flowed away about the wealthy, deserted city, so richly provided with luxuries and comforts. Like a starved herd, that keeps together crossing a barren plain, but at once on reaching rich pastures inevitably strays apart and scatters over them, the army was irresistibly lured into scattering over the wealthy town.

Moscow was without its inhabitants, and the soldiers were sucked up in her, like water into sand, as they flowed away irresistibly in all directions from the Kremlin, which they had entered first. Cavalry soldiers, who had entered a merchant's house abandoned with all its belongings, and finding stabling for their horses and to spare, yet went on to take the house next door, which seemed to them better. Many took several houses, chalking their names on them, and quarrelled and even fought with other companies for their possession. Soldiers had no sooner succeeded in securing quarters than they ran along the street to look at the town, and on hearing that everything had been abandoned, hurried off where objects of value could be carried off for nothing. The officers followed to check the soldiers, and were involuntarily lured into doing the same. In Carriage Row shops had been abandoned stocked with carriages, and the generals flocked thither to choose coaches and carriages for themselves. The few inhabitants who had stayed on invited the officers into their houses, hoping thereby to secure themselves against being robbed. Wealth there was in abundance: there seemed no end to it. Everywhere all round the parts occupied by the French there were unexplored regions unoccupied beyond, in which the French fancied there were even more riches to be found. And Moscow absorbed them further and further into herself. Just as when water flows over dry land, water and dry land alike disappear and are lost in mud, so when the hungry army entered the wealthy, deserted city, the army and the wealth of the city both perished; and fires and marauding bands sprang up where they had been.

The French ascribed the burning of Moscow *au patriotisme féroce de Rastoptchine*; the Russians to the savagery of the French. In reality, explanations of the fire of Moscow, in the sense of the conflagration being brought home to the door of any one person or group of persons, there have never been, and never could be. Moscow was burned because she was placed in conditions in which any town built of wood was bound to be burned, quite apart from the question whether there were or were not one hundred and thirty inefficient fire-engines in the town. Moscow was sure to be burned, because her inhabitants had gone away, as inevitably as a heap of straw is sure to be burned where sparks are scattered on it for several days in succession. A town of wooden houses, in which when the police and the inhabitants owning the houses are in possession of it, fires are of daily occurrence, cannot escape being burned when its inhabitants are gone and it is filled with soldiers smoking pipes, making fires in Senate-house Square of the Senate-house chairs, and cooking themselves meals twice a day. In times of peace, whenever troops are quartered on villages in any district, the number of fires in the district at once increases. How greatly must the likelihood of fires be increased in an abandoned town, built of wood, and occupied by foreign soldiers! *Le patriotisme féroce de Rastoptchine* and the savagery of the French do not come into the question. Moscow was burned through the pipes, the kitchen stoves, and camp fires, through the recklessness of the enemy's soldiers, who lived in the houses without the care of householders. Even if there were cases of incendiarism (which is very doubtful, because no one had any reason for incendiarism, and in any case such a crime is a troublesome and dangerous one), there is no need to accept incendiarism as the cause, for the conflagration would have been inevitable anyway without it.

Soothing as it was to the vanity of the French to throw the blame on the ferocity of Rastoptchin, and to that of the Russians to throw the blame on the miscreant Bonaparte, or later on to place the heroic torch in the hand of its patriot peasantry, we cannot disguise from ourselves that there could be no such direct cause of the fire, since Moscow was as certain to be burned as any village, factory, or house forsaken by its owners, and used as a temporary shelter and cooking-place by strangers. Moscow was burned by her inhabitants it is true; but not by the inhabitants who had lingered on, but by the inhabitants who had abandoned her. Moscow did not, like Berlin, Vienna, and other towns, escape harm while in the occupation of the enemy, simply because her inhabitants did not receive the French with the keys, and the bread and salt of welcome, but abandoned her.

XXVII

THE process of the absorption of the French into Moscow in a widening circle in all directions did not, till the evening of the 2nd of September, reach the quarter of the town in which Pierre was staying.

After the two last days spent in solitude and exceptional conditions, Pierre was in a condition approaching madness. One haunting idea had complete possession of him. He could not have told how or when it had come to him, but that idea had now such complete possession of him that he remembered nothing in the past, and understood nothing in the present; and everything he saw and heard seemed passing in a dream.

Pierre had left his own house simply to escape from the complicated tangle woven about him by the demands of daily life, which in his condition at that time he was incapable of unravelling. He had gone to Osip Alexyevitch's house on the pretext of sorting out the books and papers of the deceased. Simply he was in search of a quiet home of rest from the storm of life, and his memories of Osip Alexyevitch were connected in his soul with a whole world of calm, solemn, and eternal ideas, in every way the reverse of the tangled whirl of agitation into which he felt himself being drawn. He was in search of a quiet refuge, and he certainly found it in Osip Alexyevitch's study. When, in the deathlike stillness of the study, he sat with his elbows on the dusty writing-table of his deceased friend, there passed in calm and significant succession before his mental vision the impressions of the last few days, especially of the battle of Borodino, and of that overwhelming sense of his own pettiness and falsity in comparison with the truth and simplicity and force of that class of men, who were mentally referred to by him as 'they.' When Gerasim roused him from his reverie, the idea occurred to Pierre that he would take part in the defence of Moscow by the people, which was, he knew, expected. And with that object he had asked Gerasim to get him a peasant's coat and a pistol, and had told him that he intended to conceal his name, and to remain in Osip Alexyevitch's house. Then during the first day of solitude and idleness (Pierre tried several times in vain to fix his attention on the masonic manuscripts) there rose several times vaguely to his mind the idea that had occurred to him in the past of the cabalistic significance of his name in connection with the name of Bonaparte. But the idea that he, *l'Russe Besuhof*, was destined to put an end to the power of the *Beast*, had as yet only come to him as one of those dreams that flit idly through the brain leaving no trace behind. When after buying the peasant's coat, simply with the object of taking part in the defence of Moscow by the people, Pierre had met the Rostovs, and Natasha said to him, 'You are staying? Ah, how splendid that is!' the idea had flashed into his mind that it really might be splendid, even if they did take Moscow, for him to remain, and to do what had been foretold for him to do.

Next day with the simple aim of not sparing himself and not doing less than *they* would do, he had gone out to the Three Hills barrier. But when he came back, convinced that Moscow would not be defended, he suddenly felt that what had only occurred to him before as a possibility, had now become something necessary and inevitable. He must remain in Moscow, concealing his name, must meet Napoleon, and kill him, so as either to perish or to put an end to the misery of all

Europe, which was in Pierre's opinion entirely due to Napoleon alone.

Pierre knew all the details of the German student's attempt on Napoleon's life at Vienna in 1809, and knew that that student had been shot. And the danger to which he would be exposing his own life in carrying out his design excited him even more violently.

Two equally powerful feelings drew Pierre irresistibly to his design. The first was the craving for sacrifice and suffering through the sense of the common calamity, the feeling that had impelled him to go to Mozhaisk on the 25th, and to place himself in the very thick of the battle, and now to run away from his own house, to give up his accustomed luxury and comfort, to sleep without undressing on a hard sofa, and to eat the same food as Gerasim. The other was that vague and exclusively Russian feeling of contempt for everything conventional, artificial, human, for everything that is regarded by the majority of men as the highest good in the world. Pierre had for the first time experienced that strange and fascinating feeling in the Slobodsky palace, when he suddenly felt that wealth and power and life, all that men build up and guard with such effort, is only worth anything through the joy with which it can all be cast away.

It was the same feeling that impels the volunteer-recruit to drink up his last farthing, the drunken man to smash looking-glasses and window-panes for no apparent cause, though he knows it will cost him his little all; the feeling through which a man in doing things, vulgarly speaking, senseless, as it were, proves his personal force and power, by manifesting the presence of a higher standard of judging life, outside mere human limitations.

Ever since the day when Pierre first experienced this feeling in the Slobodsky palace, he had been continually under the influence of it, but it was only now that it found full satisfaction. Moreover at the present moment Pierre was supported in his design, and prevented from abandoning it, by the steps he had already taken in that direction. His flight from his own house, and his disguise, and his pistol, and his statement to the Rostovs that he should remain in Moscow,—all would have been devoid of meaning, would have been indeed absurd and laughable (a point to which Pierre was sensitive) if after all that he had simply gone out of Moscow like other people.

Pierre's physical state, as is always the case, corresponded with his moral condition. The coarse fare to which he was unused, the vodka he drank during those days, the lack of wine and cigars, his dirty, unchanged linen, and two half-sleepless nights, spent on a short sofa without bedding, all reduced Pierre to a state of nervous irritability bordering on madness.

It was two o'clock in the afternoon. The French had already entered Moscow. Pierre knew this, but instead of acting, he only brooded over his enterprise, going over all the minutest details of it. In his dreams Pierre never clearly pictured the very act of striking the blow, nor the death of Napoleon, but with extraordinary vividness and mournful enjoyment dwelt on his own end and his heroic fortitude.

'Yes, one man for all, I must act or perish!' he thought. 'Yes, I will approach . . . and then all at once . . . with a pistol or a dagger!' thought Pierre. 'But that doesn't matter. It's not I but the Hand of Providence punishes you. . . . I shall say' (Pierre pondered over the words he would utter as he killed Napoleon). 'Well, take me, execute me!' Pierre would murmur to himself, bowing his head with a sad but firm expression on his face.

While Pierre was standing in the middle of the room, musing in this fashion, the door of the study opened, and Makar Alexyevitch—always hitherto so timid—appeared in the doorway, completely transformed.

His dressing-gown was hanging open. His face was red and distorted. He was unmistakably drunk. On seeing Pierre he was for the first minute disconcerted, but observing discomfiture in Pierre's face too, he was at once emboldened by it; and with his thin, tottering legs walked into the middle of the room.

'They have grown fearful,' he said in a husky and confidential voice. 'I say: I will not surrender, I say . . . eh, sir?' He paused and suddenly catching sight of the pistol on the table, snatched it with surprising rapidity and ran out into the corridor.

Gerasim and the porter, who had followed Makar Alexyevitch, stopped him in the vestibule, and tried to get the pistol away from him. Pierre coming out of the study looked with repugnance and compassion at the half-insane old man. Makar Alexyevitch, frowning with effort, succeeded in keeping the pistol, and was shouting in a husky voice, evidently imagining some heroic scene.

'To arms! Board them! You shan't get it!' he was shouting.

'Give over, please, give over. Do me the favour, sir, please be quiet. There now, if you please, sir, . . .' Gerasim was saying, cautiously trying to steer Makar Alexyevitch by his elbows towards the door.

'Who are you? Bonaparte! . . .' yelled Makar Alexyevitch.

'That's not the thing, sir. You come into your room and rest a little. Let me have the pistol now.'

'Away, base slave! Don't touch me! Do you see?' screamed Makar Alexyevitch, brandishing the pistol. 'Run them down!'

'Take hold!' Gerasim whispered to the porter.

They seized Makar Alexyevitch by the arms and dragged him towards the door.

The vestibule was filled with the unseemly sounds of scuffling and drunken, husky gasping.

Suddenly a new sound, a shrill, feminine shriek, was heard from the porch, and the cook ran into the vestibule.

'They! Merciful heavens! ... My goodness, here they are! Four of them, horsemen!' she screamed.

Gerasim and the porter let Makar Alexyevitch go, and in the hush that followed in the corridor they could distinctly hear several hands knocking at the front door.

XXVIII

HAVING inwardly resolved that until the execution of his design, he ought to disguise his station and his knowledge of French, Pierre stood at the half-open door into the corridor, intending to conceal himself at once as soon as the French entered. But the French entered, and Pierre did not leave the door; an irresistible curiosity kept him there.

There were two of them. One—an officer, a tall, handsome man of gallant bearing; the other, obviously a soldier or officer's servant, a squat, thin, sunburnt man, with hollow cheeks and a dull expression. The officer walked first, limping and leaning on a stick. After advancing a few steps, the officer, apparently making up his mind that these would be good quarters, stopped, turned round and shouted in a loud, peremptory voice to the soldiers standing in the doorway to put up the horses. Having done this the officer, with a jaunty gesture, crooking his elbow high in the air, stroked his moustaches and put his hand to his hat.

'*Bonjour, la compagnie!*' he said gaily, smiling and looking about him.

No one made any reply.

'*Vous êtes le bourgeois?*' the officer asked, addressing Gerasim.

Gerasim looked back with scared inquiry at the officer.

'*Quartire, quartire, logement,*' said the officer, looking down with a condescending and good-humoured smile at the little man. 'The French are good lads. Don't let us be cross, old fellow,' he went on in French, clapping the scared and mute Gerasim on the shoulder. 'I say, does no one speak French in this establishment?' he added, looking round and meeting Pierre's eyes. Pierre withdrew from the door.

The officer turned again to Gerasim. He asked him to show him over the house.

'Master not here—no understand . . . me you . . .' said Gerasim, trying to make his words more comprehensible by saying them in reverse order.

The French officer, smiling, waved his hands in front of Gerasim's nose, to give him to understand that he too failed to understand him, and walked with a limp towards the door where Pierre was standing. Pierre was about to retreat to conceal himself from him, but at that very second he caught sight of Makar Alexyevitch peeping out of the open kitchen door with a pistol in his hand. With a madman's cunning, Makar Alexyevitch eyed the Frenchmen, and lifting the pistol, took aim. 'Run them down! ! !' yelled the drunkard, pressing the trigger. The French officer turned round at the scream, and at the same instant Pierre dashed at the drunken man. Just as Pierre snatched at the pistol and jerked it up, Makar Alexyevitch succeeded at last in pressing the trigger, and a deafening shot rang out, wrapping every one in a cloud of smoke. The Frenchman turned pale and rushed back to the door.

Forgetting his intention of concealing his knowledge of French, Pierre pulled away the pistol, and throwing it on the ground, ran to the officer and addressed him in French. 'You are not wounded?' he said.

'I think not,' answered the officer, feeling himself; 'but I have had a narrow escape this time,' he added, pointing to the broken plaster in the wall.

'Who is this man?' he asked, looking sternly at Pierre.

'Oh, I am really in despair at what has happened,' said Pierre quickly, quite forgetting his part. 'It is a madman, an unhappy creature, who did not know what he was doing.'

The officer went up to Makar Alexyevitch and took him by the collar.

Makar Alexyevitch pouting out his lips, nodded, as he leaned against the wall, as though dropping asleep.

'Brigand, you shall pay for it,' said the Frenchman, letting go of him. 'We are clement after victory, but we do not pardon traitors,' he added, with gloomy dignity in his face, and a fine, vigorous gesture.

Pierre tried in French to persuade the officer not to be severe with this drunken imbecile. The Frenchman listened in silence, with the same gloomy air, and then suddenly turned with a smile to Pierre. For several seconds he gazed at him mutely. His handsome face assumed an expression of melodramatic feeling, and he held out his hand.

'You have saved my life. You are French,' he said. For a Frenchman, the deduction followed indubitably. An heroic action could only be performed by a Frenchman, and to save the life of him, M. Ramballe, captain of the 13th Light Brigade, was undoubtedly a most heroic action.

But however indubitable this logic, and well grounded the conviction the officer based it on, Pierre thought well to disillusion him on the subject.

'I am Russian,' he said quickly.

'Tell that to others,' said the Frenchman, smiling and waving his finger before his nose. 'You shall tell me all about it directly,' he said. 'Charmed to meet a compatriot. Well, what are we to do with this man?' he added, applying to Pierre now as though to a comrade. If Pierre were indeed not a Frenchman, he would hardly on receiving that appellation—the most honourable in the world—care to disavow it, was what the expression and tone of the French officer suggested. To his last question Pierre explained once more who Makar Alexyevitch was. He explained that just before his arrival the drunken imbecile had carried off a loaded pistol, which they had not succeeded in getting from him, and he begged him to let his action go unpunished. The Frenchman arched his chest, and made a majestic gesture with his hand.

'You have saved my life! You are a Frenchman. You ask me to pardon him. I grant you his pardon. Let this man be released,' the French officer pronounced with rapidity and energy, and taking the arm of Pierre—promoted to be a Frenchman for saving his life—he was walking with him into the room.

The soldiers in the yard, hearing the shot, had come into the vestibule to ask what had happened, and to offer their services in punishing the offender; but the officer sternly checked them.

'You will be sent for when you are wanted,' he said. The soldiers withdrew. The orderly, who had meanwhile been in the kitchen, came in to the officer.

'Captain, they have soup and a leg of mutton in the kitchen,' he said. 'Shall I bring it up.'

'Yes, and the wine,' said the captain.

XXIX

As the French officer drew Pierre with him into the room, the latter thought it his duty to assure the captain again that he was not a Frenchman, and would have withdrawn, but the French officer would not hear of it. He was so courteous, polite, good-humoured, and genuinely grateful to him for saving his life that Pierre had not the heart to refuse, and sat down with him in the dining-room, the first room they entered. To Pierre's asseveration that he was not a Frenchman, the captain, plainly unable to comprehend how any one could refuse so flattering a title, shrugged his shoulders, and said that if he insisted in passing for a Russian, so be it, but that in spite of that he should yet feel bound to him for ever by sentiments of gratitude for the defence of his life.

If this man had been endowed with even the slightest faculty of perceiving the feelings of others, and had had the faintest inkling of Pierre's sentiments, the latter would probably have left him. But his lively impenetrability to everything not himself vanquished Pierre.

'Frenchman or Russian prince incognito,' said the Frenchman, looking at Pierre's fine, though dirty linen, and the ring on his finger; 'I owe my life to you, and I offer you my friendship. A Frenchman never forgets an insult or a service. I offer you my friendship. That's all I say.'

In the tones of the voice, the expression of the face, and the gestures of the officer, there was so much naïve good nature and good breeding (in the French sense) that Pierre unconsciously responded with a smile to his smile, as he took his outstretched hand.

'Captain Ramballe of the 13th Light Brigade, decorated for the affair of the 7th September,' he introduced himself, an irrepressible smile of complacency lurking under his moustache. 'Will you tell me now to whom I have the honour of speaking so agreeably, instead of remaining in the ambulance with that madman's ball in my body.'

Pierre answered that he would not tell him his name, and was beginning with a blush, while trying to invent a name, to speak of the reasons for which he was unable to do so, but the Frenchman hurriedly interrupted him.

'Enough!' he said. 'I understand your reasons; you are an officer ... a staff officer, perhaps. You have borne arms against us. That's not my business. I owe you my life. That's enough for me. I am at your disposal. You are a nobleman?' he added, with an intonation of inquiry. Pierre bowed.

'Your baptismal name, if you please? I ask nothing more. M. Pierre, you say? Perfect! That's all I want to know.'

When they had brought in the mutton, an omelette, a samovar, vodka, and wine from a Russian cellar brought with them by the French, Ramballe begged Pierre to share his dinner; and at once with the haste and greediness of a healthy, hungry man, set to work on the viands himself, munching vigorously with his strong teeth, and continually smacking his lips and exclaiming, *'Excellent! exquis!'* His face became flushed and perspiring. Pierre was hungry, and pleased to share the repast. Morel, the orderly, brought in a pot of hot water, and put a bottle of red wine to warm in it. He brought in too a bottle of kvass from the kitchen for them to taste. This beverage was already known to the French, and had received a nickname. They called it *limonade de cochon*, and Morel praised this 'pigs' lemonade,' which he had found in the kitchen. But as the captain had the wine they had picked up as they crossed Moscow, he left the kvass for Morel, and attacked the bottle of bordeaux. He wrapped a napkin round the bottle, and poured out wine for himself and Pierre. The wine, and the satisfaction of his hunger, made the captain even more lively, and he chatted away without a pause all dinner-time.

'Yes, my dear M. Pierre, I owe you a fine votive candle for saving me from that maniac. I have bullets enough in my body, you know. Here is one from Wagram' (he pointed to his side), 'and two from Smolensk' (he showed the scar on his cheek). 'And this leg which won't walk, as you see. It was at the great battle of la Moskowa on the 7th that I got that. *Sacré Dieu*, it was fine! You ought to have seen that; it was a deluge of fire. You cut us out a tough job; you can boast of that, my word on it! And on my word, in spite of the cough I caught, I should be ready to begin again. I pity those who did not see it.'

'I was there,' said Pierre.

'Really!' pursued the Frenchman. 'Well, so much the better. You are fine enemies, though. The great redoubt was well held, by my pipe. And you made us pay heavily for it too. I was at it three times, as I'm sitting here. Three times we were upon the cannons, and three times we were driven back like cardboard figures. Oh, it was fine, M. Pierre. Your grenadiers were superb, God's thunder. I saw them six times in succession close the ranks and march as though on parade. Fine fellows. Our king of Naples, who knows all about it, cried, Bravo! Ah, ah, soldiers like ourselves,' he said after a moment's silence. 'So much the better, so much the better, M. Pierre. Terrible in war . . . gallant, with the fair' (he winked with a smile)—'there you have the French, M. Pierre, eh?'

The captain was so naïvely and good-humouredly gay and obtuse and self-satisfied that Pierre almost winked in response, as he looked good-humouredly at him. Probably the word 'gallant' brought the captain to reflect on the state of things in Moscow.

'By the way, tell me, is it true that all the women have left Moscow? What a queer idea! What had they to fear?'

'Would not the French ladies quit Paris, if the Russians were to enter it?' said Pierre.

'Ha—ha—ha! . . .' The Frenchman gave vent to a gay, sanguine chuckle, slapping Pierre on the shoulder. 'That's a good one, that is,' he went on. 'Paris.... But Paris...'

'Paris is the capital of the world,' said Pierre, finishing the sentence for him.

The captain looked at Pierre. He had the habit of stopping short in the middle of conversation, and staring intently with his laughing, genial eyes.

'Well, if you had not told me you are a Russian, I would have wagered you were a Parisian. You have that indescribable something...' and uttering this compliment, he again gazed at him mutely.

'I have been in Paris. I spent years there,' said Pierre.

'One can see that! Paris! A man who does not know Paris is a savage... A Parisian can be told two leagues off. Paris—it is Talma, la Duschénois, Potier, the Sorbonne, the boulevards.' Perceiving that the conclusion of his phrase was somewhat of an anticlimax, he added hurriedly, 'There is only one Paris in the world.... You have been in Paris, and you remain Russian. Well, I don't think the less of you for that.'

After the days he had spent alone with his gloomy thoughts, Pierre, under the influence of the wine he had drunk, could not help taking pleasure in conversing with this good-humoured and naïve person.

'To return to your ladies, they are said to be beautiful. What a silly idea to go and bury themselves in the steppes, when the French army is in Moscow. What a chance they have lost. Your peasants are different; but you civilised people ought to know better than that. We have taken Vienna, Berlin, Madrid, Naples, Rome, Warsaw—all the capitals in the world. We are feared, but we are loved. We are worth knowing. And then the Emperor...' he was beginning, but Pierre interrupted him.

'The Emperor,' repeated Pierre, and his face suddenly wore a mournful and embarrassed look. 'What of the Emperor?'

'The Empèror? He is generosity, mercy, justice, order, genius—that is the Emperor. It is I, Ramballe, who tell you that. I was his enemy eight years ago. My father was an emigrant count. But he has conquered me, that man. He has taken hold of me. I could not resist the spectacle of the greatness and glory with which he was covering France. When I understood what he wanted, when I saw he was preparing a bed of laurels for us, I said to myself: "That is a monarch." And I gave myself up to him. Oh yes, he is the greatest man of the centuries, past and to come.'

'And is he in Moscow?' Pierre asked, hesitating and looking guilty.

The Frenchman gazed at Pierre's guilty face, and grinned.

'No, he will make his entry tomorrow,' he said, and went on with his talk.

Their conversation was interrupted by several voices shouting at the gates, and Morel coming in to tell the captain that some Würtemburg Hussars had come and wanted to put up their horses in the yard in which the captain's had been put up. The difficulty arose chiefly from the hussars not understanding what was said to them.

The captain bade the senior sergeant be brought to him, and in a stern voice asked him to what regiment he belonged, who was his commanding officer, and on what pretext he dared attempt to occupy quarters already occupied. The German, who knew very little French, succeeded in answering the first two questions, but in reply to the last one, which he did not understand, he answered in broken French and German that he was quartermaster of the regiment, and had received orders from his superior officer to occupy all the houses in the row. Pierre, who knew German, translated the German's words to the captain, and translated the captain's answer back for the Würtemburg hussar. On understanding what was said to him, the German gave in, and took his men away.

The captain went out to the entrance and gave some loud commands.

When he came back into the room, Pierre was sitting where he had been sitting before, with his head in his hands. His face expressed suffering. He really was at that moment suffering. As soon as the captain had gone out, and Pierre had been left alone, he suddenly came to himself, and recognised the position he was in. It was not that Moscow had been taken, not that these lucky conquerors were making themselves at home there and patronising him, bitterly as Pierre felt it, that tortured him at that moment. He was tortured by the consciousness of his own weakness. The few glasses of wine he had drunk, the chat with this good-natured fellow, had dissipated that mood of concentrated gloom, which he had been living in for the last few days, and which was essential for carrying out his design. The pistol and dagger and the peasant's coat were ready, Napoleon was making his entry on the morrow. Pierre felt it as praiseworthy and as beneficial as ever to slay the miscreant; but he felt now that he would not do it. He struggled against the consciousness of his own weakness, but he vaguely felt that he could not overcome it, that his past gloomy train of ideas, of vengeance, murder, and self-sacrifice, had been blown away like dust at contact with the first human being.

The captain came into the room, limping a little, and whistling some tune.

The Frenchman's chatter that had amused Pierre struck him now as revolting. And his whistling a tune, and his gait, and his gesture in twisting his moustaches, all seemed insulting to Pierre now.

'I'll go away at once, I won't say another word to him,' thought Pierre. He thought this, yet went on sitting in the same place. Some strange feeling of weakness riveted him to his place; he longed to get up and go, and could not.

The captain, on the contrary, seemed in exceedingly good spirits. He walked a couple of times up and down the room. His eyes sparkled and his moustaches slightly twitched as though he were smiling to himself at some amusing notion.

'Charming fellow the colonel of these Würtemburgers,' he said all at once. 'He's a German, but a good fellow if ever there was one. But a German.'

He sat down facing Pierre.

'By the way, you know German?'

Pierre looked at him in silence.

'How do you say "*asile*" in German?'

'*Asile?*' repeated – Pierre. '*Asile* in German is *Unterkunft*.'

'What do you say?' the captain queried quickly and doubtfully.

'*Unterkunft*,' repeated Pierre.

'*Onterkoff*,' said the captain, and for several seconds he looked at Pierre with his laughing eyes. 'The Germans are awful fools, aren't they, M. Pierre?' he concluded.

'Well, another bottle of this Moscow claret, eh? Morel, warm us another bottle!' the captain shouted gaily.

Morel brought candles and a bottle of wine. The captain looked at Pierre in the candle-light, and was obviously struck by the troubled face of his companion. With genuine regret and sympathy in his face, Ramballe approached Pierre, and bent over him.

'Eh, we are sad!' he said, touching Pierre on the hand. 'Can I have hurt you? No, really, have you anything against me?' he questioned. 'Perhaps it is owing to the situation of affairs?'

Pierre made no reply, but looked cordially into the Frenchman's eyes. This expression of sympathy was pleasant to him.

'My word of honour, to say nothing of what I owe you, I have a liking for you. Can I do anything for you? Dispose of me. It is for life and death. With my hand and my heart, I say so,' he said, slapping himself on the chest.

'Thank you,' said Pierre. The captain gazed at Pierre as he had gazed at him when he learnt the German for 'refuge,' and his face suddenly brightened.

'Ah, in that case, I drink to our friendship,' he cried gaily, pouring out two glasses of wine.

Pierre took the glass and emptied it. Ramballe emptied his, pressed Pierre's hand once more, and leaned his elbow on the table in a pose of pensive melancholy.

'Yes, my dear friend, such are the freaks of fortune,' he began. 'Who would have said I should be a soldier and captain of dragoons in the service of Bonaparte, as we used to call him. And yet here I am at Moscow with him. I must tell you, my dear fellow,' he continued in the mournful and measured voice of a man who intends to tell a long story, 'our name is one of the most ancient in France.'

And with the easy and naïve unreserve of a Frenchman, the captain told Pierre the history of his forefathers, his childhood, boyhood, and manhood, and all his relations, his fortunes, and domestic affairs. '*Ma pauvre mère*,' took, of course, a prominent part in this recital.

'But all that is only the setting of life; the real thing is love. Love! Eh, M. Pierre?' he said, warming up. 'Another glass.'

Pierre again emptied his glass, and filled himself a third.

'O women! women!' and the captain, gazing with moist eyes at Pierre, began talking of love and his adventures with the fair sex. They were very numerous, as might readily be believed, judging from the officer's conceited, handsome face and the eager enthusiasm with which he talked of women. Although all Ramballe's accounts of his love affairs were characterised by that peculiar nastiness in which the French find the unique charm and poetry of love, the captain told his stories with such genuine conviction that he was the only man who had tasted and known all the sweets of love, and he described the women he had known in such an alluring fashion that Pierre listened to him with curiosity.

It was evident that *l'amour* the Frenchman was so fond of was neither that low and simple kind of love Pierre had at one time felt for his wife, nor the romantic love, exaggerated by himself, that he felt for Natasha. For both those kinds of love Ramballe had an equal contempt – one was *l'amour des charretiers*, the other *l'amour des nigauds*. *L'amour* for which the Frenchman had a weakness consisted principally in an unnatural relation to the woman, and in combinations of monstrous circumstances which lent the chief charm to the feeling.

Thus the captain related the touching history of his love for a fascinating marquise of five-and-thirty, and at the same time for a charming, innocent child of seventeen, the daughter of the fascinating marquise. The conflict of generosity between mother and daughter, ending in the mother sacrificing herself and offering her daughter in marriage to her lover, even now, though it was a memory in the remote past, moved the captain deeply. Then he related an episode in which the husband played the part of the lover, and he—the lover—the part of the husband, and several comic episodes among his reminiscences of Germany, where *Unterkunft* means *asile*, where the husbands eat cabbage soup, and where the young girls are too flaxen-haired.

The last episode was one in Poland, still fresh in the captain's memory, and described by him with rapid gestures and a glowing face. The story was that he had saved the life of a Pole—the episode of saving life was continually cropping up in the captain's anecdotes—and that Pole had intrusted to his care his bewitching wife, a Parisian in heart, while he himself entered the French service. The captain had been happy, the bewitching Polish lady had wanted to elope with him; but moved by a magnanimous impulse, the captain had restored the wife to the husband with the words: 'I saved your life, and I save your honour.'

As he repeated these words, the captain wiped his eyes and shook himself, as though to shake off the weakness that overcame him at this touching recollection.

As men often do at a late hour at night, and under the influence of wine, Pierre listened to the captain's stories, and while he followed and understood all he told him, he was also following a train of personal reminiscences which had for some reason risen to his imagination. As he listened to those love affairs, his own love for Natasha suddenly came into his mind, and going over all the pictures of that love in his imagination, he mentally compared them with Ramballe's stories. As he heard the account of the conflict between love and duty, Pierre saw before him every detail of the meeting with the object of his love at the Suharev Tower. That meeting had not at the time made much impression on him; he had not once thought of it since. But now it seemed to him that there was something very significant and romantic in that meeting.

'Pyotr Kirillitch, come here, I recognise you'; he could hear her words now, could see her eyes, her smile, her travelling cap, and the curl peeping out below it . . . and he felt that there was something moving, touching in all that.

When he had finished his tale about the bewitching Polish lady, the captain turned to Pierre with the inquiry whether he had had any similar experience of self-sacrifice for love and envy of a lawful husband.

Pierre, roused by this question, lifted his head and felt an irresistible impulse to give expression to the ideas in his mind. He began to explain that he looked upon love for woman somewhat differently. He said he had all his life long loved one woman, and still loved her, and that that woman could never be his.

'*Tiens!*' said the captain.

Then Pierre explained that he had loved this woman from his earliest youth, but had not dared to think of her because she was too young, and he had been an illegitimate son, with no name of his own. Then when he had received a name and wealth, he had not dared think of her because he loved her too much, because he set her too high above all the world, and so even more above himself. On reaching this point, Pierre asked the captain, did he understand that.

The captain made a gesture expressing that whether he understood it or not, he begged him to proceed.

'Platonic love; moonshine . . .' he muttered. The wine he had drunk, or an impulse of frankness, or the thought that this man did not know, and never would know, any of the persons concerned in his story, or all together loosened Pierre's tongue. With faltering lips and with a faraway look in his moist eyes, he told all his story; his marriage and the story of Natasha's love for his dearest friend and her betrayal of him, and all his own simple relations with her. In response to questions from Ramballe, he told him, too, what he had at first concealed—his position in society—and even disclosed his name.

What impressed the captain more than anything else in Pierre's story was the fact that Pierre was very wealthy, that he had two palatial houses in Moscow, and that he had abandoned everything, and yet had not left Moscow, but was staying in the town concealing his name and station.

Late in the night they went out together into the street. The night was warm and clear. On the left there was the glow of the first fire that broke out in Moscow, in Petrovka. On the right a young crescent moon stood high in the sky, and in the opposite quarter of the heavens hung the brilliant comet which was connected in Pierre's heart with his love. At the gates of the yard stood Gerasim, the cook, and two Frenchmen. Pierre could hear their laughter and talk, incomprehensible to one another. They were looking at the glow of the fire burning in the town.

There was nothing alarming in a small remote fire in the immense city.

Gazing at the lofty, starlit sky, at the moon, at the comet and the glow of the fire, Pierre felt a thrill of joyous and tender emotion. 'How fair it all is! what more does one want?' he thought. And all at once, when he recalled his design, his head seemed going round; he felt so giddy that he leaned against the fence so as not to fall.

Without taking leave of his new friend, Pierre left the gate with unsteady steps, and going back to his room lay down on the sofa and at once fell asleep.

XXX

FROM various roads, and with various feelings, the inhabitants running and driving away from Moscow, and the retreating troops, gazed at the glow of the first fire that broke out in the city on the 2nd of September.

The Rostov's party stopped for that night at Mytishtchy, twenty versts from Moscow. They had started so late on the 1st of September, the road had been so blocked by wagons and troops, so many things had been forgotten, and servants sent back to get them, that they had decided to halt for the first night five versts from Moscow. The next morning they waked late, and there were again so many delays that they only reached Great Mytishtchy. At ten o'clock the Rostov family, and the wounded soldiers travelling with them, had all found places for the night in the yards and huts of the greater village. The servants, the Rostovs' coachmen, and the orderlies of the wounded officers, after settling their masters for the night, supped, fed their horses, and came out into the porch of a hut.

In the next hut lay Raevsky's adjutant with a broken wrist, and the terrible pain made him moan incessantly, and these moans had a gruesome sound in the autumn darkness of the night. On the first night this adjutant had spent the night in a building in the same yard as the hut in which the Rostovs slept. The countess declared that she had not closed her eyes all night from that moaning, and at Mytishtchy she had moved into a less comfortable hut simply to get further away from the wounded man. One of the servants noticed in the dark night sky, above the high carriage standing at the entry, another small glow of fire. One such glow had been seen long before, and every one knew it was Little Mytishtchy, which had been set on fire by Mamonov's Cossacks.

'I say, mates, there's another fire,' said the man. All of them looked towards the glow.

'Why, they told us Mamonov's Cossacks had fired Little Mytishtchy.' 'Nay! that's not Mytishtchy, it's further.' 'Look'ee, it's in Moscow seemingly.' Two of the men left the porch, went to a carriage and squatted on the step. 'It's more to the left! Why, Mytishtchy is away yonder, and that's quite the other side.'

Several more men joined the first group.

'I say it is flaring,' said one; 'that's a fire in Moscow, my friends; either in Sushtchovsky or in Rogozhsky.'

No one answered this remark. And for a good while all these men gazed in silence at the flames of this new conflagration glowing far away. An old man, the count's valet (as he was called), Danilo Terentyitch, came up to the crowd and called Mishka.

'What are you gaping at? ... The count may ask for you and nobody to be found; go and put the clothes together.'

'Oh, I only ran out for some water,' said Mishka.

'And what do you say, Danilo Terentyitch? that's a fire in Moscow, isn't it?' said one of the footmen.

Danilo Terentyitch made no reply, and for a long while all were mute again. The glow spread wider, and flickered further and further away.

'God have mercy! ... a wind and the drought ...' said a voice again.

'Look'ee, how it's spreading. O Lord! why, one can see the jackdaws! Lord, have mercy on us poor sinners!'

'They'll put it out, never fear.'

'Who's to put it out?' cried the voice of Danilo Terentyitch, silent till that moment. His voice was quiet and deliberate. 'Moscow it is, mates,' he said; 'it's she, our mother, the white city ...' his voice broke, and he suddenly burst into the sobs of old age. And it seemed as though all had been only waiting for that to grasp the import for all of that glow they were watching. Sighs were heard and muttered prayers, and the sobs of the old valet.

XXXI

THE valet on going in informed the count that Moscow was on fire. The count put on his dressing-gown and went out to look. With him went Sonya, who had not yet undressed, and Madame Schoss. Natasha and the countess were left alone within. Petya was no longer with the family; he had gone on ahead with his regiment marching to Troitsa.

The countess wept on hearing that Moscow was in flames. Natasha, pale, with staring eyes, sat on the bench under the holy images, the spot where she had first thrown herself down on entering, and took no notice of her father's words. She was listening to the never-ceasing moan of the adjutant, audible three huts away.

'Oh! how awful!' cried Sonya, coming in chilled and frightened from the yard. 'I do believe all Moscow is burning; there's an awful fire! Natasha, do look; you can see now from the window here,' she said, obviously trying to distract her friend's mind. But Natasha stared at her, as though she did not understand what was asked of her, and fixed her eyes again on the corner of the stove. Natasha had been in this petrified condition ever since the morning, when Sonya, to the amazement and anger of the countess, had for some incomprehensible reason thought fit to inform Natasha of Prince Andrey's wound, and his presence among their train. The countess had been angry with Sonya, as she was very rarely angry. Sonya had cried and begged forgiveness, and now she waited all the while on her friend, as though trying to atone for her fault.

'Look, Natasha, how frightfully it's burning,' said Sonya.

'What's burning?' asked Natasha. 'Oh yes, Moscow.'

And to get rid of Sonya, and not hurt her by a refusal, she moved her head towards the window, looked in such a way that it was evident she could see nothing, and sat down again in the same attitude as before.

'But you didn't see?'

'Yes, I really did see,' she declared in a voice that implored to be left in peace.

Both the countess and Sonya could readily understand that Moscow, the burning of Moscow, anything whatever in fact, could be of no interest to Natasha.

The count came in again behind the partition wall and lay down. The countess went up to Natasha, put the back of her hand to her head, as she did when her daughter was ill, then touched her forehead with her lips, as though to find out whether she were feverish, and kissed her.

'You are chilled? You are all shaking. You should lie down,' she said.

'Lie down? Yes, very well, I'll lie down. I'll lie down in a minute,' said Natasha.

When Natasha had been told that morning that Prince Andrey was seriously wounded, and was travelling with them, she had at the first moment asked a great many questions, how and why and where was he going; whether he were dangerously wounded, and whether she could see him. But after she had been told that she could not see him, that his wound was a serious one, but that his life was not in danger, though she plainly did not believe what was told her, she saw that she would get the same answer whatever she said, and gave up asking questions and speaking at all. All the way Natasha had sat motionless in the corner of the carriage with those wide eyes, the look in which the countess knew so well and dreaded so much. And she was sitting in just the same way now on the bench in the hut. She was brooding on some plan; she was making, or already by now had made some decision, in her own mind—that the countess knew, but what that decision was she did not know, and that alarmed and worried her.

'Natasha, undress, darling, get into my bed.'

For the countess only a bed had been made up on a bedstead. Madame Schoss and the two girls were to sleep on hay on the floor.

'No, mamma, I'll lie here on the floor,' said Natasha irritably; she went to the window and opened it. The moans of the adjutant could be heard more distinctly from the open window. She put her head out into the damp night air, and the countess saw her slender neck shaking with sobs and heaving against the window frame. Natasha knew it was not Prince Andrey moaning. She knew that Prince Andrey was in the same block of huts as they were in, that he was in the next hut just across the porch, but that fearful never ceasing moan made her sob. The countess exchanged glances with Sonya.

'Go to bed, darling, go to bed, my pet,' said the countess, lightly touching Natasha's shoulder. 'Come, go to bed.'

'Oh yes . . . I'll go to bed at once, at once,' said Natasha, hurriedly undressing, and breaking the strings of her petticoats. Dropping off her dress, and putting on a dressing-jacket, she sat down on the bed made up on the floor, tucking her feet under her, and flinging her short, fine hair over her shoulder, began plaiting it. Her thin, long, practised fingers rapidly and deftly divided, plaited, and tied up her hair. Natasha's head turned from side to side as usual as she did this, but her eyes, feverishly wide, looked straight before her with the same fixed stare. When her toilet for the night was over, Natasha sank softly down on to the sheet laid on the hay nearest the door.

'Natasha, you lie in the middle,' said Sonya.

'I'll stay here,' said Natasha. 'And do go to bed,' she added in a tone of annoyance. And she buried her face in the pillow.

The countess, Madame Schoss, and Sonya hurriedly undressed and went to bed. The lamp before the holy images was the only light left in the room. But out of doors the fire at Little Mytishtchy lighted the country up for two versts round, and there was a noisy clamour of peasants shouting at the tavern across the street, which Mamonov's Cossacks had broken into, and the moan of the adjutant could be heard unceasingly through everything.

For a long while Natasha listened to the sounds that reached her from within and without, and she did not stir. She heard at first her mother's prayers and sighs, the creaking of her bed under her, Madame Schoss's familiar, whistling snore, Sonya's soft breathing. Then the countess called to Natasha. Natasha did not answer.

'I think she's asleep, mamma,' answered Sonya.

The countess, after a brief silence, spoke again, but this time no one answered her.

Soon after this Natasha caught the sound of her mother's even breathing. Natasha did not stir, though her little bare foot, poking out below the quilt, felt frozen against the uncovered floor.

A cricket chirped in a crack, as though celebrating a victory over all the world. A cock crowed far away, and another answered close by. The shouts had died away in the tavern, but the adjutant's moaning went on still the same. Natasha sat up.

'Sonya! Are you asleep? Mamma!' she whispered. No one answered. Slowly and cautiously Natasha got up, crossed herself, and stepped cautiously with her slender, supple, bare feet on to the dirty, cold floor. The boards creaked. With nimble feet she ran like a kitten a few steps, and took hold of the cold door-handle.

It seemed to her that something with heavy, rhythmical strokes was banging on all the walls of the hut; it was the beating of her own heart, torn with dread, with love and terror.

She opened the door, stepped over the lintel, and on to the damp, cold earth of the passage outside. The cold all about her refreshed her. Her bare foot felt a man asleep; she stepped over him, and opened the door of the hut in which Prince Andrey was lying.

In that hut it was dark. A tallow candle with a great, smouldering wick stood on a bench in the further corner, by a bed, on which something was lying.

Ever since she had been told in the morning of Prince Andrey's wound and his presence there, Natasha had resolved that she must see him. She could not have said why this must be, but she knew their meeting would be anguish to her, and that made her the more certain that it must be inevitable.

All day long she had lived in the hope that at night she would see him. But now when the moment had come, a terror came over her of what she would see. How had he been disfigured? What was left of him? Was he like that unceasing moan of the adjutant? Yes, he was all over like that. In her imagination he was that awful moan of pain personified. When she caught sight of an undefined mass in the corner, and took his raised knees under the quilt for his shoulders, she pictured some fearful body there, and stood still in terror. But an irresistible force drew her forward. She made one cautious step, another, and found herself in the middle of the small hut, cumbered up with baggage. On the bench, under the holy images, lay another man (this was Timohin), and on the floor were two more figures (the doctor and the valet).

The valet sat up and muttered something. Timohin, in pain from a wound in his leg, was not asleep, and gazed, all eyes, at the strange apparition of a girl in a white night-gown, dressing-jacket, and nightcap. The valet's sleepy and frightened words: 'What is it? What do you want?' only made Natasha hasten towards the figure lying in the corner. However fearfully unlike a human shape that figure might be now, she must see him. She passed by the valet, the smouldering candle flickered up, and she saw clearly Prince Andrey, lying with his arms stretched out on the quilt, looking just as she had always seen him.

He was just the same as ever; but the flush on his face, his shining eyes, gazing passionately at her, and especially the soft, childlike neck, showing above the lay-down collar of the nightshirt, gave him a peculiarly innocent, childlike look, such as she had never seen in him before. She ran up to him and with a swift, supple, youthful movement dropped on her knees.

He smiled, and held out his hand to her.

XXXII

SEVEN days had passed since Prince Andrey had found himself in the ambulance station on the field of Borodino. All that time he had been in a state of almost continual unconsciousness. The fever and inflammation of the bowels, which had been injured, were, in the opinion of the doctor accompanying the wounded, certain to carry him off. But on the seventh day he ate with relish a piece of bread with some tea, and the doctor observed that the fever was going down. Prince Andrey had regained consciousness in the morning. The first night after leaving Moscow had been fairly warm, and Prince Andrey had spent the night in his carriage. But at Mytishtchy the wounded man had himself asked to be moved and given tea. The pain caused by moving him into the hut had made Prince Andrey groan aloud and lose consciousness again. When he had been laid on his camp bedstead, he lay a long while with closed eyes without moving. Then he opened his eyes and whispered softly, 'How about the tea?' The doctor was struck by this instance of consciousness of the little details of daily life. He felt his pulse, and to his surprise and dissatisfaction found that the pulse was stronger. The doctor's dissatisfaction was due to the fact that he felt certain from his experience that Prince Andrey could not live, and that if he did not die now, he would only die a little later with even greater suffering. With Prince Andrey was the red-nosed major of his regiment, Timohin, who had joined him in Moscow with a wound in his leg received at the same battle of Borodino. The doctor, the prince's valet, and coachman, and two orderlies were in charge of them.

Tea was given to Prince Andrey. He drank it eagerly, looking with feverish eyes at the door in front of him, as though trying to understand and recall something.

'No more. Is Timohin here?' he asked.

Timohin edged along the bench towards him.

'I am here, your excellency.'

'How is your wound?'

'Mine? All right. But how are you?'

Prince Andrey pondered again, as though he were recollecting something.

'Could not one get a book here?' he said.

'What book?'

'The Gospel! I haven't one.'

The doctor promised to get it, and began questioning the prince about his symptoms. Prince Andrey answered all the doctor's questions rationally, though reluctantly, and then said that he wanted a support put under him, as it was uncomfortable and very painful for him as he was. The doctor and the valet took off the military cloak, with which he was covered, and puckering up their faces at the sickly smell of putrifying flesh that came from the wound, began to look into the terrible place. The doctor was very much troubled about something; he made some changes, turning the wounded man over so that he groaned again, and again lost consciousness from the pain when they turned him over. He began to be delirious, and kept asking for the book to be brought and to be put under him. 'What trouble would it be to you?' he kept saying. 'I haven't it, get it me, please,—put it under me just for a minute,' he said in a piteous voice.

The doctor went outside to wash his hands.

'Ah, you have no conscience, you fellows really,' the doctor was saying to the valet, who was pouring water over his hands. 'For one minute I didn't look after you. Why, it's such suffering that I wonder how he bears it.'

'I thought we did put it under him right, by the Lord Jesus Christ,' said the valet.

Prince Andrey had for the first time grasped where he was and what was happening to him, and had recollected that he had been wounded and how, at the moment when the carriage had stopped at Mytishtchy, he had asked to be taken into the hut. Losing consciousness again from the pain, he came fully to himself once more in the hut while he was drinking tea. And thereupon again, going over in his memory all that had happened to him, the most vivid picture in his mind was of that moment at the ambulance station when at the sight of the sufferings of a man he had not liked, those new thoughts had come to him with such promise of happiness. And those thoughts—though vague now and shapeless—took possession of his soul again. He remembered that he had now some new happiness, and that that happiness had something to do with the Gospel. That was why he asked for the Gospel. But the position he had been laid in, without support under his wound, and the new change of position, put his thoughts to confusion again; and it was only in the complete stillness of the night that he came to himself again for the third time. Every one was asleep around him. A cricket was chirping across the passage; some one was shouting and singing in the street; cockroaches were rustling over the table, the holy images and the walls; a big fly flopped on his pillow and about the tallow candle that stood with a great, smouldering wick beside him.

His soul was not in its normal state. A man in health usually thinks, feels and remembers simultaneously an immense number of different things, but he has the power and the faculty of selecting one series of ideas or phenomena and concentrating all his attention on that series. A man in health can at the moment of the profoundest thought break off to say a civil word to any one who comes in, and then return again to his thoughts. Prince Andrey's soul was not in a normal condition in this respect. All the faculties of his soul were clearer and more active than ever, but they acted apart from his will. The most diverse ideas and images had possession of his mind at the same time. Sometimes his brain suddenly began to work, and with a force, clearness, and depth with which it had never been capable of working in health. But suddenly the train of thought broke off in the midst, to be replaced by some unexpected image, and the power to go back to it was wanting. 'Yes, a new happiness was revealed to me, that could not be taken away from man,' he thought, as he lay in the still, half-dark hut, gazing before him with feverishly wide, staring eyes. 'Happiness beyond the reach of material forces, outside material, external influences on man, the happiness of the soul alone, the happiness of love! To feel it is in every man's power, but God alone can know it and ordain it. But how did God ordain this law? Why the Son? . . .' And all at once that train of thought broke off, and Prince Andrey heard (not knowing whether in delirium or in actual fact he heard it) a kind of soft, whispering voice, incessantly beating time: 'Piti-pitt-piti,' and then 'i-ti-ti,' and again, 'ipiti-piti-piti,' and again 'iti-ti.' And to the sound of this murmuring music Prince Andrey felt as though a strange, ethereal edifice of delicate needles or splinters were being raised over his face, over the very middle of it. He felt that (hard though it was for him) he must studiously preserve his balance that this rising edifice might not fall to pieces; but yet it was falling to pieces, and slowly rising up again to the rhythmic beat of the murmuring music.

'It is stretching out, stretching out, and spreading and stretching out!' Prince Andrey said to himself. While he listened to the murmur and felt that edifice of needles stretching out, and rising up, Prince Andrey saw by glimpses a red ring of light round the candle, and heard the rustling of the cockroaches and the buzzing of the fly as it flopped against his pillow and his face. And every time the fly touched his face it gave him a stinging sensation, but yet it surprised him that though the fly struck him in the very centre of the rising edifice, it did not shatter it. But, apart from all this, there was one other thing of importance. That was the white thing at the door; that was a statue of the sphinx, which oppressed him too.

'But perhaps it is my shirt on the table,' thought Prince Andrey, 'and that's my legs, and that's the door, but why this straining and moving and piti-piti-iti and ti-ti and piti-piti-piti . . . Enough, cease, be still, please,' Prince Andrey besought some one wearily. And all at once thought and feeling floated to the surface again with extraordinary clearness and force.

'Yes, love (he thought again with perfect distinctness), but not that love that loves for something, to gain something, or because of something, but that love that I felt for the first time, when dying, I saw my enemy and yet loved him. I knew that feeling of love which is the very essence of the soul, for which no object is needed. And I know that blissful feeling now too. To love one's neighbours; to love one's enemies. To love everything—to love God in all His manifestations. Some one dear to one can be loved with human love; but an enemy can only be loved with divine love. And that was why I felt such joy when I felt that I loved that man. What happened to him? Is he alive? . . . Loving with human love, one may pass from love to hatred; but divine love cannot change. Nothing, not even death, nothing can shatter it. It is the very nature of the soul. And how many people I have hated in my life. And of all people none I have loved and hated more than her.' And he vividly pictured Natasha to himself, not as he had pictured her in the past, only with the charm that had been a joy to him; for the first time he pictured to himself her soul. And he understood her feeling, her sufferings, her shame, and her penitence. Now, for the first time, he felt all the cruelty of his abandonment, saw all the cruelty of his rupture with her. 'If it were only possible for me to see her once more . . . once, looking into those eyes, to say . . .'

Piti-piti-piti iti-ti, ipiti-piti—boom, the fly flapped . . . And his attention passed all at once into another world of reality and delirium, in which something peculiar was taking place. In that place the edifice was still rising, unshattered; something was still stretching out, the candle was still burning, with a red ring round it; the same shirt-sphinx still lay by the door. But besides all this, something creaked, there was a whiff of fresh air, and a new white sphinx appeared standing before the doorway. And that sphinx had the white face and shining eyes of that very Natasha he had been dreaming of just now.

'Oh, how wearisome this everlasting delirium is!' thought Prince Andrey, trying to dispel that face from his vision. But that face stood before him with the face of reality, and that face was coming closer. Prince Andrey tried to go back to the world of pure thought, but he could not, and he was drawn back into the realm of delirium. The soft murmuring voice kept up its rhythmic whisper, something was oppressing him, and rising up, and the strange face stood before him. Prince Andrey rallied all his forces to regain his senses; he stirred a little, and suddenly there was a ringing in his ears and a dimness before his eyes, and like a man sinking under water, he lost consciousness.

When he came to himself, Natasha, the very living Natasha, whom of all people in the world he most longed to love with that new, pure, divine love that had now been revealed to him, was on her knees before him. He knew that it was the real, living Natasha, and did not wonder, but quietly rejoiced. Natasha, on her knees, in terror, but without moving (she could not have moved), gazed at him, restraining her sobs. Her face was white and rigid. There was only a sort of quiver in the lower part of it.

Prince Andrey drew a sigh of relief, smiled, and held out his hand.

'You?' he said. 'What happiness!'

With a swift but circumspect movement, Natasha came nearer, still kneeling, and carefully taking his hand she bent her face over it and began kissing it, softly touching it with her lips.

'Forgive me!' she said in a whisper, lifting her head and glancing at him. 'Forgive me!'

'I love you,' said Prince Andrey.

'Forgive . . .'

'Forgive what?' asked Prince Andrey.

'Forgive me for what I di. . . id,' Natasha murmured in a hardly audible, broken whisper, and again and again she softly put her lips to his hand.

'I love thee more, better than before,' said Prince Andrey, lifting her face with his hand so that he could look into her eyes.

Those eyes, swimming with happy tears, gazed at him with timid commiseration and joyful love. Natasha's thin, pale face, with its swollen lips, was more than ugly—it looked terrible. But Prince Andrey did not see her face, he saw the shining eyes, which were beautiful. They heard talk behind them.

Pyotr, the valet, by now wide awake, had waked up the doctor. Timohin, who had not slept all night for the pain in his leg, had been long watching all that was happening, and huddled up on his bench, carefully wrapping his bare person up in the sheet.

'Why, what's this?' said the doctor, getting up from his bed on the floor. 'Kindly retire, madam.'

At that moment there was a knock at the door; a maid had been sent by the countess in search of her daughter.

Like a sleep-walker awakened in the midst of her trance, Natasha walked out of the room, and getting back to her hut, sank sobbing on her bed.

From that day at all the halts and resting-places on the remainder of the Rostovs' journey, Natasha never left Bolkonsky's side, and the doctor was forced to admit that he had not expected from a young girl so much fortitude, nor skill in nursing a wounded man.

Terrible as it was to the countess to think that Prince Andrey might (and very probably, too, from what the doctor said) die on the road in her daughter's arms, she could not resist Natasha. Although with the renewal of affectionate relations between Prince Andrey and Natasha the idea did occur that in case he recovered their old engagement would be renewed, no one—least of all Natasha and Prince Andrey—spoke of this. The unsettled question of life and death hanging, not only over Prince Andrey, but over all Russia, shut off all other considerations.

XXXIII

PIERRE waked up late on the 3rd of September. His head ached, the clothes in which he had slept without undressing fretted his body, and he had a vague sense in his heart of something shameful he had done the evening before. That something shameful was his talk with Captain Ramballe.

His watch told him it was eleven, but it seemed a particularly dull day. Pierre stood up, rubbed his eyes, and seeing the pistol with its engraved stock—Gerasim had put it back on the writing-table—Pierre remembered where he was and what was in store for him that day.

'Am I not too late already?' Pierre wondered.

No, probably *he* would not make his entry into Moscow before twelve o'clock. Pierre did not allow himself to reflect on what lay before him, but made haste to act.

Setting his clothes to rights, Pierre took up the pistol and was about to set off. But then for the first time it occurred to him to wonder how, if not in his hand, he was to carry the weapon in the street. Even under his full coat it would be hard to conceal a big pistol. It could not be put in his sash, nor under his arm, without being noticeable. Moreover, the pistol was now unloaded, and Pierre could not succeed in reloading it in time. 'The dagger will do as well,' Pierre said to himself; though, in considering how he should carry out his design, he had more than once decided that the great mistake made by the student in 1809 was that he had tried to kill Napoleon with a dagger. But Pierre's chief aim seemed to be, not so much to succeed in his project, as to prove to himself that he was not renouncing his design, but was doing everything to carry it out. Pierre hurriedly took the blunt, notched dagger in a green scabbard, which he had bought, together with the pistol, at the Suharev Tower, and hid it under his waistcoat.

Tying the sash round his peasant's coat, and pulling his cap forward, Pierre walked along the corridor, trying to avoid making a noise and meeting the captain, and slipped out into the street.

The fire, at which he had gazed so indifferently the evening before, had sensibly increased during the night. Moscow was on fire at various points. There were fires at the same time in Carriage Row, Zamoskvoryetche, the Bazaar, and Povarsky, and the timber market near Dorogomilov bridge and the barges in the river Moskva were in a blaze.

Pierre's way lay across a side street to Povarsky, and from there across Arbaty to the chapel of Nikola Yavlenny, where he had long before in his fancy fixed on the spot at which the deed ought to be done. Most of the houses had their gates and shutters closed. The streets and lanes were deserted; there was a smell of burning and smoke in the air. Now and then he met Russians with uneasy and timid faces, and Frenchmen with a look of the camp about them, walking in the middle of the road. Both looked at Pierre with surprise. Apart from his great height and stoutness, and the look of gloomy concentration and suffering in his face and whole figure, Russians stared at Pierre because they could not make out to what class he belonged. Frenchmen looked after him with surprise, because, while all other Russians stared timidly and inquisitively at them, Pierre walked by without noticing them. At the gates of a house, three Frenchmen, disputing about something with some Russians, who did not understand their meaning, stopped Pierre to ask whether he knew French.

Pierre shook his head and walked on. In another lane a sentinel, on guard by a green caisson, shouted at him, and it was only at the repetition of his menacing shout, and the sound of his picking up his gun, that Pierre grasped that he ought to have passed the street on the other side. He heard and saw nothing around him. With haste and horror he bore within him his intention as something strange and fearful to him, fearing—from the experience of the previous night—to lose it. But Pierre was not destined to carry his design in safety to the spot to which he was bending his steps. Moreover, if he had not been detained on the road, his design could not have been carried out, because Napoleon had four hours earlier left the Dorogomilov suburb, and crossed Arbaty to the Kremlin; and he was by then sitting in the royal study in the Kremlin palace in the gloomiest temper, giving circumstantial orders for immediately extinguishing the fires, preventing pillage, and reassuring the inhabitants. But Pierre knew nothing of that; entirely engrossed in what lay before him, he was suffering the anguish men suffer when they persist in undertaking a task impossible for them—not from its inherent difficulties, but from its incompatibility with their own nature. He was tortured by the dread that he would be weak at the decisive moment, and so would lose his respect for himself.

Though he saw and heard nothing around him, he instinctively found his way, and took the right turning to reach Povarsky.

As Pierre got nearer to Povarsky Street, the smoke grew thicker and thicker, and the air was positively warm from the heat of the conflagration. Tongues of flame shot up here and there behind the house-tops. He met more people in the streets, and these people were in great excitement. But though Pierre felt that something unusual was happening around him, he did not grasp the fact that he was getting near the fire. As he walked along a path, across the large open space adjoining on one side Povarsky Street, and on the other side the gardens of Prince Gruzinsky, Pierre suddenly heard close by him the sound of a woman, crying desperately. He stood still, as though awakened from a dream, and raised his head.

On the dried-up, dusty grass on one side of the path lay heaps of household belongings piled up: feather-beds, a samovar, holy images, and boxes. On the ground, near the boxes, sat a thin woman, no longer young, with long, projecting front teeth, dressed in a black cloak and cap. This woman was weeping violently, swaying to and fro, and muttering something. Two little girls, from ten to twelve years old, dressed in dirty, short frocks and cloaks were gazing at their mother, with an expression of stupefaction on their pale, frightened faces. A little boy of seven, in a coat and a huge cap, obviously not his own, was crying in an old nurse's arms. A bare-legged, dirty servant-girl was sitting on a chest; she had let down her flaxen hair, and was pulling out the singed hairs, sniffing at them. The husband, a short, stooping man, in a uniform, with little, wheel-shaped whiskers, and smooth locks of hair, peeping out from under his cap, which was stuck erect on his head, was moving the chests from under one another with an immovable face, dragging garments of some sort from under them.

The woman almost flung herself at Pierre's feet as soon as she saw him.

'Merciful heavens, good Christian folk, save me, help me, kind sir! . . . somebody help me,' she articulated through her sobs. 'My little girl! . . . My daughter! . . . My youngest girl left behind! . . . She's burnt! Oo . . . er! What a fate I have nursed thee for . . . Ooo!'

'Hush, Marya Nikolaevna,' the husband said in a low voice to his wife, evidently only to justify himself before an outsider. 'Sister must have taken her, nothing else can have happened to her!' he added.

'Monster, miscreant!' the woman screeched furiously, her tears suddenly ceasing. 'There is no heart in you, you have no feeling for your own child. Any other man would have rescued her from the fire. But he is a monster, not a man, not a father. You are a noble man,' the woman turned to Pierre sobbing and talking rapidly. 'The row was on fire—they rushed in to tell us. The girl screamed: Fire! We rushed to get our things out. Just as we were, we escaped. . . . This is all we could snatch up . . the blessed images, we look at the children, and the bed that was my dowry, and all the rest is lost. Katitchka's missing. Ooo! O Lord! . . .' and again she broke into sobs. 'My darling babe! burnt! burnt!'

'But where, where was she left?' said Pierre.

From the expression of his interested face, the woman saw that this man might help her.

'Good, kind sir!' she screamed, clutching at his legs. 'Benefactor, set my heart at rest anyway . . . Aniska, go, you slut, show the way,' she bawled to the servant-girl, opening her mouth wide in her anger, and displaying her long teeth more than ever.

'Show the way, show me, I . . . I . . . I'll do something,' Pierre gasped hurriedly.

The dirty servant-girl came out from behind the box, put up her hair, and sighing, walked on in front along the path with her coarse, bare feet.

Pierre felt as though he had suddenly come back to life after a heavy swoon. He drew his head up, his eyes began to shine with the light of life, and with rapid steps he followed the girl, overtook her, and went into Povarsky Street. The whole street was full of clouds of black smoke. Tongues of flame shot up here and there out of these clouds. A great crowd had gathered in front of the fire. In the middle of the street stood a French general, saying something to those about him. Pierre, accompanied by the servant-girl, was approaching the place where the French general stood; but the French soldiers stopped him.

'Can't pass,' a voice shouted to him.

'This way, master,' bawled the girl; 'we'll cut across Nikoliny by the lane.'

Pierre turned back, breaking into a run now and then to keep pace with her. The girl ran across the street, turned into a lane on the left, and passing three houses, turned in at a gate on the right.

'It's just here,' she said, and running across a yard, she opened a little gate in a paling-fence, and stopping short, pointed out to Pierre a small wooden lodge, which was blazing away brightly. One side of it had fallen in, the other was on fire, and flames peeped out at the window-holes and under the roof.

As Pierre went in at the little gate, he felt the rush of heat, and involuntarily stopped short.

'Which, which is your house?' he asked.

'Oooh!' wailed the servant-girl, pointing to the lodge. 'That's it, that same was our lodging. Sure, you're burnt to death, our treasure, Katitchka, my precious little missy, ooh!' wailed Aniska, at the sight of the fire feeling the necessity of giving expression to her feelings too.

Pierre darted up to the lodge, but the heat was so great that he could not help describing a curve round it, and found himself close to a big house, which was as yet only on fire on one side, at the roof. A group of French soldiers were swarming round it. Pierre could not at first make out what these Frenchmen were about, dragging something out of the house. But seeing a French soldier in front of him beating a peasant with a blunt cutlass, and taking from him a fur-lined coat, Pierre became vaguely aware that pillaging was going on here—but he had no time to dwell on the idea.

The sound of the rumble and crash of falling walls and ceilings; the roar and hiss of the flames, and the excited shouts of the crowd; the sight of the hovering clouds of smoke—here folding over into black masses, there drawing out and lighted up by gleaming sparks; and the flames—here like a thick red sheaf, and there creeping like golden fish-scales over the walls; the sense of the heat and smoke and rapidity of movement, all produced on Pierre the usual stimulating effect of a conflagration. That effect was particularly strong on Pierre, because all at once, at the sight of the fire, he felt himself set free from the ideas weighing upon him. He felt young, gay, ready, and resolute. He ran round the lodge on the side of the house, and was about to run into that part which was still standing, when he heard several voices shouting immediately above his head, followed by the crash and bang of something heavy falling close by.

Pierre looked round, and saw at the windows of the house some French soldiers, who had just dropped out a drawer of a chest, filled with some metallic objects. Some more French soldiers standing below went up to the drawer.

'Well, what does that fellow want?' one of the French soldiers shouted, referring to Pierre.

'A child in the house. Haven't you seen a child?' said Pierre.

'What's the fellow singing? Get along, do!' shouted voices; and one of the soldiers, evidently afraid Pierre might take it into his head to snatch the silver and bronzes from them, pounced on him in a menacing fashion.

'A child?' shouted a Frenchman from above. 'I did hear something crying in the garden. Perhaps it's the fellow's brat. Must be humane, you know.'

'Where is it?' asked Pierre.

'This way!' the French soldier shouted to him from the window pointing to the garden behind the house. 'Wait, I'll come down.'

And in a minute the Frenchman, a black-eyed fellow, with a patch on his cheek, in his shirt-sleeves, did in fact jump out of a window on the ground floor, and slapping Pierre on the shoulder, he ran with him to the garden. 'Make haste, you fellows,' he shouted to his comrades, 'it's beginning to get hot.' Running behind the house to a sanded path, the Frenchman pulled Pierre by the arm, and pointed out to him a circular space. Under a garden seat lay a girl of three years old, in a pink frock.

'Here's your brat. Ah, a little girl. So much the better,' said the Frenchman. 'Good-bye. Must be humane, we are all mortal, you know'; and the Frenchman, with the patch on his cheek, ran back to his comrades.

Pierre, breathless with joy, ran up to the child, and would have taken her in his arms. But seeing a stranger, the little girl—a scrofulous-looking, unattractive child, very like her mother—screamed and ran away. Pierre caught her, however, and lifted her up in his arms; she squealed in desperate fury, and tried to tear herself out of Pierre's arms with her little hands, and to bite him with her dirty, dribbling mouth. Pierre had a sense of horror and disgust, such as he had felt at contact with some little beast. But he made an effort to overcome it, and not to drop the child, and ran with it back to the big house. By now, however, it was impossible to get back by the same way; the servant-girl, Aniska, was nowhere to be seen, and with a feeling of pity and loathing, Pierre held close to him, as tenderly as he could, the piteously howling, and sopping wet baby, and ran across the garden to seek some other way out.

XXXIV

WHEN Pierre, after running across courtyards and by-lanes, got back with his burden to Prince Gruzinsky's garden, at the corner of Povarsky, he did not for the first moment recognise the place from which he had set out to look for the baby: it was so packed with people and goods, dragged out of the houses. Besides the Russian families with their belongings saved from the fire, there were a good many French soldiers here too in various uniforms. Pierre took no notice of them. He was in haste to find the family, and to restore the child to its mother, so as to be able to go back and save some one else. It seemed to Pierre that he had a great deal more to do, and to do quickly. Warmed up by the heat and running, Pierre felt even more strongly at that minute the sense of youth, eagerness, and resolution, which had come upon him when he was running to save the baby.

The child was quiet now, and clinging to Pierre's coat with her little hands, she sat on his arm, and looked about her like a little, wild beast. Pierre glanced at her now and then, and smiled slightly. He fancied he saw something touchingly innocent in the frightened, sickly little face.

Neither the official nor his wife were in the place where he had left them. With rapid steps, Pierre walked about among the crowd, scanning the different faces he came across. He could not help noticing a Georgian or Armenian family, consisting of a very old man, of a handsome Oriental cast of face, dresed in a new cloth-faced sheepskin and new boots; an old woman of a similar type; and a young woman. The latter—a very young woman—struck Pierre as a perfect example of Oriental beauty, with her sharply marked, arched, black eyebrows, her extraordinarily soft, bright colour and beautiful, expressionless, oval face. Among the goods flung down in the crowd in the grass space, in her rich satin mantle, and the bright lilac kerchief on her head, she suggested a tender, tropical plant, thrown down in the snow. She was sitting on the baggage a little behind the old woman, and her big, black, long-shaped eyes, with their long lashes, were fixed immovably on the ground. Evidently she was aware of her beauty, and fearful because of it. Her face struck Pierre, and in his haste he looked round at her several times as he passed along by the fence. Reaching the fence, and still failing to find the people he was looking for, Pierre stood still and looked round.

Pierre's figure was more remarkable than ever now with the baby in his arms, and several Russians, both men and women, gathered about him.

'Have you lost some one, good sir? Are you a gentleman yourself, or what? Whose baby is it?' they asked him.

Pierre answered that the baby belonged to a woman in a black mantle, who had been sitting at this spot with her children; and asked whether any one knew her, and where she had gone.

'Why, it must be the Anferovs,' said an old deacon addressing a pock-marked peasant woman. 'Lord, have mercy on us! Lord, have mercy on us!' he added, in his professional bass.

'The Anferovs,' said the woman. 'Why, the Anferovs have been gone since early this morning. It will either be Marya Nikolaevna's or Ivanova's.'

'He says a woman, and Marya Nikolaevna's a lady,' said a house-serf.

'You know her, then; a thin woman—long teeth,' said Pierre.

'To be sure, Marya Nikolaevna. They moved off into the garden as soon as these wolves pounced down on us,' said the woman, indicating the French soldiers.

'O Lord, have mercy on us!' the deacon added again.

'You go on yonder, they are there. It's she, for sure. She was quite beside herself with crying,' said the woman again. 'It's she. Here, this way.'

But Pierre was not heeding the woman. For several seconds he had been gazing intently at what was passing a few paces from him. He was looking at the Armenian family and two French soldiers, who had approached them. One of these soldiers, a nimble, little man, was dressed in a blue coat, with a cord tied round for a belt. He had a nightcap on his head, and his feet were bare. Another, whose appearance struck Pierre particularly, was a long, round-shouldered, fair-haired, thin man, with ponderous movements and an idiotic expression of face. He was dressed in a frieze tunic, blue trousers and big, torn, high boots. The little barefooted Frenchman in the blue coat, on going up to the Armenians, said something, and at once took hold of the old man's legs, and the old man began immediately in haste pulling off his boots. The other soldier in the tunic stopped facing the beautiful Armenian girl, with his hands in his pockets, and stared at her without speaking or moving.

'Take it, take the child,' said Pierre, handing the child to the peasant woman, and speaking with peremptory haste. 'You give her to them, you take her,' he almost shouted to the woman, setting the screaming child on the ground, and looking round again at the Frenchmen and the Armenian family. The old man was by now sitting barefoot. The little Frenchman had just taken the second boot from him, and was slapping the boots together. The old man was saying something with a sob, but all that Pierre only saw in a passing glimpse. His whole attention was absorbed by the Frenchman in the tunic, who had meanwhile, with a deliberate, swinging gait, moved up to the young woman, and taking his hands out of his pockets, caught hold of her neck.

The beautiful Armenian still sat in the same immobile pose, with her long lashes drooping, and seemed not to see and not to feel what the soldier was doing to her.

While Pierre ran the few steps that separated him from the Frenchmen, the long soldier in the tunic had already torn the necklace from the Armenian beauty's neck, and the young woman, clutching at her neck with both hands, screamed shrilly.

'Let that woman alone!' Pierre roared in a voice hoarse with rage, and seizing the long, stooping soldier by the shoulders he shoved him away. The soldier fell down, got up, and ran away. But his comrade, dropping the boots, pulled out his sword, and moved up to Pierre in a menacing attitude.

'*Voyons, pas de bêtises!*' he shouted.

Pierre was in that transport of frenzy in which he remembered nothing, and his strength was increased tenfold. He dashed at the barefoot Frenchman, and before he had time to draw his cutlass, he knocked him down, and was pommelling him with his fists. Shouts of approval were heard from the crowd around, and at the same moment a patrol of French Uhlans came riding round the corner. The Uhlans trotted up to Pierre, and the French soldiers surrounded him. Pierre had no recollection of what followed. He remembered that he beat somebody, and was beaten, and that in the end he found that his hands were tied, that a group of French soldiers were standing round him, ransacking his clothes.

'Lieutenant, he has a dagger,' were the first words Pierre grasped the meaning of.

'Ah, a weapon,' said the officer, and he turned to the barefoot soldier, who had been taken with Pierre. 'Very good, very good; you can tell all your story at the court-martial,' said the officer. And then he turned to Pierre: 'Do you know French?'

Pierre looked about him with bloodshot eyes, and made no reply. Probably his face looked very terrible; for the officer said something in a whisper, and four more Uhlans left the rest, and stationed themselves both sides of Pierre.

'Do you speak French?' the officer, keeping his distance, repeated the question. 'Call the interpreter.' From the ranks a little man came forward, in a Russian civilian dress. Pierre, from his dress and speech, at once recognised in him a French shopman from some Moscow shop.

'He doesn't look like a common man,' said the interpreter scanning Pierre.

'Oh, oh, he looks very like an incendiary,' said the officer. 'Ask him who he is,' he added.

'Who are you?' asked the interpreter in his Frenchified Russian. 'You must answer the officer.'

'I will not say who I am. I am your prisoner. Take me away,' Pierre said suddenly in French.

'Ah! ah!' commented the officer, knitting his brows; 'well, march then!'

A crowd had gathered around the Uhlans. Nearest of all to Pierre stood the pock-marked peasant woman with the child. When the patrol was moving, she stepped forward:

'Why, where are they taking you, my good soul?' she said. 'The child! what am I to do with the child if it's not theirs?' she cried.

'What does she want, this woman?' asked the officer.

Pierre was like a drunken man. His excitement was increased at the sight of the little girl he had saved.

'What does she want?' he said. 'She is carrying my daughter, whom I have just saved from the flames,' he declared. 'Good-bye!' and utterly at a loss to explain to himself the aimless lie he had just blurted out, he strode along with a resolute and solemn step between the Frenchmen.

The patrol of Uhlans was one of those that had been sent out by Durosnel's orders through various streets of Moscow to put a stop to pillage, and still more to capture the incendiaries, who in the general opinion of the French officers in the higher ranks on that day were causing the fires. Patrolling several streets, the Uhlans arrested five more suspicious characters, a shopkeeper, two divinity students, a peasant, and a house-serf—all Russians—besides several French soldiers engaged in pillage. But of all these suspicious characters, Pierre seemed to them the most suspicious of all.

When they had all been brought for the night to a big house on Zubovsky rampart, which had been fixed upon as a guardhouse, Pierre was put apart from the rest under strict guard.

PART XII

I

IN THE HIGHER circles in Petersburg the intricate conflict between the parties of Rumyantsev, of the French, of Mariya Fyodorovna, of the Tsarevitch, and the rest was going on all this time with more heat than ever, drowned, as always, by the buzzing of the court drones. But the easy, luxurious life of Petersburg, troubled only about phantasms, the reflection of life, went on its old way; and the course of that life made it a difficult task to believe in the danger and the difficult position of the Russian people. There were the same levees and balls, the same French theatre, the same court interests, the same interests and intrigues in the government service. It was only in the very highest circles that efforts were made to recollect the difficulty of the real position. There was whispered gossip of how the two Empresses had acted in opposition to one another in these difficult circumstances. The Empress Mariya Fyodorovna, anxious for the welfare of the benevolent and educational institutions under her patronage, had arrangements made for the removal of all the institutes to Kazan, and all the belongings of these establishments were already packed. The Empress Elizaveta Alexyevna on being asked what commands she was graciously pleased to give, had been pleased to reply that in regard to state matters she could give no commands, since that was all in the Tsar's hands; as far as she personally was concerned, she had graciously declared, with her characteristic Russian patriotism, that she would be the last to leave Petersburg.

On the 26th of August, the very day of the battle of Borodino, there was a *soirée* at Anna Pavlovna's, the chief attraction of which was to be the reading of the Metropolitan's letter, written on the occasion of his sending to the Tsar the holy picture of Saint Sergey. This letter was looked upon as a model of patriotic eloquence. It was to be read by Prince Vassily himself, who was famed for his fine elocution. (He used even to read aloud in the Empress's drawing-room.) The beauty of his elocution was supposed to lie in the loud, resonant voice, varying between a despairing howl and a tender whine, in which he rolled off the words quite independently of the sense, so that a howl fell on one word and a whine on others quite at random. This reading, as was always the case with Anna Pavlovna's entertainments, had a political significance. She was expecting at this *soirée* several important personages who were to be made to feel ashamed of patronising the French theatre, and to be roused to patriotic fervour. A good many people had already arrived, but Anna Pavlovna did not yet see those persons whose presence in her drawing-room was necessary, and she was therefore starting general topics of conversation before proceeding to the reading.

The news of the day in Petersburg was the illness of Countess Bezuhov. The countess had been taken ill a few days previously; she had missed several entertainments, of which she was usually the ornament, and it was said that she was seeing no one, and that instead of the celebrated Petersburg physicians, who usually attended her, she had put herself into the hands of some Italian doctor, who was treating her on some new and extraordinary method.

Everybody was very well aware that the charming countess's illness was due to inconveniences arising from marrying two husbands at once, and that the Italian doctor's treatment consisted in the removal of such inconvenience. But in the presence of Anna Pavlovna no one ventured to think about that view of the question, or even, as it were, to know what they did know about it.

'They say the poor countess is very ill. The doctor says it is *angina pectoris*.'

'*Angine?* Oh, that's a terrible illness.'

'They say the rivals are reconciled, thanks to the *angine* . . .' The word *angine* was repeated with great relish.

'I am told the old count is touching. He cried like a child when the doctor told him there was danger.'

'Oh, it would be a terrible loss. She is a fascinating woman.'

'You speak of the poor countess,' said Anna Pavlovna, coming up. 'I sent to inquire after her. I was told she was going on better. Oh, no doubt of it, she is the most charming woman in the world,' said Anna Pavlovna, with a smile at her own enthusiasm. 'We belong to different camps, but that does not prevent me from appreciating her as she deserves. She is very unhappy,' added Anna Pavlovna.

Supposing that by these last words Anna Pavlovna had slightly lifted the veil of mystery that hung over the countess's illness, one unwary young man permitted himself to express surprise that no well-known doctor had been called in, and that the countess should be treated by a charlatan, who might make use of dangerous remedies.

'Your information may be better than mine,' cried Anna Pavlovna, falling upon the inexperienced youth with sudden viciousness, 'but I have it on good authority that this doctor is a very learned and skilful man. He is the private physician of the Queen of Spain.'

And having thus annihilated the young man, Anna Pavlovna turned to Bilibin, who was talking in another group about the Austrians, and had his forehead puckeerd up in wrinkles in readiness to utter *un mot*.

'I think it is charming!' he was saying of the diplomatic note which had been sent to Vienna with the Austrian flags taken by Wittgenstein, '*le héros de Pétropol*,' as he was called at Petersburg.

'What? what was it?' Anna Pavlovna inquired, creating a silence for the *mot* to be heard, though she had in fact heard it before.

And Bilibin repeated the precise words of the diplomatic despatch he had composed.

'The Emperor sends back the Austrian flags,' said Bilibin; '*drapeaux amis et égarés qu'il a trouvés hors de la route*,' Bilibin concluded, letting the wrinkles run off his forehead.

'Charming, charming!' said Prince Vassily.

'The road to Warsaw, perhaps,' Prince Ippolit said loudly, to the general surprise. Everybody looked at him, at a loss to guess what he meant. Prince Ippolit, too, looked about him with light-hearted wonder. He had no more notion than other people what was meant by his words. In the course of his diplomatic career he had more than once noticed that words suddenly uttered in that way were accepted as highly diverting, and on every occasion he uttered in that way the first words that chanced to come to his tongue. 'May be, it will come out all right,' he thought, 'and if it doesn't, they will know how to give some turn to it.' And the awkward silence that reigned was in fact broken by the entrance of the personage of defective patriotism whom Anna Pavlovna was waiting for to convert to a better mind; and smiling, and shaking her finger at Prince Ippolit, she summoned Prince Vassily to the table, and setting two candles and a manuscript before him, she begged him to begin. There was a general hush.

'Most high and gracious Emperor and Tsar!' Prince Vassily boomed out sternly, and he looked round at his audience as though to inquire whether any one had anything to say against that. But nobody said anything. 'The chief capital city, Moscow, the New Jerusalem, receives *her* Messiah'—he threw a sudden emphasis on the '*her*'—'even as a mother in the embraces of her zealous sons, and through the gathering darkness, foreseeing the dazzling glory of thy dominion, sings aloud in triumph: ' "Hosanna! Blessed be He that cometh!" '

Prince Vassily uttered these last words in a tearful voice.

Bilibin scrutinised his nails attentively, and many of the audience were visibly cowed, as though wondering what they had done wrong. Anna Pavlovna murmured the words over beforehand, as old women whisper the prayer to come at communion: 'Let the base and insolent Goliath . . .' she whispered.

Prince Vassily continued:

'Let the base and insolent Goliath from the borders of France encompass the realm of Russia with the horrors of death; lowly faith, the sling of the Russian David, shall smite a swift blow at the head of his pride that thirsteth for blood. This holy image of the most venerable Saint Sergey, of old a zealous champion of our country's welfare, is borne to your Imperial Majesty. I grieve that my failing strength hinders me from the joy of your most gracious presence. Fervent prayers I am offering up to Heaven, and the Almighty will exalt the faithful and fulfil in His mercy the hopes of your Majesty.'

'Quel force! Quel style!' was murmured in applause of the reader and the author. Roused by this appeal, Anna Pavlovna's guests continued for a long while talking of the position of the country, and made various surmises as to the issue of the battle to be fought in a few days.

'You will see,' said Anna Pavlovna, 'that tomorrow on the Emperor's birthday we shall get news. I have a presentiment of something good.'

II

ANNA PAVLOVNA'S presentiment was in fact fulfilled. Next day, during the special service at court in honour of the Tsar's birthday, Prince Volkonsky was called out of church and received a despatch from Prince Kutuzov. This was the despatch Kutuzov had sent off on the day of the battle from Tatarinovo. Kutuzov wrote that the Russians had not retreated a single step, that the French had lost far more than our troops, that he was writing off in haste from the field of battle before he had time to collect the latest intelligence. So it had been a victory, it appeared. And at once, without leaving church, the assembled court offered up thanks to the Creator for His succour, and for the victory.

Anna Pavlovna's presentiment had been fulfilled, and the whole morning a mood of joyous festivity prevailed in the town. Every one accepted the victory as a conclusive one, and some people were already beginning to talk of Napoleon's having been taken prisoner, of his deposition, and the selection of a new sovereign for France.

At a distance from the scene of action and amid the conditions of court life, it is very difficult for events to be reflected in their true force and dimensions. Public events are involuntarily grouped about some private incident. So in this case, the courtiers' rejoicing was as much due to the fact of the news of this victory having arrived precisely on the Tsar's birthday as to the fact of the victory itself. It was like a successfully arranged surprise. Kutuzov's despatches had spoken, too, of the Russian losses, and among them had mentioned the names of Tutchkov, Bagration, and Kutaissov. The melancholy side, too, of the event was unconsciously in this Petersburg world concentrated about a single incident—the death of Kutaissov. Every one knew him, the Tsar liked him, he was young and interesting. All met that day with the words:

'How wonderful it should have happened so! Just in the Te Deum. But what a loss—Kutaissov! Ah, what a pity!'

'What did I tell you about Kutuzov?' Prince Vassily said now with the pride of a prophet. 'I always said he was the only man capable of conquering Napoleon.'

But next day no news came from the army, and the public voice began to waver. The courtiers suffered agonies over the agonies of suspense which the Tsar was suffering.

'Think of the Emperor's position!' the courtiers said; and they no longer sang the praises of Kutuzov as two days before, but upbraided him as the cause of the Tsar's uneasiness that day. Prince Vassily no longer boasted of his protégé Kutuzov, but was mute when the commander-in-chief was the subject of conversation. Moreover, on the evening of that day everything seemed to conspire to throw the Petersburg world into agitation and uneasiness: a terrible piece of news came to add to their alarms. Countess Elena Bezuhov died quite suddenly of the terrible illness which had been so amusing to talk about. At larger gatherings every one repeated the official story that Countess Bezuhov had died of a terrible attack of angina pectoris, but in intimate circles people told in detail how the Queen of Spain's own medical attendant had prescribed to Ellen small doses of a certain drug to bring about certain desired results; but that Ellen, tortured by the old count's suspecting her, and by her husband's not having answered her letter (that unfortunate, dissipated Pierre), had suddenly taken an enormous dose of the drug prescribed, and had died in agonies before assistance could be given. The story ran that Prince Vassily and the old count had been going to take proceedings against the Italian; but the latter had produced notes in his possession from the unhappy deceased of such a character that they had promptly let him go.

Conversation centred round three melancholy facts—the Tsar's state of suspense, the loss of Kutaissov, and the death of Ellen.

On the third day after Kutuzov's despatch, a country gentleman arrived in Petersburg from Moscow, and the news of the surrender of Moscow to the French was all over the town. This was awful! Think of the position of the Emperor! Kutuzov was a traitor, and, during the 'visits of condolence' paid to Prince Vassily on the occasion of his daughter's death, when he spoke of Kutuzov, whose praises he had once sung so loudly—it was pardonable in his grief to forget what he had said before—he said that nothing else was to be expected from a blind and dissolute old man.

'I only wonder how such a man could possibly be trusted with the fate of Russia.'

So long as the news was not official, it was still possible to doubt its truth; but next day the following communication arrived from Count Rastoptchin:

'Prince Kutuzov's adjutant has brought me a letter in which he asks me to furnish police-officers to escort the army to the Ryazan road. He says that he is regretfully abandoning Moscow. Sire! Kutuzov's action decides the fate of that capital and of your empire. Russia will shudder to learn of the abandonment of the city, where the greatness of Russia is centred, where are the ashes of our forefathers. I am following the army. I have had everything carried away; all that is left me is to weep over the fate of my country.'

On receiving this communication, the Tsar sent Prince Volkonsky with the following rescript to Kutuzov:

'Prince Mihail Ilarionovitch! I have received no communication from you since the 29th of August. Meanwhile I have received, by way of Yaroslavl, from the governor of Moscow the melancholy intelligence that you have decided with the army to abandon Moscow. You can imagine the effect this news has had upon me, and your silence redoubles my astonishment. I am sending herewith Staff-General Prince Volkonsky, to ascertain from you the position of the army and of the causes that have led you to so melancholy a decision.'

III

NINE days after the abandonment of Moscow, a courier from Kutuzov reached Petersburg with the official news of the surrender of Moscow. This courier was a Frenchman, Michaud, who did not know Russian, yet was, 'though a foreigner, Russian in heart and soul,' as he used to say of himself.

The Tsar at once received the messenger in his study in the palace of Kamenny island. Michaud, who had never seen Moscow before the campaign, and did not know a word of Russian, yet felt deeply moved when he came before *notre très gracieux souverain* (as he wrote) with the news of the burning of Moscow, whose flames illumined his route.

Though the sources of M. Michaud's sorrow must indeed have been different from that to which the grief of Russian people was due, Michaud had such a melancholy face when he was shown into the Tsar's study that the Tsar asked him at once:

'Do you bring me sad news, colonel?'

'Very sad, sire, the surrender of Moscow,' answered Michaud, casting his eyes down with a sigh.

'Can they have surrendered my ancient capital without a battle?' the Tsar asked quickly, suddenly flushing.

Michaud respectfully gave the message he had been commanded to give from Kutuzov, that is, that there was no possibility of fighting before Moscow, and that seeing there was no chance but either to lose the army and Moscow or to lose Moscow alone, the commander-in-chief had been obliged to choose the latter.

The Tsar listened without a word, not looking at Michaud.

'Has the enemy entered the city?' he asked.

'Yes, sire, and by now the city is in ashes. I left it all in flames,' said Michaud resolutely; but glancing at the Tsar, Michaud was horrified at what he had done. The Tsar was breathing hard and rapidly, his lower lip was twitching, and his fine blue eyes were for a moment wet with tears.

But that lasted only a moment. The Tsar suddenly frowned, as though vexed with himself for his own weakness; and raising his head he addressed Michaud in a firm voice:

'I see, colonel, from all that is happening to us that Providence requires great sacrifices of us. I am ready to submit to His will in everything; but tell me, Michaud, how did you leave the army, seeing my ancient capital thus abandoned without striking a blow? Did you not perceive discouragement?'

Seeing that his most gracious sovereign had regained his composure, Michaud too regained his; but to the Tsar's direct question of a matter of fact which called for a direct answer, he had not yet an answer ready.

'Sire, will you permit me to speak frankly, as a loyal soldier?' he said, to gain time.

'Colonel, I always expect it,' said the Tsar. 'Hide nothing from me; I want to know absolutely how it is.'

'Sire!' said Michaud, with a delicate, scarcely perceptible smile on his lips, as he had now had time to prepare his answer in the form of a light and respectful play of words. 'Sire! I left the whole army, from the commanders to the lowest soldier without exception, in extreme, desperate terror.'

'How so?' the Tsar interrupted, frowning sternly. 'My Russians let themselves be cast down by misfortune? . . . Never . . .'

This was just what Michaud was waiting for to get in his next phrases.

'Sire,' he said, with a respectful playfulness of expression, 'they fear only that your Majesty through goodness of heart may let yourself be persuaded to make peace. They burn to fight,' said the plenipotentiary of the Russian people, 'and to prove to your Majesty by the sacrifice of their lives how devoted they are . . .'

'Ah!' said the Tsar, reassured, slapping Michaud on the shoulder, with a friendly light in his eyes. 'You tranquillise me, colonel . . .'

The Tsar looked down, and for some time he was silent. 'Well, go back to the army,' he said, drawing himself up to his full height and with a genial and majestic gesture addressing Michaud, 'and tell our brave fellows, tell all my good subjects wherever you go, that when I have not a soldier left, I will put myself at the head of my dear nobility, of my good peasants, and so use the last resources of my empire. It offers me still more than my enemies suppose,' said the Tsar, more and more stirred. 'But if it should be written in the decrees of divine Providence,' he said, and his fine, mild eyes, shining with emotion, were raised towards heaven, 'that my dynasty should cease to reign on the throne of my ancestors, then after exhausting every means in my power, I would let my beard grow to here' (the Tsar put his hand half-way down his breast), 'and go and eat potatoes with the meanest of my peasants rather than sign the shame of my country and my dear people, whose sacrifice I know how to appreciate.' Uttering these words in a voice of much feeling, the Tsar turned quickly away, as though wishing to conceal from Michaud the tears that were starting into his eyes, and he walked to the further end of his study. After standing there some instants, he strode back to Michaud, and with a vigorous action squeezed his arm below the elbow. The Tsar's fine, mild face was flushed, and his eyes gleamed with energy and anger. 'Colonel Michaud, do not forget what I say to you here; perhaps one day we shall recall it with pleasure. . . . Napoleon or me,' he said, touching his breast, 'we can no longer reign together. I have learned to know him. He will not deceive me again . . .' And the Tsar paused, frowning. Hearing these words, seeing the look of firm determination in the Tsar's eyes, Michaud, though a foreigner, Russian in heart and soul, felt (as he used to recount later) at that solemn moment moved to enthusiasm by what he had just heard; and in the following phrase he sought to give expression to his own feelings and those of the Russian people, whose representative he considered himself to be.

'Sire!' he said, 'your Majesty is signing at this moment the glory of the nation and the salvation of Europe!'

With a motion of his head the Tsar dismissed Michaud.

IV

WHILE half of Russia was conquered, and the inhabitants of Moscow were fleeing to remote provinces, and one levy of militia after another was being raised for the defence of the country, we, not living at the time, cannot help imagining that all the people in Russia, great and small alike, were engaged in doing nothing else but making sacrifices, saving their country, or weeping over its downfall. The tales and descriptions of that period without exception tell us of nothing but the self-sacrifice, the patriotism, the despair, the grief, and the heroism of the Russians. In reality, it was not at all like that. It seems so to us, because we see out of the past only the general historical interest of that period, and we do not see all the personal human interests of the men of that time. And yet in reality these personal interests of the immediate present are of so much greater importance than public interests, that they prevent the public interest from ever being felt—from being noticed at all, indeed. The majority of the people of that period took no heed of the general progress of public affairs, and were only influenced by their immediate personal interests. And those very people played the most useful part in the work of the time.

Those who were striving to grasp the general course of events, and trying by self-sacrifice and heroism to take a hand in it, were the most useless members of society; they saw everything upside down, and all that they did with the best intentions turned out to be useless folly, like Pierre's regiment, and Mamonov's, that spent their time pillaging the Russian villages, like the lint scraped by the ladies, that never reached the wounded, and so on. Even those who, being fond of talking on intellectual subjects and expressing their feelings, discussed the position of Russia, unconsciously imported into their talk a shade of hypocrisy or falsity or else of useless fault-finding and bitterness against persons, whom they blamed for what could be nobody's fault.

In historical events we see more plainly than ever the law that forbids us to taste of the fruit of the Tree of Knowledge. It is only unselfconscious activity that bears fruit, and the man who plays a part in an historical drama never understands its significance. If he strives to comprehend it, he is stricken with barrenness.

The significance of the drama taking place in Russia at that time was the less easy to grasp, the closer the share a man was taking in it. In Petersburg, and in the provinces remote from Moscow, ladies and gentlemen in volunteer uniforms bewailed the fate of Russia and the ancient capital, and talked of self-sacrifice, and so on. But in the army, which had retreated behind Moscow, men scarcely talked or thought at all about Moscow, and, gazing at the burning city, no one swore to be avenged on the French, but every one was thinking of the next quarter's pay due to him, of the next halting-place, of Matryoshka the canteen-woman, and so on.

Nikolay Rostov, without any idea of self-sacrifice, simply because the war had happened to break out before he left the service, took an immediate and continuous part in the defence of his country, and consequently he looked upon what was happening in Russia without despair or gloomy prognostications. If he had been asked what he thought of the present position of Russia, he would have said that it was not his business to think about it, that that was what Kutuzov and the rest of them were for, but that he had heard that the regiments were being filled up to their full complements, and that they must therefore be going to fight for a good time longer, and that under the present circumstances he might pretty easily obtain the command of a regiment within a couple of years.

Since this was his point of view, it was with no regret at taking no part in the approaching battle, but with the greatest satisfaction—which he did not conceal, and his comrades fully understood—that he received the news of his appointment to go to Voronezh to purchase remounts for his division.

A few days before the battle of Borodino, Nikolay received the sums of money and official warrants required, and, sending some hussars on before him, he drove with posting-horses to Voronezh.

Only one who has had the same experience—that is, has spent several months continuously in the atmosphere of an army in the field—can imagine the delight Nikolay felt when he got out of the region overspread by the troops with their foraging parties, trains of provisions, and hospitals; when he saw no more soldiers, army waggons, and filthy traces of the camp, but villages of peasants and peasant women, gentlemen's country houses, fields with grazing oxen, and station-houses with sleepy overseers, he rejoiced as though he were seeing it all for the first time. What in particular remained for a long while a wonder and a joy to him was the sight of women, young and healthy, without dozens of officers hanging about every one of them; and women, too, who were pleased and flattered at an officer's cracking jokes with them.

In the happiest frame of mind, Nikolay reached the hotel at Voronezh at night, ordered everything of which he had so long been deprived in the army, and next day, after shaving with special care and putting on the full-dress uniform he had not worn for so long past, he drove off to present himself to the authorities.

The commander of the militia of the district was a civilian general, an old gentleman, who evidently found amusement in his military duties and rank. He gave Nikolay a brusque reception (supposing that this was the military manner), and cross-examining him with an important air, as though he had a right to do so, and expressed his approval and disapproval, as though called upon to give his verdict on the management of the war. Nikolay was in such high spirits that this only amused him.

From the commander of militia, he went to the governor's. The governor was a brisk little man, very affable and unpretentious. He mentioned to Nikolay the stud-farms, where he might obtain horses, recommended him to a horse-dealer in the town, and a gentleman living twenty versts from the town, who had the best horses, and promised him every assistance.

'You are Count Ilya Andreitch's son? My wife was a great friend of your mamma's. We receive on Thursdays: today is Thursday, pray come in, quite without ceremony,' said the governor, as he took leave of him.

Nikolay took a posting carriage, and making his quartermaster get in beside him, galloped straight off from the governor's to the gentleman with the stud of fine horses twenty versts away.

During the early days of his stay in Voronezh, everything seemed easy and pleasant to Nikolay, and, as is always the case, when a man is himself in a happy frame of mind, everything went well and prospered with him.

The country gentleman turned out to be an old cavalry officer, a bachelor, a great horse-fancier, a sportsman, and the owner of a smoking-room, of hundred-year-old herb-brandy, of some old Hungarian wine, and of superb horses.

In a couple of words, Nikolay had bought for six thousand roubles seventeen stallions, all perfect examples of their several breeds (as he said), as show specimens of his remounts. After dining and drinking a glass or so too much of the Hungarian wine, Rostov, exchanging kisses with the country gentleman, with whom he was already on the friendliest terms, galloped back over the most atrociously bad road in the happiest frame of mind, continually urging the driver on, so that he might be in time for the *soirée* at the governor's.

After dressing, scenting himself, and douching his head with cold water, Nikolay made his appearance at the governor's, a little late, but with the phrase, 'Better late than never,' ready on the tip of his tongue.

It was not a ball, and nothing had been said about dancing; but every one knew that Katerina Petrovna would play waltzes and écossaises on the clavichord, and that there would be dancing, and every one reckoning on it, had come dressed for a ball.

Provincial life in the year 1812 went on exactly the same as always, the only difference being that the provincial towns were livelier owing to the presence of many wealthy families from Moscow, that, as in everything going on at that time in Russia, there was perceptible in the gaiety a certain devil-may-care, desperate recklessness, and also that the small talk indispensable between people was now not about the weather and common acquaintances, but about Moscow and the army and Napoleon.

The gathering at the governor's consisted of the best society in Voronezh.

There were a great many ladies, among them several Moscow acquaintances of Nikolay's; but among the men there was no one who could be compared with the cavalier of St. George, the gallant hussar, and good-natured, well-bred Count Rostov. Among the men there was an Italian prisoner—an officer of the French army; and Nikolay felt that the presence of this prisoner gave an added lustre to him—the Russian hero. He was, as it were, a trophy of victory. Nikolay felt this, and it seemed to him as though every one looked at the Italian in the same light, and he treated the foreign officer with gracious dignity and reserve.

As soon as Nikolay came in in his full-dress uniform of an officer of hussars, diffusing a fragrance of scent and wine about him, and said himself, and heard several times said to him, the words, 'Better late than never,' people clustered round him. All eyes were turned on him, and he felt at once that he had stepped into a position that just suited him in a provincial town—a position always agreeable, but now after his long privation of such gratifications, intoxicatingly delightful—that of a universal favourite. Not only at the posting-stations, at the taverns, and in the smoking-room of the horse-breeding gentleman, had he found servant-girls flattered by his attention, but here, at the governor's assembly, there were (so it seemed to Nikolay) an inexhaustible multitude of young married ladies and pretty girls, who were only waiting with impatience for him to notice them. The ladies and the young girls flirted with him, and the old people began even from this first evening bestirring themselves to try and get this gallant young rake of an hussar married and settled down. Among the latter was the governor's wife herself, who received Rostov as though he were a near kinsman, and called him 'Nikolay.'

Katerina Petrovna did in fact proceed to play waltzes and écossaises, and dancing began, in which Nikolay fascinated the company more than ever by his elegance. He surprised every one indeed by his peculiarly free and easy style in dancing. Nikolay was a little surprised himself at his own style of dancing at that *soirée*. He had never danced in that manner at Moscow, and would indeed have regarded such an extremely free and easy manner of dancing as not correct, as bad style; but here he felt it incumbent on him to astonish them all by something extraordinary, something that they would be sure to take for the usual thing in the capital, though new to them in the provinces.

All the evening Nikolay paid the most marked attention to a blue-eyed, plump, and pleasing little blonde, the wife of one of the provincial officials. With the naïve conviction of young men who are enjoying themselves, that other men's wives are created for their special benefit, Rostov never left this lady's side, and treated her husband in a friendly way, almost as though there were a private understanding between them, as though they knew without speaking of it how capitally they, that is, how Nikolay and the wife, would get on. The husband did not, however, appear to share this conviction, and tried to take a gloomy tone with Rostov. But Nikolay's good-humoured naïveté was so limitless that at times the husband could not help being drawn into his gay humour. Towards the end of the evening, however, as the wife's face grew more flushed and animated, the husband's grew steadily more melancholy and stolid, as though they had a given allowance of liveliness between them, and as the wife's increased, the husband's dwindled.

V

WITH a smile that never left his lips, Nikolay sat bent a little forward on a low chair, and stooping close over his blonde beauty, he paid her mythological compliments.

Jauntily shifting the posture of his legs in his tight riding-breeches, diffusing a scent of perfume, and admiring his fair companion and himself and the fine lines of his legs in the tight breeches, Nikolay told the blonde lady that he wanted to elope with a lady here, in Voronezh.

'What is she like?'

'Charming, divine. Her eyes' (Nikolay gazed at his companion) 'are blue, her lips are coral, her whiteness . . .' he gazed at her shoulders, 'the shape of Diana . . .'

The husband came up to them and asked his wife gloomily what she was talking of.

'Ah! Nikita Ivanitch,' said Nikolay, rising courteously. And as though anxious for Nikita Ivanitch to take a share in his jests, he began to tell him too of his intention of running away with a blonde lady.

The husband smiled grimly, the wife gaily.

The good-natured governor's wife came up to them with a disapproving air.

'Anna Ignatyevna wants to see you, Nikolay,' she said, pronouncing the name in such a way that Rostov was at once aware that Anna Ignatyevna was a very great lady. 'Come, Nikolay. You let me call you so, don't you?'

'Oh yes, *ma tante*. Who is she?'

'Anna Ignatyevna Malvintsev. She has heard about you from her niece, how you rescued her . . . Do you guess? . . .'

'Oh, I rescued so many!' cried Nikolay.

'Her niece, Princess Bolkonsky. She is here in Voronezh with her aunt. Oho! how he blushes! Eh?'

'Not a bit of it, nonsense, *ma tante*.'

'Oh, very well, very well. Oh! oh! what a boy it is!'

The governor's wife led him up to a tall and very stout lady in a blue toque, who had just finished a game of cards with the personages of greatest consequence in the town. This was Madame Malvintsev, Princess Marya's aunt on her mother's side, a wealthy, childless widow, who always lived in Voronezh. She was standing up, reckoning her losses, when Rostov came up to her.

She dropped her eyelids with a severe and dignified air, glanced at him, and went on upbraiding the general who had been winning from her.

'Delighted, my dear boy,' she said, holding out her hand to him. 'Pray come and see me.'

After saying a few words about Princess Marya and her late father, whom Madame Malvintsev had evidently disliked, and inquiring what Nikolay knew about Prince Andrey, who was apparently also not in her good graces, the dignified old lady dismissed him, repeating her invitation to come and see her.

Nikolay promised to do so and blushed again as he took leave of Madame Malvintsev. At the mention of Princess Marya's name, Rostov experienced a sensation of shyness, even of terror, which he could not have explained to himself.

On leaving Madame Malvintsev, Rostov would have gone back to the dance, but the little governor's wife laid her plump little hand on his sleeve, and saying that she wanted to have a few words with him, led him into the divan-room; the persons in that room promptly withdrew that they might not be in her way.

'Do you know, *mon cher*,' said the governor's wife with a serious expression on her good-natured, little face, 'this is really the match for you; if you like, I will try and arrange it.'

'Whom do you mean, *ma tante*?' asked Nikolay.

'I will make a match for you with the princess. Katerina Petrovna talks of Lili, but I say, no—the princess. Do you wish it? I am sure your mamma will be grateful. Really, she is such a splendid girl, charming! And she is by no means so very plain.'

'Not at all so,' said Nikolay, as though offended at the idea. 'As for me, *ma tante*, as a soldier should, I don't force myself on any one, nor refuse anything that turns up,' said Rostov, before he had time to consider what he was saying.

'So remember then; this is no jesting matter.'

'How could it be!'

'Yes, yes,' said the governor's wife, as though talking to herself. 'And *entres autres, mon cher*, you are too assiduous with the other—the blonde. One feels sorry for the husband, really . . .'

'Oh no, we are quite friendly,' said Nikolay in the simplicity of his heart: it had never occurred to him that such an agreeable pastime for him could be other than agreeable to any one else.

'What a stupid thing I said to the governor's wife though!' suddenly came into Nikolay's mind at supper. 'She really will begin to arrange a match, and Sonya? . . .'

And on taking leave of the governor's wife, as she said to him once more with a smile, 'Well, remember then,' he drew her aside.

'But there is something . . . To tell you the truth, *ma tante* . . .'

'What is it, what is it, my dear. Come, let us sit down here.'

Nikolay had a sudden desire, an irresistible impulse to talk of all his most secret feelings (such as he would never have spoken of to his mother, to his sister, to an intimate friend) to this woman, who was almost a stranger. Whenever Nikolay thought afterwards of this uncalled-for outburst of inexplicable frankness—though it had most important consequences for him—it seemed to him (as it always seems to people in such cases) that it had happened by chance, through a sudden fit of folly. But at the same time this outburst of frankness, together with other insignificant events, had consequences of immense importance to him and to all his family.

'It's like this, *ma tante*. It has long been *maman*'s wish to marry me to an heiress; but the mere idea of it—marrying for money—is revolting to me.'

'Oh yes, I can understand that,' said the governor's wife.

'But Princess Bolkonsky, that's a different matter. In the first place, I'll tell you the truth, I like her very much, I feel drawn to her, and then, ever since I came across her in such a position, so strangely, it has often struck me, that it was fate. Only think: mamma has long been dreaming of it, but I had never happened to meet her before—it always so happened that we didn't meet. And then when my sister, Natasha, was engaged to her brother, of course it was impossible to think of a match between us then. It seems it was to happen that I met her first just when Natasha's engagement had been broken off; and well, everything afterwards . . . So you see how it is. I have never said all this to any one, and I never shall. I only say it to you.'

The governor's wife pressed his elbow gratefully.

'Do you know Sophie, my cousin? I love her; I have promised to marry her, and I am going to marry her . . . So you see it's no use talking of such a thing,' Nikolay concluded lamely, flushing crimson.

'My dearest boy, how can you talk so? Why, Sophie hasn't a farthing, and you told me yourself that your papa's affairs are terribly straitened. And your *maman*? It would kill her—for one thing. Then Sophie, if she is a girl of any heart, what a life it would be for her! Your mother in despair, your position ruined . . . No, my dear, Sophie and you ought to realise that.'

Nikolay did not speak. It was comforting to him to hear these arguments.

'All the same, *ma tante*, it cannot be,' he said, with a sigh, after a brief silence. 'And besides would the princess accept me? And again she is in mourning; can such a thing be thought of?'

'Why, do you suppose I am going to marry you out of hand on the spot? There are ways of doing everything,' said the governor's wife.

'What a match-maker you are, *ma tante* . . .' said Nikolay, kissing her plump little hand.

VI

ON reaching Moscow, after her meeting with Rostov at Bogutcharovo, Princess Marya had found her nephew there with his tutor, and a letter from Prince Andrey, directing her what route to take to her aunt, Madame Malvintsev's at Voronezh. The arrangements for the journey, anxiety about her brother, the organisation of her life in a new house, new people, the education of her nephew—all of this smothered in Princess Marya's heart that feeling as it were of temptation, which had tormented her during her father's illness and after his death, especially since her meeting with Rostov.

She was melancholy. Now after a month had passed in quiet, undisturbed conditions, she felt more and more deeply the loss of her father, which was connected in her heart with the downfall of Russia. She was anxious: the thought of the dangers to which her brother—the one creature near to her now left—was being exposed was a continual torture to her. She was worried too by the education of her nephew, which she was constantly feeling herself unfitted to control. But at the bottom of her heart there was an inward harmony, that arose from the sense that she had conquered in herself those dreams and hopes of personal happiness, that had sprung up in connection with Rostov.

When the governor's wife called on Madame Malvintsev the day after her *soirée*, and, talking over her plans with her, explaining that though under present circumstances a formal betrothal was of course not to be thought of, yet they might bring the young people together, and let them get to know one another, and having received the aunt's approval, began to speak of Rostov in Princess Marya's presence, singing his praises, and describing how he had blushed on hearing the princess's name, her emotion was not one of joy, but of pain. Her inner harmony was destroyed, and desires, doubts, self-reproach, and hope sprang up again.

In the course of the two days that followed before Rostov called, Princess Marya was continually considering what her behaviour ought to be in regard to Rostov. At one time, she made up her mind that she would not come down into the drawing-room when he came to see her aunt, that it was not suitable for her in her deep mourning to receive visitors. Then she thought this would be rude after what he had done for her. Then the idea struck her that her aunt and the governor's wife had views of some sort upon her and Rostov; their words and glances had seemed at times to confirm this suspicion. Then she told herself that it was only her own depravity that could make her think this of them: could they possibly fail to realise that in her position, still wearing the heaviest mourning, such match-making would be an insult both to her and to her father's memory? On the supposition that she would go down to see him, Princess Marya imagined the words he would say to her, and she would say to him; and at one moment, those words seemed to her undeservedly frigid, at the next, they struck her as carrying too much meaning. Above all she dreaded the embarrassment, which she felt would be sure to overcome her, and betray her, as soon as she saw him.

But when, on Sunday after matins, the footman came into the drawing-room to announce that Count Rostov had called, the princess showed no sign of embarrassment, only a faint flush came into her cheeks, and her eyes shone with a new, radiant light.

'You have seen him, aunt?' said Princess Marya, in a composed voice, not knowing herself how she could be externally so calm and natural.

When Rostov came into the room, the princess dropped her head for an instant, as though to give time for their visitor to greet her aunt; and then at the very moment when Nikolay turned to her, she raised her head and met his gaze with shining eyes. With a movement full of dignity and grace, she rose with a joyous smile, held out her delicate, soft hand to him, and spoke in a voice in which for the first time there was the thrill of deep, womanly chest notes. Mademoiselle Bourienne, who was in the drawing-room, gazed at Princess Marya with bewildered surprise. The most accomplished coquette herself, she could not have manœuvred better on meeting a man whom she wanted to attract.

'Either black suits her wonderfully, or she really has grown better looking without my noticing it. And above all, such tact and grace!' thought Mademoiselle Bourienne.

Had Princess Marya been capable of reflection at that moment, she would have been even more astonished than Mademoiselle Bourienne at the change that had taken place in her. From the moment she set eyes on that sweet, loved face, some new force of life seemed to take possession of her, and to drive her to speak and act apart from her own will. From the time Rostov entered the room, her face was transformed. Just as when a light is kindled within a carved and painted lantern, the delicate, intricate, artistic tracery comes out in unexpected and impressive beauty, where all seemed coarse, dark, and meaningless before; so was Princess Marya's face transformed. For the first time all the pure, spiritual, inner travail in which she had lived till then came out in her face. All her inner searchings of spirit, her self-reproach, her sufferings, her striving for goodness, her resignation, her love, her self-sacrifice—all this was radiant now in those luminous eyes, in the delicate smile, in every feature of her tender face.

Rostov saw all this as clearly as though he had known her whole life. He felt that he was in the presence of a creature utterly different from and better than all those he had met up to that moment, and, above all, far better than he was himself.

The conversation was of the simplest and most insignificant kind. They talked of the war, unconsciously, like every one else, exaggerating their sadness on that subject; they talked of their last meeting—and Nikolay then tried to turn the subject; they talked of the kind-hearted governor's wife, of Nikolay's relations, and of Princess Marya's.

Princess Marya did not talk of her brother, but turned the conversation, as soon as her aunt mentioned Prince Andrey. It was evident that of the troubles of Russia she could speak artificially, but her brother was a subject too near her heart, and she neither would nor could speak lightly of him. Nikolay noticed this, as indeed with a keenness of observation not usual with him, he noticed every shade of Princess Marya's character, and everything confirmed him in the conviction that she was an altogether rare and original being.

Nikolay, like Princess Marya, had blushed and been embarrassed, when he heard the princess spoken of, and even when he thought of her; but in her presence he felt perfectly at ease, and he said to her not at all what he had prepared beforehand to say to her, but what came into his mind at the moment, and always quite appropriately.

As visitors always do where there are children, Nikolay, in a momentary silence during his brief visit, had recourse to Prince Andrey's little son, caressing him, and asking him if he would like to be an hussar. He took the little boy in his arms, began gaily whirling him round, and glanced at Princess Marya. With softened, happy, shy eyes, she was watching the child she loved in the arms of the man she loved. Nikolay caught that look too, and as though he divined its significance, flushed with delight, and fell to kissing the child with simple-hearted gaiety.

Princess Marya was not going into society at all on account of her mourning, and Nikolay did not think it the proper thing to call on them again. But the governor's wife still persisted in her match-making, and repeating to Nikolay something flattering Princess Marya had said of him, and *vice versa*, kept urging that Rostov should declare himself to Princess Marya. With this object, she arranged that the young people should meet at the reverend father's before Mass.

Though Rostov did tell the governor's wife that he should make no sort of declaration to Princess Marya, he promised to be there.

Just as at Tilsit Rostov had not allowed himself to doubt whether what was accepted by every one as right were really right, so now after a brief but sincere struggle between the effort to order his life in accordance with his own sense of right, and humble submission to circumstances, he chose the latter, and yielded himself to the power, which, he felt, was irresistibly carrying him away. He knew that to declare his feelings to Princess Marya after his promise to Sonya would be what he called base. And he knew that he would never do a base thing. But he knew too (it was not what he knew, but what he felt at the bottom of his heart), that in giving way now to the force of circumstances and of the people guiding him, he was not only doing nothing wrong, but was doing something very, very grave, something of more gravity than anything he had done in his life.

After seeing Princess Marya, though his manner of life remained externally the same, all his former pleasures lost their charm for him, and he often thought of her. But he never thought of her, as he had thought of all the young girls he had met in society, nor as he had long, and sometimes with enthusiasm, thought of Sonya. Like almost every honest-hearted young man, he had thought of every young girl as of a possible future wife, had adapted to them in his imagination all the pictures of domestic felicity: the white morning wrapper, the wife behind the samovar, the wife's carriage, the little ones, mamma and papa, their attitude to one another, and so on, and so on. And these pictures of the future afforded him gratification. But when he thought of Princess Marya, to whom the match-makers were trying to betroth him, he could never form any picture of his future married life with her. Even if he tr: .. to do so, it all seemed incoherent and false. And it only filled him with dread.

VII

THE terrible news of the battle of Borodino, of our losses in killed and wounded, and the even more terrible news of the loss of Moscow reached Voronezh in the middle of September. Princess Marya, learning of her brother's wound only from the newspapers, and having no definite information about him, was preparing (so Nikolay heard, though he had not seen her) to set off to try and reach Prince Andrey.

On hearing the news of the battle of Borodino and of the abandonment of Moscow, Rostov felt, not despair, rage, revenge nor any such feeling, but a sudden weariness and vexation with everything at Voronezh, and a sense of awkwardness and uneasy conscience. All the conversations he listened to seemed to him insincere; he did not know what to think of it all, and felt that only in the regiment would all become clear to him again. He made haste to conclude the purchase of horses, and was often without good cause ill-tempered with his servant and quartermaster.

Several days before Rostov's departure there was a thanksgiving service in the cathedral for the victory gained by the Russian troops, and Nikolay went to the service. He was a little behind the governor, and was standing through the service meditating with befitting sedateness on the most various subjects. When the service was concluding, the governor's wife beckoned him to her.

'Did you see the princess?' she said, with a motion of her hand towards a lady in black standing behind the choir.

Nikolay recognised Princess Marya at once, not so much from the profile he saw under her hat as from the feeling of watchful solicitude, awe, and pity which came over him at once. Princess Marya, obviously buried in her own thoughts, was making the last signs of the cross before leaving the church.

Nikolay gazed in wonder at her face. It was the same face he had seen before; there was the same general look of refined, inner, spiritual travail; but now there was an utterly different light in it. There was a touching expression of sadness, of prayer and of hope in it. With the same absence of hesitation as he had felt before in her presence, without waiting for the governor's wife to urge him, without asking himself whether it were right, whether it were proper for him to address her here in church, Nikolay went up to her, and said he had heard of her trouble and grieved with his whole heart to hear of it. As soon as she heard his voice, a vivid colour glowed in her face, lighting up at once her joy and her sorrow.

'One thing I wanted to tell you, princess,' said Rostov, 'that is, that if Prince Andrey Nikolaevitch were not living, since he is a colonel, it would be announced immediately in the gazettes.'

The princess looked at him, not comprehending his words, but comforted by the expression of sympathetic suffering in his face.

'And I know from so many instances that a wound from a splinter' (the papers said it was from a grenade) 'is either immediately fatal or else very slight,' Nikolay went on. 'We must hope for the best, and I am certain . . .'

Princess Marya interrupted him.

'Oh, it would be so aw . . .' she began, and her emotion choking her utterance, she bent her head with a graceful gesture, like everything she did in his presence, and glancing gratefully at him followed her aunt.

That evening Nikolay did not go out anywhere, but stayed at home to finish some accounts with the horse-vendors. By the time he had finished his work it was rather late to go out anywhere, but still early to go to bed, and Nikolay spent a long while walking up and down the room, thinking over his life, a thing that he rarely did.

Princess Marya had made an agreeable impression on him at Bogutcharovo. The fact of his meeting her then in such striking circumstances, and of his mother having at one time pitched precisely on her as the wealthy heiress suitable for him, had led him to look at her with special attention. During his stay at Voronezh, that impression had become, not merely a pleasing, but a very strong one. Nikolay was impressed by the peculiar, moral beauty which he discerned in her at this time. He had, however, been preparing to go away, and it had not entered his head to regret that in leaving Voronezh he was losing all chance of seeing her. But his meeting with Princess Marya that morning in church had, Nikolay felt, gone more deeply to his heart than he had anticipated and more deeply than he desired for his peace of mind. That pale, delicate, melancholy face, those luminous eyes, those soft, gracious gestures, and, above all, the deep and tender melancholy expressed in all her features, agitated him and drew his sympathy. In men Rostov could not bear an appearance of higher, spiritual life (it was why he did not like Prince Andrey), he spoke of it contemptuously as philosophy, idealism; but in Princess Marya it was just in that melancholy, showing all the depth of a spiritual world, strange and remote to Nikolay, that he found an irresistible attraction.

'She must be a marvellous girl! An angel, really!' he said to himself. 'Why am I not free? Why was I in such a hurry with Sonya?' And involuntarily he compared the two: the poverty of the one and the wealth of the other in those spiritual gifts, which Nikolay was himself without and therefore prized so highly. He tried to picture what would have happened if he had been free, and in what way he would have made her an offer and she would have become his wife. No, he could not imagine that. A feeling of dread came over him and that picture would take no definite shape. With Sonya he had long ago made his picture of the future, and it was all so simple and clear, just because it was all made up and he knew all there was in Sonya. But with Princess Marya he could not picture his future life, because he did not understand her—he simply loved her.

There was something light-hearted, something of child's play in his dreams of Sonya. But to dream of Princess Marya was difficult and a little terrible.

'How she was praying!' he thought. 'One could see that her whole soul was in her prayer. Yes, it was that prayer that moves mountains, and I am convinced that her prayer will be answered. Why don't I pray for what I want?' he bethought himself. 'What do I want? Freedom, release from Sonya. She was right,' he thought of what the governor's wife had said, 'nothing but misery can come of my marrying her. Muddle, mamma's grief . . . our position . . . a muddle, a fearful muddle! Besides, I don't even love her. No, I don't love her in the right way. My God! take me out of this awful, hopeless position!' he began praying all at once. 'Yes, prayer will move mountains, but one must believe, and not pray, as Natasha and I prayed as children for the snow to turn into sugar, and then ran out into the yard to try whether it had become sugar. No; but I am not praying for trifles now,' he said, putting his pipe down in the corner and standing with clasped hands before the holy picture. And softened by the thought of Princess Marya, he began to pray as he had not prayed for a long while. He had tears in his eyes and a lump in his throat when Lavrushka came in at the door with papers.

'Blockhead! bursting in when you're not wanted!' said Nikolay, quickly changing his attitude.

'A courier has come,' said Lavrushka in a sleepy voice, 'from the governor, a letter for you.'

'Oh, very well, thanks, you can go!'

Nikolay took the two letters. One was from his mother, the other from Sonya. He knew them from the handwriting, and broke open Sonya's letter first. He had hardly read a few lines when his face turned white and his eyes opened wide in dismay and joy. 'No, it's not possible!' he said aloud. Unable to sit still, he began walking to and fro in the room, holding the letter in both hands as he read it. He skimmed through the letter, then read it through once and again, and shrugging his shoulders and flinging up his hands, he stood still in the middle of the room with wide-open mouth and staring eyes. What he had just been praying for with the assurance that God would answer his prayer had come to pass; but Nikolay was astounded at it as though it were something extraordinary, and as though he had not expected it, and as though the very fact of its coming to pass so quickly proved that it had not come from God, to whom he had been praying, but was some ordinary coincidence.

The knot fastening his freedom, that had seemed so impossible to disentangle, had been undone by this unexpected and, as it seemed to Nikolay, uncalled-for letter from Sonya. She wrote that their late misfortunes, the loss of almost the whole of the Rostovs' property in Moscow, and the countess's frequently expressed desire that Nikolay should marry Princess Bolkonsky, and his silence and coldness of late, all taken together led her to decide to set him free from his promise, and to give him back complete liberty.

'It would be too painful to me to think that I could be a cause of sorrow and discord in the family which has overwhelmed me with benefits,' she wrote; 'and the one aim of my love is the happiness of those I love, and therefore I beseech you, Nicolas, to consider yourself free, and to know that in spite of everything, no one can love you more truly than your—SONYA.'

Both letters were from Troitsa. The other letter was from the countess. It described the last days in Moscow, the departure, the fire and the loss of the whole of their property. The countess wrote too that Prince Andrey had been among the train of wounded soldiers who had travelled with them. He was still in a very critical condition, but that the doctor said now that there was more hope. Sonya and Natasha were nursing him.

With this letter Nikolay went next day to call on Princess Marya. Neither Nikolay nor Princess Marya said a word as to all that was implied by the words: 'Natasha is nursing him'; but thanks to this letter, Nikolay was brought suddenly into intimate relations, almost those of a kinsman, with the princess.

Next day Rostov escorted Princess Marya as far as Yaroslavl, and a few days later he set off himself to join his regiment.

VIII

SONYA'S letter to Nikolay, that had come as an answer to his prayer, was written at Troitsa. It had been called forth in the following way. The idea of marrying Nikolay to a wealthy heiress had taken more and more complete possession of the old countess's mind. She knew that Sonya was the great obstacle in the way of this. And Sonya's life had of late, and especially after the letter in which Nikolay described his meeting with Princess Marya at Bogutcharovo, become more and more difficult in the countess's house. The countess never let slip an opportunity for making some cruel or humiliating allusion to Sonya. But a few days before they set out from Moscow the countess, distressed and overwrought by all that was happening, sent for Sonya, and instead of insistence and upbraiding, besought her with tears and entreaties to repay all that had been done for her by sacrificing herself, and breaking off her engagement to Nikolay. 'I shall have no peace of mind till you make me this promise,' she said.

Sonya sobbed hysterically, answered through her sobs that she would do anything, that she was ready for anything; but she did not give a direct promise, and in her heart she could not bring herself to what was demanded of her. She had to sacrifice herself for the happiness of the family that had brought her up and provided for her. To sacrifice herself for others was Sonya's habit. Her position in the house was such that only by way of sacrifice could she show her virtues, and she was used to sacrificing herself and liked it. But in every self-sacrificing action hitherto she had been happily conscious that by her very self-sacrifice she was heightening her value in the eyes of herself and others, and becoming worthier of Nikolay, whom she loved beyond everything in life. But now her sacrifice would consist in the renunciation of what constituted for her the whole reward of sacrifice, and the whole meaning of life. And for the first time in her life she felt bitterness against the people who had befriended her only to torment her more poignantly: she felt envy of Natasha, who had never had any experience of the kind, who had never been required to make sacrifices, and made other people sacrifice themselves for her, and was yet loved by every one. And for the first time Sonya felt that there was beginning to grow up out of her quiet, pure love for Nikolay a passionate feeling, which stood above all principles, and virtue, and religion. And under the influence of that passion, Sonya, whose life of dependence had unconsciously trained her to reserve, gave the countess vague, indefinite answers, avoided talking with her, and resolved to wait for a personal interview with Nikolay, not to set him free, but, on the contrary, to bind him to her for ever.

The fuss and the horror of the Rostovs' last days in Moscow had smothered the gloomy thoughts that were weighing on Sonya. She was glad to find an escape from them in practical work. But when she heard of Prince Andrey's presence in their house, in spite of all the genuine compassion she felt for him, and for Natasha, a joyful and superstitious feeling that it was God's will that she should not be parted from Nikolay took possession of her. She knew Natasha loved no one but Prince Andrey, and had never ceased to love him. She knew that brought together now, under such terrible circumstances, they would love one another again; and that then, owing to the relationship that would (in accordance with the laws of the Orthodox Church) exist between them, Nikolay could not be married to Princess Marya. In spite of all the awfulness of what was happening during the last day or two in Moscow and the first days of the journey, that feeling, that consciousness of the intervention of Providence in her personal affairs, was a source of joy to Sonya. At the Troitsa monastery the Rostovs made the first break in their journey.

In the hostel of the monastery three big rooms were assigned to the Rostovs, one of which was occupied by Prince Andrey. The wounded man was by this time a great deal better. Natasha was sitting with him. In the next room were the count and the countess reverently conversing with the superior, who was paying a visit to his old acquaintances and patrons. Sonya was sitting with them, fretted by curiosity as to what Prince Andrey and Natasha were saying. She heard the sounds of their voices through the door. The door of Prince Andrey's room opened. Natasha came out with an excited face, and not noticing the monk, who rose to meet her, and pulled back his wide sleeve off his right hand, she went up to Sonya and took her by the arm.

'Natasha, what are you about? Come here,' said the countess.

Natasha went up to receive the blessing, and the superior counselled her to turn for aid to God and to His saint.

Immediately after the superior had gone out, Natasha took her friend by the arm, and went with her into the empty third room.

'Sonya, yes, he will live,' she said. 'Sonya, how happy I am, and how wretched! Sonya, darling, everything is just as it used to be. If only he were going to live. He cannot, . . . because . . . be . . . cause . . .' and Natasha burst into tears.

'Yes! I knew it would be! Thank God,' said Sonya. 'He will live.'

Sonya was no less excited than her friend, both by the latter's grief and fears, and by her own personal reflections, of which she had spoken to no one. Sobbing, she kissed and comforted Natasha. 'If only he were to live!' she thought. After weeping, talking a little, and wiping their tears, the two friends went towards Prince Andrey's door. Natasha, cautiously opening the door, glanced into the room. Sonya stood beside her at the half-open door.

Prince Andrey was lying raised high on three pillows. His pale face looked peaceful, his eyes were closed, and they could see his quiet, regular breathing.

'Ah, Natasha!' Sonya almost shrieked all of a sudden, clutching at her cousin's arm, and moving back away from the door.

'What! what is it?' asked Natasha.

'It's the same, the same, you know . . .' said Sonya, with a white face and quivering lips.

Natasha softly closed the door and walked away with Sonya to the window, not yet understanding what she was talking of.

'Do you remember,' said Sonya, with a scared and solemn face, 'do you remember when I looked into the mirror for you . . . at Otradnoe at Christmas time . . . Do you remember what I saw?' . . .

'Yes, yes,' said Natasha, opening her eyes wide, and vaguely recalling that Sonya had said something then about seeing Prince Andrey lying down.

'Do you remember?' Sonya went on. 'I saw him then, and told you all so at the time, you and Dunyasha. I saw him lying on a bed,' she said, at each detail making a gesture with her lifted finger, 'and that he had his eyes shut, and that he was covered with a pink quilt, and that he had his hands folded,' said Sonya, convinced as she described the details she had just seen that they were the very details she had *seen* then. At the time she had seen nothing, but had said she was seeing the first thing that came into her head. But what she had invented then seemed to her now as real a memory as any other. She not only remembered that she had said at the time that he looked round at her and smiled, and was covered with something red, but was firmly convinced that she had seen and said at the time, that he was covered with a pink quilt—yes, pink—and that his eyes had been closed.

'Yes, yes, pink it was,' said Natasha, who began now to fancy too that she remembered her saying it was a pink quilt, and saw in that detail the most striking and mysterious point in the prediction.

'But what does it mean?' said Natasha dreamily.

'Ah, I don't know, how extraordinary it all is!' said Sonya, clutching at her head.

A few minutes later, Prince Andrey rang his bell, and Natasha went in to him; while Sonya, in a state of excitement and emotion such as she had rarely experienced, remained in the window, pondering over all the strangeness of what was happening.

That day there was an opportunity of sending letters to the army, and the countess wrote a letter to her son.

'Sonya,' said the countess, raising her head from her letter, as her niece passed by her. 'Sonya, won't you write to Nikolenka?' said the countess, in a soft and trembling voice; and in the tired eyes, that looked at her over the spectacles, Sonya read all that the countess meant by those words. Those eyes expressed entreaty and dread of a refusal and shame at having to beg, and readiness for unforgiving hatred in case of refusal.

Sonya went up to the countess, and kneeling down, kissed her hand.

'I will write, mamma,' she said.

Sonya was softened, excited, and moved by all that had passed that day, especially by the mysterious fulfilment of her divination, which she had just seen. Now, when she knew that in case of the renewal of Natasha's engagement to Prince Andrey, Nikolay could not be married to Princess Marya, she felt with delight a return of that self-sacrificing spirit in which she was accustomed and liked to live. And with tears in her eyes, and with a glad sense of performing a magnanimous action, she sat down, and several times interrupted by the tears that dimmed her velvety black eyes, she wrote the touching letter the reception of which had so impressed Nikolay.

IX

IN the guard-room to which Pierre had been taken, the officer and soldiers in charge treated him with hostility, but at the same time with respect. Their attitude to him betrayed both doubt who he might be—perhaps a person of great importance—and hostility, in consequence of the personal conflict they had so recently had with him.

But when on the morning of the next day the guard was relieved, Pierre felt that for his new guard—both officers and soldiers—he was no longer an object of the same interest as he had been to those who had taken him prisoner. And, indeed, in the big, stout man in a peasant's coat, the sentinels in charge next day saw nothing of the vigorous person who had fought so desperately with the pillaging soldier and the convoy, and had uttered that solemn phrase about saving a child; they saw in him only number seventeen of the Russian prisoners who were to be detained for some reason by order of the higher authorities. If there were anything peculiar about Pierre, it lay on in his undaunted air of concentrated thought, and in the excellent French in which, to the surprise of the French, he expressed himself. In spite of that, Pierre was put that day with the other suspicious characters who had been apprehended, since the room he had occupied was wanted for an officer.

All the Russians detained with Pierre were persons of the lowest class. And all of them, recognising Pierre as a gentleman, held aloof from him all the more for his speaking French. Pierre mournfully heard their jeers at his expense.

On the following evening, Pierre learned that all the prisoners (and himself probably in the number) were to be tried for incendiarism. The day after, Pierre was taken with the rest to a house where were sitting a French general with white moustaches, two colonels, and other Frenchmen with scarfs on their shoulders. With that peculiar exactitude and definiteness, which is always employed in the examination of prisoners and is supposed to preclude all human weaknesses, they put questions to Pierre and the others, asking who he was, where he had been, with what object, and so on.

These questions, leaving on one side the essence of the living fact, and excluding all possibility of that essence being discovered, like all questions, indeed, in legal examinations, aimed only at directing the channel along which the examining officials desired the prisoner's answers to flow, so as to lead him to the goal of the inquiry—that is, to conviction. So soon as he began to say anything that was not conducive to this aim, then they pulled up the channel, and the water might flow where it would. Moreover, Pierre felt, as the accused always do feel at all trials, a puzzled wonder why all these questions were asked him. He had a feeling that it was only out of condescension, out of a sort of civility, that this trick of directing the channel of their replies was made use of. He knew he was in the power of these men, that it was only by superior force that he had been brought here, that it was only superior force that gave them the right to exact answers to their questions, that the whole aim of the proceeding was to convict him. And, therefore, since they had superior force, and they had the desire to convict him, there seemed no need of the network of questions and the trial. It was obvious that all the questions were bound to lead up to his conviction. To the inquiry what he was doing when he was apprehended, Pierre replied with a certain tragic dignity that he was carrying back to its parents a child he had 'rescued from the flames.' Why was he fighting with the soldiers? Pierre replied that he was defending a woman, that the defence of an insulted woman was the duty of every man, and so on . . . He was pulled up; this was irrelevant. With what object had he been in the courtyard of a burning house where he had been seen by several witnesses? He answered that he was going out to see what was going on in Moscow. He was pulled up again. He had not been asked, he was told, where he was going, but with what object he was near the fire. Who was he? The first question was repeated, to which he had said he did not want to answer. Again he replied that he could not answer that.

'Write that down, that's bad. Very bad,' the general with the white whiskers and the red, flushed face said to him sternly.

On the fourth day, fire broke out on the Zubovsky rampart.

Pierre was moved with thirteen of the others to a coach-house belonging to a merchant's house on the Crimean Ford. As he passed through the street, Pierre could hardly breathe for the smoke, which seemed hanging over the whole city. Fires could be seen in various directions. Pierre did not at that time grasp what was implied by the burning of Moscow, and he gazed with horror at the fires.

In a coach-house behind a house in the Crimean Ford, Pierre spent another four days, and in the course of those four days he learned, from the conversation of the French soldiers, that all the prisoners in detention here were every day awaiting the decision of their fate by a marshal. Of what marshal, Pierre could not ascertain from the soldiers. For the soldiers, this marshal was evidently the highest and somewhat mysterious symbol of power.

These first days, up to the 8th of September, when the prisoners were brought up for a second examination, were the most painful for Pierre.

X

ON the 8th of September, there came into the prisoners' coach-house an officer of very great consequence, judging by the respectfulness with which he was addressed by the soldiers on guard. This officer, probably some one on the staff, held a memorandum in his hand, and called over all the Russians' names, giving Pierre the title of 'the one who will not give his name.' And with an indolent and indifferent glance at all the prisoners, he gave the officer on guard orders to have them decently dressed and in good order before bringing them before the marshal. In an hour a company of soldiers arrived, and Pierre with the thirteen others was taken to the Virgin's Meadow. It was a fine day, sunny after rain, and the air was exceptionally clear. The smoke did not hang low over the town as on the day when Pierre had been taken from the guard-room of the Zubovsky rampart; the smoke rose up in columns into the pure air. Flames were nowhere to be seen; but columns of smoke were rising up on all sides, and all Moscow, all that Pierre could see, was one conflagration. On all sides he saw places laid waste, with stoves and pipes left standing in them, and now and then the charred walls of a stone house.

Pierre stared at the fires, and did not recognise parts of the town that he knew well. Here and there could be seen churches that had not been touched by the fire. The Kremlin uninjured, rose white in the distance, with towers and Ivan the Great. Close at hand, the cupola of the Monastery of the New Virgin shone brightly, and the bells for service rang out gaily from it. Those bells reminded Pierre that it was Sunday and the festival of the birth of the Virgin Mother. But there seemed to be no one to keep this holiday; on all sides they saw the ruin wrought by the fires, and the only Russians they met were a few tattered and frightened-looking people, who hid themselves on seeing the French.

It was evident that the Russian nest was in ruins and destroyed; but with this annihilation of the old Russian order of life, Pierre was unconsciously aware that the French had raised up over this ruined nest an utterly different but strong order of their own. He felt this at the sight of the regular ranks of the boldly and gaily marching soldiers who were escorting him and the other prisoners; he felt it at the sight of some important French official in a carriage and pair, driven by a soldier, whom they met on their way. He felt it at the gay sounds of regimental music, which floated across from the left of the meadow; and he had felt it and realised it particularly strongly from the memorandum the French officer had read in the morning when he called over the prisoners' names. Pierre was taken by one set of soldiers, led off to one place, and thence to another, with dozens of different people. It seemed to him that they might have forgotten him, have mixed him up with other people. But no; his answers given at the examination came back to him in the form of the designation, 'the one who will not give his name.' And under this designation, which filled Pierre with dread, they led him away somewhere, with unhesitating conviction written on their faces that he and the other prisoners with him were the right ones, and that they were being taken to the proper place. Pierre felt himself an insignificant chip that had fallen under the wheel of a machine that worked without a hitch, though he did not understand it.

Pierre was led with the other prisoners to the right side of the Virgin's Meadow, not far from the monastery, and taken up to a big, white house with an immense garden. It was the house of Prince Shtcherbatov, and Pierre had often been inside it in former days to see its owner. Now, as he learnt from the talk of the soldiers, it was occupied by the marshal, the Duke of Eckmühl.

They were led up to the entrance, and taken into the house, one at a time. Pierre was the sixth to be led in. Through a glass-roofed gallery, a vestibule, and a hall, all familiar to Pierre, he was led to the long, low-pitched study, at the door of which stood an adjutant.

Davoust was sitting at a table at the end of the room, his spectacles on his nose. Pierre came close up to him. Davoust, without raising his eyes, was apparently engaged in looking up something in a document that lay before him. Without raising his eyes, he asked softly: 'Who are you?'

Pierre was mute because he was incapable of articulating a word. Davoust was not to Pierre simply a French general; to Pierre, Davoust was a man notorious for his cruelty. Looking at the cold face of Davoust, which, like a stern teacher, seemed to consent for a time to have patience and await a reply, Pierre felt that every second of delay might cost him his life. But he did not know what to say. To say the same as he had said at the first examination he did not dare; to disclose his name and his position would be both dangerous and shameful.

Pierre stood mute. But before he had time to come to any decision, Davoust raised his head, thrust his spectacles up on his forehead, screwed up his eyes, and looked intently at Pierre.

'I know this man,' he said, in a frigid, measured tone, obviously reckoning on frightening Pierre. The chill that had been running down Pierre's back seemed to clutch his head in a vice.

'General, you cannot know me, I have never seen you.'

'It is a Russian spy,' Davoust interrupted, addressing another general in the room, whom Pierre had not noticed. And Davoust turned away. With an unexpected thrill in his voice, Pierre began speaking with sudden rapidity.

'*Non, monseigneur*,' he said, suddenly recalling that Davoust was a duke, 'you could not know me. I am a militia officer, and I have not quitted Moscow.'

'Your name?' repeated Davoust.

'Bezuhov.'

'What proof is there that you are not lying?'

'*Monseigneur!*' cried Pierre in a voice not of offence but of supplication.

Davoust lifted his eyes and looked intently at Pierre. For several seconds they looked at one another, and that look saved Pierre. In that glance, apart from all circumstances of warfare and of judgment, human relations arose between these two men. Both of them in that one instant were vaguely aware of an immense number of different things, and knew that they were both children of humanity, that they were brothers.

At the first glance when Davoust raised his head from his memorandum, where men's lives and doings were marked off by numbers, Pierre was only a circumstance, and Davoust could have shot him with no sense of an evil deed on his conscience; but now he saw in him a man. He pondered an instant.

'How will you prove to me the truth of what you say?' said Davoust coldly.

Pierre thought of Ramballe, and mentioned his name and regiment and the street and house where he could be found.

'You are not what you say,' Davoust said again.

In a trembling, breaking voice, Pierre began to bring forward proofs of the truth of his testimony.

But at that moment an adjutant came in and said something to Davoust.

Davoust beamed at the news the adjutant brought him, and began buttoning up his uniform. Apparently he had completely forgotten about Pierre. When an adjutant reminded him of the prisoner, he nodded in Pierre's direction with a frown, and told them to take him away. But where were they to take him—Pierre did not know: whether back to the shed or the place prepared for their execution which his companion had pointed out to him as they passed through the Virgin's Meadow.

He turned his head and saw that the adjutant was repeating some question.

'Yes, of course!' said Davoust. But what that 'yes' meant, Pierre could not tell.

Pierre did not remember how or where he went, and how long he was going. In a condition of complete stupefaction and bewilderment, seeing nothing around him, he moved his legs in company with the others till they all stopped, and he stopped.

There was one idea all this time in Pierre's head. It was the question: Who, who was it really that was condemning him to death? It was not the men who had questioned him at the first examination; of them not one would or obviously could do so. It was not Davoust, who had looked at him in such a human fashion. In another minute Davoust would have understood that they were doing wrong, but the adjutant who had come in at that moment had prevented it. And that adjutant had obviously had no evil intent, but he might have stayed away. Who was it, after all, who was punishing him, killing him, taking his life—his, Pierre's, with all his memories, his strivings, his hopes, and his ideas? Who was doing it? And Pierre felt that it was no one's doing. It was discipline, and the concatenation of circumstances. Some sort of discipline was killing him, Pierre, robbing him of life, of all, annihilating him.

XI

FROM Prince Shtcherbatov's house the prisoners were taken straight downhill across the Virgin's Meadow to the left of the monastery of the Virgin, and led to a kitchen garden, in which there stood a post. A big pit had been dug out near the post, and the freshly turned-up earth was heaped up by it. A great crowd of people formed a semicircle about the pit and the post. The crowd consisted of a small number of Russians and a great number of Napoleon's soldiers not on duty: there were Germans, Italians, and Frenchmen in various uniforms. To the right and left of the post stood rows of French soldiers, in blue uniforms, with red epaulettes, in Hessians and shako. The prisoners were stood in a certain order, in accordance with a written list (Pierre was sixth) and led up to the post. Several drums suddenly began beating on both sides of them, and Pierre felt as though a part of his soul was being torn away from him by that sound. He lost all power of thought and reflection. He could only see and hear. And there was only one desire left in him, the desire that the terrible thing that was to be done should be done more quickly. Pierre looked round at his companions and scrutinised them.

The two men at the end were shaven convicts; one tall and thin, the other a swarthy, hirsute, muscular fellow with a flattened nose. The third was a house-serf, a man of five-and-forty, with grey hair and a plump, well-fed figure. The fourth was a peasant, a very handsome fellow with a full, flaxen beard and black eyes. The fifth was a factory hand, a thin, sallow lad of eighteen, in a dressing-gown.

Pierre heard the Frenchmen deliberating how they were to be shot, singly, or two at a time. 'Two at a time,' a senior officer answered coldly. There was a stir in the ranks of the soldiers, and it was evident that every one was in haste and not making haste, as people do when they are getting through some job every one can understand, but as men hasten to get something done that is inevitable, but is disagreeable and incomprehensible.

A French official wearing a scarf came up to the right side of the file of prisoners, and read aloud the sentence in Russian and in French.

Then two couples of French soldiers came up to the prisoners by the instruction of an officer, and took the two convicts who stood at the head. The convicts went up to the post, stopped there, and while the sacks were being brought, they looked dumbly about them, as a wild beast at bay looks at the approaching hunter. One of them kept on crossing himself, the other scratched his back and worked his lips into the semblance of a smile. The soldiers with hurrying fingers bandaged their eyes, put the sacks over their heads and bound them to the post.

A dozen sharpshooters, with muskets, stepped out of the ranks with a fine, regular tread, and halted eight paces from the post. Pierre turned away not to see what was coming. There was a sudden bang and rattle that seemed to Pierre louder than the most terrific clap of thunder, and he looked round. There was a cloud of smoke, and the French soldiers, with trembling hands and pale faces, were doing something in it by the pit. The next two were led up. These two, too, looked at every one in the same way, with the same eyes, dumbly, and in vain, with their eyes only begging for protection, and plainly unable to understand or believe in what was coming. They could not believe in it, because they only knew what their life was to them, and so could not understand, and could not believe, that it could be taken from them.

Pierre tried not to look, and again turned away; but again a sort of awful crash smote his hearing, and with the sound he saw smoke, blood, and the pale and frightened faces of the Frenchmen, again doing something at the post, and balking each other with their trembling hands. Pierre, breathing hard, looked about him as though asking, 'What does it mean?' The same question was written in all the eyes that met Pierre's eyes. On all the faces of the Russians, on the faces of the French soldiers and officers, all without exception, he read the same dismay, horror, and conflict as he felt in his own heart. 'But who is it doing it there really? They are all suffering as I am! Who is it? who?' flashed for one second through Pierre's mind. 'Sharpshooters of the eighty-sixth forward!' some one shouted. The fifth prisoner standing beside Pierre was led forward—alone. Pierre did not understand that he was saved; that he and all the rest had been brought here simply to be present at the execution. With growing horror, with no sense of joy or relief, he gazed at what was being done. The fifth was the factory lad in the loose gown. As soon as they touched him, he darted away in terror and clutched Pierre (Pierre shuddered and tore himself away from him). The factory lad could not walk. He was held up under the arms and dragged along, and he screamed something all the while. When they had brought him to the post he was suddenly quiet. He seemed suddenly to have grasped something. Whether he grasped that it was no use to scream, or that it was impossible for men to kill him, he stood at the post, waiting to be bound like the others, and like a wild beast under fire looked about him with glittering eyes.

Pierre could not make himself turn away and close his eyes. The curiosity and emotion he felt, and all the crowd with him, at this fifth murder reached its highest pitch. Like the rest, this fifth man seemed calm. He wrapped his dressing-gown round him, and scratched one bare foot with the other.

When they bound up his eyes, of himself he straightened the knot, which hurt the back of his head; then, when they propped him against the blood-stained post, he staggered back, and as he was uncomfortable in that position, he shifted his attitude, and leaned back quietly, with his feet put down symmetically. Pierre never took his eyes off him, and did not miss the slightest movement he made.

The word of command must have sounded, and after it the shots of the eight muskets. But Pierre, however earnestly he tried to recollect it afterwards, had not heard the slightest sound from the shots. He only saw the factory lad suddenly fall back on the cords, saw blood oozing in two places, and saw the cords themselves work loose from the weight of the hanging body, and the factory lad sit down, his head falling unnaturally, and one leg bent under him. Pierre ran up to the post. No one hindered him. Men with pale and frightened faces were doing something round the factory lad. There was one old whiskered Frenchman, whose lower jaw twitched all the while as he untied the cords. The body sank down. The soldiers, with clumsy haste, dragged it from the post and shoved it into the pit.

All of them clearly knew, beyond all doubt, that they were criminals, who must make haste to hide the traces of their crime.

Pierre glanced into the pit and saw that the factory lad was lying there with his knees up close to his head, and one shoulder higher than the other. And that shoulder was convulsively, rhythmically rising and falling. But spadefuls of earth were already falling all over the body. One of the soldiers, in a voice of rage, exasperation, and pain, shouted to Pierre to stand aside. But Pierre did not understand him, and still stood at the post, and no one drove him away.

When the pit was quite filled up, the word of command was heard. Pierre was taken back to his place, and the French troops, standing in ranks on both sides of the post, faced about, and began marching with a measured step past the post. The twenty-four sharpshooters, standing in the middle of the circle, with uncharged muskets, ran back to their places as their companies marched by them.

Pierre stared now with dazed eyes at these sharpshooters, who were running two together out of the circle. All of them had joined their companies except one. A young soldier, with a face of deathly pallor, still stood facing the pit on the spot upon which he had shot, his shako falling backwards off his head, and his fuse dropping on to the ground. He staggered like a drunken man, taking a few steps forward, and then a few back, to keep himself from falling. An old under-officer ran out of the ranks, and, seizing the young soldier by the shoulder, dragged him to his company. The crowd of Frenchmen and Russians began to disperse. All walked in silence, with downcast eyes.

'That will teach them to set fire to the places,' said some one among the French. Pierre looked round at the speaker, and saw that it was a soldier who was trying to console himself somehow for what had been done, but could not. Without finishing his sentence, he waved his hand and went on.

XII

AFTER the execution Pierre was separated from the other prisoners and left alone in a small, despoiled, and filthy church.

Towards evening a patrol sergeant, with two soldiers, came into the church and informed Pierre that he was pardoned, and was now going to the barracks of the prisoners of war. Without understanding a word of what was said to him, Pierre got up and went with the soldiers. He was conducted to some sheds that had been rigged up in the upper part of the meadow out of charred boards, beams, and battens, and was taken into one of them. Some twenty persons of various kinds thronged round Pierre. He stared at them, with no idea of what these men were, why they were here, and what they wanted of him. He heard the words they said to him, but his mind made no kind of deduction or interpretation of them; he had no idea of their meaning. He made some answer, too, to the questions asked him, but without any notion who was hearing him, or how they would understand his replies. He gazed at faces and figures, and all seemed to him equally meaningless.

From the moment when Pierre saw that fearful murder committed by men who did not want to do it, it seemed as though the spring in his soul, by which everything was held together and given the semblance of life, had been wrenched out, and all seemed to have collapsed into a heap of meaningless refuse. Though he had no clear apprehension of it, it had annihilated in his soul all faith in the beneficent ordering of the universe, and in the soul of men, and in his own soul, and in God. This state of mind Pierre had experienced before, but never with such intensity as now. When such doubts had come upon him in the past they had arisen from his own fault. And at the very bottom of his heart Pierre had been aware then that salvation from that despair and from these doubts lay in his own hands. But now he felt that it was not his fault that the world was collapsing before his eyes, and that nothing was left but meaningless ruins. He felt that to get back to faith in life was not in his power.

Around him in the darkness stood men. Probably they found something very entertaining in him. They were telling him something, asking him something, then leading him somewhere, and at last he found himself in a corner of the shed beside men of some sort, who were talking on all sides, and laughing.

'And so, mates . . . that same prince who' (with a special emphasis on the last word) . . . some voice was saying in the opposite corner of the shed.

Sitting in the straw against the wall, mute and motionless, Pierre opened, and then closed, his eyes. As soon as he shut his eyes he saw the fearful face of the factory lad, fearful especially from its simplicity, and the faces of the involuntary murderers, still more fearful in their uneasiness. And he opened his eyes again and stared blankly about him in the darkness.

Close by him a little man was sitting bent up, of whose presence Pierre was first aware from the strong smell of sweat that rose at every movement he made. This man was doing something with his feet in the darkness, and although Pierre did not see his face, he was aware that he was continually glancing at him. Peering intently at him in the dark, Pierre made out that the man was undoing his foot-gear. And the way he was doing it began to interest Pierre.

Undoing the strings in which one foot was tied up, he wound them neatly off, and at once set to work on the other leg, glancing at Pierre. While one hand hung up the first leg-binder, the other was already beginning to untie the other leg. In this way, deftly, with rounded, effective movements following one another without delay, the man unrolled his leg-wrappers and hung them up on pegs driven in over-head, took out a knife, cut off something, shut the knife up, put it under his bolster, and settling himself more at his ease, clasped his arms round his knees, and stared straight at Pierre. Pierre was conscious of something pleasant, soothing, and rounded off in those deft movements, in his comfortable establishment of his belongings in the corner, and even in the very smell of the man, and he did not take his eyes off him.

'And have you seen a lot of trouble, sir? Eh?' said the little man suddenly. And there was a tone of such friendliness and simplicity in the sing-song voice that Pierre wanted to answer, but his jaw quivered, and he felt the tears rising. At the same second, leaving no time for Pierre's embarrassment to appear, the little man said, in the same pleasant voice:

'Ay, darling, don't grieve,' he said, in that tender, caressing sing-song in which old Russian peasant women talk. 'Don't grieve, dearie; trouble lasts an hour, but life lasts for ever! Ay, ay, my dear. And we get on here finely, thank God; nothing to vex us. They're men, too, and bad and good among them,' he said; and, while still speaking, got with a supple movement on his knees to his feet, and clearing his throat walked away.

'Hey, the hussy, here she is!' Pierre heard at the end of the shed the same caressing voice. 'Here she is, the hussy; she remembers me! There, there, lie down!' And the soldier, pushing down a dog that was jumping up on him, came back to his place and sat down. In his hands he had something wrapped up in a cloth.

'Here, you taste this, sir,' he said, returning to the respectful tone he had used at first, and untying and handing to Pierre several baked potatoes. 'At dinner we had soup. But the potatoes are first-rate!'

Pierre had eaten nothing the whole day, and the smell of the potatoes struck him as extraordinarily pleasant. He thanked the soldier and began eating.

'But why so, eh?' said the soldier smiling, and he took one of the potatoes. 'You try them like this.' He took out his clasp-knife again, cut the potato in his hand into two even halves, and sprinkled them with salt from the cloth, and offered them to Pierre.

'The potatoes are first-rate,' he repeated. 'You taste them like that.'

It seemed to Pierre that he had never eaten anything so good.

'No, I am all right,' said Pierre; 'but why did they shoot those poor fellows? ... The last was a lad of twenty.'

'Tss ... tss ...' said the little man. 'Sin, indeed, ... sin ...' he added quickly, just as though the words were always ready in his mouth and flew out of it by accident; he went on: 'How was it, sir, you came to stay in Moscow like this?'

'I didn't think they would come so soon. I stayed by accident,' said Pierre.

'But how did they take you, darling; from your home?'

'No, I went out to see the fire, and then they took me up and brought me to judgment as an incendiary.'

'Where there's judgment, there there's falsehood,' put in the little man.

'And have you been here long?' asked Pierre, as he munched the last potato.

'I? On Sunday they took me out of the hospital in Moscow.'

'Who are you, a soldier?'

'We are soldiers of the Apsheron regiment. I was dying of fever. We were never told anything. There were twenty of us lying sick. And we had never a thought, never a guess of how it was.'

'Well, and are you miserable here?' asked Pierre.

'Miserable, to be sure, darling. My name's Platon, surname Karataev,' he added, evidently to make it easier for Pierre to address him. 'In the regiment they called me "the little hawk." How can one help being sad, my dear? Moscow—she's the mother of cities. One must be sad to see it. Yes, the maggot gnaws the cabbage, but it dies before it's done; so the old folks used to say,' he added quickly.

'What, what was that you said?' asked Pierre.

'I?' said Karataev. 'I say it's not by our wit, but as God thinks fit,' said he, supposing that he was repeating what he had said. And at once he went on: 'Tell me, sir, and have you an estate from your fathers? And a house of your own? To be sure, your cup was overflowing! And a wife, too? And are your old parents living?' he asked, and though Pierre could not see him in the dark, he felt that the soldier's lips were puckered in a restrained smile of kindliness while he asked these questions. He was evidently disappointed that Pierre had no parents, especially that he had not a mother.

'Wife for good counsel, mother-in-law for kind welcome, but none dear as your own mother!' said he. 'And have you children?' he went on to ask. Pierre's negative reply seemed to disappoint him again, and he added himself: 'Oh well, you are young folks; please God, there will be. Only live in peace and concord.'

'But it makes no difference now,' Pierre could not help saying.

'Ah, my dear man,' rejoined Platon, 'the beggar's bag and the prison walls none can be sure of escaping.' He settled himself more comfortably, and cleared his throat, evidently preparing himself for a long story. 'So it was like this, dear friend, when I used to be living at home,' he began, 'we had a rich heritage, a great deal of land, the peasants were well off, and our house—something to thank God for, indeed. Father used to go out to reap with six of us. We got along finely. Something like peasants we were. It came to pass . . .' and Platon Karataev told a long story of how he had gone into another man's copse for wood, and had been caught by the keeper, how he had been flogged, tried, and sent for a soldier. 'And do you know, darling,' said he, his voice changing from the smile on his face, 'we thought it was a misfortune, while it was all for our happiness. My brother would have had to go if it hadn't been for my fault. And my younger brother had five little ones; while I, look you, I left no one behind but my wife. I had a little girl, but God had taken her before I went for a soldier. I went home on leave, I must tell you. I find them all better off than ever. The yard full of beasts, the women folk at home, two brothers out earning wages. Only Mihailo, the youngest, at home. Father says all his children are alike; whichever finger's pricked, it hurts the same. And if they hadn't shaved Platon for a soldier then, Mihailo would have had to go. He called us all together—would you believe it—made us stand before the holy picture. Mihailo, says he, come here, bend down to his feet; and you, women, bow down; and you, grandchildren. Do you understand? says he. Yes, so you see, my dear. Fate acts with reason. And we are always passing judgment; that's not right, and this doesn't suit us. Our happiness, my dear, is like water in a drag-net; you drag, and it is all puffed up, but pull it out and there's nothing. Yes, that's it.' And Platon moved to a fresh seat in the straw.

After a short pause, Platon got up.

'Well, I dare say, you are sleepy?' he said, and he began rapidly crossing himself, murmuring:

'Lord Jesus Christ, holy Saint Nikola, Frola and Lavra; Lord Jesus

Christ, holy Saint Nikola, Frola and Lavra; Lord Jesus Christ—have mercy and save us!' he concluded, bowed down to the ground, got up, sighed, and sat down on his straw. 'That's right. Let me lie down like a stone, O God, and rise up like new bread!' he murmured, and lay down, pulling his military coat over him.

'What prayer was that you recited?' asked Pierre.

'Eh?' said Platon (he was already half asleep). 'Recited? I prayed to God. Don't you pray, too?'

'Yes, I do,' said Pierre. 'But what was it you said—Frola and Lavra?'

'Eh, to be sure,' Platon answered quickly. 'They're the horses' saints. One must think of the poor beasts, too,' he said. 'Why, the little hussy, she's curled up. You're warm, child of a bitch!' he said, feeling the dog at his feet; and, turning over again, he fell asleep at once.

Outside shouting and wailing could be heard somewhere far away, and through the cracks in the walls could be seen the glow of fire; but within the shed all was dark and hushed. For a long while Pierre did not sleep, and lay with open eyes in the darkness, listening to Platon snoring rhythmically as he lay beside him, and he felt that the world that had been shattered was rising up now in his soul, in new beauty, and on new foundations that could not be shaken.

XIII

IN this shed, where Pierre spent four weeks, there were twenty-three soldiers, three officers, and two civilian functionaries, all prisoners.

They were all misty figures to Pierre afterwards, but Platon Karataev remained for ever in his mind the strongest and most precious memory, and the personification of everything Russian, kindly, and round. When next day at dawn Pierre saw his neighbour, his first impression of something round was fully confirmed; Platon's whole figure in his French military coat, girt round the waist with cord, in his forage-cap and bast shoes, was roundish, his head was perfectly round, his back, his chest, his shoulders, even his arms, which he always held as though he were about to embrace something, were round in their lines; his friendly smile and big, soft, brown eyes, too, were round.

Platon Karataev must have been over fifty to judge by his stories of the campaigns in which he had taken part. He did not himself know and could not determine how old he was. But his strong, dazzlingly white teeth showed in two unbroken semicircles whenever he laughed, as he often did, and all were good and sound: there was not a grey hair in his beard or on his head, and his whole frame had a look of suppleness and of unusual hardiness and endurance.

His face had an expression of innocence and youth in spite of the curving wrinkles on it; his voice had a pleasant sing-song note. But the great peculiarity of his talk was its spontaneity and readiness. It was evident that he never thought of what he was saying, or of what he was going to say; and that gave a peculiar, irresistible persuasiveness to his rapid and genuine intonations.

His physical powers and activity were such, during the first period of his imprisonment, that he seemed not to know what fatigue or sickness meant. Every evening as he lay down to sleep, he said: 'Let me lie down, Lord, like a stone; let me rise up like new bread'; and every morning on getting up, he would shake his shoulder in the same way, saying: 'Lie down and curl up, get up and shake yourself.' And he had, in fact, only to lie down in order to sleep at once like a stone, and he had but to shake himself to be ready at once, on waking, without a second's delay, to set to work of some sort; just as children, on waking, begin at once playing with their toys. He knew how to do everything, not particularly well, but not badly either. He baked, and cooked, and sewed, and planed, and cobbled boots. He was always busy, and only in the evenings allowed himself to indulge in conversation, which he loved, and singing. He sang songs, not as singers do, who know they are listened to, but sang, as the birds' sing obviously, because it was necessary to him to utter those sounds, as it sometimes is to stretch or to walk about; and those sounds were always thin, tender, almost feminine, melancholy notes, and his face as he uttered them was very serious.

Being in prison, and having let his beard grow, he had apparently cast off all the soldier's ways that had been forced upon him and were not natural to him, and had unconsciously relapsed into his old peasant habits.

'A soldier discharged is the shirt outside the breeches again,' he used to say. He did not care to talk of his life as a soldier, though he never complained, and often repeated that he had never once been beaten since he had been in the service. When he told stories, it was always by preference of his old and evidently precious memories of 'his life as a 'Christian,' as he pronounced the word 'krestyan,' or peasant. The proverbial sayings, of which his talk was full, were not the bold, and mostly indecent, sayings common among soldiers, but those peasant saws, which seem of so little meaning looked at separately, and gain all at once a significance of profound wisdom when uttered appropriately.

Often he would say something directly contrary to what he had said before, but both sayings were equally true. He liked talking, and talked well, adorning his speech with caressing epithets and proverbial sayings, which Pierre fancied he often invented himself. But the great charm of his talk was that the simplest incidents—sometimes the same that Pierre had himself seen without noticing them—in his account of them gained a character of seemliness and solemn significance. He liked to listen to the fairy tales which one soldier used to tell—always the same ones over and over again—in the evenings, but most of all he liked to listen to stories of real life. He smiled gleefully as he listened to such stories, putting in words and asking questions, all aiming at bringing out clearly the moral beauty of the action of which he was told. Attachments, friendships, love, as Pierre understood them, Karataev had none; but he loved and lived on affectionate terms with every creature with whom he was thrown in life, and especially so with man—not with any particular man, but with the men who happened to be before his eyes. He loved his dog, loved his comrades, loved the French, loved Pierre, who was his neighbour. But Pierre felt that in spite of Karataev's affectionate tenderness to him (in which he involuntarily paid tribute to Pierre's spiritual life), he would not suffer a moment's grief at parting from him. And Pierre began to have the same feeling towards Karataev.

To all the other soldiers Platon Karataev was the most ordinary soldier; they called him 'little hawk,' or Platosha; made good-humoured jibes at his expense, sent him to fetch things. But to Pierre, such as he appeared on that first night—an unfathomable, rounded-off, and everlasting personification of the spirit of simplicity and truth —so he remained to him for ever.

Platon Karataev knew nothing by heart except his prayers. When he talked, he did not know on beginning a sentence how he was going to end it.

When Pierre, struck sometimes by the force of his remarks, asked him to repeat what he had said, Platon could never recall what he had said the minute before, just as he could never repeat to Pierre the words of his favourite song. There came in, 'My own little birch-tree,' and 'My heart is sick,' but there was no meaning in the words. He did not understand, and could not grasp the significance of words taken apart from the sentence. Every word and every action of his was the expression of a force uncomprehended by him, which was his life. But his life, as he looked at it, had no meaning as a separate life. It had meaning only as a part of a whole, of which he was at all times conscious. His words and actions flowed from him as smoothly, as inevitably, and as spontaneously, as the perfume rises from the flower. He could not understand any value or significance in an act or a word taken separately.

XIV

ON hearing from Nikolay that her brother was at Yaroslavl with the Rostovs, Princess Marya, in spite of her aunt's efforts to dissuade her, prepared at once to go to him and to go not alone, but with her nephew; whether this were difficult or not, whether it were possible or not, she did not inquire, and did not care to know: it was her duty not only to be herself at the side of her—perhaps, dying—brother, but to do everything possible to take his son to him, and she prepared to set off. If Prince Andrey had not himself communicated with her, Princess Marya put that down either to his being too weak to write, or to his considering the long journey too difficult and dangerous for her and his son.

Within a few days Princess Marya was ready for the journey. Her equipage consisted of her immense travelling coach in which she had come to Voronezh, and a covered trap and a waggon. She was accompanied by Mademoiselle Bourienne, Nikolushka, with his tutor, the old nurse, three maids, Tihon, a young valet, and a courier, whom her aunt was sending with her.

To travel by the usual route to Moscow was not to be thought of, and the circuitous route which Princess Marya was obliged to take by Lipetsk, Ryazan, Vladimir, and Shuya was very long; from lack of posting horses difficult; and in the neighbourhood of Ryazan, where they were told the French had begun to appear, positively dangerous.

During this difficult journey, Mademoiselle Bourienne, Dessalle, and Princess Marya's servants were astonished at the tenacity of her will and her energy. She was the last to go to rest, the first to rise, and no difficulty could daunt her. Thanks to her activity and energy, which infected her companions, she was towards the end of the second week close upon Yaroslavl.

The latter part of her stay in Voronezh had been the happiest period in Princess Marya's life. Her love for Rostov was not then a source of torment or agitation to her. That love had by then filled her whole soul and become an inseparable part of herself, and she no longer struggled against it. Of late Princess Marya was convinced—though she never clearly in so many words admitted it to herself—that she loved and was beloved. She had been convinced of this by her last interview with Nikolay when he came to tell her that her brother was with the Rostovs. Nikolay did not by one word hint at the possibility now (in case of Prince Andrey's recovery) of his engagement to Natasha being renewed, but Princess Marya saw by his face that he knew and thought of it. And in spite of that, his attitude to her—solicitous, tender, and loving—was so far from being changed, that he seemed overjoyed indeed that now a sort of kinship between him and Princess Marya allowed him to give freer expression to his loving friendship, as Princess Marya sometimes thought it. Princess Marya knew that she loved for the first and last time in her life, and felt that she was loved, and she was happy and at peace in that relation.

But this happiness on one side of her spiritual nature was far from hindering her from feeling intense grief on her brother's account. On the contrary, her spiritual peace on that side enabled her to give herself more completely to her feeling for her brother. This feeling was so strong at the moment of setting out from Voronezh that all her retinue were persuaded, looking at her careworn, despairing face, that she would certainly fall ill on the journey. But the very difficulties and anxieties of the journey, which Princess Marya tackled with such energy, saved her for the time from her sorrow and gave her strength.

As is always the case on a journey, Princess Marya thought of nothing but the journey itself, forgetting what was its object. But on approaching Yaroslavl, when what might await her—and not now at the end of many days, but that very evening—became clear to her mind again, her agitation reached its utmost limits.

When the courier, whom she had sent on ahead to find out in Yaroslavl where the Rostovs were staying, and in what condition Prince Andrey was, met the great travelling coach at the city gate he was frightened at the terribly pale face that looked out at him from the window.

'I have found out everything, your excellency: the Rostovs are staying in the square, in the house of a merchant, Bronnikov. Not far off, right above the Volga,' said the courier.

Princess Marya looked into his face with frightened inquiry, not understanding why he did not answer her chief question: How was her brother? Mademoiselle Bourienne put this question for the princess.

'How is the prince?' she asked.

'His excellency is staying in the same house with them.'

'He is living, then,' thought the princess; and she softly asked, 'How is he?'

'The servants say, "No change."'

What was meant by 'no change' the princess did not inquire, and with a passing, hardly perceptible, glance at little seven-year-old Nikolushka, sitting before her, delighted at the sight of the town, she bowed her head, and did not raise it again till the heavy carriage—rumbling, jolting, and swaying from side to side—came to a standstill. The carriage-steps were let down with a crash.

The carriage-door was opened. On the left was water—a broad river;

on the right, entrance steps. At the entrance were people, servants, and a rosy-faced girl with a thick coil of black hair, who smiled at her in an unpleasantly affected way, as it seemed to Princess Marya (it was Sonya). The princess ran up the steps; the girl, smiling affectedly, said, 'This way! this way!' and the princess found herself in the vestibule, facing an elderly woman of an Oriental type of face, who came rapidly to meet her, looking moved. It was the countess. She embraced Princess Marya, and proceeded to kiss her.

'My child,' she said, 'I love you, and have known you a long while.'

In spite of her emotion, Princess Marya knew it was the countess, and that she must say something to her. Not knowing how she did it, she uttered some polite French phrases in the tone in which she had been addressed, and asked, 'How is he?'

'The doctor says there is no danger,' said the countess; but as she said it she sighed, and turned her eyes upwards, and this gesture contradicted her words.

'Where is he? Can I see him; can I?' asked the princess.

'In a minute; in a minute, my dear. Is this his son?' she said, turning to Nikolushka, who came in with Dessalle. 'We shall find room for every one; the house is large. Oh, what a charming boy!'

The countess led the princess into the drawing-room. Sonya began to converse with Mademoiselle Bourienne. The countess caressed the child. The old count came into the room to welcome the princess. He was extraordinarily changed since Princess Marya had seen him last. Then he had been a jaunty, gay, self-confident old gentleman, now he seemed a pitiful, bewildered creature. As he talked to the princess, he was continually looking about him, as though asking every one if he were doing the right thing. After the destruction of Moscow and the loss of his property, driven out of his accustomed rut, he had visibly lost the sense of his own importance, and felt that there was no place for him in life.

In spite of her one desire to see her brother without loss of time, and her vexation that at that moment, when all she wanted was to see him, they should entertain her conventionally with praises of her nephew, the princess observed all that was passing around her, and felt it inevitable for the time to fall in with the new order of things into which she had entered. She knew that all this was inevitable, and it was hard for her, but she felt no grudge against them for it.

'This is my niece,' said the countess, presenting Sonya; 'you do not know her, princess?'

Princess Marya turned to her, and trying to smother the feeling of hostility that rose up within her at the sight of this girl, she kissed her.

But she felt painfully how out of keeping was the mood of every one around her with what was filling her own breast.

'Where is he?' she asked once more, addressing them all.

'He is downstairs; Natasha is with him,' answered Sonya, flushing. 'We have sent to ask. You are tired, I expect, princess?'

Tears of vexation came into Princess Marya's eyes. She turned away and was about to ask the countess again where she could see him, when she heard at the door light, eager steps that sounded to her full of gaiety. She looked round and saw, almost running in, Natasha—that Natasha whom she had so disliked when they met long before in Moscow.

But Princess Marya had hardly glanced at Natasha's face before she understood that here was one who sincerely shared her grief, and was therefore her friend. She flew to meet her, and embracing her, burst into tears on her shoulder.

As soon as Natasha, sitting by Prince Andrey's bedside, heard of Princess Marya's arrival, she went softly out of the room with those swift steps that to Princess Marya sounded so light-hearted, and ran to see her.

As she ran into the room, her agitated face wore one expression—an expression of love, of boundless love for him, for her, for all that was near to the man she loved—an expression of pity, of suffering for others, and of passionate desire to give herself up entirely to helping them. It was clear that at that moment there was not one thought of self, of her own relation to him, in Natasha's heart.

Princess Marya with her delicate intuition saw all that in the first glance at Natasha's face, and with mournful relief wept on her shoulder.

'Come, let us go to him, Marie,' said Natasha, drawing her away into the next room.

Princess Marya lifted up her head, dried her eyes, and turned to Natasha. She felt that from her she would learn all, would understand all. 'How . . .' she was beginning, but stopped short. She felt that no question nor answer could be put into words. Natasha's face and eyes would be sure to tell her all more clearly and more profoundly.

Natasha looked at her, but seemed to be in dread and in doubt whether to say or not to say all she knew; she seemed to feel that before those luminous eyes, piercing to the very bottom of her heart, it was impossible not to tell the whole, whole truth as she saw it. Natasha's lip suddenly twitched, ugly creases came round her mouth, and she broke into sobs, hiding her face in her hands.

Princess Marya knew everything.

But still she could not give up hope, and asked in words, though she put no faith in them:

'But how is his wound? What is his condition altogether?'

'You . . . you will see that,' was all Natasha could say.

They sat a little while below, near his room, to control their tears and go in to him with calm faces.

'How has the whole illness gone? Has he been worse for long? When did *this* happen?' Princess Marya asked.

Natasha told her that at first there had been danger from inflammation and the great pain, but that that had passed away at Troitsa, and the doctor had only been afraid of one thing—gangrene. But the risk of that, too, was almost over. When they reached Yaroslavl, the wound had begun to suppurate (Natasha knew all about suppuration and all the rest of it), and the doctor had said that the suppuration might follow the regular course. Fever had set in. The doctor had said this fever was not so serious. 'But two days ago,' Natasha began, 'all of a sudden *this* change came . . .' She struggled with her sobs. 'I don't know why, but you will see the change in him.'

'He is weaker? thinner? . . .' queried the princess.

'No, not that, but worse. You will see. O Marie, he is too good, he cannot, he cannot live, because . . .'

XV

WHEN Natasha opened the door with her practised hands, letting her pass in before her, Princess Marya felt the sobs rising in her throat. However much she prepared herself, however much she tried to compose herself, she knew that she would not be able to see him without tears.

She understood what Natasha had meant by the words: *two days ago this change came*. She interpreted it as meaning that he had suddenly grown softer, and that that softening, that tenderness, was the sign of death. As she approached the door, she saw already in her imagination that face of the little Andryusha, as she had known it in childhood, tender, gentle, softened, as it was so rarely, and as it affected her so strongly. She felt sure he would say soft, tender words to her like those her father had uttered on his deathbed, and that she would not be able to bear it, and would break into sobs at them. But sooner or later, it must be, and she went into the room. Her sobs seemed rising higher and higher in her throat as with her short-sighted eyes she distinguished his figure more and more clearly, and now she saw his face and met his eyes.

He was lying on a couch, propped up with cushions, in a squirrel-lined dressing-gown. He was thin and pale. One thin, transparently white hand held a handkerchief, with the other he was softly fingering the delicate moustache that had grown long. His eyes gazed at them as they came in.

On seeing his face and meeting his eyes, Princess Marya at once slackened the rapidity of her step and felt the tears dried up and the sobs checked. As she caught the expression of his face and eyes, she felt suddenly shy and guilty.

'But how am I in fault?' she asked herself. 'In being alive and thinking of the living while I! . . .' his cold, stern eyes seemed to answer.

In the profound, not outward- but inward-looking gaze there was something almost like hostility as he deliberately scanned his sister and Natasha. He kissed his sister's hand, while she kissed his, as their habit was.

'How are you, Marie; how did you manage to get here?' he said, in a voice as even and as aloof as the look in his eyes. If he had uttered a shriek of despair, that shriek would have been to Princess Marya less awful than the sound of his voice.

'And you have brought Nikolushka?' he said, as evenly and deliberately, with an evident effort to recollect things.

'How are you now?' said Princess Marya, wondering herself at what she was saying.

'That, my dear, you must ask the doctor,' he said, and evidently making another effort to be affectionate, he said with his lips only (it was obvious he was not thinking of what he was saying):

'Thank you, my dear, for coming.'

Princess Marya pressed his hand. He gave a hardly perceptible frown at the pressure of her hand. She was silent, and she did not know what to say. She understood the change that had come over him two days ago. In his words, in his tone, above all in his eyes—those cold, almost antagonistic eyes—could be felt that aloofness from all things earthly that is so fearful to a living man. It was evidently with difficulty that he understood anything living; but yet it seemed that he did not understand what was living, not because he had lost the power of understanding, but because he understood something else that the living did not and could not understand, and that entirely absorbed him.

'Yes, see how strangely fate has brought us together again,' he said, breaking the silence, and pointing to Natasha. 'She is nursing me.'

Princess Marya heard him, and could not understand what he was saying. He, Prince Andrey, with his delicate, tender intuition, how could he say that before the girl whom he loved, and who loved him! If he had any thought of living, he could not have said that in that slightingly cold tone. If he had not known he was going to die, how could he have failed to feel for her, how could he speak like that before her! There could be but one explanation of it—that was, that it was all of no moment to him now, and of no moment because something else, more important, had been revealed to him.

The conversation was frigid and disconnected, and broke off at every moment.

'Marie came by Ryazan,' said Natasha.

Prince Andrey did not notice that she called his sister Marie. And Natasha, calling her by that name before him, for the first time became aware of it herself.

'Well?' said he.

'She was told that Moscow had been burnt to the ground, all of it, entirely. That it looks as though . . .'

Natasha stopped. It was impossible to talk. He was obviously making an effort to listen, and yet he could not.

'Yes; it's burnt, they say,' he said. 'That's a great pity,' and he gazed straight before him, his fingers straying heedlessly about his moustache.

'And so you met Count Nikolay, Marie?' said Prince Andrey, suddenly, evidently trying to say something to please them. 'He wrote here what a great liking he took to you,' he went on, simply and calmly, plainly unable to grasp all the complex significance his words had for living people. 'If you liked him, too, it would be a very good thing . . . for you to get married,' he added, rather more quickly, apparently pleased at finding at last the words he had been seeking. Princess Marya heard his words, but they had no significance for her except as showing how terribly far away he was now from everything living.

'Why talk of me?' she said calmly, and glanced at Natasha. Natasha, feeling her eyes on her, did not look at her. Again all of them were silent.

'Andrey, would you . . .' Princess Marya said suddenly in a shaky voice, 'would you like to see Nikolushka? He is always talking of you.'

For the first time Prince Andrey smiled a faintly perceptible smile, but Princess Marya, who knew his face so well, saw with horror that it was a smile not of joy, not of tenderness for his son, but of quiet, gentle irony at his sister's trying what she believed to be the last resource for rousing him to feeling.

'Yes, I shall be very glad to see Nikolushka. Is he quite well?'

When they brought in little Nikolushka, who gazed in dismay at his father, but did not cry, because nobody else was crying, Prince Andrey kissed him, and obviously did not know what to say to him.

When they had taken the child away, Princess Marya went up to her brother once more, kissed him, and unable to control herself any longer, began to weep.

He looked at her intently.

'You weep for Nikolushka?' he asked.

Princess Marya nodded through her tears.

'Marie, you know the Gos . . .' he began, but suddenly paused.

'What do you say?'

'Nothing. You mustn't weep here,' he said, looking at her with the same cold eyes.

When Princess Marya wept he knew that she was weeping that Nikolushka would be left without a father. With a great effort he tried to come back again to life, and to put himself at their point of view.

'Yes, it must seem sad to them,' he thought. 'But how simple it is!'

'"They sow not, neither do they reap, but your Father feedeth them,"' he said to himself, and he wanted to say it to his sister. But no, they would understand it in their own way; they would not understand! 'What they cannot understand is that these feelings that they set store by—all our feelings, all these thoughts, which seem of so much importance to us—that they are all not wanted! We cannot understand each other!' and he was silent.

Prince Andrey's little son was seven years old. He could hardly read—he knew nothing. He passed through much after that day, gaining knowledge, observation, experience. But if he had possessed at that time all the mental faculties he acquired afterwards, he could not have had a truer, a deeper comprehension of all the significance of the scene he saw passing between his father, Princess Marya, and Natasha than he had now. He understood it all, and without weeping, went out of the room, in silence went up to Natasha, who had followed him out; glanced shyly at her with his beautiful, dreamy eyes: his uplifted, rosy upper lip quivered; he leaned his head against her, and burst into tears.

From that day he avoided Dessalle, avoided the countess, who would have petted him, and either sat alone, or shyly joined Princess Marya and Natasha, whom he seemed to love even more than his aunt, and bestowed shy and gentle caresses upon them.

When Princess Marya left her brother's side, she fully understood all that Natasha's face had told her. She spoke no more to Natasha of hope of saving his life. She took turns with her by his bedside, and she shed no more tears, but prayed without ceasing, turning in spirit to the Eternal and Unfathomable whose presence was palpable now, hovering over the dying man.

XVI

PRINCE ANDREY did not only know that he would die, but felt indeed that he was dying; that he was already half-dead. He experienced a sense of aloofness from everything earthly, and a strange and joyous lightness in his being. Neither impatient, nor troubled, he lay awaiting what was before him. . . . The menacing, the eternal, the unknown, and remote, the presence of which he had never ceased to feel during the whole course of his life, was now close to him, and—from that strange lightness of being, that he experienced—almost comprehensible and palpable.

In the past he had dreaded the end. Twice he had experienced that terribly agonising feeling of the dread of death, of the end, and now he had ceased to understand it.

The first time he had experienced that feeling when the grenade was rotating before him, and he looked at the stubble, at the bushes, at the sky, and knew that death was facing him. When he had come to himself after his wound, and instantly, as though set free from the cramping bondage of life, there had sprung up in his soul that flower of love, eternal, free, not dependent on this life, he had no more fear, and no more thought, of death.

In those hours of solitary suffering and half-delirium that he spent afterwards, the more he passed in thought into that new element of eternal love, revealed to him, the further he unconsciously travelled from earthly life. To love everything, every one, to sacrifice self always for love, meant to love no one, meant not to live this earthly life. And the further he penetrated into the element of love, the more he renounced life, and the more completely he annihilated that fearful barrier that love sets up between life and death. Whenever, during that first period, he remembered that he had to die, he said to himself: 'Well, so much the better.'

But after that night at Mytishtchy, when in his half-delirium she, whom he had longed for, appeared before him, and when pressing her hand to his lips, he wept soft, happy tears, love for one woman stole unseen into his heart, and bound him again to life. And glad and disturbing thoughts began to come back to him. Recalling that moment at the ambulance station, when he had seen Kuragin, he could not now go back to his feeling then. He was fretted by the question whether he were alive. And he dared not ask.

His illness went through its regular physical course; but what Natasha had called 'this change' had come upon him two days before Princess Marya's arrival. It was the last moral struggle between life and death, in which death gained the victory. It was the sudden consciousness that life, in the shape of his love for Natasha, was still precious to him, and the last and vanquished onslaught of terror before the unknown.

It happened in the evening. He was, as usually after dinner, in a slightly feverish condition, and his thoughts were particularly clear. Sonya was sitting at the table. He fell into a doze. He felt a sudden sense of happiness.

'Ah, she has come in!' he thought.

Natasha had, in fact, just come in with noiseless steps, and was sitting in Sonya's place.

Ever since she had been looking after him he had always felt this physical sense of her presence. She was in a low chair beside him, knitting a stocking, and sitting so as to screen the light of the candle from him. She had learned to knit since Prince Andrey had once said to her that no one made such a good sick-nurse as an old nurse who knitted stockings, and that there was something soothing about knitting. Her slender fingers moved the needles rapidly with a slight click, and the dreamy profile of her drooping head could be clearly seen by him. She made a slight movement; the ball rolled off her knee. She started, glanced round at him, and, screening the light with her hand, bent over with a cautious, supple, and precise movement, picked up the ball, and sat back in the same attitude as before.

He gazed at her without stirring, and saw that after her movements she wanted to draw a deep breath, but did not dare to, and breathed with careful self-restraint.

At the Troitsa monastery they had spoken of the past, and he had told her that if he were to live he should thank God for ever for his wound, which had brought them together again; but since then they had never spoken of the future.

'Could it be, or could it not?' he was wondering now as he watched her and listened to the slight steel click of the needles. 'Can fate have brought us together so strangely only for me to die? . . . Can the truth of life have been revealed to me only for me to have spent my life in falsity? I love her more than anything in the world! But what am I to do if I love her?' he said, and suddenly he unconsciously moaned from the habit he had fallen into in the course of his sufferings.

Hearing the sound, Natasha laid down her stocking, and bent closer to him, and suddenly noticing his shining eyes, went up to him with a light step and stooped down.

'You are not asleep?'

'No; I have been looking at you for a long while. I felt when you came in. No one but you gives me the same soft peace . . . the same light. I want to weep with gladness!'

Natasha moved closer to him. Her face beamed with rapturous delight.

'Natasha, I love you too much! More than everything in the world!'

'And I?' She turned away for a second. 'Why too much?' she said.

'Why too much? . . . Well, what do you think, what do you feel in your heart, your whole heart, am I going to live? What do you think?'

'I am sure of it; sure of it!' Natasha almost cried out, taking both his hands with a passionate gesture.

He was silent for a while.

'How good it would be!' And taking her hand, he kissed it.

Natasha was happy and deeply stirred; and she recollected at once that this must not be, and that he must have quiet.

'But you are not asleep,' she said, subduing her joy. 'Try and sleep . . . please, do.'

He pressed her hand and let it go, and she moved back to the candle, and sat down again in the same position as before. Twice she glanced round at him; his eyes were bright as she met them. She set herself a task on her stocking, and told herself she would not look round till she had finished it.

He did, in fact, soon after shut his eyes and fall asleep. He did not sleep long, and woke up suddenly in a cold sweat of alarm.

As he fell asleep he was still thinking of what he had been thinking about all the time—of life and of death. And most of death. He felt that he was closer to it.

'Love? What is love?' he thought.

'Love hinders death. Love is life. All, all that I understand, I understand only because I love. All is, all exists only because I love. All is bound up in love alone. Love is God, and dying means for me a

particle of love, to go back to the universal and eternal source of love.'
These thoughts seemed to him comforting. But they were only thoughts.
Something was wanting in them; there was something one-sided and
personal, something intellectual; they were not self-evident. And there
was uneasiness, too, and obscurity. He fell asleep.

He dreamed that he was lying in the very room in which he was
lying in reality, but that he was not ill, but quite well. Many people
of various sorts, indifferent people of no importance, were present. He
was talking and disputing with them about some trivial matter. They
seemed to be preparing to set off somewhere. Prince Andrey had a dim
feeling that all this was of no consequence, and that he had other
matters of graver moment to think of, but still he went on uttering
empty witticisms of some sort that surprised them. By degrees all
these people began to disappear, and the one thing left was the question of closing the door. He got up and went towards the door
to close it and bolt it. *Everything* depended on whether he were in
time to shut it or not. He was going, he was hurrying, but his legs
would not move, and he knew that he would not have time to shut
the door, but still he was painfully straining every effort to do so. And
an agonising terror came upon him. And that terror was the fear of
death; behind the door stood *It*. But while he is helplessly and clumsily
struggling towards the door, that something awful is already pressing
against the other side of it, and forcing the door open. Something not
human—death—is forcing the door open, and he must hold to it. He
clutches at the door with a last straining effort—to shut it is impossible,
at least to hold it—but his efforts are feeble and awkward; and, under
the pressure of that awful thing, the door opens and shuts again.

Once more *It* was pressing on the door from without. His last,
supernatural efforts are vain, and both leaves of the door are noiselessly opened. *It* comes in, and it is *death*. And Prince Andrey died.

But at the instant when in his dream he died, Prince Andrey recollected that he was asleep; and at the instant when he was dying, he
made an effort and waked up.

'Yes, that was death. I died and waked up. Yes, death is an awakening,' flashed with sudden light into his soul, and the veil that had till
then hidden the unknown was lifted before his spiritual vision. He
felt, as it were, set free from some force that held him in bondage, and
was aware of that strange lightness of being that had not left him
since.

When he waked up in a cold sweat and moved on the couch, Natasha
went up and asked him what was the matter. He did not answer, and
looked at her with strange eyes, not understanding her.

That was the change that had come over him two days before Princess Marya's arrival. The doctor said that from that day the wasting fever had assumed a more serious aspect, but Natasha paid little heed to what the doctor said; she saw the terrible moral symptoms, that for her were far more convincing.

With his awakening from sleep that day there began for Prince Andrey an awakening from life. And in relation to the duration of life it seemed to him not more prolonged than the awakening from sleep in relation to the duration of a dream. There was nothing violent or terrible in this relatively slow awakening.

His last days and hours passed in a simple and commonplace way. Princess Marya and Natasha, who never left his side, both felt that. They did not weep nor shudder, and towards the last they both felt they were waiting not on him (he was no more, he had gone far away from them), but on the nearest memory of him—his body. The feelings of both of them were so strong that the external, horrible side of death did not affect them, and they did not find it needful to work up their grief. They did not weep either in his presence nor away from him, and they never even talked of him together. They felt that they could not express in words what they understood.

They both saw that he was slowly and quietly slipping further and further away from them, and both knew that this must be so, and that it was well. He received absolution and extreme unction; every one came to bid him good-bye. When his son was brought in to him, he pressed his lips to him and turned away, not because it was painful or sad to him (Princess Marya and Natasha saw that), but simply because he supposed he had done all that was required of him. But he was told to give him his blessing, he did what was required, and looked round as though to ask whether there was anything else he must do. When the body, deserted by the spirit, passed through its last struggles, Princess Marya and Natasha were there.

'It is over!' said Princess Marya, after the body had lain for some moments motionless, and growing cold before them. Natasha went close, glanced at the dead eyes, and made haste to shut them. She closed them, and did not kiss them, but hung over what was the nearest memory of him. 'Where has he gone? Where is he now? ...'

When the body lay, dressed and washed, in the coffin on the table, every one came to take leave of him, and every one cried. Nikolushka cried from the agonising bewilderment that was rending his heart. The countess and Sonya cried from pity for Natasha, and from grief that he was gone. The old count cried because he felt that he too must soon take the same terrible step.

Natasha and Princess Marya wept too now. But they did not weep for their personal sorrow; they wept from the emotion and awe that filled their souls before the simple and solemn mystery of death that had been accomplished before their eyes.

PART XIII

I

THE COMBINATION of causes of phenomena is beyond the grasp of the human intellect. But the impulse to seek causes is innate in the soul of man. And the human intellect, with no inkling of the immense variety and complexity of circumstances conditioning a phenomenon, any one of which may be separately conceived of as the cause of it, snatches at the first and most easily understood approximation, and says here is the cause. In historical events, where the actions of men form the subject of observation, the most primitive conception of a cause was the will of the gods, succeeded later on by the will of those men who stand in the historical foreground—the heroes of history. But one had but to look below the surface of any historical event, to look, that is, into the movement of the whole mass of men taking part in that event, to be convinced that the will of the hero of history, so far from controlling the actions of the multitude, is continually controlled by them. It may be thought that it is a matter of no importance whether historical events are interpreted in one way or in another. But between the man who says that the peoples of the West marched into the East, because Napoleon willed they should do so, and the man who says that that movement came to pass because it was bound to come to pass, there exists the same difference as between the men who maintained that the earth was stationary and the planets revolved about it, and the men who said that they did not know what holds the earth in its place, but they did know that there were laws controlling its motions and the motions of the other planets. Causes of historical events—there are not and cannot be, save the one cause of all causes. But there are laws controlling these events; laws partly unknown, partly accessible to us. The discovery of these laws is only possible when we entirely give up looking for a cause in the will of one man, just as the discovery of the laws of the motions of the planets has only become possible since men have given up the conception of the earth being stationary.

After the battle of Borodino, and the taking and burning of Moscow, historians consider the most important episode of the war of 1812 to be the movement of the Russian army from the Ryazan to the Kaluga road and to the Tarutino camp, the so-called oblique march behind Krasnaya Pahra. Historians ascribe the credit of this stroke of genius to various persons, and dispute to whom it is rightfully due. Even foreign, even French historians, admit the genius of the Russian generals when they mention this flank march. But why military writers, and others following their lead, assume this oblique movement to be a project profoundly planned by some one person for the deliverance of Russia and the overthrow of Napoleon it is very difficult to see. It is difficult in the first place to see wherein the profound wisdom and genius of this march lies; for no great intellectual effort is needed to guess that the best position for an army, when not being attacked, is where supplies are most plentiful. And every one, even a stupid boy of thirteen, could have guessed that the most advantageous position for the army in 1812, after the retreat from Moscow, would be on the Kaluga road. And so one cannot understand, in the first place, what conclusions led the historians to see some deep wisdom in this manoeuvre. Secondly, it is even more difficult to understand why the historians ascribe to this manoeuvre the deliverance of Russia and the overthrow of the French; for, had other circumstances preceded, accompanied, or followed it, this flank movement might as well have led to the destruction of the Russian army and the deliverance of the French. If the position of the Russian army did, in fact, begin to improve from the time of that march, it does not at all follow that the improvement was caused by it.

That oblique march might have been not simply of no use; it might have led to the destruction of the Russian army, but for the conjunction of other circumstances. What would have happened if Moscow had not been burnt? If Murat had not lost sight of the Russians? If Napoleon had not remained inactive? If, as Bennigsen and Barclay advised, the Russians had given battle near Krasnaya Pahra? What would have happened if the French had attacked the Russians when they were marching behind Pahra? What would have happened if later on Napoleon, on reaching Tarutino, had attacked the Russians with one-tenth of the energy with which he had attacked them at Smolensk? What would have happened if the French had marched to Petersburg? ... On any of these hypotheses, the oblique march might have led to ruin instead of to safety.

The third point, most difficult of all to understand, is that students of history seem intentionally to refuse to see that this march cannot be ascribed to any one man, that no one foresaw it at any time, that, like the retreat to Fili, the manoeuvre was, in reality, never conceived of by any one in its entirety, but arose step by step, incident by incident, moment by moment from a countless multitude of the most diverse circumstances, and is only conceived of in its entirety, when it is an accomplished fact, and has become the past.

At the council at Fili the accepted idea among the Russians—the course taken for granted in fact—was retreat in a direct line back, that is, along the Nizhni road. Evidence of this is that the majority of votes at the council were for adopting this course, and the commander-in-chief's famous conversation after the council with Lansky, the head of the commissariat department, is an even more striking proof of it. Lansky submitted to the commander-in-chief that the chief supplies for the army were stored along the Oka, in the Tula and Kazan provinces, and that if they retreated along the Nizhni road, the army would be cut off from its supplies by the broad river Oka, across which transport in the early winter was impossible. This was the first proof of the necessity of departing from the course that had at first seemed the most natural one, the retreat along the Nizhni road. The army kept more to the south along the Ryazan road, closer to its supplies. Later on the inactivity of the French, who positively lost sight of the Russian army, anxiety for the defence of the Tula arsenal, and above all, the advantage of being near their supplies led the army to turn even more to the south, to the Tula road. After crossing by a forced march behind Pahra to the Tula road, the generals of the Russian army intended to remain at Podolsk, and had no idea of the Tarutino position. But an infinite number of circumstances, among them the reappearance of French troops on the scene, and plans for giving battle, and most of all, the abundance of supplies in Kaluga, led our army to turn even more to the south, and to pass from the Tula to the Kaluga road to Tarutino, a central position between their lines of communication with their supplies. Just as it is impossible to answer the question at what date Moscow was abandoned, it is impossible too to say precisely when and by whom it was decided to move the army to Tarutino. It was only after the army, through the action of innumerable infinitesimally small forces, had been brought to Tarutino, that people began to protest to themselves that that was the course they had desired, and had long foreseen as the right one.

II

THE famous oblique movement consisted simply in this. The Russian troops, which had been retreating directly back from the French, as soon as the French attack ceased, turned off from that direction, and seeing they were not pursued, moved naturally in the direction where they were drawn by the abundance of supplies.

If we imagine, instead of generals of genius at the head of the Russian army, an army acting alone, without leadership of any kind, such an army could have done nothing else but move back again towards Moscow, describing a semicircle through the country that was best provided with necessaries, and where supplies were most plentiful.

So natural was this oblique movement from the Nizhni to the Ryazan, Tula, and Kaluga road, that that direction was the one taken by the flying bands of marauders from the Russian army, and the one which the authorities in Petersburg insisted upon Kutuzov's taking. At Tarutino Kutuzov received what was almost a reprimand from the Tsar for moving the army to the Ryazan road, and he was directed to take up the very position facing Kaluga, in which he was encamped at the time when the Tsar's letter reached him.

After recoiling in the direction of the shock received during the whole campaign, and at the battle of Borodino, the ball of the Russian army, as the force of that blow spent itself, and no new blow came, took the direction that was natural for it.

Kutuzov's merit lay in no sort of military genius, as it is called, in no strategic manoeuvre, but in the fact that he alone grasped the significance of what had taken place. He alone grasped even then the significance of the inactivity of the French army; he alone persisted in maintaining that the battle of Borodino was a victory; he alone—the man who from his position as commander-in-chief might have been expected to be the first to be eager for battle—he alone did everything in his power to hold the Russian army back from useless fighting.

The wild beast wounded at Borodino lay where the fleeing hunter had left him; but whether alive and strong, or only feigning, the hunter knew not. All at once a moan was heard from the creature. The moan of that wounded creature, the French army, that betrayed its hopeless plight, was the despatch of Lauriston to the camp of Kutuzov with overtures for peace.

Napoleon, with his conviction that not what was right was right, but whatever came into his head was right, wrote to Kutuzov the first words that occurred to his mind, words that had no meaning at all.

'M. LE PRINCE KOUTOUZOFF,' he wrote, 'I am sending you one of my aides-de-camp to converse with you on various interesting subjects. I desire that your highness will put faith in what he says, especially when he expresses the sentiments of esteem and particular consideration that I have long entertained for your person. This letter having no other object, I pray God to have you in His holy and powerful keeping.

(Signed) NAPOLEON.

'*Moscow, October* 30, 1812.'

'I should be cursed by posterity if I were regarded as the first instigator of any sort of settlement. *Tel est l'esprit actuel de ma nation,*' answered Kutuzov, and went on doing everything in his power to hold the army back from advance.

A month spent by the French army in pillaging Moscow, and by the Russian army quietly encamped at Tarutino, brought about a change in the relative strength of the two armies, a change both in spirit and in numbers, which was all to the advantage of the Russians. Although the position of the French army and its numbers were unknown to the Russians, as soon as their relative strength had changed, a great number of signs began to show that an attack would be inevitable. Among the causes that contributed to bring about this result were Lauriston's mission, and the abundance of provisions at Tarutino, and the reports that were continually coming in from all sides of the inactivity and lack of discipline in the French army, and the filling up of our regiments by recruits, and the fine weather, and the long rest enjoyed by the Russian soldiers, and the impatience to do the work for which they have been brought together, that always arises in troops after repose, and curiosity to know what was going on in the French army, of which they had so long seen nothing, and the daring with which the Russian outposts dashed in among the French encamped at Tarutino, and the news of the easy victories gained by bands of peasants and free-lances over the French, and the envy aroused by them, and the desire of revenge, that every man cherished at heart so long as the French were in Moscow; and—stronger than all—the vague sense growing up in every soldier's heart that the relative strength of the armies had changed, and the preponderance was now on our side. The relative strength of the armies had really changed, and advance had become inevitable. And at once, as surely as the chimes in a clock begin to beat and play when the hand has made the full round of the dial, was this change reflected in the increased activity, and bustle and stir of wheels within wheels in the higher spheres.

III

THE Russian army was commanded by Kutuzov and his staff and by the Tsar from Petersburg. Before the news of the abandonment of Moscow had reached Petersburg, a detailed plan of the whole campaign had been drawn up and sent to Kutuzov for his guidance. In spite of the fact that this plan had been made on the supposition that Moscow was still in our hands, it was approved by the staff, and accepted as the plan to be carried out. Kutuzov simply wrote that directions from a distance were always difficult to carry out. And to solve any difficulties that might arise, fresh instructions were sent, together with newer persons, whose duty it was to be to keep a watch on his movements, and to report upon them.

Apart from these new authorities, the whole staff of generals in the Russian army was now transformed. The places of Bagration, who had been killed, and Barclay, who had taken offence and retired, had to be filled. The question was deliberated with the greatest seriousness: whether A should be put in B's place, and B in the place of D, or whether, on the other hand, D in A's place, and so on, as though the matter affected anything whatever except the satisfaction of A and B and D.

In consequence of Kutuzov's hostility to the head officer of his staff, Bennigsen, and the presence of confidential advisers of the Tsar, and these various new appointments, the struggle of parties at headquarters was even more complicated than usual. A was trying to undermine B's position, D to undermine C's position, and so on, in all the possible combinations and permutations. In all these conflicting currents the object of intrigue was for the most part the management of the war, which all these men supposed they were controlling, though it did, in fact, follow its inevitable course quite apart from their action, a course that never corresponded with their schemes, but was the outcome of the forces interacting in the masses. All these schemes, thwarting and stultifying one another, were simply accepted in the higher spheres as the correct reflection of what was bound to come to pass.

'Prince Mihail Ilarionovitch!' the Tsar wrote on the 2nd of October, a letter received by Kutuzov after the battle of Tarutino. 'From the 2nd of September Moscow has been in the hands of the enemy. Your last reports were dated the 20th; and in the course of all this time since, no attempt has been made to act against the enemy, and to relieve the ancient capital, and you have even, from your last reports, retreated further. Serpuhov is by now occupied by a detachment of the enemy, and Tula, with its famous arsenal, of such importance to the army, is in danger. From the reports received from General Wintzengerode, I see that a corps of the enemy, ten thousand strong, is marching along the Petersburg road. Another, numbering some thousands, is already close upon Dmitrov. A third is advancing along the Vladimir road. A fourth force of considerable strength is stationed between Ruza and Mozhaisk. Napoleon himself was in Moscow on the 25th. In face of these facts, with the enemy's forces split up into these detached bodies, and Napoleon himself with his guards in Moscow, is it possible that the enemy's forces confronting you are too strong to permit of your acting on the offensive? One may, with far more probability, assume that you are being pursued by detachments, or at most a corps by far inferior to the army under your command. It would seem that taking advantage of these circumstances, you might with advantage have attacked forces inferior in strength to your army, and have destroyed them, or at least have forced them to retreat, and have kept in our hands a considerable part of the province now occupied by the enemy, and thereby have averted all danger from Tula and the other towns of the interior. You will be responsible, if the enemy is able to send a considerable body of men to Petersburg, to menace that capital, in which it has been impossible to keep any great number of troops; for with the army under your command, acting with energy and decision, you have ample means at your disposal for averting such a calamity. Recollect that you have still to answer to your humiliated country for the loss of Moscow. You have had experience of my readiness to reward you. That readiness is no less now, but Russia and I have the right to expect from you all the energy, decision, and success, which your intellect, your military talents, and the valour of the troops under your command should guarantee us.'

But while this letter, proving that the change in the relative strength of the armies was by now reflected in opinion at Petersburg, was on its road, Kutuzov had been unable to hold the army back, and a battle had already been fought.

On the 2nd of October, a Cossack Shapovalov, out scouting, shot one hare and wounded a second. Shapovalov was led on in pursuit of the game far into the forest, and came across the left flank of Murat's army, which was encamped and quite off guard. The Cossack told his comrades with laughter the tale of how he had all but fallen into the hands of the French. The ensign, who heard the story, repeated it to his superior officer. The Cossack was sent for and questioned. The officers of the Cossacks wanted to take advantage of this to carry off some horses from the French, but one of them, who was intimate with some of the higher authorities in the army, mentioned the incident to a general on the staff. On the staff the position of late had been strained to the utmost. A few days previously, Yermolov had gone to Bennigsen and besought him to use his influence with the commander-in-chief to bring about an attack.

'If I did not know you, I should suppose you did not desire that result. I have only to advise one course for his highness to be sure to adopt the opposite one,' answered Bennigsen.

The news brought by the Cossack, confirmed by scouts, proved conclusively that the time was ripe. The strained string broke, and the wheels of the clock whirred, and the chimes began to strike. In spite of all his supposed power, his intellect, his experience, and his knowledge of men, Kutuzov, taking into consideration the note from Bennigsen, who was sending a personal report on the subject to the Tsar, the desire expressed by all the generals alike, the desire assumed by them to be the Tsar's wish, and the news brought by the Cossack, could hold back the inevitable movement no longer, and gave orders for what he regarded as useless and mischievous—gave his assent, in fact, to the accomplished fact.

IV

THE note submitted by Bennigsen, and the report sent in by the Cossacks of the enemy's left flank being unguarded, were simply the last straws that showed the inevitability of giving the signal for advance, and it was arranged to advance to attack on the 5th of October.

On the morning of the 4th, Kutuzov signed the disposition of the forces. Toll read it to Yermolov, proposing that he should superintend the further instructions for carrying it out.

'Very good, very good, I haven't time just now,' said Yermolov, and he hurried out of the cottage. The arrangement of the troops as drawn up by Toll was an excellent one. The disposition had been written out, as at Austerlitz, though not in German:

'The First Column marches here and there, the Second Column occupies this place,' and so on.

On paper all these columns were in their proper place at a fixed time and annihilated the enemy. Everything had been, as in all such cases, carefully thought of, and as in all such cases not a single column did reach its right place at the right time. When a sufficient number of copies of the disposition were ready, an officer was summoned and sent off to give them to Yermolov, that he might see that instructions were given in accordance with them. A young officer of the horseguards, in waiting on Kutuzov, set off for Yermolov's quarters, delighted at the importance of the commission with which he was intrusted.

'Not at home,' Yermolov's servant told him. The officer of the horse-guards set off to the quarters of the general, with whom Yermolov was often to be found.

'Not here, nor the general either,' he was told.

The officer mounted his horse again and rode off to another general's.

'No, not at home.'

'If only I don't get into trouble for the delay! How annoying!' thought the officer.

He rode all over the camp. One man told him he had seen Yermolov riding away in company with some other generals; another said he was sure to be at home again by now. The officer was hunting him till six o'clock in the evening without stopping for dinner. Yermolov was nowhere to be found, and no one knew where he was. The officer took a hasty meal at a comrade's, and trotted back to the advance guard to see Miloradovitch. Miloradovitch, too, was not at home, but there he was told that he was at a ball at General Kikin's and that, most likely, Yermolov was there too.

'But where is that?'

'At Etchkino, that way,' said an officer of the Cossacks, pointing out to him a country house in the far distance.

'Out there! beyond our lines!'

'Two regiments of our fellows have been sent out to the outposts, and there is a spree going on there now, fine doings! Two bands, three choruses of singers.'

The officer rode out beyond our lines to Etchkino. While yet a long way off, he heard the gay sounds of a soldier's dance tune sung in chorus.

'In the meadows . . . in the meadows,' he heard with a whistle and string music, drowned from time to time in a roar of voices. The officer's spirits, too, rose at these sounds, but at the same time he was in terror lest he should be held responsible for having so long delayed giving the important message entrusted to him. It was by now nearly nine o'clock. He dismounted and walked up to the entrance of a big manor-house that had been left uninjured between the French and the Russian lines. Footmen were bustling about with wines and edibles in the vestibule and the buffet. Choruses were standing under the windows. The officer was led up to a door, and he saw all at once all the most important generals in the army, among them the big, impressive figure of Yermolov. All the generals were standing in a semicircle, laughing loudly, their uniforms unbuttoned, and their faces flushed and animated. In the middle of the room a handsome, short general with a red face, was smartly and jauntily executing the steps of the *trepak*.

'Ha, ha, ha! Bravo, Nikolay Ivanovitch! ha, ha! ...'

The officer felt doubly guilty in breaking in at such a moment with important business, and he would have waited; but one of the generals caught sight of him, and hearing what he had come for, told Yermolov. The latter, with a frowning face, came out to the officer, and hearing his story, took the papers from him without a word.

'Do you suppose it was by chance that he was not at home?' said a comrade of the officer's who was on the staff, speaking of Yermolov that evening. 'That's all stuff and nonsense; it was all done on purpose. To play a trick on Konovnitsyn. You see, there'll be a pretty kettle of fish tomorrow!'

V

THE decrepit old man, Kutuzov, had bade them wake him early next day, and in the early morning he said his prayers, dressed, and with a disagreeable consciousness that he had to command in a battle of which he did not approve, he got into his carriage and drove from Letashevka, five versts behind Tarutino, to the place where the attacking columns were to be gathered together. Kutuzov drove along, dropping asleep and waking up again, and listening to hear whether that were the sound of shots on the right, whether the action had not begun. But everything was still quiet. A damp and cloudy autumn day was dawning. As he approached Tarutino, Kutuzov noticed cavalry soldiers leading their horses to a watercourse across the road along which he was driving. Kutuzov looked at them, stopped his carriage, and asked what regiment did they belong to. They belonged to a column which was to have been far away in front in ambush.

'A mistake, perhaps,' thought the old commander-in-chief. But as he drove on further, Kutuzov saw infantry regiments with their arms stacked, and the soldiers in their drawers busy cooking porridge and fetching wood. He sent for their officer. The officer submitted that no command to advance had been given.

'No command...' Kutuzov began, but he checked himself at once, and ordered the senior officer to be summoned to him. Getting out of the carriage, with drooping head he walked to and fro in silence, breathing heavily. When the general staff officer, Eichen, for whom he had sent, arrived, Kutuzov turned purple with rage, not because that officer was to blame for the mistake, but because he was an object of sufficient importance for him to vent his wrath on. And staggering and gasping, the old man fell into that state of fury in which he would sometimes roll on the ground in frenzy, and flew at Eichen, shaking his fists, and shouting abuse in the language of the gutter. Another officer, Captain Brozin, who was in no way to blame, happening to appear, suffered the same fate.

'What will the blackguards do next? Shoot them! The scoundrels!' he shouted hoarsely, shaking his fist and staggering. He was in a state of actual physical suffering. He, his highness the commander-in-chief, who was assured by every one that no one in Russia had ever had such power as he, he put into this position—made a laughing-stock to the whole army. 'Worrying myself, praying over today, not sleeping all night, and thinking about everything—all for nothing!' he thought about himself. 'When I was a mere boy of an officer no one would have dared to make a laughing-stock of me like this . . . And now!' He was in a state of physical suffering, as though from corporal punishment, and could not help expressing it in wrathful and agonised outcries. But soon his strength was exhausted, and looking about him, feeling that he had said a great deal that was unjust, he got into his carriage and drove back in silence.

His wrath once spent did not return again, and Kutuzov, blinking feebly, listened to explanations and self-justifications (Yermolov himself did not put in an appearance till next day), and to the earnest representations of Bennigsen, Konovnitsyn, and Toll that the battle that had not come off should take place on the following day. And again Kutuzov had to acquiesce.

VI

NEXT day the troops were massed in their appointed places by the evening, and were moving forward in the night. It was an autumn night with a sky overcast by purplish-black clouds, but free from rain. The earth was damp, but not muddy, and the troops advanced noiselessly, except for a hardly audible jingling now and then from the artillery. They were forbidden to talk aloud, to smoke or to strike a light; the horses were kept from neighing. The secrecy of the enterprise increased its attractiveness. The men marched on gaily. Several columns halted, stacked their guns in piles, and lay down on the chilly ground, supposing they had reached their destination. Other columns (the majority) marched all night long, and arrived somewhere, unmistakably not where they were meant to be.

Count Orlov-Denisov with his Cossacks (the detachment of least importance of the lot) was the only one that reached the right place at the right time. This detachment halted at the extreme edge of a forest, on a path from the village of Stromilovo to Dmitrovskoe.

Before dawn Count Orlov, who had fallen asleep, was waked up. A deserter from the French camp was brought to him. It was a Polish under-officer of Poniatovsky's corps. This under-officer explained in Polish that he had deserted because he had been insulted in the service; because he ought long ago to have been an officer, and was braver than any of them, and so he had thrown them up and wanted to punish them. He said that Murat was camping for the night a verst from them, and that if they would give him a convoy of a hundred men he would take him alive. Count Orlov-Denisov took council with his comrades. The proposition was too alluring to be refused. Every one clamoured to go, every one advised making the attempt. After many disputes and confabulations, it was settled that Major-General Grekov, with two regiments of Cossacks, should go with the Polish deserter.

'Now, remember,' said Count Orlov-Denisov to the Polish deserter, as he dismissed him, 'if you have been lying, I will have you shot like a dog, but if it's true, a hundred crowns.'

The deserter made no reply to these words, and with a resolute air mounted his horse and rode off with Grekov's men, who were hurriedly gathered together. They disappeared into the wood. Count Orlov, shivering from the freshness of the dawning morning, and excited by the enterprise he had undertaken on his own responsibility, came out of the wood, accompanying Grekov, and began scrutinising the enemy's camp, faintly visible now in the deceptive light of the approaching dawn and the smouldering camp-fires. On the open copse on Count Orlov-Denisov's right our columns ought to have been visible. Count Orlov-Denisov looked in that direction; but although they could have been seen even if a long distance away, these columns were not in sight. Count Orlov-Denisov fancied, and his adjutant, who was extremely long-sighted, confirmed the idea, that they were beginning to move in the French camp.

'Oh, of course it's too late,' said Count Orlov, staring at the camp. As so often happens when the man in whom we are putting faith is no longer before our eyes, it all seemed at once perfectly clear and obvious to him that the deserter had been playing them false, that he had been telling them lies, and was only spoiling the whole attack by removing these two regiments, which he was leading away—God only knew where! As if it were possible to capture the general out of such a mass of troops.

'No doubt he was lying, that scoundrel,' said the Count.

'We can turn them back,' said one of the suite, who was feeling just the same mistrust in the undertaking as he gazed at the camp.

'Ah! Yes... what do you think, or shall we leave them? Or not?'

'Do you command them to return?'

'To return, yes, to return!' Count Orlov said, with sudden decision, looking at his watch; 'it will be too late; it's quite light.'

And an adjutant galloped into the wood after Grekov. When Grekov came back, Count Orlov-Denisov, excited by giving up this enterprise, and by vainly waiting for the infantry columns, which still did not appear, and by the enemy's being so near (every man in his detachment was feeling the same), resolved to attack.

In a whisper he gave the command: 'Mount!'

The men got into their places, crossed themselves... 'In God's name, off!'

'Hurrah!' rang out in the wood, and the Cossacks, with spears lowered, flew gaily, one hundred after another, across the stream into the camp, as though they were being shot out of a sack.

One desperate, frightened scream from the first Frenchman who caught sight of the Cossacks, and every creature in the camp, undressed and half-asleep, was running away, abandoning cannons, muskets, and horses.

If the Cossacks had pursued the French without regard to what they left all around and behind them, they could have captured Murat and all there was there. Their commanding officers tried to make them do so. But there was no making the Cossacks budge when they had got booty and prisoners. No one heeded the word of command. They had taken fifteen hundred prisoners, thirty-eight cannons, flags, and, what was of most consequence in the eyes of the Cossacks, horses, saddles, coverings, and various other objects. All of this they wanted to see after, to secure the prisoners and the cannons, to divide the booty, to shout at and even fight with one another over the spoils; and all this absorbed the Cossacks' attention. The Frenchmen, finding themselves not pursued further, began to rally; they formed into companies and began firing. Orlov-Denisov still expected the other columns to arrive, and did not advance further.

Meanwhile, in accordance with the disposition—*'die erste Colonne marschirt,'* and so on—the infantry regiments of the belated columns, under the command of Bennigsen and the direction of Toll, had started off in due course, and had, in the usual way, arrived somewhere, but not where they were intended to arrive. In the usual way too, the soldiers, who had set off gaily, began to halt; there were murmurs of dissatisfaction and a sense of muddle, and they were marched back to some point. Adjutants and generals galloped to and fro, shouting angrily, quarrelling, declaring they had come utterly wrong and were too late, upbraiding some one, and so on; and finally, all washed their hands of the business in despair, and marched on simply in order to get somewhere. 'We must arrive somewhere sooner or later!' And so they did, in fact, arrive somewhere, but not where they were wanted. And some did even reach their destination, but reached it so late that their doing so was of no use at all, and only resulted in their being fired at for nothing. Toll, who in this battle played the part of Weierother in the battle of Austerlitz, galloped with unflagging energy from one part of the field to another, and found everything at sixes and sevens everywhere. So, for instance, he found Bagovut's corps in the wood, when it was broad daylight, though the corps ought to have been there long before, and to have gone to support Orlov-Denisov. Disappointed and excited at the failure, and supposing some one must be to blame for it, Toll galloped up to the general in command of the corps, and began sternly reprimanding him, declaring that he deserved to be shot. Bagovut, a sturdy old general of placid disposition, had been worried too by all the delays, the muddles, and the contradictory orders, and, to the amazement of everybody, he flew into a violent rage, quite out of keeping with his character, and said some very nasty things to Toll.

'I am not going to be taught my duty by anybody, but I can face death with my men as well as any one,' he said, and he marched forward with one division. The valiant Bagovut, not considering in his excitement whether his advance into action now with a single division was likely to be of use or not, marched his men straight forward into the enemy's fire.

Danger, shells, and bullets were just what he wanted in his fury. One of the first bullets killed him, the other bullets killed many of his men. And his division remained for some time under fire for no object whatever.

VII

MEANWHILE another column was to have fallen upon the French in the centre, but of this column Kutuzov was in command. He knew very well that nothing but muddle would come of this battle, begun against his will, and, as far as it was in his power, he held his forces back. He did not move.

Kutuzov rode mutely about on his grey horse, making languid replies to the suggestions for an attack.

'You can all talk about attacking, but you don't see that we don't know how to execute complicated manœuvres,' he said to Miloradovitch, who was begging to be allowed to advance.

'We couldn't take Murat alive in the morning, nor be in our places in time; now there's nothing to be done!' he said to another.

When it was reported to Kutuzov that there were now two battalions of Poles in the rear of the French, where according to the earlier reports of the Cossacks there had been none, he took a sidelong glance behind him at Yermolov, to whom he had not spoken since the previous day.

'Here they are begging to advance, proposing projects of all sorts, and as soon as you get to work, there's nothing ready, and the enemy, forewarned, takes his measures.'

Yermolov half closed his eyelids, and faintly smiled, as he heard those words. He knew that the storm had blown over him, and that Kutuzov would not go beyond that hint.

'That's his little joke at my expense,' said Yermolov softly, poking Raevsky, near him, with his knee.

Soon after that, Yermolov moved forward to Kutuzov and respectfully submitted:

'The time has not passed, your highness; the enemy has not gone away. If you were to command an advance? Or else the guards won't have a sight of smoke.'

Kutuzov said nothing, but when news was brought him that Murat's troops were in retreat, he gave orders for an advance; but every hundred paces he halted for three-quarters of an hour.

The whole battle was confined to what had been done by the Cossacks of Orlov-Denisov; the rest of the troops simply lost a few hundreds of men for nothing.

In consequence of this battle, Kutuzov received a diamond decoration; Bennigsen, too, was rewarded with diamonds and a hundred thousand roubles; and the other generals, too, received agreeable recognition according to their rank, and more changes were made on the staff.

'That's how things are always done among us, everything topsy-turvy!' the Russian officers and generals said after the battle of Tarutino; just as they say it nowadays, with an assumption that some stupid person had muddled everything, while *we* would have managed quite differently. But the men who speak like this either do not understand what they are talking of, or intentionally deceive themselves. Every battle—Tarutino, Borodino, Austerlitz—fails to come off as those who planned it expected it to do. That is inevitable.

An innumerable collection of freely acting forces (and nowhere is a man freer than on the field of battle, where it is a question of life and death) influence the direction taken by a battle, and that can never be known beforehand and never corresponds with the direction of any one force.

If many forces are acting simultaneously in different directions on any body, the direction of its motion will not correspond with any one of the forces, but will always follow a middle course, the summary of them, what is expressed in mechanics by the diagonal of the parallelogram of forces.

If in the accounts given us by historians, especially by French ones, we find that wars and battles appear to follow a definite plan laid down beforehand, the only deduction we can make from that is that these accounts are not true.

The battle of Tarutino obviously failed to attain the aim which Toll had in view: to lead the army into action in accordance with his disposition of the troops, or the aim which Count Orlov-Denisov may have had: to take Murat prisoner; or the aim of destroying at one blow the whole corps, which Bennigsen and others may have entertained; or the aim of the officer who desired to distinguish himself under fire; or the Cossack, who wanted to obtain more booty than he did attain, and so on. But if we regard the object of the battle as what was actually accomplished by it, and what was the universal desire of all Russians (the expulsion of the French from Russia and the destruction of their army), it will be perfectly evident that the battle of Tarutino, precisely in consequence of its incongruities, was exactly what was wanted at that period of the campaign. It is difficult or impossible to imagine any issue of that battle more in accordance with that object than its actual result. With the very smallest effort, in spite of the greatest muddle, and with the most trifling loss, the most important results in the whole campaign were obtained—the transition was made from retreat to attack, the weakness of the French was revealed, and the shock was given which was all that was needed to put Napoleon's army to flight.

VIII

NAPOLEON enters Moscow after the brilliant victory *de la Moskowa*: there can be no doubt of the victory, since the French are left in possession of the field of battle. The Russians retreat and leave Moscow —well stocked with provisions, arms, implements, and countless riches —in the hands of Napoleon. The Russian army, of one-half the strength of the French, during the course of a whole month makes no effort to attack. Napoleon's position is most brilliant. One would have supposed that no great genius was needed with an army of double the strength to fall upon the Russian forces and destroy them, to negotiate an advantageous peace; or, in case of negotiations being refused, to make a menacing march upon Petersburg, or even, in case of failure in this, to return to Smolensk or to Vilna, or to remain in Moscow, to retain, in short, the brilliant position in which the French army now found themselves. To do all this it was only necessary to take the simplest and easiest measures: to keep the soldiers from pillage, to prepare winter clothes (of which there was a supply in Moscow amply sufficient for the whole army), and regularly to collect the provisions, of which the supply in Moscow was, on the showing of the French historians, sufficient to feed the whole army for six months. Napoleon, the greatest of all military geniuses, with absolute power, as historians assert, over the army, did nothing of all this.

Far from doing anything of the sort, he used his power to select out of all the various courses open to him the stupidest and most pernicious of all. Of all the different things Napoleon might have done—spending the winter in Moscow, going to Petersburg, going to Nizhni-Novgorod, going back a little more to the north or to the south, by the road Kutuzov afterwards took—no course one can imagine could have been more ruinous for his army (as the sequel proved) than the one Napoleon actually did adopt; that is, the course of staying in Moscow till October, letting the troops plunder the town, then in hesitation leaving a garrison behind, marching out of Moscow, going to meet Kutuzov and not giving battle, turning to the right and going as far as Maley Yaroslavets, again refusing to risk a battle, and finally retreating, not by the road Kutuzov had taken, but by Mozhaisk and the Smolensk route through devastated country. Let the most skilful tacticians, supposing that Napoleon's object was the destruction of his army, try and devise a series of actions which could, apart from any measures that might be taken by the Russian forces, have ensured with such certainty the complete destruction of the whole French army as the course taken by Napoleon.

This the genius Napoleon did. But to say that Napoleon ruined his army because he wanted to do so, or because he was very stupid, would be just as unjust as to say that Napoleon got his troops to Moscow because he wanted to, and because he was very clever and a great genius.

In both cases his personal activity, having no more force than the personal activity of every soldier, was merely coincidental with the laws by which the event was determined.

Quite falsely (and simply because the sequel did not justify Napoleon's actions) do historians represent Napoleon's faculties as flagging at Moscow. Just as before, and afterwards in the year 1813, he used all his powers and faculties to do the best for himself and his army, Napoleon's activity at this time was no less marvellous than in Egypt, in Italy, in Austria, and in Prussia. We do not know with any certainty how real was the genius of Napoleon in Egypt, where forty centuries looked down upon his greatness, because all his great exploits there are recounted to us by none but Frenchmen. We cannot judge with certainty of his genius in Austria and Prussia, as the accounts of his doings there must be drawn from French and German sources. And the unaccountable surrender of corps of soldiers without a battle, and of fortresses without a siege, must dispose Germans to postulate Napoleon's genius as the unique explanation of the war as it was waged in Germany. But we have, thank God, no need to plead his genius to cloak our shame. We have paid for the right to look facts simply and squarely in the face, and that right we will not give up.

His activity in Moscow was as marvellous and as full of genius as anywhere else. Command upon command and plan upon plan was continually being issued by him from the time he entered Moscow to the time he left it. The absence of the citizens and of a deputation, and even the burning of Moscow, did not daunt him. He did not lose sight of the welfare of his army, nor of the doings of the enemy, nor of the welfare of the people of Russia, nor the conduct of affairs at Paris, nor of diplomatic negotiations as to the terms of peace.

IX

ON the military side, immediately on entering Moscow, Napoleon gives General Sebastiani strict orders to keep a watch on the movements of the Russian army, sends detachments along the various roads, and charges Murat to find Kutuzov. Then he gives careful instructions for the fortification of the Kremlin; then he makes a plan of the coming campaign over the whole map of Russia; that was a work of genius, indeed. On the diplomatic side, Napoleon summons to his presence Captain Yakovlev, who had been robbed and reduced to rags and did not know how to get out of Moscow, expounds to him minutely his whole policy and his magnanimity; and after writing a letter to the Emperor Alexander, in which he considers it his duty to inform his friend and brother that Rastoptchin had performed his duties very badly in Moscow, he despatches Yakovlev with it to Petersburg.

Expounding his views and his magnanimity with equal minuteness to

Tutolmin, he despatches that old man too to Petersburg to open negotiations.

On the judicial side, orders were issued, immediately after the fires broke out, for the guilty persons to be found and executed. And the miscreant Rastoptchin was punished by the order to set fire to his houses.

On the administrative side, Moscow was presented with a constitution. A municipal council was instituted, and the following proclamation was issued: —

'CITIZENS OF MOSCOW!

'Your misfortunes have been cruel, but his Majesty the Emperor and King wishes to put an end to them. Terrible examples have shown you how he punishes crime and breach of discipline. Stern measures have been taken to put an end to disorder and to restore public security. A paternal council, chosen from among yourselves, will compose your municipality or town council. It will care for you, for your needs and your interests. The members of it will be distinguished by a red ribbon, which they will wear across the shoulder, and the mayor will wear a white sash over it. But except when discharging their duties, they will wear only a red ribbon round the left arm.

'The city police are established on their former footing, and they are already restoring order. The government has appointed two general commissioners, or superintendents of police, and twenty commissioners, or police inspectors, stationed in the different quarters of the town. You will recognise them by the white ribbon they will wear round the left arm. Several churches of various denominations have been opened, and divine service is performed in them without hindrance. Your fellow-citizens are returning every day to their dwellings, and orders have been given that they should find in them the aid and protection due to misfortune. These are the measures which the government has adopted to restore order and alleviate your position; but to attain that end, it is necessary that you should unite your efforts with them; should forget, if possible, the misfortunes you have suffered; should look hopefully at a fate that is not so cruel; should believe that a shameful death inevitably awaits those guilty of violence against your persons or your deserted property, and consequently leaves no doubt that they will be preserved, since such is the will of the greatest and most just of monarchs. Soldiers and citizens of whatever nation you may be! Restore public confidence, the source of the prosperity of a state; live like brothers, give mutual aid and protection to one another; unite in confounding the projects of the evil-minded; obey the civil and military authorities, and your tears will soon cease to flow.'

On the commissariat side, Napoleon issued orders for all the troops to enter Moscow in turn, *à la maraude*, to gather supplies for themselves; so that in that way the army was provided with supplies for the future.

On the religious side, Napoleon ordered the priests to be brought back, and services to be performed again in the churches.

With a view to encouraging commerce and providing supplies for the troops, the following notice was placarded everywhere:—

'PROCLAMATION.

'You, peaceable inhabitants of Moscow, artisans, and working men, who have been driven out of the city by the disturbance, and you, scattered tillers of the soil, who are still kept in the fields by groundless terror, hear! Tranquillity is returning to this capital, and order is being restored in it. Your fellow-countrymen are coming boldly out of their hiding-places, seeing that they are treated with respect. Every act of violence against them or their property is promptly punished. His Majesty the Emperor and King protects them, and he reckons none among you his enemies but such as disobey his commands. He wishes to put an end to your trouble, and to bring you back to your homes and your families. Co-operate with his beneficent designs and come to us without apprehension. Citizens! Return with confidence to your habitations; you will soon find the means of satisfying your needs! Artisans and industrious handicraftsmen! Return to your employment; houses, shops, and guards to protect them are awaiting you, and you will receive the payment due to you for your toil! And you, too, peasants, come out of the forests where you have been hiding in terror, return without fear to your huts in secure reliance on finding protection. Markets have been established in the city, where peasants can bring their spare stores and country produce. The government has taken the following measures to secure freedom of sale for them: (1) From this day forward, peasants, husbandmen, and inhabitants of the environs of Moscow can, without any danger, bring their goods of any kind to two appointed markets—namely, the Mohovaya and the Ohotny Ryad. (2) Goods shall be bought from them at such a price as seller and buyer shall agree upon together; but if the seller cannot get what he asks for as a fair price, he will be at liberty to take his goods back to his village, and no one can hinder his doing so on any pretext whatever. (3) Every Sunday and Wednesday are fixed for weekly market days: to that end a sufficient number of troops will be stationed on Tuesdays and Saturdays along all the high roads at such a distance from the town as to protect the carts coming in. (4) Similar measures will be taken that the peasants with their carts and horses may meet with no hindrance on their homeward way. (5) Steps will be immediately taken to re-establish the ordinary shops.

'Inhabitants of the city and of the country, and you workmen and handicraftsmen of whatever nationality you may be! You are called upon to carry out the paternal designs of his Majesty the Emperor and King, and to co-operate with him for the public welfare. Lay your respect and confidence at his feet, and do not delay to unite with us!'

With a view to keeping up the spirits of the troops and the people, reviews were continually being held, and rewards were distributed.

The Emperor rode about the streets and entertained the inhabitants; and in spite of his preoccupation with affairs of state, visited in person the theatre set up by his orders.

As regards philanthropy, too—the fairest jewel in the conqueror's crown—Napoleon did everything that lay within him. On the benevolent institutions he ordered the inscription to be put up, '*Maison de ma mère*,' thereby combining a touching filial sentiment with a monarch's grandeur of virtue. He visited the Foundling Home; and as he gave the orphans he had saved his white hands to kiss, he conversed graciously with Tutolmin. Then, as Thiers eloquently recounts, he ordered his soldiers' pay to be distributed among them in the false Russian notes he had counterfeited: —

'Reinforcing the use of these methods by an act worthy of him and of the French army, he had assistance distributed to those who had suffered loss from the fire. But as provisions were too precious to be given to strangers, mostly enemies, Napoleon preferred to furnish them with money for them to provide themselves from without, and ordered paper roubles to be distributed among them.'

With a view to maintaining discipline in the army, orders were continually being issued for severely punishing nonfulfilment of military duty and for putting an end to pillaging.

X

BUT, strange to say, all these arrangements, these efforts and plans, which were no whit inferior to those that had been made on similar occasions before, never touched the root of the matter; like the hands on the face of a clock, when detached from the mechanism, they turned aimlessly and arbitrarily, without catching the wheels.

The plan of campaign, that work of genius, of which Thiers says, that his genius never imagined anything more profound, more skilful, and more admirable, and entering into a polemical discussion with M. Fenn, proves that the composition of this work of genius is to be referred, not to the 4th, but to the 15th of October—that plan never was and never could be put into execution, because it had nothing in common with the actual facts of the position. The fortification of the Kremlin, for which it was necessary to pull down la Mosquée (as Napoleon called the church of Vassily the Blessed) turned out to be perfectly useless. The mining of the Kremlin was only of use for carrying out the desire the Emperor expressed on leaving Moscow, to blow up the Kremlin, like a child that beats the floor against which it has hurt itself. The pursuit of the Russian army, on which Napoleon laid so much stress, led to an unheard-of result. The French generals lost sight of the sixty thousand men of the Russian army, and it was only, in the words of Thiers, thanks to the skill, and apparently also the genius, of Murat that they succeeded at last in finding, like a lost pin, this army of sixty thousand men.

On the diplomatic side, all Napoleon's expositions of his magnanimity and justice, both to Tutolmin and to Yakovlev (the latter was principally interested in finding himself a greatcoat and a conveyance for travelling) turned out to be fruitless. Alexander would not receive these envoys, and made no reply to the message they brought.

On the side of law, of order, after the execution of the supposed incendiaries, the other half of Moscow was burnt down.

The establishment of a municipal council did not check pillage, and was no benefit to any one but the few persons, who were members of it, and were able on the pretext of preserving order to plunder Moscow on their own account, or to save their own property from being plundered.

On the religious side, the difficulty had so easily been settled by Napoleon's visit to a mosque in Egypt, but here similar measures led to no results whatever. Two or three priests, picked up in Moscow, did attempt to carry out Napoleon's desire; but one of them was slapped in the face by a French soldier during the service, and in regard to the other, the following report was made by a French official: 'The priest, whom I had discovered and invited to resume saying the Mass, cleaned and closed the church. In the night they came again to break in the doors, break the padlocks, tear the books, and commit other disorders.'

As for the encouragement of commerce, the proclamation to 'industrious artisans and peasants,' met with no response at all. Industrious artisans there were none in Moscow, and the peasants set upon the messengers who ventured too far from the town with this proclamation and killed them.

The attempts to entertain the people and the troops with theatres were equally unsuccessful. The theatres set up in the Kremlin and Poznyakov's house were closed again immediately, because the actors and actresses were stripped of their belongings by the soldiers.

Even philanthropy did not bring the desired results. Moscow was full of paper money, genuine and counterfeit, and the notes had no value. The French, accumulating booty, cared for nothing but gold. The counterfeit notes, which Napoleon so generously bestowed on the unfortunate, were of no value, and even silver fell below its standard value in relation to gold.

But the most striking example of the ineffectiveness of all efforts made by the authorities was Napoleon's vain endeavour to check plunder, and to maintain discipline.

Here are reports sent in by the military authorities:

'Pillage continues in the city, in spite of the orders to stop it. Order is not yet restored, and there is not a single merchant carrying on trade in a lawful fashion. But the canteen-keepers permit themselves to sell the fruits of pillage.

'Part of my district continues to be a prey to the pillaging of the soldiers of the 3rd corps, who, not satisfied with tearing from the poor wretches, who have taken refuge in the underground cellars, the little they have left, have even the ferocity to wound them with sword-cuts, as I have seen in several instances.

'Nothing new, but that the soldiers give themselves up to robbery and plunder. October 9th.

'Robbery and pillage continue. There is a band of robbers in our district, which would need strong guards to arrest it. October 11th.

'The Emperor is exceedingly displeased that, in spite of the strict orders to stop pillage, bands of marauders from the guards are continually returning to the Kremlin. In the Old Guards, the disorder and pillaging have been more violent than ever last night and today. The Emperor sees, with regret, that the picked soldiers, appointed to guard his person, who should set an example to the rest, are losing discipline to such a degree as to break into the cellars and stores prepared for the army. Others are so degraded that they refuse to obey sentinels and officers on guard, abuse them, and strike them.

'The chief marshal of the palace complains bitterly that, in spite of repeated prohibitions, the soldiers continue to commit nuisances in all the courtyards, and even before the Emperor's own windows.'

The army, like a herd of cattle run wild, and trampling underfoot the fodder that might have saved them from starvation, was falling to pieces, and getting nearer to its ruin with every day it remained in Moscow.

But it did not move.

It only started running when it was seized by panic fear at the capture of a transport on the Smolensk road and the battle of Tarutino. The news of the battle of Tarutino reached Napoleon unexpectedly in the middle of a review, and aroused in him—so Thiers tells us—a desire to punish the Russians, and he gave the order for departure that all the army was clamouring for.

In their flight from Moscow, the soldiers carried with them all the plunder they had collected. Napoleon, too, carried off his own private *trésor*. Seeing the great train of waggons, loaded with the booty of the army, Napoleon was alarmed (as Thiers tells us). But with his military experience he did not order all unnecessary waggons of goods to be burnt, as he had done with a marshal's baggage on the way to Moscow. He gazed at those carts and carriages, filled with soldiers, and said that it was very well, that those conveyances would come in useful for provisions, the sick, and the wounded.

The plight of the army was like the plight of a wounded beast, that feels its death at hand, and knows not what it is doing. Studying the intricate manœuvres and schemes of Napoleon and his army from the time of entering Moscow up to the time of the destruction of that army is much like watching the death struggles and convulsions of a beast mortally wounded. Very often the wounded creature, hearing a stir, rushes to meet the hunter's shot, runs forward and back again, and itself hastens its end. Napoleon under the pressure of his army did likewise. Panic-stricken at the rumour of the battle of Tarutino, like a wild beast, the army made a rush towards the shot, reached the hunter, and ran back again; and at last, like every wild creature took the old familiar track, that was the worst and most disastrous way for it.

Napoleon is represented to us as the leader in all this movement, just as the figurehead in the prow of a ship to the savage seems the force that guides the ship on its course. Napoleon in his activity all this time was like a child, sitting in a carriage, pulling the straps within it, and fancying he is moving it along.

XI

EARLY in the morning of the 6th of October, Pierre came out of the shed, and when he went back, he stood in the doorway, playing with the long bandy-legged, purplish-grey dog, that jumped about him. This dog lived in their shed, sleeping with Karataev, though it sometimes went off on its own account into the town, and came back again. It had probably never belonged to any one, and now it had no master, and no name. The French called it Azor; the soldier who told stories called it Femgalka; Karataev called it 'Grey-coat,' and sometimes 'Floppy.' The lack of a master, of a name, of any particular breed, and even of a definite colour, by no means troubled the purplish-grey dog. Its fluffy tail stood up firm and round like a plume; its bandy legs served it so well that often, as though disdaining to use all four, it would hold one hind-leg gracefully up, and run very quickly and smartly on three paws. Everything was a source of satisfaction to it. At one moment, it was barking with joy, then it would bask in the sun, with a dreamy and thoughtful air, then it would frolic about, playing with a chip or a straw.

Pierre's attire now consisted of a dirty, tattered shirt, the sole relic left of his previous wardrobe, a pair of soldier's drawers, tied with string round the ankles by Karataev's advice, for the sake of warmth, a full peasant's coat and a peasant's cap. Physically Pierre had changed greatly during this period. He no longer seemed stout, though he still had that look of solidity and strength that was characteristic of the Bezuhov family. The lower part of his face was overgrown with beard and moustaches; his long, tangled hair, swarming with lice, formed a mat of curls on his head. His eyes had a look of firmness, calm, and alert readiness, such as had never been seen in Pierre's face before. All his old slackness, which had shown even in his eyes, was replaced now by a vigorous, alert look of readiness for action and for resistance. His feet were bare.

Pierre looked over the meadow, across which waggons and men on horseback were moving that morning, then far away beyond the river, then at the dog, who was pretending to be meaning to bite him in earnest, then at his bare feet, which he shifted with pleasure from one position to another, moving the dirty, thick, big toes. And every time he looked at his bare feet, a smile of eager self-satisfaction flitted across his face. The sight of those bare feet reminded him of all he had passed through and learned during this time; and the thought of that was sweet to him.

The weather had for several days been still and clear, with light frosts in the mornings—the so-called 'old granny's summer.'

It was warm out of doors in the sunshine, and that warmth was particularly pleasant, with the bracing freshness of the morning frost still in the air.

Over everything, over all objects near and far, lay that magical, crystal-clear brightness, which is only seen at that time in the autumn. In the distance could be seen the Sparrow Hills, with the village, the church, and the great white house. And the leafless trees, and the sand and the stones and roofs of the houses, the green spire of the church, and the angles of the white house in the distance, all stood out in the most delicate outlines with unnatural distinctness in the limpid air. Close at hand stood the familiar ruins of a half-burnt mansion, occupied by French soldiers, with lilac bushes still dark-green by the fence. And even this charred and ruined house, which looked revoltingly hideous in bad weather, had a sort of soothing comeliness in the clear, still brightness.

A French corporal, in a smoking-cap, with his coat comfortably unbuttoned, came round the corner of the shed, with a short pipe between his teeth, and with a friendly wink, approached Pierre.

'What sunshine, *hein* M. Kiril?' (This was what all the French soldiers called Pierre.) 'One would say it was spring.' And the corporal leaned against the door, and offered Pierre his pipe, though he was always offering it, and Pierre always declined it.

'If one were marching in weather like this,' he began.

Pierre questioned him what he had heard of the departure of the French, and the corporal told him that almost all the troops were setting out, and that today instructions were expected in regard to the prisoners. In the shed in which Pierre was, one of the Russian soldiers, Sokolov, was dangerously ill, and Pierre told the corporal that something ought to be done about this soldier. The corporal said that Pierre might set his mind at rest, that they had both travelling and stationary hospitals for such cases, that instructions would be given in regard to the sick, and that in fact every possible contingency was provided for by the authorities.

'And then, M. Kiril, you have only to say a word to the captain, you know. Oh, he is a man who never forgets anything. Speak to the captain when he makes his round; he will do anything for you.'

The captain of whom the corporal spoke used often to have long conversations with Pierre, and did him all kinds of favours.

'You see, St. Thomas,' he said to me the other day, 'Kiril is a man of education, who speaks French; he is a Russian lord who has had troubles, but he is a man. And he understands . . . If he wants anything, let him tell me, he shall not meet with a refusal. When one has studied, one likes education, you see, and well-bred people. It's for your own sake I tell you that, M. Kiril. In the affair that happened the other day, if it hadn't been for you, things would have ended badly.'

(The corporal was alluding to a fight a few days before between the prisoners and the French soldiers, in which Pierre had succeeded in pacifying his companions.) After chatting a little time longer the corporal went away.

Several of the prisoners had heard Pierre talking to the corporal, and they came up immediately to ask what the latter had said. While Pierre was telling his companions what the corporal had said about setting off from Moscow, a thin, sallow, ragged French soldier came up to the door of the shed. With a shy and rapid gesture he put his fingers to his forehead by way of a salute, and addressing Pierre, asked him if the soldier, Platoche, who was making a shirt for him were in this shed.

The French soldiers had been provided with linen and leather a week previously, and had given out the materials to the Russian prisoners to make them boots and shirts.

'It's ready, darling, it's ready!' said Karataev, coming out with a carefully folded shirt. On account of the heat and for greater convenience in working, Karataev was wearing nothing but a pair of drawers and a tattered shirt, as black as the earth. He had tied a wisp of bast round his hair, as workmen do, and his round face looked rounder and more pleasing than ever.

'Punctuality is own brother to good business. I said Friday, and so I have done it,' said Platon, smiling and displaying the shirt he had made.

The Frenchman looked about him uneasily, and as though overcoming some hesitation, rapidly slipped off his uniform and put on the shirt. Under his uniform he had no shirt, but a long, greasy, flowered silk waistcoat next his bare, yellow, thin body. The Frenchman was evidently afraid that the prisoners, who were looking at him, would laugh at him, and he made haste to put his head through the shirt. None of the prisoners said a word. 'To be sure, it fits well,' Platon observed, pulling the shirt down. The Frenchman, after putting his head and arms through, looked down at the shirt, and examined the stitching without lifting his eyes.

'Well, darling, this isn't a tailor's, you know, and I had no proper sewing materials, and there's a saying without the right tool you can't even kill a louse properly,' said Karataev, still admiring his own handiwork.

'Very good, thanks; but you must have some stuff left . . .' said the Frenchman.

'It will be more comfortable as it wears to your body,' said Karataev, still admiring his work. 'There, you'll be nice and comfortable.'

'Thanks, thanks, old fellow; but what is left . . .?' repeated the Frenchman, giving Karataev a paper note. 'Give me the pieces that are over.'

Pierre saw that Platon did not want to understand what the Frenchman said, and he looked on without interfering. Karataev thanked him for the rouble and went on admiring his own work. The Frenchman persisted in asking for what was left, and asked Pierre to translate what he said.

'What does he want with the pieces?' said Karataev. 'They would have made me capital leg wrappers. Oh well, God bless the man.'

And, looking suddenly crestfallen and melancholy, Karataev took a bundle of remnants out of his bosom and gave it to the Frenchman without looking at him. 'Ach-ma!' he cried, and walked away. The Frenchman looked at the linen, he hesitated, glanced inquiringly at Pierre, and as though Pierre's eyes had told him something:

'Here, Platoche!' he cried in a shrill voice, suddenly blushing. 'Keep them yourself,' he said, and giving him the remnants, he turned and went out.

'There, look'ee now,' said Karataev, shaking his head. 'They say they're not Christians, but they have souls too. It's true what the old folks used to say: a sweating hand is an open hand, but a dry hand is closefisted. His own back's bare, and yet he has given me this.' Karataev paused for a while, smiling dreamily and gazing at the cuttings of linen. 'But first-rate leg binders they'll make me, my dear,' he added, as he went back into the shed.

XII

FOUR weeks had passed since Pierre had been taken prisoner. Although the French had offered to transfer him from the common prisoners' shed to the officers', he had remained in the same shed as at first.

In Moscow, wasted by fire and pillage, Pierre passed through hardships almost up to the extreme limit of privation that a man can endure. But, owing to his vigorous health and consitution, of which he had hardly been aware till then; and still more, owing to the fact that these privations came upon him so gradually that it was impossible to say when they began, he was able to support his position, not only with ease, but with positive gladness. And it was just at this time that he attained that peace and content with himself, for which he had always striven in vain before. For long years of his life he had been seeking in various directions for that peace, that harmony with himself, which had struck him so much in the soldiers at Borodino. He had sought for it in philanthropy, in freemasonry, in the dissipations of society, in wine, in heroic feats of self-sacrifice, in his romantic love for Natasha; he had sought it by the path of thought; and all his researches and all his efforts had failed him. And now without any thought of his own, he had gained that peace and that harmony with himself simply through the horror of death, through hardships, through what he had seen in Karataev. Those fearful moments that he had lived through during the execution had, as it were, washed for ever from his imagination and his memory the disturbing ideas and feelings that had once seemed to him so important. No thought came to him of Russia, of the war, of politics, or of Napoleon. It seemed obvious to him that all that did not concern him, that he was not called upon and so was not able to judge of all that. 'Russia and summer never do well together,' he repeated Karataev's words, and those words soothed him strangely. His project of killing Napoleon, and his calculations of the cabalistic numbers, and of the beast of the Apocalypse struck him now as incomprehensible and positively ludicrous. His anger with his wife, and his dread of his name being disgraced by her, seemed to him trivial and amusing. What business of his was it, if that woman chose to lead somewhere away from him the life that suited her tastes? What did it matter to any one—least of all to him—whether they found out or not that their prisoner's name was Count Bezuhov.

He often thought now of his conversation with Prince Andrey, and agreed fully with his friend, though he put a somewhat different construction on his meaning. Prince Andrey had said and thought that happiness is only negative, but he had said this with a shade of bitterness and irony. It was as though in saying this he had expressed another thought—that all the strivings towards positive happiness, that are innate in us, were only given us for our torment. But Pierre recognised the truth of the main idea with no such undercurrent of feeling. The absence of suffering, the satisfaction of needs, and following upon that, freedom in the choice of occupation, that is, of one's manner of life, seemed to Pierre the highest and most certain happiness of man. Only here and now for the first time in his life Pierre fully appreciated the enjoyment of eating when he was hungry, of drinking when he was thirsty, of sleep when he was sleepy, of warmth when he was cold, of talking to a fellow creature when he wanted to talk and to hear men's voices. The satisfaction of his needs—good food, cleanliness, freedom—seemed to Pierre now that he was deprived of them to be perfect happiness; and the choice of his occupation, that is, of his manner of life now that that choice was so limited, seemed to him such an easy matter that he forgot that a superfluity of the conveniences of life destroys all happiness in satisfying the physical needs, while a great freedom in the choice of occupation, that freedom which education, wealth, and position in society had given him, makes the choice of occupations exceedingly difficult, and destroys the very desire and possibility of occupation.

All Pierre's dreams now turned to the time when he would be free. And yet, in all his later life, Pierre thought and spoke with enthusiasm of that month of imprisonment, of those intense and joyful sensations that could never be recalled, and above all of that full, spiritual peace, of that perfect, inward freedom, of which he had only experience at that period.

On the first day, when, getting up early in the morning, he came out of the shed into the dawn, and saw the cupolas and the crosses of the New Monastery of the Virgin, all still in darkness, saw the hoar frost on the long grass, saw the slopes of the Sparrow Hills and the wood-clad banks of the encircling river vanishing into the purple distance, when he felt the contact of the fresh air and heard the sounds of the rooks flying out of Moscow across the fields, and when flashes of light suddenly gleamed out of the east and the sun's rim floated triumphantly up from behind a cloud, and cupolas and crosses and hoar frost and the horizon and the river were all sparkling in the glad light, Pierre felt a new feeling of joy and vigour in life such as he had never experienced before.

And that feeling had not left him during the whole period of his imprisonment, but on the contrary had gone on growing in him as the hardships of his position increased.

· That feeling—of being ready for anything, of moral alertness—was strengthened in Pierre by the high opinion in which he began to be held by his companions very soon after he entered the shed. His knowledge of languages, the respect shown him by the French, the good-nature with which he gave away anything he was asked for (he received the allowance of three roubles a week, given to officers among the prisoners), the strength he showed in driving nails into the wall, the gentleness of his behaviour to his companions, and his capacity—which seemed to them mysterious—of sitting stockstill doing nothing and plunged in thought, all made him seem to the soldiers a rather mysterious creature of a higher order. The very peculiarities that in the society he had previously lived in had been a source of embarrassment, if not of annoyance—his strength, his disdain for the comforts of life, his absent-mindedness, his good-nature—here among these men gave him the prestige almost of a hero. And Pierre felt that their view of him brought its duties.

XIII

ON the night of the 6th of October, the march of the retreating French army began: kitchens and shanties were broken up, waggons were packed, and troops and trains of baggage began moving.

At seven o'clock in the morning an escort of French soldiers in marching order, in shakoes, with guns, knapsacks, and huge sacks, stood before the sheds and a running fire of eager French talk, interspersed with oaths, was kept up all along the line.

In the shed they were ready, dressed and belted and shod, only waiting for the word of command to come out. The sick soldier, Sokolov, pale and thin, with blue rings round his eyes, sat alone in his place, without boots or out-of-door clothes on. His eyes, that looked prominent from the thinness of his face, gazed inquiringly at his companions, who took no notice of him, and he uttered low groans at regular intervals. It was evidently not so much his sufferings—he was ill with dysentery—as the dread and grief of being left alone that made him groan.

Pierre was shod with a pair of slippers that Karataev had made for him out of the leather cover of a tea-chest, brought him by a Frenchman for soling his boots. With a cord tied round for a belt, he went up to the sick man, and squatted on his heels beside him.

'Come, Sokolov, they are not going away altogether, you know. They have a hospital here. Very likely you will be better off than we others,' said Pierre.

'O Lord! it will be the death of me! O Lord!' the soldier groaned more loudly.

'Well, I will ask them again in a minute,' said Pierre, and getting up, he went to the door of the shed. While Pierre was going to the door, the same corporal, who had on the previous day offered Pierre a pipe, came in from outside, accompanied by two soldiers. Both the corporal and the soldiers were in marching order, with knapsacks on and shakoes, with straps buttoned, that changed their familiar faces.

The corporal had come to the door so as to shut it in accordance with the orders given him. Before getting them out, he had to count over the prisoners.

'Corporal, what is to be done with the sick man?' Pierre was beginning, but at the very moment that he spoke the words he doubted whether it were the corporal he knew or some stranger—the corporal was so unlike himself at that moment. Moreover, at the moment Pierre was speaking, the roll of drums was suddenly heard on both sides. The corporal scowled at Pierre's words, and uttering a meaningless oath, he slammed the door. It was half-dark now in the shed; the drums beat a sharp tattoo on both sides, drowning the sick man's groans.

'Here it is! ... Here it is again!' Pierre said to himself, and an involuntary shudder ran down his back. In the changed face of the corporal, in the sound of his voice, in the stimulating and deafening din of the drums, Pierre recognised that mysterious, unsympathetic force which drove men, against their will, to do their fellow-creatures to death; that force, the effect of which he had seen at the execution. To be afraid, to try and avoid that force, to appeal with entreaties or with exhortations to the men who were serving as its instruments, was useless. That Pierre knew now. One could but wait and be patient. Pierre did not go near the sick man again, and did not look round at him. He stood at the door of the shed in silence, scowling.

When the doors of the shed were opened, and the prisoners, huddling against one another like a flock of sheep, crowded in the entry, Pierre pushed in front of them, and went up to the very captain who was, so the corporal had declared, ready to do anything for him. The captain was in marching trim, and from his face, too, there looked out the same 'it' Pierre had recognised in the corporal's words and in the roll of the drums.

'*Filez, filez!*' the captain was saying, frowning sternly, and looking at the prisoners crowding by him.

Pierre knew his effort would be in vain, yet he went up to him.

'Well, what is it?' said the officer, scanning him coldly, as though he did not recognise him. Pierre spoke of the sick prisoner.

'He can walk, damn him!' said the captain.

'*Filez, filez!*' he went on, without looking at Pierre.

'Well, no, he is in agony...!' Pierre was beginning.

'*Voulez-vous bien?*'... shouted the captain, scowling malignantly.

'Dram-da-da-dam, dam-dam,' rattled the drums, and Pierre knew that the mysterious force had already complete possession of those men, and that to say anything more now was useless.

The officers among the prisoners were separated from the soldiers and ordered to march in front.

The officers, among whom was Pierre, were thirty in number; the soldiers three hundred.

These officers, who had come out of other sheds, were all strangers to Pierre, and much better dressed than he was. They looked at him in his queer foot-gear with aloof and mistrustful eyes. Not far from Pierre walked a stout major, with a fat, sallow, irascible countenance. He was dressed in a Kazan gown, girt with a linen band, and obviously enjoyed the general respect of his companion prisoners. He held his tobacco-pouch in one hand thrust into his bosom; with the other he pressed the stem of his pipe. This major, panting and puffing, grumbled angrily at every one for pushing against him, as he fancied, and for hurrying when there was no need of hurry, and for wondering when there was nothing to wonder at. Another, a thin, little officer, addressed remarks to every one, making conjectures where they were being taken now, and how far they would go that day. An official, in felt high boots and a commissariat uniform, ran from side to side to get a good view of the results of the fire in Moscow, making loud observations on what was burnt, and saying what this or that district of the town was as it came into view. A third officer, of Polish extraction by his accent, was arguing with the commissariat official, trying to prove to him that he was mistaken in his identification of the various quarters of Moscow.

'Why dispute?' said the Major angrily. 'Whether it's St. Nikola or St. Vlas, it's no matter. You see that it's all burnt, and that's all about it. . . . Why are you pushing, isn't the road wide enough?' he said, angrily addressing a man who had passed behind him and had not pushed against him at all.

'Aie, aie, aie, what have they been doing?' the voices of the prisoners could be heard crying on one side and on another as they looked at the burnt districts. 'Zamoskvoryetche, too, and Zubovo, and in the Kremlin. . . . Look, there's not half left. Why, didn't I tell you all Zamoskvoryetche was gone, and so it is.'

'Well, you know it is burnt, well, why argue about it?' said the major.

Passing through Hamovniky (one of the few quarters of Moscow that had not been burnt) by the church, the whole crowd of prisoners huddled suddenly on one side, and exclamations of horror and aversion were heard.

'The wretches! The heathens! Yes; a dead man; a dead man; it is . . . They have smeared it with something.'

Pierre, too, drew near the church, where was the object that had called forth these exclamations, and he dimly discerned something leaning against the fence of the church enclosure. From the words of his companions, who saw better than he did, he learnt that it was the dead body of a man, propped up in a standing posture by the fence, with the face smeared with soot.

'Move on, damn you! Go on, thirty thousand devils!' . . . They heard the escort swearing, and the French soldiers, with fresh vindictiveness, used the flat sides of their swords to drive on the prisoners, who had lingered to look at the dead man.

XIV

THROUGH the lanes of Hamovniky, the prisoners marched alone with their escort, a train of carts and waggons, belonging to the soldiers of the escort, following behind them. But as they came out to the provision shops they found themselves in the middle of a huge train of artillery, moving with difficulty, and mixed up with private baggage-waggons.

At the bridge itself the whole mass halted, waiting for the foremost to get across. From the bridge the prisoners got a view of endless trains of baggage-waggons in front and behind. On the right, where the Kaluga road turns by Neskutchny Gardens, endless files of troops and waggons stretched away into the distance. These were the troops of Beauharnais's corps, which had set off before all the rest. Behind, along the riverside, and across Kamenny bridge, stretched the troops and transport of Ney's corps.

Davoust's troops, to which the prisoners belonged, were crossing by the Crimean Ford, and part had already entered Kaluga Street. But the baggage-trains were so long that the last waggons of Beauharnais's corps had not yet got out of Moscow into the Kaluga Street, while the vanguard of Ney's troops had already emerged from Bolshaya Ordynka.

After crossing the Crimean Ford, the prisoners moved a few steps at a time and then halted, and again moved forward, and the crowd of vehicles and people grew greater and greater on all sides. After taking over an hour in crossing the few hundred steps which separates the bridge from Kaluga Street and getting as far as the square where the Zamoskvoryetche streets run into Kaluga Street, the prisoners were jammed in a close block and kept standing for several hours at the cross roads. On all sides there was an unceasing sound, like the roar of the sea, of rumbling wheels, and tramping troops, and incessant shouts of anger and loud abuse. Pierre stood squeezed against the wall of a charred house, listening to that sound, which in his imagination melted off into the roll of drums.

Several of the Russian officers clambered up on to the wall of the burnt house by which Pierre stood so as to get a better view.

'The crowds! What crowds! . . . They have even loaded goods on the cannons! Look at the furs! . . .' they kept saying. 'I say, the vermin, they have been pillaging. . . . Look at what that one has got behind, on the cart. . . . Why, they are holy pictures, by God! . . . Those must be Germans. And a Russian peasant; by God! . . . Ah; the wretches! . . . See, how he's loaded; he can hardly move! Look, I say, chaises; they have got hold of them, too! . . . See, he has perched on the boxes. Heavens! . . . They have started fighting! . . . That's right; hit him in the face! We shan't get by before evening like this. Look, look! . . . Why that must surely be Napoleon himself. Do you see the horses! with the monograms and a crown! That's a portable house. He has dropped his sack, and doesn't see it. Fighting again. . . . A woman with a baby, and good-looking, too! Yes, I dare say; that's the way they will let you pass. . . . Look; why, there's no end to it. Russian wenches, I do declare they are. See how comfortable they are in the carriages!'

Again a wave of general curiosity, as at the church in Hamovniky, carried all the prisoners forward towards the road, and Pierre, thanks to his height, saw over the heads of the others what attracted the prisoners' curiosity. Three carriages were blocked between caissons, and in them a number of women with rouged faces, decked out in flaring colours, were sitting closely packed together, shouting something in shrill voices.

From the moment when Pierre had recognised the manifestation of that mysterious force, nothing seemed to him strange or terrible; not the corpse with its face blacked for a jest, not these women hurrying away, nor the burnt ruins of Moscow. All that Pierre saw now made hardly any impression on him—as though his soul, in preparation for a hard struggle, refused to receive any impression that might weaken it.

The carriages of women drove by. They were followed again by carts, soldiers, waggons, soldiers, carriages, soldiers, caissons, and again soldiers, and at rare intervals women.

Pierre did not see the people separately; he saw only their movement.

All these men and horses seemed, as it were, driven along by some unseen force. During the hour in which Pierre watched them they all were swept out of the different streets with the same one desire to get on as quickly as possible. All of them, alike hindered by the rest, began to get angry and to fight. The same oaths were bandied to and fro, and white teeth flashed, and every frowning face wore the same look of reckless determination and cold cruelty, which had struck Pierre in the morning in the corporal's face, while the drums were beating.

It was almost evening when the officer in command of their escort rallied his men, and with shouts and oaths forced his way in among the baggage-trains; and the prisoners, surrounded on all sides, came out on the Kaluga road.

They marched very quickly without pausing, and only halted when the sun was setting. The baggage-carts were moved up close to one another, and the men began to prepare for the night. Every one seemed ill-humoured and dissatisfied. Oaths, angry shouts, and fighting could be heard on all sides till a late hour. A carriage, which had been following the escort, had driven into one of their carts and run a shaft into it. Several soldiers ran up to the cart from different sides; some hit the carriage horses on the head as they turned them round, others were fighting among themselves, and Pierre saw one German seriously wounded by a blow from the flat side of a sword on his head.

It seemed as though now when they had come to a standstill in the midst of the open country, in the cold twilight of the autumn evening, all these men were experiencing the same feeling of unpleasant awakening from the hurry and eager impulse forward that had carried them all away at setting off. Now standing still, all as it were grasped that they knew not where they were going, and that there was much pain and hardship in store for them on the journey.

At this halting-place, the prisoners were even more roughly treated by their escort than at starting. They were for the first time given horse-flesh to eat.

In every one of the escort, from the officers to the lowest soldier, could be seen a sort of personal spite against every one of the prisoners, in surprising contrast with the friendly relations that had existed between them before.

This spite was increased when, on counting over the prisoners, it was discovered that in the bustle of getting out of Moscow one Russian soldier had managed to run away by pretending to be seized with colic. Pierre had seen a Frenchman beat a Russian soldier unmercifully for moving too far from the road, and heard the captain, who had been his friend, reprimanding an under-officer for the escape of the prisoner, and threatening him with court-martial. On the under-officer's urging that the prisoner was ill and could not walk, the officer said that their orders were to shoot those who should lag behind. Pierre felt that that fatal force which had crushed him at the execution, and had been imperceptible during his imprisonment, had now again the mastery of his existence. He was afraid; but he felt, too, that as that fatal force strove to crush him, there was growing up in his soul and gathering strength a force of life that was independent of it. Pierre supped on soup made of rye flour and horseflesh, and talked a little with his companions.

Neither Pierre nor any of his companions talked of what they had seen in Moscow, nor of the harsh treatment they received from the French, nor of the orders to shoot them, which had been announced to them. As though in reaction against their more depressing position, all were particularly gay and lively. They talked of personal reminiscences, of amusing incidents they had seen as they marched, and avoided touching on their present position.

The sun had long ago set. Stars were shining brightly here and there in the sky; there was a red flush, as of a conflagration on the horizon, where the full moon was rising, and the vast, red ball seemed trembling strangely in the grey darkness. It became quite light. The evening was over, but the night had not yet begun. Pierre left his new companions and walked between the camp-fires to the other side of the road, where he had been told that the common prisoners were camping. He wanted to talk to them. On the road a French sentinel stopped him and bade him go back.

Pierre did go back, but not to the camp-fire where his companions were, but to an unharnessed waggon where there was nobody. Tucking his legs up under him, and dropping his head, he sat down on the cold ground against the waggon wheel, and sat there a long while motionless, thinking. More than an hour passed by. No one disturbed Pierre. Suddenly he burst into such a loud roar of his fat, good-humoured laughter, that men looked round on every side in astonishment at this strange and obviously solitary laughter. 'Ha, ha, ha!' laughed Pierre. And he talked aloud to himself. 'The soldier did not let me pass. They have taken me—shut me up. They keep me prisoner. Who is "me"? Me? Me—my immortal soul! Ha, ha, ha! . . . Ha, ha, ha! . . .' he laughed, with the tears starting into his eyes.

A man got up and came to see what this strange, big man was laughing at all by himself. Pierre left off laughing, got up, walked away from the inquisitive intruder, and looked about him.

The immense, endless bivouac, which had been full of the sound of crackling fires and men talking, had sunk to rest; the red camp-fires burnt low and dim. High overhead in the lucid sky stood the full moon. Forests and fields, that before could not be seen beyond the camp, came into view now in the distance. And beyond those fields and forests could be seen the bright, shifting, alluring, boundless distance. Pierre glanced at the sky, at the far-away, twinkling stars. 'And all that is mine, and all that is in me, and all that is I!' thought Pierre. 'And all this they caught and shut up in a shed closed in with boards!' He smiled and went to lie down to sleep beside his companions.

XV

EARLY in October another messenger came to Kutuzov from Napoleon with overtures for peace and a letter, falsely professing to come from Moscow, though Napoleon was in fact not far ahead of Kutuzov on the old Kaluga road. Kutuzov answered this letter as he had done the first one, brought him by Lauriston; he said that there could be no question of peace.

Soon after this Dorohov's irregulars, which were moving on the left of Tarutino, sent a report that French troops had appeared at Fominskoe, that these troops were of Broussier's division, and that that division, being separate from the rest of the army, might easily be cut to pieces. The soldiers and officers again clamoured for action. The staff generals, elated by the easy victory of Tarutino, urged on Kutuzov that Dorohov's suggestion should be acted upon.

Kutuzov did not consider any action necessary. A middle course, as was inevitable, was adopted; a small detachment was sent to Fominskoe to attack Broussier.

By strange chance this appointment, a most difficult and most important one, as it turned out to be later, was given to Dohturov, that modest little general, whom no one has depicted to us making plans of campaign, dashing at the head of regiments, dropping crosses about batteries, or doing anything of the kind; whom people looked on and spoke of as lacking decision and penetration, though all through the Russian wars with the French, from Austerlitz to the year 1813, we always find him in command where the position is particularly difficult. At Austerlitz he was the last to remain at the ford of Augest, rallying the regiments, saving what he could, when all was flight and ruin, and not a single other general was to be found in the rearguard. When ill with fever, he marched with twenty thousand men to Smolensk to defend the town against the whole of Napoleon's army. In Smolensk he had only just fallen asleep at the Malahovsky gates in a paroxysm of fever when he was waked by the cannonade of Smolensk, and Smolensk held out a whole day. At Borodino when Bagration was killed, and nine-tenths of the men of our left flank had been slain, and the fire of all the French artillery was turned upon it, Kutuzov made haste to recall another general he had sent by mistake, and sent there no other than Dohturov, who was said to be lacking in decision and penetration.

And unpretentious little Dohturov went there, and Borodino became the greatest glory of the Russian arms. And many of its heroes have been celebrated in prose and verse, but of Dohturov hardly a word. Again Dohturov was sent to Fominskoe, and from there to Maley Yaroslavets, the place where the last battle was fought with the French, and where it is plain the final destruction of the French army really begun. And again many heroes and men of genius are described to us in accounts of this period of the campaign, but of Dohturov nothing is said, or but few words of dubious praise. This silence in regard to Dohturov is the plainest testimony to his merits.

It is natural that a man who does not understand the working of a machine should suppose, when he sees it in action, that a shaving that has fallen into it by chance, and flaps about in it, hindering its progress, is the most important part of the mechanism. Any one who does not understand the construction of the machine cannot conceive that this shaving is only clogging and spoiling it, while the little cog-wheel, which turns noiselessly, is one of the most essential parts of the machine.

On the 10th of October Dohturov had marched half-way to Fominskoe, and halted at the village of Aristovo, making every preparation for exactly carrying out the orders given him. On the same day the whole French army, after reaching in its spasmodic rush as far as Murat's position, seemingly with the object of giving battle, suddenly, with no apparent cause, turned off to the left to the new Kaluga road, and began marching into Fominskoe, where Broussier had before been alone. Dohturov had under his command at the time only Dorohov's troops and the two small detachments of Figner and Seslavin.

On the evening of the 11th of October, Seslavin came to the general at Aristovo with a French prisoner of the Guards. The prisoner said that the troops that had reached Fominskoe that day were the advance guard of the whole army; that Napoleon was with them; that the whole army had marched out of Moscow five days before. The same evening a house-serf coming from Borovsk brought word that he had seen an immense army entering that town. Dorohov's Cossacks reported that they had seen the French guards marching along the road to Borovsk. From all this it was evident that where they had expected to find one division there was now the whole army of the French, marching from Moscow in an unexpected direction—along the old Kaluga road. Dohturov was unwilling to take any action, as it was not clear to him now where his duty lay. He had received instructions to attack Fominskoe. But there had then been only Broussier at Fominskoe, and now the whole French army was there. Yermolov wanted to act on his own judgment, but Dohturov insisted that he must have instructions from his highness the commander-in-chief. It was resolved to send a report to the staff.

For this purpose they chose a capable officer, Bolhovitinov, who was to take a written report, and to explain the whole matter verbally. At midnight Bolhovitinov received his despatch and his verbal instructions, and galloped off to headquarters, accompanied by a Cossack with spare horses.

XVI

IT was a dark, warm autumn night. Rain had been falling for the last four days. Changing horses twice, Bolhovitinov galloped in an hour and a half thirty versts over a muddy, slippery road. He reached Letashevko after one o'clock in the night. Dismounting at a hut, on the hurdle fence of which was the inscription 'Headquarters of the Staff,' and letting his horse go, he walked into the dark entry.

'The general on duty at once! Very important!' he cried to some one, who jumped up, wheezing in the darkness.

'His honour has been very unwell since the evening; he has not slept for three nights,' an orderly's voice whispered, interposing. 'You must wake the captain first.'

'Very important from General Dohturov,' said Bolhovitinov, feeling for the opened door and going in.

The orderly went in before him, and began waking some one up. 'Your honour, your honour, a courier.'

'What? what? from whom?' said a sleepy voice.

'From Dohturov and from Alexey Petrovitch. Napoleon is at Fominskoe,' said Bolhovitinov, not seeing the speaker in the darkness, but assuming from the voice that it was not Konovnitsyn.

The man who had been waked yawned and stretched. 'I don't want to wake him,' he said, fumbling for something. 'He's ill! Perhaps it's only a rumour.'

'Here is the report,' said Bolhovitinov. 'My instructions are to give it at once to the general on duty.'

'Wait a minute, I'll strike a light. What do you do with things, damn you!' said the sleepy voice addressing the orderly. The speaker was Shtcherbinin, Konovnitsyn's adjutant. 'I have found it, I have found it,' he added.

The orderly struck a light, Shtcherbinin felt for a candlestick.

'Ah, the nasty beasts!' he said with disgust.

By the light of the sparks in the tinderbox Bolhovitinov had a glimpse of Shtcherbinin's youthful face, and in a corner another man asleep. This was Konovnitsyn.

When the tinder broke first into a blue and then into a red flame, Shtcherbinin lighted a tallow candle—the cockroaches that had been gnawing it ran away in all directions—and looked at the messenger. Bolhovitinov was bespattered all over, and on rubbing his face with his sleeve, had smudged that too with mud.

'But who sends the report?' said Shtcherbinin, taking the packet.

'The news is certain,' said Bolhovitinov. 'Prisoners and Cossacks and spies, all tell the same story.'

'Well there's no help for it, we must wake him,' said Shtcherbinin, getting up and going to the sleeping man who wore a nightcap and was covered up with a military cloak. 'Pyotr Petrovitch!' he said. Konovnitsyn did not stir. 'Wanted at headquarters!' he said with a smile, knowing these words would be sure to wake him. And the head in the nightcap was in fact lifted at once. Konovnitsyn's strong, handsome face, with feverishly swollen cheeks, still wore for an instant a far-away, dreamy look, but he gave a sudden start and his face resumed its customary expression of calmness and strength.

'Well, what is it? From whom?' he asked at once, but with no haste, blinking at the light. Hearing what the officer had to tell him, Konovnitsyn broke open the packet and read it. He had hardly read it before he dropped his feet in worsted stockings on to the earth floor and began putting on his boots. Then he took off the nightcap, and combing his hair, put on a forage cap.

'Did you get here quickly? Let us go to his highness.'

Konovnitsyn understood at once that the news was of great importance, and that they must lose no time. As to whether it were good news or bad, he had no opinion and did not even put the question to himself. That did not interest him. He looked at the whole subject of the war, not with his intellect, not with his reason, but with something different. In his heart he had a deep, unaltered conviction that all would be well, yet that he ought not to believe in this, and still more ought not to say so, but ought simply to do his duty. And that he did do, giving all his energies to it.

Pyotr Petrovitch Konovnitsyn, like Dohturov, is simply as a formality included in the list of the so-called heroes of 1812 with the Barclays, Raevskys, Yermolovs, Platovs and Miloradovitchs. Like Dohturov, he had the reputation of being a man of very limited capacities and information; and, like Dohturov, he never proposed plans of campaign, but was always to be found in the most difficult position. Ever since he had been appointed the general on duty, he had slept with his door open, and given orders to be waked on the arrival of any messenger. In battle he was always under fire, so that Kutuzov even reproached him for it, and was afraid to send him to the front. Like Dohturov, he was one of those inconspicuous cogwheels, which, moving without creaking or rattling, make up the most essential part of the machine.

Coming out of the hut into the damp, dark night, Konovnitsyn frowned, partly from his headache getting worse, and partly from the disagreeable thought that occurred to him of the stir this would make in all the nest of influential persons on the staff; of its effect on Bennigsen in particular, who since the battle of Tarutino had been at daggers drawn with Kutuzov; of the suppositions and discussions and orders and counter orders. And the presentiment of all that was disagreeable to him, though he knew it to be inevitable.

Toll, to whom he went to communicate the news, did in fact begin at once expounding his views on the situation to the general who shared his abode; and Konovnitsyn, after listening in weary silence, reminded him that they must go to his highness.

XVII

LIKE all old people, Kutuzov slept little at night. He often dropped into sudden naps during the daytime, but at night he lay on his bed without undressing, and generally not asleep but thinking.

He was lying like that now on his bedstead, his huge, heavy, misshapen head leaning on his fat hand. He was thinking with his one eye wide open, gazing into the darkness.

Since Bennigsen, who was in correspondence with the Tsar and had more weight than all the rest of the staff, had avoided him, Kutuzov was more at ease so far as not being compelled to lead his soldiers into useless offensive operations. The lesson of Tarutino and the day before the battle, a memory that rankled in Kutuzov's mind, must, he thought, have its effect on them too.

'They ought to understand that we can but lose by taking the offensive. Time and patience, these are my champions!' thought Kutuzov. He knew the apple must not be picked while it was green. It will fall of itself when ripe, but if you pick it green, you spoil the apple and the tree and set your teeth on edge. Like an experienced hunter, he knew the beast was wounded, wounded as only the whole force of Russia could wound it; but whether to death or not, was a question not yet solved. Now from the sending of Lauriston and Bertemy, and from the reports brought by the irregulars, Kutuzov was almost sure that the wound was a deadly one. But more proof was wanted; he must wait.

'They want to run and look how they have wounded him. Wait a bit, you will see. Always manœuvres, attacks,' he thought. 'What for? Anything to distinguish themselves. As though there were any fun in fighting. They are like children from whom you can never get a sensible view of things because they all want to show how well they can fight. But that's not the point now. And what skilful manœuvres all these fellows propose! They think that when they have thought of two or three contingencies (he recalled the general plan from Petersburg) that they have thought of all of them. And there is no limit to them!'

The unanswered question, whether the wound dealt at Borodino were mortal or not, had been for a whole month hanging over Kutuzov's head. On one side, the French had taken possession of Moscow. On the other side, in all his being, Kutuzov felt beyond all doubt that the terrible blow for which, together with all the Russians, he had strained all his strength must have been mortal. But in any case proofs were wanted, and he had been waiting for them now a month, and as time went on he grew more impatient. As he lay on his bed through sleepless nights, he did the very thing these younger generals did, the very thing he found fault with in them. He imagined all possible contingencies, just like the younger generation, but with this difference that he based no conclusion on these suppositions, and that he saw these contingencies not as two or three, but as thousands. The more he pondered, the more of them he saw. He imagined all sorts of movements of Napoleon's army, acting as a whole or in part, on Petersburg, against him, to out-flank him (that was what he was most afraid of), and also the possibility that Napoleon would fight against him with his own weapon, that he would stay on in Moscow waiting for him to move. Kutuzov even imagined Napoleon's army marching back to Medyn and Yuhnov. But the one thing he could not foresee was what happened—the mad, convulsive stampede of Napoleon's army during the first eleven days of its march from Moscow—the stampede that made possible what Kutuzov did not yet dare to think about, the complete annihilation of the French. Dorohov's report of Broussier's division, the news brought by the irregulars of the miseries of Napoleon's army, rumours of preparations for leaving Moscow, all confirmed the supposition that the French army was beaten and preparing to take flight. But all this was merely supposition, that seemed of weight to the younger men, but not to Kutuzov. With his sixty years' experience he knew how much weight to attach to rumours; he knew how ready men are when they desire anything to manipulate all evidence so as to confirm what they desire; and he knew how readily in that case they let everything of an opposite significance pass unheeded. And the more

Kutuzov desired this supposition to be correct, the less he permitted himself to believe it. This question absorbed all his spiritual energies. All the rest was for him the mere customary performance of the routine of life. Such a customary performance and observance of routine were his conversations with the staff-officers, his letters to Madame de Staël that he wrote from Tarutino, his French novels, distribution of rewards, correspondence with Petersburg, and so on. But the destruction of the French, which he alone foresaw, was the one absorbing desire of his heart.

On the night of the 11th of October he lay leaning on his arm and thinking of that.

There was a stir in the next room, and he heard the steps of Toll, Konovnitsyn and Bolhovitinov.

'Hey, who is there? Come in, come in! Anything new?' the commander-in-chief called to them.

While a footman lighted a candle, Toll told the drift of the news.

'Who brought it?' asked Kutuzov, with a face that impressed Toll when the candle was lighted by its frigid sternness.

'There can be no doubt of it, your highness.'

'Call him, call him here!'

Kutuzov sat with one leg out of bed and his unwieldy, corpulent body propped on the other leg bent under him. He screwed up his one seeing eye to get a better view of the messenger, as though he hoped in his face to read what he cared to know.

'Tell me, tell me, my dear fellow,' he said to Bolhovitinov, in his low, aged voice, pulling the shirt together that had come open over his chest. 'Come here, come closer. What news is this you have brought me? Eh? Napoleon has marched out of Moscow? Is it truly so? Eh?'

Bolhovitinov began repeating in detail the message that had been given him.

'Tell me, make haste, don't torture me,' Kutuzov interrupted him.

Bolhovitinov told him all and paused, awaiting instructions. Toll was beginning to speak, but Kutuzov checked him. He tried to say something, but all at once his face began to work, to pucker; waving his hand at Toll, he turned the other way to the corner of the hut, which looked black with the holy pictures. 'Lord, my Creator! Thou hast heard our prayer . . .' he said in a trembling voice, clasping his hands. 'Russia is saved. I thank Thee, O Lord.' And he burst into tears.

XVIII

FROM that time up to the end of the campaign, all Kutuzov's activity was limited to trying by the exercise of authority, by guile and by entreaties, to hold his army back from useless attacks, manœuvres, and skirmishes with the perishing enemy. Dohturov marched to Maley Yaroslavets, but Kutuzov lingered with the main army, and gave orders for the clearing of the Kaluga, retreat beyond which seemed to Kutuzov quite possible.

Everywhere Kutuzov retreated, but the enemy, without waiting for him to retire, fled back in the opposite direction.

Napoleon's historians describe to us his skilful manœuvres at Tarutino, and at Maley Yaroslavets, and discuss what would have happened if Napoleon had succeeded in making his way to the wealthy provinces of the south.

But to say nothing of the fact that nothing hindered Napoleon from marching into these southern provinces (since the Russian army left the road open), the historians forget that nothing could have saved Napoleon's army, because it carried within itself at that time the inevitable germs of ruin. Why should that army, which found abundant provisions in Moscow and could not keep them, but trampled them underfoot, that army which could not store supplies on entering Smolensk, but plundered at randon, why should that army have mended its ways in the Kaluga province, where the inhabitants were of the same Russian race as in Moscow, and where fire had the same aptitude for destroying whatever they set fire to.

The army could not have recovered itself any way. From the battle of Borodino and the sacking of Moscow it bore within itself, as it were, the chemical elements of dissolution.

The men of what had been an army fled with their leaders, not knowing whither they went, Napoleon and every soldier with him filled with one desire: to make his own escape as quickly as might be from the hopeless position of which all were dimly aware.

At the council in Maley Yaroslavets, when the French generals, affecting to be deliberating, gave various opinions as to what was to be done, the opinion of the blunt soldier, Mouton, who said what all were thinking, that the only thing to do was to get away as quick as possible, closed every one's mouth; and no one, not even Napoleon, could say anything in opposition to this truth that all recognised.

But though everybody knew that they must go, there was still a feeling of shame left at acknowledging they must fly. And some external shock was necessary to overcome that shame. And that shock came when it was needed. It was *le Hourra de l'Empereur*, as the French called it.

On the day after the council, Napoleon, on the pretext of inspecting the troops and the field of a past and of a future battle, rode out early in the morning in the midst of the lines of his army with a suite of marshals and an escort. The Cossacks, who were in search of booty, swept down on the Emperor, and all but took him prisoner. What saved Napoleon from the Cossacks that day was just what was the ruin of the French army, the booty, which here as well as at Tarutino tempted the Cossacks to let their prey slip. Without taking any notice of Napoleon, they dashed at the booty, and Napoleon succeeded in getting away.

When *les enfants du Don* might positively capture the Emperor himself in the middle of his army, it was evident that there was nothing else to do but to fly with all possible haste by the nearest and the familiar road. Napoleon, with his forty years and his corpulence, had not all his old resourcefulness and courage, and he quite took the hint; and under the influence of the fright the Cossacks had given him, he agreed at once with Mouton, and gave, as the historians tell us, the order to retreat along the Smolensk road.

The fact that Napoleon agreed with Mouton, and that the army did not retreat in that direction, does not prove that his command decided that retreat, but that the forces acting on the whole army and driving it along the Mozhaisk road were simultaneously acting upon Napoleon too.

XIX

WHEN a man finds himself in movement, he always invents a goal of that movement. In order to walk a thousand versts, a man must believe that there is some good beyond those thousand versts. He needs a vision of a promised land to have the strength to go on moving. The promised land for the French on their march into Russia was Moscow; on their retreat it was their own country. But their country was too far; and a man walking a thousand versts must inevitably put aside his final goal and say to himself every day that he is going to walk forty versts to a resting-place where he can sleep; and before the first halt that resting-place has eclipsed the image of the final goal, and all his hopes and desires are concentrated on it. All impulses manifest in the individual are always greatly exaggerated in a crowd.

For the French, marching back along the old Smolensk road, the final goal, their own country, was too remote, and the nearer goal on which all hopes and desires, enormously intensified by the influence of the crowd, were concentrated, was Smolensk.

It was not because the soldiers knew that there were plentiful supplies in Smolensk and reinforcements, nor because they were told so (on the contrary, the generals and Napoleon himself knew that the supplies there were scanty), but because this was the only thing that could give them the strength to move and to bear their present hardships, that they—those that knew better and those that did not alike—deceived themselves, and rushed to Smolensk as to a land of promise.

When they got out on the high road, the French fled to their imagined goal with extraordinary energy and unheard-of rapidity. Apart from the common impulse that bound the crowds of Frenchmen together into one whole and gave them a certain momentum, there was another cause that held them together, that cause was their immense number. As in the physical law of gravitation, the immense mass of them drew the separate atoms to itself. They moved in their mass of hundreds of thousands like a whole state.

Every man among them longed for one thing only—to surrender and be taken prisoner, to escape from all the horrors and miseries of his actual position. But on one hand the momentum of the common impulse towards Smolensk drew each individual in the same direction. On the other hand, it was out of the question for a corps to surrender to a squadron; and although the French took advantage of every convenient opportunity to straggle away from one another, and on the smallest decent pretext to be taken prisoners, those opportunities did not always occur. Their very number, and their rapid movement in such a closely-packed mass, deprived them of such possibilities, and made it not only difficult but impossible for the Russians to stop that movement into which the whole energy of that great mass was thrown. No mechanical splitting up of the body could accelerate beyond certain limits the process of dissolution that was going on within it.

A snowball cannot be melted instantaneously. There is a certain limit of time within which no application of heat can thaw the snow. On the contrary, the greater the heat, the harder the snow that is left.

Of the Russian generals no one but Kutuzov understood this. When the flight of the French army took its final direction along the Smolensk road, then what Kutuzov had foreseen on the night of the 11th of October began to come to pass. All the generals and officers of the Russian army were eager to distinguish themselves, to cut off the enemy's retreat, to overtake, to capture, to fall upon the French, and all clamoured for action.

Kutuzov alone used all his powers (and the powers of any commander-in-chief are far from great) to resist this clamour for attack.

He could not tell them what we can say now: he could not ask them what was the object of fighting and obstructing the road and losing our men, and inhumanely persecuting the poor wretches, when one-third of that army melted away of itself without a battle between Moscow and Vyazma. But drawing from the stores of his aged wisdom what they could understand, he told them of the golden bridge, and they laughed at him, slandered him, pushed on and dashed forward, exulting over the wounded beast.

Near Vyazma, Yermolov, Miloradovitch, Platov, and others, finding themselves in the neighbourhood of the French, could not resist the desire to cut them off and to fall upon two French corps. In sending to inform Kutuzov of their project, they slipped a blank sheet of paper into the envelope instead of the despatch.

And in spite of Kutuzov's efforts to restrain the army, our soldiers attacked the French and tried to bar their way. The infantry regiments, we are told, marched to attack them with music and beating of drums, and slew and were slain by thousands.

But as for cutting off their retreat—none were cut off nor turned aside. And the French army, brought into closer cohesion by danger, and slowly melting as it went, kept still on its fatal way to Smolensk.

PART XIV

I

THE BATTLE of Borodino with the occupation of Moscow and the flight of the French, that followed without any more battles, is one of the most instructive phenomena in history.

All historians are agreed that the external activity of states and peoples in their conflicts finds expression in wars; that the political power of states and peoples is increased or diminished as the immediate result of success or defeat in war.

Strange are the historical accounts that tell us how some king or emperor, quarrelling with another king or emperor, levies an army, fights a battle with the army of his foe, gains a victory, kills three, five, or ten thousand men, and consequently subdues a state and a whole people consisting of several millions; and incomprehensible it seems that the defeat of an army, one hundredth of the whole strength of a people, should force that people to submit. Yet all the facts of history (so far as we know it) confirm the truth of the statement, that the successes or defeats of a nation's army are the causes or, at least, the invariable symptoms of the increase or diminution of the power of a nation. An army gains a victory, and immediately the claims of the conquering people are increased to the detriment of the conquered. An army is defeated, and at once the people loses its rights in proportion to the magnitude of the defeat; and if its army is utterly defeated, the people is completely conquered. So (according to history) it has been from the most ancient times up to the present. All Napoleon's earlier wars serve as illustrations of the rule. As the Austrian armies were defeated, Austria was deprived of her rights, and the rights and power of France were increased. The victories of the French at Jena and at Auerstadt destroyed the independent existence of Prussia.

But suddenly, in 1812, the French gained a victory before Moscow. Moscow was taken, and in consequence of that, with no subsequent battles, not Russia, but the French army of six hundred thousand, and then Napoleonic France itself ceased to exist. To strain the facts to fit the rules of history, to maintain that the field of Borodino was left in the hands of the Russians, or that after the evacuation of Moscow, there were battles that destroyed Napoleon's army—is impossible.

After the victory of the French at Borodino, there was no general engagement, nor even a skirmish of any great importance, yet the French army ceased to exist. What is the meaning of it? If it had been an example from the history of China, we could have said it was not an historical fact (the resource of historians, when anything will not fit in with their rules). If it had occurred in a conflict on a small scale, in which only small numbers of soldiers had taken part, we might have looked upon it as an exception. But all this took place before the eyes of our fathers, for whom it was a question of life and death for their country; and the war was on a larger scale than any wars we know of.

The sequel of the campaign of 1812—from Borodino to the final expulsion of the French—has proved that victories are not always a cause nor even an invariable sign of conquest; it has proved that the force that decides the fate of peoples does not lie in military leaders, nor even in armies and battles, but in something else.

The French historians, who describe the position of the French troops before they marched out of Moscow, assert that everything was in good order in the Grande Armee, except the cavalry, the artillery, and the transport, and that there was no forage for the horses and cattle. There was no remedy for this defect, because the peasants of the surrounding country burned their hay rather than let the French have it.

Victory did not bring forth its usual results, because the peasants, Karp and Vlas, by no means persons of heroic feelings (after the French evacuation, they hurried with their carts to pillage Moscow), and the immense multitude of others like them burnt their hay rather than bring it to Moscow, however high the prices offered them.

Let us imagine two men, who have come out to fight a duel with swords in accordance with all the rules of the art of swordsmanship. The fencing has lasted for some time. All at once one of the combatants, feeling that he is wounded, grasping that it is no joking matter, but a question of life and death, flings away his sword, and snatching up the first cudgel that comes handy, begins to brandish that. But let us imagine that the combatant, who has so sensibly made use of the best and simplest means for the attainment of his object, should be inspired by the traditions of chivalry to try and disguise the real cause of the conflict and should persist in declaring that he had been victor in the duel in accordance with all the rules of swordsmanship. One can imagine what confusion and obscurity would arise from his description of the duel!

The duellist, who insisted on the conflict being fought in accordance with the principles of the fencer's art, stands for the French; his opponent, who flung away his sword and snatched up a cudgel, did like the Russians; and the attempted description of the duel in accordance with the rules of swordsmanship has been given us by the historians of the war.

From the time of the burning of Smolensk a war began which did not follow any of the old traditions of warfare. The burning of towns and villages, the retreat after every battle, the blow dealt at Borodino and followed by retreat, the burning of Moscow, the capture of marauders, the seizing of transports,—the whole of the irregular warfare was a departure from the rules.

Napoleon was aware of it, and from the time when he stood waiting in Moscow in the correct pose of the victorious fencer, and instead of his opponent's sword, saw the bludgeon raised against him, he never ceased complaining to Kutuzov and to the Emperor Alexander that the war was being conducted contrary to all the rules of war. (As though any rules existed for the slaughter of men!)

In spite of the complaints of the French that they did not keep to the rules, in spite of the fact that the Russians in the highest positions felt it somehow shameful to be fighting with a cudgel, and wanted to take up the correct position *en quarte* or *en tierce*, to make a skilful thrust, *en prime* and so on, the cudgel of the people's war was raised in all its menacing and majestic power; and troubling itself about no question of any one's tastes or rules, about no fine distinctions, with stupid simplicity, with perfect consistency, it rose and fell and belaboured the French till the whole invading army had been driven out.

And happy the people that will not, as the French did in 1813, saluting according to the rules, gracefully and cautiously offer the sword hilt to the magnanimous conqueror. Happy the people who, in the moment of trial, asks no questions how others would act by the recognised rules in such cases, but with ease and directness picks up the first cudgel that comes handy and deals blows with it, till resentment and revenge give way to contempt and pity.

II

ONE of the most conspicuous and advantageous departures from the so-called rules of warfare is the independent action of men acting separately against men huddled together in a mass. Such independent activity is always seen in a war that assumes a national character. In this kind of warfare, instead of forming in a crowd to attack a crowd, men disperse in small groups, attack singly and at once fly, when attacked by superior forces, and then attack again, when an opportunity presents itself. Such were the methods of the guerillas in Spain; of the mountain tribes in the Caucasus, and of the Russians in 1812.

War of this kind has been called partisan warfare on the supposition that this name defined its special significance. But this kind of warfare does not follow any rules of war, but is in direct contradiction to a well-known rule of tactics, regarded as infallible. That rule lays it down that the attacking party must concentrate his forces in order to be stronger than his opponent at the moment of conflict.

Partisan warfare (always successful, as history testifies) acts in direct contradiction of this rule.

Military science assumes that the relative strength of forces is identical with their numerical proportions. Military science maintains that the greater the number of soldiers, the greater their strength. *Les gros bataillons ont toujours raison.*

To say this is as though one were in mechanics to say that forces were equal or unequal simply because the masses of the moving bodies were equal or unequal.

Force (the volume of motion) is the product of the mass into the velocity.

In warfare the force of armies is the product of the mass multiplied by something else, an unknown x.

Military science, seeing in history an immense number of examples in which the mass of an army does not correspond with its force, and in which small numbers conquer large ones, vaguely recognise the existence of this unknown factor, and try to find it sometimes in some geometrical disposition of the troops, sometimes in the superiority of weapons, and most often in the genius of the leaders. But none of those factors yield results that agree with the historical facts.

One has but to renounce the false view that glorifies the effect of the activity of the heroes of history in warfare in order to discover this unknown quantity, x.

X is the spirit of the army, the greater or less desire to fight and to face dangers on the part of all the men composing the army, which is quite apart from the question whether they are fighting under leaders of genius or not, with cudgels or with guns that fire thirty times a minute. The men who have the greater desire to fight always put themselves, too, in the more advantageous position for fighting. The spirit of the army is the factor which multiplied by the mass gives the product of the force. To define and express the significance of this unknown factor, the spirit of the army, is the problem of science.

This problem can only be solved when we cease arbitrarily substituting for that unknown factor *x* the conditions under which the force is manifested, such as the plans of the general, the arming of the men and so on, and recognise this unknown factor in its entirety as the greater or less desire to fight and face danger. Then only by expressing known historical facts in equations can one hope from comparison of the relative value of this unknown factor to approach its definition. Ten men, or battalions or divisions are victorious fighting with fifteen men or battalions or divisions, that is, they kill or take prisoner all of them while losing four of their own side, so that the loss has been four on one side and fifteen on the other. Consequently, four of one side have been equivalent to fifteen on the other, and consequently $4x = 15y$. Consequently $\frac{z}{y} \frac{15}{4}$. This equation does not give us the value of the unknown factors, but it does give us the ratio between their values. And from the reduction to such equations of various historical units (battles, campaigns, periods of warfare) a series of numbers are obtained, in which there must be and may be discovered historical laws.

The strategic principle, that armies should act in masses on the offensive, and should break up into smaller groups for retreat, unconsciously confirms the truth that the force of an army depends on its spirit. To lead men forward under fire needs more discipline (which can only be attained by marching in masses) than is needed for self-defence when attacked. But this rule, which leaves out of sight the spirit of the army, is continually proving unsound, and is strikingly untrue in practice in all national wars, when there is a great rise or fall in the spirit of the armies.

The French, on their retreat in 1812, though they should, by the laws of tactics, have defended themselves in detached groups, huddled together in a crowd, because the spirit of the men had sunk so low that it was only their number that kept them up. The Russians should, on the contrary, by the laws of tactics, have attacked them in a mass, but in fact attacked in scattered companies, because the spirit of the men ran so high that individual men killed the French without orders, and needed no compulsion to face hardships and dangers.

III

THE so-called 'partisan' warfare had begun with the enemy's entrance into Smolensk. Before the irregular warfare was officially recognised by our government many thousands of the enemy's soldiers—straggling, marauding, or foraging parties—had been slain by Cossacks and peasants, who killed these men as instinctively as dogs set upon a stray mad dog. Denis Davydov was the first to feel with his Russian instinct the value of this terrible cudgel which belaboured the French, and asked no questions about the etiquette of the military art; and to him belongs the credit of the first step toward the recognition of this method of warfare.

The first detachment of irregulars—Davydov's—was formed on the 24th of August, and others soon followed. In the latter stages of the campaign these detachments became more and more numerous.

The irregulars destroyed the Grande Armee piecemeal. They swept up the fallen leaves that were dropping of themselves from the withered tree, and sometimes they shook the tree itself. By October, when the French were fleeing to Smolensk, there were hundreds of these companies, differing widely from one another in number and in character. Some were detachments that followed all the usual routine of an army, with infantry, artillery, staff-officers, and all the conveniences of life. Some consisted only of Cossacks, mounted men. Others were small bands of men, on foot and also mounted. Some consisted of peasants, or of landowners and their serfs, and remained unknown. There was a deacon at the head of such a band, who took several hundred prisoners in a month. There was the village elder's wife, Vassilisa, who killed hundreds of the French.

The latter part of October was the time when this guerilla warfare reached its height. That period of this warfare, in which the irregulars were themselves amazed at their own audacity, were every moment in dread of being surrounded and captured by the French, and never unsaddling, hardly dismounting, hid in the woods, in momentary expectation of pursuit, was already over. The irregular warfare had by now taken definite shape; it had become clear to all the irregulars what they could, and what they could not, accomplish with the French. By now it was only the commanders of detachments marching with staff-officers according to the rules at a distance from the French who considered much impossible. The small bands of irregulars who had been at work a long while, and were at close quarters with the French, found it possible to attempt what the leaders of larger companies did not dare to think of doing. The Cossacks and the peasants, who crept in among the French, thought everything possible now.

On the 22nd of October, Denisov, who was a leader of a band of irregulars, was eagerly engaged in a typical operation of this irregular warfare. From early morning he had been with his men moving about the woods that bordered the high road, watching a big convoy of cavalry ggage and Russian prisoners that had dropped behind the other French troops, and under strong escort—as he learned from his scouts and from prisoners—was making its way to Smolensk. Not only Denisov and Dolohov (who was also a leader of a small band acting in the same district) were aware of the presence of this convoy. Some generals in command of some larger detachments, with staff-officers also, knew of this convoy, and, as Denisov said, their mouths were watering for it. Two of these generals—one a Pole, the other a German—had almost at the same time sent to Denisov an invitation to join their respective detachments in attacking the convoy.

'No, friend, I wasn't born yesterday!' said Denisov, on reading these documents; and he wrote to the German that in spite of his ardent desire to serve under so brilliant and renowned a general, he must deprive himself of that happiness because he was already under the command of the Polish general. To the Pole he wrote the same thing, informing him that he was already serving under the command of the German.

Having thus disposed of that difficulty, Denisov, without communicating on the subject to the higher authorities, intended with Dolohov to attack and carry off this transport with his own small force. The transport was, on the 22nd of October, going from the village of Mikulino to the village of Shamshevo. On the left side of the road between Mikulino and Shamshevo there were great woods, which in places bordered on the road, and in places were a verst or more from the road. Denisov, with a small party of followers, had been the whole day riding about in these woods, sometimes plunging into their centre, and sometimes coming out at the edge, but never losing sight of the moving French. In the morning, not far from Mikulino, where the wood ran close to the road, the Cossacks of Denisov's party had pounced on two French waggonloads of saddles, stuck in the mud, and had carried them off into the wood. From that time right on to evening, they had been watching the movements of the French without attacking them. They wanted to avoid frightening them, and to let them go quietly on to Shamshevo, and then, joining Dolohov (who was to come that evening to a trysting-place in the wood, a verst from Shamshevo, to concert measures with them), from two sides to fall at dawn like an avalanche of snow on their heads, and to overcome and capture all of them at a blow.

Six Cossacks had been left behind, two versts from Mikulino, where the wood bordered the road. They were to bring word at once as soon as any fresh columns of French came into sight.

In front of Shamshevo, Dolohov was in the same way to watch the road to know at what distance there were other French troops. With the transport there was supposed to be fifteen hundred men. Denisov had two hundred men, and Dolohov might have as many more. But superiority in numbers was no obstacle to Denisov. There was only one thing that he still needed to know, and that was what troops these were; and for that object Denisov needed to take a 'tongue' (that is, some man belonging to that column of the enemy). The attack on the waggons in the morning was all done with such haste that they killed all the French soldiers in charge of the waggons, and captured alive only a little drummer-boy, who had straggled away from his own regiment, and could tell them nothing certain about the troops forming the column.

To make another descent upon them, Denisov thought, would be to risk alarming the whole column, and so he sent on ahead to Shamshevo a peasant, Tihon Shtcherbatov, to try if he could capture at least one of the French quartermasters from the vanguard.

IV

IT was a warm, rainy, autumn day. The sky and the horizon were all of the uniform tint of muddy water. Sometimes a mist seemed to be falling, and sometimes there was a sudden downpour of heavy, slanting rain.

Denisov, in a long cape and a high fur cap, both streaming with water, was riding a thin, pinched-looking, thoroughbred horse. With his head aslant, and his ears pricked up, like his horse, he was frowning at the driving rain, and anxiously looking before him. His face, which had grown thin, and was covered with a thick, short, black beard, looked wrathful.

Beside Denisov, wearing also a long cape and a high cap, and mounted on a sleek, sturdy Don horse, rode the esaul, or hetman of the Cossacks—Denisov's partner in his enterprises.

The esaul, Lovaisky, a third man, also in a cape, and a high cap, was a long creature, flat as a board, with a pale face, flaxen hair, narrow, light eyes, and an expression of calm self-confidence both in his face and his attitude. Though it was impossible to say what constituted the peculiarity of horse and rider, at the first glance at the esaul and at Denisov, it was evident that Denisov was both wet and uncomfortable; that Denisov was a man sitting on a horse; while the esaul seemed as comfortable and calm as always, and seemed not a man sitting on a horse, but a man forming one whole with a horse—a single being enlarged by the strength of two.

A little ahead of them walked a peasant-guide, soaked through and through in his grey full coat and white cap.

A little behind, on a thin, delicate Kirghiz pony, with a flowing tail and mane, and a mouth flecked with blood, rode a young officer in a blue French military coat. Beside him rode an hussar, with a boy in a tattered French uniform and blue cap, perched upon his horse behind him. The boy held on to the hussar with hands red with cold, and kept moving his bare feet, trying to warm them, and lifting his eyebrows, gazed about him wonderingly. This was the French drummer, who had been taken in the morning.

Along the narrow, muddy, cut-up forest-track there came hussars in knots of three and four at a time, and then Cossacks; some in capes, some in French cloaks; others with horse-cloths pulled over their heads. The horses, chestnut and bay, all looked black from the soaking rain. Their necks looked strangely thin with their drenched manes, and steam rose in clouds from them. Clothes, saddles, and bridles, all were sticky and swollen with the wet, like the earth and the fallen leaves with which the track was strewn. The men sat huddled up, trying not to move, so as to keep warm the water that had already reached their skins, and not to let any fresh stream of cold rain trickle in anywhere under their seat, or at their knees or necks. In the midst of the file of Cossacks two waggons, drawn by French horses, and Cossack saddle-horses hitched on in front, rumbled over stumps and branches, and splashed through the ruts full of water.

Denisov's horse, in avoiding a puddle in the track, knocked his rider's knee against a tree.

'Ah, devil!' Denisov cried angrily; and showing his teeth, he struck his horse three times with his whip, splashing himself and his comrades with mud. Denisov was out of humour, both from the rain and hunger (no one had eaten anything since morning); and, most of all, from having no news of Dolohov, and from no French prisoner having been caught to give him information.

'We shall never have such another chance to fall on the transport as today. To attack them alone would be risky, and to put it off to another day—some one of the bigger leaders will carry the booty off from under our noses,' thought Denisov, continually looking ahead, and fancying he saw the messenger from Dolohov he expected.

Coming out into a clearing from which he could get a view to some distance on the right, Denisov stopped.

'There's some one coming,' he said.

The esaul looked in the direction Denisov was pointing to.

'There are two men coming—an officer and a Cossack. Only I

wouldn't be *prepositive* that is the colonel himself,' said the esaul, who loved to use words that were unfamiliar to the Cossacks. The two figures, riding downhill, disappeared from sight, and came into view again a few minutes later. The foremost was an officer, dishevelled looking, and soaked through, with his trousers tucked up above his knees; he was lashing his horse into a weary gallop. Behind him a Cossack trotted along, standing up in his stirrups. This officer, a quite young boy, with a broad, rosy face and keen, merry eyes, galloped up to Denisov, and handed him a sopping packet.

'From the general,' he said. 'I must apologise for its not being quite dry....'

Denisov, frowning, took the packet and broke it open.

'Why, they kept telling us it was so dangerous,' said the officer, turning to the esaul while Denisov was reading the letter. 'But Komarov'—and he indicated the Cossack—'and I were prepared. We have both two pisto... But what's this?' he asked, seeing the French drummer-boy. 'A prisoner? You have had a battle already? May I talk to him?'

'Rostov! Petya!' Denisov cried at that moment, running through the packet that had been given him. 'Why, how was it you didn't say who you were?' and Denisov, turning with a smile, held out his hand to the officer. This officer was Petya Rostov.

Petya had been all the way preparing himself to behave with Denisov as a grown-up person and an officer should do, making no reference to their previous acquaintance. But as soon as Denisov smiled at him, Petya beamed at once, blushed with delight, and forgetting all the formal demeanour he had been intending to preserve, he began telling him how he had ridden by the French, and how glad he was he had been given this commission, and how he had already been in a battle at Vyazma, and how a certain hussar had distinguished himself in it.

'Well, I am glad to see you,' Denisov interrupted him, and his face looked anxious again.

'Mihail Feoklititch,' he said to the esaul, 'this is from the German again, you know. He' (Petya) 'is in his suite.' And Denisov told the esaul that the letter, which had just been brought, repeated the German general's request that they would join him in attacking the transport. 'If we don't catch them by tomorrow, he'll snatch them from under our noses,' he concluded.

While Denisov was talking to the esaul, Petya, disconcerted by Denisov's cold tone, and imagining that that tone might be due to the condition of his trousers, furtively pulled them down under his cloak, trying to do so unobserved, and to maintain as martial an air as possible.

'Will your honour have any instructions to give me?' he said to Denisov, putting his hand to the peak of his cap, and going back to the comedy of adjutant and general, which he had prepared himself to perform, 'or should I remain with your honour?'

'Instructions? . . .' said Denisov absently. 'Well, can you stay till tomorrow?'

'Ah, please . . . May I stay with you?' cried Petya.

'Well, what were your instructions from your general—to go back at once?' asked Denisov.

Petya blushed.

'Oh, he gave me no instructions. I think I may?' he said interrogatively.

'All right, then,' said Denisov. And turning to his followers, he directed a party of them to go to the hut in the wood, which they had fixed on as a resting-place, and the officer on the Kirghiz horse (this officer performed the duties of an adjutant) to go and look for Dolohov, to find out where he was, and whether he were coming in the evening.

Denisov himself, with the esaul and Petya, intended to ride to the edge of the wood near Shamshevo to have a look at the position of the French, where their attack next day was to take place.

'Come, my man,' he said to their peasant guide, 'take us to Shamshevo.'

Denisov, Petya, and the esaul, accompanied by a few Cossacks and the hussar with the prisoner, turned to the left and crossed a ravine towards the edge of the wood.

V

THE rain was over, but a mist was falling and drops of water dripped from the branches of the trees. Denisov, the esaul, and Petya, in silence, followed the peasant in the pointed cap, who, stepped lightly and noiselessly in his bast shoes over roots and wet leaves, led them to the edge of the wood.

Coming out on the road, the peasant paused, looked about him, and turned towards a thin screen of trees. He stood still at a big oak, still covered with leaves, and beckoned mysteriously to them.

Denisov and Petya rode up to him. From the place where the peasant was standing the French could be seen. Just beyond the wood a field of spring corn ran sharply downhill. On the right, across a steep ravine, could be seen a little village and a manor-house with the roofs broken down. In that village and in the house and all over the high ground in the garden, by the wells and the pond, and all along the road uphill from the bridge to the village, not more than five hundred yards away, crowds of men could be seen in the shifting mist. They could distinctly hear their foreign cries at the horses pulling the baggage uphill and their calls to one another.

'Give me the prisoner here,' said Denisov, in a low voice, never taking his eyes off the French.

A Cossack got off his horse, lifted the boy down, and came with him to Denisov. Denisov, pointing to the French, asked the boy what troops they were. The boy, thrusting his chilled hands into his pockets and raising his eyebrows, looked in dismay at Denisov, and in spite of his unmistakable desire to tell all he knew, he was confused in his answers, and merely repeated Denisov's questions. Denisov, frowning, turned away from him, and addressing the esaul, told him his own views on the matter.

Petya, turning his head rapidly, looked from the drummer to Denisov, and from the esaul to the French in the village and on the road, trying not to miss anything of importance.

'Whether Dolohov comes or not, we must take them. . . . Eh?' said Denisov, his eyes sparkling merrily.

'It is a convenient spot,' said the esaul.

'We will send the infantry down below, by the marshes,' Denisov went on. 'They will creep up to the garden; you dash down with the Cossacks from there'—Denisov pointed to the wood beyond the village—'and I from here with my hussars. And at a shot . . .'

'It won't do to go by the hollow; it's a bog,' said the esaul. 'The horses will sink in, you must skirt round more to the left. . . .'

While they were talking in undertones, there was the crack of a shot and a puff of white smoke in the hollow below near the pond, and the voices of hundreds of Frenchmen half-way up the hill rose in a ringing shout, as though in merry chorus. At the first minute both Denisov and the esaul darted back. They were so near that they fancied they were the cause of that shot and those shouts. But they had nothing to do with them. A man in something red was running through the marshes below. The French were evidently firing and shouting at him.

'Why, it's our Tihon,' said the esaul.

'It's he! it's he!'

'The rogue,' said Denisov.

'He'll get away!' said the esaul, screwing up his eyes.

The man they called Tihon, running up to the little river, splashed into it, so that the water spurted up round him, and disappearing for an instant, scrambled out on all fours, looking dark from the water, and ran on. The French, who had been pursuing him, stopped.

'Well, he's a smart fellow, said the esaul.

'The beast,' said Denisov, with the same expression of vexation. 'And what has he been about all this time?'

'Who is he?' asked Petya.

'It's our scout. I sent him to catch a "tongue" for us.'

'Ah, to be sure,' said Petya, nodding at Denisov's first word, as though he knew all about it, though he did not understand a word.

Tihon Shtcherbatov was one of the most useful men among Denisov's followers. He was a peasant of the village of Pokrovskoe, near Gzhat. Denisov had come to Pokrovskoe early in his operations as a guerilla leader, and sending, as he always did, for the village elder, asked him what he knew about the French.

The village elder had answered, as all village elders always did answer, that he knew nothing about them, and had seen nothing of them. But when Denisov explained to him that his object was to kill the French, and inquired whether no French had strayed into his village, the village elder replied that there had been some *miroders* certainly, but that the only person who took any heed of such things was Tishka Shtcherbatov. Denisov ordered Tihon to be brought before him, and praising his activity, said in the presence of the elder a few words about the devotion to the Tsar and the Fatherland and the hatred of the French that all sons of the Fatherland must cherish in their hearts.

'We don't do any harm to the French,' said Tihon, evidently scared at Denisov's words. 'It's only, you know, just a bit of fun for the lads and me. The *miroders* now—we have killed a dozen or so of them, but we have done no harm else . . .'

Next day, when Denisov was leaving Pokrovskoe, having forgotten all about this peasant, he was told that Tihon was with his followers, and asked to be allowed to remain with them. Denisov bade them let him stay.

At first Tihon undertook the rough work of making fires, fetching water, skinning horses, and so on, but he soon showed great zeal and capacity for guerilla warfare. He would go after booty at night, and never failed to bring back French clothes and weapons, and when he was bidden, he would bring back prisoners too. Denisov took Tihon from his menial work, and began to employ him on expeditions, and to reckon him among the Cossacks.

Tihon did not like riding, and always went on foot, yet never lagged behind the cavalry. His weapons were a musket, which he carried rather as a joke, a pike, and an axe, which he used as skilfully as a wolf does its teeth—catching fleas in its coat and crunching thick bones with them equally easily. With equal precision Tihon swinging his axe split logs, or, taking it by the head, cut thin skewers or carved spoons. Among Denisov's followers, Tihon was on a special footing of his own. When anything particularly disagreeable or revolting had to be done—to put one's shoulder to a waggon stuck in the mud, to drag a horse out of a bog by the tail, to flay a horse, to creep into the midst of the French, to walk fifty versts in a day—every one laughed, and looked to Tihon to do it.

'No harm will come to him; the devil; he's a stalwart beast,' they used to say of him.

One day a Frenchman he had captured wounded Tihon with a pistol-shot in the fleshy part of the back. This wound, which Tihon treated only by applications of vodka—internal and external—was the subject of the liveliest jokes through the whole party, and Tihon lent himself readily to their jests.

'Well, old chap, you won't do that again! Are you crook-backed!' laughed the Cossacks; and Tihon, assuming a doleful face, and grimacing to pretend he was angry, would abuse the French with the most comical oaths. The effect of the incident on Tihon was that he rarely afterwards brought prisoners in.

Tihon was the bravest and most useful man of the lot. No one discovered so many opportunities of attack, no one captured or killed so many Frenchmen. And consequently he was the favourite subject of all the gibes of the Cossacks and the hussars, and readily fell in with the position.

Tihon had been sent overnight by Denisov to Shamshevo to capture a 'tongue.' But either because he was not satisfied with one French prisoner, or because he had been asleep all night, he had crept by day into the bushes in the very middle of the French, and, as Denisov had seen from the hill, had been discovered by them.

VI

AFTER talking a little while longer with the esaul about the next day's attack, which Denisov seemed to have finally decided upon after seeing how near the French were, he turned his horse's head and rode back.

'Now, my boy, we will go and dry ourselves,' he said to Petya.

As he came near the forester's hut, Denisov stopped, looking into the wood before him. A man in a short jacket, bast shoes, and a Kazan hat, with a gun across his shoulder, and an axe in his belt, was striding lightly through the forest with long legs and long arms swinging at his side. Catching sight of Denisov, he hastily flung something into the bushes, and taking off his sopped hat, the brim of which drooped limply, he walked up to his commanding officer.

This was Tihon. His pock-marked and wrinkled face, with little slits of eyes, beamed with self-satisfaction and merriment. He held his head high, and looked straight at Denisov as though he were suppressing a laugh.

'Well, where have you been?' said Denisov.

'Where have I been? I have been after the French,' Tihon answered boldly and hastily, in a husky, but mellow bass.

'Why did you creep in in the daytime? Ass! Well, why didn't you catch one?'

'Catch one I did,' said Tihon.

'Where is he, then?'

'I caught one at the very first at daybreak,' Tihon went on, setting his feet down wider apart, in their flat, turned-up bast shoes; 'and I took him into the wood too. I see he's no good. So, thinks I, better go and get another, rather more the proper article.'

'Ay, the rogue, so that's how it is,' said Denisov to the esaul. 'Why didn't you bring that one?'

'Why, what was the use of bringing him in?' Tihon broke in, hurriedly and angrily. 'A worthless fellow! Don't I know what sort you want?'

'Ah, you brute! ... Well?'

'I went to get another,' Tihon went on. 'I crept up in this way in the wood, and I lay down.' With a sudden, supple movement, Tihon lay down on his stomach, to show how he had done this. 'One turned up,' he went on, 'I seized him like this,' Tihon jumped up swiftly and lightly. '"Come along to the colonel," says I. He set up such a shouting; and then I saw four of them. And they rushed at me with their sabres. I went at them like this with my axe. "What are you about?" says I. "Christ be with you,"' cried Tihon, waving his arms and squaring his chest with a menacing scowl.

'Oh yes, we saw from the hill how you gave them the slip, through the pools,' said the esaul, screwing up his sparkling eyes.

Petya had a great longing to laugh, but he saw that all the others refrained from laughing. He kept looking rapidly from Tihon's face to the face of the esaul and Denisov, not knowing what to make of it all.

'Don't play the fool,' said Denisov, coughing angrily. 'Why didn't you bring the first man?'

Tihon began scratching his back with one hand and his head with the other, and all at once his countenance expanded into a beaming, foolish grin, showing the loss of a tooth that had given him his name, Shtcherbatov (*i.e.* lacking a tooth). Denisov smiled, and Petya went off into a merry peal of laughter, in which Tihon himself joined.

'Why, he was no good at all,' said Tihon. 'He was so badly dressed, how could I bring him? And a coarse fellow, your honour. Why, says he, "I'm a general's son," says he, "I'm not going."'

'Ugh, you brute!' said Denisov. 'I wanted to question him...'

'Oh, I did question him,' said Tihon. 'He said he didn't know much. "There are a lot of our men," says he, "but they are all poor creatures; that's all you can say for them. Give a good shout," says he, "and you can take them all,"' Tihon concluded, with a merry and determined look at Denisov.

'Mind, I'll give you a good hundred lashes that will teach you to play the fool,' said Denisov sternly.

'Why be angry,' said Tihon, 'because I haven't seen your sort of Frenchmen? As soon as it gets dark, I'll catch whatever kind you like, three of them I'll bring.'

'Well, come along,' said Denisov, and all the way to the forester's hut he was silent, frowning angrily.

Tihon was walking behind, and Petya heard the Cossacks laughing with him and at him about a pair of boots that he had thrown into the bushes.

When the laughter roused by Tihon's words and smile had passed, and Petya understood for a moment that Tihon had killed the man, he had an uneasy feeling. He looked round at the boy prisoner, and there was a sudden pang in his heart. But that uneasiness only lasted a moment. He felt it incumbent on him to hold his head high, and with a bold and important air to question the esaul about the next day's expedition, that he might not be unworthy of the company in which he found himself.

The officer Denisov had sent to Dolohov met him on the way with the news that everything was going well with Dolohov, and that he was coming himself immediately.

Denisov at once became more cheerful, and beckoned Petya to him.

'Come, tell me about yourself,' he said.

VII

ON leaving Moscow, Petya had parted from his parents to join his regiment, and shortly afterwards had been appointed an orderly in attendance on a general who was in command of a large detachment.

From the time of securing his commission, and even more since joining a regiment in active service, and taking part in the battle of Vyazma, Petya had been in a continual state of happy excitement at being grown-up, and of intense anxiety not to miss any opportunity of real heroism. He was highly delighted with all he had seen and experienced in the army, but, at the same time, he was always fancying that wherever he was not, there the most real and heroic exploits were at that very moment being performed. And he was in constant haste to be where he was not.

On the 21st of October, when his general expressed a desire to send some one to Denisov's company, Petya had so piteously besought him to send him, that the general could not refuse. But, as he was sending him off, the general recollected Petya's foolhardy behaviour at the battle of Vyazma, when, instead of riding by way of the road to take a message, Petya had galloped across the lines under the fire of the French, and had there fired a couple of pistol-shots. Recalling that prank, the general explicitly forbade Petya's taking part in any enterprise whatever that Denisov might be planning. This was why Petya had blushed and been disconcerted when Denisov asked him if he might stay. From the moment he set off till he reached the edge of the wood, Petya had fully intended to do his duty steadily, and to return at once. But when he saw the French, and saw Tihon, and learned that the attack would certainly take place that night, with the rapid transition from one view to another, characteristic of young people, he made up his mind that his general, for whom he had till that moment had the greatest respect, was a poor stick, and only a German, that Denisov was a hero, and the esaul a hero, and Tihon a hero, and that it would be shameful to leave them at a moment of difficulty.

It was getting dark when Denisov, with Petya and the esaul reached the forester's hut. In the half-dark they could see saddled horses, Cossacks and hussars, rigging up shanties in the clearing, and building up a glowing fire in a hollow near, where the smoke would not be seen by the French. In the porch of the little hut there was a Cossack with his sleeves tucked up, cutting up a sheep. In the hut, three officers of Denisov's band were setting up a table made up of doors. Petya took off his wet clothes, gave them to be dried, and at once set to work to help the officers in fixing up a dining-table.

In ten minutes the table was ready and covered with a napkin. On the table was set vodka, a flask of rum, white bread, and roast mutton, and salt.

Sitting at the table with the officers, tearing the fat, savoury mutton with greasy fingers, Petya was in a childishly enthusiastic condition of tender love for all men and a consequent belief in the same feeling for himself in others.

'So what do you think, Vassily Fyodorovitch,' he said to Denisov, 'it won't matter my staying a day with you, will it?' And without waiting for an answer, he answered himself: 'Why, I was told to find out, and here I am finding out . . . Only you must let me go into the middle . . . into the real . . . I don't care about rewards . . . But I do want . . .' Petya clenched his teeth and looked about him, tossing his head and waving his arm.

'Into the real, real thing . . .' Denisov said, smiling.

'Only, please, do give me a command of something altogether, so that I really might command,' Petya went on. 'Why, what would it be to you? Ah, you want a knife?' he said to an officer, who was trying to tear off a piece of mutton. And he gave him his pocket-knife.

The officer praised the knife.

'Please keep it. I have several like it . . .' said Petya, blushing. 'Heavens! Why, I was quite forgetting,' he cried suddenly. 'I have some capital raisins, you know the sort without stones. We have a new canteen-keeper, and he does get first-rate things. I bought ten pounds of them. I'm fond of sweet things. Will you have some?' . . . And Petya ran out to his Cossack in the porch, and brought in some panniers in which there were five pounds of raisins. 'Please take some.'

'Don't you need a coffee-pot?' he said to the esaul; 'I bought a famous one from our canteen-keeper! He has first-rate things. And he's very honest. That's the great thing. I'll be sure and send it you. Or perhaps your flints are worn out; that does happen sometimes. I brought some with me, I have got them here . . .' he pointed to the panniers. 'A hundred flints. I bought them very cheap. You must please take as many as you want or all, indeed . . .' And suddenly, dismayed at the thought that he had let his tongue run away with him, Petya stopped short and blushed.

He began trying to think whether he had been guilty of any other blunders. And running through his recollections of the day the image of the French drummer-boy rose before his mind.

'We are enjoying ourselves, but how is he feeling? What have they done with him? Have they given him something to eat? Have they been nasty to him?' he wondered.

But thinking he had said too much about the flints, he was afraid to speak now.

'Could I ask about him?' he wondered. 'They'll say: he's a boy himself, so he feels for the boy. I'll let them see tomorrow whether I'm a boy! Shall I feel ashamed if I ask?' Petya wondered. 'Oh, well! I don't care,' and he said at once, blushing and watching the officers' faces in dread of detecting amusement in them:

'Might I call that boy who was taken prisoner, and give him something to eat . . . perhaps . . .'

'Yes, poor little fellow,' said Denisov, who clearly saw nothing to be ashamed of in this reminder. 'Fetch him in here. His name is Vincent Bosse. Fetch him in.'

'I'll call him,' said Petya.

'Yes, do. Poor little fellow,' repeated Denisov.

Petya was standing at the door as Denisov said this. He slipped in between the officers and went up to Denisov.

'Let me kiss you, dear old fellow,' he said. 'Ah, how jolly it is! how splendid!' And, kissing Denisov, he ran out into the yard.

'Bosse! Vincent!' Petya cried, standing by the door.

'Whom do you want, sir?' said a voice out of the darkness. Petya answered that he wanted the French boy, who had been taken prisoner that day.

'Ah! Vesenny?' said the Cossack.

His name Vincent had already been transformed by the Cossacks into Vesenny, and by the peasants and the soldiers into Visenya. In both names there was a suggestion of the spring—vesna—which seemed to them to harmonise with the figure of the young boy.

'He's warming himself there at the fire. Ay, Visenya! Visenya!' voices called from one to another with laughter in the darkness. 'He is a sharp boy,' said an hussar standing near Petya. 'We gave him a meal not long ago. He was hungry, terribly.'

There was a sound of footsteps in the darkness, and the drummer-boy came splashing through the mud with his bare feet towards the door.

'Ah, that's you!' said Petya. 'Are you hungry? Don't be afraid, they won't hurt you,' he added shyly and cordially touching his hand. 'Come in, come in.'

'Thank you,' answered the drummer, in a trembling, almost childish voice, and he began wiping the mud off his feet on the threshold. Petya had a great deal he longed to say to the drummer-boy, but he did not dare. He stood by him in the porch, moving uneasily. Then he took his hand in the darkness and squeezed it. 'Come in, come in,' he repeated, but in a soft whisper.

'Oh, if I could only do something for him!' Petya was saying inwardly, and opening the door he ushered the boy in before him.

When the drummer-boy had come into the hut, Petya sat down at some distance from him, feeling that it would be lowering his dignity to take much notice of him. But he was feeling the money in his pocket and wondering whether it would do to give some to the drummer-boy.

VIII

DENISOV gave orders for the drummer-boy to be given some vodka and mutton, and to be put into a Russian dress, so that he should not be sent off with the other prisoners, but should stay with his band. Petya's attention was diverted from the boy by the arrival of Dolohov. He had heard a great many stories told in the army of Dolohov's extraordinary gallantry and of his cruelty to the French. And therefore from the moment Dolohov entered the hut Petya could not take his eyes off him, and flinging up his head, he assumed a more and more swaggering air, that he might not be unworthy of associating even with a hero like Dolohov.

Dolohov's appearance struck Petya as strange through its simplicity.

Denisov was dressed in a Cossack coat; he had let his beard grow, and had a holy image of Nikolay, the wonder-worker, on his breast. His whole manner of speaking and all his gestures were suggestive of his peculiar position. Dolohov, on the contrary, though in old days he had worn a Persian dress in Moscow, looked now like the most correct officer of the Guards. He was clean-shaven; he wore the wadded coat of the Guards with a St. George medal on a ribbon, and a plain forage cap, put on straight on his head. He took his wet cloak off in the corner and, without greeting any one, went straight up to Denisov and began at once asking questions about the matter in hand. Denisov told him of the designs the larger detachment had upon the French convoy, of the message Petya had brought, and the answer he had given to both generals. Then he told him all he knew of the position of the French.

'That's so. But we must find out what troops they are, and what are their numbers,' said Dolohov; 'we must go and have a look at them. We can't rush into the thing without knowing for certain how many there are of them. I like to do things properly. Come, won't one of you gentlemen like to come with me to pay them a call in their camp. I have an extra uniform with me.'

'I, I . . . I'll come with you!' cried Petya.

'There's not the slightest need for you to go,' said Denisov, addressing Dolohov; 'and as for him I wouldn't let him go on any account.'

'That's good!' cried Petya; 'why shouldn't I go? . . .'

'Why, because there's no reason to.'

'Oh, well, excuse me . . . because . . . because . . . I'm going, and that's all. You will take me?' he cried, turning to Dolohov.

'Why not? ...' Dolohov answered, absently, staring into the face of the French drummer-boy.

'Have you had that youngster long?' he asked Denisov.

'We caught him today, but he knows nothing; I have kept him with us.'

'Oh, and what do you do with the rest?' said Dolohov.

'What do I do with them? I take a receipt for them, and send them off!' cried Denisov, suddenly flushing. 'And I make bold to say that I haven't a single man's life on my conscience. Is there any difficulty in your sending thirty, or three hundred men, under escort, to the town rather than stain—I say so bluntly—one's honour as a soldier.'

'It's all very well for this little count here at sixteen to talk of such refinements,' Dolohov said, with a cold sneer; 'but it's high time for you to drop all that.'

'Why, I am not saying anything, I only say that I am certainly going with you,' said Petya shyly.

'But for me and you, mate, it's high time to drop such delicacy,' Dolohov went on, apparently deriving peculiar gratification from talking on a subject irritating to Denisov. 'Why have you kept this lad,' he said, 'except because you are sorry for him? Why, we all know how much your receipts are worth. You send off a hundred men and thirty reach the town. They die of hunger or are killed on the way. So isn't it just as well to make short work of them?'

The esaul, screwing up his light-coloured eyes, nodded his head approvingly.

'That's not my affair, no need to discuss it. I don't care to have their lives on my conscience. You say they die. Well, let them. Only not through my doing.'

Dolohov laughed.

'Who prevented their taking me twenty times over? But you know if they do catch me—and you too with your chivalrous sentiments—it will just be the same—the nearest aspen-tree.' He paused. 'We must be getting to work, though. Send my Cossack here with the pack. I have two French uniforms. Well, are you coming with me?' he asked Petya.

'I? Yes, yes, of course,' cried Petya, blushing till the tears came into his eyes, and glancing at Denisov.

While Dolohov had been arguing with Denisov what should be done with prisoners, Petya had again had that feeling of discomfort and nervous hurry; but again he had not time to get a clear idea of what they were talking about. 'If that's what is thought by grown-up men, famous leaders, then it must be so, it must be all right,' he thought. 'And the great thing is, that Denisov shouldn't dare to imagine that I must obey him, that he can order me about. I shall certainly go with Dolohov into the French camp. He can go, and so can I!'

To all Denisov's efforts to dissuade him from going, Petya replied that he too liked doing things properly and not in haphazard fashion, and that he never thought about danger to himself.

'For, you must admit, if we don't know exactly how many men there are there, it might cost the life of hundreds, and it is only we two, and so I very much wish it, and I shall certainly, most certainly go, and don't try to prevent me,' he said; 'it won't be any use . . .'

IX

PETYA and Dolohov, after dressing up in French uniforms and shakos, rode to the clearing from which Denisov had looked at the French camp, and coming out of the wood, descended into the hollow in the pitch darkness. When they had ridden downhill, Dolohov bade the Cossacks accompanying him to wait there, and set off at a smart trot along the road towards the bridge. Petya, faint with excitement, trotted along beside him.

'If we are caught, I won't be taken alive. I have a pistol,' whispered Petya.

'Don't speak Russian,' said Dolohov, in a rapid whisper, and at that moment they heard in the dark the challenge: 'Who goes there?' and the click of a gun.

The blood rushed into Petya's face, and he clutched at his pistol.

'Uhlans of the Sixth Regiment,' said Dolohov, neither hastening nor slackening his horse's pace.

The black figure of a sentinel stood on the bridge.

'The password?'

Dolohov reined in his horse, and advanced at a walking pace.

'Tell me, is Colonel Gerrard here?' he said.

'Password?' repeated the sentinel, making no reply and barring their way.

'When an officer makes his round, sentinels don't ask him for the password . . .' cried Dolohov, suddenly losing his temper and riding straight at the sentinel. 'I ask you is the colonel here?'

And not waiting for an answer from the sentinel, who moved aside, Dolohov rode at a walking pace uphill.

Noticing the black outline of a man crossing the road, Dolohov stopped the man, and asked where the colonel and officers were. The man, a soldier with a sack over his shoulder, stopped, came close up to

Dolohov's horse, stroking it with his hand, and told them in a simple and friendly way that the colonel and the officers were higher up the hill, on the right, in the courtyard of the farm, as he called the little manor-house.

After going further along the road, from both sides of which they heard French talk round the camp-fires, Dolohov turned into the yard of the manor-house. On reaching the gate, he dismounted and walked towards a big, blazing fire, round which several men were sitting, engaged in loud conversation. There was something boiling in a cauldron on one side, and a soldier in a peaked cap and blue coat, kneeling in the bright glow of the fire, was stirring it with his ramrod.

'He's a tough customer,' said one of the officers, sitting in the shadow on the opposite side of the fire.

'He'll make them run, the rabbits' (a French proverb), said the other, with a laugh.

Both paused, and peered into the darkness at the sound of the steps of Petya and Dolohov approaching with their horses.

'*Bonjour, messieurs!*' Dolohov called loudly and distinctly.

There was a stir among the officers in the shadow, and a tall officer with a long neck came round the fire and went up to Dolohov.

'Is that you, Clément?' said he. 'Where the devil . . .' but becoming aware of his mistake, he did not finish, and with a slight frown greeted Dolohov as a stranger, and asked him what he could do for him. Dolohov told him that he and his comrade were trying to catch up their regiment, and asked, addressing the company in general, whether the officers knew anything about the Sixth Regiment. No one could tell them anything about it; and Petya fancied the officers began to look at him and Dolohov with unfriendly and suspicious eyes.

For several seconds no one spoke.

'If you're reckoning on some soup, you have come too late,' said a voice from behind the fire, with a smothered laugh.

Dolohov answered that they had had supper, and wanted to push on further that night.

He gave their horses to the soldier who was stirring the pot, and squatted down on his heels beside the officer with the long neck. The latter never took his eyes off Dolohov, and asked him again what regiment did he belong to.

Dolohov appeared not to hear the question. Making no answer he lighted a short French pipe that he took from his pocket, and asked the officers whether the road ahead of them were safe from Cossacks.

'The brigands are everywhere,' answered an officer from behind the fire.

Dolohov said that the Cossacks were only a danger for stragglers like himself and his comrade; 'he supposed they would not dare to attack large detachments,' he added inquiringly.

No one replied.

'Well, now he will come away,' Petya was thinking every moment, as he stood by the fire listening to the talk.

But Dolohov took up the conversation that had dropped, and proceeded to ask them point blank how many men there were in their battalion, how many battalions they had, and how many prisoners.

When he asked about the Russian prisoners, Dolohov added:

'Nasty business dragging those corpses about with one. It would be better to shoot the vermin,' and he broke into such a strange, loud laugh, that Petya fancied the French must see through their disguise at once, and he involuntarily stepped back from the fire.

Dolohov's words and laughter elicited no response, and a French officer whom they had not seen (he lay rolled up in a coat), sat up and whispered something to his companion. Dolohov stood up and called to the men, who held their horses.

'Will they give us the horses or not?' Petya wondered, unconsciously coming closer to Dolohov.

They did give them the horses. '*Bonsoir, messieurs,*' said Dolohov.

Petya tried to say '*Bonsoir,*' but he could not utter a sound. The officers were whispering together. Dolohov was a long while mounting his horse, who would not stand still; then he rode out of the gate at a walking pace. Petya rode beside him, not daring to look round, though he was longing to see whether the French were running after him or not.

When they came out on to the road, Dolohov did not turn back towards the open country, but rode further along into the village.

At one spot he stood still, listening. 'Do you hear?' he said. Petya recognised the sound of voices speaking Russian, and saw round the camp-fire the dark outlines of Russian prisoners. When they reached the bridge again, Petya and Dolohov passed the sentinel, who, without uttering a word, paced gloomily up and down. They came out to the hollow where the Cossacks were waiting for them.

'Well now, good-bye. Tell Denisov, at sunrise, at the first shot,' said Dolohov, and he was going on, but Petya clutched at his arm.

'Oh!' he cried, 'you are a hero! Oh! how splendid it is! how jolly! How I love you!'

'That's all right,' answered Dolohov, but Petya did not let go of him, and in the dark Dolohov made out that he was bending over to him to be kissed. Dolohov kissed him, laughed, and turning his horse's head, vanished into the darkness.

X

ON reaching the hut in the wood, Petya found Denisov in the porch. He was waiting for Petya's return in great uneasiness, anxiety, and vexation with himself for having let him go.

'Thank God!' he cried. 'Well, thank God!' he repeated, hearing Petya's ecstatic account. 'And damn you, you have prevented my sleeping!' he added. 'Well, thank God; now, go to bed. We can still get a nap before morning.'

'Yes ... no,' said Petya. 'I'm not sleepy yet. Besides, I know what I am; if once I go to sleep, it will be all up with me. And besides, it's not my habit to sleep before a battle.'

Petya sat for a little while in the hut, joyfully recalling the details of his adventure, and vividly imagining what was coming next day. Then, noticing that Denisov had fallen asleep, he got up and went out of doors.

It was still quite dark outside. The rain was over, but the trees were still dripping. Close by the hut could be seen the black outlines of the Cossacks' shanties and the horses tied together. Behind the hut there was a dark blur where two waggons stood with the horses near by, in the hollow there was a red glow from the dying fire. The Cossacks and the hussars were not all asleep; there mingled with the sound of the falling drops and the munching of the horses, the sound of low voices, that seemed to be whispering.

Petya came out of the porch, looked about him in the darkness, and went up to the waggons. Some one was snoring under the waggons, and saddled horses were standing round them munching oats. In the dark Petya recognised and approached his own mare, whom he called Karabach, though she was in fact of a Little Russian breed.

'Well, Karabach, tomorrow we shall do good service,' he said, sniffing her nostrils and kissing her.

'Why, aren't you asleep, sir?' said a Cossack, sitting under the waggon.

'No; but ... Lihatchev—I believe that's your name, eh? You know I have only just come back. We have been calling on the French.' And Petya gave the Cossack a detailed account, not only of his adventure, but also of his reasons for going, and why he thought it better to risk his life than to do things in a haphazard way.

'Well, you must be sleepy; get a little sleep,' said the Cossack.

'No, I am used to it,' answered Petya. 'And how are the flints in your pistols—not worn out? I brought some with me. Don't you want any? Do take some.'

The Cossack popped out from under the waggon to take a closer look at Petya.

'For, you see, I like to do everything carefully,' said Petya. 'Some men, you know, leave things to chance, and don't have things ready, and then they regret it. I don't like that.'

'No, to be sure,' said the Cossack.

'Oh, and another thing, please, my dear fellow, sharpen my sabre for me; I have blunt . . .' (but Petya could not bring out a lie) . . . 'it has never been sharpened. Can you do that?'

'To be sure I can.'

Lihatchev stood up, and rummaged in the baggage, and Petya stood and heard the martial sound of steel and whet-stone He clambered on to the waggon, and sat on the edge of it. The Cossack sharpened the sabre below.

'Are the other brave fellows asleep?' said Petya.

'Some are asleep, and some are awake, like us.'

'And what about the boy?'

'Vesenny? He's lying yonder in the hay. He's sleeping well after his fright. He was so pleased.'

For a long while after that Petya sat quiet, listening to the sounds. There was a sound of footsteps in the darkness, and a dark figure appeared.

'What are you sharpening?' asked a man coming up to the waggon.

'A sabre for the gentleman here.'

'That's a good thing,' said the man, who seemed to Petya to be an hussar. 'Was the cup left with you here?'

'It's yonder by the wheel.' The hussar took the cup. 'It will soon be daylight,' he added, yawning, as he walked off.

Petya must, one would suppose, have known that he was in a wood, with Denisov's band of irregulars, a verst from the road; that he was sitting on a waggon captured from the French; that there were horses fastened to it; that under it was sitting the Cossack Lihatchev sharpening his sabre; that the big, black blur on the right was the hut, and the red, bright glow below on the left the dying camp-fire; that the man who had come for the cup was an hussar who was thirsty. But Petya knew nothing of all that, and refused to know it. He was in a fairyland, in which nothing was like the reality. The big patch of shadow might be a hut certainly, but it might be a cave leading down into the very depths of the earth. The red patch might be a fire, but it might be the eye of a huge monster. Perhaps he really was sitting now on a waggon, but very likely he was sitting not on a waggon, but on a fearfully high tower, and if he fell off, he would go on flying to the earth for a whole day, for a whole month—fly and fly for ever and never reach it. Perhaps it was simply the Cossack Lihatchev sitting under the waggon; but very likely it was the kindest, bravest, most wonderful and splendid man in the world whom no one knew of. Perhaps it really was an hussar who had come for water and gone into the hollow; but perhaps he had just vanished, vanished altogether and was no more.

Whatever Petya had seen now, it would not have surprised him. He was in a land of fairy, where everything was possible.

He gazed at the sky. The sky too was an enchanted realm like the earth. It had begun to clear, and the clouds were scudding over the tree-tops, as though unveiling the stars. At times it seemed as though they were swept away, and there were glimpses of clear, black sky between them. At times these black patches looked like storm-clouds. At times the sky seemed to rise high, high overhead, and then again to be dropping down so that one could reach it with the hand.

Petya closed his eyes and began to nod. The branches dripped. There was a low hum of talk and the sound of some one snoring. The horses neighed and scuffled.

'Ozheeg, zheeg, ozheeg, zheeg...' hissed the sabre on the whetstone; and all at once Petya seemed to hear harmonious music, an orchestra playing some unfamiliar, solemnly sweet hymn. Petya was as musical by nature as Natasha, and far more so than Nikolay; but he had had no musical training, and never thought about music, so that the melody that came unexpectedly into his mind had a special freshness and charm for him. The music became more and more distinct. The melody grew and passed from one instrument to another. There was being played what is called a fugue, though Petya had not the slightest idea of what was meant by a fugue. Each instrument—one like a violin, others like flutes, but fuller and more melodious than violins and flutes—played its part, and before it had finished the air, melted in with another, beginning almost the same air, and with a third and a fourth; and all mingled into one harmony, and parted again, and again mingled into solemn church music, and then into some brilliant and triumphant song of victory.

'Oh yes, of course I am dreaming,' Petya said to himself, nodding forward. 'It is only in my ears. Perhaps, though, it's my own music. Come, again. Strike up, my music! Come!...'

He closed his eyes. And from various directions the sounds began vibrating as though from a distance, began to strike up, to part, and to mingle again, all joined in the same sweet and solemn hymn. 'Ah how exquisite! As much as I want, and as I like it!' Petya said to himself. He tried to conduct this immense orchestra.

'Come, softly, softly, now!' And the sounds obeyed him. 'Come, now fuller, livelier! More and more joyful!' And from unknown depths rose the swelling, triumphant sounds. 'Now, voices, join in!' Petya commanded. And at first in the distance he heard men's voices, then women's. The voices swelled into rhythmic, triumphant fullness. Petya felt awe and joy as he drank in their marvellous beauty.

With the triumphant march of victory mingled the song of the voices, and the drip of the branches and the zheeg, zheeg, zheeg of the sabre on the whetstone; and again the horses neighed and scuffled, not disturbing the harmony, but blending into it. How long it lasted, Petya could not tell; he was enjoying it, and wondering all the while at his own enjoyment, and regretting he had no one to share it with. He was waked by the friendly voice of Lihatchev.

'It's ready, your honour, you can cut the Frenchman in two now.'

Petya waked up.

'Why, it's light already; it's really getting light,' he cried. The horses, unseen before, were visible to the tails now, and through the leafless boughs there could be seen a watery light. Petya shook himself, jumped up, took a rouble out of his pocket, and gave it to Lihatchev, brandished his sabre to try it, and thrust it into the scabbard. The Cossacks were untying the horses and fastening the saddlegirths.

'And here is the commander,' said Lihatchev.

Denisov came out of the hut, and calling to Petya, bade him get ready.

XI

RAPIDLY in the twilight the men picked out their horses, tightened saddlegirths, and formed into parties. Denisov stood by the hut, giving the last orders. The infantry of the detachment moved on along the road, hundreds of feet splashing through the mud. They quickly vanished among the trees in the mist before the dawn. The esaul gave some order to the Cossacks. Petya held his horse by the bridle, eagerly awaiting the word of command to mount. His face glowed from a dip in cold water, and his eyes gleamed. He felt a chill running down his back, and a kind of rapid, rhythmic throbbing all over.

'Well, have you everything ready?' said Denisov. 'Give us our horses.'

They brought the horses up. Denisov was vexed with the Cossack because the saddlegirths were slack, and swore at him as he mounted his horse. Petya put his foot in the stirrup. The horse, as its habit was, made as though to nip at his leg; but Petya leaped into the saddle, unconscious of his own weight, and looking round at the hussars moving up from behind in the darkness, he rode up to Denisov.

'Vassily Fyodorovitch, you will trust me with some commission? Please . . . for God's sake . . .' he said. Denisov seemed to have forgotten Petya's existence. He looked round at him.

'One thing I beg of you,' he said sternly, 'to obey me and not to put yourself forward.'

All the way Denisov did not say another word to Petya; he rode on in silence. By the time that they reached the edge of the wood, it was perceptibly getting light in the open country. Denisov whispered something to the esaul, and the Cossacks began riding by Petya and Denisov. When they had all passed on, Denisov put spurs to his horse, and rode downhill. Slipping and sinking back on their haunches, the horses slid down into the hollow with their riders. Petya kept beside Denisov. The tremor all over him was growing more intense. It was getting lighter and lighter, but the mist hid objects at a distance. When he had reached the bottom, Denisov looked back and nodded to the Cossack beside him.

'The signal,' he said. The Cossack raised his arm, and a shot rang out. At the same moment they heard the tramp of horses galloping in front, shouts from different directions, and more shots.

The instant that he heard the first tramp of hoofs and shouts, Petya gave the rein to his horse, and lashing him on, galloped forward, heedless of Denisov, who shouted to him. It seemed to Petya that it suddenly became broad daylight, as though it were midday, at the moment when he heard the shot. He galloped to the bridge. The Cossacks were galloping along the road in front. At the bridge he jostled against a Cossack who had lagged behind, and he galloped on. In front Petya saw men of some sort—the French he supposed—running across the road from right to left. One slipped in the mud under his horse's legs.

Cossacks were crowding about a hut, doing something. A fearful scream rose out of the middle of the crowd. Petya galloped up to this crowd, and the first thing he saw was the white face and trembling lower jaw of a Frenchman, who had clutched hold of a lance aimed at his breast.

'Hurrah! . . . Mates . . . ours . . .' shouted Petya, and giving the rein to his excited horse, he galloped on down the village street.

He heard firing in front. Cossacks, hussars, and tattered Russian prisoners, running up from both sides of the road, were all shouting something loud and unintelligible. A gallant-looking Frenchman, in a blue coat, with a red, frowning face, and no cap, was keeping back the hussars with a bayonet. By the time that Petya galloped up, the Frenchman had fallen. 'Too late again,' flashed through Petya's brain, and he galloped to the spot where he heard the hottest fire. The shots came from the yard of the manor-house where he had been the night before with Dolohov. The French were ambushing there behind the fence in among the bushes of the overgrown garden, and firing at the Cossacks who were crowding round the gates. As he rode up to the gates, Petya caught a glimpse in the smoke of Dolohov's white, greenish face, as he shouted something to the men. 'Go round. Wait for the infantry!' he was shouting, just as Petya rode up to him.

'Wait? . . . Hurrah! . . .' shouted Petya, and without pausing a moment, he galloped towards the spot where he heard the shots and where the smoke was the thickest. There came a volley of shots with the sound of bullets whizzing by and thudding into something. The Cossacks and Dolohov galloped in at the gates after Petya. In the thick, hovering smoke the French flung down their arms and ran out of the bushes to meet the Cossacks, or fled downhill towards the pond. Petya was galloping on round the courtyard, but instead of holding the reins, he was flinging up both arms in a strange way, and slanting more and more to one side in the saddle. The horse stepped on to the ashes of the fire smouldering in the morning light, and stopped short. Petya fell heavily on the wet earth. The Cossacks saw his arms and legs twitching rapidly, though his head did not move. A bullet had passed through his brain.

After parleying with the French senior officer, who came out of the house with a handkerchief on a sword to announce that they surrendered, Dolohov got off his horse and went up to Petya, who lay motionless with outstretched arms.

'Done for,' he said frowning, and walked to the gate to Denisov, who was riding towards him.

'Killed?' cried Denisov, even from a distance recognising the familiar, unmistakably lifeless posture in which Petya's body was lying.

'Done for,' Dolohov repeated, as though the utterance of those words afforded him satisfaction; and he walked rapidly towards the prisoners, whom the Cossacks were hurriedly surrounding. 'No quarter!' he shouted to Denisov. Denisov made no reply. He went up to Petya, got off his horse, and with trembling hands turned over the blood-stained, mud-spattered face that was already turning white.

'I'm fond of sweet things. They are capital raisins, take them all,' came into his mind. And the Cossacks looked round in surprise at the sound like the howl of a dog, that Denisov uttered as he turned away, walked to the fence and clutched at it.

Among the Russian prisoners rescued by Denisov and Dolohov was Pierre Bezuhov.

XII

T H E party of prisoners, of whom Pierre was one, was on the 22nd of October not with the troops and transport, in whose company they had left Moscow, though no fresh instructions in regard to them had been given by the French authorities. Half of the transport with stores of biscuit, which had followed them during the early stages of the march, had been carried off by the Cossacks, the other half had got away in front. Of the cavalry soldiers on foot, who had marched in front of the prisoners, not one was left; they had all disappeared. The artillery, which the prisoners had seen in front during the early stages, was now replaced by the immense train of Marshal Junot's baggage, convoyed by an escort of Westphalians. Behind the prisoners came a transport of cavalry accoutrements.

The French had at first marched in three columns, but from Vyazma they had formed a single mass. The symptoms of lack of discipline, which Pierre had observed at the first halt outside Moscow, had by now reached their extreme limits.

The road along which they marched was strewn on both sides with the carcases of dead horses. The tattered soldiers, stragglers from different regiments, were continually changing, joining the column as it marched, and dropping behind it again. Several times there had been false alarms, and the soldiers of the convoy had raised their guns, and fired and fled, trampling one another underfoot. Then they had rallied again, and abused one another for their causeless panic.

These three bodies, travelling together—the cavalry transport, the convoy of prisoners, and Junot's baggage transport—still made up a complete separate whole, though each of its three parts was rapidly dwindling away.

Of the cavalry transport, which had at first consisted of one hundred and twenty waggons, only sixty were left; the rest and been carried off or abandoned. Several waggonloads of Junot's baggage, too, had been discarded or captured. Three waggons had been attacked and pillaged by stragglers from Davoust's regiment. From the talk he overheard among the Germans, Pierre learned that a more careful watch was kept over this baggage-train than over the prisoners, and that one of their comrades, a German, had been shot by order of the marshal himself because a silver spoon belonging to the marshal had been found in the soldier's possession.

The convoy of prisoners had dwindled even more than the other two convoys. Of the three hundred and thirty men who had started from

Moscow there were now less than a hundred left. The prisoners were a burden even more irksome to the soldiers than the cavalry stores and Junot's baggage. The saddles and Junot's spoons they could understand might be of some use, but why cold and starving soldiers should stand as sentinels, keeping guard over Russians as cold and starving, who were continually dying and being left on the road, and whom they had orders to shoot—it was not only incomprehensible, but revolting. And the soldiers of the escort, apparently afraid in the miserable plight they were in themselves, to give way to the pity they felt for the prisoners, for fear of making their own lot harder, treated them with marked moroseness and severity.

At Dorogobuzh the soldiers of the escort had gone off to plunder their own stores, leaving the prisoners locked in a stable, and several prisoners had burrowed under the wall and run away, but they were caught by the French and shot.

The arrangement, made at the start from Moscow, that the officers among the prisoners should march separately from the common soldiers, had long been given up. All who could walk marched together; and at the third stage Pierre had rejoined Karataev and the bow-legged, purple-grey dog, who had chosen Karataev for her master.

On the third day after leaving Moscow, Karataev had a return of the fever, which had kept him in the Moscow hospital, and as Karataev's strength failed, Pierre held more aloof from him. Pierre could not have said why it was, but from the time Karataev fell sick, he had to make an effort to force himself to go near him. And when he did go near him and heard the subdued moans, which Karataev often uttered, as he lay at the halting-places, and smelt the increasing odour from the sick man, Pierre moved further away from him and did not think about him.

In captivity in the shed that had been his prison, Pierre had learned, not through his intellect, but through his whole being, through life, that man is created for happiness, that happiness lies in himself, in the satisfaction of his natural, human cravings; that all unhappiness is due, not to lack of what is needful, but to superfluity. But now, during the last three weeks of the march, he had learned another new and consolatory truth—he had learned that there is nothing terrible to be dreaded in the world. He had learned that just as there is no position in the world in which a man can be happy and perfectly free, so too there is no position in which he need be unhappy and in bondage. He had found out that there is a limit to suffering and a limit to freedom, and that that limit is very soon reached; that the man who suffered from a crumpled petal in his bed of roses, suffered just as much as he suffered now, sleeping on the bare, damp earth, with one side getting chilled as the other side got warm; that when in former days he had put on his tight dancing-shoes, he had suffered in just the same way as now, when he walked quite barefoot (his foot-gear had long since fallen to pieces), with his feet covered with sores. He learned that when he had—by his own freewill, as he had fancied—married his wife, he had been no more free than now when he was locked up for the night in a stable. Of all that he did himself afterwards call sufferings, though at the time he hardly felt them so, the chief was the state of his bare, blistered, sore feet. The horse-flesh was savoury and nourishing, the saltpetre flavour given it by the gunpowder they used instead of salt was positively agreeable; there was no great degree of cold, it was always warm in the daytime on the march, and at night there were the camp-fires, and the lice that devoured him helped to keep him warm. One thing was painful in the earlier days—that was his feet.

On the second day of the march, as he examined his blisters by the camp-fire, Pierre thought he could not possibly walk on them; but when they all got up, he set off limping, and later on, when he got warm, he walked without pain, though his feet looked even more terrible that evening. But he did not look at them, and thought of something else.

Only now Pierre grasped all the force of vitality in man, and the saving power innate in man, of transferring his attention, like the safety-valve in steam-engines, that lets off the superfluous steam so soon as its pressure exceeds a certain point.

He did not see and did not hear how the prisoners that lagged behind were shot, though more than a hundred of them had perished in that way. He did not think about Karataev, who was getting weaker every day, and would obviously soon fall a victim to the same fate. Still less did Pierre think about himself. The harder his lot became, the more terrible his future, the more independent of his present plight were the glad and soothing thoughts, memories, and images that occurred to him.

XIII

AT midday on the 22nd, Pierre was walking along the muddy, slippery road uphill, looking at his feet and at the unevenness of the road. From time to time he glanced at the familiar crowd around him, and then again at his feet. Both that crowd and those feet were alike his and familiar to him. The purplish, bandy-legged, grey dog was running merrily along at the side of the road; sometimes picking up a hind leg, and skipping along on three paws as a sign of content and briskness, or barking at the crows that perched on the carrion. The grey dog was sleeker and merrier than in Moscow. All around lay the flesh of different animals—from men to horses—in different stages of decomposition, and the marching soldiers prevented wolves from coming near it, so that the grey dog could feast to her heart's content.

Rain had been falling since early morning; and it seemed continually as though in another minute it would cease and the sky would clear, when, after a short break, the rain came on again more heavily. The road, saturated with rain, could soak up no more, and streams flowed along the ruts.

Pierre walked, looking from side to side, counting his steps, and reckoning them off in threes on his fingers. Inwardly addressing the rain, he said to it, 'Now then, come on then, pelt away!'

It seemed to him that he was thinking of nothing at all; but somewhere deep down his soul was pondering something grave and consolatory. That something was the subtlest, spiritual deduction arising from his talk the night before with Karataev.

Getting chilled by the dying fire on the previous night's halt, Pierre had got up and moved to the next fire, which was burning better. There Platon was sitting, with a coat put over his head, like a priest's chasuble. In his flexible, pleasant voice, feeble now from illness, he was telling the soldiers a story Pierre had heard already. It was past midnight, the time when Karataev's fever usually abated, and he was particularly lively. As he drew near the fire and heard Platon's weak, sickly voice, and saw his piteous mien in the bright firelight, Pierre felt a pang at heart. He was frightened at his own pity for this man, and would have gone away, but there was no other fire to go to, and trying not to look at Platon, he sat down by it.

'Well, how is your fever?' he asked.

'How is my fever? Weep over sickness, and God won't give you death,' said Karataev, and he went back at once to the story he had begun.

'And so, brother,' he went on with a smile on his thin, white face, and a peculiar, joyful light in his eyes, 'And so, brother...'

Pierre had heard the story long before. Karataev had told it to him about six times already, and always with special joyful emotion. But well as Pierre knew the story, he listened to it now as though it were something new, and the subdued ecstasy, which Karataev evidently felt in telling it, infected Pierre too.

It was the story of an old merchant, who had lived in good works and in the fear of God with his family, and had made a journey one day with a companion, a rich merchant, to Makary.

Both the merchants had put up at an inn and gone to sleep; and next day the rich merchant had been found robbed, and with his throat cut. A knife, stained with blood, was found under the old merchant's pillow. The merchant was tried, sentenced to be flogged, and to have his nostrils slit—all according to the law in due course, as Karataev said—and sent to hard labour.'

'And so, brother' (it was at this point in the story that Pierre found Karataev) 'ten years or more passed by after that. The old man lives on in prison. He submits, as is fitting; he does nothing wrong. Only he prays to God for death. Very well. And so at night-time they are gathered together, the convicts, just as we are here, and the old man with them. And so they fall to talking of what each is suffering for, and how he has sinned against God. One tells how he took a man's life, another two, another had set fire to something, and another was a runaway just for no reason. So they began asking the old man, "What," they say, "are you suffering for, grandfather?" "I am suffering, dear brethren," says he, "for my own sins, and for other men's sin. I have not taken a life, nor taken other men's goods, save what I have bestowed on poorer brethren. I was a merchant, dear brethren, and I had great wealth.' And he tells them this and that, and how the whole thing had happened. "For myself," says he, "I do not grieve. God has chastened me. The only thing," says he, "I am sorry for my old wife and my children." And so the old man fell a-weeping. And it so happened that in that company there was the very man, you know, who had killed the merchant. "Where did it happen, grandfather?" says he. "When and in what month?" and so he asked him all about it. His heart began to ache. He goes up to the old man like this—and falls down at his feet. "You are suffering for me, old man," says he. "It's the holy truth; this man is tormented innocently, for nothing, lads," says he. "I did that deed," says he, "and put the knife under his head when he was asleep. Forgive me, grandfather, for Christ's sake!" says he.'

Karataev paused, smiling blissfully, and gazing at the fire, as he rearranged the logs.

'The old man, he says, "God forgive you," says he, "but we are all sinners before God," says he. "I am suffering for my own sins." And he wept with bitter tears. What do you think, darling?' said Karataev, his ecstatic smile growing more and more radiant, as though the great charm and whole point of his story lay in what he was going to tell now, 'what do you think, darling, that murderer confessed of himself to the police. "I have killed six men," says he (for he was a great criminal), "but what I am most sorry for is this old man. Let him not weep through my fault.' He confessed. It was written down, and a paper sent off to the right place. The place was far away. Then came a trial. Then all the reports were written in due course, by the authorities, I mean. It was brought to the Tsar. Then a decree comes from the Tsar to let the merchant go free; to give him the recompense they had awarded him. The paper comes; they fall to looking for the old man. Where was that old man who had suffered innocently? The paper had come from the Tsar, and they fell to looking for him.' Karataev's lower jaw quivered. 'But God had pardoned him already—he was dead! So it happened, —darling!' Karataev concluded, and he gazed a long while straight before him, smiling silently.

Not the story itself, but its mysterious import, the ecstatic gladness that beamed in Karataev's face as he told it, the mysterious significance of that gladness vaguely filled and rejoiced Pierre's soul now.

XIV

'To your places!' a voice shouted suddenly.

There was a cheerful stir among the prisoners and convoy soldiers, and an air of expecting something festive and solemn. Shouted commands could be heard on all sides, and a party of well-dressed cavalry soldiers on good horses came trotting up from the left, making a circuit round the prisoners. Every face wore the look of nervousness commonly seen at the approach of men in authority. The prisoners huddled together and were shoved out of the way. The convoy soldiers formed in ranks.

'The Emperor! The Emperor! The marshal! the duke! ...' and the sleek cavalry soldiers had hardly ridden by when a carriage rattled up drawn by grey horses. Pierre had a passing glimpse of the serene, handsome, fat, white face of a man in a three-cornered hat. It was one of the marshals. The marshal's eye was caught by Pierre's big, striking figure; and in the expression with which he frowned and looked away Pierre fancied he saw pity and the desire to conceal it.

The general in charge of the transport whipped up his lean horse, and galloped after the carriage with a red, panic stricken face. Several officers met in a group; the soldiers came round them. All had excited and uneasy faces.

'What did he say? What was it he said? ...' Pierre heard.

While the marshal was driving by, the prisoners had been hustled together into one group, and Pierre caught sight of Karataev, whom he had not yet seen that morning. He was sitting, wrapped in his little military coat, leaning against a birch-tree. His face still wore the same look of joyous emotion as when he had been telling the story of the merchant, but it had another expression too, a look of subdued solemnity.

Karataev looked at Pierre with his kindly, round eyes, that were bright now with tears, and there was an unmistakable appeal in them. He evidently wanted to say something to him. But Pierre was in too great dread for himself. He made as though he had not seen that look, and hastily walked away.

When the prisoners set off again Pierre looked back. Karataev was sitting under the birch-tree by the edge of the road, and two Frenchmen were bending over him in conversation. Pierre did not look again. He went on limping up the hill.

There was the sound of a shot behind, at the spot where Karataev was sitting. Pierre heard that shot distinctly, but at the moment that he heard it, he recalled that he had not finished reckoning up how many stages were left to Smolensk, the calculation he had begun before the marshal rode by. And he began to reckon. Two French soldiers ran by Pierre, one holding a still smoking gun. They were both pale, and in the expression of their faces—one of them glanced timidly at Pierre—there was something like what he had seen in the young soldier at the execution in Moscow. Pierre looked at the soldier and remembered how, the day before yesterday, that man had burnt his shirt in drying it before the fire, and how the others had laughed at him.

The dog began to howl behind at the spot where Karataev was sitting. 'Silly creature! what is she howling for?' thought Pierre.

The prisoners, his companions marching at his side, like him, refrained from looking back to the place whence came the sound of the shot and the dog's howl. There was a set look on all their faces.

XV

THE cavalry transport, and the prisoners, and the marshal's baggage-train, halted at the village of Shamshevo. All crowded together round the camp-fire. Pierre went up to a fire, ate some roast horse-flesh, lay down with his back to the fire, and at once fell asleep. He fell into the same sort of sleep that he had slept at Mozhaisk, after the battle of Borodino.

Again the facts of real life mingled with his dreams; and again some one, himself or some one else, was uttering thoughts in his ear, and the same thoughts, indeed, as had come in his dream at Mozhaisk.

Life is everything. Life is God. All is changing and moving, and that motion is God. And while there is life, there is the joy of the consciousness of the Godhead. To love life is to love God. The hardest and the most blessed thing is to love this life in one's sufferings, in undeserved suffering.

'Karataev!' flashed into Pierre's mind. And all at once there rose up, as vivid as though alive, the image, long forgotten, of the gentle old teacher, who had given Pierre geography lessons in Switzerland. 'Wait a minute,' the old man was saying. And he was showing Pierre a globe. This globe was a living, quivering ball, with no definite limits. Its whole surface consisted of drops, closely cohering together. And those drops were all in motion, and changing, several passing into one, and then one splitting up again into many. Every drop seemed striving to spread, to take up more space, but the others, pressing upon it, sometimes absorbed it, sometimes melted into it.

'This is life,' the old teacher was saying.

'How simple it is and how clear,' thought Pierre. 'How was it I did not know that before? God is in the midst, and each drop strives to expand, to reflect Him on the largest scale possible. And it grows, and is absorbed and crowded out, and on the surface it disappears, goes back into the depths, and falls not to the surface again. That is how it is with him, with Karataev; he is absorbed and has disappeared.'

'You understand, my child,' said the teacher.

'You understand, damn you!' shouted a voice, and Pierre woke up.

He raised his head and sat up. A French soldier was squatting on his heels by the fire. He had just shoved away a Russian soldier, and was roasting a piece of meat on the end of a ramrod. His sinewy, lean, hairy, red hands, with short fingers, were deftly turning the ramrod. His brown, morose face, with its sullen brows, could be clearly seen in the light of the glowing embers.

'It's just the same to him,' he muttered, quickly addressing a soldier standing behind him. 'Brigand! go!'

And the soldier, turning the ramrod, glanced gloomily at Pierre. The latter turned away, gazing into the shadows. A Russian soldier, the one who had been pushed away, was sitting near the fire, patting something with his hand. Looking more closely, Pierre saw the grey dog, who was sitting by the soldier, wagging her tail.

'Ah, she has come . . .' said Pierre. 'And Plat . . .' he was beginning, but he did not go on. All at once, instantly in close connection, there rose up the memory of the look Platon had fixed upon him, as he sat under the tree, of the shot heard at that spot, of the dog's howl, of the guilty faces of the soldiers as they ran by, of the smoking gun, of Karataev's absence at that halting-place; and he was on the point of fully realising that Karataev had been killed, but at the same instant, at some mysterious summons, there rose up the memory of a summer evening he had spent with a beautiful Polish lady on the verandah of his house at Kiev. And nevertheless, making no effort to connect the impressions of the day, and to deduce anything from them, Pierre closed his eyes, and the picture of the summer night in the country mingled with the thought of bathing and of that fluid, quivering globe, and he seemed to sink deep down into water, so that the waters closed over his head.

Before sunrise he was wakened by loud and rapid shots and outcries. The French were flying by him.

'The Cossacks!' one of them shouted, and a minute later a crowd of Russians were surrounding Pierre. For a long while Pierre could not understand what had happened to him. He heard all about him his comrades' wails of joy.

'Mates! our own folk! brothers!' the old soldiers cried weeping, as they embraced the Cossacks and the hussars. The hussars and the Cossacks crowded round the prisoners, pressing on them clothes, and boots, and bread. Pierre sat sobbing in their midst, and could not utter one word; he hugged the first soldier who went up to him, and kissed him, weeping.

Dolohov was standing at the gates of a dilapidated house, letting the crowd of unarmed Frenchmen pass by him. The French, excited by all that had happened, were talking loudly among themselves; but as they passed before Dolohov, who stood switching his boots with his riding-whip, and watching them with his cold, glassy eyes, that boded nothing good, their talk died away. One of Dolohov's Cossacks stood on the other side, counting the prisoners, and marking off the hundreds with a chalk mark on the gate.

'How many?' Dolohov asked him.

'The second hundred,' answered the Cossack.

'*Filez, filez,*' said Dolohov, who had picked up the expression from the French; and when he met the eyes of the passing prisoners, his eyes gleamed with a cruel light.

With a gloomy face Denisov, holding his high Cossack hat in his hand, was walking behind the Cossacks, who were bearing to a hole freshly dug in the garden the body of Petya Rostov.

XVI

FROM the 28th of October, when the frosts began, the flight of the French assumed a more tragic aspect, from the men being frozen or roasted to death by the camp-fires, while the Emperor, and kings, and dukes, still drove on with their stolen booty in fur cloaks and closed carriages. But in its essentials, the process of the flight and disintegration of the French army went on unchanged.

From Moscow to Vyazma of the seventy-three thousands of the French army (not reckoning the Guards, who had done nothing but pillage all through the war), only thirty-six thousand were left, though only five thousand had been killed in battle. Here we have the first term of a progression, by which the remaining terms are determined with mathematical exactness. The French army went on melting away and disappearing in the same ratio from Moscow to Vyazma, from Vyazma to Smolensk, from Smolensk to the Berezina, from the Berezina to Vilna, apart from the greater or less degree of cold, the pursuit and barring of the way, and all other conditions taken separately. After Vyazma, instead of three columns, the French troops formed a single mass, and so they marched on to the end. This is how Berthier wrote to the Emperor (we know that generals feel it permissible to depart rather widely from the truth in describing the condition of their armies): —

'I think it my duty to report to your Majesty the condition of the various corps under my observation on the march the last two or three days. They are almost disbanded. Hardly a quarter of the men remain with the flags of their regiments; the rest wander off on their own account in different directions, trying to seek food and to escape discipline. All think only of Smolensk, where they hope to recover. During the last few days many soldiers have been observed to throw away their cartridges and muskets. In such a condition of affairs, whatever your further plans may be, the interests of your Majesty's service make it essential to muster the army at Smolensk, and to rid them of ineffectives, such as cavalrymen without horses, as well as superfluous baggage and a part of the artillery, which is now out of proportion with the numbers of the effective army. Supplies and some days' rest are essential: the soldiers are exhausted by hunger and fatigue; during the last few days many have died by the roadside or in the bivouacs. This state of things is growing continually worse, and if steps are not quickly taken for averting the danger, we shall be exposed to the risk of being unable to control the army in the event of a battle.

'November 9. Thirty versts from Smolensk.'

After struggling into Smolensk, the promised land of their dreams, the French killed one another fighting over the food there, sacked their own stores, and when everything had been pillaged, they ran on further. All hastened on, not knowing whither or for what end they were going; least of all knew that great genius, Napoleon, since there was no one to give him orders. But still he and those about him clung to their old habits: wrote commands, letters, reports, orders of the day; called each other your majesty, *mon frère, Prince d'Eckmühl, roi de Naples,* and so on. But the orders and reports were all on paper: no attempt was made to carry them out, because they could not be carried out. And although they addressed each other as 'majesty,' 'highness,' and *'mon cousin,'* they all felt that they were pitiful and loathsome creatures, who had done a great wrong, for which they had now to pay the penalty. And in spite of their pretence of caring for the army, each was thinking only of himself, and how to make his escape as quickly as possible to safety.

XVII

THE actions of the Russian and French armies during the retreat from Moscow to the Niemen resembled a game of Russian blindman's buff, in which there are two players, both with their eyes bandaged, and one rings a bell at intervals to let the other know of his whereabouts. At first he rings his bell with no fear of his opponent; but when he begins to find himself in a difficult position, he runs away as noiselessly as he can from his opponent, and often supposing he is running away from him, walks straight into his arms.

At first Napoleon's army made its whereabouts known—that was in the early period of the retreat along the Kaluga road—but afterwards, when they had taken to the Smolensk road, they ran holding the tongue of the bell; and often supposing they were running away, ran straight towards the Russians.

Owing to the rapidity of the flight of the French, and of the Russians after them, and the consequent exhaustion of the horses, the chief means of keeping a close watch on the enemy's position—by means of charges of cavalry—was out of the question. Moreover, in consequence of the frequent and rapid changes of position of both armies, what news did come always came too late. If information arrived on the second that the army of the enemy had been in a certain place on the first, by the third, when the information could be acted upon, the army was already two days' march further, and in quite a different position.

One army fled, the other pursued. From Smolensk, there were a number of different roads for the French to choose from; and one would have thought that, as they stayed there four days, the French might have found out where the enemy was, have thought out some advantageous plan, and undertaken something new. Yet after a halt of four days, the crowds of them ran back; again not to right or to left, but, with no manœuvres or plans, along their old road—the worst one—by Krasnoe and Orsha, along their beaten track.

Expecting the enemy in their rear and not in front, the French ran, straggling out, and getting separated as far as twenty-four hours' march from one another. In front of all fled the Emperor, then the kings, then the dukes. The Russian army, supposing Napoleon would take the road to the right beyond the Dnieper—the only sensible course—turned also to the right, and came out on the high road at Krasnoe. And here, just as in the game of blindman, the French came bearing straight down on our vanguard. Seeing the enemy unexpectedly, the French were thrown into confusion, stopped short from the suddenness of the fright, but then ran on again, abandoning their own comrades in their rear. Then for three days, the separate parts of the French army passed, as it were, through the lines of the Russian army: first the viceroy's troops, then Davoust's, and then Ney's. They all abandoned one another, abandoned their heavy baggage, their artillery, and half their men, and fled, making semicircles to the right to get round the Russians by night.

Ney was the last, because in spite, or perhaps in consequence, of their miserable position, with a child's impulse to beat the floor that has bruised it, he lingered to demolish the walls of Smolensk, which had done nobody any harm. Ney, who was the last to pass with his corps of ten thousand, reached Napoleon at Orsha with only a thousand men, having abandoned all the rest, and all his cannons, and made his way by stealth at night, under cover of the woods, across the Dneiper.

From Orsha they fled on along the road to Vilna, still playing the same game of blindman with the pursuing army. At Berezina again, they were thrown into confusion, many were drowned, many surrendered, but those that got across the river, fled on.

Their chief commander wrapped himself in a fur cloak, and getting into a sledge, galloped off alone, deserting his companions. Who ever could, ran away too, and those who could not—surrendered or died.

XVIII

ONE might have supposed that the historians, who ascribe the actions of the masses to the will of one man, would have found it impossible to explain the retreat of the French on their theory, considering that they did everything possible during this period of the campaign to bring about their own ruin, and that not a single movement of that rabble of men, from their turning into the Kaluga road up to the flight of the commander from his army, showed the slightest trace of design.

But no! Mountains of volumes have been written by historians upon this campaign, and in all of them we find accounts of Napoleon's masterly arrangements and deeply considered plans; of the strategy with which the soldiers were led, and the military genius showed by the marshals.

The retreat from Maley Yaroslavets, when nothing hindered Napoleon from passing through a country abundantly furnished with supplies, and the parallel road was open to him, along which Kutuzov afterwards pursued him—this wholly unnecessary return by a road through devastated country is explained to us as due to various sagacious considerations. Similar reasons are given us for Napoleon's retreat from Smolensk to Orsha. Then we have a description of his heroism at Krasnoe, when he is reported to have prepared to give battle, and to take the command, and coming forward with a birch stick in his hand, to have said:

'Long enough I have been an emperor, it is time now to be a general!

Yet in spite of this, he runs away immediately afterwards, abandoning the divided army in the rear to the hazards of destiny.

Then we have descriptions of the greatness of some of the marshals, especially of Ney—a greatness of soul that culminated in his taking a circuitous route by the forests across the Dneiper, and fleeing without his flags, his artillery, and nine-tenths of his men into Orsha.

And lastly, the final departure of the great Emperor from his heroic army is represented by the historians as something great—a stroke of genius.

Even that final act of running away—which in homely language would be described as the lowest depth of baseness, such as every child is taught to feel ashamed of—even that act finds justification in the language of the historians.

When it is impossible to stretch the elastic thread of historical argument further, when an action is plainly opposed to what all humanity is agreed in calling right and justice, the historians take refuge in the conception of greatness. Greatness would appear to exclude all possibility of applying standards of right and wrong. For the great man—nothing is wrong. There is no atrocity which could be made a ground for blaming a great man.

'*C'est grand!*' cry the historians; and at that word good and bad have ceased to be, and there are only '*grand*' and not '*grand*'. '*Grand*' is equivalent to good, and not '*grand*' to bad. To be *grand* is to their notions the characteristic of certain exceptional creatures, called by them heroes. And Napoleon, wrapping himself in his warm fur cloak and hurrying home away from men, who were not only his comrades, but (in his belief) brought there by his doing, feels *que c'est grand*; and his soul is content.

'*Du sublime au ridicule il n'y a qu'un pas,*' he says (he sees something grand in himself). And the whole world has gone on for fifty years repeating: Sublime! Grand! Napoleon the Great.

'*Du sublime au ridicule il n'y a qu'un pas.*'

And it never enters any one's head that to admit a greatness, immeasurable by the rule of right and wrong, is but to accept one's own nothingness and immeasurable littleness.

For us, with the rule of right and wrong given us by Christ, there is nothing for which we have no standard. And there is no greatness where there is not simplicity, goodness, and truth.

XIX

WHAT Russian reader has not known an irksome feeling of annoyance, dissatisfaction, and perplexity, when he reads the accounts of the latter period of the campaign of 1812? Who has not asked himself: How was it all the French were not captured or cut to pieces, when all the three Russian armies were surrounding them in superior numbers, when the French were a disorderly, starving, and freezing rabble, and the whole aim of the Russians (so history tells us) was to check, to cut off, and to capture all the French?

How was it that the Russian army, that with inferior numbers had fought the battle of Borodino, failed in its aim of capturing the French, when the latter were surrounded on three sides? Can the French be so immensely superior to us that we are not equal to beating them, when we have surrounded them with forces numerically superior? How could that have come to pass? History (what passes by that name) answers these questions by saying that that came to pass because Kutuzov, and Tormasov, and Tchitchagov, and this general and that failed to carry out certain manoeuvres.

But why did they fail to carry them out? And how was it, if they really were responsible for not attaining the aim set before them, that they were not tried and punished for their shortcomings? But even if we admit that Kutuzov and Tchitchagov and the others were responsible for the non-success of the Russians, it is still impossible to understand why, in the position the Russian troops were in at Krasnoe and the Berezina, on both occasions with numerically superior forces, the French army and marshals were not taken prisoners, if that really was the aim of the Russians.

The explanation of this phenomenon given by the Russian military historians—that Kutuzov hindered the attack—is insufficient, because we know that Kutuzov was not able to restrain the troops from attacking at Vyazma and Tarutino. Why was it that the Russian army, that with inferior forces, gained a victory at Borodino over the enemy in full strength, was unsuccessful at Krasnoe and the Berezina, when fighting in superior numbers against the undisciplined crowds of the French.

If the aim of the Russians really was to cut off Napoleon and his marshals, and to take them prisoners, and that aim was not only frustrated, but all attempts at attaining it were every time defeated in the most shameful way, this last period of the war is quite correctly represented by the French as a series of victories for them, and quite incorrectly represented by the Russians as redounding to our glory.

The Russian military historians, so far as they recognise the claims of logic, are forced to this conclusion, and in spite of their lyric eulogies of Russian gallantry and devotion, and all the rest of it, they are reluctantly obliged to admit that the retreat of the French from Moscow was a series of victories for Napoleon and of defeats for Kutuzov.

But putting patriotic vanity entirely aside, one cannot but feel that there is an inherent discrepancy in this conclusion, seeing that the series of Russian defeats was followed by the destruction of their enemy, and the deliverance of their country.

The source of this discrepancy lies in the fact that historians, studying events in the light of the letters of the sovereigns and of generals, of narratives, reports, projects, and so on, have assumed quite falsely that the plan of that period of the campaign of 1812 was to cut off and capture Napoleon and his marshals and his army.

Such a plan never was, and could not have been, the aim of the Russian army, because it had no meaning, and its attainment was utterly out of the question.

There was no object in such a plan. In the first place, because Napoleon's army was flying in disorder at its utmost possible speed out of Russia; that is to say, doing the very thing that every Russian most desired. What object was there in conducting all sorts of operations against the French when they were running away as fast as they could already? Secondly, it would have been idle to stop men on the road, whose whole energies were bent on flight. Thirdly, it would have been absurd to lose men in destroying the French army when it was already, without external interference, perishing at such a rate that, without any obstruction of their road, not more than one hundredth of its original number succeeded in crossing the frontier in December.

Fourthly, it was absurd to desire to take prisoners the Emperor, kings, and dukes, since the possession of such prisoners would have greatly enhanced the difficulty of the Russian position, as was recognised by the most clear-sighted diplomatists of the time (J. Maistre and others). Still more absurd would have been the desire to capture the French army when it had dwindled to one-half before reaching Krasnoe, and a division of convoys had to be given up to guard a corps of prisoners, while the Russian soldiers themselves had not always full rations, and the prisoners they did take died of hunger.

Any plan of cutting off and capturing Napoleon and his army, however carefully thought out, would have been like the action of a gardener who, after driving out a herd of cattle that had been trampling his beds, should run out to belabour the cattle about the head. The only thing that could be said in justification of his proceeding would be that he was great incensed. But the authors of this supposed plan cannot plead even this excuse, since theirs were not the gardens that had been trampled.

And, besides being absurd, to cut off the retreat of Napoleon's army was also impossible.

It was impossible, in the first place, because, since experience shows that the movement of columns in a single battlefield at five versts' distance never coincides with the plan of their movements, the probability that Tchitchagov, Kutuzov, and Wittgenstein would all reach an appointed spot in time was so remote that it practically amounted to impossibility. As Kutuzov in fact regarded it when he said that manœuvres planned at great distances do not produce the results expected of them.

Secondly, it was impossible, because to paralyse the force of inertia with which Napoleon's army was rebounding back along its track, incomparably greater forces were needed than those the Russians had at their command.

Thirdly, it was impossible, because the military expression, to cut off, has really no meaning. One may cut off a slice of bread, but not an army. To cut off an army—that is, to bar its road—is impossible, because there are always many places by which the men can make a circuit to get out, and there is always the night, during which nothing can be done; a fact of which the military strategists might have been convinced by the examples of Krasnoe and Berezina. One can never take a prisoner unless he agrees to be taken, just as one can never catch a swallow, though of course it is possible if it settles on one's hand. One can take a prisoner who will surrender, as the Germans did, in accordance with the rules of strategy and tactics. But the French soldiers very wisely did not feel it incumbent on them to do so, since death from cold and hunger awaited them as much if taken prisoner, as if persisting in their flight.

The fourth and chief reason why it was impossible is that war was waged in 1812 under conditions more terrible than ever since the world has existed; and the Russian troops strained every nerve in the pursuit of the French, and could not have done more without perishing themselves.

The Russian army lost in its march from Tarutino to Krasnoe fifty thousand sick or stragglers, that is, a number equal to the population of a large provincial town. Half of the army was lost without a battle.

At this period of the campaign the soldiers were without boots or fur-lined coats, on half rations, without vodka, camping out at night for months in the snow with fifteen degrees of frost; while there were only seven or eight hours of daylight, and the rest was night; where discipline could exert the same influence, and men were put in peril of death, not for a few hours, as on the field of battle, but for whole months together were keeping up a struggle every moment with death from cold and hunger. And of this period of the campaign, when half the army perished in one month, the historians tell us that Miloradovitch ought to have made an oblique march in one direction, and Tormasov in another, and Tchitchagov ought to have advanced to this point (the men advancing knee-deep in the snow), and that so and so pushed through and cut the French off, and so on, and so on.

The Russian soldiers did all that could or ought to have been done to attain an end worthy of the people, and half of them died in doing it. They are not to blame because other Russians, sitting in warm rooms at home, proposed that they should do the impossible.

All this strange discrepancy between the facts and the accounts of historians, so difficult to understand today, arises simply from this, that the historians wrote the history of the noble sentiments and fine speeches of various generals, and not the history of the events themselves.

They attach great consequence to the words of Miloradovitch, to the honours bestowed on this general or that, and the proposals made by them. But the question of the fifty thousand men who lay in the hospitals and graveyards does not even interest them, for it does not come within the scope of their researches.

And yet we have but to turn away from researches among the reports and plans of the generals, and to look into the movements of those hundred thousand men who took direct immediate part in the events; and all the questions that seemed insoluble before can be readily and certainly explained with extraordinary ease and simplicity.

The plan of cutting off Napoleon and his army never existed save in the imagination of some dozen men. It could not have existed because it was absurd and could not be carried out.

The people had a single aim: to clear their country of the invaders. That aim was effected primarily of itself, since the French were flying, and all that was necessary was not to check their flight. It was promoted, too, by the irregular warfare kept up by the people destroying the French army piecemeal; and thirdly, by the great Russian army following in the rear of the French, ready to use force in case there were any pause in their retreat.

The Russian army had to act as a whip urging on a fleeing animal. And the experienced driver knew that it was better to keep the whip raised as a menace than to bring it down on the creature's back.

PART XV

I

WHEN A MAN sees an animal dying, a horror comes over him. What he is himself—his essence, visibly before his eyes, perishes—ceases to exist. But when the dying creature is a man, and a man dearly loved, then, besides the horror at the extinction of life, what is felt is a rending of the soul, a spiritual wound, which, like a physical wound, is sometimes mortal, sometimes healed, but always aches and shrinks from contact with the outer world, that sets it smarting.

After Prince Andrey's death, Natasha and Princess Marya both alike felt this. Crushed in spirit, they closed their eyes under the menacing cloud of death that hovered about them, and dared not look life in the face. Carefully they guarded their open wounds from every rough and painful touch. Everything—the carriage driving along the street, the summons to dinner, the maid asking which dress to get out; worse still —words of faint, feigned sympathy—set the wound smarting, seemed an insult to it, and jarred on that needful silence in which both were trying to listen to the stern, terrible litany that had not yet died away in their ears, and to gaze into the mysterious, endless vistas that seemed for a moment to have been unveiled before them.

Only alone together were they safe from such outrage and pain. They said little to one another. When they did speak, it was about the most trivial subjects. And both equally avoided all mention of anything connected with the future.

To admit the possibility of a future seemed to them an insult to his memory. Still more circumspectly did they avoid in their talk all that could be connected with the dead man. It seemed to them that what they had felt and gone through could not be expressed in words. It seemed to them that every allusion in words to the details of his life was an outrage on the grandeur and holiness of the mystery that had been accomplished before their eyes.

The constant restraint of speech and studious avoidance of everything that might lead to words about him, these barriers, fencing off on all sides what could not be spoken of, brought what they were feeling even more clearly and vividly before their minds.

But pure and perfect sorrow is as impossible as pure and perfect joy. From the isolation of her position, as the guardian and foster-mother of her nephew, and independent mistress of her own destinies, Princess Marya was the first to be called back to life from that world of mourning in which she lived for the first fortnight. She received letters from her relations which had to be answered; the room in which Nikolushka had been put was damp, and he had begun to cough. Alpatitch came to Yaroslavl with accounts. He had suggestions to make, and advised Princess Marya to move to Mscow to the house in Vozdvizhenka, which was uninjured, and only needed some trifling repairs. Life would not stand still, and she had to live. Painful as it was for Princess Marya to come out of that world of solitary contemplation, in which she had been living till then, and sorry, and, as it were, conscience-stricken, as she felt at leaving Natasha alone, the duties of daily life claimed her attention, and against her own will she had to give herself up to them. She went through the accounts with Alpatitch, consulted Dessalle about her little nephew, and began to make preparations for moving to Moscow.

Natasha was left alone, and from the time that Princess Marya began to busy herself with preparations for her journey, she held aloof from her too.

Princess Marya asked the countess to let Natasha come to stay with her in Moscow; and both mother and father eagerly agreed to her suggestion, for they saw their daughter's physical strength failing every day, and they hoped that change of scene and the advice of Moscow doctors might do her good.

'I am not going anywhere,' answered Natasha, when the suggestion was made to her; 'all I ask is, please let me alone,' she said, and she ran out of the room, hardly able to restrain tears more of vexation and anger than of sorrow.

Since she felt herself deserted by Princess Marya, and alone in her grief, Natasha had spent most of her time alone in her room, huddled up in a corner of her sofa. While her slender, nervous fingers were busy twisting or tearing something, she kept her eyes fixed in a set stare on the first object that met them. This solitude exhausted and tortured her; but it was what she needed. As soon as any one went in to her, she got up quickly, changed her attitude and expression, and picked up a book or some needlework, obviously waiting with impatience for the intruder to leave her.

It seemed to her continually that she was on the very verge of understanding, of penetrating to the mystery on which her spiritual vision was fastened with a question too terrible for her to bear.

One day towards the end of December, Natasha, thin and pale, in a black woollen gown, with her hair fastened up in a careless coil, sat perched up in the corner of her sofa, her fingers nervously crumpling and smoothing out the ends of her sash, while she gazed at the corner of the door.

She was inwardly gazing whither he had gone, to that further shore. And that shore, of which she had never thought in old days, which had seemed to her so far away, so incredible, was now closer to her, and more her own, more comprehensible than this side of life, in which all was emptiness and desolation or suffering and humiliation.

She was gazing into that world where she knew he was. But she could not see him, except as he had been here on earth. She was seeing him again as he had been at Mytishtchy, at Troitsa, at Yaroslavi.

She was seeing his face, hearing his voice, and repeating his words, and words of her own that she had put into his mouth; and sometimes imagining fresh phrases for herself and him which could only have been uttered in the past.

Now she saw him as he had once been, lying on a low chair in his velvet, fur-lined cloak, his head propped on his thin, pale hand. His chest looked fearfully hollow, and his shoulders high. His lips were firmly closed, his eyes shining, and there was a line on his white brow that came and vanished again. There was a rapid tremor just perceptible in one foot. Natasha knew he was struggling to bear horrible pain. 'What was that pain like? Why was it there? What was he feeling? How did it hurt?' Natasha had wondered. He had noticed her attention, raised his eyes, and, without smiling, began to speak.

'One thing would be awful,' he had said: 'to bind oneself for ever to a suffering invalid. It would be an everlasting torture.' And he had looked with searching eyes at her. Natasha, as she always did, had answered without giving herself time to think; she had said: 'It can't go on like this, it won't be so, you will get well—quite well.'

She was seeing him now as though it were the first time, and going through all she had felt at that time. She recalled the long, mournful, stern gaze he had given her at those words, and she understood all the reproach and the despair in that prolonged gaze.

'I agreed,' Natasha said to herself now, 'that it would be awful if he were to remain always suffering. I said that then only because it would be so awful for him, but he did not understand it so. He thought that it would be awful *for me*. Then he still wanted to live, and was afraid of death. And I said it so clumsily, so stupidly. I was not thinking that. I was thinking something quite different. If I had said what I was thinking, I should have said: "Let him be dying, dying all the time before my eyes, and I should be happy in comparison with what

I am now." Now . . . there is nothing, no one. Did he know that? No. He did not know, and never will know it. And now it can never, never be made up for.'

And again he was saying the same words; but this time Natasha in her imagination made him a different answer. She stopped him, and said: 'Awful for you, but not for me. You know that I have nothing in life but you, and to suffer with you is the greatest happiness possible for me.' And he took her hand and pressed it, just as he had pressed it on that terrible evening four days before his death. And in her imagination she said to him other words of tenderness and love, which she might have said then, which she only said now. . . . 'I love thee! . . . thee . . . I love, love thee . . .' she said, wringing her hands convulsively, and setting her teeth with bitter violence . . .

And a sweeter mood of sorrow was coming over her, and tears were starting into her eyes; but all at once she asked herself: 'To whom was she saying that? Where is he, and what is he now?'

And again everything was shrouded in chill, cruel doubt, and again, frowning nervously, she tried to gaze into that world where he was. And now, now, she thought, she was just penetrating the mystery . . . But at that instant, when the incomprehensible, it seemed, was being unveiled before her eyes, a loud rattle at the door handle broke with a painful shock on her hearing. Her maid, Dunyasha, rushed quickly and abruptly into the room with frightened eyes, that took no heed of her.

'Come to your papa, make haste,' Dunyasha said, with a strange, excited expression. 'A misfortune . . . Pyotr Ilyitch . . . a letter,' she gasped out, sobbing.

II

THE feeling of aloofness from all the world, that Natasha experienced at this time, she felt in an even more marked degree with the members of her own family. All her own family, her father and mother and Sonya, were so near her, so every day and ordinary that every word they uttered, every feeling they expressed, was jarring in the world in which she had lived of late. She felt more than indifference, positive hostility to them. She heard Dunyasha's words of Pyotr Ilyitch, of a misfortune, but she did not understand them.

'What misfortune could they have, what misfortune is possible to them? Everything goes on in its old, regular, easy way with them,' Natasha was saying inwardly.

As she went into the drawing-room, her father came quickly out of the countess's room. His face was puckered up and wet with tears. He had evidently run out of the room to give vent to the sobs that were choking him. Seeing Natasha, he waved his arms in despair, and went off into violent, miserable sobs, that convulsed his soft, round face.

'Pet . . . Petya . . . Go, go in, she's calling . . .' And sobbing like a child, he tottered with feeble legs to a chair, and almost dropped on to it, hiding his face in his hands.

An electric shock seemed to run all through Natasha. Some fearful pain seemed to stab her to the heart. She felt a poignant anguish; it seemed to her that something was being rent within her, and she was dying. But with the pain she felt an instant release from the seal that shut her out of life. At the sight of her father, and the sound of a fearful, husky scream from her mother through the door, she instantly forgot herself and her own sorrow.

She ran up to her father, but he feebly motioned her towards her mother's door. Princess Marya, with a white face and quivering lower jaw, came out and took Natasha's hand, saying something to her. Natasha neither saw nor heard her. With swift steps she went towards the door, stopped for an instant as though struggling with herself, and ran in to her mother.

The countess was lying down in a low chair in a strange, awkward attitude; she was beating her head against the wall. Sonya and some maid-servants were holding her by the arms.

'Natasha, Natasha! . . .' the countess was screaming. 'It's not true, not true . . . it's false . . . Natasha!' she screamed, pushing the maids away. 'All of you go away, it's not true! Killed! . . . ha, ha, ha! . . . not true! . . .'

Natasha knelt down on the low chair, bent over her mother, embraced her, with surprising strength lifted her up, turned her face to her, and pressed close to her.

'Mamma! . . . darling! . . . I'm here, dearest mamma,' she whispered to her, never ceasing for a second.

She would not let her mother go; she struggled tenderly with her, asked for pillows and water, unbuttoned and tore open her mother's dress. 'Dearest . . . my darling . . . Mamma . . . my precious,' she whispered without pausing, kissing her head, her hands, her face, and feeling the tears streaming in irrepressible floods over her nose and cheeks.

The countess squeezed her daughter's hand, closed her eyes, and was quieter for a moment. All at once she sat up with unnatural swiftness, looked vacantly round, and seeing Natasha, began hugging her head to her with all her might. Natasha's face involuntarily worked with the pain, as her mother turned it towards her, and gazed a long while into it. 'Natasha, you love me,' she said, in a soft, confiding whisper. 'Natasha, you won't deceive me? You will tell me the whole truth?'

Natasha looked at her with eyes swimming with tears, and in her face seemed only imploring her love and forgiveness.

'Mamma . . . darling,' she kept repeating, putting forth all the strength of her love to try somehow to take a little of the crushing load of sorrow off her mother on to herself.

And again in the helpless struggle with reality, the mother, refusing to believe that she could live while her adored boy, just blossoming into life, was dead, took refuge from reality in the world of delirium.

Natasha had no recollection of how she spent that day and that night, and the following day and the following night. She did not sleep, and did not leave her mother's side. Natasha's love, patient and persistent, seemed to enfold the countess on all sides every second, offering no explanation, no consolation, simply beckoning her back to life.

On the third night the countess was quiet for a few minutes, and Natasha closed her eyes, her head propped on the arm of the chair. The bedstead creaked; Natasha opened her eyes. The countess was sitting up in bed, and talking softly.

'How glad I am you have come home. You are tired, won't you have tea?' Natasha went up to her. 'You have grown so handsome and manly,' the countess went on, taking her daughter's hand.

'Mamma, what are you saying . . . ?'

'Natasha, he is gone, he is no more.' And embracing her daughter, the countess for the first time began to weep.

III

PRINCESS MARYA put off her departure. Sonya and the count tried to take Natasha's place, but they could not. They saw that she was the only one who could keep the mother from the frenzy of despair. For three weeks Natasha never left her mother's side, slept on a lounge in her room, made her drink and eat, and without pause talked to her, talked because her tender, loving voice was the only thing that soothed the countess.

The wound in the mother's heart could never be healed. Petya's death had torn away half of her life. When the news of Petya's death reached her, she was a fresh-looking, vigorous woman of fifty; a month later she came out of her room an old woman, half dead and with no more interest in life. But the wound that half killed the countess, that fresh wound, brought Natasha back to life.

A spiritual wound that comes from a rending of the spirit is like a physical wound, and after it has healed externally, and the torn edges are scarred over, yet, strange to say, like a deep physical injury, it only heals inwardly by the force of life pushing up from within.

So Natasha's wound healed. She believed that her life was over. But suddenly her love for her mother showed her that the essence of her life—love—was still alive within her. Love was awakened, and life waked with it.

The last days of Prince Andrey had been a close bond between Natasha and Princess Marya. This fresh trouble brought them even closer together. Princess Marya put off her departure, and for the last three weeks she had been looking after Natasha, as though she were a sick child. Those weeks spent by Natasha in her mother's room had completely broken down her health.

One day Princess Marya noticed that Natasha was shivering with a feverish chill, and brought her away to her own room, and tucked her up in her bed in the middle of the day. Natasha lay down, but when Princess Marya, having let down the blinds, was about to leave the room, Natasha called her to her.

'I'm not sleepy, Marie; stay with me.'

'You are tired; try and go to sleep.'

'No, no. Why did you bring me away? She will ask for me.'

'She is much better. She was talking much more like herself today,' said Princess Marya.

Natasha lay on the bed, and in the half-dark room she tried to make out Princess Marya's face.

'Is she like him?' Natasha wondered. 'Yes; like and unlike. But she is original, different, a quite new, unknown person. And she likes me. What is there in her heart? Everything good. But what is it like? What are her thoughts like? How does she look on me? Yes; she is nice!'

'Masha,' she said, shyly drawing her hand towards her. 'Masha, you mustn't think I'm horrid. No? Masha, darling! How I love you! Let us be quite, quite friends.' And embracing her, Natasha fell to kissing her hands and face.

Princess Marya was abashed and overjoyed at this demonstration of feeling.

From that day there sprang up between Princess Marya and Natasha one of those tender and passionate friendships which can only exist between women. They were continually kissing each other and saying tender things to one another, and they spent the greater part of their time together. If one went away, the other was uneasy and hastened to join her. They felt more harmony together with each other than apart, each with herself. There sprang up between them a feeling stronger than friendship; that was the feeling of life being only possible in each other's company.

Sometimes they did not speak for hours together. Sometimes, as they lay in their beds, they would begin to talk, and talked till morning. They talked, for the most part, of their own remote past. Princess Marya told her of her childhood, of her mother, of her father, of her dreams. And Natasha, who had in the past turned away with calm acceptance of her non-comprehension of that life of devotion and resignation, of the idealism of Christian self-sacrifice, grew to love Princess Marya's past, and to understand that side of life of which she had had no conception before. She had no thought of imitating that resignation and self-sacrifice in her own life, because she was accustomed to look for other joys in life; but she understood and loved in another that virtue that had been till now beyond her ken. Princess Marya, too, as she listened to Natasha's stories of her childhood and early girlhood, had a glimpse of a side of life she had known nothing of, of faith in life and in the enjoyment of life.

They still refrained from talking of *him*, that they might not, as it seemed to them, desecrate the exalted feeling in their hearts; but this reticence led them, though they would not have believed it, into gradually forgetting him.

Natasha had grown thin and pale, and was physically so weak that every one was continually talking about her health, and she was glad it was so. Yet sometimes she was suddenly seized, not simply by a dread of death, but by a dread of sickness, of ill-health, of losing her good looks; and sometimes she unconsciously examined her bare arm, marvelling at its thinness, or peeped in the looking-glass in the morning at her pinched face, and was touched by its piteous look. It seemed to her that this was as it should be, and yet she felt afraid and mournful at it.

One day she ran upstairs quickly, and was painfully short of breath. Immediately she made some pretext for going down again, and ran upstairs again, to try her strength and put herself to the test.

Another day she called Dunyasha, and her voice broke. She called her once more, though she heard her coming—called her in the deep chest-voice with which she used to sing, and listened to the sound.

She knew it not, and would not have believed it; yet though the layer of mould under which she fancied that her soul was buried seemed unbroken, the delicate, tender, young blades of grass were already pushing through it, and were destined to take root, and so to hide the grief that had crushed her under their living shoots that it would soon be unseen and forgotten. The wound was healing from within.

Towards the end of January Princess Marya set off for Moscow, and the count insisted on Natasha going with her to consult the doctors.

IV

AFTER the engagement at Vyazma, where Kutuzov could not restrain his troops in their desire to break through, to cut off and all the rest of it, the further march of the flying French, and of the Russians flying after them, continued as far as Krasnoe without a battle. The flight was so rapid that the Russian army racing after the French could not catch them up; the horses of the cavalry and artillery broke down, and information as to the movements of the French was always very uncertain.

The Russian soldiers were so exhausted by this unbroken march at the rate of forty versts a day that they were unable to quicken their pace.

To form an idea of the degree of exhaustion of the Russian army, one need only grasp clearly what is meant by the fact that while losing no more than five thousand killed and wounded, and not a hundred prisoners, the Russian army, which had left Tarutino a hundred thousand strong, numbered only fifty thousand on reaching Krasnoe.

The rapidity of the Russian pursuit had as disintegrating an effect on the Russian army as the flight of the French had on their army. The only difference was that the Russian army moved at its own will, free from the menace of annihilation that hung over the French, and that the sick and stragglers of the French were left in the hands of their enemy, while Russian stragglers were at home among their own people. The chief cause of the wasting of Napoleon's army was the rapidity of its movements, and an indubitable proof of that is to be seen in the corresponding dwindling of the Russian army.

Just as at Tarutino and at Vyazma, all Kutuzov's energies were directed to preventing—so far as it lay in his power—any arrest of the fatal flight of the French from being checked (as the Russian generals in Petersburg, and also in the army, wished it to be). He did all he could to urge on the flight of the French, and to slacken the speed of his own army.

In addition to the exhaustion of the men, and the immense losses due to the rapidity of their movements, Kutuzov saw another reason for slackening the pace, and not being in a hurry. The object of the Russian army was the pursuit of the French. The route of the French was uncertain, and therefore the more closely our soldiers followed on the heels of the French, the greater the distances they had to traverse. It was only by following at a considerable distance that they could take advantage of short cuts across the ziz-zags made by the French in their course. All the skilful manœuvres suggested by the generals were based on forced marches at accelerated speed, while the only rational object to be aimed at was the diminution of the strain put on the men. And this was the object to which all Kutuzov's efforts were directed during the whole campaign from Moscow to Vilna,—not casually, not fitfully, but so consistently that he never once lost sight of it.

Not through reason, not by science, but with all his Russian heart and soul, Kutuzov felt and knew, as every Russian soldier felt it, that the French were vanquished, that their foes were in flight, and that they must see them off. But at the same time he felt with his soldiers, as one man, all the sufferings of that march, unheard of at such speed and in such weather.

But the generals, especially those not Russian, burning to distinguish themselves, to dazzle people, to take some duke or king prisoner for some incomprehensible reason—those generals thought that then, when any battle was sickening and meaningless, was the very time for fighting battles and conquering somebody. Kutuzov simply shrugged his shoulders when they came to him one after another with projects of manœuvres with the ill-shod, half-clothed, and half-starved soldiers, whose numbers had in one month dwindled to one-half without a battle, and who would even, under the most favourable circumstances, have a longer distance to traverse before they reached the frontier than they had come already.

This desire on the part of the generals to distinguish themselves, to execute manœuvres, to attack, and to cut off the enemy, was particularly conspicuous whenever the Russian army did come into contact with the French.

So it was at Krasnoe, where they had expected to find one of the three columns of the French, and stumbled upon Napoleon himself with sixteen thousand troops. In spite of all Kutuzov's efforts to avoid this disastrous engagement, and to keep his men safe for three days at Krasnoe, there was a slaughter of the disordered bands of the French by the exhausted soldiers of the Russian army.

Toll wrote out a disposition: first column to advance to this spot, and so on. And as always, what was done was not at all in accordance with that disposition. Prince Eugene of Würtemburg kept up a fire from the hills on the mob of French as they raced by, and asked for reinforcements, which did not come. In the nights the French dispersed to get round the Russians, hid themselves in the woods, and all that could struggled on again.

Miloradovitch, who declared that he had no wish to know anything about the commissariat arrangements of his detachment, who could never be found when he was wanted, that *chevalier sans peur et sans reproche*, as he called himself, always eager for parleys with the French, sent messengers to demand their surrender, wasted time, and did not carry out the orders given him.

'I make you a present of that column, lads,' he said to his men, pointing out the French to his cavalry. And the cavalry, with spur and sabre, urged their broken-down horses into a trot, and with immense effort reached the column he had bestowed on them, that is to say, a mob of frozen, numb, and starving Frenchmen. And the column laid down their weapons and surrendered, which was what they had been longing to do for weeks past.

At Krasnoe there were taken twenty-six thousand prisoners, a hundred cannons, a stick of some sort, which was promptly dubbed a 'marshal's baton.' And the generals disputed among themselves who had gained most distinction in the action, and were delighted at it, though they were full of regret at not having captured Napoleon or some marshal and hero, and blamed one another, and above all Kutuzov, for failing to do so.

These men, drawn on by their own passions, were but the blind instruments of the most melancholy law of necessity; but they believed themselves heroes, and imagined that what they were doing was the noblest and most honourable achievement. They blamed Kutuzov, and declared that from the very beginning of the campaign he had prevented them from conquering Napoleon; that he thought of nothing but his own sensual gratifications, and would not advance out of Polotnyany Zavody because he was comfortable there; that he had checked the advance at Krasnoe; that he had completely lost his head when he heard Napoleon was near; that one might really suppose he had a secret understanding with Napoleon, that he had been bought over[1] by him, and so on and so on.

And not only contemporaries, misled by their own passions, have spoken thus. Posterity and history have accepted Napoleon as *grand*, while foreign writers have called Kutuzov a crafty, dissolute, weak, intriguing old man; and Russians have seen in him a nondescript being, a sort of puppet, only of use owing to his Russian name...

[1] Wilson's *Letters*.

V

IN 1812 and in 1813 Kutuzov was openly accused of blunders. The Tsar was dissatisfied with him. And in a recent history [1] inspired by promptings from the highest quarters, Kutuzov is spoken of as a designing, intriguing schemer, who was panic-stricken at the name of Napoleon, and guilty through his blunders at Krasnoe and Berezina of robbing the Russian army of the glory of complete victory over the French. Such is the lot of men not recognised by Russian intelligence as 'great men', *grands hommes*; such is the destiny of those rare and always solitary men who divining the will of Providence submit their personal will to it. The hatred and contempt of the crowd is the punishment of such men for their comprehension of higher laws.

Strange and terrible to say, Napoleon, the most insignificant tool of history, who never even in exile displayed one trait of human dignity, is the subject of the admiration and enthusiasm of the Russian historians; in their eyes he is a *grand homme*.

Kutuzov, the man who from the beginning to the end of his command in 1812, from Borodino to Vilna, was never in one word or deed false to himself, presents an example exceptional in history of self-sacrifice and recognition in the present of the relative value of events in the future. Kutuzov is conceived of by the historians as a nondescript, pitiful sort of creature, and whenever they speak of him in the year 1812, they seem a little ashamed of him.

And yet it is difficult to conceive of an nistorical character whose energy could be more invariably directed to the same unchanging aim. It is difficult to imagine an aim more noble and more in harmony with the will of a whole people. Still more difficult would it be to find an example in history where the aim of any historical personage has been so completely attained as the aim towards which all Kutuzov's efforts were devoted in 1812.

Kutuzov never talked of 'forty centuries looking down from the Pyramids,' of the sacrifices he was making for the fatherland, of what he meant to do or had done. He did not as a rule talk about himself, played no sort of part, always seemed the plainest and most ordinary man, and said the plainest and most ordinary things. He wrote letters to his daughters and to Madame de Staël, read novels, liked the company of pretty women, made jokes with the generals, the officers, and the soldiers, and never contradicted the people, who tried to prove anything to

[1] Bogdanovitch's *History of the Year 1812:* The character of Kutuzov, and criticism of the unsatisfactory results of Kutuzov's battles.

him. When Count Rastoptchin galloped up to him at Yauzsky bridge, and reproached him personally with being responsible for the loss of Moscow, and said: 'Didn't you promise not to abandon Moscow without a battle?' Kutuzov answered: 'And I am not abandoning Moscow without a battle,' although Moscow was in fact already abandoned. When Araktcheev came to him from the Tsar to say that Yermolov was to be appointed to the command of the artillery, Kutuzov said: 'Yes, I was just saying so myself,' though he had said just the opposite a moment before. What had he, the one man who grasped at the time all the vast issues of events, to do in the midst of that dull-witted crowd? What did he care whether Count Rastoptchin put down the disasters of the capital to him or to himself? Still less could he be concerned by the question which man was appointed to the command of the artillery.

This old man, who through experience of life had reached the conviction that the thoughts and words that serve as its expression are never the motive force of men, frequently uttered words, which were quite meaningless—the first words that occurred to his mind.

But heedless as he was of his words, he never once throughout all his career uttered a single word which was inconsistent with the sole aim for the attainment of which he was working all through the war. With obvious unwillingness, with bitter conviction that he would not be understood, he more than once, under the most different circumstances, gave expression to his real thought. He first differed from all about him after the battle of Borodino, which he alone persisted in calling a victory, and this view he continued to assert verbally and in reports and to his dying day. He alone said that *the loss of Moscow is not the loss of Russia*. In answer to the overtures for peace, his reply to Lauriston was: *There can be no peace, for such is the people's will*. He alone during the retreat of the French said that *all our manœuvres are unnecessary; that everything is being done of itself better than we could desire; that we must give the enemy a 'golden bridge'; that the battles of Tarutino, of Vyazma, and of Krasnoe, were none of them necessary; that we must keep some men to reach the frontier with; that he wouldn't give one Russian for ten Frenchmen*. And he, this intriguing courtier, as we are told, who lied to Araktcheev to propitiate the Tsar, he alone dared to face the Tsar's displeasure by telling him at Vilna that *to carry the war beyond the frontier would be mischievous and useless*.

But words alone would be no proof that he grasped the significance of events at the time. His actions—all without the slightest deviation—were directed towards the one three-fold aim: first, to concentrate all his forces to strike a blow at the French; secondly, to defeat them; and thirdly, to drive them out of Russia, alleviating as far as was possible the sufferings of the people and the soldiers in doing so.

He, the lingerer Kutuzov, whose motto was always 'Time and Patience,' the sworn opponent of precipitate action, he fought the battle of Borodino, and made all his preparations for it with unwonted solemnity. Before the battle of Austerlitz he foretold that it would be lost, but at Borodino, in spite of the conviction of the generals that the battle was a defeat, in spite of the fact, unprecedented in history, of his army being forced to retreat after the victory, he alone declared in opposition to all that it was a victory, and persisted in that opinion to his dying day. He was alone during the whole latter part of the campaign in insisting that there was no need of fighting now, that it was a mistake to cross the Russian frontier and to begin a new war. It is easy enough now that all the events with their consequences lie before us to grasp their significance, if only we refrain from attributing to the multitude the aims that only existed in the brains of some dozen or so of men.

But how came that old man, alone in opposition to the opinion of all, to gauge so truly the importance of events from the national standard, so that he never once was false to the best interests of his country?

The source of this extraordinary intuition into the significance of contemporary events lay in the purity and fervour of patriotic feeling in his heart.

It was their recognition of this feeling in him that led the people in such a strange manner to pick him out, an old man out of favour, as the chosen leader of the national war, against the will of the Tsar. And this feeling alone it was to which he owed his exalted position, and there he exerted all his powers as commander-in-chief not to kill and maim men, but to save them and have mercy on them.

This simple, modest, and therefore truly great figure, could not be cast into the false mould of the European hero, the supposed leader of men, that history has invented.

To the flunkey no man can be great, because the flunkey has his own flunkey conception of greatness.

VI

THE 5th of November was the first day of the so-called battle of Krasnoe.

Many had been the blunders and disputes among the generals, who had not reached their proper places, many the contradictory orders carried to them by adjutants, but towards evening it was clear that the enemy were everywhere in flight, and that there would not and could not be a battle. In the evening Kutuzov set out from Krasnoe towards Dobroe, to which place the headquarters had that day been removed.

It had been a clear, frosty day. Kutuzov, mounted on his fat, white little horse, was riding towards Dobroe, followed by an immense suite of generals, whispering their dissatisfaction behind his back. Seven thousand French prisoners had been taken that day, and all along the road they met parties of them, crowding to warm themselves round the camp-fires. Not far from Dobroe they heard a loud hum of talk from an immense crowd of tattered prisoners, bandaged and wrapped up in rags of all sorts, standing in the road near a long row of unharnessed French cannons. At the approach of the commander-in-chief the buzz of talk died away, and all eyes were fixed upon Kutuzov, who moved slowly along the road, wearing a white cap with a red band, and a wadded overcoat, that set in a hunch on his round shoulders. One of the generals began explaining to Kutuzov where the prisoners and the guns had been taken.

Kutuzov seemed absorbed in anxious thought, and did not hear the general's words. He screwed up his eyes with an air of displeasure, and gazed intently at the figures of the prisoners, who presented a particularly pitiable appearance. The majority of the French soldiers were disfigured by frost-bitten cheeks and noses, and almost all of them had red, swollen, and streaming eyes.

One group of Frenchmen was standing close by the road, and two soldiers, one with his face covered with sores, were tearing at a piece of raw meat with their hands. There was something bestial and horrible in the cursory glance they cast on the approaching generals, and the frenzied expression with which the soldier with the sore face, after a glance at Kutuzov, turned away and went on with what he was doing.

Kutuzov looked a long while intently at those two soldiers; frowning more than before, he half-closed his eyelids, and shook his head thoughtfully. Further on, he noticed a Russian soldier, who was saying something friendly to a French prisoner, laughing and clapping him on the shoulder. Kutuzov shook his head again with the same expression.

'What do you say?' he asked the general, who was trying to draw the commander-in-chief's attention to the French flags, that were set up in front of the Preobrazhensky regiment.

'Ah, the flags!' said Kutuzov, rousing himself with evident difficulty from the subject absorbing his thoughts. He looked about him absently.

Thousands of eyes were gazing at him from all sides, waiting for his words.

He came to a standstill before the Preobrazhensky regiment, sighed heavily and closed his eyes. One of the suite beckoned to the soldiers holding the flags to come up and set up the flagstaffs around the commander-in-chief. Kutuzov was silent for a few seconds. Then with obvious reluctance, yielding to the obligations of his position, he raised his head and began to speak. Crowds of officers gathered round him. He scanned the circle of officers with an attentive eye, recognising some of them.

'I thank you all!' he said, addressing the soldiers, and then again turning to the officers. In the deep stillness that prevailed all round him, his slowly articulated words were distinctly audible: 'I thank you all for your hard and faithful service. The victory is complete, and Russia will not forget you. Your glory will be for ever!' He paused, looking about him.

'Lower; bow his head lower,' he said to the soldier, who was holding the French eagle, and had accidentally lowered it before the Preobrazhensky standard.

'Lower, lower, that's it. Hurrah, lads!' he said, his chin moving quickly as he turned to the soldiers.

'Hurrah-rah-rah!' thousands of voices roared.

While the soldiers were shouting, Kutuzov, bending forward in his saddle, bowed his head, and his eyes gleamed with a mild and, as it were, ironical light.

'And now, brothers...' he said, when the shouts had died away.

And all at once his face and expression changed: it was not the commander-in-chief speaking now, but a simple, aged man, who plainly wanted to say something most important now to his comrades.

'And now, brothers. I know it's hard for you, but there's no help for it! Have a little patience; it won't last much longer. We will see our visitors off, and then we will rest. The Tsar won't forget your services. It's hard for you, but still you are at home; while they—you see what they have come to,' he said, pointing to the prisoners. 'Worse than the lowest beggars. While they were strong, we did not spare ourselves, but now we can even spare them. They too are men. Eh, lads?'

He looked about him. And in the unflinching, respectfully wondering eyes staring persistently at him, he read sympathy with his words. His face grew brighter and brighter with the gentle smile of old age, that brought clusters of wrinkles at the corners of his mouth and his eyes. He paused and dropped his head, as though in doubt.

'But after all said and done, who asked them to come here? It serves them right, the b—— b——,' he said suddenly, lifting his head. And swinging his riding-whip, he rode off at a gallop, accompanied for the first time during the whole campaign by gleeful guffaws and roars of hurrah from the men, as they moved out of rank.

The words uttered by Kutuzov were hardly understood by the soldiers. No one could have repeated the field-marshal's speech at first of such solemnity, and towards the end of such homely simplicity. But the meaning at the bottom of his words, they understood very well, and the same feeling of solemn triumph in their victory, together with pity for the enemy and the sense of the justice of their cause—expressed, too, with precisely the same homely coarseness—lay at the bottom of every soldier's heart, and found a vent in delighted shouts, that did not cease for a long while. When one of the generals addressed the commander-in-chief after this, asking whether he desired his carriage, Kutuzov broke into a sudden sob in replying. He was evidently deeply moved.

VII

IT was getting dusk on the 8th of November, the last day of the battle of Krasnoe, when the soldiers reached their halting place for the night. The whole day had been still and frosty, with now and then a few light flakes of snow. Towards evening the sky began to grow clearer. Through the snowflakes could be seen a dark, purplish, starlit sky, and the frost was growing more intense.

A regiment of musketeers, which had left Tarutino three thousand strong, but had now dwindled to nine hundred, was among the first to reach the halting-place, a village on the high road. The quartermasters, on meeting the regiment, reported that all the cottages were full of sick and dead Frenchmen, cavalry, and staff-officers. There was only one cottage left for the colonel of the regiment.

The colonel went on to his cottage. The regiment passed through the village, and stacked their guns up at the furthest cottages along the road.

Like a huge, many-legged monster, the regiment set to work preparing its food and lodging for the night. One party of soldiers trudged off, knee-deep in the snow, into the birch copse, on the right of the village, and the ring of axes and cutlasses, the crash of breaking branches, and the sounds of merry voices were immediately heard coming thence. Another group were busily at work all round the regimental baggage-waggons, which were drawn up altogether. Some fed the horses, while others got out cooking-pots and biscuits. A third section dispersed about the village, getting the cottages ready for the staff-officers, carrying out the dead bodies of the French lying in the huts, and dragging away boards, dry wood, and straw from the thatch roofs, to furnish fuel for their fires and materials for the shelters they rigged up.

Behind the huts at the end of the village fifteen soldiers were trying with merry shouts to pull down the high wattle wall of a barn from which they had already removed the roof.

'Now then, a strong pull, altogether!' shouted the voices; and in the dark the huge, snow-sprinkled boards of the wall began to give. The lower stakes of the wattle cracked more and more often, and at last the wattle heaved over, together with the soldiers, who were hanging on to it. A loud shout and roar of coarse merriment followed.

'Work at it in twos! give us a lever here! that's it. Where are you coming to?'

'Now, altogether.... But wait, lads! ... With a shout!'

All were silent, and a low voice of velvety sweetness began singing a song. At the end of the third verse, as the last note died away, twenty voices roared out in chorus, 'O-O-O-O-O! It's coming! Pull away! Heave away, lads! . . .' but in spite of their united efforts the wall hardly moved, and in the silence that followed the men could be heard panting for breath.

'Hi, you there, of the sixth company! You devils, you! Lend us a hand.... We'll do you a good turn one day!'

Twenty men of the sixth company, who were passing, joined them, and the wattle wall, thirty-five feet in length, and seven feet in breadth, was dragged along the village street, falling over, and cutting the shoulders of the panting soldiers.

'Go on, do. . . . Heave away, you there. . . . What are you stopping for? Eh, there?' . . .

The merry shouts of unseemly abuse never ceased.

'What are you about?' cried a peremptory voice, as a sergeant ran up to the party. 'There are gentry here; the general himself's in the hut here, and you devils, you curs, you! I'll teach you!' shouted the sergeant, and sent a swinging blow at the back of the first soldier he could come across. 'Can't you go quietly?'

The soldiers were quiet. The soldier who had received the blow began grumbling, as he rubbed his bleeding face, which had been scratched by his being knocked forward against the wattle.

'Ay, the devil; how he does hit a fellow! Why, he has set all my face bleeding,' he said in a timid whisper, as the sergeant walked away. 'And you don't enjoy it, eh?' said a laughing voice; and the soldiers, moderating their voices, moved on. As they got out of the village they began talking as loudly again, interspersing their talk with the same meaningless oaths.

In the hut by which the soldiers had passed there were assembled the chief officers in command, and an eager conversation was going on over their tea about that day's doings and the manoeuvres proposed for the next. The plan was to execute a flank movement to the left, to cut off and capture the viceroy.

By the time the soldiers had dragged the fence to its place they found blazing fires, cooking supper on all sides. The firewood was crackling, the snow was melting, and the black shadows of soldiers were flitting to and fro all over the space between trampled down in the snow.

Axes and cutlasses were at work on all sides. Everything was done without a word of command being given. Wood was piled up for a supply of fuel through the night, shanties were being rigged up for the officers, pots were being boiled, and arms and accoutrements set to rights.

The wattle wall was set up in a semicircle to give shelter from the north, propped up by stakes, and before it, was built a camp-fire. They beat the tattoo-call, counted over their number, had supper, and settled themselves round the fires—some repairing their foot-gear, some smoking pipes, others stripped naked trying to steam the lice out of their clothes.

VIII

ONE would naturally have expected that in the almost inconceivably wretched conditions in which the Russian soldiers were placed at that time—without thick boots, without fur-coats, without a roof over their heads in the snow, with a frost of eighteen degrees, often without full rations—they must have presented a most melancholy and depressing spectacle.

It was quite the opposite. Never under the most favourable material conditions had the army worn a livelier and more cheerful aspect. This was due to the fact that every element that showed signs of depression or weakness was sifted every day out of the army. All the physically and morally weak had long ago been left behind. What was left was the pick of the army—in strength of body and of spirit.

The camp-fire of the eighth company, screened by their wattle fence, attracted a greater crowd than any. Two sergeants were sitting by it, and the fire was blazing more brightly than any of them. They insisted on logs being brought in return for the right of sitting under the screen.

'Ho, Makyev, hullo . . . are you lost, or have the wolves eaten you? Fetch some wood,' shouted a red-faced, red-haired soldier, screwing up his eyes, and blinking from the smoke, but not moving back from the fire.

'You run, Crow, and fetch some wood,' he cried, addressing another soldier. The red-headed man was not a non-commissioned officer, not a corporal, but he was a sturdy fellow, and so he gave orders to those who were weaker than himself. A thin, little soldier, with a sharp nose, who was called the 'Crow,' got up submissively, and was about to obey; but at that moment there stepped into the light of the fire the slender, handsome figure of a young soldier, carrying a load of wood.

'Give it here. Well, that's something like!'

They broke up the wood and threw it on, blew up the fire with their mouths, and fanned it with the skirts of their coats, and the flame began to hiss and crackle. The soldiers drew nearer the fire and lighted their pipes. The handsome young soldier who had brought in the wood put his arms akimbo, and began a smart and nimble shuffle with his frozen feet as he stood.

'Ah, mother dear, the dew is cold, but yet it is fine, and a musketeer!' ∴ . he began singing, with a sort of hiccup at each syllable of the song.

'Hey, his soles are flying off!' cried the red-haired man, noticing that the dancer's soles were loose. 'He's a rare devil for dancing!'

The dancer stopped, tore off the loose leather, and flung it in the fire.

'You're right there, brother,' said he, and sitting down he took out of his knapsack a strip of French blue cloth, and began binding it round his foot. 'It's the steam that warps them,' he added, stretching his feet out to the fire.

'They'll soon serve us new ones. They say when we finish them off, we are all to have a double lot of stuff.'

'I say, that son of a bitch, Petrov, has sneaked off, it seems,' said a sergeant.

'It's a long while since I've noticed him,' said the other.

'Oh, well, a poor sort of soldier . . .'

'And in the third company, they were saying, there were nine men missing at the roll-call yesterday.'

'Well, but after all, when one's feet are frozen, how's one to walk?'

'Oh, stuff and nonsense!' said the sergeant.

'Why, do you want to do the same?' said an old soldier, reproachfully addressing the man who had talked of frozen feet.

'Well, what do you think?' the sharp-nosed soldier, called 'Crow', said suddenly, in a squeaking and quavery voice, turning himself on one elbow behind the fire. 'If a man's sleek and fat, he just grows thin, but for a thin man it's death. Look at me, now! I have no strength left,' he said, with sudden resolution, addressing a sergeant. 'Say the word for me to be sent off to the hospital. I'm one ache with rheumatism, and one only gets left behind just the same...'

'There, that's enough; that's enough,' said the sergeant calmly.

The soldier was silent, and the conversation went on.

'There's a rare lot of these Frenchies have been taken today; but not a pair of boots on one of them, one may say, worth having; no, not worth mentioning,' one of the soldiers began, starting a new subject.

'The Cossacks had stripped them of everything. We cleaned a hut for the colonel, and carried them out. It was pitiful to see them, lads,' said the dancer. 'We overhauled them. One was alive, would you believe it, muttering something in their lingo.'

'They're a clean people, lads,' said the first. 'White—why, as white as a birch-tree, and brave they are, I must say, and gentlemen, too.'

'Well, what would you expect? Soldiers are taken from all classes with them.'

'And yet they don't understand a word we say,' said the dancer, with a wondering smile. 'I says to him, "Of what kingdom are you?" and he mutters away his lingo. A strange people!'

'I'll tell you a wonderful thing, mates,' went on the man who had expressed surprise at their whiteness. 'The peasants about Mozhaisk were telling how, when they went to take away the dead where the great battle was, why, their bodies had been lying there a good month. Well, they lay there, as white and clean as paper, and not a smell about them.'

'Why, from the cold, eh?' asked one.

'You're a clever one! Cold, indeed! Why, it was hot weather. If it had been from the cold, our men, too, wouldn't have rotted. But they say, go up to one of ours, and it would all be putrified and maggoty. They tie handkerchiefs round their noses, and drag them off, turning their faces away, so they say. They can't help it. But they're white as paper; not a smell about them.'

There was a general silence.

'Must be from the feeding,' said the sergeant: 'they are gorged like gentry.'

No one replied.

'That peasant at Mozhaisk, where the battle was, was saying that they were fetched from ten villages round, and at work there for twenty days, and couldn't get all the dead away. A lot of those wolves, says he . . .'

'That was something like a battle,' said an old soldier. 'The only one worth mentioning; everything since . . . it's simply tormenting folks for nothing.'

'Oh, well, uncle, we did attack them the day before yesterday. But what's one to do? They won't let us get at them. They were so quick at laying down their arms, and on their knees. *Pardon!*—they say. And that's only one example. They have said twice that Platov had taken Polion himself. He catches him, and lo! he turns into a bird in his hands and flies away and away. And as to killing him, no manner of means of doing it.'

'You're a sturdy liar, Kiselov, by the look of you!'

'Liar, indeed! It's the holy truth.'

'Well, if you ask me, I'd bury him in the earth, if I caught him. Yes, with a good aspen cudgel. The number of folk he has destroyed!'

'Any way, we shall soon make an end of him; he won't come again,' said the old soldier, yawning.

The conversation died away; the soldiers began making themselves comfortable for the night.

'I say, what a lot of stars; how they shine! One would say the women had been laying out their linen!' said a soldier admiring the Milky Way.

'That's a sign of a good harvest, lads!'

'We shall want a little more wood.'

'One warms one's back, and one's belly freezes. That's queer.'

'O Lord!'

'What are you shoving for—is the fire only for you, eh? See . . . there he sprawls.'

In the silence that reigned snoring could be heard from a few who had gone to sleep. The rest turned themselves to get warm by the fire, exchanging occasional remarks. From a fire a hundred paces away came a chorus of merry laughter.

'They are guffawing in the fifth company,' said a soldier. 'And what a lot of them there!'

A soldier got up and went off to the fifth company.

'There's a bit of fun!' he said, coming back. 'Two Frenchies have come. One's quite frozen, but the other's a fine plucky fellow! He's singing songs.'

'O-O! must go and look . . .' Several soldiers went across to the fifth company.

IX

THE fifth company was bivouacking close up to the birch copse. An immense camp-fire was blazing brightly in the middle of the snow, lighting up the rime-covered boughs of the trees.

In the middle of the night the soldiers had heard footsteps and the cracking of branches in the copse.

'A bear, lads,' said one soldier.

All raised their heads and listened; and out of the copse there stepped into the bright light of the fire two strangely garbed human figures, clinging to one another. These were two Frenchmen, who had been hiding in the wood. Hoarsely articulating something in a tongue incomprehensible to the soldiers, they approached the fire. One, wearing an officer's hat, was rather the taller, and seemed utterly spent. He tried to sit down by the fire, but sank on to the ground. The other, a little, stumpy man, with a kerchief bound round his cheeks, was stronger. He held his companion up, and said something pointing to his mouth. The soldiers surrounded the Frenchmen, laid a coat under the sick man, and brought both of them porridge and vodka. The exhausted French officer was Ramballe; the little man bandaged up in the kerchief was his servant, Morel.

When Morel had drunk some vodka and eaten a bowl of porridge, he suddenly passed into a state of morbid hilarity, and kept up an incessant babble with the soldiers, who could not understand him. Ramballe refused food, and leaning on one elbow by the fire, gazed dumbly with red, vacant eyes at the Russian soldiers. At intervals he uttered a prolonged groan and then was mute again. Morel, pointing to his shoulders, gave the soldiers to understand that this was an officer, and that he needed warmth. A Russian officer, who had come up to the fire, sent to ask the colonel whether he would take a French officer into his warm cottage. When they came back and said that the colonel bade them bring the officer, they told Ramballe to go to him. He got up and tried to walk, but staggered, and would have fallen had not a soldier standing near caught him.

'What? You don't want to, eh?' said a soldier addressing Ramballe with a jocose wink.

'Eh, you fool! It's no time for your fooling. A peasant, a real peasant,' voices were heard on all sides blaming the jocose soldier. The others surrounded Ramballe. Two of them held him up under the arms and carried him to the cottage. Ramballe put his arms round the soldiers' necks, and as they lifted him he began wailing plaintively.

'O you good fellows! O my kind, kind friends. These are men! O my brave, kind friends'; and like a child he put his head down on the soldier's shoulder.

Meanwhile Morel was sitting in the best place surrounded by the soldiers.

Morel, a little, thickset Frenchman, with swollen, streaming eyes, was dressed in a woman's jacket and had a woman's kerchief tied over his forage cap. He was evidently tipsy, and with one arm thrown round the soldier sitting next him, he was singing a French song in a husky, broken voice. The soldiers simply held their sides as they looked at him.

'Now then, now then, teach it me; how does it go? I'll catch it in no time. How was it?' said the soldier Morel was hugging, who was one of the singers and fond of a joke.

'*Vive Henri Quatre! Vive ce roi vaillant!* . . .' sang Morel, winking. '*Ce diable à quatre* . . .'

'*Vi-va-ri-ka! Viff-se-ru-va-ru! Si-dya-blya-ka!* . . .' repeated the soldier, waving his hand and catching the tune correctly.

'Bravo! Ho-ho-ho-ho!' a hoarse guffaw of delight rose on all sides. Morel, wrinkling up his face, laughed too.

'Come, strike up, more, more!'

'*Qui eut le triple talent de boire, de battre, et d'être un vert galant.*'

'That sounds well too. Now, Zaletaev! . . .'

'*Kyu*,' Zaletaev articulated with effort. '*Kyu-yu-yu* . . .' he sang, puckering up his lips elaborately; '*le-trip-ta-la-de-boo-de-ba-ce-detra-va-ga-la.*'

'That's fine! That's a fine Frenchman, to be sure! oy . . . ho-ho-ho. Well, do you want some more to eat?'

'Give him some porridge; it'll take him some time to satisfy his hunger.'

They gave him more porridge, and Morel, laughing, attacked a third bowlful. There were gleeful smiles on the faces of all the young soldiers watching him. The old soldiers, considering it beneath their dignity to show interest in such trifles, lay on the other side of the fire, but now and then one would raise himself on his elbow and glance with a smile at Morel.

'They are men, too,' said one, rolling himself up in his coat. 'Even the wormwood has its roots.'

'O Lord! What lots of stars! It's a sign of frost . . .' And all sank into silence.

The stars, as though they knew no one would see them now, were twinkling brightly in the black sky. Flaring up and growing dim again, and quivering, they seemed to be busily signalling some joyful mystery to each other.

X

THE French army went on melting away at a regularly increasing rate. And the crossing of the Berezina, of which so much has been written, was only one of the intermediate stages of the destruction of the army, and by no means the decisive episode of the campaign. The reason that so much has been written about Berezina on the French side is that at the broken-down bridge of Berezina the woes, which had till then come upon them in a sort of regular succession, were suddenly concentrated there in a single moment—in one tragic catastrophe, which remained printed on the memory of all. On the Russian side, the reason that so much has been made of Berezina was simply that at Petersburg, far away from the theatre of war, a plan had been devised (again by Pfuhl of all people) for catching Napoleon in a strategic snare on the banks of the Berezina. Every one was convinced that the plan would come off exactly as arranged, and so they insisted that Berezina had in any case been the scene of the final ruin of the French. In reality the results of Berezina were less ruinous to the French in loss of cannons and prisoners than was the fighting at Krasnoe, as statistics prove.

The sole significance of the disaster of Berezina lies in the fact that it proved obviously and unmistakably how misleading were all plans for cutting off the enemy's retreat; and the one possible course of action was that which was supported by Kutuzov and the mass of the Russian army—simply to follow on the enemy's track. The crowd of French soldiers fled with continually accelerating velocity, with all their energies directed to the attainment of their goal. It was fleeing like a wounded beast and could not be stopped on the way. This was proved, not so much by the construction of the crossing, as by what happened at the bridges. When the bridges were broken down, unarmed soldiers, camp-followers from Moscow, women with children, who were with the French transport, all under the influence of *vis inertiae*, dashed forward for the boats, or rushed into the frozen water, instead of surrendering.

Their impulse was a reasonable one. The position of fugitives and of pursuers was equally wretched. By remaining with his own men, each hoped for the help of comrades in misfortune, for a definite place of his own among them. By surrendering to the Russians, he found himself in the same wretched circumstances, but placed on a lower level than others as regards the satisfaction of his vital needs. The French had no need of authentic evidence that half of the prisoners—whom the Russians were unable to look after, however much they desired to save them—were dying of cold and hunger. They felt that it could not but be so. The most humane Russian officers, even those naturally warmly disposed to the French, Frenchmen in the Russian service, could do nothing for the prisoners. They perished from the wretched plight in which the Russians were themselves placed. Bread and clothing could not be taken from the starving, necessary soldiers to give it to Frenchmen—not hated, not obnoxious, nor in any way to blame—but simply superfluous. Some did even do this; but it was only an exception.

Behind them lay certain destruction; before them lay hope. Their ships were burnt; there was no hope of safety but in keeping together and in flight, and all the forces of the French were bent on this united flight.

The more precipitate the flight of the French, and the more wretched the plight of those left behind (especially after Berezina, on which great hopes had been set, owing to the Petersburg plan), the more violent were the attacks made by the Russian generals on one another, and still more on Kutuzov. Assuming that the failure of the Petersburg plan would be ascribed to him, the dissatisfaction with him, contempt of him, and jeering at him became more and more pronounced. This contempt and jeering was of course expressed in respectful form—in such a form that Kutuzov could not even ask what he was accused of. They did not talk to him seriously; they submitted their reports and asked for his decisions with an air of performing a melancholy ceremony, while they winked behind his back, and at every step tried to deceive him. It was accepted as a recognised thing by all those men that it was useless talking to the old man, simply because they could not understand him. They took it for granted that he could never comprehend the deep significance of their plans, that he would answer them with his phrases (they fancied they were only meaningless phrases) about a golden bridge, and about the impossibility of going beyond the frontier with a crowd of barefoot beggars. And everything he said—for instance, that they must wait for provisions, or that the men had no boots—all was so simple; while everything they proposed was so complicated and so clever, that it was obvious to them that he was stupid and in his dotage, while they were military officers of genius, without authority to take the lead. The dissatisfaction and malicious gossip of the staff reached its utmost limits after the brilliant admiral, the favourite hero of Petersburg, Wittgenstein, had joined the army. Kutuzov saw it, and simply sighed and shrugged his shoulders. Only once, after Berezina, he lost his temper and wrote to Bennigsen, who was in private correspondence with the Tsar, the following note:

'I beg your Most High Excellency on the receipt of this letter to retire to Kaluga, on account of your attacks of ill-health, and there to await the further commands of His Majesty the Emperor.'

But this dismissal of Bennigsen was followed by the arrival on the scene of the Grand Duke Konstantin Pavlovitch, who had received a command at the beginning of the campaign, and had been removed from the army by Kutuzov. Now the Grand Duke on rejoining the army informed Kutuzov of the Tsar's dissatisfaction at the poor successes of our troops, and the slowness of their progress. The Tsar himself intended to be with the army in a few days.

The old man, as experienced in court methods as in warfare—who in the August of that year had been chosen commander-in-chief against the Tsar's will, who had dismissed the Grand Duke and heir-apparent from the army, and acting on his own authority, in opposition to the Tsar's will, had decreed the abandonment of Moscow—understood at once now that his day was over, that his part was played out, and that his supposed power was no more. And not only from the attitude of the court did he see this. On one side he saw the war—that war in which he had played his part—was over, and he felt that his work was done. On the other hand, at this very time, he began to be sensible of the physical weariness of his aged frame, and the necessity of physical rest.

On the 29th of November, Kutuzov reached Vilna—his dear Vilna, as he used to call it. Twice during his military career he had been governor of Vilna.

In that wealthy town, which had escaped injury, Kutuzov found old friends and old associations, as well as the comforts of which he had been so long deprived. And at once turning his back on all military and political cares, he plunged into the quiet routine of his accustomed life, so far as the passions raging all round him would permit. It was as though all that was being done, and had still to be done, in the world of history, was no concern of his now.

Tchitchagov was one of the generals most zealous in advocating attack and cutting off the enemy's retreat; he had at first suggested making a diversion in Greece and then in Warsaw, but was never willing to go where he was commanded to go. Tchitchagov, who was notorious for the boldness of his remarks to the Tsar, considered Kutuzov was under an obligation to him, because when he had been sent in 1811 to conclude peace with Turkey over Kutuzov's head, and found on arriving that peace had already been concluded, he had frankly admitted to the Tsar that the credit of having concluded peace belonged to Kutuzov.

This Tchitchagov was the first to meet Kutuzov at Vilna, at the castle where the latter was to stay. Wearing a naval uniform with a dirk, and holding his forage cap under his arm, he handed the commander-in-chief the military report and the keys of the town. The contemptuously respectful attitude of youth to old age in its dotage was expressed in the most marked manner in all the behaviour of Tchitchagov, who was aware of the disfavour into which Kutuzov had fallen.

In conversation with Tchitchagov, Kutuzov happened to say that his carriages, packed with china, that had been carried off by the enemy at Borisovo, had been recovered unhurt, and would be restored to him.

'You mean to say I have nothing to eat out of? On the contrary, I can provide everything for you, even if you want to give dinner-parties,' Tchitchagov protested, getting hot. Every word he had uttered had been with the motive of proving his own rectitude, and so he imagined that Kutuzov too was preoccupied with the same desire. Shrugging his shoulders and smiling his subtle, penetrating smile, Kutuzov answered:

'I mean to say to you what I do say to you. Nothing more.'

In opposition to the Tsar's wishes, Kutuzov kept the greater part of the troops in Vilna. He was said by all the persons about him to be getting much weaker, and breaking down physically during his stay in Vilna. He took no interest in the business of the army, left everything to his generals, and spent the time of waiting for the Tsar in social dissipation.

The Tsar with his suite—Count Tolstoy, Prince Volkonsky, Araktcheev, and the rest—left Petersburg on the 7th of December, and reached Vilna on the 11th, and drove straight up to the castle in his travelling sledge. In spite of the intense cold, there were some hundred generals and staff-officers in full parade uniform, and a guard of honour of the Semyonovsky regiment standing before the castle.

A courier, galloping up to the castle with steaming horses in advance of the Tsar, shouted: 'He is coming!'

Konovnitsyn rushed into the vestibule to inform Kutuzov, who was waiting in the porter's little room within.

A minute later the big, heavy figure of the old man in full parade uniform, his breast covered with orders, and a scarf drawn tight about his bulky person, walked with a rolling gait on to the steps. He put his cocked hat on, with the flat side foremost, took his gloves in his hand, and going sideways with difficulty down the steps, took in his hand the report, that had been prepared to give the Tsar.

Bustle and hurry and whispering, another set of three horses dashing furiously up, and all eyes were turned on the approaching sledge, in which the figures of the Tsar and Volkonsky could already be distinguished.

From the habit of fifty years, all this had a physically agitating effect on the old man. He felt himself over with nervous haste, set his hat straight, and, pulling himself together and standing erect at the very moment when the Tsar, stepping out of the sledge, turned his eyes upon him, he handed him the report, and began speaking in his measured, ingratiating voice.

The Tsar scanned Kutuzov from head to foot in a rapid glance, frowned for an instant; but at once overcoming his feelings, went up to him, and opening his arms, embraced the old general. Again, through old habitual association of ideas, arousing some deep feeling in his own heart, this embrace had its usual effect on Kutuzov: he gave a sob.

The Tsar greeted the officers and the Semyonovsky guard of honour; and once more shaking hands with the old man, he went with him into the castle.

When he was alone with the commander-in-chief, the Tsar gave expression to his displeasure at the slowness of the pursuit of the enemy, and the blunders made at Krasnoe and the Berezina, and to his views as to the coming campaign abroad. Kutuzov made no observation or explanation. The same expression of unreasoning submission with which seven years before he had listened to the Tsar's commands on the field of Austerlitz remained fixed now on his face.

When Kutuzov had left the room, and with downcast head walked across the reception-hall with his heavy, waddling step, a voice stopped him.

'Your highness,' said some one.

He raised his head, and looked into the face of Count Tolstoy, who stood facing him with a small object on a silver dish. Kutuzov seemed for some time unable to grasp what was wanted of him.

All at once he seemed to recollect himself; a faint smile gleamed on his podgy face, and with a low, respectful bow, he picked up the object on the dish. It was the Order of St. George of the first rank.

XI

THE next day the commander-in-chief gave a dinner and a ball, which the Tsar honoured with his presence.

Kutuzov had received the Order of St. George of the first rank; the

Tsar had shown him the highest marks of respect, but every one was aware that the Tsar was displeased with the commander-in-chief. The proprieties were observed, and the Tsar set the first example in doing so. But every one knew that the old man was in fault, and had shown his incapacity. When, in accordance with the old custom of Catherine's time, Kutuzov gave orders for the captured standards to be lowered at the Tsar's feet on his entering the ball-room, the Tsar frowned with vexation, and muttered words, which some heard as: 'The old comedian.'

The Tsar's displeasure was increased at Vilna by Kutuzov's obvious unwillingness or incapacity to see the importance of the approaching campaign.

When next morning the Tsar said to the officers gathered about him: 'You have not only saved Russia, you have saved Europe,' every one knew at once that the war was not over.

Kutuzov alone refused to see this, frankly gave it as his opinion that no fresh war could improve the position of Russia, or add to her glory; that it could but weaken her position, and cast her down from that high pinnacle of glory at which in his view Russia was standing now. He tried to show the Tsar the impossibility of levying fresh troops, and talked of the hardships the people were suffering, the possibility of failure, and so on.

Such being his attitude on the subject, the commander-in-chief could naturally be looked upon only as a hindrance and a drag on the progress of the coming campaign.

To avoid friction with the old man, the obvious resource was—as with him at Austerlitz and with Barclay at the beginning of the war—to withdraw all real power from the commander-in-chief, without disturbing him by any open explanation on the matter, and to transfer it to the Tsar.

With this object, the staff was gradually transformed, and all the real power of Kutuzov's staff was removed and transferred to the Tsar. Toll, Konovnitsyn, and Yermolov received new appointments. Every one talked openly of the commander-in-chief's great weakness and failing health.

He was bound to be in failing health, so as to make way for his successor. And his health was, in fact, failing.

Just as naturally, as simply, and as gradually as Kutuzov had come to the Court of Exchequer at Petersburg out of Turkey to raise the militia, and then to take the command of the army just at the time when he was needed, did a new commander come now to replace him, when his part was played.

The war of 1812, in addition to its national significance, dear to every Russian heart, was to take a new European character.

The movement of men from west to east was to be followed by a movement from east to west, and this new war needed a new representative, with other aims and other qualities, and moved by impulses different from Kutuzov's.

For the movement from east to west, and the establishment of the position of peoples, Alexander was needed just as Kutuzov was needed for the deliverance and the glory of Russia.

Kutuzov did not see what was meant by Europe, the balance of power, and Napoleon. He could not understand all that.

After the enemy had been annihilated, Russia had been delivered and raised to the highest pinnacle of her glory, the representative of the Russian people, a Russian of the Russians, had no more left to do. Nothing was left for the representative of the national war but to die. And he did die.

XII

As is generally the case, Pierre only felt the full strain of the physical hardships and privations he had suffered as a prisoner, when they were over. After he had been rescued, he went to Orel, and two days after getting there, as he was preparing to start for Kiev, he fell ill and spent three months laid up at Orel. He was suffering, so the doctors said, from a bilious fever. Although they treated him by letting blood and giving him drugs, he recovered.

Everything that had happened to Pierre from the time of his rescue up to his illness had left hardly any impression on his mind. He had only a memory of dark grey weather, sometimes rainy and sometimes sunshiny, of internal physical aches, of pain in his feet and his side. He remembered a general impression of the misery and suffering of men, remembered the worrying curiosity of officers and generals, who questioned him about his imprisonment, the trouble he had to get horses and a conveyance; and more than all he remembered his own dullness of thought and of feeling all that time.

On the day of his rescue he saw the dead body of Petya Rostov. The same day he learned that Prince Andrey had lived for more than a month after the battle of Borodino, and had only a short time before died at Yaroslavl in the Rostovs' house. The same day Denisov, who had told Pierre this piece of news, happened to allude in conversation to the death of Ellen, supposing Pierre to have been long aware of it. All this had at the time seemed to Pierre only strange. He felt that he could not take in all the bearings of these facts. He was at the time simply in haste to get away from these places where men were slaughtering each other to some quiet refuge where he might rest and recover his faculties, and think over all the new strange things he had learned.

But as soon as he reached Orel, he fell ill. On coming to himself after his illness, Pierre saw waiting on him two of his servants, Terenty and Vaska, who had come from Moscow, and the eldest of his cousins, who was staying at Pierre's estate in Elets, and hearing of his rescue and his illness had come to nurse him.

During his convalescence Pierre could only gradually recover from the impressions of the last few months, which had become habitual. Only by degrees could he become accustomed to the idea that there was no one to drive him on tomorrow, that no one would take his warm bed from him, and that he was quite sure of getting his dinner, and tea, and supper. But for a long while afterwards he was always in his dreams surrounded by his conditions as a prisoner.

And only in the same gradual way did Pierre grasp the meaning of the news he had heard since his escape: of the death of Prince Andrey, of the death of his wife, and of the overthrow of the French.

The joyful sense of freedom—that full, inalienable freedom inherent in man, of which he had first had a consciousness at the first halting-place outside Moscow—filled Pierre's soul during his convalescence. He was surprised that this inner freedom, independent as it was of all external circumstances, was now as it were decked out in a luxury, a superfluity of external freedom. He was alone in a strange town without acquaintances. No one made any demands on him; no one sent him anywhere. He had all he wanted; the thought of his wife, that had in old days been a continual torture to him, was no more, since she herself was no more.

'Ah, how happy I am! how splendid it is!' he said to himself, when a cleanly covered table was moved up to him, with savoury-smelling broth, or when he got into his soft, clean bed at night, or when the thought struck him that his wife and the French were no more. 'Ah, how good it is! how splendid!' And from old habit he asked himself the question, 'Well, and what then? what am I going to do?' And at once he answered himself: 'I am going to live. Ah, how splendid it is!'

What had worried him in old days, what he had always been seeking to solve, the question of the object of life, did not exist for him now. That seeking for an object in life was over for him now; and it was not fortuitously or temporarily that it was over. He felt that there was no such object, and could not be. And it was just the absence of an object that gave him that complete and joyful sense of freedom that at this time made his happiness.

He could seek no object in life now, because now he had faith—not faith in any sort of principles, or words, or ideas, but faith in a living, ever palpable God. In old days he had sought Him in the aims he set before himself. That search for an object in life had been only a seeking after God; and all at once in his captivity he had come to know, not through words or arguments, but by his own immediate feeling, what his old nurse had told him long before: that God is here, and everywhere. In his capacity he had come to see that the God in Karataev was grander, more infinite, and more unfathomable than the Architect of the Universe recognised by the masons. He felt like a man who finds what he has sought at his feet, when he has been straining his eyes to seek it in the distance. All his life he had been looking far away over the heads of all around him, while he need not have strained his eyes, but had only to look in front of him.

In old days he had been unable to see the great, the unfathomable, and the infinite in anything. He had only felt that it must be somewhere, and had been seeking it. In everything near and comprehensible, he had seen only what was limited, petty, everyday, and meaningless. He had armed himself with the telescope of intellect, and gazed far away into the distance, where that petty, everyday world, hidden in the mists of distance, had seemed to him great and infinite, simply because it was not clearly seen. Such had been European life, politics, freemasonry, philosophy, and philanthropy in his eyes. But even then, in moments which he had looked on as times of weakness, his thought had penetrated even to these remote objects, and then he had seen in them the same pettiness, the same ordinariness and meaninglessness.

Now he had learnt to see the great, the eternal, and the infinite in everything; and naturally therefore, in order to see it, to revel in its contemplation, he flung aside the telescope through which he had hitherto been gazing over men's heads, and looked joyfully at the ever-changing, ever grand, unfathomable, and infinite life around him. And the closer he looked at it, the calmer and happier he was. The terrible question that had shattered all his intellectual edifices in old days, the question: What for? had no existence for him now. To that question, What for? he had now always ready in his soul the simple answer: Because there is a God, that God without whom not one hair of a man's head falls.

XIII

PIERRE was hardly changed in his external habits. In appearance he was just the same as before. He was, as he had always been, absent-minded, and seemed preoccupied with something of his own, something apart from what was before his eyes. The difference was that in old days, when he was unconscious of what was before his eyes, or what was being said to him, he would seem with painfully knitted brows to be striving unsuccessfully to discern something far away from him. He was just as unconcious now of what was said to him, or of what was before him. But now with a faint, apparently ironical smile, he gazed at what was before him, or listened to what was said, though he was obviously seeing and hearing something quite different. In old days he had seemed a good-hearted man, but unhappy. And so people had unconsciously held a little aloof from him. Now a smile of joy in life was continually playing about his mouth, and his eyes were bright with sympathy for others, and the question: Were they all as happy as he? And people felt at ease in his presence.

In old days he had talked a great deal, and had got hot when he talked, and he had listened very little. Now he was rarely carried away in conversation, and knew how to listen, so that people were very ready to tell him the inmost secrets of their hearts.

The princess, who had never liked Pierre, and had cherished a particularly hostile feeling towards him, since after the old count's death she had felt herself under obligation to him, had come to Orel with the intention of proving to him that in spite of his ingratitude she felt it her duty to nurse him, but after a short time she felt, to her own surprise and annoyance, that she was growing fond of him. Pierre did nothing to try and win his cousin's favour; he simply looked at her with curiosity. In old days she had felt that there was mockery and indifference in his eyes, and she had shrunk into herself before him, as she did before other people, and had shown him only her aggressive side. Now she felt on the contrary as though he were delving into the most secret recesses of her life. It was at first mistrustfully, and then with gratitude, that she let him see now the latent good side of her character.

The most artful person could not have stolen into the princess's confidence more cunningly, by arousing her recollections of the best time of her youth, and showing sympathy with them. And yet all Pierre's artfulness consisted in seeking to please himself by drawing out human qualities in the bitter, hard, and, in her own way, proud princess.

'Yes, he is a very, very good-hearted fellow when he is not under bad influence, but under the influence of people like me,' thought the princess.

The change that had taken place in Pierre was noticed in their own way by his servants too—Terenty and Vaska. They considered that he had grown much more good-natured. Often after undressing his master, and wishing him good night, Terenty would linger with his boots and his clothes in his hand, in the hope that his master would begin a conversation with him. And as a rule Pierre kept Terenty, seeing he was longing for a chat.

'Come, tell me, then . . . how did you manage to get anything to eat?' he would ask. And Terenty would begin his tales of the destruction of Moscow and of the late count, and would stand a long while with the clothes, talking away or listening to Pierre; and it was with a pleasant sense of his master's close intimacy with him and affection for him that he finally withdrew.

The doctor, who was attending Pierre, and came to see him every day, though he thought it his duty as a doctor to pose as a man every minute of whose time is of value for suffering humanity, used to sit on with him for hours together, repeating his favourite anecdotes and observations on the peculiarities of patients in general, and of ladies in particular.

'Yes, it's a pleasure to talk to a man like that; it's not what we are used to in the provinces,' he would say.

In Orel there happened to be several French prisoners, and the doctor brought one of them, a young Italian officer, to see Pierre.

This officer became a frequent visitor, and the princess used to laugh at the tender feelings the Italian expressed for Pierre.

It was obvious that the Italian was never happy but when he could see Pierre, and talk to him, and tell him all about his own past, his home life, and his love, and pour out his indignation against the French, and especially against Napoleon.

'If all Russians are the least bit like you,' he used to say to Pierre, 'it is sacrilege to make war on a people like yours. You who have suffered so much at the hands of the French, have not even a grudge against them.'

And Pierre had won the Italian's passionate devotion simply by drawing out what was best in his soul and admiring it.

During the latter part of Pierre's stay in Orel, he received a visit from an old acquaintance, Count Villarsky, the freemason, who had introduced him to the lodge in 1807. Villarsky had married a Russian heiress, who had great estates in the Orel province, and he was filling a temporary post in the commissariat department in the town.

Though Villarsky had never been very intimately acquainted with Bezuhov, on hearing that he was in Orel, he called upon him with those demonstrations of friendliness and intimacy that men commonly display on meeting one another in the desert. Villarsky was dull in Orel, and was delighted to meet a man of his own circle, who had, as he supposed, the same interests as he had.

But to his surprise, Villarsky noticed soon that Pierre had quite dropped behind the times, and had, as he defined it himself to Pierre, sunk into apathy and egoism.

'You are stagnating,' he said to him.

But in spite of that, Villarsky felt much more at home with Pierre now than he had done in the past, and came every day to see him. As Pierre watched Villarsky, and listened to him now, it seemed strange and incredible to him to think that he had very lately been the same sort of person himself.

Villarsky was a married man with a family, whose time was taken up in managing his wife's property, in performing his official duties, and in looking after his family. He regarded all these duties as a drawback in his life, and looked on them all with contempt, because they were all directed to securing his own personal welfare and that of his family. Military, administrative, political, and masonic questions were continually engrossing his attention. And without criticising this view or attempting to change it, Pierre watched this phenomenon—so strange, yet so familiar to him—with the smile of gentle, delighted irony that was now habitual with him.

In Pierre's relations with Villarsky, with his cousin, with the doctor, and with all the people he met now, there was a new feature that gained him the goodwill of all. This was the recognition of the freedom of every man to think, to feel, and to look at things in his own way; the recognition of the impossibility of altering a man's conviction by words. This legitimate individuality of every man's views, which had in old days troubled and irritated Pierre, now formed the basis of the sympathetic interest he felt in people. The inconsistency, sometimes the complete antagonism of men's views with their own life or with one another, delighted Pierre, and drew from him a gentle and mocking smile.

In practical affairs Pierre suddenly felt now that he had the centre of gravity that he had lacked in former days. In the past every money question, especially requests for money, to which as a very wealthy man he was particularly liable, had reduced him to a state of helpless agitation and perplexity. 'Ought I to give or not to give?' he used to ask himself. 'I have money and he needs it. But some one else needs it more. Who needs it more? And perhaps both are impostors?' And of all these suppositions he had in old days found no satisfactory solution, and gave to all as long as he had anything to give. In old days he had been in the same perplexity over every question relating to his property when one person told him he ought to act in one way and another advised something else.

Now to his own surprise he found that he had no more doubt or hesitation on all such questions. Now there was a judge within him settling what he must do and what he must not, by some laws of which he was himself unaware.

He was just as unconcerned about money matters as before; but now he unhesitatingly knew what he ought to do and what he ought not to do. The first application of that new power within him was in the case of a prisoner, a French colonel, who called on him, talked very freely of his own great exploits, and finally delivered himself of a request that was more like a demand, that he should give him four thousand francs to send to his wife and children. Pierre refused to do so without the slightest difficulty or effort, and wondered himself afterwards that it had been so easy and simple to do what had in old days seemed so hopelessly difficult. At the same time as he refused the French colonel, he made up his mind that he must certainly resort to some stratagem when he left Orel to induce the Italian officer to accept assistance, of which he stood in evident need. A fresh proof to Pierre of his greater certainty in regard to practical matters was the settlement of the question of his wife's debts, and of the rebuilding of his Moscow house and villas in the suburbs.

His head steward came to him in Orel, and with him Pierre went into a general review of his financial position. The fire of Moscow had cost Pierre, by the steward's account, about two millions.

The chief steward to console him for these losses presented a calculation he had made, that Pierre's income, far from being diminished, would be positively increased if he were to refuse to pay the debts left by the countess—which he could not be forced to pay—and if he were not to restore his Moscow houses and the villa near Moscow, which had cost him eighty thousand to keep up, and brought in nothing.

'Yes, yes, that's true,' said Pierre, with a beaming smile.

'Yes, yes, I don't need any of them. I have been made much richer by the destruction of the city.'

But in January Savelitch came from Moscow, talked to him of the position of the city, of the estimate the architect had sent in for restoring the house, and the villa in the suburbs, speaking of it as a settled matter. At the same time Pierre received letters from Prince Vassily and other acquaintances in Petersburg, in which his wife's debts were mentioned. And Pierre decided that the steward's plan that he had liked so much was not the right one, and that he must go to Petersburg to wind up his wife's affairs, and must rebuild in Moscow. Why he ought to do so, he could not have said; but he was convinced that he ought. His income was diminished by one-fourth owing to this decision. But it had to be so; he felt that.

Villarsky was going to Moscow, and they agreed to make the journey together.

During the whole period of his convalescence in Orel, Pierre had enjoyed the feeling of joyful freedom and life. But when he found himself on this journey on the open road, and saw hundreds of new faces, that feeling was intensified. During the journey he felt like a schoolboy in the holidays. All the people he saw—the driver, the overseer of the posting station, the peasants on the road, or in the village—all had a new significance for him. The presence and the observations of Villarsky, who was continually deploring the poverty and the ignorance and the backwardness of Russia, compared with Europe, only heightened Pierre's pleasure in it. Where Villarsky saw deadness, Pierre saw the extraordinary mighty force of vitality, the force which sustained the life of that homogeneous, original, and unique people over that immense expanse of snow. He did not contest Villarsky's opinions, and smiled gleefully, as he listened, appearing to agree with him as the easiest means of avoiding arguments which could lead to nothing.

XIV

J U S T as it is difficult to explain why the ants hurry back to a scattered ant-hill, some dragging away from it bits of refuse, eggs, and corpses, while others run back again, and what is their object in crowding together, overtaking one another, fighting with each other, so it would be hard to give the reasons that induced the Russians, after the departure of the French, to flock back to the place which had been known as Moscow. But just as looking at the ants hurrying about a ruined ant-heap, one can see by the tenacity, the energy, and the multitude of the busy insects that though all else is utterly destroyed, there is left something indestructible and immaterial that was the whole strength of the colony, so too Moscow in the month of October, though without its governing authorities, without its churches, without its holy things, without its wealth and its houses, was still the same Moscow as it had been in August. Everything was shattered except something immaterial, but mighty and indestructible.

The motives of the people, who rushed from all parts to Moscow after it was evacuated by the enemy, were of the most varied and personal kind, and at first mostly savage and brutal impulses. Only one impulse was common to all—the attraction to the place which had been called Moscow in order to set their energies to work there.

Within a week there were fifteen thousand persons in Moscow, within a fortnight twenty-five thousand; and so it went on. The number went on mounting and mounting till by the autumn of 1813 it had reached a figure exceeding the population of the city in 1812.

The first Russians to enter Moscow were the Cossacks of Wintzengerode's detachment, the peasants from the nearest villages and the residents who had fled from Moscow and concealed themselves in the environs. On entering the ruined city, and finding it pillaged, the Russians fell to pillaging it too. They continued the work begun by the French. Trains of peasants' waggons drove into Moscow to carry away to the villages all that had been abandoned in the ruined Moscow houses and streets. The Cossacks carried off what they could to their tents; the householders collected all they could out of other houses, and removed it to their own under the pretence that it was their property.

But the first pillaging parties were followed by others; and every day as the numbers pillaging increased, the work of plunder became more difficult and assumed more definite forms.

The French had found Moscow deserted but with all the forms of an organically normal town life still existent, with various branches of trades and crafts, of luxury, and political government and religion. These forms were lifeless but they still existed. There were markets, shops, stores, corn-exchanges, and bazaars—most of them stocked with goods. There were factories and trading establishments. There were palaces and wealthy houses filled with articles of luxury. There were hospitals, prisons, courts, churches, and cathedrals. The longer the French remained, the more these forms of town life perished, and at the end all was lost in one indistinguishable, lifeless scene of pillage.

The longer the pillaging of the French lasted, the more complete was the destruction of the wealth of Moscow and of the forces of the pillagers. The longer the pillaging lasted that was carried on by the Russians on their first return to the capital, and the more there were taking part in it, the more rapidly was the wealth of Moscow and the normal life of the town re-established.

Apart from those who came for plunder, people of all sorts, drawn thither, some by curiosity, some by the duties of office, some by self-interests—householders, priests, officials, high and low, traders, artisans, and peasants—flowed back to Moscow from all sides, as the blood flows to the heart.

Within a week the peasants who had come with empty carts to carry off goods were detained by the authorities, and compelled to carry dead bodies out of the town. Other peasants, who had heard of their companions' discomfiture, drove into the town with wheat, and oats, and hay, knocking down each others' prices to a figure lower than it had been in former days. Gangs of carpenters, hoping for high wages, were arriving in Moscow every day; and on all sides there were new houses being built, or old half-burnt ones being repaired. Tradesmen carried on their business in booths. Cook-shops and taverns were opened in fire-blackened houses. The clergy held services in many churches that had escaped the fire. Church goods that had been plundered were restored as offerings. Government clerks set up their baize-covered tables and pigeon-holes of papers in little rooms. The higher authorities and the police organised a distribution of the goods left by the French. The owners of houses in which a great many of the goods plundered from other houses had been left complained of the injustice of all goods being taken to the Polygonal Palace. Others maintained that the French had collected all the things from different houses to one spot, and that it was therefore unfair to restore to the master of the house the things found in it. The police were abused and were bribed; estimates for government buildings that had been burnt were reckoned at ten times their value; and appeals for help were made. Count Rastoptchin wrote his posters again.

XV

AT the end of January Pierre arrived in Moscow and settled in the lodge of his mansion, as that had escaped the fire. He called on Count Rastoptchin and several acquaintances, and was intending in three days to set off to Petersburg. Every one was triumphant at victory; the ruined and reviving city was bubbling over with life. Every one was glad to see Pierre; everybody was eager to see him, and to ask him about all he had seen. Pierre had a particularly friendly feeling towards every one he met. But unconsciously he was a little on his guard with people to avoid fettering his freedom in any way. To all the questions put to him—important or trivial—whether they asked him where he meant to live, whether he were going to build, when he was starting for

Petersburg, or whether he could take a parcel there for some one, he answered, 'Yes, very possibly,' 'I dare say I may,' and so on.

He heard that the Rostovs were in Kostroma, and the thought of Natasha rarely came to his mind, and when it did occur to him it was as a pleasant memory of time long past. He felt himself set free, not only from the cares of daily life, but also from that feeling which, it seemed to him, he had voluntarily brought upon himself.

The third day after his arrival in Moscow he learnt from the Drubetskoys that Princess Marya was in Moscow. The death, the sufferings, and the last days of Prince Andrey had often engaged Pierre's thoughts, and now recurred to him with fresh vividness. He heard at dinner that Princess Marya was in Moscow, and living in her own house in Vosdvizhenka, which had escaped the fire, and he went to call upon her the same evening.

On the way to Princess Marya's Pierre's mind was full of Prince Andrey, of his friendship for him, of the different occasions when they had met, and especially of their last interview at Borodino.

'Can he possibly have died in the bitter mood he was in then? Was not the meaning of life revealed to him before death?' Pierre wondered. He thought of Karataev, of his death, and unconsciously compared those two men, so different, and yet alike, in the love he had felt for both, and in that both had lived, and both were dead.

In the most serious frame of mind Pierre drove up to the old prince's house. The house had remained entire. There were traces to be seen of the havoc wrought in it, but the character of the house was unchanged. The old footman met Pierre with a stern face, that seemed to wish to make the guest feel that the absence of the old prince did make no difference in the severe routine of the household, and said that the princess had retired to her own apartments, and received on Sundays.

'Take my name to her; perhaps she will see me,' said Pierre.

'Yes, your excellency,' answered the footman; 'kindly walk into the portrait-gallery.'

A few minutes later the footman returned accompanied by Dessalle. Dessalle brought a message from the princess that she would be very glad to see Pierre, and begged him, if he would excuse the lack of ceremony to come upstairs to her apartment.

In a low-pitched room, lighted by a single candle, he found the princess, and some one with her in a black dress. Pierre recollected that the princess had always had lady-companions of some sort with her, but who those companions were, and what they were like, he did not remember. 'That is one of her companions,' he thought, glancing at the lady in the black dress.

The princess rose swiftly to meet him, and held out her hand.

'Yes,' she said, scrutinising his altered face, after he had kissed her hand; 'so this is how we meet again. He often talked of you at the last,' she said, turning her eyes from Pierre to the companion with a sort of bashfulness that struck him.

'I was so glad to hear of your safety. It was the only piece of good news we had had for a long time.'

Again the princess glanced still more uneasily at the companion, and would have spoken;.but Pierre interrupted her.

'Only imagine, I knew nothing about him,' he said. 'I believed he had been killed. All I have heard has been through others, at third-hand. I only know that he fell in with the Rostovs. . . . What a strange stroke of destiny!'

Pierre talked rapidly, eagerly. He glanced once at the companion's face, saw attentively friendly, inquiring eyes fixed upon him; and as often happens, while talking, he vaguely felt that this lady-companion in the black dress was a good, kind, friendly creature, who need be no hindrance to his talking freely to Princess Marya.

But as he uttered the last words about the Rostovs, the embarrassment in Princess Marya's face became even more marked. Again her eyes shifted from Pierre's face to the face of the lady in the black dress, and she said:

'You don't recognise her?'

Pierre glanced once more at the pale, thin face of her companion, with its black eyes and strange mouth. Something very near to him, long forgotten, and more than sweet, gazed at him out of those intent eyes.

'But no, it cannot be,' he thought. 'That stern, thin, pale face that looks so much older? It cannot be she. It cannot be she. It is only a reminder of it.'

But at that moment Princess Marya said, 'Natasha!'

And the face with the intent eyes—painfully, with effort, like a rusty door opening—smiled, and through that opened door there floated to Pierre a sudden, overwhelming rush of long-forgotten bliss, of which, especially now, he had no thought. It breathed upon him, overwhelmed him, and swallowed him up entirely. When she smiled, there could be no doubt. It was Natasha, and he loved her.

In that first minute Pierre unwittingly betrayed to her and to Princess Marya, and most of all to himself, the secret of which he had been himself unaware. He flushed joyfully, and with agonising distress. He tried to conceal his emotion. But the more he tried to conceal it, the more clearly—more clearly than if he had uttered the most definite words—he betrayed to himself, and to her, and to Princess Marya, that he loved her.

'No, it is nothing; it's the sudden surprise,' Pierre thought. But as soon as he tried to go on with the conversation with Princess Marya, he glanced again at Natasha, and a still deeper flush spread over his face, and a still more violent wave of rapture and terror flooded his heart. He stammered in his speech, and stopped short in the middle of a sentence.

Pierre had not noticed Natasha because he had never expected to see her here; but he had not recognised her because the change that had taken place in her since he had seen her was immense. She had grown thin and pale. But it was not that that made her unrecognisable. No one would have recognised her at the moment when he entered, because when he first glanced at her there was no trace of a smile in the eyes that in old days had always beamed with a suppressed smile of the joy of life. They were intent, kindly eyes, full of mournful inquiry, and nothing more.

Pierre's embarrassment was not reflected in a corresponding embarrassment in Natasha, but only in a look of pleasure, that faintly lighted up her whole face.

XVI

'SHE has come to stay with me,' said Princess Marya. 'The count and the countess will be here in a few days. The countess is in a terrible state. But Natasha herself had to see the doctors. They made her come away with me.'

'Yes. Is there a family without its own sorrow?' said Pierre, turning to Natasha. 'You know it happened the very day we were rescued. I saw him. What a splendid boy he was!'

Natasha looked at him, and, in answer to his words, her eyes only opened wider and grew brighter.

'What can one say, or think, to give comfort?' said Pierre. 'Nothing. Why had he to die, such a noble boy, so full of life?'

'Yes; in these days it would be hard to live without faith . . .' said Princess Marya.

'Yes, yes. That is true, indeed,' Pierre put in hurriedly.

'How so?' Natasha asked, looking intently into Pierre's eyes.

'How so?' said Princess Marya. 'Why, only the thought of what awaits . . .'

Natasha, not heeding Princess Marya's words, looked again inquiringly at Pierre.

'And because,' Pierre went on, 'only one who believes that there is a God guiding our lives can bear such a loss as hers, and . . . yours,' said Pierre.

Natasha opened her mouth, as though she would say something, but she suddenly stopped.

Pierre made haste to turn away from her, and to address Princess Marya again with a question about the last days of his friend's life. Pierre's embarrassment had by now almost disappeared, but at the same time he felt that all his former freedom had vanished too. He felt that there was now a judge criticising every word, every action of his; a judge whose verdict was of greater consequence to him than the verdict of all the people in the world. As he talked now he was considering the impression his words were making on Natasha as he uttered them. He did not intentionally say what might please her; but whatever he said, he looked at himself from her point of view.

With the unwillingness usual in such cases, Princess Marya began telling Pierre of the position in which she had found her brother. But Pierre's questions, his eagerly restless glance, his face quivering with emotion, gradually induced her to go into details which she shrank, for her own sake, from recalling to her imagination.

'Yes, yes, . . .' said Pierre, bending forward over Princess Marya, and eagerly drinking in her words. 'Yes, yes. So he found peace? He was softened? He was always striving with his whole soul for one thing only: to be entirely good, so that he could not dread death. The defects that were in him—if he had any—did not come from himself. So he was softened?' he said.

'What a happy thing that he saw you again,' he said to Natasha, turning suddenly to her, and looking at her with eyes full of tears.

Natasha's face quivered. She frowned, and for an instant dropped her eyes. For a moment she hesitated whether to speak or not to speak.

'Yes, it was a great happiness,' she said in a low, deep voice; 'for me it was certainly a great happiness.' She paused. 'And he . . . he . . . he told me he was longing for it the very moment I went in to him . . .' Natasha's voice broke. She flushed, squeezed her hands against her knees and suddenly, with an evident effort to control herself, she lifted her head and began speaking rapidly:

'We knew nothing about it when we were leaving Moscow. I did not dare ask about him. And all at once Sonya told me he was with us. I could think of nothing, I had no conception in what state he was; all I wanted was to see him—to be with him,' she said, trembling and breathless. And not letting them interrupt her, she told all that she had never spoken of to any one before; all she had gone through in those three weeks of their journey and their stay in Yaroslavl.

Pierre heard her with parted lips and eyes full of tears fastened upon her. As he listened to her, he was not thinking of Prince Andrey, nor of death, nor of what she was saying. He heard her voice and only pitied her for the anguish she was feeling now in telling him.

The princess, frowning in the effort to restrain her tears, sat by Natasha's side and heard for the first time the story of those last days of her brother's and Natasha's love.

To speak of that agonising and joyous time was evidently necessary to Natasha.

She talked on, mingling up the most insignificant details with the most secret feelings of her heart, and it seemed as though she could never finish. Several times she said the same thing twice.

Dessalle's voice was heard at the door asking whether Nikolushka might come in to say good-night. 'And that is all, all . . .' said Natasha. She got up quickly at the moment Nikolushka was coming in, and almost running to the door, knocked her head against it as it was hidden by the portière, and with a moan, half of pain, half of sorrow, she rushed out of the room.

Pierre gazed at the door by which she had gone out, and wondered why he felt suddenly alone in the wide world.

Princess Marya roused him from his abstraction, calling his attention to her nephew who had just come into the room.

The face of Nikolushka, so like his father, had such an effect on Pierre at this moment of emotional tension, that, after kissing the child, he got up himself, and taking out his handkerchief, walked away to the window. He would have taken leave, but Princess Marya would not let him go.

'No, Natasha and I often do not go to bed till past two, please stay a little longer. We will have supper. Go downstairs, we will come in a moment.'

Before Pierre went down, the princess said to him: 'It is the first time she has talked of him like this.'

XVII

PIERRE was conducted into the big, lighted-up dining-room. In a few minutes he heard footsteps and the princess and Natasha came into the room. Natasha was calm, though the stern, unsmiling expression had come back again now into her face. Princess Marya, Natasha, and

Pierre all equally experienced that feeling of awkwardness which usually follows when a serious and deeply felt conversation is over. To continue on the same subject is impossible; to speak of trivial matters seems desecration, and to be silent is unpleasant, because one wants to talk, and this silence seems a sort of affectation. In silence they came to the table. The footmen drew back and pushed up the chairs. Pierre unfolded his cold dinner napkin, and making up his mind to break the silence he glanced at Natasha and at Princess Marya. Both had plainly reached the same decision at the same moment; in the eyes of both there gleamed a satisfaction with life, and an admission that there was gladness in it as well as sorrow.

'Do you drink vodka, count?' said Princess Marya, and those words at once dispelled the shadows of the past.

'Tell us about yourself,' said Princess Marya; 'such incredibly marvellous stories are being told about you.'

'Yes,' answered Pierre, with the gentle smile of irony that had now become habitual with him. 'I myself am told of marvels that I never dreamed of. Marya Abramovna invited me to come and see her and kept telling me what had happened to me, or ought to have happened. Stepan Stepanovitch too instructed me how I was to tell my story. Altogether I have noticed that to be an interesting person is a very easy position (I am now an interesting person); people invite me and then tell me all about it.'

Natasha smiled and was about to say something.

'We have been told that you lost two millions in Moscow. Is that true?'

'Oh, I am three times as rich,' said Pierre. In spite of the strain on his fortune, of his wife's debts, and the necessity of rebuilding, Pierre still said that he had become three times as rich.

'What I have undoubtedly gained,' he said, 'is freedom . . .' he was beginning seriously; but on second thoughts he did not continue, feeling that it was too egoistic a subject.

'And you are building?'

'Yes, such are Savelitch's orders.'

'Tell me, you had not heard of the countess's death when you stayed on in Moscow?' said Princess Marya; and she flushed crimson at once, conscious that in putting this question to him after his mention of 'freedom,' she was ascribing a significance to his words which was possibly not intended.

'No,' answered Pierre, obviously unconscious of any awkwardness in the interpretation Princess Marya had put on his allusion to his freedom. 'I heard of it in Orel, and you cannot imagine how it affected me. We were not an exemplary couple,' he said quickly, glancing at Natasha and detecting in her face curiosity as to how he would speak of his wife. 'But her death affected me greatly. When two people quarrel, both are always in fault. And one becomes terribly aware of one's shortcomings towards any one who is no more. And then such a death . . . apart from friends and consolation. I felt very sorry for her,' he concluded, and noticed with satisfaction a glad look of approval on Natasha's face.

'And so you are once more an eligible *parti*,' said Princess Marya.

Pierre flushed suddenly crimson; and for a long while he tried not to look at Natasha. When he did venture to glance at her, her face was cold and severe, even, he fancied, disdainful.

'But did you really see and talk to Napoleon, as we have been told?' said Princess Marya.

Pierre laughed.

'Not once, never. Every one always imagines that to be a prisoner is equivalent to being on a visit to Napoleon. I never saw, never even heard anything about him. I was in much lower company.'

Supper was over, and Pierre, who had at first refused to talk about his captivity, was gradually drawn into telling them about it.

'But it is true that you stayed behind to kill Napoleon?' Natasha asked him with a slight smile. 'I guessed that at the time when we met you by the Suharev Tower; do you remember?'

Pierre owned that it was so; and from that question was led on by Princess Marya's, and still more by Natasha's, questions to give a detailed account of his adventures.

At first he told his story with that tone of gentle irony that he always had now towards men and especially towards himself. But as he came to describe the horrors and sufferings he had seen, he was drawn on unawares, and began to speak with the suppressed emotion of a man living again in imagination through the intense impressions of the past.

Princess Marya looked from Pierre to Natasha with a gentle smile. In all he told them she saw only Pierre and his goodness. Natasha, her head supported in her hand, and her face changing continually with the story, watched Pierre, never taking her eyes off him, and was in imagination passing through all he told her with him. Not only her eyes, but her exclamations and the brief questions she put showed Pierre that she understood from his words just what he was trying to convey by them. It was evident that she understood, not only what he said, but also what he would have liked to say and could not express in words. The episode of the child and of the woman in whose defence he was taken prisoner, Pierre described in this way. 'It was an awful scene, children abandoned, some in the midst of the fire . . . Children were dragged out before my eyes . . . and women, who had their things pulled off them, earrings torn off . . .'

Pierre flushed and hesitated. 'Then a patrol came up and all who were not pillaging, all the men, that is, they took prisoner. And me with them.'

'I am sure you are not telling us all; I am sure you did something,' said Natasha, and after a moment's pause, 'something good.'

Pierre went on with his story. When he came to the execution, he would have passed over the horrible details of it, but Natasha insisted on his leaving nothing out.

Pierre was beginning to tell them about Karataev; he had risen from the table and was walking up and down, Natasha following him with her eyes.

'No,' he said, stopping short in his story, 'you cannot understand what I learned from that illiterate man—that simple creature.'

'No, no, tell us,' said Natasha. 'Where is he now?'

'He was killed almost before my eyes.'

And Pierre began to describe the latter part of their retreat, Karataev's illness (his voice shook continually) and then his death.

Pierre told the tale of his adventures as he had never thought of them before. He saw now as it were a new significance in all he had been through. He experienced now in telling it all to Natasha that rare happiness given to men by women when they listen to them—not by *clever* women, who, as they listen, are either trying to remember what they are told to enrich their intellect and on occasion to repeat it, or to adapt what is told them to their own ideas and to bring out in haste the clever comments elaborated in their little mental factory. This rare happiness is given only by those real women, gifted with a faculty for picking out and assimilating all that is best in what a man shows them. Natasha, though herself unconscious of it, was all rapt attention; she did not lose one word, one quaver of the voice, one glance, one twitching in the facial muscles, one gesture of Pierre's. She caught the word before it was uttered and bore it straight to her open heart, divining the secret import of all Pierre's spiritual travail.

Princess Marya understood his story and sympathised with him, but she was seeing now something else that absorbed all her attention. She saw the possibility of love and happiness between Natasha and Pierre. And this idea, which struck her now for the first time, filled her heart with gladness.

It was three o'clock in the night. The footmen, with melancholy and severe faces, came in with fresh candles, but no one noticed them.

Pierre finished his story. With shining, eager eyes Natasha still gazed intently and persistently at him, as though she longed to understand something more, that perhaps he had left unsaid. In shamefaced and happy confusion, Pierre glanced at her now and then, and was thinking what to say now to change the subject. Princess Marya was mute. It did not strike any of them that it was three o'clock in the night, and time to be in bed.

'They say: sufferings are misfortunes,' said Pierre. 'But if at once, this minute, I was asked, would I remain what I was before I was taken prisoner, or go through it all again, I should say, for God's sake let me rather be a prisoner and eat horse-flesh again. We imagine that as soon as we are torn out of our habitual path all is over, but it is only the beginning of something new and good. As long as there is life, there is happiness. There is a great deal, a great deal before us. That I say to you,' he said, turning to Natasha.

'Yes, yes,' she said, answering something altogether different, 'and I too would ask for nothing better than to go through it all again.'

Pierre looked intently at her.

'Yes, and nothing more,' Natasha declared.

'Not true, not true,' cried Pierre. 'I am not to blame for being alive and wanting to live; and you the same.'

All at once Natasha let her head drop into her hands, and burst into tears.

'What is it, Natasha?' said Princess Marya.

'Nothing, nothing.' She smiled through her tears to Pierre. 'Goodnight, it's bedtime.'

Pierre got up, and took leave.

Natasha, as she always did, went with Princess Marya into her bedroom. They talked of what Pierre had told them. Princess Marya did not give her opinion of Pierre. Natasha, too, did not talk of him.

'Well, good-night, Marie,' said Natasha. 'Do you know I am often afraid that we don't talk of him' (she meant Prince Andrey), 'as though we were afraid of desecrating our feelings, and so we forget him.'

Princess Marya sighed heavily, and by this sigh acknowledged the justice of Natasha's words; but she did not in words agree with her.

'Is it possible to forget?' she said.

'I was so glad to tell all about it today; it was hard and painful, and yet I was glad to . . . Very glad,' said Natasha; 'I am sure that he really loved him. That was why I told him . . . it didn't matter my telling him?' she asked suddenly, blushing.

'Pierre? Oh, no! How good he is,' said Princess Marya.

'Do you know, Marie,' said Natasha, suddenly, with a mischievous smile, such as Princess Marya had not seen for a long while on her face. 'He has become so clean and smooth and fresh; as though he had just come out of a bath; do you understand? Out of a moral bath. Isn't it so?'

'Yes,' said Princess Marya. 'He has gained a great deal.'

'And his short jacket, and his cropped hair; exactly as though he had just come out of a bath . . papa used sometimes . . .'

'I can understand how *he*' (Prince Andrey) 'cared for no one else as he did for him,' said Princess Marya.

'Yes, and he is so different from him. They say men are better friends when they are utterly different. That must be true; he is not a bit like him in anything, is he?'

'Yes, and he is such a splendid fellow.'

'Well, good-night,' answered Natasha. And the same mischievous smile lingered a long while as though forgotten on her face.

XVIII

FOR a long while Pierre could not sleep that night. He walked up and down his room, at one moment frowning, deep in some difficult train of thought, at the next shrugging his shoulders and shaking himself, and at the next smiling blissfully.

He thought of Prince Andrey, of Natasha, of their love, and at one moment was jealous of her past, and at the next reproached himself, and then forgave himself for the feeling. It was six o'clock in the morning, and still he paced the room.

'Well, what is one to do, if there's no escaping it? What is one to do? It must be the right thing, then,' he said to himself; and hurriedly undressing, he got into bed, happy and agitated, but free from doubt and hesitation.

'However strange, however impossible such happiness, I must do everything that we may be man and wife,' he said to himself.

Several days previously Pierre had fixed on the following Friday as the date on which he would set off to Petersburg. When he waked up next day it was Thursday, and Savelitch came to him for orders about packing the things for the journey.

'To Petersburg? What is Petersburg? Who is in Petersburg?' he unconsciously asked, though only of himself. 'Yes, some long while ago, before this happened, I was meaning for some reason to go to Petersburg,' he recalled. 'Why was it? And I shall go, perhaps. How kind he is, and how attentive, how he remembers everything!' he thought, looking at Savelitch's old face. 'And what a pleasant smile!' he thought.

'Well, and do you still not want your freedom, Savelitch?' asked Pierre.

'What should I want my freedom for, your excellency? With the late count—the Kingdom of Heaven to him—we got on very well, and under you, we have never known any unkindness.'

'Well, but your children?'

'My children too will do very well, your excellency; under such masters one can get all right.'

'Well, but my heirs?' said Pierre. 'All of a sudden I shall get married . . . It might happen, you know,' he added, with an involuntary smile.

'And I make bold to say, a good thing too, your excellency.'

'How easy he thinks it,' thought Pierre. 'He does not know how terrible it is, how perilous. Too late or too early . . . It is terrible!'

'What are your orders? Will you be pleased to go tomorrow?' asked Savelitch.

'No; I will put it off a little. I will tell you later. You must excuse the trouble I give you,' said Pierre, and watching Savelitch's smile, he thought how strange it was, though, that he should not know there was no such thing as Petersburg, and that *that* must be settled before everything.

'He really does know, though,' he thought; 'he is only pretending. Shall I tell him? What does he think about it? No, another time.'

At breakfast, Pierre told his cousin that he had been the previous evening at Princess Marya's, and had found there—could she fancy whom—Natasha Rostov.

The princess looked as though she saw nothing more extraordinary in that fact than if Pierre had seen some Anna Semyonovna.

'You know her?' asked Pierre.

'I have seen the princess,' she answered, 'and I had heard they were making a match between her and young Rostov. That would be a very fine thing for the Rostovs; I am told they are utterly ruined.'

'No, I meant, do you know Natasha Rostov?'

'I heard at the time all about that story. Very sad.'

'She does not understand, or she is pretending,' thought Pierre. 'Better not tell her either.'

. The princess, too, had prepared provisions for Pierre's journey.

'How kind they all are,' thought Pierre, 'to trouble about all this now, when it certainly can be of no interest to them. And all for my sake; that is what's so marvellous.'

The same day a police officer came to see Pierre, with an offer to send a trusty agent to the Polygonal Palace to receive the things that were today to be restored among the owners.

'And this man too,' thought Pierre, looking into the police officer's face, 'what a nice, good-looking officer, and how good-natured! To trouble about such trifles *now*. And yet they say he is not honest, and takes bribes. What nonsense! though after all why shouldn't he take bribes? He has been brought up in that way. They all do it. But such a pleasant, good-humoured face, and he smiles when he looks at me.'

Pierre went to Princess Marya's to dinner. As he drove through the streets between the charred wrecks of houses, he admired the beauty of those ruins. The chimneys of stoves, and the tumbledown walls of houses stretched in long rows, hiding one another, all through the burnt quarters of the town, and recalled to him the picturesque ruins of the Rhine and of the Colosseum. The sledge-drivers and men on horseback, the carpenters at work on the frames of the houses, the hawkers and shopkeepers all looked at Pierre with cheerful, beaming faces, and seemed to him to say: 'Oh, here he is! We shall see what comes of it.'

On reaching Princess Marya's house, Pierre was beset by a sudden doubt whether it were true that he had been there the day before, and had really seen Natasha and talked to her. 'Perhaps it was all my own invention, perhaps I shall go in and see no one.' But no sooner had he entered the room than in his whole being, from his instantaneous loss of freedom, he was aware of her presence. She was wearing the same black dress, that hung in soft folds, and had her hair arranged in the same way, but she was utterly different. Had she looked like this when he came in yesterday, he could not have failed to recognise her.

She was just as he had known her almost as a child, and later when betrothed to Prince Andrey. A bright, questioning light gleamed in her eyes; there was a friendly and strangely mischievous expression in her face.

Pierre dined, and would have spent the whole evening with them; but Princess Marya was going to vespers, and Pierre went with them.

Next day Pierre arrived early, dined with them, and stayed the whole evening. Although Princess Marya and Natasha were obviously glad to see their visitor, and although the whole interest of Pierre's life was now centred in that house, by the evening they had said all they had to say, and the conversation passed continually from one trivial subject to another and often broke off altogether. Pierre stayed so late that evening that Princess Marya and Natasha exchanged glances, plainly wondering whether he would not soon go. Pierre saw that, but he could not go away. He began to feel it irksome and awkward, but still he sat on because he *could not* get up and go.

Princess Marya, foreseeing no end to it, was the first to get up, and complaining of a sick headache, she began saying good-night.

'So you are going tomorrow to Petersburg?' she said.

'No, I am not going,' said Pierre hurriedly, with surprise and a sort of resentment in his tone. 'No . . . yes, to Petersburg. Tomorrow, perhaps; but I won't say good-bye. I shall come to see if you have any commissions to give me,' he added, standing before Princess Marya, turning very red, and not taking leave.

Natasha gave him her hand and retired. Princess Marya, on the contrary, instead of going away, sank into an armchair, and with her luminous, deep eyes looked sternly and intently at Pierre. The weariness she had unmistakably betrayed just before had now quite passed off. She drew a deep, prolonged sigh, as though preparing for a long conversation.

As soon as Natasha had gone, all Pierre's confusion and awkwardness instantly vanished, and were replaced by excited eagerness.

He rapidly moved a chair close up to Princess Marya. 'Yes, I wanted to tell you,' he said, replying to her look as though to words. 'Princess, help me. What am I to do? Can I hope? Princess, my dear friend, listen to me. I know all about it. I know I am not worthy of her; I know that it is impossible to talk of it now. But I want to be a brother to her. No, not that, I don't, I can't . . .' He paused and passed his hands over his face and eyes. 'It's like this,' he went on, making an evident effort to speak coherently. 'I don't know since when I have loved her. But I have loved her alone, only her, all my life, and I love her so that I cannot imagine life without her. I cannot bring myself to ask for her hand now; but the thought that, perhaps, she might be my wife and letting slip this opportunity . . . opportunity . . . is awful. Tell me, can I hope? Tell me, what am I to do? Dear princess,' he said, after a brief pause, touching her hand as she did not answer.

'I am thinking of what you have just told me,' answered Princess Marya. 'This is what I think. You are right that to speak to her of love now . . .' The princess paused. She had meant to say that to speak to her of love now was impossible; but she stopped, because she had seen during the last three days by the sudden change in Natasha that she would by no means be offended if Pierre were to avow his love, that, in fact, it was the one thing she desired.

'To speak to her now . . . is out of the question,' she nevertheless said.

'But what am I to do?'

'Trust the matter to me,' said Princess Marya. 'I know . . .'

Pierre looked into her eyes.

'Well, well . . .' he said.

'I know that she loves . . . that she will love you,' Princess Marya corrected herself.

She had hardly uttered the words, when Pierre leaped up, and with a face of consternation clutched at Princess Marya's hand.

'What makes you think so? You think I may hope? You think so? . . .'

'Yes, I think so,' said Princess Marya, smiling. 'Write to her parents. And leave it to me. I will tell her when it is possible. I desire it to come to pass. And I have a feeling in my heart that it will be so.'

'No, it cannot be! How happy I am! But it cannot be! . . . How happy I am! No, it cannot be!' Pierre kept saying, kissing Princess Marya's hands.

'You should go to Petersburg; it will be better. And I will write to you,' she said.

'To Petersburg? I am to go? Yes, very well, I will go. But I can come and see you tomorrow?'

Next day Pierre came to say good-bye. Natasha was less animated than on the preceding days; but sometimes that day, looking into her eyes, Pierre felt that he was vanishing away, that he and she were no more, that there was nothing but happiness. 'Is it possible? No, it cannot be,' he said to himself at every glance she gave, every gesture, every word, that filled his soul with gladness.

When, on saying good-bye, he took her thin, delicate hand he unconsciously held it somewhat longer in his own.

'Is it possible that that hand, that face, those eyes, all that treasure of womanly charm, so far removed from me, is it possible it may all one day be my own for ever, as close and intimate as I am to myself? No, it's surely impossible? . . .'

'Good-bye, count,' she said to him aloud. 'I shall so look forward to seeing you again,' she added in a whisper.

And those simple words, and the look in the eyes and the face, that accompanied them, formed the subject of inexhaustible reminiscences, interpretations, and happy dreams for Pierre during two whole months. 'I shall look forward to seeing you again.' 'Yes, yes, how did she say it? Yes. "I shall so look forward to seeing you again." Oh, how happy I am! How can it be that I am so happy!' Pierre said to himself.

XIX

THERE was nothing in Pierre's soul now like what had passed within him in similar circumstances during the time of his being betrothed to Ellen.

He did not go over, as he had then, with a sickening sense of shame the words he had uttered; he did not say to himself: 'Oh, why did I not say that, and why, oh why, did I say then: I love you.' Now, on the contrary, every word of hers and of his own, he went over in his imagination with every detail of look and smile, and wanted to add nothing, to take nothing away, he longed only to hear it over again. As for doubts—whether what he contemplated doing was right or wrong—there was never a trace of them now. Only one terrible doubt sometimes assailed his mind. Was it not all a dream? Was not Princess Marya mistaken? Am I not too conceited and self-confident? I believe in it; but all at once—and it's what is sure to happen—Princess Marya tells her; and she smiles and answers: 'How queer! He has certainly made a mistake. Doesn't he know that he is a man, a mere man, while I? . . . I am something altogether different, higher?'

This doubt alone often beset Pierre. He made no plans of any sort now. The happiness before him seemed to him so incredible that the only thing that mattered was to bring it to pass, and nothing could be beyond. Everything else was over.

A joyful, unexpected frenzy, of which Pierre had believed himself incapable, seized upon him. The whole meaning of life, not for him only, but for all the world, seemed to him centred in his love and the possibility of her loving him. Sometimes all men seemed to him to be absorbed in nothing else than his future happiness. It seemed to him sometimes that they were all rejoicing as he was himself, and were only trying to conceal that joy, by pretending to be occupied with other interests. In every word and gesture he saw an allusion to his happiness. He often surprised people by his significant and blissful looks and smiles, that seemed to express some secret understanding with them. But when he realised that people could not know of his happiness, he pitied them from the bottom of his heart, and felt an impulse to try to make them somehow understand that all that they were interested in was utter nonsense and trifles not deserving of attention.

When suggestions were made to him that he should take office under government, or when criticisms of any sort on general, political questions, or on the war, were made before him, on the supposition that one course of events or another would affect the happiness of all men, he listened with a gentle smile of commiseration, and astounded the persons conversing with him by his strange observations. But both those persons, who seemed to Pierre to grasp the true significance of life, that is, his feeling, and those luckless wretches who obviously had no notion of it—all at this period appeared to Pierre in the radiant light of his own glowing feeling; so that on meeting any one, he saw in him without the slightest effort everything that was good and deserving of love.

As he looked through his dead wife's papers and belongings, he had no feeling towards her memory but one of pity that she had not known the happiness he knew now. Prince Vassily, who was particularly haughty just then, having received a new post and a star, struck him as a pathetic and kind-hearted old man, very much to be pitied.

Often afterwards Pierre recalled that time of happy insanity. All the judgments he formed of men and circumstances during that period remained for ever true to him. Far from renouncing later on those views of men and things, on the contrary, in inner doubts and contradictions, he flew back to the view he had had during that time of madness; and that view always turned out to be a true one.

'Perhaps,' he thought, 'I did seem strange and absurd then; but I was not so mad then as I seemed. On the contrary, I was cleverer and had more insight then than at any time, and I understood everything worth understanding in life, because . . . I was happy.'

Pierre's madness showed itself in his not waiting, as in old days, for those personal grounds, which he had called good qualities in people, in order to love them; but as love was brimming over in his heart he loved men without cause, and so never failed to discover incontestable reasons that made them worth loving.

XX

FROM that first evening, when Natasha had said to Princess Marya, with a gaily mocking smile, that he looked exactly, yes, exactly, as if he had come out of a bath with his short jacket and his 'cropped hair—from that minute something hidden and unrecognised by herself, yet irresistible, awakened in Natasha's soul.

Everything—face, gait, eyes, voice—everything was at once transformed in her. To her own surprise, the force of life and hopes of happiness floated to the surface and demanded satisfaction. From that first evening Natasha seemed to have forgotten all that had happened to her.

From that time she never once complained of her position; she said not one word about the past, and was not afraid of already making light-hearted plans for the future. She spoke little of Pierre; but when Princess Marya mentioned him, a light that had long been dim gleamed in her eyes, and her lips curved in a strange smile.

The change that took place in Natasha at first surprised Princess Marya; but when she understood what it meant, that change mortified her. 'Can she have loved my brother so little that she can so soon forget him?' thought Princess Marya, when she thought over it alone. But when she was with Natasha she was not vexed with her, and did not blame her. The awakened force of life that had regained possession of Natasha was obviously so irresistible and so unexpected by herself, that in Natasha's presence Princess Marya felt that she had no right to blame her even in her heart.

Natasha gave herself up with such completeness and sincerity to her new feeling that she did not even attempt to conceal that she was not now sorrowful, but glad and happy.

When Princess Marya had returned to her room that night after her interview with Pierre, Natasha met her on the threshold.

'He has spoken? Yes? He has spoken?' she repeated. And a joyful, and at the same time piteous, expression, that begged forgiveness for its joy, was in Natasha's face. 'I wanted to listen at the door; but I knew you would tell me.'

Ready as Princess Marya was to understand and to be touched by the expression with which Natasha looked at her, and much as she felt for her agitation, yet her words for the first moment mortified her. She thought of her brother and his love.

'But what is one to do? She cannot help it,' thought Princess Marya; and with a sad and somewhat severe face she repeated to Natasha all Pierre had said to her. Natasha was stupefied to hear he was going to Petersburg. 'To Petersburg!' she repeated, as though unable to take it in.

But looking at the mournful expression of Princess Marya's face she divined the cause of her sadness, and suddenly burst into tears.

'Marie,' she said, 'tell me what I am to do. I am afraid of being horrid. Whatever you say, I will do; tell me . . .'

'You love him?'

'Yes!' whispered Natasha.

'What are you crying for, then? I am very glad for you,' said Princess Marya, moved by those tears to complete forgiveness of Natasha's joy.

'It will not be soon . . . some day. Only think how happy it will be when I am his wife and you marry Nikolay!'

'Natasha, I have begged you not to speak of that. Let us talk of you.' Both were silent.

'Only why go to Petersburg?' cried Natasha suddenly, and she hastened to answer herself. 'No, no; it must be so . . . Yes, Marie? It must be . . .'

EPILOGUE

PART I

I

SEVEN years had passed by. The storm-tossed, historic ocean of Europe was subsiding within its shores. It seemed to have grown calm; but the mysterious forces moving humanity (mysterious, because the laws controlling their action are unknown to us) were still at work.

Although the surface of the ocean of history seemed motionless, the movement of humanity was as uninterrupted as the flow of time. Various series of groups of men were joining together and separating; the causes were being prepared that would bring about the formation and the dissolution of empires and the migrations of peoples.

The ocean of history was not now, as before, tossed violently from one shore to the other; it was seething in its depths. Historical figures were not dashing abruptly from one side to the other; now they seemed to be rotating on the same spot. The historical figures, that had in the preceding years at the head of armies reflected the movement of the masses, commanding wars, and marches, and battles, now reflected that movement in political and diplomatic combinations, statutes, and treaties.

This tendency on the part of the figures of history, the historians call the reaction.

In describing the part played by these historical personages, the historians criticise them severely, supposing them to be the cause of what they call the *reaction*. All the celebrated persons of that period, from Alexander and Napoleon to Madame de Staël, Foty, Schelling, Fichte, Chateaubriand, and so on, receive the severest criticism at their hands, and are acquitted or condemned according as they worked for *progress* or for *reaction*.

In Russia, too, so they tell us, a reaction was taking place at that period, and the person chiefly to blame for that reaction was Alexander I.—the same Alexander who, by their own account, was chiefly responsible for the liberal movement at the beginning of his reign, and for the saving of Russia.

In modern Russian literature there is no one, from the schoolboy essay writer to the learned historian, who would not throw his stone at Alexander for the unprincipled acts of this later period of his reign.

'He should have acted in such and such a way. On that occasion he acted well, and on that other, he acted ill. He behaved splendidly in the beginning of his reign and during 1812; but he did ill in giving a constitution to Poland, in making the Holy Alliance, in letting Araktcheev have power, in encouraging Golitsin and mysticism; and later on, in encouraging Shishkov, and Foty. He acted wrongly in interfering with the army on active service; he acted wrongly in cashiering the Semyonovsky regiment, and so on.'

One might cover ten pages in enumerating all the faults found in him by the historians, on the assumption that they possess a knowledge of what is for the good of humanity.

What do these criticisms mean?

Do not the very actions for which the historians applaud Alexander I, such as the liberalism of the early part of his reign, the struggle with Napoleon, the firmness shown in 1812, and the campaign of 1813, proceed from those very sources—the circumstances of birth and breeding and life that made Alexander's personality what it was—from which proceed also the acts for which he is censured by the historians, such as the Holy Alliance, the restoration of Poland, the reaction from 1820 onward?

What is the substance of the charge brought in these criticisms? It is a charge brought against an historical personage standing at the highest possible pinnacle of human power, as it were, in the focus where all the rays of history concentrated their blinding light upon him; a personage subjected to the strongest influences of intrigue, deceit, flattery, and self-deception, inseparable from power; a personage who felt himself at every moment of his life responsible for all that was being done in Europe; and a personage, not an invented character, but a live creature, like any other man, with his own personal idiosyncrasies, and passions and impulses towards goodness, beauty, and truth. And the charge brought against this personage is not that he was not virtuous (the historians have no reproach to make against him on this score), but that he, living fifty years ago, had not the same views as to the good of humanity as those held today by a professor who has, from his youth up, been engaged in study, *i.e.* in reading books, listening to lectures, and making notes of those books and those lectures in a note-book.

But even if we assume that Alexander I, fifty years ago, was mistaken in his view of what was for the good of peoples, we can hardly help assuming that the historian, criticising Alexander, will, after a certain lapse of time, prove to be also incorrect in his view of what is for the good of humanity. It is the more natural and inevitable to assume this because, watching the development of history, we see that with every year, with every new writer, the view of what is for the good of humanity is somewhat shifted; so that what did seem good, after ten years, is regarded as harmful, and *vice versa*. That is not all. We even find in history the views of contemporaries as to what was good, and what was harmful, utterly opposed to one another. Some regard the giving of a constitution to Poland, and the Holy Alliance, as highly to the credit of Alexander; while others regard the same actions as a slur on his name.

It is impossible to say of the careers of Alexander and of Napoleon that they were beneficial or harmful, seeing that we cannot say wherein the benefit or harm of humanity lies. If any one dislikes the career of either, he only dislikes it from its incompatibility with his own limited conception of what is the good of humanity. Even though I regard as good the preservation of my father's house in Moscow in 1812, or the glory of the Russian army, or the flourishing of the Petersburg or some other university, or the independence of Poland, or the supremacy of Russia, or the balance of European power, or a special branch of European enlightenment—progress—yet I am bound to admit that the activity of any historical personage had, apart from such ends, other ends more general and beyond my grasp.

But let us suppose that so-called science has the power of conciliating all contradictions, and has an invariable standard of good and bad by which to try historical personages and events.

Let us suppose that Alexander could have acted quite differently. Let us assume that, in accordance with the prescription of those who censure him, and who profess a knowledge of the final end of the movement of humanity, he could have followed that programme of nationalism, of freedom, of equality, and of progress (there seems to be no other) which his modern critics would have selected for him. Let us suppose that programme could have been possible, and had actually been formulated at that time, and that Alexander could have acted in accordance with it. What, then, would have become of the activity of all the persons who were opposing the tendency of the government of that day—of the activity which, in the opinion of the historians, was good and beneficial? There would have been none of that activity; there would have been no life; there would have been nothing.

Once admit that human life can be guided by reason, and all possibility of life is annihilated.

II

IF one admits, as historians do, that great men lead humanity to the attainments of certain ends, such as the aggrandisement of Russia or of France, or the balance of power, or the diffusion of the ideas of the revolution, or of general progress, or anything else you like, it becomes impossible to explain the phenomena of history apart from the conceptions of *chance* and *genius*.

If the object of the European wars of the beginning of this century had been the aggrandisement of Russia, that object might have been attained without any of the preceding wars, and without invasion of foreign territory.

If the object were the aggrandisement of France, that aim might have been attained apart from the revolution and the empire. If the object were the diffusion of ideas, the printing of books would have attained that object much more effectually than soldiers. If the object were the progress of civilisation, one may very readily assume that there are other more effectual means of diffusing civilisation than the slaughter of men and the destruction of their property.

Why did it come to pass in this way and no other? Because it happened so. '*Chance* created the position; *genius* took advantage of it,' says history.

But what is *chance*? What is *genius*?

The words *chance* and *genius* mean nothing actually existing, and so cannot be defined. These words merely denote a certain stage in the comprehension of phenomena. I do not know how some phenomenon is brought about; I believe that I cannot know; consequently I do not want to know and talk of *chance*. I see a force producing an effect out of proportion with the average effect of human powers; I do not understand how this is brought about, and I talk about *genius*.

To a flock of sheep the sheep who is every evening driven by the shepherd into a special pen to feed, and becomes twice as fat as the rest, must seem to be a genius. And the circumstance that every evening that sheep does not come into the common fold, but into a special pen full of oats, and that that same sheep grows fat and is killed for mutton, must present itself to the minds of the other sheep as a singular conjunction of genius with a whole series of exceptional chances.

But the sheep need only cease to assume that all that is done to them is with a view to the attainment of their sheepish ends; they need only admit that the events that occur to them may have ends beyond their ken, and they will at once see a unity and a coherence in what happens with the fatted sheep. Even though they will not know for what end he is fattened, at least they will know that all that happens to him does not happen by chance, and they will have no need to resort to the conception of *chance*, nor to the conception of *genius*.

It is only by renouncing all claims to knowledge of an immediate comprehensible aim, and acknowledging the final aim to be beyond our ken, that we see a consistent whole in the life of historical persons. The cause is then revealed to us of that effect produced by them out of proportion with the common powers of humanity, and we have no need of the words *chance* and *genius*.

We have only to admit that the object of the convulsions of the European nations is beyond our knowledge, and that we know only the facts, consisting mainly of murders committed at first in France, then in Italy, then in Africa, in Prussia, in Austria, in Spain, and in Russia, and that the movements from west to east and from east to west constitute the essence and end of those events, and we shall not need to see something exceptional—*genius*—in the characters of Napoleon and of Alexander, and shall indeed be unable to conceive of those persons as being in any way different from everybody else. And far from having to explain as *chance* those petty events, which made those men what they were, it will be clear to us that all those petty details were inevitable.

When we give up all claim to a knowledge of the final end, we shall clearly perceive that just as we cannot invent any flower or seed more truly appropriate to a plant than those it produces, so we cannot imagine any two persons, with all their past in such complete congruity, down to the smallest details, with the part they were destined to play.

III

THE underlying essentially significant feature of the European events of the beginning of the present century is the military movement of masses of European peoples from west to east, and again from east to west. The original movement was that from west to east. That the peoples of the west might be able to accomplish the military march upon Moscow, which they did accomplish, it was essential (1) that they should be combined in a military group of such a magnitude as to be able to withstand the resistance of the military group of the east; (2) that they should have renounced all their established traditions and habits; and (3) that they should have at their head a man able to justify in his own name and theirs the perpetration of all the deception, robbery, and murder that accompany that movement.

And to start from the French Revolution, that old group of insufficient magnitude is broken up; the old habits and traditions are destroyed; step by step a group is elaborated of new dimensions, new habits, and new traditions; and the man is prepared, who is to stand at the head of the coming movement, and to take upon himself the whole responsibility of what has to be done.

A man of no convictions, no habits, no traditions, no name, not even a Frenchman, by the strangest freaks of chance, as it seems, rises above the seething parties of France, and without attaching himself to any one of them, advances to a prominent position.

The incompetence of his colleagues, the weakness and insignificance of his opponents, the frankness of the deception, and the dazzling and self-confident limitation of the man raise him to the head of the army. The brilliant personal qualities of the soldiers of the Italian army, the disinclination to fight of his opponents, and his childish insolence and conceit gain him military glory. Innumerable so-called *chance* circumstances attend him everywhere. The disfavour into which he falls with the French Directorate turns to his advantage. His efforts to avoid the path ordained for him are unsuccessful; he is not received into the Russian army, and his projects in Turkey come to nothing.

During the wars in Italy he was several times on the verge of destruction, and was every time saved in an unexpected fashion. The Russian troops—the very troops which were able to demolish his glory—owing to various diplomatic considerations, do not enter Europe until he is there.

On his return from Italy, he finds the government in Paris in that process of dissolution in which all men who are in the government are inevitably effaced and nullified. And an escape for him from that perilous position offers itself in the shape of an aimless, groundless expedition to Africa. Again the same so-called *chance* circumstances accompany him. Malta, the impregnable, surrenders without a shot being fired; the most ill-considered measures are crowned with success. The enemy's fleet, which later on does not let one boat escape it, now lets a whole army elude it. In Africa a whole series of outrages is perpetrated on the almost unarmed inhabitants. And the men perpetrating these atrocities, and their leader most of all, persuade themselves that it is noble, it is glory, that it is like Cæsar and Alexander of Macedon, and that it is fine.

That ideal of *glory* and of *greatness*, consisting in esteeming nothing one does wrong, and glorying in every crime, and ascribing to it an incomprehensible, supernatural value—that ideal, destined to guide this man and those connected with him, is elaborated on a grand scale in

Africa. Whatever he does succeeds. The plague does not touch him. The cruelty of murdering his prisoners is not remembered against him. His childishly imprudent, groundless, and ignoble departure from Africa, abandoning his comrades in misfortune, does him good service; and again the enemy's fleet lets him twice slip through their hands. At the moment when, completely intoxicated by the success of his crimes and ready for the part he has to play, he arrives in Paris entirely without any plan, the disintegration of the Republican government, which might have involved him in its ruin a year before, has now reached its utmost limit, and his presence, a man independent of parties, can now only aid his elevation.

He has no sort of plan; he is afraid of everything; but all parties clutch at him and insist on his support.

He alone—with the ideal of glory and greatness he has acquired in Italy and Egypt, with his frenzy of self-adoration, with his insolence in crime, and his frankness in mendacity—he alone can justify what has to be accomplished.

He is needed for the place that awaits him, and so, almost apart from his own volition, and in spite of his uncertainty, the lack of plan, and the blunders he commits, he is drawn into a conspiracy that aims at seizing power ; and that conspiracy is crowned with success.

He is dragged into the assembly of the rulers. In alarm he tries to flee, believing himself in danger; pretends to faint, says the most senseless things that should have been his ruin. But the rulers of France, once proud and discerning, now feeling their part is over, are even more panic-stricken than he, and fail to utter the words they should have pronounced to preserve their power and crush him.

Chance, millions of *chances*, give him power; and all men, as though in league together, combine to confirm that power. *Chance* circumstances create the characters of the rulers of France, who cringe before him,; *chance* creates the character of Paul I, who acknowledges his authority; *chance* causes the plot against him to strengthen his power instead of shaking it. *Chance* throws the Duc d'Enghien into his hands and accidentally impels him to kill him, thereby convincing the crowd by the strongest of all arguments that he has the right on his side since he has the might. *Chance* brings it to pass that though he strains every nerve to fit out an expedition against England, which would unmistakably have led to his ruin, he never puts this project into execution, and happens to fall upon Mack with the Austrians, who surrender without a battle. *Chance* and *genius* give him the victory at Austerlitz; and by *chance* it comes to pass that all men, not only the French, but all the countries of Europe except England, which takes no part in the events that are to be accomplished, forget their old horror and aversion for his crimes, and now recognise the power he has gained by them, acknowledge the title he has bestowed upon himself, and accept his ideal of greatness and glory, which seems to every one something fine and rational.

As though practising and preparing themselves for the great movement before them, the forces of the west make several dashes—in 1805, 1806, 1807 and 1809—into the east, growing stronger and more numerous. In 1811 a group of men formed in France is joined by an enormous group from the peoples of Central Europe. As the numbers of the great mass increase, the power of justification of the man at the head of the movement gathers more and more force. During the ten years of the preparatory period preceding the great movement, this man forms relations with all the crowned heads of Europe. The sovereigns of the world, stripped bare by him, can oppose no rational ideal to the senseless Napoleonic ideal of *glory* and greatness. They vie with one another in demonstrating to him their insignificance. The King of Prussia sends his wife to sue for the good graces of the great man; the Emperor of Austria considers it a favour for this man to take the daughter of the Kaisers to his bed. The Pope, the guardian of the faith of the peoples, uses religion to aid the great man's elevation. Napoleon does not so much prepare himself for the part he is to play as all around him lead him on to take upon himself the responsibility of what is being done and is to be done. There is no act, no crime, no petty deceit which he would not commit, and which would not be at once represented on the lips of those about him as a great deed. The most suitable fête the Germans could think of in his honour was the celebration of Jena and Auerstadt. Not only is he great; his forefathers, his brothers, his stepchildren, and his brothers-in-law are great too. Everything is done to deprive him of the last glimmering of reason, and to prepare him for his terrible part. And when he is ready, his forces too are in readiness.

The invading army flows towards the east and reaches its final goal: Moscow. The ancient city is taken; the Russian army suffers greater losses than were ever suffered by the opposing armies in the previous wars from Austerlitz to Wagram. But all at once, instead of that *chance* and *genius*, which had so consistently led him hitherto by an interrupted series of successes to his destined goal, an immense number of *chance* circumstances occur of an opposite kind from the cold caught at Borodino to the spark that fired Moscow; and instead of *genius* there was shown a folly and baseness unexampled in history.

The invading army flees away, turns back and flees again; and all the chances now are consistently not for but against him.

Then there follows the opposing movement from east to west, with a remarkable similarity to the eastward movement from the west that had preceded it. There were similar tentative movements westward as had in 1805, 1807 and 1809 preceded the great eastward movement. There was the same cohesion together of all into one group of immense numbers; the same adherence of the peoples of Central Europe to the movement; the same hesitation midway, and the same increased velocity as the goal was approached.

Paris, the furthest goal, was reached. Napoleon's government and armies are shattered. Napoleon himself is of no further consequence; all his actions are obviously paltry and mean; but again inexplicable chance comes in. The allies detest Napoleon, in whom they see the cause of all their troubles. Stripped of his power and his might, convicted of frauds and villanies, he should have been seen by them as he had been ten years before, and was a year later—a brigand outside the pale of the law. But by some strange freak of chance no one sees it. His part is not yet played out. The man who ten years back, and one year later, was looked on as a miscreant outside the law, was sent by them to an island two days' journey from France, given to him as his domain, with guards and millions of money, as though to pay him for some service he had done.

IV

THE commotion among the peoples begins to subside. The waves of the great tempest begin to abate, and eddies begin to be formed about the calmer surface where diplomatists are busy, fancying the calm is their work.

But all at once the quiet sea is convulsed again. The diplomatists imagine that they, their disagreements, are the cause of this fresh disturbance; they look for wars between their sovereigns; the position seems insoluble. But the storm they feel brewing does not come from the quarter where they look for it. It rises again from the same starting point—Paris. The last backwash of the westward movement follows— the backwash which was to solve the seemingly inextricable diplomatic difficulties, and to put an end to the military unrest of the period.

The man who has devastated France comes back to France alone, with no project, and no soldiers. Any policeman can arrest him; but by a strange freak of chance no one does seize him, but all meet with enthusiasm the man they have been cursing but a day before, and will curse again within a month.

That man is needed for the last act winding up the drama.

The act is performed.

The last part is played. The actor is bidden to undress, and wash off his powder and paint; he will be needed no more.

And for several years this man, in solitude on his island, plays his pitiful farce to himself, intrigues and lies, justifying his conduct when a justification is no longer needed, and shows all the world what the thing was men took for power when an unseen hand guided it.

The stage manager, when the drama was over, and the puppet stripped, showed him to us.

'Look what you believed in! Here he is! Do you see now that it was not he but I that moved you.'

But blinded by the force of the movement men for long could not perceive that.

Even more coherence and inevitability is to be seen in the life of Alexander I, the personage who stood at the head of the counter-movement from east westward.

What was needed for the man who, to the exclusion of others, should stand at the head of that movement from the east westward?

There was needed a sense of justice, an interest in the affairs of Europe, but a remote one, not obscured by petty interests, a moral pre-eminence over his peers—the sovereigns of the time; there was needed a gentle and attractive personal character; there was needed too a personal grievance against Napoleon. And all that is to be seen in Alexander I; it was all prepared beforehand by the innumerable so-called *chance* circumstances of his previous life, by his education and the liberalism of the beginning of his reign, and the counsellors around, and Austerlitz, and Tilsit, and Erfurt.

During the war in defence of the country this personage is inactive; he is not needed. But as soon as a general European war becomes inevitable, at the given moment, he is in his place, and bringing the European peoples together he leads them to the goal.

The goal is reached. After the last war of 1815 Alexander finds himself at the highest possible pinnacle of human power. How does he use it?

While Napoleon in his exile was drawing up childish and lying schemes of the blessings he would have showered on humanity if he had had the power, Alexander, the pacificator of Europe, the man who, from his youth up, had striven for nothing but the good of the people, the first champion of liberal reforms in his country, now when he seemed to possess the greatest possible power, and consequent possibility of doing good to his people, felt his work was done, and God's hand was laid upon him, and recognising the nothingness of that semblance of power, turned from it, gave it up to despicable men, and men he despised, and could only say:

'Not to us, not to us, but to Thy Name! I too am a man like all of you; let me live like a man, and think of my soul and of God.'

Just as the sun and every atom of ether is a sphere complete in itself, and at the same time is only a part of a whole inconceivable to man through its vastness, so every individuality bears within it its own ends, and yet bears them so as to serve general ends unfathomable by man.

A bee settling on a flower has stung a child. And the child dreads bees, and says the object of the bee is to sting people. A poet admires the bee, sipping honey from the cup of the flower, and says the object of the bee is to sip the nectar of the flower. A beekeeper, noticing that the bee gathers pollen and brings it to the hive, says that the object of the bee is to gather honey. Another beekeeper, who has studied the life of the swarm more closely, says the bee gathers honey to feed the young ones, and to rear a queen, that the object of the bee is the perpetuation of its race. The botanist observes that the bee flying with the pollen fertilises the pistil, and in this he sees the object of the bee. Another, watching the hybridisation of plants, sees that the bee contributes to that end also, and he may say that the bee's object is that. But the final aim of the bee is not exhausted by one or another, or a third aim, which the human intellect is capable of discovering. The higher the human intellect rises in the discovery of such aims, the more obvious it becomes that the final aim is beyond its reach.

All that is within the reach of man is the observation of the analogy of the life of the bee with other manifestations of life. And the same is true with the final aims of historical persons and of nations.

V

NATASHA'S marriage to Bezuhov, which took place in 1813, was the last happy event in the family of the old Rostovs. Count Ilya Andreivitch died the same year; and as is always the case, with the death of the father the family was broken up.

The events of the previous year: the burning of Moscow and the flight from that city; the death of Prince Andrey and Natasha's despair; the death of Petya and the grief of the countess fell like one blow after another on the old count's head. He seemed not to understand, and to feel himself incapable of understanding, the significance of all these events, and figuratively speaking, bowed his old head to the storm, as though expecting and seeking fresh blows to make an end of him. By turns he seemed scared and distraught, and then unnaturally lively and active.

Natasha's marriage for a time occupied him on its external side. He arranged dinners and suppers in honour of it, and obviously tried to be cheerful; but his cheerfulness was not infectious as in old days, but, on the contrary, aroused the commiseration of those who knew and liked him.

After Pierre and his wife had left, he collapsed and began to complain of depression. A few days later he fell ill and took to his bed. In spite of the doctor's assurances, he knew from the first days of his illness that he would never get up again. For a whole fortnight the countess sat in a low chair by his pillow, never taking off her clothes. Every time she gave him his medicine, he mutely kissed her hand, weeping. On the last day, sobbing, he begged forgiveness of his wife, and of his absent son, too, for squandering their property, the chief sin that lay on his conscience. After receiving absolution and the last unction, he quietly died; and next day a crowd of acquaintances, come to pay the last debt of respect to the deceased, filled the Rostovs' hired lodgings. All those acquaintances, who had so often dined and danced in his house, and had so often laughed at his expense, were saying now with the same inward feeling of contrition and self-reproach, as though seeking to justify themselves: 'Yes, whatever he may have been, he was a splendid man. One doesn't meet such men nowadays . . . And who has not his weaknesses? . . .'

It was precisely when the count's fortunes were so irretrievably embroiled that he could not conceive how, in another year, it would end, that he suddenly died.

Nikolay was with the Russian army in Paris when the news of his father's death reached him. He at once applied for his discharge, and without waiting for it, obtained leave and went to Moscow. Within a month after the count's death the financial position had been made perfectly clear, astounding every one by the immense sum of various petty debts, the existence of which no one had suspected. The debts were more than double the assets of the estate.

The friends and relations advised Nikolay to refuse to accept his inheritance. But Nikolay looked on such a refusal as a slur on the honoured memory of his father; and so he would not hear of such a course, and accepted the inheritance with the obligation of paying the debts.

The creditors, who had so long been silent, held in check during the old count's lifetime by the vague but powerful influence of his easy good-nature, all beset Nikolay at once. There seemed, as so often happens, a sort of rivalry among them, which should get paid first; and the very people, such as Mitenka and others, who held promissory notes, not received in discharge of debts, but as presents, were now the most importunate of the creditors. They would give Nikolay no peace and no respite, and those who had shown pity for the old man, who was responsible for their losses (if they really had lost money by him), were now ruthless in their persecution of the young heir, who was obviously guiltless as far as they were concerned, and had voluntarily undertaken to pay them.

Not one of the plans that Nikolay resorted to was successful: the estate was sold by auction at half its value, and half the debts remained still unpaid. Nikolay accepted a loan of thirty thousand roubles offered him by his brother-in-law Bezuhov; and paid that portion of the debts that he recognised as genuine obligations. And to avoid being thrown into prison for the remainder, as the creditors threatened, he once more entered the government service.

To return to the army, where at the next promotion he would have been colonel, was out of the question, because his mother now clung to her son as her one hold on life. And so in spite of his disinclination to remain in Moscow, in the midst of a circle of acquaintances who had known him in former days, in spite of his distaste for the civil service, he accepted a civilian post in Moscow, and taking off his beloved uniform, established himself in a little lodging in Sivtsevoy Vrazhok with his mother and Sonya.

Natasha and Pierre were living at this period in Petersburg, and had no very distinct idea of Nikolay's position. After having borrowed money from his brother-in-law, Nikolay did his utmost to conceal his poverty-stricken position from him. His situation was rendered the more difficult, as with his twelve hundred roubles of salary he had not only to keep himself, Sonya, and his mother, but to keep his mother in such a way that she would not be sensible of their poverty. The countess could not conceive of life being possible without the luxurious surroundings to which she had been accustomed from her childhood; and without any idea of its being difficult for her son, she was continually insisting on having a carriage, which they had not, to send for a friend, or an expensive delicacy for herself, or wine for her son, or money to buy a present, as a surprise for Natasha, for Sonya, or for Nikolay himself.

Sonya kept house, waited on her aunt, read aloud to her, bore with her caprices and her secret dislike, and helped Nikolay to conceal from the old countess their poverty-stricken position. Nikolay felt himself under a debt of gratitude to Sonya that he could never repay, for all she did for his mother; he admired her patience and devotion, but he tried to keep himself aloof from her.

In his heart he seemed to feel a sort of grudge against her for being too perfect, and for there being no fault to find with her. She had all the good qualities for which people are valued, but little of what would have made him love her. And he felt that the more he valued her the less he loved her. He had taken her at her word when she had written to him giving him his freedom, and now he behaved with her as though what had passed between them had been long, long ago forgotten, and could never under any circumstances be renewed.

Nikolay's position was becoming worse and worse. His hope of laying by something out of his salary proved to be an idle dream. Far from saving anything, he was even running up some small debts to satisfy his mother's exigencies. There seemed no means of escape from his position. The idea of marrying a rich heiress, which his female relatives suggested, was repulsive to him. The only other solution of his difficulties—the death of his mother—never entered his head. He desired nothing, and hoped for nothing; and at the bottom of his heart he took a stern and gloomy satisfaction in the unrepining endurance of his position. He tried to avoid his old acquaintances, with their commiseration and their mortifying offers of assistance; shunned every sort of entertainment and amusement; and even at home did nothing but play patience with his mother, pace silently about the room, and smoke pipe after pipe. He seemed studiously to maintain in himself that gloomy temper, which alone enabled him to bear his position.

VI

A T the beginning of the winter Princess Marya arrived in Moscow. From the gossip of the town she heard of the position of the Rostovs, and of how 'the son was sacrificing himself for his mother,' as the gossips said. 'It is just what I expected of him,' Princess Marya said to herself, finding in it a delightful confirmation of her love for him. Remembering her intimate relations with the whole family—almost as one of themselves—she thought it her duty to call on them. But thinking of her relations with Nikolay in Voronezh, she was afraid of doing so. A few weeks after her arrival in Moscow, she did, however, make an effort, and went to see the Rostovs.

Nikolay was the first to meet her, since it was impossible to reach the countess's room without passing through his room. Instead of the expression of delight Princess Marya had expected to see on his face at the first glance at her, he met her with a look of chilliness, stiffness, and pride that she had never seen before. Nikolay inquired after her health, conducted her to his mother, and, after staying five minutes, went out of the room.

When Princess Marya left the countess, Nikolay again met her, and with marked formality and stiffness led her to the hall. He made no reply to her remarks about the countess's health. 'What is it to you? Leave me in peace,' his expression seemed to say.

'And why should she stroll in here? What does she want? I can't endure these ladies and all these civilities!' he said aloud before Sonya, obviously unable to restrain his vexation, after the princess's carriage had rolled away from the house.

'Oh, how can you talk like that, *Nicolas*,' said Sonya, hardly able to conceal her delight. 'She is so kind, and *maman* is so fond of her.'

Nikolay made no reply, and would have liked to say no more about Princess Marya. But after her visit the old countess talked about her several times every day.

She sang her praises; insisted that her son should go and see her; expressed a wish to see more of her; and yet was always out of temper when she had been talking of her.

Nikolay tried to say nothing when his mother talked of Princess Marya, but his silence irritated her.

'She is a very good and conscientious girl,' she would say, 'and you must go and call on her. Any way, you will see some one; and it is dull for you, I expect, with us.'

'But I don't wish at all to, mamma.'

'Why, you wanted to see people and now you don't wish it. I really don't understand you, my dear. At one minute you are dull, and the next you suddenly don't care to see any one.'

'Why, I never said I was dull.'

'Why, you said yourself you did not even wish to see her. She is a very good girl, and you always liked her; and now all of a sudden you have some reasons or other. Everything is kept a secret from me.'

'Not at all, mamma.'

'If I were to beg you to do something unpleasant, but as it is, I simply beg you to drive over and return her call. Why, civility demands it, I should suppose . . . I have begged you to do so, and now I will meddle no further since you have secrets from your mother.'

'But I will go, if you wish it.'

'It's nothing to me; it's for your sake I wish it.'

Nikolay sighed, and bit his moustache, and dealt the cards, trying to draw his mother's attention to another subject.

Next day, and the third, and the fourth, the same conversation was repeated again and again.

After her visit to the Rostovs, and the unexpectedly cold reception she had met with from Nikolay, Princess Marya acknowledged to herself that she had been right in not wanting to be the first to call.

'It was just what I expected,' she said to herself, summoning her pride to her aid. 'I have no concern with him, and I only wanted to see the old lady, who was always kind to me, and to whom I am under obligations for many things.'

But she could not tranquillise herself with these reflections: a feeling akin to remorse fretted her, when she thought of her visit. Although she was firmly resolved not to call again on the Rostovs, and to forget all about it, she was continually feeling herself in an undefined position. And when she asked herself what it was that worried her, she was obliged to admit that it was her relation to Rostov. His cold, ceremonious tone did not proceed from his feeling for her (of that she was convinced); but that tone covered something. What that something was, she wanted to see clearly, and till then she felt that she could not be at peace.

In the middle of the winter she was sitting in the schoolroom, supervising her nephew's lessons, when the servant announced that Rostov was below. With the firm determination not to betray her secret, and not to manifest any embarrassment, she summoned Mademoiselle Bourienne, and with her went into the drawing-room.

At the first glance at Nikolay's face, she saw that he had come merely to perform the obligations of civility, and she determined to keep to the tone he adopted towards her.

They talked of the health of the countess, of common acquaintances, of the latest news of the war, and when the ten minutes required by propriety had elapsed, Nikolay got up to say good-bye.

With the aid of Mademoiselle Bourienne, Princess Marya had kept up the conversation very well. But at the very last moment, just when he was getting up, she was so weary of talking of what did not interest her, and she was so absorbed in wondering why to her alone so little joy had been vouchsafed in life, that in a fit of abstraction, she sat motionless, gazing straight before her with her luminous eyes, and not noticing that he was getting up.

Nikolay looked at her, and anxious to appear not to notice her abstraction, he said a few words to Mademoiselle Bourienne, and again glanced at the princess. She was sitting in the same immovable pose, and there was a look of suffering on her soft face. He felt suddenly sorry for her, and vaguely conscious that he might be the cause of the sadness he saw in her face. He longed to help her, to say something pleasant to her, but he could not think what to say to her.

'Good-bye, princess,' he said. She started, flushed, and sighed heavily.

'Oh, I beg your pardon,' she said, as though waking from sleep. 'You are going already, count; well, good-bye! Oh, the cushion for the countess?'

'Wait a minute, I will fetch it,' said Mademoiselle Bourienne, and she left the room.

They were both silent, glancing at each other now and then.

'Yes, princess,' said Nikolay at last, with a mournful smile, 'it seems not long ago, but how much has happened since the first time we met at Bogutcharovo. We all seemed in such trouble then, but I would give a great deal to have that time back ... and there's no bringing it back.'

Princess Marya was looking intently at him with her luminous eyes, as he said that. She seemed trying to divine the secret import of his words, which would make clear his feeling towards her.

'Yes, yes,' she said, 'but you have no need to regret the past, count. As I conceive of your life now, you will always think of it with satisfaction, because the self-sacrifice in which you are now ...'

'I cannot accept your praises,' he interrupted hurriedly; 'on the contrary, I am always reproaching myself; but it is an uninteresting and cheerless subject.'

And again the stiff and cold expression came back into his face. But Princess Marya saw in him again now the man she had known and loved, and it was to that man only she was speaking now.

'I thought you would allow me to say that,' she said. 'I have been such intimate friends with you ... and with your family, and I thought you would not feel my sympathy intrusive; but I made a mistake,' she said. Her voice suddenly shook. 'I don't know why,' she went on, recovering herself, 'you used to be different, and ...'

'There are thousands of reasons *why*.' (He laid special stress on the word *why*.) 'I thank you, princess,' he added softly. 'It is sometimes hard ...'

'So that is why! That is why!' an inner voice was saying in Princess Marya's soul. 'Yes, it was not only that gay, kind, and frank gaze, not only that handsome exterior I loved in him; I divined his noble, firm, and self-sacrificing soul,' she said to herself.

'Yes, he is poor now, and I am rich ... Yes, it is only that ... Yes, if it were not for that ...' And recalling all his former tenderness, and looking now at his kind and sad face, she suddenly understood the reason of his coldness.

'Why, count, why?' she almost cried all at once, involuntarily moving nearer to him. 'Why, do tell me. You must tell me.' He was mute. 'I do not know, count, your *why*,' she went on. 'But I am sad, I . . . I will own that to you. You mean for some reason to deprive me of our old friendship. And that hurts me.' There were tears in her eyes and in her voice. 'I have had so little happiness in my life that every loss is hard for me . . . Excuse me, good-bye,' she suddenly burst into tears, and was going out of the room.

'Princess! stay, for God's sake,' he cried, trying to stop her. 'Princess!'

She looked round. For a few seconds they gazed mutely in each other's eyes, and the remote and impossible became all at once close at hand, possible and inevitable.

VII

IN the autumn of 1813, Nikolay married Princess Marya, and with his wife, and mother, and Sonya, took up his abode at Bleak Hills.

Within four years he had paid off the remainder of his debts without selling his wife's estates, and coming into a small legacy on the death of a cousin, he repaid the loan he had borrowed from Pierre also.

In another three years, by 1820, Nikolay had so well managed his pecuniary affairs that he was able to buy a small estate adjoining Bleak Hills, and was opening negotiations for the repurchase of his ancestral estate of Otradnoe, which was his cherished dream.

Though he took up the management of the land at first from necessity, he soon acquired such a passion for agriculture, that it became his favourite and almost his exclusive interest. Nikolay was a plain farmer, who did not like innovations, especially English ones, just then coming into vogue, laughed at all theoretical treatises on agriculture, did not care for factories, for raising expensive produce, or for expensive imported seed. He did not, in fact, make a hobby of any one part of the work, but kept the welfare of the *estate* as a whole always before his eyes. The object most prominent to his mind in the estate was not the azote nor the oxygen in the soil or the atmosphere, not a particular plough nor manure, but the principal agent by means of which the azote and the oxygen and the plough and the manure were all made effectual—that is, the labourer, the peasant. When Nikolay took up the management of the land, and began to go into its different branches, the peasant attracted his chief attention. He looked on the peasant, not merely as a tool, but also as an end in himself, and as his critic. At first he studied the peasant attentively, trying to understand what he wanted, what he thought good and bad; and he only made a pretence of making arrangements and giving orders, while he was in reality learning from the peasants their methods and their language and their views of what was good and bad. And it was only when he understood the tastes and impulses of the peasant, when he had learned to speak his speech and to grasp the hidden meaning behind his words, when he felt himself in alliance with him, that he began boldly to direct him—to perform, that is, towards him the office expected of him. And Nikolay's management produced the most brilliant results.

On taking over the control of the property, Nikolay had at once by some unerring gift of insight appointed as bailiff, as village elder, and as delegate the very men whom the peasants would have elected themselves, had the choice been in their hands, and the authority once given them was never withdrawn. Before investigating the chemical constituents of manure, or going into 'debit and credit' (as he liked sarcastically to call book-keeping), he found out the number of cattle the peasants possessed, and did his utmost to increase the number. He kept the peasants' families together on a large scale, and would not allow them to split up into separate households. The indolent, the dissolute, and the feeble he was equally hard upon and tried to expel them from the community. At the sowing and the carrying of the hay and corn, he watched over his own and the peasants' fields with absolutely equal care. And few landowners had fields so early and so well sown and cut, and few had such crops as Nikolay.

He did not like to have anything to do with the house-serfs, he called them *parasites*, and everybody said that he demoralised and spoiled them. When any order had to be given in regard to a house-serf, especially when one had to be punished, he was always in a state of indecision and asked advice of every one in the house. But whenever it was possible to send a house-serf for a soldier in place of a peasant, he did so without the smallest compunction. In all his dealings with the peasants, he never experienced the slightest hesitation. Every order he gave would, he knew, be approved by the greater majority of them.

He never allowed himself either to punish a man by adding to his burdens, or to reward him by lightening his tasks simply at the prompting of his own wishes. He could not have said what his standard was of what he ought and ought not to do; but there was a standard firm and rigid in his soul.

Often talking of some failure or irregularity, he would complain of 'our Russian peasantry,' and he imagined that he could not bear the peasants.

But with his whole soul he did really love 'our Russian peasantry,' and their ways; and it was through that he had perceived and adopted the only method of managing the land which could be productive of good results.

Countess Marya was jealous of this passion of her husband's for agriculture, and regretted she could not share it. But she was unable to comprehend the joys and disappointments he met with in that world apart that was so alien to her. She could not understand why he used to be so particularly eager and happy when after getting up at dawn and spending the whole morning in the fields or the threshing-floor he came back to tea with her from the sowing, the mowing, or the harvest. She could not understand why he was so delighted when he told her with enthusiasm of the well-to-do, thrifty peasant Matvey Ermishin, who had been up all night with his family, carting his sheaves, and had all harvested when no one else had begun carrying. She could not understand why, stepping out of window on to the balcony, he smiled under his moustaches and winked gleefully when a warm, fine rain began to fall on his young oats that were suffering from the drought, or why, when a menacing cloud blew over in mowing or harvest time, he would come in from the barn red, sunburnt, and perspiring, with the smell of wormwood in his hair, and rubbing his hands joyfully would say: 'Come, another day of this and my lot, and the peasants' too, will all be in the barn.'

Still less could she understand how it was that with his good heart and everlasting readiness to anticipate her wishes, he would be thrown almost into despair when she brought him petitions from peasants or their wives who had appealed to her to be let off tasks, why it was that he, her good-natured Nikolay, obstinately refused her, angrily begging her not to meddle in his business. She felt that he had a world apart, that was intensely dear to him, governed by laws of its own which she did not understand.

Sometimes trying to understand him she would talk to him of the good work he was doing in striving for the good of his serfs; but at this he was angry and answered: 'Not in the least; it never even entered my head; and for their good I would not lift my little finger. That's all romantic nonsense and old wives' cackle—all that doing good to one's neighbour. I don't want our children to be beggars; I want to build up our fortunes in my lifetime; that is all. And to do that one must have discipline, one must have strictness . . . So there!' he would declare, clenching his sanguine fist. 'And justice too—of course,' he would add, 'because if the peasant is naked and hungry, and has but one poor horse, he can do no good for himself or me.'

And doubtless because Nikolay did not allow himself to entertain the idea that he was doing anything for the sake of others, or for the sake of virtue, everything he did was fruitful. His fortune rapidly increased; the neighbouring serfs came to beg him to purchase them, and long after his death the peasantry preserved a reverent memory of his rule. 'He was a master . . . The peasants' welfare first and then his own. And to be sure he would make no abatements. A real good master —that's what he was!'

VIII

THE one thing that sometimes troubled Nikolay in his government of his serfs was his hasty temper and his old habit, acquired in the hussars, of making free use of his fists. At first he saw nothing blameworthy in this, but in the second year of his married life his views on that form of correction underwent a sudden change.

One summer day he had sent for the village elder who had taken control at Bogutcharovo on the death of Dron. The man was accused of various acts of fraud and neglect. Nikolay went out to the steps to see him, and at the first answers the village elder made, shouts and blows were heard in the hall. On going back indoors to lunch, Nikolay went up to his wife, who was sitting with her head bent low over her embroidery frame, and began telling her, as he always did, everything that had interested him during the morning, and among other things about the Bogutcharovo elder. Countess Marya, turning red and pale and setting her lips, sat in the same pose, making no reply to her husband.

'The insolent rascal,' he said, getting hot at the mere recollection. 'Well, he should have told me he was drunk, he did not see . . . Why, what is it, Marie?' he asked all at once.

Countess Marya raised her head, trying to control her lips.

'What is it? What is wrong, my darling? . . .' His plain wife always looked her best when she was in tears. She never wept for pain or anger, but always from sadness and pity. And when she wept her luminous eyes gained an indescribable charm.

As soon as Nikolay took her by the hand, she was unable to restrain herself, and burst into tears.

'Nikolay, I saw . . . he was in fault, but you, why did you! Nikolay!' and she hid her face in her hands.

Nikolay did not speak; he flushed crimson, and walking away from her, began pacing up and down in silence. He knew what she was crying about, but he could not all at once agree with her in his heart that what he had been used to from childhood, what he looked upon as a matter of course, was wrong. 'It's sentimental nonsense, old wives' cackle—or is she right?' he said to himself. Unable to decide that question, he glanced once more at her suffering and loving face, and all at once he felt that she was right, and that he had known himself to be in fault a long time before.

'Marie,' he said softly, going up to her: 'it shall never happen again; I give you my word. Never,' he repeated in a shaking voice, like a boy begging forgiveness.

The tears flowed faster from his wife's eyes. She took his hand and kissed it.

'Nikolay, when did you break your cameo?' she said to change the subject, as she scrutinised the finger on which he wore a ring with a cameo of Laocoon.

'Today; it was all the same thing. O Marie, don't remind me of it!' He flushed again. 'I give you my word of honour that it shall never happen again. And let this be a reminder to me for ever,' he said, pointing to the broken ring.

From that time forward, whenever in interviews with his village elders and foremen he felt the blood rush to his face and his fists began to clench, Nikolay turned the ring round on his finger and dropped his eyes before the man who angered him. Twice a year, however, he would forget himself, and then, going to his wife, he confessed, and again promised that this would really be the last time.

'Marie, you must despise me,' he said to her. 'I deserve it.'

'You must run away, make haste and run away if you feel yourself unable to control yourself,' his wife said mournfully, trying to comfort him.

In the society of the nobility of the province Nikolay was respected but not liked. The local politics of the nobility did not interest him. And in consequence he was looked upon by some people as proud and by others as a fool. In summer his whole time from the spring sowing to the harvest was spent in looking after the land. In the autumn he gave himself up with the same business-like seriousness to hunting, going out for a month or two at a time with his huntsmen, dogs, and horses on hunting expeditions. In the winter he visited their other properties and spent his time in reading, chiefly historical books, on which he spent a certain sum regularly every year. He was forming for himself, as he used to say, a serious library, and he made it a principle to read through every book he bought. He would sit over his book in his study with an important air; and what he had at first undertaken as a duty became an habitual pursuit, which afforded him a special sort of gratification in the feeling that he was engaged in serious study.

Except when he went on business to visit their other estates, he spent the winter at home with his family, entering into all the petty cares and interests of the mother and children. With his wife he got on better and better, every day discovering fresh spiritual treasures in her.

From the time of Nikolay's marriage Sonya had lived in his house. Before their marriage, Nikolay had told his wife all that had passed between him and Sonya, blaming himself and praising her conduct. He begged Princess Marya to be kind and affectionate to his cousin. His wife was fully sensible of the wrong her husband had done his cousin; she felt herself too guilty towards Sonya; she fancied her wealth had influenced Nikolay in his choice, could find no fault in Sonya, and wished to love her. But she could not like her, and often found evil feelings in her soul in regard to her, which she could not overcome.

One day she was talking with her friend Natasha of Sonya and her own injustice towards her.

'Do you know what,' said Natasha; 'you have read the Gospel a great deal; there is a passage there that applies to Sonya.'

'What is it?' Countess Marya asked in surprise.

'"To him that hath shall be given, and to him that hath not shall be taken even that that he hath," do you remember? She is the one that hath not; why, I don't know; perhaps she has no egoism. I don't know; but from her is taken away, and everything has been taken away. I am sometimes awfully sorry for her. I used in the old days to want Nikolay to marry her; but I always had a sort of presentiment that it would not happen. She is a *barren flower*, you know, like what one finds among the strawberry flowers. Sometimes I am sorry for her, and sometimes I think she does not feel it as we should have felt it.'

And although Countess Marya argued with Natasha that those words of the Gospel must not be taken in that sense, looking at Sonya, she agreed with the explanation given by Natasha. It did seem really as though Sonya did not feel her position irksome, and was quite reconciled to her fate as a *barren flower*. She seemed to be fond not so much of people as of the whole family. Like a cat, she had attached herself not to persons, but to the house. She waited on the old countess, petted and spoiled the children, was always ready to perform small services, which she seemed particularly clever at; but all she did was unconsciously taken for granted, without much gratitude....

The Bleak Hills house had been built up again, but not on the same scale as under the old prince.

The buildings, begun in days of straitened means, were more than simple. The immense mansion on the old stone foundation was of wood, plastered only on the inside. The great rambling house, with its unstained plank floors, was furnished with the simplest rough sofas and chairs and tables made of their own birch-trees by the labour of their serf carpenters. The house was very roomy, with quarters for the house-serfs and accommodation for visitors.

The relations of the Rostovs and the Bolkonskys would sometimes come on visits to Bleak Hills with their families, sixteen horses and dozens of servants, and stay for months. And four times a year—on the name-days and birthdays of the master and mistress—as many as a hundred visitors would be put up for a day or two. The rest of the year the regular life of the household went on in unbroken routine, with its round of duties, and of teas, breakfasts, dinners, and suppers, all provided out of home-grown produce.

IX

It was on the eve of St. Nikolay's day, the 5th of December 1820. That year Natasha with her husband and children had been staying at Bleak Hills since the beginning of autumn. Pierre was in Petersburg, where he had gone on private business of his own, as he said, for three weeks. He had already been away for six, and was expected home every minute.

On this 5th of December there was also staying with the Rostovs Nikolay's old friend, the general on half-pay, Vassily Fedorovitch Denisov.

Next day visitors were coming in celebration of his name-day, and Nikolay knew that he would have to take off his loose Tatar coat, to put on a frockcoat, and narrow boots with pointed toes, and to go to the new church he had built, and there to receive congratulations, and to offer refreshments to his guests, and to talk about the provincial elections and the year's crops. But the day before he considered he had a right to spend as usual. Before dinner-time Nikolay had gone over the bailiff's accounts from the Ryazan estate, the property of his wife's nephew; written two business letters, and walked through the corn barns, the cattleyard, and the stables. After taking measures against the general drunkenness he expected next day among his peasants in honour of the fête, he came in to dinner, without having had a moment's conversation alone with his wife all day. He sat down to a long table laid with twenty covers, at which all the household were assembled, consisting of his mother, old Madame Byelov, who lived with her as a companion, his wife and three children, their governess and tutor, his wife's nephew with his tutor, Sonya, Denisov, Natasha, her three children, their governess, and Mihail Ivanitch, the old prince's architect, who was living out his old age in peace at Bleak Hills.

Countess Marya was sitting at the opposite end of the table. As soon as her husband sat down to the table, from the gesture with which he took up his table-napkin and quickly pushed back the tumbler and wine-glass set at his place, she knew that he was out of humour, as he sometimes was, particularly before the soup, and when he came straight in to dinner from his work. Countess Marya understood this mood in her husband very well, and when she was herself in a good temper, she used to wait quietly till he had swallowed his soup, and only then began to talk to him and to make him admit that he had no reason to be out of temper. But today she totally forgot this principle of hers; she had a miserable sense of his being vexed with her without cause, and she felt wretched. She asked him where he had been. He answered. She asked again whether everything were going well on the estate. He frowned disagreeably at her unnatural tone, and made a hasty reply.

'I was right then,' thought Countess Marya, 'and what is he cross with me for?' In the tone of his answer she read ill-will towards her and a desire to cut short the conversation. She felt that her words were unnatural; but she could not restrain herself, and asked a few more questions.

The conversation at dinner, thanks to Denisov, soon became general and animated, and she did not say more to her husband. When they rose from table, and according to custom came up to thank the old countess, Countess Marya kissed her husband, offering him her hand, and asked why he was cross with her.

'You always have such strange ideas; I never thought of being cross,' he said.

But that word *always* answered her: Yes, I am angry, and I don't choose to say.

Nikolay lived on such excellent terms with his wife that even Sonya and the old countess, who from jealousy would have been pleased to see disagreement between them, could find nothing to reproach them with; but there were moments of antagonism even between them. Sometimes, particularly just after their happiest periods, they had a sudden feeling of estrangement and antagonism; that feeling was most frequent during the times when Countess Marya was with child. They happened to be just now at such a period of antagonism.

'Well, *messieurs et mesdames*,' said Nikolay loudly, and with a show of cheerfulness (it seemed to his wife that this was on purpose to mortify her), 'I have been since six o'clock on my legs. Tomorrow will be an infliction, so today I'll go and rest.' And saying nothing more to Countess Marya, he went off to the little divan-room, and lay down on the sofa.

'That's how it always is,' thought his wife. 'He talks to everybody but not to me, I see that I am repulsive to him, especially in this condition.' She looked down at her high waist and then into the looking-glass at her sallow and sunken face, in which the eyes looked bigger than ever.

And everything jarred upon her: Denisov's shout and guffaw and Natasha's chatter, and above all the hasty glance Sonya stole at her.

Sonya was always the first excuse Countess Marya pitched on for her irritability.

After sitting a little while with her guests, not understanding a word they were saying, she slipped out and went to the nursery.

The children were sitting on chairs playing at driving to Moscow, and invited her to join them. She sat down and played with them, but the thought of her husband and his causeless ill-temper worried her all the time. She got up, and walked with difficulty on tiptoe to the little divan-room.

'Perhaps he is not asleep. I will speak plainly to him,' she said to herself. Andryusha, her elder boy, followed her on tiptoe, imitating her. His mother did not notice him.

'Dear Marie, I believe he is asleep; he was so tired,' said Sonya, meeting her in the next room (it seemed to Countess Marya that she was everywhere). 'Andryusha had better not wake him.'

Countess Marya looked round, saw Andryusha behind her, felt that Sonya was right, and for that reason flushed angrily, and with evident difficulty restrained herself from a cruel retort. She said nothing, and, so as not to obey her, let Andryusha follow her, but signed to him to be quiet, and went up to the door. Sonya went out by the other door. From the room where Nikolay was asleep, his wife could hear his even breathing, every tone of which was so familiar. As she listened to it, she could see his smooth, handsome brow, his moustaches, the whole face she had so often gazed at in the stillness of the night when he was asleep. Nikolay suddenly stirred and cleared his throat. And at the same instant Andryusha shouted from the door, 'Papa, mamma's here!' His mother turned pale with dismay and made signs to the boy. He was quiet, and there followed a terrible silence that lasted a minute. She knew how Nikolay disliked being waked. Suddenly she heard him stir and clear his throat again, and in a tone of displeasure he said:

'I'm never given a moment's peace. Marie, is it you? Why did you bring him here?'

'I only came to look ... I did not see ... I'm so sorry ...'

Nikolay coughed and said no more. His wife went away, and took her son back to the nursery. Five minutes later little, black-eyed, three-year-old Natasha, her father's favourite, hearing from her brother that papa was asleep, and mamma in the next room, ran in to her father, unnoticed by her mother.

The black-eyed little girl boldly rattled at the door, and her fat, little feet ran with vigorous steps up to the sofa. After examining the position of her father, who was asleep with his back to her, she stood on tiptoe and kissed the hand that lay under his head. Nikolay turned round to her with a smile of tenderness on his face.

'Natasha, Natasha!' he heard his wife whisper in dismay from the door. 'Papa is sleepy.'

'No, mamma, he isn't sleepy,' little Natasha answered with conviction. 'He's laughing.'

Nikolay set his feet down, got up, and picked his little daughter up in his arms.

'Come in, Masha,' he said to his wife. She went in and sat down beside him.

'I did not see him run in after me,' she said timidly. 'I just looked in . . .'

Holding his little girl on one arm, Nikolay looked at his wife, and noticing her guilty expression, he put the other arm round her and kissed her on the hair.

'May I kiss mamma?' he asked Natasha. The little girl smiled demurely. 'Again,' she said, with a peremptory gesture, pointing to the spot where Nikolay had kissed her mother.

'I don't know why you should think I am cross,' said Nikolay, replying to the question which he knew was in his wife's heart.

'You can't imagine how unhappy, how lonely, I am when you are like that. It always seems to me . . .'

'Marie, hush, nonsense! You ought to be ashamed,' he said gaily.

'It seems to me that you can't care for me; that I am so ugly . . . at all times, and now in this . . .'

'Oh, how absurd you are! It's not those who are handsome we love, but those we love who are handsome. It is only Malvinas and such heroines who are loved because they are beautiful. And do you suppose I love my wife? Oh no, I don't love you, but only . . . I don't know how to tell you. When you are away, and any misunderstanding like this comes between us, I feel as though I were lost, and can do nothing. Why, do I love my finger? I don't love it, but only try cutting it off . . .'

'No, I don't feel like that, but I understand. Then you are not angry with me?'

'I am awfully angry!' he said, smiling, and getting up, and smoothing his hair, he began pacing up and down the room.

'Do you know, Marie, what I have been thinking?' he began, beginning at once now that peace was made between them, thinking aloud before his wife. He did not inquire whether she were disposed to listen; that did not matter to him. An idea occurred to him; and so it must to her, too. And he told her that he meant to persuade Pierre to stay with them till the spring.

Countess Marya listened to him, made some comments, and then in her turn began thinking her thoughts aloud. Her thoughts were of the children.

'How one can see the woman in her already, she said in French, pointing to little Natasha. 'You reproach us women for being illogical. You see in her our logic. I say, papa is sleepy; and she says, no, he's laughing. And she is right,' said Countess Marya, smiling blissfully.

'Yes, yes,' and Nikolay, lifting up his little girl in his strong arm, raised her high in the air, sat her on his shoulder, holding her little feet, and began walking up and down with her. There was just the same look of thoughtless happiness on the faces of father and daughter.

'But do you know, you may be unfair. You are too fond of this one,' his wife whispered in French.

'Yes, but what can I do? ... I try not to show it ...'

At that moment there was heard from the hall and the vestibule the sound of the block of the door, and footsteps, as though some one had arrived.

'Somebody has come.'

'I am sure it is Pierre. I will go and find out,' said Countess Marya, and she went out of the room.

While she was gone Nikolay allowed himself to gallop round the room with his little girl. Panting for breath, he quickly lowered the laughing child, and hugged her to his breast. His capers made him think of dancing; and looking at the childish, round, happy little face, he wondered what she would be like when he would be an old man, taking her out to dances, and he remembered how his father used to dance Daniel Cooper and the mazurka with his daughter.

'It is he, it is he, Nikolay!' said Countess Marya, returning a few minutes later. 'Now our Natasha is herself again. You should have seen her delight, and what a scolding he came in for at once for having outstayed his time. Come, let us go; make haste; come along! You must part at last,' she said, smiling, as she looked at the little girl nestling up to her father. Nikolay went out, holding his daughter by the hand.

Countess Marya lingered behind.

'Never, never could I have believed,' she murmured to herself, 'that one could be so happy.' Her face lighted up with a smile; but at the same moment she sighed, and a soft melancholy came into her thoughtful glance. It was as though, apart from the happiness she was feeling there was another happiness unattainable in this life, which she could not help remembering at that moment.

X

NATASHA was married in the early spring of 1813, and by 1820 she had three daughters and a son. The latter had been eagerly desired, and she was now nursing him herself. She had grown stouter and broader, so that it was hard to recognise in the robust-looking young mother the slim, mobile Natasha of old days. Her features had become more defined, and wore an expression of calm softness and serenity. Her face had no longer that ever-glowing fire of eagerness that had once constituted her chief charm. Now, often her face and body were all that was to be seen, and the soul was not visible at all. All there was to be seen in her was a vigorous, handsome, and fruitful mother. Only on rare occasions now the old fire glowed in her again. That happened only when, as now, her husband returned after absence, when a sick child recovered, or when she spoke to Countess Marya of Prince Andrey (to her husband she never spoke of Prince Andrey, fancying he might be jealous of her love for him), or on the rare occasions when something happened to attract her to her singing, which she had entirely laid aside since her marriage. And at those rare moments, when the old fire glowed again, she was more attractive, with her handsome, fully-developed figure, than she had ever been in the past.

Since her marriage Natasha and her husband had lived in Moscow, in Petersburg, on their estate near Moscow, and at her mother's; that is to say, at Nikolay's. The young Countess Bezuhov was little seen in society, and those who had seen her there were not greatly pleased with her. She was neither charming nor amiable. It was not that Natasha was fond of solitude (she could not have said whether she liked it or not; she rather supposed indeed that she did not); but as she was bearing and nursing children, and taking interest in every minute of her husband's life, she could not meet all these demands on her except by renouncing society. Every one who had known Natasha before her marriage marvelled at the change that had taken place in her, as though it were something extraordinary. Only the old countess, with her mother's insight, had seen that what was at the root of all Natasha's wild outbursts of feeling was simply the need of children and a husband of her own, as she often used to declare, more in earnest than in joke, at Otradnoe. The mother was surprised at the wonder of people who did not understand Natasha, and repeated that she had always known that she would make an exemplary wife and mother.

'Only she does carry her devotion to her husband and children to an extreme,' the countess would say; 'so much so, that it's positively foolish.'

Natasha did not follow the golden rule preached by so many prudent persons, especially by the French, that recommends that a girl on marrying should not neglect herself, should not give up her accomplishments, should think even more of her appearance than when a young girl, and should try to fascinate her husband as she had fascinated him before he was her husband. Natasha, on the contrary, had at once abandoned all her accomplishments, of which the greatest was her singing. She gave that up just because it was such a great attraction. Natasha troubled herself little about manners or delicacy of speech; nor did she think of showing herself to her husband in the most becoming attitudes and costumes, nor strive to avoid worrying him by being over-exacting. She acted in direct contravention of all those rules. She felt that the arts of attraction that instinct had taught her to use before would have seemed only ludicrous to her husband, to whom she had from the first moment given herself up entirely, that is with her whole soul, not keeping a single corner of it hidden from him. She felt that the tie that bound her to her husband did not rest on those romantic feelings which had attracted him to her, but rested on something else undefined, but as strong as the tie that bound her soul to her body.

To curl her hair, put on a crinoline, and sing songs to attract her husband would have seemed to her as strange as to deck herself up so as to please herself. To adorn herself to please others might perhaps have been agreeable to her—she did not know—but she had absolutely no time for it. The chief reason why she could not attend to her singing, nor to her dress, nor to the careful choice of her words was that she simply had no time to think of those things.

It is well known that man has the faculty of entire absorption in one subject, however trivial that subject may appear to be. And it is well known that there is no subject so trivial that it will not grow to infinite proportions if concentrated attention be devoted to it.

The subject in which Natasha was completely absorbed was her family, that is, her husband, whom she kept such a hold on so that he should belong entirely to her, to his home and her children, whom she had to carry, to bear, to nurse and to bring up.

And the more she put, not her mind only, but her whole soul, her whole being, into the subject that absorbed her, the more that subject seemed to enlarge under her eyes, and the feebler and the more inadequate her own powers seemed for coping with it, so that she concentrated them all on that one subject, and still had not time to do all that seemed to her necessary.

There were in those days, just as now, arguments and discussions on the rights of women, on the relations of husband and wife, and on freedom and rights in marriage, though they were not then, as now, called *questions*. But those questions had no interest for Natasha, in fact she had absolutely no comprehension of them.

Those questions, then as now, existed only for those persons who see in marriage only the satisfaction the married receive from one another, that is, only the first beginnings of marriage and not all its significance, which lies in the family.

Such discussions and questions of today, like the question how to get the utmost possible gratification out of one's dinner, then, as now, did not exist for persons for whom the object of dinner is nourishment, and the object of wedlock is family.

If the end of dinner is the nourishment of the body, the man who eats two dinners obtains possibly a greater amount of pleasure, but he does not attain the object of it, since two dinners cannot be digested by the stomach.

If the end of marriage is the family, the person who prefers to have several wives and several husbands may possibly derive a great deal of satisfaction therefrom, but will not in any case have a family. If the end of dinner is nourishment and the end of marriage is the family, the whole question is only solved by not eating more than the stomach can digest and not having more husbands or wives than as many as are needed for the family, that is, one wife and one husband. Natasha needed a husband. A husband was given her; and her husband gave her a family. And she saw no need of another better husband, and indeed, as all her spiritual energies were devoted to serving that husband and his children, she could not picture, and found no interest in trying to picture, what would have happened had things been different.

Natasha did not care for society in general, but she greatly prized the society of her kinsfolk—of Countess Marya, her brother, her mother, and Sonya. She cared for the society of those persons to whom she could rush in from the nursery in a dressing-gown with her hair down; to whom she could, with a joyful face, show a baby's napkin stained yellow instead of green, and to receive their comforting assurances that that proved that baby was now really better.

Natasha neglected herself to such a degree that her dresses, her untidy hair, her inappropriately blurted-out words, and her jealousy—she was jealous of Sonya, of the governess, of every woman, pretty and ugly—were a continual subject of jests among her friends. The general opinion was that Pierre was tied to his wife's apron strings, and it really was so. From the earliest days of their marriage Natasha had made plain her claims. Pierre had been greatly surprised at his wife's view—to him a completely novel idea—that every minute of his life belonged to her and their home. He was surprised at his wife's demands, but he was flattered by them, and he acquiesced in them.

Pierre was so far under petticoat government that he did not dare to be attentive, or even to speak with a smile, to any other woman; did not dare to go to dine at the club, without good reason, simply for entertainment; did not dare spend money on idle whims, and did not dare to be away from home for any long time together, except on business, in which his wife included his scientific pursuits. Though she understood nothing of the latter, she attached great consequence to them. To make up for all this Pierre had complete power in his own house to dispose of the whole household, as well as of himself, as he chose. In their own home Natasha made herself a slave to her husband; and the whole household had to go on tiptoe if the master were busy reading or writing in his study. Pierre had only to show the slightest preference, for what he desired to be at once carried out. He had but to express a wish and Natasha jumped up at once and ran for what he wanted.

The whole household was ruled by the supposed directions of the master, that is, by the wishes of Pierre, which Natasha tried to guess. Their manner of life and place of residence, their acquaintances and ties, Natasha's pursuits, and the bringing up of the children—all followed, not only Pierre's expressed wishes, but even the deductions Natasha strove to draw from the ideas he explained in conversation with her. And she guessed very correctly what was the essential point of Pierre's wishes, and having once guessed it she was steadfast in adhering to it: even when Pierre himself would have veered round she opposed him with his own weapons.

In the troubled days that Pierre could never forget, after the birth of their first child, they had tried three wet nurses, one after another, for the delicate baby, and Natasha had fallen ill with anxiety. At the time Pierre had explained to her Rousseau's views on the unnaturalness and harmfulness of a child being suckled by any woman but its own mother, and told her he fully agreed with those views. When the next baby was born, in spite of the opposition of her mother, the doctors, and even of her husband himself, who all looked on it as something unheard of, and injurious, she insisted on having her own way, and from that day had nursed all her children herself. It happened very often in moments of irritability that the husband and wife quarrelled; but long after their dispute Pierre had, to his own delight and surprise, found in his wife's actions, as well as words, that very idea of his with which she had quarrelled. And he not only found his own idea, but found it purified of all that was superfluous, and had been evoked by the heat of argument in his own expression of the idea.

After seven years of married life, Pierre had a firm and joyful consciousness that he was not a bad fellow, and he felt this because he saw himself reflected in his wife. In himself he felt all the good and bad mingled together, and obscuring one another. But in his wife he saw reflected only what was really good; everything not quite good was left out. And this result was not reached by the way of logical thought, but by way of a mysterious, direct reflection of himself.

XI

TWO months previously, Pierre was already settled at the Rostovs' when he received a letter from a certain Prince Fyodor, urging him to come to Petersburg for the discussion of various important questions that were agitating the Petersburg members of a society, of which Pierre had been one of the chief founders.

Natasha read this letter, as she did indeed all her husband's letters, and bitterly as she always felt his absence, she urged him herself to go to Petersburg. To everything appertaining to her husband's intellectual, abstract pursuits, she ascribed immense consequence, though she had no understanding of them, and she was always in dread of being a hindrance to her husband in such matters. To Pierre's timid glance of inquiry after reading the letter, she replied by begging him to go, and all she asked was that he would fix an absolutely certain date for his return. And leave of absence was given him for four weeks.

Ever since the day fixed for his return, a fortnight before, Natasha had been in a continual condition of alarm, depression, and irritability.

Denisov, a general on the retired list, very much dissatisfied at the present position of public affairs, had arrived during that fortnight, and he looked at Natasha with melancholy wonder, as at a bad likeness of a person once loved. A bored, dejected glance, random replies, and incessant talk of the nursery was all he saw and heard of his enchantress of old days.

All that fortnight Natasha had been melancholy and irritable, especially when her mother, her brother, Sonya, or Countess Marya tried to console her by excusing Pierre, and inventing good reasons for his delay in returning.

'It's all nonsense, all idiocy,' Natasha would say; 'all his projects that never lead to anything, and all those fools of societies,' she would declare of the very matters in the immense importance of which she firmly believed. And she would march off to the nursery to nurse her only boy, the baby Petya.

No one could give her such sensible and soothing consolation as that little three months' old creature, when it lay at her breast, and she felt the movement of its lips and the snuffling of its nose. That little creature said to her: 'You are angry, you are jealous, you would like to punish him, you are afraid, but here am I—I am he. Here, I am he . . .' And there was no answering that. It was more than true.

Natasha had so often during that fortnight had recourse to her baby for comfort, that she had over-nursed him, and he had fallen ill. She was terrified at his illness, but still this was just what she needed. In looking after him, she was able to bear her uneasiness about her husband better.

She was nursing the baby when Pierre's carriage drove noisily up to the entrance, and the nurse, knowing how to please her mistress, came inaudibly but quickly to the door with a beaming face.

'He has come?' asked Natasha in a rapid whisper, afraid to stir for fear of waking the baby, who was dropping asleep.

'He has come, ma'am,' whispered the nurse.

The blood rushed to Natasha's face, and her feet involuntarily moved; but to jump up and run was out of the question. The baby opened its little eyes again, glanced, as though to say, 'You are here,' and gave another lazy smack with its lips.

Cautiously withdrawing her breast, Natasha dandled it, handed it to the nurse, and went with swift steps towards the door. But at the door she stopped as though her conscience pricked her for being in such haste and joy to leave the baby, and she looked back. The nurse, with her elbows raised, was lifting the baby over the rail of the cot.

'Yes, go along, go along, ma'am, don't worry, run along,' whispered the nurse, smiling with the familiarity that was common between nurse and mistress.

With light steps Natasha ran to the vestibule. Denisov, coming out of the study into the hall with a pipe in his mouth, seemed to see Natasha again for the first time. A vivid radiance of joy shed streams of light from her transfigured countenance.

'He has come!' she called to him, as she flew by, and Denisov felt that he was thrilled to hear that Pierre had come, though he did not particularly care for him. Running into the vestibule, Natasha saw a tall figure in a fur cloak fumbling at his scarf.

'He! he! It's true. Here he is,' she said to herself, and darting up to him, she hugged him, squeezing her head to his breast, and then drawing back, glanced at the frosty, red, and happy face of Pierre. 'Yes, here he is; happy, satisfied . . .'

And all at once she remembered all the tortures of suspense she had passed through during the last fortnight. The joy beaming in her face vanished; she frowned, and a torrent of reproaches and angry words broke upon Pierre.

'Yes, you are all right, you have been happy, you have been enjoying yourself . . . But what about me! You might at least think of your children. I am nursing, my milk went wrong . . . Petya nearly died of it. And you have been enjoying yourself. Yes, enjoying yourself . . .'

Pierre knew he was not to blame, because he could not have come sooner. He knew this outburst on her part was unseemly, and would be all over in two minutes. Above all, he knew that he was himself happy and joyful. He would have liked to smile, but dared not even think of that. He made a piteous, dismayed face, and bowed before the storm.

'I could not, upon my word. But how is Petya?'

'He is all right now, come along. Aren't you ashamed? If you could see what I am like without you, how wretched I am . . .'

'Are you quite well?'

'Come along, come along,' she said, not letting go of his hand. And they went off to their rooms. When Nikolay and his wife came to look for Pierre, they found him in the nursery, with his baby son awake on his broad right hand, dandling him. There was a gleeful smile on the baby's broad face and open, toothless mouth. The storm had long blown over, and a bright, sunny radiance of joy flowed all over Natasha's face, as she gazed tenderly at her husband and son.

'And did you have a good talk over everything with Prince Fyodor?' Natasha was saying.

'Yes, capital.'

'You see, he holds his head up' (Natasha meant the baby). 'Oh, what a fright he gave me. And did you see the princess? Is it true that she is in love with that . . .'

'Yes, can you fancy . . .'

At that moment Nikolay came in with his wife. Pierre, not letting go of his son, stooped down, kissed them, and answered their inquiries.

But it was obvious that in spite of the many interesting things they had to discuss, the baby, with the wobbling head in the little cap, was absorbing Pierre's whole attention.

'How sweet he is!' said Countess Marya, looking at the baby and playing with him. 'That's a thing I can't understand, Nikolay,' she said, turning to her husband, 'how it is you don't feel the charm of these exquisite little creatures?'

'Well, I don't, I can't,' said Nikolay, looking coldly at the baby. 'Just a morsel of flesh. Come along, Pierre.'

'The great thing is, that he is really a devoted father,' said Countess Marya, apologising for her husband, 'but only after a year or so . . .'

'Oh, Pierre is a capital nurse,' said Natasha; 'he says his hand is just made for a baby's back. Just look.'

'Oh yes, but not for this,' Pierre cried laughing, and hurriedly snatching up the baby, he handed him back to his nurse.

XII

As in every real family, there were several quite separate worlds living together in the Bleak Hills house, and while each of these preserved its own individuality, they made concessions to one another, and mixed into one harmonious whole. Every event that occurred in the house was alike important and joyful or distressing to all those circles. But each circle had its own private grounds for rejoicing or mourning at every event quite apart from the rest.

So Pierre's arrival was a joyful and important event, reflected as such in all the circles of the household.

The servants, the most infallible judges of their masters, because they judge them, not from their conversation and expression of their feelings, but from their actions and their manner of living, were delighted at Pierre's return, because they knew that when he was there, the count, their master, would not go out every day to superintend the peasants on the estate, and would be in better temper and spirits, and also because they knew there would be valuable presents for all of them for the fête day.

The children and their governesses were delighted at Bezuhov's return, because no one drew them into the general social life of the house as Pierre did. He it was who could play on the clavichord that écossaise (his one piece), to which, as he said, one could dance all possible dances; and he was quite sure, too, to have brought all of them presents.

Nikolinka Bolkonsky, who was now a thin, delicate, intelligent boy of fifteen, with curly light hair and beautiful eyes, was delighted because Uncle Pierre, as he called him, was the object of his passionate love and adoration. No one had instilled a particular affection for Pierre into Nikolinka, and he only rarely saw him. Countess Marya, who had brought him up, had done her utmost to make Nikolinka love her husband, as she loved him; and the boy did like his uncle, but there was a scarcely perceptible shade of contempt in his liking of him. Pierre he adored. He did not want to be an hussar or a Cavalier of St. George like his Uncle Nikolay; he wanted to be learned, clever, and kind like Pierre. In Pierre's presence there was always a happy radiance on his face, and he blushed and was breathless when Pierre addressed him. He never missed a word that Pierre uttered, and afterwards alone or with Dessalle recalled every phrase, and pondered its exact significance. Pierre's past life, his unhappiness before 1812 (of which, from the few words he had heard, he had made up a vague, romantic picture), his adventures in Moscow, and captivity with the French, Platon Karataev (of whom he had heard from Pierre), his love for Natasha (whom the boy loved too with quite a special feeling), and, above all, his friendship with his father, whom Nikolinka did not remember, all made Pierre a hero and a saint in his eyes.

From the phrases he had heard dropped about his father and Natasha, from the emotion with which Pierre spoke of him, and the circumspect, reverent tenderness with which Natasha spoke of him, the boy, who was only just beginning to form his conceptions of love, had gathered the idea that his father had loved Natasha, and had bequeathed her at his death to his friend. That father, of whom the boy had no memory, seemed to him a divine being, of whom one could have no clear conception, and of whom he could not think without a throbbing heart and tears of sorrow and rapture.

And so the boy too was happy at Pierre's arrival.

The guests in the house were glad to see Pierre, for he was a person who always enlivened every party, and made its different elements mix well together.

The grown-up members of the household were glad to see a friend who always made daily life run more smoothly and easily.

The old ladies were pleased both at the pressents he brought them, and still more at Natasha's being herself again.

Pierre felt the various views those different sets of people took of him, and made haste to satisfy the expectations of all of them.

Though he was the most absent-minded and forgetful of men, by the help of a list his wife made for him, he had bought everything, not forgetting a single commission from his mother-in-law or brother-in-law, nor the presents of a dress for Madame Byelov and toys for his nephews.

In the early days of his married life his wife's expectation that he should forget nothing he had undertaken to buy had struck him as strange, and he had been impressed by her serious chagrin when after his first absence he had returned having forgotten everything. But in time he had grown used to this. Knowing that Natasha gave him no commissions on her own account, and for others only asked him to get things when he had himself offered to do so, he now took a childish pleasure, that was a surprise to himself, in those purchases of presents for all the household, and never forgot anything. If he incurred Natasha's censure now, it was only for buying too much, and paying too much for his purchases. To her other defects in the eyes of the world—good qualities in Pierre's eyes—her untidiness and negligence, Natasha added that of stinginess.

Ever since Pierre had begun living a home life, involving increased expenses in a large house, he had noticed to his astonishment that he was spending half what he had spent in the past, and that his circumstances, somewhat straitened latterly, especially by his first wife's debts, were beginning to improve.

Living was much cheaper, because his life was coherent, the most expensive luxury in his former manner of life, that is, the possibility of a complete change in it at any moment, Pierre had not now, and had no desire for. He felt that his manner of life was settled now once for all till death; that to change it was not in his power, and therefore that manner of life was cheaper.

With a beaming, smiling countenance, Pierre was unpacking his purchases.

'Look!' he said, unfolding a piece of material like a shopman. Natasha was sitting opposite him with her eldest girl on her knee, and she turned her sparkling eyes from her husband to what he was showing her.

'That's for Madame Byelov? Splendid.' She touched it to feel the goodness of the material. 'It must have been a rouble a yard?'

Pierre mentioned the price.

'Very dear,' said Natasha. 'Well, how pleased the children will be and *maman* too. Only you shouldn't have bought me this,' she added, unable to suppress a smile, as she admired the gold and pearl comb, of a pattern just then coming into fashion.

'Adèle kept on at me to buy it,' said Pierre.

'When shall I wear it?' Natasha put it in her coil of hair. 'It will do when I have to bring little Masha out; perhaps they will come in again then. Well, let us go in.'

And gathering up the presents, they went first into the nursery, and then in to see the countess.

The countess, as her habit was, was sitting playing patience with Madame Byelov when Pierre and Natasha went into the drawing-room with parcels under their arms.

The countess was by now over sixty. Her hair was completely grey, and she wore a cap that surrounded her whole face with a frill. Her face was wrinkled, her upper lip had sunk, and her eyes were dim.

After the deaths of her son and her husband that had followed so quickly on one another, she had felt herself a creature accidentally forgotten in this world, with no object and no interest in life. She ate and drank, slept and lay awake, but she did not live. Life gave her no impressions. She wanted nothing from life but peace, and that peace she could find only in death. But until death came to her she had to go on living—that is, using her vital forces. There was in the highest degree noticeable in her what may be observed in very small children and in very old people. No external aim could be seen in her existence; all that could be seen was the need to exercise her various capacities and propensities. She had to eat, to sleep, to think, to talk, to weep, to work, to get angry, and so on, simply because she had a stomach, a brain, muscles, nerves, and spleen. All this she did not at the promptings of any external motive, as people do in the full vigour of life, when the aim towards which they strive screens from our view that other aim of exercising their powers. She only talked because she needed to exercise her lungs and her tongue. She cried like a child, because she needed the physical relief of tears, and so on. What for people in their full vigour is a motive, with her was obviously a pretext.

Thus in the morning, especially if she had eaten anything too rich the night before, she sought an occasion for anger, and pitched on the first excuse—the deafness of Madame Byelov.

From the other end of the room she would begin to say something to her in a low voice.

'I fancy it is warmer today, my dear,' she would say in a whisper. And when Madame Byelov replied: 'To be sure, they have come,' she would mutter angrily: 'Mercy on us, how deaf and stupid she is!'

Another excuse was her snuff, which she fancied either too dry, or too moist, or badly pounded. After these outbursts of irritability, a bilious hue came into her face. And her maids knew by infallible tokens when Madame Byelov would be deaf again, and when her snuff would again be damp, and her face would again be yellow. Just as she had to exercise her spleen, she had sometimes to exercise her remaining faculties; and for thought the pretext was patience. When she wanted to cry, the subject of her tears was the late count. When she needed excitement, the subject was Nikolay and anxiety about his health. When she wanted to say something spiteful, the pretext was the Countess Marya. When she required exercise for her organs of speech—this was usually about seven o'clock, after she had had her after-dinner rest in a darkened room—then the pretext was found in repetition of anecdotes, always the same, and always to the same listeners.

The old countess's condition was understood by all the household, though no one ever spoke of it, and every possible effort was made by every one to satisfy her requirements. Only rarely a mournful half-smile passed between Nikolay, Pierre, Natasha, and Countess Marya that betrayed their comprehension of her condition.

But those glances said something else besides. They said that she had done her work in life already, that she was not all here in what was seen in her now, that they would all be the same, and that they were glad to give way to her, to restrain themselves for the sake of this poor creature, once so dear, once as full of life as they. *Memento mori*, said those glances.

Only quite heartless and stupid people and little children failed to understand this, and held themselves aloof from her.

XIII

WHEN Pierre and his wife came into the drawing-room, the countess happened to be in her customary condition of needing the mental exercise of a game of patience, and therefore, although from habit she uttered the words she always repeated on the return of Pierre or her son after absence: 'It was high time, high time, my dear boy; we have been expecting you a long while. Well, thank God, you are here.' And on the presents being given her, pronounced another stock phrase: 'It's not the gift that is precious, my dear. . . . Thank you for thinking of an old woman like me. . . .' It was evident that Pierre's entrance at that moment was unwelcome, because it interrupted her in dealing her cards. She finished her game of patience, and only then gave her attention to the presents. The presents for her consisted of a card-case of fine workmanship, a bright blue Sèvres cup with a lid and a picture of shepherdesses on it, and a gold snuff-box with the count's portrait on it, which Pierre had had executed by a miniature-painter in Petersburg. The countess had long wished to have this; but just now she had no inclination to weep, and so she looked unconcernedly at the portrait, and took more notice of the card-case.

'Thank you, my dear, you are a comfort to me,' she said, as she always did. 'But best of all, you have brought yourself back. It has been beyond everything; you must really scold your wife. She is like one possessed without you. She sees nothing, thinks of nothing,' she said as usual. 'Look, Anna Timofyevna,' she added, 'what a card-case my son has brought us.'

Madame Byelov admired the present, and was enchanted with the dress material.

Pierre, Natasha, Nikolay, Countess Marya, and Denisov had a great deal they wanted to talk about, which was not talked of before the old countess; not because anything was concealed from her, but simply because she had dropped so out of things, that if they had begun to talk freely before her they would have had to answer so many questions put by her at random, and to repeat so many things that had been repeated to her so many times already; to tell her that this person was dead and that person was married, which she could never remember. Yet they sat as usual at tea in the drawing-room, and Pierre answered the countess's quite superfluous questions, which were of no interest even to her, and told her that Prince Vassily was looking older, and that Countess Marya Alexeyevna sent her kind regards and remembrances, etc.

Such conversation, of no interest to any one, but inevitable, was kept up all tea-time. All the grown-up members of the family were gathered about the round tea-table with the samovar, at which Sonya presided. The children with their tutors and governesses had already had tea, and their voices could be heard in the next room. At tea every one sat in their own habitual places. Nikolay sat by the stove at a little table apart, where his tea was handed him. An old terrier bitch, with a perfectly grey face, Milka, the daughter of the first Milka, lay on a chair beside him. Denisov, with streaks of grey in his curly hair, moustaches, and whiskers, wearing his general's coat unbuttoned, sat beside Countess Marya. Pierre was sitting between his wife and the old countess. He was telling what he knew might interest the old lady and be intelligible to her. He talked of external social events and of the persons who had once made up the circle of the old countess's contemporaries, and had once been a real living circle of people, but were now for the most part scattered about the world, and, like her, living out their remnant of life, gleaning up the stray ears of wheat they had sown in life. But they, these contemporaries, seemed to the old countess to make up the only real world that was worth considering. By Pierre's eagerness, Natasha saw that his visit had been an interesting one, that he was longing to tell them about it, but dared not speak freely before the countess. Denisov, not being a member of the family, did not understand Pierre's circumspectness, and, moreover, being dissatisfied with the course of events, took a very great interest in all that was going forward at Petersburg. He was continually trying to get Pierre to tell him about the recent scandal about the Semyonovsky regiment, or about Araktcheev, or about the Bible Society. Pierre was sometimes led on into beginning to talk about those subjects, but Nikolay and Natasha always brought him back to the health of Prince Ivan and Countess Marya Antonovna.

'Well, what is all this idiocy, Gossner and Madame Tatarinov,' Denisov asked, 'is that still going on?'

'Going on?' said Pierre. 'Worse than ever. The Bible Society is now the whole government.'

'What is that, *mon cher ami*?' asked the old countess, who, having drunk her tea, was obviously seeking a pretext for ill-humour after taking food. 'What are you saying about the government? I don't understand that.'

'Why, you know, *maman*,' put in Nikolay, who knew how to translate things into his mother's language. 'Prince Alexander Nikolaevitch Golitsin has founded a society, so he has great influence they say.'

'Araktcheev and Golitsin,' said Pierre incautiously, 'are practically the government now. And what a government! They see conspiracy in everything, they are afraid of everything.'

'What, Prince Alexander Nikolaevitch found fault with! He is a most estimable man. I used to meet him in old days at Marya Antonovna's,' said the countess in an aggrieved tone. And still more aggrieved by the general silence, she went on, 'Nowadays people find fault with every one. A Gospel Society, what harm is there in that?' and she got up (everyone rose too), and with a severe face sailed out to her table in the adjoining divan-room.

In the midst of the mournful silence that followed, they heard the sound of children's voices and laughter from the next room. There was evidently some joyful excitement afoot among the children.

'Finished, finished!' the gleeful shriek of little Natasha was heard above all the rest. Pierre exchanged glances with Countess Marya and Nikolay (Natasha he was looking at all the time), and he smiled happily.

'Delightful music!' he said.

'Anna Makarovna has finished her stocking,' said Countess Marya.

'Oh, I'm going to have a look at them,' said Pierre, jumping up. 'You know,' he said, stopping at the door, 'why it is I so particularly love that music—it is what first lets me know that all's well. As I came today, the nearer I got to home, the greater my panic. As I came into the vestibule, I heard Andryusha in peals of laughter, and then I knew all was well...'

'I know, I know that feeling,' Nikolay chimed in. 'I mustn't come—the stockings are a surprise in store for me.'

Pierre went in to the children, and the shrieks and laughter were louder than ever. 'Now, Anna Makarovna,' cried Pierre's voice, 'here in the middle of the room and at the word of command—one, two, and when I say three, you stand here. You in my arms. Now, one two...' there was complete silence. 'Three!' and an enthusiastic roar of children's voices rose in the room. 'Two, two!' cried the children.

They meant the two stockings, which, by a secret only known to her, Anna Makarovna used to knit on her needles at once. She always made a solemn ceremony of pulling one stocking out of the other in the presence of the children when the pair was finished.

XIV

SOON after this the children came in to say good-night. The children kissed every one, the tutors and governesses said good-night and went away. Dessalle alone remained with his pupil. The tutor whispered to his young charge to come downstairs.

'No, M. Dessalle, I will ask my aunt for leave to stay,' Nikolinka Bolkonsky answered, also in a whisper.

'*Ma tante*, will you let me stay?' said Nikolinka, going up to his aunt. His face was full of entreaty, excitement, and enthusiasm. Countess Marya looked at him and turned to Pierre.

'When you are here, there is no tearing him away...' she said.

'I will bring him directly, M. Dessalle. Good-night,' said Pierre, giving his hand to the Swiss tutor, and he turned smiling to Nikolinka. 'We have not seen each other at all yet. Marie, how like he is growing,' he added, turning to Countess Marya.

'Like my father?' said the boy, flushing crimson and looking up at Pierre with rapturous, shining eyes.

Pierre nodded to him, and went on with the conversation that had been interrupted by the children. Countess Marya had some canvas embroidery in her hands; Natasha sat with her eyes fixed on her husband. Nikolay and Denisov got up, asked for pipes, smoked, and took cups of tea from Sonya, still sitting with weary pertinacity at the samovar, and asked questions of Pierre. The curly-headed, delicate boy, with his shining eyes, sat unnoticed by any one in a corner. Turning the curly head and the slender neck above his laydown collar to follow Pierre's movements, he trembled now and then, and murmured something to himself, evidently thrilled by some new and violent emotion.

The conversation turned on the scandals of the day in the higher government circles, a subject in which the majority of people usually find the chief interest of home politics. Denisov, who was dissatisfied with the government on account of his own disappointments in the service, heard with glee of all the follies, as he considered them, that were going on now in Petersburg, and made his comments on Pierre's words in harsh and in cutting phrases.

'In old days you had to be a German to be anybody, nowadays you have to dance with the Tatarinov woman and Madame Krüdner, to read . . . Eckartshausen, and the rest of that crew. Ugh! I would let good old Bonaparte loose again! He would knock all the nonsense out of them. Why, isn't it beyond everything to have given that fellow Schwartz the Semyonovsky regiment?' he shouted.

Though Nikolay had not Denisov's disposition to find everything amiss, he too thought it dignified and becoming to criticise the government, and he believed that the fact, that A. had been appointed minister of such a department, and B had been made governor of such a province, and the Tsar had said this, and the minister had said that, were all matters of the greatest importance. And he thought it incumbent upon him to take an interest in the subject and to question Pierre about it. So the questions put by Nikolay and Denisov kept the conversation on the usual lines of gossip about the higher government circles.

But Natasha, who knew every thought and expression in her husband, saw that Pierre all the while wanted to lead the conversation into another channel, and to open his heart on his own idea, the idea which he had gone to Petersburg to consult his new friend Prince Fyodor about. She saw too that he could not lead up to this, and she came to the rescue with a question: How had he settled things with Prince Fyodor?

'What was that?' asked Nikolay.

'All the same thing over and over again,' said Pierre, looking about him. 'Every one sees that things are all going so wrong that they can't be endured, and that it's the duty of all honest men to oppose it to the utmost of their power.'

'Why, what can honest men do?' said Nikolay, frowning slightly. 'What can be done?'

'Why, this . . .'

'Let us go into the study,' said Nikolay.

Natasha, who had a long while been expecting to be fetched to her baby, heard the nurse calling her, and went off to the nursery. Countess Marya went with her. The men went to the study, and Nikolinka Bolkonsky stole in, unnoticed by his uncle, and sat down at the writing-table, in the dark by the window.

'Well, what are you going to do?' said Denisov.

'Everlastingly these fantastic schemes,' said Nikolay.

'Well,' Pierre began, not sitting down, but pacing the room, and coming to an occasional standstill, lisping and gesticulating rapidly as he talked. 'This is the position of things in Petersburg: the Tsar lets everything go. He is entirely wrapped up in this mysticism' (mysticism Pierre could not forgive in anybody now). 'All he asks for is peace; and he can only get peace through these men of no faith and no conscience, who are stifling and destroying everything, Magnitsky and Araktcheev, and *tutti quanti* . . . You will admit that if you did not look after your property yourself, and only asked for peace and quiet, the crueller your bailiff were, the more readily you would attain your object,' he said, turning to Nikolay.

'Well, but what is the drift of all this?' said Nikolay.

'Why, everything is going to ruin. Bribery in the law-courts, in the army nothing but coercion and drill: exile—people are being tortured, and enlightenment is suppressed. Everything youthful and honourable —they are crushing! Everybody sees that it can't go on like this. The strain is too great, and the string must snap,' said Pierre (as men always do say, looking into the working of any government so long as governments have existed). 'I told them one thing in Petersburg.'

'Told whom?' asked Denisov.

'Oh, you know whom,' said Pierre, with a meaning look from under his brows, 'Prince Fyodor and all of them. Zeal in educational and philanthropic work is all very good of course. Their object is excellent and all the rest of it; but in present circumstances what is wanted is something else.'

At that moment Nikolay noticed the presence of his nephew. His face fell; he went up to him.

'Why are you here?'

'Oh, let him be,' said Pierre, taking hold of Nikolay's arm; and he went on. 'That's not enough, I told them; something else is wanted now. While you stand waiting for the string to snap every moment; while every one is expecting the inevitable revolution, as many people as possible should join hands as closely as they can to withstand the general catastrophe. All the youth and energy is being drawn away and dissipated. One lured by women, another by honours, a third by display or money—they are all going over to the wrong side. As for independent, honest men, like you and me—there are none of them left. I say: enlarge the scope of the society: let the *mot d'ordre* be not loyalty only, but independence and action.'

Nikolay, leaving his nephew, had angrily moved out a chair, and sat down in it. As he listened to Pierre, he coughed in a dissatisfied way, and frowned more and more.

'But action with what object?' he cried. 'And what attitude do you take up to the government?'

'Why, the attitude of supporters! The society will perhaps not even be a secret one, if the government will allow it. So far from being hostile to the government, we are the real conservatives. It is a society of *gentlemen*, in the full significance of the word. It is simply to prevent Pugatchov from coming to massacre my children and yours, to prevent Araktcheev from transporting me to a military settlement, that we are joining hands, with the sole object of the common welfare and security.'

'Yes; but it's a secret society, and consequently a hostile and mischievous society, which can only lead to evil.'

'Why so? Did the *Tugend-bund* which saved Europe (people did not yet venture to believe that Russia had saved Europe) lead to evil? A *Tugend-bund* it is, an alliance of virtue; it is love and mutual help; it is what Christ preached on the cross . . .'

Natasha, coming into the room in the middle of the conversation, looked joyfully at her husband. She was not rejoicing in what he was saying. It did not interest her indeed, because it seemed to her that it was all so excessively simple, and that she had known it long ago. She fancied this, because she knew all that it sprang from—all Pierre's soul. But she was glad looking at his eager, enthusiastic figure.

Pierre was watched with even more rapturous gladness by the boy with the slender neck in the laydown collar, who had been forgotten by all of them. Every word Pierre uttered set his heart in a glow, and his fingers moving nervously, he unconsciously picked up and broke to pieces the sticks of sealing-wax and pens on his uncle's table.

'It's not at all what you imagine, but just such a society as the German *Tugend-bund* is what I propose.'

'Well, my boy, that's all very well for the sausage-eaters—a *Tugend-bund*—but I don't understand it, and I can't even pronounce it,' Denisov's loud, positive voice broke in. 'Everything's rotten and corrupt; I agree there; only your *Tugend-bund* I don't understand, but if one is dissatisfied,—a *bunt* now' (*i.e.* riot or mutiny), '*je suis votre homme!*'

Pierre smiled, Natasha laughed; but Nikolay knitted his brows more than ever, and began arguing with Pierre that no revolution was to be expected, and that the danger he talked of had no existence but in his imagination. Pierre maintained his view, and as his intellectual faculties were keener and more resourceful, Nikolay was soon at a loss for an answer. This angered him still more, as in his heart he felt convinced, not by reasoning, but by something stronger than reasoning, of the indubitable truth of his own view.

'Well, let me tell you,' he said, getting up and nervously setting his pipe down in the corner, and then flinging it away; 'I can't prove it you. You say everything is all rotten, and there will be a revolution; I don't see it; but you say our oath of allegiance is a conditional thing, and as to that, let me tell you, you are my greatest friend, you know that, but you make a secret society, you begin working against the government—whatever it may be, I know it's my duty to obey it. And if Araktcheev bids me march against you with a squadron and cut you down, I shan't hesitate for a second, I shall go. And then you may think what you like about it.'

An awkward silence followed these words. Natasha was the first to break it by defending her husband and attacking her brother. Her defence was weak and clumsy. But it attained her object. The conversation was taken up again, and no longer in the unpleasantly hostile tone in which Nikolay's last words had been spoken.

When they all got up to go in to supper, Nikolinka Bolkonsky went up to Pierre with a pale face and shining, luminous eyes.

'Uncle Pierre . . . you . . . no . . . If papa had been alive . . . he would have been on your side?' he asked.

Pierre saw in a flash all the original, complicated and violent travail of thought and feeling that must have been going on independently in this boy during the conversation. And recalling all he had been saying, he felt vexed that the boy should have heard him. He had to answer him, however.

'I believe he would,' he said reluctantly, and he went out of the study.

The boy looked down, and then for the first time seemed to become aware of the havoc he had been making on the writing-table. He flushed hotly and went up to Nikolay.

'Uncle, forgive me; I did it—not on purpose,' he said, pointing to the fragments of sealing-wax and pens.

Nikolay bounded up angrily. 'Very good, very good,' he said, throwing the bits of pens and sealing-wax under the table. And with evident effort mastering his fury, he turned away from him.

'You ought not to have been here at all,' he said.

XV

AT supper no more was said of politics and societies, but a conversation turned on the subject most agreeable to Nikolay—reminiscences of 1812. Denisov started the talk, and Pierre was particularly cordial and amusing. And the party broke up on the friendliest terms. Nikolay, after undressing in his study, and giving instructions to his steward, who was awaiting him, went in his dressing-gown to his bedroom, and found his wife still at her writing-table: she was writing something.

'What are you writing, Marie?' asked Nikolay. Countess Marya flushed. She was afraid that what she was writing would not be understood and approved by her husband.

She would have liked to conceal what she was writing from him, and at the same time she was glad he had caught her, and she had to tell him.

'It's my diary, Nikolay,' she said, handing him a blue notebook, filled with her firm, bold handwriting.

'A diary!'... said Nikolay, with a shade of mockery, and he took the note-book. He saw written in French:

'*December 4.*—Andryusha' (their elder boy) 'would not be dressed when he waked up this morning, and Mademoiselle Louise sent for me. He was naughty and obstinate. I tried threatening him, but he only got more ill-tempered. Then I undertook to manage him, left him, and helped nurse get the other children up, and told him I did not love him. For a long while he was quiet, as though he were surprised. Then he rushed out to me in his night-shirt, and sobbed so that I could not soothe him for a long while. It was clear that what distressed him most was having grieved me. Then, when I gave him his report in the evening, cried piteously again as he kissed me. One can do anything with him by tenderness.'

'What is his report?' asked Nikolay.

'I have begun giving the elder ones little marks in the evening of how they have behaved.'

Nikolay glanced at the luminous eyes watching him, and went on turning over, and read the diary. Everything in the children's lives was noted down in it that seemed to the mother of interest as showing the character of the children, or leading to general conclusions as to methods of bringing them up. It consisted mostly of the most trifling details; but they did not seem so either to the mother or the father, as he now, for the first time, read this record of his children's lives. On the 5th of December there was the note:

'Mitya was naughty at table. Papa said he should have no pudding. He had none; but he looked so miserably and greedily at the others while they were eating. I believe that punishing them by depriving them of sweet things only develops greediness. Must tell Nikolay.'

Nikolay put the book down and looked at his wife. The luminous eyes looked at him doubtfully, to see whether he approved or not. There could be no doubt of Nikolay's approval, of his enthusiastic admiration of his wife.

Perhaps there was no need to do it so pedantically; perhaps there was no need of it at all, thought Nikolay; but this untiring, perpetual spiritual effort, directed only at the children's moral welfare, enchanted him. If Nikolay could have analysed his feelings, he would have found that the very groundwork of his steady and tender love and pride in his wife was always this feeling of awe at her spirituality, at that elevated moral world that he could hardly enter, in which his wife always lived.

He was proud that she was so clever and so good, recognising his own insignificance beside her in the spiritual world, and he rejoiced the more that she, with her soul, not only belonged to him, but was a part of his very self.

'I quite, quite approve, my darling!' he said, with a significant air. 'And,' after a brief pause, he added, 'And I have behaved badly today. You were not in the study. Pierre and I were arguing, and I lost my temper. I couldn't help it. He is such a child. I don't know what would become of him if Natasha didn't keep him at her apron-strings. Can you imagine what he went to Petersburg about? . . . They have made a . . .'

'Yes, I know,' said Countess Marya. 'Natasha told me.'

'Oh, well, you know, then,' Nikolay went on, getting hot at the mere recollection of the discussion. 'He wants to persuade me that it's the duty of every honest man to work against the government when one's sworn allegiance and duty. . . . I am sorry you were not there. As it was, they all fell upon me, Denisov, and Natasha, too. . . . Natasha is too amusing. We know she twists him round her little finger, but when it comes to discussion—she hasn't an idea to call her own—she simply repeats his words,' added Nikolay, yielding to that irresistible impulse that tempts one to criticise one's nearest and dearest. Nikolay was unaware that what he was saying of Natasha might be said word for word of himself in relation to his wife.

'Yes, I have noticed that,' said Countess Marya.

'When I told him that duty and sworn allegiance come before everything, he began arguing God knows what. It was a pity you were not there. What would you have said?'

'To my thinking, you were quite right. I told Natasha so. Pierre says that every one is suffering, and being ill-treated and corrupted, and that it's our duty to help our neighbours. Of course, he is right,' said Countess Marya; 'but he forgets that we have other nearer duties, which God Himself has marked out for us, and that we may run risks for ourselves, but not for our children.'

'Yes, yes, that's just what I told him,' cried Nikolay, who actually fancied he had said just that. 'And they had all their say out about loving one's neighbour, and Christianity, and all the rest of it, before Nikolinka, who had slipped in there, and was pulling all my things to pieces.'

'Ah, do you know, Nikolay, I am so often worried about Nikolinka,' said Countess Marya. 'He is such an exceptional boy. And I am afraid I neglect him for my own. All of us have our children; we all have our own ties; while he has nobody. He is always alone with his thoughts.'

'Well, I don't think you have anything to reproach yourself with on his account. Everything the fondest mother could do for her son you have done, and are doing, for him. And of course I am glad you do. He is a splendid boy, splendid! This evening he was lost in a sort of dream listening to Pierre. And only fancy, we got up to go into supper. I look; and there he has broken everything on my table to fragments, and he told me of it at once. I have never known him tell a fib. He's a splendid boy!' repeated Nikolay, who did not in his heart like Nikolinka, but always felt moved to acknowledge that he was a splendid fellow.

'Still I am not the same as a mother,' said Countess Marya. 'I feel that it's not the same, and it worries me. He's a wonderful boy; but I am awfully afraid for him. Companionship will be good for him.'

'Oh, well, it's not for long; next summer I shall take him to Petersburg,' said Nikolay. 'Yes, Pierre always was, and always will be, a dreamer,' he went on, returning to the discussion in the study, which had evidently worked on his feelings. 'Why, what concern is all that of mine—Araktcheev's misdoings, and all the rest of it—what concern was it of mine, when at the time of our marriage I had so many debts that they were going to put me in prison, and a mother who couldn't see it or understand it. And then you, and the children, and my work. It's not for my own pleasure I am from morning to night looking after the men, or in the counting-house. No, I know I must work to comfort my mother, repay you, and not leave my children in beggary, as I was left myself.'

Countess Marya wanted to tell him that man does not live by bread alone; that he attached too much importance to this *work*. But she knew that she must not say this, and that it would be useless. She only took his hand and kissed it. He accepted this gesture on his wife's part as a sign of assent and approval of his words, and after a few moments of silent thought he went on thinking aloud.

'Do you know, Marie,' he said, 'Ilya Mitrofanitch' (this was a steward of his) 'was here today from the Tambov estate, and he tells me they will give eighty thousand for the forest.' And with an eager face Nikolay began talking of the possibility of buying Otradnoe back within a very short time. 'Another ten years of life, and I shall leave the children . . . in a capital position.'

Countess Marya listened to her husband, and understood all he said to her. She knew that when he was thus thinking aloud, he would sometimes ask what he had been saying, and was vexed when he noticed she had been thinking of something else. But she had to make a great effort to attend, because she did not feel the slightest interest in what he was saying to her. She looked at him, and though she would not exactly think of other things, her feelings were elsewhere. She felt a submissive, tender love for this man, who could never understand all that she understood; and she seemed, for that very reason, to love him the more, with a shade of passionate tenderness. Apart from that feeling, which absorbed her entirely, and prevented her from following the details of her husband's plans, thoughts kept floating through her brain that had nothing in common with what he was saying. She thought of her nephew (what her husband had said of his excitement over Pierre's talk had made a great impression on her), and various traits of his tender, sensitive character rose to her mind; and while she thought of her nephew, she thought, too, of her own children. She did not compare her nephew with her own children, but she compared her own feeling for him, and her feeling for her children, and felt, with sorrow, that in her feeling for Nikolinka there was something wanting.

Sometimes the idea had occurred to her that this difference was due to his age; but she felt guilty towards him, and in her soul vowed to amend, and to do the impossible, that is, in this life, to love her husband, and her children, and Nikolinka, and all her fellow-creatures, as Christ loved men. Countess Marya's soul was always striving towards the infinite, the eternal, and the perfect, and so she could never be at peace. A stern expression came into her face from that hidden, lofty suffering of the spirit, weighed down by the flesh. Nikolay gazed at her. 'My God! What will become of us, if she dies, as I dread, when she looks like that?' he thought, and standing before the holy images, he began to repeat his evening prayer.

XVI

NATASHA, as soon as she was alone with her husband, had begun talking too, as only husband and wife can talk, that is, understanding and communicating their thoughts to each other, with extraordinary clearness and rapidity, by a quite peculiar method opposed to all the rules of logic, without the aid of premises, deductions, and conclusions. Natasha was so used to talking to her husband in this fashion that a logical sequence of thought on Pierre's part was to her an infallible symptom of something being out of tune between them. When he began arguing, talking reasonably and calmly, and when she was led on by his example into doing the same, she knew it would infallibly lead to a quarrel.

From the moment they were alone together and Natasha, with wide-open, happy eyes, crept softly up to him and suddenly, swiftly seizing his head, pressed it to her bosom, saying, 'Now you're all mine, mine! You shan't escape!' that conversation began that contravened every rule of logic, especially because they talked of several different subjects at once. This discussion of all sorts of things at once, far from hindering clearness of comprehension, was the surest token that they understood one another fully.

As in a dream everything is uncertain, meaningless, and contradictory except the feeling that directs the dream, so in this communion of ideas, apart from every law of reason, what is clear and consecutive is not what is said, but the feeling that prompts the words.

Natasha talked to Pierre of the daily round of existence at her brother's; told him how she had suffered and been half-dead without him; and that she was fonder of Marie than ever, and Marie was better in every way than she was. In saying this Natasha was quite sincere in acknowledging Marie's superiority, but at the same time she expected Pierre to prefer her to Marie and all other women, and now, especially after he had been seeing a great many women in Petersburg, to tell her so anew. In response to Natasha's words, Pierre told her how intolerable he had found the evening parties and dinners with ladies in Petersburg.

'I have quite lost the art of talking to ladies,' he said; 'it was horribly tiresome. Especially as I was so busy.'

Natasha looked intently at him, and went on. 'Marie, now she is wonderful!' she said. 'The insight she has into children. She seems to see straight into their souls. Yesterday, for instance, Mitenka was naughty...'

'And isn't he like his father?' Pierre put in.

Natasha knew why he made this remark about Mitenka's likeness to Nikolay. He disliked the thought of his dispute with his brother-in-law, and was longing to hear what she thought about it.

'It's a weakness of Nikolay's, that if anything is not generally accepted, he will never agree with it. And I see that that's just what you value to *ouvrir une carrière*,' she said, repeating a phrase Pierre had once uttered.

'No, the real thing is that to Nikolay,' said Pierre, 'thoughts and ideas are an amusement, almost a pastime. Here he's forming a library and has made it a rule not to buy a new book till he has read through the last he has bought—Sismondi and Rousseau and Montesquieu,' Pierre added with a smile. 'You know how I——,' he was beginning to soften his criticism; but Natasha interrupted, giving him thereby to understand that that was not necessary.

'So you say ideas to him are not serious...'

'Yes, and to me nothing else is serious. All the while I was in Petersburg, I seemed to be seeing every one in a dream. When I am absorbed by an idea, nothing else is serious.'

'Oh, what a pity I didn't see your meeting with the children,' said Natasha. 'Which was the most pleased? Liza, of course?'

'Yes,' said Pierre, and he went on with what interested him. 'Nikolay says we ought not to think. But I can't help it. To say nothing of the fact (I can say so to you) that in Petersburg I felt that the whole thing would go to pieces without me, every one pulled his own way. But I succeeded in bringing them all together; and then my idea is so clear and simple. I don't say we ought to work against so and so. We may be mistaken. But I say: let those join hands who care for the good cause, and let our one standard be energy and honesty. Prince Sergey is a capital fellow, and clever.'

Natasha would have had no doubt that Pierre's idea was a grand idea, but that one thing troubled her. It was his being her husband. 'Is it possible that a man of such value, of such importance to society, is at the same time my husband? How can it have happened?' She wanted to express this doubt to him. 'Who are the persons who could decide positively whether he is so much cleverer than all of them?' she wondered, and she went over in imagination the people who were very much respected by Pierre. There was nobody whom, to judge by his own account, he had respected so much as Platon Karataev.

'Do you know what I am thinking about?' she said. 'About Platon Karataev. What would he have said? Would he have approved of you now?'

Pierre was not in the least surprised at this question. He understood the connection of his wife's ideas.

'Platon Karataev?' he said, and he pondered, evidently trying sincerely to picture what Karataev's judgment would have been on the subject. 'He would not have understood, and yet, perhaps, he would.'

'I like you awfully!' said Natasha all at once. 'Awfully! awfully!'

'No, he wouldn't have approved,' said Pierre, musing. 'What he would have approved of is our home life. He did so like to see seemliness, happiness, peace in everything, and I could have shown him all of us with pride. You talk about separation. But you would not believe what a special feeling I have for you after separation . . .'

'And, besides, . . .' Natasha was beginning.

'No, not so. I never leave off loving you. And one couldn't love more; but it's something special. . .' He did not finish, because their eyes meeting said the rest.

'What nonsense,' said Natasha suddenly, 'it all is about the honeymoon and that the greatest happiness is at first. On the contrary, now is much the best. If only you wouldn't go away. Do you remember how we used to quarrel? And I was always in the wrong. It was always my doing. And what we quarrelled about—I don't remember even.'

'Always the same thing,' said Pierre smiling. 'Jea . . .'

'Don't say it, I can't hear it,' cried Natasha, and a cold, vindictive light gleamed in her eyes. 'Did you see her?' she added after a pause.

'No; and if I had, I shouldn't have known her.'

They were silent.

'Oh! do you know, when you were talking in the study, I was looking at you,' said Natasha, obviously trying to drive away the cloud that had come between them. 'And do you know you are as like him as two drops of water, like the boy.' That was what she called her baby son. 'Ah, it's time I went to him. . . . But I am sorry to go away.'

They were both silent for some seconds. Then all at once, at the same moment, they turned to each other and began talking. Pierre was beginning with self-satisfaction and enthusiasm, Natasha with a soft, happy smile. Interrupting each other, both stopped, waiting for the other to go on.

'No, what is it? Tell me, tell me.'

'No, you tell me, it wasn't anything, only nonsense,' said Natasha.

Pierre said what he had been going to say. It was the sequel to his complacent reflections on his success in Petersburg. It seemed to him at that moment that he was destined to give a new direction to the progress of the whole of Russian society and of the whole world.

'I only meant to say that all ideas that have immense results are always simple. All my idea really is that if vicious people are united and form a power, honest men must do the same. It's so simple, you see.'

'Yes.'

'But what were you going to say?'

'Oh, nothing, nonsense.'

'No, say it though.'

'Oh, nothing, only silly nonsense,' said Natasha, breaking into a more beaming smile than ever. 'I was only going to tell you about Petya. Nurse came up to take him from me today, he laughed and puckered up his face and squeezed up to me—I suppose he thought he was hiding. He's awfully sweet. . . . There he is crying. Well, good-bye!' and she ran out of the room.

Meanwhile, below in Nikolinka Bolkonsky's bedroom a lamp was burning as usual (the boy was afraid of the dark and could not be cured of this weakness). Dessalle was asleep with his head high on his four pillows, and his Roman nose gave forth rhythmic sounds of snoring. Nikolinka had just waked up in a cold sweat, and was sitting up in bed, gazing with wide-open eyes straight before him. He had been waked by a fearful dream. In his dream his Uncle Pierre and he in helmets, such as appeared in the illustrations in his Plutarch, were marching at the head of an immense army. This army was made up of slanting, white threads that filled the air like those spider-webs that float in autumn and that Dessalle used to call *le fil de la Vierge*. Ahead of them was glory, which was something like those threads too, only somewhat more opaque. They—he and Pierre—were flying lightly and happily nearer and nearer to their goal. All at once the threads that moved them seemed to grow weak and tangled; and it was all difficult. And Uncle Nikolay stood before them in a stern and menacing attitude.

'Have you done this?' he said, pointing to broken pens and sticks of sealing-wax. 'I did love you, but Araktcheev has bidden me, and I will kill the first that moves forward.'

Nikolinka looked round for Pierre; but Pierre was not there. Instead of Pierre, there was his father—Prince Andrey—and his father had no shape or form, but he was there; and seeing him, Nikolinka felt the weakness of love; he felt powerless, limp, and relaxed. His father caressed him and pitied him, but his Uncle Nikolay was moving down upon them, coming closer and closer. A great horror came over Nikolinka, and he waked up.

'My father!' he thought. (Although there were two very good portraits of Prince Andrey in the house, Nikolinka never thought of his father in human form.) 'My father has been with me, and has caressed me. He approved of me; he approved of Uncle Pierre. Whatever he might tell me, I would do it. Mucius Scaevola burnt his hand. But why should not the same sort of thing happen in my life? I know they want me to study. And I am going to study. But some day I shall have finished, and then I will act. One thing only I pray God for, that the same sort of thing may happen with me as with Plutarch's men, and I will act in the same way. I will do more. Every one shall know of me, shall love me, and admire me.' And all at once Nikolinka felt his breast heaving with sobs, and he burst into tears.

'Are you ill?' he heard Dessalle's voice.

'No,' answered Nikolinka, and he lay back on his pillow. 'How good and kind he is; I love him!' He thought of Dessalle. 'But Uncle Pierre! Oh, what a wonderful man! And my father? Father! Father! Yes, I will do something that even *he* would be content with . . .'

PART II

I

THE SUBJECT OF history is the life of peoples and of humanity. To catch and pin down in words—that is, to describe directly the life, not only of humanity, but even of a single people, appears to be impossible.

All the ancient historians employed the same method for describing and catching what is seemingly elusive—that is, the life of a people. They described the career of individual persons ruling peoples; and their activity was to them an expression of the activity of the whole people.

The questions. In what way individual persons made nations act in accordance with their will, and by what the will of those individuals themselves was controlled, the ancients answered, By the will of God; which in the first case made the nation subject to the will of one chosen person, and, in the second, guided the will of that chosen monarch to the ordained end.

For the ancients these questions were solved by faith in the immediate participation of the Deity in the affairs of mankind.

Modern history has theoretically rejected both those positions. One would have thought that rejecting the convictions of the ancients of men's subjection to the Deity, and of a defined goal to which nations are led, modern history should have studied, not the manifestations of power, but the causes that go to its formation. But modern history has not done that. While in theory rejecting the views of the ancients, it follows them in practice.

Instead of men endowed with divine authority and directly led by the will of the Deity, modern history has set up either heroes, endowed with extraordinary, superhuman powers, or simply men of the most varied characteristics, from monarchs to journalists, who lead the masses. Instead of the old aim, the will of the Deity, that to the old historians seemed the end of the movements of peoples, such as the Gauls, the Greeks, and the Romans, modern history has advanced aims of its own—the welfare of the French, the German, or the English people, or its highest pitch of generalisation, the civilisation of all humanity, by which is usually meant the people inhabiting a small, north-western corner of the great mother-earth.

Modern history has rejected the faiths of the ancients, without putting any new conviction in their place; and the logic of the position has forced the historians, leaving behind them the rejected, divine right of kings and fate of the ancients, to come back by a different path to the same point again: to the recognition, that is (1), that peoples are led by individual persons; and (2) that there is a certain goal towards which humanity and the peoples constituting it are moving.

In all the works of the more modern historians, from Gibbon to Buckle, in spite of their apparent differences and the apparent novelty of their views, these two old inevitable positions lie at the basis of the argument.

In the first place the historian describes the conduct of separate persons who, in his opinion, lead humanity (one regards as such only monarchs, military generals, and ministers of state; another includes besides, monarchs, orators, scientific men, reformers, philosophers, and poets). Secondly, the goal towards which humanity is being led is known to the historian. To one this goal is the greatness of the Roman, or the Spanish, or the French state; for another, it is freedom, equality, a certain sort of civilisation in a little corner of the world called Europe.

In 1789 there was a ferment in Paris: it grew and spread, and found expression in the movement of peoples from west to east. Several times that movement is made to the east, and comes into collision with a counter-movement from east westwards. In the year 1812 it reaches its furthest limit, Moscow, and then, with a remarkable symmetry, the counter-movement follows from east to west; drawing with it, like the first movement, the peoples of Central Europe. The counter-movement reaches the starting-point of the first movement—Paris—and subsides.

During this period of twenty years an immense number of fields are not tilled; houses are burned; trade changes its direction; millions of men grow poor and grow rich, and change their habitations; and millions of Christians, professing the law of love, murder one another.

What does all this mean? What did all this proceed from? What induced these people to burn houses and to murder their fellow-creatures? What were the causes of these events? What force compelled men to act in this fashion? These are the involuntary and most legitimate questions that, in all good faith, humanity puts to itself when it stumbles on memorials and traditions of that past age of restlessness.

To answer these questions the common-sense of humanity turns to the science of history, the object of which is the self-knowledge of nations and of humanity.

Had history retained the view of the ancients, it would have said: The Deity, to reward or to punish His people, gave Napoleon power, and guided his will for the attainment of His own divine ends. And that answer would have been complete and clear. One might believe or disbelieve in the divine significance of Napoleon. For one who believed in it, all the history of that period would have been comprehensible, and there would have been nothing contradictory in it.

But modern history cannot answer in that way. Science does not accept the view of the ancients as to the direct participation of the Deity in the affairs of mankind, and therefore must give other answers.

Modern history, in answer to these questions, says: 'You want to know what this movement means, what it arose from, and what force produced these events? Listen.

'Louis XIV was a very haughty and self-willed man; he had such and such mistresses, and such and such ministers, and he governed France badly. Louis's successors, too, were weak men, and they, too, governed France badly. And they had such and such favourites, and such and such mistresses. Moreover, there were certain men writing books at this period. At the end of the eighteenth century there were some two dozen men in Paris who began to talk all about men being equal and free. This led people all over France to fall to hewing and hacking at each other. These people killed the king and a great many more. At that time there was in France a man of genius—Napoleon. He conquered every one everywhere, that is, he killed a great many people, because he was a very great genius. And for some reason he went to kill the Africans; and killed them so well, and was so cunning and clever, that on returning to France he bade every one obey him. And they all did obey him. After being made Emperor he went to kill people in Italy, Austria, and Prussia. And there, too, he killed a great many. In Russia there was an Emperor, Alexander, who was resolved to re-establish order in Europe, and so made war with Napoleon. But in 1807 he suddenly made friends with him, and in 1811 he quarrelled again, and again they began killing a great many people. And Napoleon took six hundred thousand men into Russia, and conquered Moscow, and then he suddenly ran away out of Moscow, and then the Emperor Alexander, aided by the counsels of Stein and others, united Europe for defence against the destroyer of her peace. All Napoleon's allies suddenly became his enemies; and the united army advanced against the fresh troops raised by Napoleon. The allies vanquished Napoleon; entered Paris; forced Napoleon to abdicate, and sent him to the island of Elba, not depriving him, however, of the dignity of Emperor, showing him, in fact, every respect, although five years before, and one year later, he was regarded by every one as a brigand outside the pale of the law. And Louis XVIII, who, till then, had been a laughing-stock to the French and the allies, began to reign. Napoleon shed tears before the Old Guard, abdicated the throne, and went into exile. Then the subtle, political people and diplomatists (conspicuous among them Talleyrand, who succeeded in sitting down in a particular chair before any one else, and thereby extended the frontiers of France) had conversations together at Vienna, and by these conversations made nations happy or unhappy. All at once the diplomatists and monarchs all but quarrelled; they were on the point of again commanding their armies to kill one another; but at that time Napoleon entered France with a battalion, and the French, who had been hating him, at once submitted to him. But the allied monarchs were angry at this, and again went to war with the French. And the genius, Napoleon, was conquered; and suddenly recognising that he was a brigand, they took him to the island of St. Helena. And on that rock the exile, parted from the friends of his heart, and from his beloved France, died a lingering death, and bequeathed all his great deeds to posterity. And in Europe the reaction followed, and all the sovereigns began oppressing their subjects again.'

It would be quite a mistake to suppose that this is mockery—a caricature of historical descriptions. On the contrary, it is a softened-down picture of the contradictory and random answers, that are no answers, given by *all* history, from the compilers of memoirs and of histories of separate states to general histories, and the new sort of histories of the *culture* of that period.

What is strange and comic in these answers is due to the fact that modern history is like a deaf man answering questions which no one has asked him.

If the aim of history is the description of the movement of humanity and of nations, the first question which must be answered, or all the rest remains unintelligible, is the following: What force moves nations? To meet this question modern history carefully relates that Napoleon was a very great genius, and that Louis XIV was very haughty, or that certain writers wrote certain books.

All this may very well be so, and humanity is ready to acquiesce in it; but it is not what it asks about. All that might be very interesting if we recognised a divine power, based on itself and always alike, guiding its peoples through Napoleons, Louis, and writers; but we do not acknowledge such a power, and therefore before talking about Napoleons, and Louis, and great writers, we must show the connection existing between those persons and the movement of the nations. If another force is put in the place of the divine power, then it should be explained what that force consists of, since it is precisely in that force that the whole interest of history lies.

History seems to assume that this force is taken for granted of itself, and is known to every one. But in despite of every desire to admit this new force as known, any one who reads through very many historical works cannot but doubt whether this new force, so differently understood by the historians themselves, is perfectly well known to every one.

II

WHAT is the force that moves nations?

Biographical historians, and historians writing of separate nations, understand this force as a power residing in heroes and sovereigns. According to their narratives, the events were entirely due to the wills of Napoleons, of Alexanders, or, generally speaking, of those persons who form the subject of historical memoirs. The answers given by historians of this class to the question as to the force which brings about events are satisfactory, but only so long as there is only one historian for any event. But as soon as historians of different views and different nationalities begin describing the same event, the answers given by them immediately lose all their value, as this force is understood by them, not only differently, but often in absolutely opposite ways. One historian asserts that an event is due to the power of Napoleon; another maintains that it is produced by the power of Alexander; a third ascribes it to the influence of some third person. Moreover, historians of this class contradict one another even in their explanation of the force on which the influence of the same person is based. Thiers, a Bonapartist, says that Napoleon's power rested on his virtue and his genius; Lanfrey, a Republican, declares that it rested on his duplicity and deception of the people. So that historians of this class, mutually destroying each other's position, at the same time destroy the conception of the force producing events, and give no answer to the essential question of history.

Writers of universal history, who have to deal with all the nations at once, appear to recognise the incorrectness of the views of historians of separate countries as to the force that produces events. They do not recognise this force as a power pertaining to heroes and sovereigns, but regard it as the resultant of many forces working in different directions. In describing a war or the subjugation of a people, the writer of general history seeks the cause of the event, not in the power of one person, but in the mutual action on one another of many persons connected with the event.

The power of historical personages conceived as the product of several forces, according to this view, can hardly, one would have supposed, be regarded as a self-sufficient force independently producing events. Yet writers of general history do in the great majority of cases employ the conception of power again as a self-sufficient force producing events and standing in the relation of cause to them. According to their exposition now the historical personage is the product of his time, and his power is only the product of various forces, now his power is the force producing events. Gervinus, Schlosser, for instance, and others, in one place, explain that Napoleon is the product of the Revolution, of the ideas of 1789, and so on; and in another plainly state that the campaign of 1812 and other events not to their liking are simply the work of Napoleon's wrongly directed will, and that the very ideas of 1789 were arrested in their development by Napoleon's arbitrary rule. The ideas of the Revolution, the general temper of the age produced Napoleon's power. The power of Napoleon suppressed the ideas of the Revolution and the general temper of the age.

This strange inconsistency is not an accidental one. It confronts us at every turn, and, in fact, whole works upon universal history are made up of consecutive series of such inconsistencies. This inconsistency is due to the fact that after taking a few steps along the road of analysis, these historians have stopped short half-way.

To find the component forces that make up the composite or resultant force, it is essential that the sum of the component parts should equal the resultant. This condition is never observed by historical writers, and consequently, to explain the resultant force, they must inevitably admit, in addition to those insufficient contributory forces, some further unexplained force that affects also the resultant action.

The historian describing the campaign of 1813, or the restoration of the Bourbons, says bluntly that these events were produced by the will of Alexander. But the philosophic historian Gervinus, controverting the view of the special historian of those events, seeks to prove that the campaign of 1813 and the restoration of the Bourbons was due not only to Alexander, but also to the work of Stein, Metternich, Madame de Staël, Talleyrand, Fichte, Chateaubriand, and others. The historian obviously analyses the power of Alexander into component forces. Talleyrand, Chateaubriand, and so on, and the sum of these component forces, that is, the effect on one another of Chateaubriand, Talleyrand, Madame de Staël, and others is obviously not equal to the resultant effect, that is, the phenomenon of millions of Frenchmen submitting to the Bourbons. Such and such words being said to one another by Chateaubriand, Madame de Staël, and others, only affects their relation to one another, and does not account for the submission of millions. And therefore to explain how the submission of millions followed from their relation to one another, that is, how from component forces equal to a given quantity A, there followed a resultant equal to a thousand times A, the historian is inevitably bound to admit that force of power, which he has renounced, accepting it in the resultant force, that is, he is obliged to admit an unexplained force that acts on the resultant of those components. And this is just what the philosophic historians do. And consequently they not only contradict the writers of historical memoirs, but also contradict themselves.

Country people who have no clear idea of the cause of rain say, The wind has blown away the rain, or the wind is blowing up for rain, according as they are in want of rain or of fair weather. In the same way, philosophic historians at times, when they wish it to be so, when it fits in with their theory, say that power is the result of events; and at times, when they want to prove something else, they say power produces the events.

A third class of historians, the writers of the so-called history of culture, following on the lines laid down by the writers of universal history who sometimes accept writers and ladies as forces producing events, yet understand that force quite differently. They see that force in so-called culture, in intellectual activity. The historians of culture are quite consistent as regards their prototypes—the writers of universal history—for if historical events can be explained by certain persons having said certain things to one another, why not explain them by certain persons having written certain books? Out of all the immense number of tokens that accompany every living phenomenon, these historians select the symptom of intellectual activity, and assert that this symptom is the cause. But in spite of all their endeavours to prove that the cause of events lies in intellectual activity, it is only by a great stretch that one can agree that there is anything in common between intellectual activity and the movement of peoples. And it is altogether impossible to admit that intellectual activity has guided the actions of men, for such phenomena as the cruel murders of the French Revolution, resulting from the doctrine of the equality of man, and the most wicked wars and massacres arising from the Gospel of love, do not confirm this hypothesis.

But even admitting that all the cunningly woven arguments with which these histories abound are correct, admitting that nations are governed by some indefinite force called an *idea*—the essential question of history still remains unanswered; or to the power of monarchs and the influence of counsellors and other persons, introduced by the philosophic historian, another new force is now joined—the *idea*, the connection of which with the masses demands explanation. One can understand that Napoleon had power and so an event came to pass; with some effort one can even conceive that Napoleon together with other influences was the cause of an event. But in what fashion a book, *Le Contrat Social*, led the French to hack each other to pieces cannot be understood without an explanation of the causal connection of this new force with the event.

There undoubtedly exists a connection between all the people living at one time, and so it is possible to find some sort of connection between the intellectual activity of men and their historical movements, just as one may find a connection between the movements of humanity and commerce, handicrafts, gardening, and anything you like. But why intellectual activity should be conceived of by the historians of culture as the cause or the expression of a whole historical movement, it is hard to understand. Historians can only be led to such a conclusion by the following considerations: (1) That history is written by learned men; and so it is natural and agreeable to them to believe that the pursuit of their calling is the basis of the movement of the whole of humanity, just as a similar belief would be natural and agreeable to merchants, agriculturists, or soldiers (such a belief on their part does not find expression simply because merchants and soldiers don't write history); and (2) that spiritual activity, enlightenment, civilisation, culture, ideas are all vague, indefinite conceptions, under cover of which they can conveniently use phrases having a less definite signification, and so easily brought under any theory.

But to say nothing of the inner dignity of histories of this kind (possibly they are of use for some one or for something), the histories of culture, towards which all general histories tend more and more to approximate, are noteworthy from the fact that though they give a serious and detailed analysis of various religious, philosophic, and political doctrines as causes of events, every time they have to describe an actual historical event, as, for instance, the campaign of 1812, they unconsciously describe it as the effect of the exercise of power, frankly saying that that campaign was the work of Napoleon's will. In saying this, the historians of culture unconsciously contradict themselves, or prove that the new force they have invented is not the expression of historical events, and that the sole means of explaining history is by that power which they had apparently rejected.

III

A STEAM-ENGINE moves. The question is asked, How is it moved? A peasant answers, It is the devil moving it. Another man says, The steam-engine moves because the wheels are going round. A third maintains that the cause of the motion is to be found in the smoke floated from it by the wind.

The peasant's contention is irrefutable. To refute him some one must prove to him that there is no devil, or another peasant must explain that it is not a devil, but a German who moves the steamer. Then from their contradictory views they see that both are wrong. But the man who says the cause is the movement of the wheels refutes himself, seeing that having once entered on the path of analysis, he ought to proceed further and further along it; he ought to explain the cause of the wheels moving. And he has not to stop in his search for a cause till he finds the ultimate cause of the movement of the steam-engine in the steam compressed in the boiler. As for the man who explained the movement of the steam-engine as due to the smoke being blown back from it, he has simply noticed that the wheel explanation was insufficient, and pitching on the first accompanying symptom, gave that out as his cause.

The only conception which can explain the movement of the steamer is the conception of a force equal to the movement that is seen.

The only conception by means of which the movements of nations can be explained is a conception of a force equal to the whole movement of the nations.

Yet under this conception there are included by various historians forces of the most various kind, and all unequal to the movement that is seen. Some see in it a force directly pertaining to heroes, as the peasant sees the devil in the steam-engine. Others, a force resulting from several other forces, like the movement of the wheels; a third class, intellectual influence, like the smoke.

So long as histories are written of individual persons—whether they are Cæsars and Alexanders, or Luthers and Voltaires—and not the history of *all*, without one exception, *all* the people taking part in an event, there is no possibility of describing the movement of humanity without a conception of a force impelling men to direct their activity to one end. And the only conception of this kind familiar to historians is power.

This conception is the sole handle by means of which the material of history, as at present expounded, can be dealt with; and the historian who should, like Buckle, break off this handle, without discovering any other means of dealing with historical material, would only be depriving himself of the last chance of dealing with it. The necessity of the conception of the exercise of power to explain the phenomena of history is most strikingly shown by the very writers of universal history and the history of culture, who, after professedly rejecting the conception of power, inevitably resort to it at every step.

Historical science in relation to the questions of humanity has hitherto been like money in circulation—paper notes and metal coins. The historical memoirs and histories of separate peoples are like paper money. They may pass and be accepted, doing their part without mischief to any one, and even being useful, so long as no question arises as to their value. One has only to forget the question how the will of heroes produces events, and Thiers's histories will be interesting, instructive, and will, moreover, not be devoid of a certain poetry. But just as a doubt of the stability of paper money arises, either because from the ease of making it, too much is put into circulation, or because of a desire to replace it by gold, so a doubt of the real value of history of this kind arises either because too many such histories appear, or because some one in the simplicity of his heart asks: By what force did Napoleon do that?—that is, wishes to change the current paper for the pure gold of a true conception.

The writers of general history and the history of culture are like men who, recognising the inconvenience of paper money, should decide to make instead of paper notes, jingling coin of metal not of the density of gold. And such coin would be jingling coin, and only jingling coin. A paper note might deceive the ignorant; but coin not of precious metal could deceive no one. Just as gold is only gold when it is of value, not only for exchange, but also for use, so the writers of universal history will only prove themselves of real value when they are able to answer the essential question of history: What is power? These historians give contradictory answers to this question, while the historians of culture altogether evade it, answering something quite different. And as counters in imitation of gold can only be used in a community of persons who agree to accept them for gold, or who are ignorant of the true character of gold, so do the historians who do not answer the essential questions of humanity serve for some objects of their own as current coin at the universities and with that crowd of readers—fond of serious reading, as they call it.

IV

SINCE, history has abandoned the views of the ancients as to the divine subjection of the will of a people to one chosen vessel, and the subjection of the will of that chosen vessel to the Deity, it cannot take a single step without encountering contradictions. It must choose one of two alternatives: either to return to its old faith in the direct intervention of the Deity in the affairs of humanity; or to find a definite explanation of that force producing historical events that is called power.

To return to the old way is out of the question: the old faith is shattered, and so an explanation must be found of the meaning of power.

Napoleon commanded an army to be raised, and to march out to war. This conception is so familiar to us, we are so accustomed to this idea, that the question why six hundred thousand men go out to fight when Napoleon utters certain words seems meaningless to us. He had the power, and so the commands he gave were carried out.

This answer is completely satisfactory if we believe that power has been given from God. But as soon as we do not accept that, it is essential to define what this power is of one man over others.

This power cannot be that direct power of the physical ascendancy of a strong creature over a weak one, that ascendancy based on the application or the threat of the application of physical force—like the power of Hercules. Nor can it be based on the ascendancy of moral force, as in the simplicity of their hearts several historians suppose, maintaining that the leading historical figures are heroes—that is, men endowed with a special force of soul and mind called genius. This power cannot be based on the ascendancy of moral force, for, to say nothing of historical heroes, like Napoleon, concerning whose moral qualities opinions greatly differ, history proves to us that neither Louis XI, not Metternich, who governed millions of men, had any marked characteristics of moral force, but that they were, on the contrary, in most respects morally weaker than any one of the millions of men they governed.

If the source of power lies not in the physical and not in the moral characteristics of the person possessing, it is evident that the source of this power must be found outside the person—in those relations in which the person possessing the power stands to the masses.

That is precisely how power is interpreted by the science of law, that cash bank of history, that undertakes to change the historical token money of power for sterling gold.

Power is the combined wills of the masses, transferred by their expressed or tacit consent to the rulers chosen by the masses.

In the domain of the science of law, made up of arguments on how a state and power ought to be constructed, if it were possible to construct it, all this is very clear; but in its application to history this definition of power calls for elucidation.

The science of law regards the state and power, as the ancients regarded fire, as something positively existing. But for history the state and power are merely phenomena, just as for the physical science of today fire is not an element, but a phenomenon.

From this fundamental difference in the point of view of history and of the science of law, it comes to pass that the science of law can discuss in detail how in the scientific writer's opinion power should be organised, and what is power, existing immovable outside the conditions of time; but to historical questions as to the significance of power, undergoing visible transformation in time, it can give no answer.

If power is the combined will of the masses transferred to their rulers, is Pugatchof a representative of the will of the masses? If he is not, how then is Napoleon I such a representative? Why is it that Napoleon III, when he was seized at Boulogne, was a criminal, and afterwards those who had been seized by him were criminals?

In palace revolutions—in which sometimes two or three persons only take part—is the will of the masses transferred to a new person? In international relations, is the will of the masses of the people transferred to their conqueror? In 1808 was the will of the Rhine Alliance league transferred to Napoleon? Was the will of the mass of the Russian people transferred to Napoleon in 1809, when our army in alliance with the French made war upon Austria?

These questions may be answered in three ways: (1) By maintaining that the will of the masses is always unconditionally delegated over to that ruler or those rulers whom they have chosen, and that consequently every rising up of new power, every struggle against the power once delegated, must be regarded as a contravention of the real power.

Or (2) by maintaining that the will of the masses is delegated to the rulers, under certain definite conditions, and by showing that all restrictions on, conflicts with, and even abolition of power are due to non-observance of the rulers of those conditions upon which power was delegated to them.

Or (3) by maintaining that the will of the masses is delegated to the rulers conditionally, but that the conditions are uncertain and undefined, and that the rising up of several authorities, and their conflict and fall, are due only to the more or less complete fulfilment of the rulers of the uncertain conditions upon which the will of the masses is transferred from one set of persons to another.

In these three ways do historians explain the relation of the masses to their rulers.

Some historians—those most distinctively biographers and writers of memoirs, of whom we have spoken above—failing in the simplicity of their hearts to understand the question as to the meaning of power, seem to believe that the combined will of the masses is delegated to historical leaders unconditionally, and therefore, describing any such authority, these historians assume that that authority is the one absolute and real one, and that every other force, opposing that real authority, is not authority, but a violation of authority, and unlawful violence.

Their theory fits in well with primitive and peaceful periods of history; but in its application to complicated and stormy periods in the life of nations, when several different authorities rise up simultaneously and struggle together, the inconvenience arises that the legitimist historian will assert that the National Assembly, the Directorate, and Bonaparte were only violations of real authority; while the Republican and the Bonapartist will maintain, one that the Republic, and the other that the Empire were the real authority, and that all the rest was a violation of authority. It is evident that the explanations given by these historians, being mutually contradictory, can satisfy none but children of the tenderest age.

Recognising the deceptiveness of this view of history, another class of historians assert that authority rests on the conditional delegation of the combined will of the masses to their rulers, and that historical leaders possess power only on condition of carrying out the programme which the will of the people has by tacit consent dictated to them. But what this programme consists of, those historians do not tell us, or if they do, they continually contradict one another.

In accordance with his view of what constitutes the goal of the movements of a people, each historian conceives of this programme, as, for instance, the greatness, the wealth, the freedom, or the enlightenment of the citizens of France or some other kingdom. But putting aside the contradictions between historians as to the nature of such a programme, and even supposing that one general programme to exist for all, the facts of history almost always contradict this theory.

If the conditions on which power is vested in rulers are to be found in the wealth, freedom, and enlightenment of the people, how is it that kings like Louis XIV and John IV lived out their reigns in peace, while kings like Louis XVI and Charles I were put to death by their peoples? To this question these historians reply, that the effect of the actions of

Louis XIV contrary to the programme were reacted upon Louis XVI. But why not reflected on Louis XIV and Louis XV? Why precisely on Louis XVI? And what limit is there to such reflection? To these questions there is and can be no reply. Nor does this view explain the reason that the combined will of a people remains for several centuries vested in its rulers and their heirs, and then all at once during a period of fifty years is transferred to a Convention, a Directory, to Napoleon, to Alexander, to Louis XVIII, again to Napoleon, to Charles X, to Louis Philippe, to a republican government, and to Napoleon III. To explain these rapid transferences of the people's will from one person to another, especially when complicated by international relations, wars, and alliances, these historians are unwillingly obliged to allow that a proportion of these phenomena are not normal transferences of the will of the people, but casual incidents, depending on the cunning, or the blundering, or the craft, or the weakness of a diplomatist or a monarch, or the leader of a party. So that the greater number of the phenomena of history—civil wars, revolutions, wars—are regarded by these historians as not being produced by the delegation of the freewill of the people, but as being produced by the wrongly directed will of one or several persons, that is, again by a violation of authority. And so by this class of historians, too, historical events are conceived of as exceptions to their theory.

These historians are like a botanist who, observing that several plants grow by their seed parting into two cotyledons, or seed-leaves, should insist that everything that grows only grows by parting into two leaves; and that the palm-tree and the mushroom, and even the oak, when it spreads its branches in all directions in its mature growth, and has lost all semblance to its two seed-leaves, are departures from their theory of the true law of growth. A third class of historians admit that the will of the masses is vested in historical leaders conditionally, but say that those conditions are not known to us. They maintain that historical leaders have power only because they are carrying out the will of the masses delegated to them.

But in that case, if the force moving the peoples lies not in their historical leaders, but in the people themselves, where is the significance of those historical leaders?

Historical leaders are, so those historians tell us, the self-expression of the will of the masses; the activity of the historical leaders serves as a type of activity of the masses.

But in that case the question arises, Does all the activity of historical leaders serve as an expression of the will of the masses, or only a certain side of it? If all the life-activity of historical leaders serves as an expression of the will of the masses, as some indeed believe, then the biographies of Napoleons and Catherines, with all the details of court scandal, serve as the expression of the life of their peoples, which is an obvious absurdity. If only one side of the activity of an historical leader serves as the expression of the life of a people, as other supposed philosophical historians believe, then to define what side of the activity of an historical leader does express the life of a people, one must know first what the life of the people consists of.

Being confronted with this difficulty, historians of this class invent the most obscure, intangible, and general abstraction, under which to class the greatest possible number of events, and declare that in this abstraction is to be found the aims of the movements of humanity. The most usual abstractions accepted by almost all historians are: freedom, equality, enlightenment, progress, civilisation, culture. Postulating some such abstraction as the goal of the movements of humanity, the historians study those persons who have left the greatest number of memorials behind them—kings, ministers, generals, writers, reformers, popes, and journalists—from the point of view of the effect those persons in their opinion had in promoting or hindering that abstraction. But as it is nowhere proven that the goal of humanity really is freedom, equality, enlightenment, or civilisation, and as the connection of the masses with their rulers and with the leaders of humanity only rests on the arbitrary assumption that the combined will of the masses is always vested in these figures which attract our attention—the fact remains that the activity of the millions of men who move from place to place, burn houses, abandon tilling the soil, and butcher one another, never does find expression in descriptions of the activity of some dozen persons, who do not burn houses, never have tilled the soil, and do not kill their fellow-creatures.

History proves this at every turn. Is the ferment of the peoples of the west towards the end of the last century, and their rush to the east, explained by the activity of Louis XIV, Louis XV, and Louis XVI, or their mistresses and ministers, or by the life of Napoleon, of Rousseau, of Diderot, of Beaumarchais, and others?

The movement of the Russian people to the east, to Kazan and Siberia, is that expressed in the details of the morbid life of John IV and his correspondence with Kurbsky?

Is the movement of the peoples at the time of the Crusades explained by the life and activity of certain Godfreys and Louis and their ladies?

It has remained beyond our comprehension that movement of the peoples from west to east, without an object, without leadership, with a crowd of tramps following Peter the Hermit. And even more incomprehensible is the cessation of that movement, when a rational and holy object for the expeditions had been clearly set up by historical leaders—that is, the deliverance of Jerusalem.

Popes, kings, and knights urged the people to set free the Holy Land. But the people did not move, because that unknown cause, which had impelled them before to movement, existed no longer. The history of the Godreys and the Minnesingers evidently cannot be regarded as an epitome of the life of the peoples. And the history of the Godfreys and the Minnesingers has remained the history of those knights and those Minnesingers, while the history of the life of the peoples and their impulses has remained unknown.

Even less explanatory of the life of the peoples is the history of the lives of writers and reformers.

The history of culture offers us as the impelling motives of the life of the people the circumstances of the lives or the ideas of a writer or a reformer. We learn that Luther had a hasty temper and uttered certain speeches; we learn that Rousseau was distrustful and wrote certain books; but we do not learn what made the nations cut each other to pieces after the Reformation, or why men guillotined each other during the French Revolution.

If we unite both these kinds of history together as do the most modern historians, then we shall get histories of monarchs and of writers, but not a history of the life of nations.

V

THE life of nations is not contained in the life of a few men, since the connection between those few men and the nations has not been found. The theory that this connection is based on the delegation of the combined will of a people to its historical leaders is an hypothesis, not supported by the testimony of history.

The theory of the delegation of the combined will of the masses to historical personages may perhaps explain a great deal in the domain of the science of law, and is possibly essential for its purposes. But in its application to history, as soon as revolutions, wars, civil disturbances arise, as soon as history begins in fact—this theory explains nothing.

This theory appears irrefutable, just because the act of delegating the will of the people can never be verified, since it has never existed.

Whatever event might take place, and whoever might be taking the lead in such an event, the theory can always say that such a person took the lead in bringing about that event because the combined will was vested in him.

The answers given by this theory to historical questions are like the answers of a man who, watching the movements of a flock, should pay no attention to the varying quality of the pasturage in different parts of the field, nor to the actions of the shepherd, but should look for the causes of the flock taking this or that direction simply in the animal that happened to be foremost in it.

'The flock moves in this direction because the animal in front leads it, and the combined will of all the other animals is delegated to the leader of the flock.' Such is the answer given by the first class of historians, who suppose an unconditional delegation of will to the authority.

'If the animals leading the flock are changed for others, it is due to the fact that the combined will of all the beasts is transferred from one leader to another owing to the fact that the first leader did not follow the direction chosen by all the flock.' Such is the reply of those historians who assume that the combined will of the masses is vested in their rulers on conditions which they regard as unknown. (With this method of observation it very often happens that the observer, judging from the direction chosen by him, reckons as leaders those who, when the direction of the masses is changed, are not in front, but on one side, and even sometimes the hindmost.)

'If the beasts that are foremost are constantly being changed, and the direction taken by the flock too is continually changing, that is due to the fact that to attain a certain direction known to us the beasts delegate their wills to those beasts which attract our attention, and to study the movements of the flock we ought to observe all the noticeable animals that are moving on all sides of the flock.' So say the third class of historians, who accept all historical characters as the expression of their age from monarchs to journalists.

The theory of the transference of the will of the masses to historical characters is only a paraphrase—only a restatement of the question in other words.

What is the cause of historical events? Power.

What is power? Power is the combined will of the masses vested in one person.

On what conditions are the wills of the masses vested in one person? On condition of that person's expressing the will of all men. That is, power is power. That is, power is a word the meaning of which is beyond our comprehension.

If the domain of human knowledge were confined to abstract reasoning alone, then, after subjecting the explanation of power given by science to criticism, humanity would come to the conclusion that power is only a word, and that it has no existence in reality. But for the knowledge of phenomena, man has besides abstract reasoning another instrument—experience—by which he verifies the results of reasoning. And experience tells him that power is not merely a word, but an actually existing phenomenon.

To say nothing of the fact that not a single account of the combined action of men can omit the conception of power, the reality of power is shown us, not only by history, but by observation of contemporary events.

Whenever an event takes place, a man or men appear by whose will the event is conceived to have been accomplished. Napoleon III gives an order, and the French go to Mexico. The Prussian King and Bismarck give certain orders, and troops go to Bohemia. Napoleon I gives a command, and soldiers march into Russia. Alexander I gives a command, and the French submit to the Bourbons. Experience shows us that whatever event takes place, it is always connected with the will of one or of several men, who decreed it should be so.

Historians, from the old habit of recognising Divine intervention in the affairs of humanity, are inclined to look for the cause of events in the exercise of the will of the person endowed with power; but this conclusion is not confirmed either by reason or by experience.

On one side reason shows that the expression of the will of a man—his words, in fact, are only a part of the general activity expressed in an event, such as a revolution or a war, and therefore without the assumption of an incomprehensible, supernatural force—a miracle—it cannot be admitted that these words can be the immediate cause of the movements of millions of men.

On the other side, even if one admits that words may be the cause of an event, history shows us that the expression of the will of historical personages in the great majority of cases does not lead to any effect at all—that is, that their commands are often not carried out, and, in fact, sometimes the very opposite of what they have commanded is done.

Without admitting divine intervention in the affairs of humanity, we cannot accept power as a cause of events.

Power, from the point of view of experience, is only the dependence—existing between the expression of the will of a person and the carrying out of that will by others.

To explain the conditions of that dependence, we have, first of all, to reinstate the conception of the expression of will, referring it to man, and not to the Deity.

If the Deity gives a command, expresses His will, as the history of the ancients tells us, the expression of that will is independent of time, and is not called forth by anything, as the Deity is not connected with the event. But when we speak of commands that are the expression of the will of men, acting in time and connected with one another, we must, if we are to understand the connection of the command with the event, restore (1) the conditions of all the circumstances that took place, the dynamic continuity in time both of the event and of the person commanding it; and (2) the condition of the inevitable connection in which the person commanding stands with those who carry out his command.

VI

ONLY the expression of the will of the Deity, not depending on time, can relate to a whole series of events that have to take place during several years or centuries; and only the Deity, acting by His will alone, not affected by any cause, can determine the direction of the movement of humanity. Man acts in time, and himself takes part in the event.

Restoring the first condition that was omitted, the condition of time, we perceive that no single command can be carried out apart from preceding commands that have made the execution of the last command possible.

Never is a single command given quite independently and arbitrarily, nor does it cover a whole series of events. Every command is the sequel to some other; and it never relates to a whole course of events, but only to one moment in those events.

When we say, for instance, that Napoleon commanded the army to go to fight, we sum up in one single expression a series of consecutive commands, depending one upon another. Napoleon could not command a campaign against Russia, and never did command it. He commanded one day certain papers to be written to Vienna, to Berlin, and to Petersburg; next day, certain decrees and instructions to the army, the fleet, and the commissariat, and so on and so on—millions of separate commands, making up a whole series of commands, corresponding to a series of events leading the French soldiers to Russia.

Napoleon was giving commands all through his reign for an expedition to England. On no one of his undertakings did he waste so much time and so much effort, and yet not once during his reign was an attempt made to carry out his design. Yet he made an expedition against Russia, with which, according to his repeatedly expressed conviction, it was to his advantage to be in alliance; and this is due to the fact that his commands in the first case did not, and in the second did, correspond with the course of events.

In order that a command should certainly be carried out, it is necessary that the man should give a command that can be carried out. To know what can and what cannot be carried out is impossible, not only in the case of Napoleon's campaign against Russia, in which millions took part, but even in the case of the simplest event, since millions of obstacles may always arise to prevent its being carried out. Every command that is carried out is always one out of a mass of commands that are not carried out. All the impossible commands are inconsistent with the course of events and are not carried out. Only those which are possible are connected with consecutive series of commands, consistent with series of events, and they are carried out.

Our false conception that the command that precedes an event is the cause of an event is due to the fact that when the event has taken place and those few out of thousands of commands, which happen to be consistent with the course of events, are carried out, we forget those which were not, because they could not be, carried out. Apart from that, the chief source of our error arises from the fact that in the historical account a whole series of innumerable, various, and most minute events, as, for instance, all that led the French soldiers to Russia, are generalised into a single event, in accordance with the result produced by that series of events; and by a corresponding generalisation a whole series of commands too is summed up into a single expression of will.

We say: Napoleon chose to invade Russia and he did so. In reality we never find in all Napoleon's doings anything like an expression of that design: what we find is a series of commands or expressions of his will of the most various and undefined tendency. Out of many series of innumerable commands of Napoleon not carried out, one series of commands for the campaign of 1812 was carried out; not from any essential difference between the commands carried out and those not carried out, but simply because the former coincided with the course of events that led the French soldiers into Russia; just as in stencil-work one figure or another is sketched, not because the colours are laid on this side or in that way, but because on the figure cut out in stencil colours are laid on all sides.

So that examining in time the relation of commands to events, we find that the command can never in any case be the cause of the event, but that a certain definite dependence exists between them. To understand of what this dependence consists, it is essential to restore the other circumstances lost sight of, a condition accompanying any command issuing not from the Deity, but from man. That circumstance is that the man giving the comand is himself taking part in the event.

That relation of the commanding person to those he commands is indeed precisely what is called power. That relation may be analysed as follows.

For common action, men always unite in certain combinations, in which, in spite of the difference of the objects aimed at by common action, the relation between the men taking a part in the action always remains the same.

Uniting in these combinations, men always stand in such a relation to one another that the largest number of men take a greater direct share, and a smaller number of men a less direct share in the combined action for which they are united. Of all such combinations in which men are organised for the performance of common action, one of the most striking and definite examples is the army.

Every army is composed of members of lower military standing—the private soldiers, who are always the largest proportion of the whole; of members of a slightly higher military standing—corporals and non-commissioned officers, who are fewer in number than the privates; of still higher officers, whose numbers are even less; and so on, up to the chief military command of all, which is concentrated in one person.

The military organisation may be with perfect accuracy compared to the figure of a cone, the base of which, with the largest diameter, consists of privates; the next higher and smaller plane, of the lower officers; and so on up to the apex of the cone, which will be the commander-in-chief.

The soldiers, who are the largest number, form the lowest plane and the base of the cone. The soldier himself does the stabbing and hacking, and burning and pillaging, and always receives commands to perform these acts from the persons in the plane next above. He himself never gives a command. The non-commissioned officer (these are fewer in number) more rarely performs the immediate act than the soldier; but he gives commands. The officer next above him still more rarely acts directly himself, and still more frequently commands. The general does nothing but command the army, and hardly ever makes use of a weapon. The commander-in-chief never takes direct part in the action itself, and simply makes general arrangements as to the movements of the masses. A similar relation exists in every combination of persons for common action—in agriculture, commerce, and in every department of activity.

And so without artificially analysing all the converging planes of the cone and ranks of the army or classes or ranks of any department whatever, or public undertaking, from lower to higher, a law comes into existence, by which men always combine together for the performance of common action in such relation that the more directly they take part in action, the less they command, and the greater their numbers; and the less direct the part they take in the common action, the more they command, and the fewer they are in number; passing in that way from the lower strata up to a single man at the top, who takes least direct share in the action, and devotes his energy more than all the rest to giving commands.

This is the relation of persons in command to those whom they command, and it constitutes the essence of the conception of what is called power.

Restoring the conditions of time under which all events take place, we found that a command is carried out only when it relates to a corresponding course of events. Restoring the essential condition of connection between the persons commanding and fulfilling the commands, we have found that by their very nature the persons commanding take the smallest part in the action itself, and their energy is exclusively directed to commanding.

VII

WHEN some event takes place, men express their opinions and desires in regard to the event, and as the event proceeds from the combined action of many men, some one of the opinions or desires expressed is certain to be at least approximately fulfilled. When one of the opinions expressed is fulfilled, that opinion is connected with the event as the command preceding it.

Men are dragging a log. Every man expresses his opinion as to how and where to drag it. The men drag the log off; and it turns out that it has been done just as one of them advised. He gave the command then. This is commanding and power in its primitive aspect.

The man who did most work with his arms could think least what he was doing, reflect least what might come of the common action, and so command least. The man who commanded most could obviously, from his greater verbal activity, act less vigorously with his arms. In a larger assembly of men, combining their energies to one end, the class of those persons who take the less direct share in the common work the more their energy is turned to command, is still more sharply defined.

When a man acts alone, he always carries within him a certain series of considerations, that have, as he supposes, directed his past conduct, and that serve to justify to him his present action, and to lead him to make projects for his future activity.

Assemblies of men act in the same way, only leaving to those who do not take direct part in the action to invent considerations, justifications, and projects concerning their combined activity.

For causes, known or unknown to us, the French begin to chop and hack at each other. And to match the event, it is accompanied by its justification in the expressed wills of certain men, who declare it essential for the good of France, for the cause of freedom, of equality. Men cease slaughtering one another, and that event is accompanied by the justification of the necessity of centralisation of power, of resistance to Europe, and so on. Men march from west to east, killing their fellow-creatures, and this event is accompanied by phrases about the glory of France, the baseness of England, and so on. History teaches us that those justifications for the event are devoid of all common sense, that they are inconsistent with one another, as, for instance, the murder of a man as a result of the declaration of his rights, and the murder of millions in Russia for the abasement of England. But those justifications have an incontestable value in their own day.

They remove moral responsibility from those men who produce the events. At the time they do the work of brooms, that go in front to clear the rails for the train: they clear the path of men's moral responsibility. Apart from those justifications, no solution could be found for the most obvious question that occurs to one at once on examining any historical event; that is, How did millions of men come to combine to commit crimes, murders, wars, and so on?

Under the existing complex forms of political social life in Europe, can any event be imagined which would not have been prescribed, decreed, commanded by some sovereigns, ministers, parliaments, or newspapers? Is there any sort of combined action which could not find justification in political unity, or in patriotism, or in the balance of power, or in civilisation? So that every event that occurs inevitably coincides with some expressed desire, and receiving justification, is regarded as the result of the will of one or more persons.

Whichever way the ship steers its course, there will always be seen ahead of it the flow of the waves it cleaves. To the men in the ship the movement of those waves will be the only motion perceptible.

It is only by watching closely, moment by moment, the movement of that flow, and comparing it with the movement of the ship, that we are convinced that every moment that flowing by of the waves is due to the forward movement of the ship, and that we have been led into error by the fact that we are ourselves moving too.

We see the same thing, watching moment by moment the movement of historical personages (that is, restoring the inevitable condition under which all action takes place—the condition of the continuity of motion in time), and not losing sight of the necessary connection of historical figures with the masses.

Whatever happens, it always appears that that was foreseen and decreed. Whichever way the ship turns, the waves gurgle in front of it, and neither guiding nor accelerating its movement, will seem to us at a distance to be moving arbitrarily and guiding the course of the ship.

Examining only those expressions of the will of historical characters which related to events as commands, historians have assumed that the events were dependent on the commands. Examining the events themselves, and that connection in which the historical characters stand with the masses, we have found that historical characters and their commands are dependent on the events. An incontestable proof of this deduction is to be found in the fact that, however many commands may be given, the event does not take place if there is no other cause to produce it. But as soon as an event does take place—whatever it may be—out of the number of all the expressions of the will of different persons, there are always some which, from their meaning and time of utterance, are related to the events as commands.

Having reached this conclusion, we can directly and positively answer these two essential questions of history:

1. What is power?
2. What force produces the movements of peoples?

1. Power is a relation of a certain person to other persons, in which that person takes the less direct share in an act, the more he expresses opinions, theories, and justifications of the combined action.

2. The movement of peoples is not produced by the exercise of power, nor by intellectual activity, nor even by a combination of the two, as historians have supposed; but by the activity of *all* the men taking part in the event, who are always combined in such a way that those who take most direct part in the action take the smallest share in responsibility for it, and *vice versa*.

In its moral aspect the cause of the event is conceived of as power; in its physical aspect as those who were subject to that power. But since moral activity is inconceivable apart from physical, the cause of the event is found in neither the one nor the other, but in the conjunction of the two.

Or, in other words, the conception of cause is not applicable to the phenomenon we are examining.

In our final analysis we are brought to the circle of infinity, to that utmost limit, to which the human intellect is brought in every department of thought, if it is not merely playing with its subject. Electricity produces heat; heat produces electricity. Atoms are attracted; atoms are repelled.

Speaking of the mutual relations of heat and of electricity and of atoms, we cannot say why it is so, and we say it is so because it is unthinkable otherwise; because it must be so; because it is a law. The same thing applies also to historical phenomena. Why does a war or a revolution come to pass? We do not know. We only know that to bring either result to pass, men form themselves into a certain combination in which all take part; and we say that this is so because it is unthinkable otherwise; because it is a law.

VIII

IF history had to deal with external phenomena, the establishment of this simple and obvious law would be sufficient, and our argument would be at an end. But the law of history relates to man. A particle of matter cannot tell us that it does not feel the inevitability of attraction and repulsion, and that the law is not true. Man, who is the subject of history, bluntly says: I am free, and so I am not subject to law.

The presence of the question of the freedom of the will, if not openly expressed, is felt at every step in history.

All seriously thinking historians are involuntarily led to this question. All the inconsistencies, and the obscurity of history, and the false path that science has followed, is due to that unsolved question.

If the will of every man were free, that is, if every man could act as he chose, the whole of history would be a tissue of disconnected accidents.

If one man only out of millions once in a thousand years had the power of acting freely, that is, as he chose, it is obvious that a single free act of that man in opposition to the laws governing human action would destroy the possibility of any laws whatever governing all humanity.

If there is but one law controlling the actions of men, there can be no free will, since men's will must be subject to that law.

In this contradiction lies the question of the freedom of the will, which from the most ancient times has occupied the best intellects of mankind, and has from the most ancient times been regarded as of immense importance.

Looking at man as a subject of observation from any point of view—theological, historical, ethical, philosophical—we find a general law of necessity to which he is subject like everything existing. Looking at him from within ourselves, as what we are conscious of, we feel ourselves free.

This consciousness is a source of self-knowledge utterly apart and independent of reason. Through reason man observes himself; but he knows himself only through consciousness.

Apart from consciousness of self, any observation and application of reason is inconceivable.

To understand, to observe, to draw conclusions, a man must first of all be conscious of himself as living. A man knows himself as living, not otherwise than as willing, that is, he is conscious of his free will. Man is conscious of his will as constituting the essence of his life, and he cannot be conscious of it except as free.

If subjecting himself to his own observation, a man perceives that his will is always controlled by the same law (whether he observes the necessity of taking food, or of exercising his brain, or anything else), he cannot regard this never-varying direction of his will otherwise than as a limitation of it. If it were not free, it could not be limited. A man's will seems to him to be limited just because he is not conscious of it except as free. You say: I am not free. But I have lifted and dropped my hand. Everybody understands that this illogical reply is an irrefutable proof of freedom.

This reply is an expression of a consciousness not subject to reason.

If the consciousness of freedom were not a separate source of self-knowledge apart from reason, it would be controlled by reasoning and experience. But in reality such control never exists, and is inconceivable.

A series of experiments and arguments prove to every man that he, as an object of observation, is subject to certain laws, and the man submits to them, and never, after they have once been pointed out to him, controverts the law of gravitation or of impenetrability. But the same series of experiments and arguments proves to him that the complete freedom of which he is conscious in himself is impossible; that every action of his depends on his organisation, on his character, and the motives acting on him. But man never submits to the deductions of these experiments and arguments.

Learning from experience and from reasoning that a stone falls to the ground, a man unhesitatingly believes this; and in all cases expects the law he has learnt to be carried out.

But learning just as incontestably that his will is subject to laws, he does not, and cannot, believe it.

However often experience and reasoning show a man that in the same circumstances, with the same character, he does the same thing as before, yet on being led the thousandth time in the same circumstances, with the same character, to an action that always ends in the same way, he feels just as unhesitatingly convinced that he can act as he chooses, as ever. Every man, savage and sage alike, however incontestably reason and experience may prove to him that it is impossible to imagine two different courses of action under precisely the same circumstances, yet feels that without this meaningless conception (which constitutes the essence of freedom) he cannot conceive of life. He feels that, however impossible it may be, it is so; seeing that, without that conception of freedom, he would be not only unable to understand life, but could not live for a single instant.

He could not live because all men's instincts, all their impulses in life, are only efforts to increase their freedom. Wealth and poverty, health and disease, culture and ignorance, labour and leisure, repletion and hunger, virtue and vice, are all only terms for greater or less degrees of freedom.

To conceive a man having no freedom is impossible except as a man deprived of life.

If the idea of freedom appears to the reason a meaningless contradiction, like the possibility of doing two actions at a single moment of time, or the possibility of an effect without a cause, that only proves that consciousness is not subject to reason.

That unwavering, irrefutable consciousness of freedom, not influenced by experience and argument, recognised by all thinkers, and felt by all men without exception, that consciousness without which no conception of man is reliable, constitutes the other side of the question.

Man is the creation of an Almighty, All-good, and All-wise God. What is sin, the conception of which follows from man's consciousness of freedom? That is the question of theology.

Men's actions are subject to general and invariable laws, expressed in statistics. What is man's responsibility to society the conception of which follows from his consciousness of freedom? That is the question of jurisprudence.

A man's actions follow from his innate character and the motives acting on him. What is conscience and the sense of right and wrong in action that follows from the consciousness of freedom? That is the question of ethics.

Man in connection with the general life of humanity is conceived as governed by the laws that determine that life. But the same man, apart from that connection, is conceived of as free. How is the past life of nations and of humanity to be regarded—as the product of the free or not free action of men? That is the question of history.

Only in our conceited age of the popularisation of knowledge, thanks to the most powerful weapon of ignorance—the diffusion of printed matter—the question of the freedom of the will has been put on a level, on which it can no longer be the same question. In our day the majority of so-called advanced people—that is, a mob of ignoramuses—have accepted the result of the researches of natural science, which is occupied with one side only of the question, for the solution of the whole question.

There is no soul and no freewill, because the life of man is expressed in muscular movements, and muscular movements are conditioned by nervous activity. There is no soul and no freewill, because at some unknown period of time we came from apes, they say, and write, and print. Not at all suspecting that thousands of years ago all religions and all thinkers have admitted—have never, in fact, denied—that same law of necessity, which they are now so strenuously trying to prove by physiology and comparative zoology. They do not see that natural science can do no more in this question than serve to illumine one side of it. The facts that, from the point of view of observation, the reason and the will are but secretions of the brain, and that man, following the general law of development, may have developed from lower animals at some unknown period of time, only illustrates in a new aspect the truth, recognised thousands of years ago by all religious and philosophic theories, that man is subject to the laws of necessity. It does not advance one hair's-breadth the solution of the question, which has another opposite side, founded on the consciousness of freedom.

If men have descended from apes at an unknown period of time, that is as comprehensible as that they were fabricated out of a clod of earth at a known period of time (in the one case the date is the unknown quantity, in the other the method of fabrication); and the question how to reconcile man's consciousness of freewill with the law of necessity to which he is subject cannot be solved by physiology and zoology, seeing that in the frog, the rabbit, and the monkey we can observe only muscular and nervous activity, while in man we find muscular and nervous activity plus consciousness.

The scientific men and their disciples who suppose they are solving this question are like plasterers set to plaster one side of a church wall, who, in the absence of the chief superintendent of their work, should in the excess of their zeal plaster over the windows, and the holy images, and the woodwork, and the scaffolding, and rejoice that from their plasterers' point of view everything was now so smooth and even.

IX

THE question of freewill and necessity holds a position in history different from its place in other branches of knowledge, because in history, the question relates, not to the essential nature of the will of man, but to the representation of the manifestations of that will in the past and under certain conditions.

History, in regard to the solution of this question, stands to the other sciences in the position of an experimental science to speculative sciences.

The subject of history is not the will of man, but our representation of its action.

And so the insoluble mystery of the union of the two antinomies of freedom and necessity does not exist for history as it does for theology, ethics, and philosophy. History deals with the representation of the life of man, in which the union of those two antinomies is accomplished.

In actual life every historical event, every human action, is quite clearly and definitely understood, without a sense of the slightest contradiction in it, although every event is conceived of partly as free, and partly as necessary.

To solve the problem of combining freedom and necessity and the question what constitutes the essence of those two conceptions, the philosophy of history can and ought to go to work in a direction opposite to that taken by the other sciences. Instead of first defining the ideas of freedom and necessity in themselves, and then ranging the phenomena of life under those definitions, history must form the definition of the ideas of freewill and necessity from the immense multitude of phenomena in her domain that are always dependent on those two elements.

Whatever presentation of the activity of one man or of several persons we examine, we always regard it as the product partly of that man or men's freewill, partly of the laws of necessity.

Whether we are discussing the migrations of peoples and the inroads of barbarians, or the government of Napoleon III, or the action of some man an hour ago in selecting one direction for his walk out of several, we see nothing contradictory in it. The proportion of freedom and necessity guiding the actions of those men is clearly defined for us.

Very often our conception of a greater or less degree of freedom differs according to the different points of view from which we regard the phenomenon.

But every human action is always alike conceived by us as a certain combination of freewill and necessity.

In every action we investigate, we see a certain proportion of freedom and a certain proportion of necessity. And whatever action we investigate, the more necessity we see the less freedom, and the more freedom the less necessity.

The proportion of freedom to necessity is decreased or increased, according to the point of view from which the act is regarded; but there always remains an inverse ratio between them.

A drowning man clutching at another and drowning him, or a hungry mother starved by suckling her baby and stealing food, or a man trained to discipline who at the word of command kills a defenceless man, all seem less guilty—that is, less free and more subject to the law of necessity to one who knows the circumstances in which they are placed, and more free to one who did not know that the man was himself drowning, that the mother was starving, that the soldier was on duty, and so on. In the same way a man who has twenty years ago committed a murder and afterwards has gone on living calmly and innocently in society seems less guilty, and his acts seem more subject to the law of necessity, to one who looks at his act after the lapse of twenty years than to one looking at the same act the day after it was perpetrated. And just in the same way the act of a madman, a drunkard, or a man labouring under violent excitement seems less free and more inevitable to one who knows the mental condition of the man who performed the action, and more free and less inevitable to one who does not know it. In all such cases the conception of freedom is increased or diminished, and that of necessity correspondingly diminished or increased, according to the point of view from which the action is regarded. So that the more necessity is seen in it the less freedom. And *vice versa*.

Religion, the common sense of humanity, the science of law, and history itself understand this relation between necessity and freewill.

All cases, without exception, in which our conception of freewill and necessity varies depend on three considerations:

1. The relation of the man committing the act to the external world.
2. His relation to time.
3. His relation to the causes leading to the act.

In the first case the variation depends on the degree to which we see the man's relation to the external world, on the more or less clear idea we form of the definite position occupied by the man in relation to everything co-existing with him. It is this class of considerations that makes it obvious to us that the drowning man is less free and more subject to necessity than a man standing on dry ground; and that makes the actions of a man living in close connection with other people in a thickly populated district, bound by ties of family, official duties, or business undertaking, seem undoubtedly less free than those of a man living in solitude and seclusion.

If we examine a man alone, apart from his relations to everything around him, every action of his seems free to us. But if we see any relation of his to anything surrounding, if we perceive any connection between him and anything else, a man speaking to him, a book read by him, the work he is employed in, even the air he breathes, or the light that falls on the objects around him, we perceive that every one of those circumstances has its influence on him, and controls at least one side of his activity. And the more we perceive of those influences, the smaller the idea we form of his freedom, and the greater our conception of the necessity to which he is subject.

2. The second cause of variation is due to the degree of distinctness with which the man's position in time is perceived, the clearness of the notion formed by us of the place the man's action fills in time. It is owing to this class of considerations that the fall of the first man, leading to the origin of the human race, seems to us obviously less free than the marriage of any one of our contemporaries. It is owing to this class of considerations that the life and acts of men who lived years go cannot seem to me as free as the life of my contemporaries, the consequences of whose acts are still unknown to me.

The variation in our conception of freewill in this connection depends on the interval of time that has elapsed between the action and our criticism of it.

If I examine an act I have committed a moment ago in approximately the same circumstances as I am placed in now, my act appears to me indubitably free. But if I examine an act I have committed a month ago, then being placed in other circumstances, I cannot help recognising that had not that act been committed, much that is good and agreeable, and even inevitable, resulting from that act, could not have taken place. If I reflect on a still more remote action, performed ten years or more ago, the consequences of my act are even plainer to me, and it will be difficult for me to conceive what would have happened if that action had not taken place. The further back I go in my reminiscences, or what is the same thing, the further forward in my criticism of them, the more doubtful becomes my view of the freedom of my action.

We find precisely the same ratio of variation in our views of the element of freewill in the general affairs of men in history. A contemporary event we conceive of as undoubtedly the doing of all the men we know of concerned in it. But with a more remote event, we see its inevitable consequences, which prevent our conceiving of anything else as possible. And the further back we go in the examination of events, the less arbitrary they seem to us.

The Austro-Prussian war appears to us to be undoubtedly the result of the crafty acts of Bismarck and so on.

The Napoleonic wars, though more doubtful, appear to us the effect of the freewill of the leading heroes of those wars. But in the Crusades we see an event, filling its definite place in history, without which the modern history of Europe is inconceivable, although to the chroniclers of the Crusades, those events appeared simply due to the will of a few persons. In the migrations of peoples it never occurs to any one now that the renewal of the European world depended on a caprice of Attila's. The more remote in history the subject of our observations, the more doubtful we feel of the freewill of the persons concerned in the event, and the more obvious is the law of necessity in it.

3. The third element influencing our judgment is the degree to which we can apprehend that endless chain of causation demanded by the reason, in which every phenomenon comprehended, and so every act of man, must have its definite place, as a result of past and a cause of future acts.

This is the element that causes our acts and those of others to appear to us on one side more free the less we know of the physiological, psychological, and historical laws deduced from observation, and the less thoroughly the physiological, psychological, or historical cause of the act has been investigated by us, and on the other hand the less simple the act observed and the less complex the character and mind of the man whose action we are examining.

When we have absolutely no understanding of the causes of an action —whether vicious or virtuous or simply non-moral—we ascribe a greater element of freewill to it. In the case of a crime, we are more urgent in demanding punishment for the act; in the case of a virtuous act, we are warmer in our appreciation of its merits. In cases of no moral bearing, we recognise more individuality, originality, and independence in it. But if only one of the innumerable causes of the act is known to us, we recognise a certain element of necessity, and are less ready to exact punishment for the crime, to acknowledge merit in the virtuous act, or freedom in the apparent originality. The fact that the criminal was reared in vicious surroundings softens his fault in our eyes. The self-sacrifice of a father, of a mother, or self-sacrifice with the possibility of reward is more comprehensible than gratuitous self-sacrifice, and so is regarded by us as less deserving of sympathy and less the work of freewill. The founder of a sect, of a party, or the inventor impresses us less when we understand how and by what the way was paved for his activity. If we have a large range of experiments, if our observation is continually directed to seeking correlations in men's actions between causes and effects, their actions will seem to us more necessary and less free, the more accurately we connect causes and effects. If the actions investigated are simple, and we have had a vast number of such actions under observation, our conception of their inevitability will be even more complete. The dishonest conduct of the son of a dishonest father, the misbehaviour of women, who have been led into certain surroundings, the relapse of the reformed drunkard into drunkenness, and so on, are instances of conduct which seems to us to be less free the better we understand their cause. If the man himself whose conduct we are examining is on the lowest stage of mental development, like a child, a madman, or a simpleton, then when we know the causes of the act and the simplicity of the character and intelligence, we see so great an element of necessity, and so little freewill, that we can foretell the act that will follow, as soon as we know the cause bound to bring it forth.

In all legislative codes the exoneration of crime or admission of mitigating circumstances rests only on those three classes of consideration. The guilt is conceived as greater or less according to the greater or lesser knowledge of the conditions in which the man judged is placed, the greater or less interval of time between the perpetration of the crime and the judgment of it, and the greater or less comprehension of the causes that led to the act.

X

A N D thus our conception of freewill and necessity is gradually diminished or increased according to the degree of connection with the external world, the degree of remoteness in time, and the degree of dependence on causes which we see in the phenomenon of man's life that we examine. So that if we examine the case of a man in which the connection with the external world is better known, the interval of time between the examination and the act greater, and the causes of the action easier to comprehend, we form a conception of a greater element of necessity and less of freewill. If we examine a man in a less close dependence on external conditions, if his action is committed at a moment nearer the present, and the causes leading him to it are beyond our ken, we form a conception of a less element of necessity and a greater element of freewill in his action.

But in neither case, however we shift our point of view, however clear we make to ourselves the connection in which the man is placed with the external world, or however fully comprehensible it may appear to us, however long or short a period of time we select, however explicable or unfathomable the causes of the act may be to us, we can never conceive of complete freewill, nor of complete necessity in any action.

1. However carefully we imagine a man excluded from the influence of the external world, we can never form a conception of freedom in space. Every act of man's is inevitably limited by what surrounds him and by his own body. I raise my arm and let it fall. My action seems to me free; but asking myself could I raise my arm in any direction, I see that I moved it in the direction in which there was least hindrance to the action arising from bodies around me or from the construction of my own body. I chose one out of all the possible directions, because in that direction I met with least hindrance. For my action to be entirely free, it would have to meet with no hindrance in any direction. To conceive a man quite free, we have to conceive him outside of space which is obviously impossible.

2. However near we bring the time of criticism to the time of action, we can never form a conception of freedom in time. For if I examine an act committed a second ago, I must still recognise that it is not free, since the act is irrevocably linked to the moment at which it was committed. Can I lift my arm? I lift it; but I ask myself: Could I not have lifted my arm in that moment of time that has just passed? To convince myself of that, I do not lift my arm the next moment. But I am not abstaining from lifting it that first moment of which I asked myself the question. The time has gone by and to detain it was not in my power, and the hand which I then raised and the air in which I raised it are not the same as the hand I do not raise now or the air in which I do not now raise it. The moment in which the first movement took place is irrevocable, and in that moment I could only perform one action, and whatever movement I had made, that movement could have been the only one. The fact that the following moment I abstained from lifting my arm did not prove that I could have abstained from lifting it. And since my movement could only be one in one moment of time, it could have been no other. To conceive it to oneself as free, one must conceive it in the present on the boundary between the past and the future, that is, outside time, which is impossible.

3. However we increase the degree of difficulty of comprehending the causes of the act, we never reach a conception of complete freewill, that is, absolute absence of cause. Though the cause of the expression of will in any act of our own or another's may be beyond our ken, it is the first impulse of the intellect to presuppose and seek a cause, without which no phenomenon is conceivable. I raise my arm in order to per-

form an act independent of any cause, but the fact that I want to perform an act independent of any cause is the cause of my action.

But even if by conceiving a man entirely excluded from external influence, and exercising only a momentary act in the present, not called forth by any cause, we were to reduce the element of necessity to an infinitesimal minimum equivalent to nil, we should even then not have reached a conception of complete freewill in a man; for a creature uninfluenced by the external world, outside of time, and independent of cause, is no longer a man.

In the same way we can never conceive a human action subject only to necessity without any element of freewill.

1. However we increase our knowledge of the conditions of space in which a man is placed, that knowledge can never be complete since the number of these conditions is infinitely great, seeing that space is infinite. And so long as not *all* the conditions that may influence a man are defined, the circle of necessity is not complete, and there is still a loophole for freewill.

2. Though we may make the period of time intervening between an act and our criticism of it as long as we choose, that period will be finite, and time is infinite, and so in this respect too the circle of necessity is not complete.

3. However easy the chain of causation of any act may be to grasp, we shall never know the whole chain, since it is endless, and so again we cannot attain absolute necessity.

But apart from that, even if, reducing the minimum of freewill till it is equivalent to nil, we were to admit in some case—as, for instance, that of a dying man, an unborn babe, an idiot—a complete absence of freewill, we should in so doing have destroyed the very conception of man, in the case we are examining; since as soon as there is no freewill, there is no man. And therefore the conception of the action of a man subject only to the law of necessity, without the smallest element of freewill, is as impossible as the conception of a completely free human action.

Thus to conceive a human action subject only to the law of necessity without freewill, we must assume a knowledge of an *infinite* number of conditions in space, an *infinitely* long period of time, and an *infinite* chain of causation.

To conceive a man perfectly free, not subject to the law of necessity, we must conceive a man *outside of space, outside of time,* and *free from all dependence on cause.*

In the first case, if necessity were possible without freewill, we should be brought to a definition of the laws of necessity in the terms of the same necessity, that is, to mere form without content.

In the second case, if freewill were possible without necessity, we should come to unconditioned freewill outside of space, and time, and cause, which by the fact of its being unconditioned and unlimited would be nothing else than content without form.

We should be brought in fact to these two fundamental elements. of which man's whole cosmic conception is made up—the incomprehensible essence of life and the laws that give form to that essence.

Reason says (1) space with all the forms given it by its visibility—matter—is infinite, and is not thinkable otherwise.

2. Time is infinite movement without one moment of rest, and it is not otherwise thinkable.

3. The connection of cause and effect has no beginning, and can have no end.

Consciousness says: 1. I alone am, and all that exists is only I; consequently I include space.

2. I measure moving time by the unchanging moment of the present, in which alone I am conscious of myself living; consequently I am outside of time, and

3. I am outside of cause, since I feel myself the cause of every phenomenon of my life.

Reason gives expression to the laws of necessity. Consciousness gives expression to the reality of freewill.

Freedom unlimited by anything is the essence of life in man's consciousness. Necessity without content is man's reason with its three forms of thought.

Freewill is what is examined: Necessity is what examines. Freewill is content: Necessity is form.

It is only by the analysis of the two sources of knowledge, standing to one another in the relation of form and content, that the mutually exclusive, and separately inconceivable ideas of freewill and necessity are formed.

Only by their synthesis is a clear conception of the life of man gained.

Outside these two ideas—in their synthesis mutually definitive as form and content—no conception of life is possible.

All that we know of men's life is only a certain relation of freewill to necessity, that is, of consciousness to the laws of reason.

All that we know of the external world of nature is only a certain relation of the forces of nature to necessity, or of the essence of life to the laws of reason.

The forces of the life of nature lie outside us, and not subject to our consciousness; and we call these forces gravitation, inertia, electricity, vital force, and so on. But the force of the life of man is the subject of our consciousness, and we call it freewill.

But just as the force of gravitation—in itself incomprehensible, though felt by every man—is only so far understood by us as we know the laws of necessity to which it is subject (from the first knowledge that all bodies are heavy down to Newton's law), so too the force of freewill, unthinkable in itself, but recognised by the consciousness of every man, is only so far understood as we know the laws of necessity to which it is subject (from the fact that every man dies up to the knowledge of the most complex economic or historic laws).

All knowledge is simply bringing the essence of life under the laws of reason.

Man's freewill is distinguished from every other force by the fact that it is the subject of man's consciousness. But in the eyes of reason it is not distinguished from any other force.

The forces of gravitation, of electricity, or of chemical affinity, are only distinguished from one another by being differently defined by reason. In the same way the force of man's freewill is only distinguished by reason from the other forces of nature by the definition given it by reason. Freedom will apart from necessity, that is, apart from the laws of reason defining it, is in no way different from gravitation, or heat, or the force of vegetation; for reason, it is only a momentary, indefinite sensation of life.

And as the undefined essence of the force moving the heavenly bodies, the undefined essence of the force of heat, of electricity, or of chemical affinity, or of vital force, forms the subject of astronomy, physics, chemistry, botany, zoology, and so on, so the essence of the force of freewill forms the subject matter of history. But even as the subject of every science is the manifestation of that unknown essence of life, yet that essence itself can only be the subject of metaphysics, so too the manifestation of the force of freewill in space, and time, and dependence on cause, forms the subject of history, but freewill itself is the subject of metaphysics.

In the experimental sciences, what is known to us we call the laws of necessity; what is unknown to us we call vital force. Vital force is simply an expression for what remains unexplained by what we know of the essence of life. So in history what is known to us we call the laws of necessity; what is unknown, we call freewill. Freewill is for history simply an expression for what remains unexplained by the laws of men's life that we know.

XI

HISTORY examines the manifestations of man's freewill in connection with the external world in time and in dependence on cause, that is, defines that freedom by the laws of reason; and so history is only a science in so far as that freedom is defined by those laws.

To history the recognition of the freewills of men as forces able to influence historical events, that is, not subject to laws, is the same as it would be to astronomy the recognition of freewill in the movements of the heavenly bodies.

This recognition destroys the possibility of the existence of laws, that is, of any science whatever. If there is so much as one body moving at its freewill, the laws of Kepler and of Newton are annulled, and every conception of the movement of the heavenly bodies is destroyed. If there is a single human action due to freewill, no historical law exists, and no conception of historical events can be formed.

For history there exist lines of movement of human wills, one extremity of which vanishes in the unknowable, and at the other extremity of which in space, in time, and in dependence on cause, there moves men's consciousness of freewill in the present.

The more this curve of movement is analysed before our eyes, the clearer is the laws of its movement. To discover and define those laws is the problem of history.

From the point of view from which the science of history now approaches its subject, by the method it now follows, seeking the causes of phenomena in the freewill of men, the expression of laws by science is impossible; since however we limit the freewill of men, so long as we recognise it as a force not subject to law, the existence of law becomes impossible.

Only limiting this element of freewill to infinity, that is, regarding it as an infinitesimal minimum, we are convinced of the complete unattainability of causes, and then, instead of seeking causes, history sets before itself the task of seeking laws.

The seeking of those laws has been begun long ago, and the new lines of thought which history must adopt are being worked out simultaneously with the self-destruction towards which the old-fashioned history is going, for ever dissecting and dissecting the causes of phenomena.

All human sciences have followed the same course. Reaching infinitesimals, mathematics, the most exact of the sciences, leaves the process of analysis and enters on a new process of approximating to summing up the unknown infinitesimals. Forsaking the conception of cause, mathematics seeks law, that is, properties common to all unknown, infinitesimal quantities.

The other sciences, too, have followed the same course, though under another form. When Newton formulated the law of gravitation, he did not say that the sun or the earth has the property of attraction. He said that all bodies—from the greatest to the smallest—have the property of attracting one another; that is, leaving on one side the question of the cause of the movements of bodies, he expressed the property common to all bodies, from the infinitely great to the infinitely small. The natural sciences do the same thing; leaving on one side the question of cause, they seek for laws. History, too, is entering on the same course. And if the subject of history is to be the study of the movements of peoples and of humanity, and not episodes from the lives of individual men, it too is bound to lay aside the idea of cause, and to seek the laws common to all the equal and inseparably interconnected, infinitesimal elements of freewill.

XII

EVER since the law of Copernicus was discovered and proved, the mere recognition that not the sun, but the earth moves, has destroyed the whole cosmography of the ancients. By disproving the law, it might have been possible to retain the old conception of the movements of the heavenly bodies; but without disproving it, it would seem to be impossible to continue studying the Ptolemaic worlds. But as a fact even after the discovery of the law of Copernicus, the Ptolemaic worlds long continued to be a subject of study.

Ever since the first person said and proved that the number of births or crimes is subject to mathematical laws, that certain geographical and politico-economical laws determine this or that form of government, that certain relations of the population to the soil lead to migrations of peoples—from that moment the foundations on which history was built were destroyed in their essence.

By disproving those new laws, the old view of history might have been retained. But without disproving them, it would seem impossible to continue studying historical events, merely as the arbitrary product of the freewill of individual men. For if a certain type of government is established, or a certain movement of peoples takes place in consequence of certain geographical, ethnographical, or economic conditions, the freewill of those persons who are described to us as setting up that type of government or leading that movement cannot be regarded as the cause.

And yet history goes on being studied as of old, side by side with laws of statistics, of geography, of political economy, of comparative philology and geology, that flatly contradict its assumptions.

The struggle between the new views and the old was long and stubborn in physical philosophy. Theology stood on guard over the old view, and accused the new view of violating revelation. But when truth gained the day, theology established itself as firmly as ever on a new basis.

As long and as obstinate is the conflict today between the old and the new view of history; and in the same way theology stands on guard over the old view, and accuses the new of attacking revelation.

In both cases on both sides, the struggle rouses evil passions and stifles truth. On one side there is dread and regret at demolishing the edifice that has been raised by the ages; on the other, the passion for destruction.

To the men who fought against the new truths of physical philosophy, it seemed that if they were to admit that truth, it would shatter faith in God, in the creation of the firmament, in the miracle of Joshua, the son of Nun. To the champions of the laws of Copernicus and Newton, to Voltaire, for instance, it seemed that the laws of astronomy were destructive of religion, and the latter made use of the law of gravitation as a weapon against religion.

So now it seems that we have but to admit the law of necessity to shatter the conception of the soul, of good, of evil, and all the political and ecclesiastical edifices reared on the basis of those conceptions.

So too, like Voltaire in his day, the champions of the law of necessity use the law as a weapon against religion, though, like the law of Copernicus in astronomy, the law of necessity in history, far from destroying, even strengthens the foundation on which political and ecclesiastical edifices are reared.

Just as then in the question of astronomy, now in the question of history, the whole difference of view rested on the recognition or nonrecognition of an absolute unit as a measure of visible phenomena. For astronomy, this was the immobility of the earth; in history, the independence of personality—freewill.

Just as in astronomy the difficulty of admitting the motion of the earth lay in the immediate sensation of the earth's stationariness and of the planet's motion, so in history the difficulty of recognising the subjection of the personality to the laws of space and time and causation lies in the difficulty of surmounting the direct sensation of the independence of one's personality. But just as in astronomy, the new view said, 'It is true, we do not feel the movement of the earth, but, if we admit its immobility, we are reduced to absurdity, while admitting its movement, we are led to laws'; so in history, the new view says, 'It is true, we do not feel our dependence, but admitting our freewill, we are led to absurdity; admitting our dependence on the external world, time, and cause, we are led to laws.'

In the first case, we had to surmount the sensation of an unreal immobility in space, and to admit a motion we could not perceive of by sense. In the present case, it is as essential to surmount a consciousness of an unreal freedom and to recognise a dependence not perceived by our senses.

THE END